Encantada

The Pirate Chronicles

Maria del Mar

ISBN 978-1-962363-08-2 (Paperback)
ISBN 978-1-962363-09-9 (Ebook)

"A Woman's Worth"
Emi April Music In ©
Lellow Productions ©
Krucialkeys2 Life Music©
Phoenix Rose
Lyrics Provided by Gracenote

Inquiries and Book Orders should be addressed to:

Leavitt Peak Press
17901 Pioneer Blvd Ste L #298, Artesia, California 90701
Phone #: 2092191548

"Where are we going?"

Marina asked her sister for what seemed to be the hundredth time. Salomé shrugged her shoulders, her frown deepening. It had started out as a spectacularly beautiful day. The ocean was glassy beneath their craft. But where before the sky above them had been clear as a picture, it was now the setting of thunderclouds moving around as if in a ritual dance. Both girls looked up, distracted by a moment by the swirling of clouds. The sun seemed to be fighting a losing battle against the impending darkness. The wind was blowing steadily. But the girls knew. Soon. You could even smell the rain in the air. Whitecaps were gently forming sporadically, here and there. It would storm soon. And it seemed to them that they were on a small boat headed out to the middle of nowhere.

Salomé took a good look at her companions. The two young men stood at the front of the boat laughing at something that immediately got snatched by the wind. They all knew each other from college. Quentin Matthews was a Big Man On Campus. He was a junior, all around sports guy, member of many teams, owner of many hearts.

There's something wrong with him, Marina thought. She glanced at the other young man. Todd Lowell. *This one's evil.* The thought came out of nowhere, making the girl shiver. She looked away, hiding her eyes behind her favorite reflector sunglasses, drawing in a shaky breath, when she felt Todd look over his shoulder at them. *You couldn't tell just by looking at him*, she thought sadly. Marina had seen both young men around. They were Joe Cool and his brother when they were together. You couldn't miss them at school, and you couldn't avoid them outside. All you had to do was follow the trail of drooling girls. But they were not of their circle of friends. As a matter of fact, she wasn't quite sure of how she and Salomé ended up in the company of these particular young men to begin with, anyway. The only connection she could make was that they were acquaintances of Jackson's, Salomé's brother.

Where the hell is Jackson, anyway?

The motor on the boat shifted, the sound changing to a lower pitch. The girls looked ahead of them to what seemed to be some sort of island. The crystal water changed color, becoming turquoise as they approached the shore, leaving the indigo depths behind them.

Salomé shot Marina a glance and faked a smile. "Finally! I thought we'd never get --- where are we, anyway?"

"Paradise," Todd answered, wiggling his eyebrows in a most lecherous way, the smirk on his face leaving no doubt as to his meaning. The boys jumped into the water with a war yell, and splashed ashore.

The girls looked at each other.

"This isn't good, Salo," Marina said anxiously. "This isn't right. Something is dead wrong."

"I know," Salomé conceded. "Let's figure it out." She jerked her head at the two men yelling in the water. "Keep your eyes and ears open, girl. Cover me", she hissed, pushing the other girl in front of her.

Marina knew better than to ask any questions. She moved quickly to the front of the boat and studied the situation. The guys had anchored quickly as they beached. The water reached their waists. Marina wasn't as tall as they were, but she wasn't small either. She stopped carefully on the side of the boat, and turned around to descend the steps into the water. One hand grasped the railing, while the other held on to the bundle on top of her head. The water was so shallow it was warm. It hit the hem of her shorts and crept up, filling her navel, reaching to just beneath her breasts. She took off her sunglasses with one hand, held her bag with both hands high in the air, and submerged to the top of her head. *It's nice and cool and quiet down here.* She came back up with a big smile, water streaming down her tan skin, bikini top outlining her breasts, as it clung to her dripping skin. *I have to put a shirt on*, she thought suddenly, catching sight of the boys' attention on her. "This is nice, you guys," Marina called out. "Where is everybody else?" She noticed them pretend not to hear her as they came up on the sand. *Do not get close to these guys.* She heard a splash and turned to see her sister come up behind her.

Salomé winked at her and shot a look over her shoulder at the young men. The girls reached the beach, moving naturally together, putting discreet distance between the guys and themselves. Salomé made a big show of spreading their blankets and towels on the sand, while Marina hastily slipped a T- shirt over her head, taking refuge in the small protection it gave her.

"You boys hungry?" Salomé asked. The response was immediate. "Starving!" cried Quentin.

"What have you got?" asked Todd.

The girls showed them. Out came fruit, bread, cheese, bottles of water. Marina knew they had brought a bottle of wine with them, but chose to stay quiet when it didn't surface. They sat around together, munching contentedly, just enjoying the peace and quiet. A radio had been left playing on board, the music heard from a distance as it came across the water. Conversation was minimal, just words to fill the occasional awkward silence. For the most part, each one was lost in his or her own thoughts. Salomé and Marina got to their feet afterwards, occupying themselves in the mundane task of picking up. Trash was bagged to be taken away in the boat, while blankets and towels were folded once more, and stashed once again in their bags.

Todd stretched, a relaxed grin splitting his face. He reached for the bag of garbage. "We'll take this. Don't want to leave it here, littering the beach."

"Yeah," Quentin added. "We left something on the boat, but we'll be right back."

The girls sat on the shore to wait as the guys made their way back to the boat, hooting and hollering, splashing each other, finally throwing the bag inside the boat before hauling themselves overboard.

"What do you think is up?" Salomé asked.

Marina glanced at her and turned her attention back to the boat. "I don't know," she answered. "I thought the whole gang was supposed to be here, but I don't think anybody else is coming. What do you know about this trip?"

"I thought Jackson set it up. He is going to go ballistic when he finds out that we're here alone with these two and nobody else."

"So, what's the plan?" Marina asked.

"I'm going to confront them," Salomé answered. "Just keep your radar on and don't let them close enough to touch you."

Marina nodded. They fell silent for a while, waiting. The day had grown increasingly darker, the whitecaps in the distance growing more distinct as the ocean prepared itself to start churning. The salt was thick in the air, leaving a slick coat of moisture on the girls' skin. Salomé doodled aimlessly in the sand, eyes fastened on the bobbing craft in front of them.

"Look!" Marina grabbed her friend's arm suddenly. She nodded towards the boat.

Salomé followed her gaze. She sat upright as she realized what they were looking at. A laugh escaped her. "Ladies and gentlemen," she crowed softly, "the play is now in session. It is Quentin up at bat. He looks around, lifts his head, bat is up in the air. Will he do it? Yes! He did it! From the intensity coming from the players, I would say they are smoking a bat! Back to you, Marina."

Marina pretended to hold a microphone. "Thank you, Salomé. As you see, Quentin is off and running with the smoking bat. He is dragging on it again and --- oh! That boy's *mamá* never taught him any manners. He needs to share!" They started giggling, eyes never leaving the boys. "But, wait! What is this? Could it be --- I'm not sure, Salomé, what do you think?"

"I am looking closely, Marina. This has been quite an interesting turn of events. The bobbing of the head is quite unmistakable, however."

The girls stared. Quentin seemed to be putting out what they were smoking. Todd was intent on something in his lap. As the two girls watched, he dipped his head down. They saw his shoulders heave suddenly as he flung his head back, hands to his face, fingers rubbing his nose. Laughter rumbled over the water. Quentin looked over his shoulder at them as Todd dipped his head again. The boat rocked as

Quentin stood and grabbed a couple of bottles of beer. He turned and tossed one at Todd. The bottle was received with a laugh as it was caught in mid-air. Bottles were opened and heads were flung back as they drank. Todd reached into his pocket and held something out in his hand, offering it to Quentin. The taller boy peered down and said something, laughing. The banter went back and forth for a few moments, but Quentin firmly shook his head no. Todd shrugged his shoulders and popped something into his mouth, washing it down with a drink of his beer.

The girls turned towards each other. Their eyes met and held, each one's thoughts racing fast and furious behind them.

"This doesn't look good, baby," Marina whispered. "Be prepared," Salomé whispered back.

They got to their feet and began scouring the beach, looking for anything that could be used as a weapon. They began picking seashells bleaching in the sand, while locating where the driftwood was.

"Here we come, girls," called Todd.

Salomé grabbed a stick of driftwood she had been eyeing. It was a little heavy and seemed solid, long, like a walking staff, but easy to swing. Marina followed suit and stood to one side, feet braced apart, watching with apprehension as the boys reached them.

Our Father, who art in Heaven, hallowed be thy name.

Quentin grinned. "Ready for some fun, girls?" He grabbed his crotch and leered at them.

Todd stretched a hand out towards them. "Dessert, ladies?"

"No, thank you," Marina glared at them.

Thy kingdom come, thy will be done, on Earth as it is in Heaven.

"What do you guys think you are doing, anyway?" Salomé demanded. The mood shifted as the boys circled them. "Why, what do you mean, Salomé? We just want to have a little fun."

"Not with us," Marina shot back.

Give us this day, our daily bread.

Todd laughed. "What's the matter ---"

"Nothing's the matter," Salomé interrupted, "because nothing is going to happen."

"Where is Jackson?" Marina demanded.

And forgive us our trespasses as we forgive those who trespass against us.

The boys' smiles faded as they stared at the girls. "He couldn't make it," Quentin offered.

Salomé squinted her eyes hard at the young man, making his heart skip a beat. "You lie," she hissed.

"No, really," Todd insisted. "He asked us to apologize on his behalf, but he had something to do at the last moment." ***Lead us not into temptation.*** "Pants on fire," Marina sang out.

"My brother will go postal on your asses when I tell him you brought us all the way out here by ourselves," Salomé informed him.

Quentin reached out a hand towards them. The girls took a step back at the same time, sticks coming up.

But deliver us from Evil.

A laugh died on the boy's lips as he took in the situation. "We won't hurt you, ladies."

"No," Salomé agreed. "But *we* will hurt *you*."

"Since this isn't a date," Marina explained, "there will be no rape."

Amen.

The four young people stood, glaring at each other. Todd made a sound of disgust. "As you wish, ladies," he sneered. "Now, let's see how you make your way back."

"*Whatever!*" Salomé shouted. "You wouldn't *dare* leave us stranded out here!"

Todd threw back his head and laughed. When he looked back at them, his eyes were dead. His answer was soft. "*Try me.*"

Marina stepped forward. "Take us back, Todd. We'll take care of this ---"

"*Forget that, bitch!*" Todd screamed suddenly. "You think you are so much better than me?" Another laugh escaped his throat. A sharp sound that caused the girls' blood to run cold. "Well, let's see how long it takes you to swim back."

"Don't do this, Todd," Salomé warned. She was furious. Her chest heaved with her pounding heart as horror began to dawn on her. Fear cooled her skin like ghost fingers tickling their way up her bare arms.

Quentin looked aghast at his friend. "Come on, man, what is wrong with you?"

Todd jabbed a finger at his chest. "*You* have a choice, however. Come with *me* or stay with *them*." He looked back at the girls and shrugged. "Either way, *I* am out of here." He looked at his friend. "*And I don't give a fuck.*" He headed towards the boat.

Quentin felt his heart sink. He looked at the girls. "I'll be back for you."

Marina gasped, fear hitting her in the stomach. *Oh, my God!* "You're just going to leave us here?"

Todd glared at her. "Spread your legs, baby," he sneered.

"*Fuck you!*" she screamed at him.

"You are not," he shot back, "but somebody else will." He laughed. "Tonight. In a nice warm bed. While you lay under the stars," he taunted.

"*Do not do this!*" Salomé screamed.

Quentin jumped in. "Todd, don't do this, man. What if something happens to them?"

Todd turned back to look at his friend once more. His eyes bore deep into the other one's eyes, making his skin crawl with fear. "I don't think you heard me right." His voice was low, paused and deliberate. "*I don't give a fuck.*" Todd turned his back on them and strode into the water, swimming away with a bold stroke.

Quentin looked at the girls again. He looked scared. His hand went up helplessly towards them and he let it drop. "I'll be back," he told them, and went to join his friend.

The girls watched helplessly as the boys got on the boat and sailed away.

They looked at each other. "Now what?" Salomé asked.

Marina sighed. "Well, it looks like we'll be in for a long wait, so let's go exploring." They looked around. "It's going to storm soon."

Storm. It had been a verb to them for years. Ever since their families took their summer vacation together with a trip to the Grand Canyon. It stormed then, too. Spectacularly. And it reaf-

firmed the loving life bond between the two families. Four parents
--- loving, together parents --- with three children between them. Of
these three children, two looked at each other now. Tears came to
their eyes, hands blindly seeking each other, grasping as their foreheads touched. They closed their eyes, chanting under their breaths.
It's cool, it's okay, we'll be fine. The girls pushed against each other like
mountain goat kids butting heads, transferring energy from one to
the other. Fingers locked as they stepped back, opening their eyes to
see, blinking back tears to smile.

"You okay?" Salomé asked.

"No." Marina stepped up to her. They met in a warm embrace
and let go. "Now I am." She smiled, wiping away her tears. Shaking
her head slowly, she sighed, her hair whipping around her shoulders.

Salomé looked around them. At their backs, the ocean rumbled
louder as the surf pounded on the sand. Ahead of them lay endless
beach, the jungle to their right ending in cliffs. "What do you say we
hit those rocks?"

"Sounds good to me. We might find a cave."

"Let us go."

They walked along the shore, carrying their things, taking their
time, just out for a stroll. It would be a long wait. And from the look
of things, their rescue wouldn't be today.

The storm was almost upon them. Sand blasted their faces in
stinging sheets as to their right, the palm trees bent, bracing themselves against the wind where the jungle began. They got to the bottom of the rock face and looked up. As Marina had predicted, halfway up was an opening. The girls looked at each other.

Salomé grinned and put her arm around her sister's shoulders.
"You got it going on, girl!"

Marina laughed. She spotted a trail to the left of the rock and
walked towards it. They ran uphill.

There was a cave. Just as they had thought. But it was more
than that. It was a cave, but it was more like a... *place*! Like someone's place. It was not too deep, the far wall just visible from the
entrance. Large enough to stay in comfortably, with room left over.
Large enough to hold several people. A place with enough areas to

do assorted activities. A place to cook in, a place to sleep in. The girls walked in, holding hands, looking around them cautiously. Putting their bags down, they walked around warily watching the entrance. They found candles, matches, and blankets. They stepped back outside.

Salomé shook her head. "I don't know about this, Marina. What if whoever left all that stuff comes back?" She shivered, biting her lip. "I want to be found, but I really don't want to be *caught* here, you know what I mean?"

Marina closed her eyes and turned her face up to the rapidly darkening sky. The first drops fell. Big, fat, heavy, splatting drops of hundreds of thousands of molecules of blessed rain. Her arms outstretched, she opened herself up to the sky. Channeling her energy, she then proceeded to do a mental scan of her body and her aura, before throwing it outwards to her surroundings. No danger presented itself. Rain fell harder. Stinging. Slamming against her eyelids, her forehead. Marina opened her eyes and looked at her sister. "Nobody is coming." She nodded towards the entrance. "Let's go or we'll drown out here."

Salomé laughed and shook her head slowly back and forth, her long black hair whipping around her face, shaking off the rain in a losing battle. Brown hands reached up to gather it and squeeze the water out as they stepped back inside. Salomé once again turned on a flashlight that had just before brought to light the secrets the cave had to reveal. They lit the candles they found against the back wall and spaced them out.

"It is kind of spooky if you think about it," Marina agreed, hands on hips, nodding her head slowly as she looked about her. "But if you look carefully, you realize that everything is so still --- this stuff has been here for a long time." She hesitated. Salomé looked at her and waited. "Although," she continued slowly, waving her hands in the air, "nobody has been here for a long time." She frowned.

Salomé nodded, understanding. "So, whoever left the stuff, just left it."

She shrugged. "Whatever. Looks like we're here for the night."

They found a pile of blankets that didn't smell too much, since the continuous air flow of ocean breeze had kept them as fresh as possible, under the circumstances. They made their crashing quarters first, each girl making a nest of some sorts to lay on when night came. Then they dug into their bags. Out came the wine that had so conveniently and mysteriously disappeared when the boys had been present. Containers of water, a roll of toilet paper, jars of fresh roasted peanuts, plums, cheese, and half a loaf of bread. Just enough for them to have a nice dinner. They would deal with the rest in the morning.

So they ate, drank, laughed. They stepped outside, sheltered from the increasing wind, to relieve their bodies. Once done, the girls proceeded to bury all evidence of their biological functions in the jungle floor. Feeling a little better physically, at least, they came back inside. Finally, they lay down side by side in their respective beds. Their hands sought each other in comfort, as they stared up at the cave ceiling.

Salomé let go of Marina's hand and sat up. "I can't do this, straight," she mumbled. Marina sat up on her elbows and watched Salomé's distorted shadow dance on the walls as she fumbled in her bag. The young woman found what she was looking for and turned to her sister, brandishing what is hereby known as dessert. "*Voila,*" whispered Salomé, eyes dancing, smile flashing. Marina smiled as the joint shone white in the candlelight.

So they smoked, laughed, pretended, The ganja doing its magic, the girls felt better. They did a spiritual dance of whispered secrets and murmured dreams. The familiar soul-searching of best friends. It felt really good that night in that cave, remembering a shared childhood with endless love and extreme gratitude. And then it got better. Louder, funnier, sillier. More intense, more teasing, more laughter.

They forgot. Not completely. Not consciously. Just for a moment. But they did. They forgot.

The girls finished smoking, drank some water and remarked on the storm outside. Mindless chitchat as they remembered. The absurd, dangerous predicament they were in was not going away.

Before long, they found themselves on their backs once again. This time, the cave ceiling was darker, as the candles struggled to stay alive. Outside the wind had shifted, sending in a small, sharp draft that slithered around the cave walls.

Salomé sighed deeply. "Okay, Marina, let's talk. What are we going to do, baby?"

Marina shrugged in the dark. "Don't know. There's nothing we can do until morning, anyway."

"You're right," agreed Salomé. "Do you think they'll be long in coming to the rescue?"

Marina thought about it. "What do you think?"

Salomé's voice was low and husky as it came back. "Child, once Jackson finds out what went down, that boy will race trains, bullets, and leap over tall buildings in a single bound to get to us."

"Yeah, he is."

"If he doesn't go to jail for killing those two jerks!"

"Ssshhh, baby. Don't get yourself upset."

"Marina..."

"I know..."

"...what if..."

"Jackson doesn't find out..."

"...at least in time to save us..."

"...alive"

"Maybe?"

"No, *mami*, it's not going down like that..."

"Jackson will come."

"No matter what."

" He will. Our parents would kill him..."

"Jackson will come."

"Todd, man, we've got to talk." Quentin thrust his fingers through his short hair, on the border of panic.

Todd looked at him, his eyes dead. "There is nothing to talk about."

"Yes, dude, there is. What if sometihing happens to those girls, man? I will not go down for something I didn't do." Quentin stood up in disgust, pacing like a caged animal. "You better fix this, Todd. I know those people's parents. They don't play." Turning on his heel, he strode to the door. "Just fix it, man."

"Wait!" Todd reached his side and put his hand on his arm. "Where the hell do you think you're going?"

Quentin looked down pointedly at the other boy's hand. Todd retreived it slowly, not breaking eye contact. Quentin opened the door. "I'm going to go out and find Jackson."

"Why, dude?"

"Because he's going to come looking for me."

The elevator was slow in coming, giving Quentin precious time to think. Things had gotten crazy, out of control. Todd was sick. He realized he'd known for a while, but the guy wasn't all bad. He just had problems. Quentin's eyes glazed as he watched the numbers light up at the elevator's ascent. *Nothing is as powerful as the truth*, he thought to himself. The number for his floor lit up, and he could hear the elevator coast to a stop. The box hissed as the doors slid open. Out stepped the only occupant.

It was a tall black man. His energy was overpowering as it followed him off the elevator. Muscles strained against his shirt, the hem just clearing the waist of his faded jeans. The hi-tops on his feet spoke volumes of endless basketball games. A small gold cross hung around his neck, and small gold hoops graced his ears. The man's face was smooth and beautiful. His eyes were the palest brown, almost yellow with specks in its depths. Feline like a big cat's. His hair was so black it shone blue, light caught in the neat even corn rows that clung to his scalp. His voice was low, a smooth rumble. "Hey."

Quentin felt his heart skip a beat, and he swallowed. He nodded his head. "Jackson…"

Jackson stepped up to him. "Hey, what's going on, man? Have you seen my sisters?"

Quentin nodded. "Yes." He stepped backwards and turned around, going back the way he had come from. "You better follow me."

Jackson followed him. He knew better than to ask any questions. Nobody had seen his girls for hours, though, and everything kept coming back to the young man in front of him. He stopped as they reached a door at the end of the hallway. Quentin looked over his shoulder at him before opening the door and stepping inside. Once again, Jackson followed him. At first glance, the room seemed to be empty. Then he caught sight of Todd. "Hey, man, what's going on?"

Todd jumped in surprise. He laughed. "That was quick," he said, looking at Quentin. "Remind me to ask you, whenever I need something in a rush."

Jackson moved forward. "Cut the bullshit, man. Where are my sisters?" Quentin threw himself into the nearest armchair, jerking his head at Todd.

"Let Romeo tell you."

Todd shook his head in disgust. "Aw, fuck it! I'm a grown man." He glared at Quentin before turning to look at Jackson. "I fucked up, man. I really fucked up. There's nothing I can do to fix it, right now."

Jackson stepped forward. "What did you do, man?"

"We just took them to this small island for a picnic, but we kind of tricked them." Todd stopped and swallowed, watching Jackson's face grow more ominous with each word. He was amazed at the words coming out of his mouth, but truth be told, he was a smart man. And Jackson looked like he could kill him. "We had a nice civilized picnic, and then we pulled some macho bullshit on them. I got pissed off and just left them there."

"*What?*"

Todd took a step backwards. "I know!" His hand reached out, pleading. "It was a stupid thing to do. I just lost it, man! But there's a storm out there, and there is nothing we can do until the morning. I could take you out there, myself ---"

"*Fuck you!*" Jackson put a hand on his chest and shoved him. "Don't leave town, man," he threatened. Turning to leave, he grabbed Quentin by the shirt, on his way out the door. "You and I are going to have a talk." Dragging the other boy behind him, Jackson reached the elevators once again. He heaved Quentin to his feet in front of him, and shook him hard. "Start talking," he growled.

Quentin closed his eyes for a moment. "It's just like Todd said. We had a nice lunch, and then we spoiled it by insinuating they should have sex with us." He stepped back, afraid of the black man. "They wouldn't have any of it, and Todd lost it. He just left them there, man! There was nothing I could do to stop it. But I had a choice, Jackson. I could either stay with them, or come back with him." Quentin held up a hand. "I came back, because I"m their only shot at being rescued. I can take you to them, man. But Todd's right. With that storm, there is no way we can get out there."

"Is there shelter for them?" Jackson demanded.

"I don't know, man, not for sure. There must be, though. There was a beach with a jungle behind it, and down the shore there were rock cliffs..."

Jackson cut him off abruptly. "See you in the morning," he said. "You are taking me to this island, no matter what the weather."

Outside the cave, the storm continued to rage. Black clouds puffed up larger in the night sky, swirling around each other, trying to outdo one another. Palms bent in sacrifice, bracing themselves, fronds blowing back in the wind. The jungle was thunderous with the downpour. Creeks and rivers overflowed, water seeking water as it raced on the jungle floor, rushing downhill to the sea. Small saplings bent, some breaking, some cowering. The oldest trees raised their branches higher in surrender, turning their leaves over to receive the rain, trembling in tune with the storm itself. Pines swayed every which way, needles shimmying like fringe on a dress. Rocks soaked luxuriously. The sand on the beach bubbled, getting swamped. And then, as the storm reached its peak, something spectacular happened. The ocean began churning, creating a whirlpool. There were no waves as we know them. Just immense masses of water chasing each other around faster and faster in a circular motion. Up above, a space opened in the clouds, matching the breadth of the liquid whirlpool, creating its counterpart in wind. The funnel that originated as a result began small. A mere thread of water reaching up to heaven. And as the night roared, it seemed to take life of its own. The funnel grew bigger and wider, turning faster, penetrating the clouds around it in a frenzy, its point of origin making a hole in the ocean, spinning out of control. The water flew up into the sky like a runaway train, disappearing. The jungle held its breath as the whole night trembled around it. Lightning flashed in cascading waves, erratic and out of control, breathtaking in its momentary display of energy and light. The sky retaliated. The rumble that followed culminated in a groundshaking explosion, the planet itself seeming to reverberate from the force. And then the sky opened up, the water hanging suspended for a moment. A ripple of energy spread over the ocean and unto the beach, enshrouding the jungle and the cave in the cliff, where girls dreamed of a brother coming to the rescue and of home. Time shifted. The sky let go. Water fell in sheets. It cascaded back to where it had come from, rushing to get home. The ocean seemed to embrace the water, as a mother forgives a child its wayward ways. And as everything returned back to its rightful place, as the madness dissolved and energy restored itself, the sky opened up once again. Then it rained.

It rained.

"*They are here.*" The words were soft, so he pretended not to hear them. The woman smiled to herself and continued rocking in her chair. Her hands were busy, slow with her creation as she sang to herself.

He was her son. Her beautiful baby boy. The young man was sitting on the floor, intent on his drawings. Candlelight danced on his features as he frowned at the paper in his hands. He was tall and muscular for his age, adulthood having arrived finally. His hands were big and strong as they clenched in fists while he stretched, broad shoulders rippling darkly, neck craning, head thrown back. The white soft cotton of his cutoff pants seemed to glow aganist his dark skin. Outside, the rain was merciless on their hut. Good thing he had repaired the roof this week, he thought with a sigh, only to do it again as soon as this was over. He looked closely at the papers in front of him once again.

Finally, he looked at his mother. "So, *Mamá...*"

"Yes, baby?"

He turned to look at her. "These visitors you are expecting, they are here already, you say?"

The woman stilled her hands for a moment, putting her work down in her lap gently. Her face was still unlined, but her eyes were ancient with wisdom, glowing with green fire like a cat in the night. Witch's eyes. Her hair lay in long dreads around her beautiful face, in assorted ropes, like a primitive Medusa. Beautiful gold hoops hung from her ears, a present from his father. Shells and beads and feathers adorned her neck, framing her chest, where her old heart beat steadily, a present from him. She smiled. "That's what I said." She reached out a hand, bangles slipping down her arm gently to her wrist.

The young man held on to the pictures for a moment, eyes dancing in mischief as they met his mother's. "All right, *Mamá*. What can you tell me about these people?"

"There's two," she answered, without missing a beat. "Two beautiful young women. Smart. They have schooling. One of them is dark skinned, long black hair. She likes to laugh this one. Sings like an angel. Sharp and beautiful, like a brand new blade. Men fall over for her, but her looks disguise her brain. Things will change quickly with this one. Her name is found in that book Padre Ignacio carries around all the time," she added with a wink.

The boy rolled his eyes. "That's the Bible, *Mamá*." He laughed at her. It was an old game between them, since in actuality Padre Ignacio was much respected in their family. He looked back down at the papers and held up one of the pictures.

His mother nodded her head and smiled, meeting her beautiful son's eyes. "The other one," she continued, "is a gift from God. She will bring enlightenment and courage. Women will change on this island, and therefore, so will men. She will singlehandedly create an economy for this island, like it has never seen before. These sea dogs will throw themselves at her feet, and..." she drifted off, for a moment, staring into space, pursuing a thought only she could see. When she met her son's eyes, hers glowed with an inner fire. "... people will be freed, baby."

"Can you tell me her name?"

"No, baby, not her real name, I don't get things like that," she laughed before continuing. "Her skin is bronzed and her hair has sunlight caught in it. She dances and loves with all her soul. She will stay. She is a child of the ocean."

His heart skip a beat, as he looked down at his drawing of the other girl. He had grown up hearing stories about these mysterious visitors that had graced their island throughout the years. Some had stayed a while, others had left immediately, and still others died trying. But he had never seen his mother speak with such passion as she did about these. They would probably be the only visitors he would meet in his lifetime, and he was fit to be tied from excitement, although he was old enough now to show a more mature side of himself. Excitement prowled around his stomach, and the hair on his arms stood on end. He smiled to himself. "Well, *Mamá*, in that case, I should better try to sleep a little. I will need energy to go to them in the morning."

"Yes, baby," she answered, standing up to walk him to the door,. With adulthood had come independence, and he now lived in his own hut close by. She took him in her arms in a close goodnight hug. She buried her face in his neck, stealing a quick snuggle as she inhaled his scent. He chuckled and drew back to look at her. She touched the picture of Salomé. "This one will bring more. She is very loved and will be missed fiercely." Taking the other piece of paper, she squinted at the outline of the second girl. "This one will stay," she repeated with a smile. Water misted around them under the eaves of the house, as the rain roared on. She brushed back the dreadlocks from his face. Her voice came out in a whisper. "Free, Caribe...

It was still dark as night when he woke up some time later. Still raining, Nature was not done yet. This time, the water fell with less intensity, although steadily. The morning air felt cooler than usual. Caribe stepped out in the rain and felt his way to the familiar path that led him out of the village. He could find his way with his eyes closed, and his step was firm on the slick jungle floor. Finally, he reached his destination. Outside the cave, he hesitated. The sky had grown a lighter shade of black over the ocean, but it was still dark enough to scare someone. And that, he did not want to do. It was bad enough having to deal with all the explanations he had to make. Shaking his head, he decided to wait for them. He headed down the trail to the beach. The rain was softer now, just a nice drizzle, a gentle wind pushing it around. Caribe sighed. With a last look up at the cave, he followed the shoreline. Out over the ocean, the sky struggled to paint pink and orange through the clouds, trying to erase the remaining darkness. On the beach, a small conch shell tumbled in the white froth. Caribe bent down and picked it up. His thought was exasperated. *One.*

Inside the cave, the girls stirred. It was gloomy, but light enough to make out the shapes of things. Marina sat up and stretched, her hands moving to her face to stifle a yawn. Finally remembering where she was, she gasped and shook the girl beside her. "Salo! Salo! ", she hissed. "It's morning, *mami.*"

Salomé stood up slowly and stepped out unto the middle of the cave. She turned in a slow circle, hands rubbing her arms in the cool air. "I don't think they'll come this early. The ocean must be wild after last night's storm."

Marina joined her. "Maybe," she agreed slowly. "But maybe it's as flat as a mirror."

Salomé giggled and hooked an arm through hers. "Well, let's go look."

Outside, it was still drizzling. Out over the horizon, the sky screamed in streaks of orange and scarlet. Marina sighed. "Red sky at morning..." she murmured.

Salomé hugged her arm. "Yeah, yeah..."

They walked to the top of the bluff and sat down. It was slowly getting lighter, and more revealed itself. The cliff sloped gradually to the beach. Down below, the jungle ended abruptly, a distance from the shoreline. Although the foliage that faced the ocean was struggling to reflect some of the morning light, the jungle itself was sinister in the wispy fog. The girls sat close together, arms around drawn up knees, chins on folded hands. They were silent for a while, each one lost in her own thoughts. Suddenly, Marina sat up straight, eyes fastened on an object on the beach. "Salo, look!" she whispered urgently. "Look! Look! Do you see?"

Salomé's eyes followed her friend's pointing finger. She gasped. "Oh, my God! " she whispered back. "There's a guy down there! Let's go talk to him!"

The girls flew to their feet and ran back into the cave. Once inside, they looked around for their bags. The candles and matches were right where they had left them. So were the blankets and assorted objects. But their bags were nowhere to be found. They looked around them, perplexed, hands on hips. "Do you remember where we put them?" Marina asked, pulling up one end of the blanket she had slept on, and letting it flutter back to the ground. Nothing here.

Salomé shook her head. "No," she said slowly. "This is too weird." She fumbled blindly into the pile of clothes next to her. "I don't know who these were meant for," she said, stepping into a skirt. "But they're clean and they fit," she continued, slipping a camisole over her head, the other girl following her lead. She looked around her one last time, excitement overpowering her. "Let's just go, Marina. I want to catch up with this guy before he disappears. Let's go and check him out."

Marina laughed. "Lead the way."

They went back down the same path they had taken yester-day, giggling and whispering urgently. As they reached the sand, they stopped, looking down the shore. The young man seemed to have turned around, and headed back their way. They stopped and looked at him approach. Salomé smiled. "Looks like the boy's got it going on."

Marina raised her eyebrows and smacked her lips. "Yes," she agreed, "he sure does." The girls fell silent as he drew nearer. Suddenly, he was standing in front of them. They all smiled.

Salomé was the first one to break their silence. "Hi," she smiled, holding out her hand. He took it in his and squeezed it firmly. "I'm Salomé. What's your name?"

"Caribe." He turned to Marina and cocked his head to one side, as he took her hand in turn.

"Marina." *Wow!* She stared, mesmerized as his dreadlocks shimmered in the misty rain. "Where are the others?"

He hated to lie, but he was prepared for that and just about every other question they could ask him. He shrugged. "They are all looking in the wrong direction." He stepped between them and started to walk off into the jungle. The girls stared after him. "Come on," he called over his shoulder. "The others will be surprised when they see you." You have no idea, he added to himself.

Marina and Salomé looked at each other. Marina had already sent out her invisible antennae, to see if she could pick up any negative vibration from the young man. No threat presented itself, everything was clear. The girls shrugged and stared after the young man. Predictably, they followed him.

The trail was lush and voluptuous, wet and vibrating in the pale daylight. The girls looked around them, minding where their bare feet stepped, keeping track of the male in front of them.

Salomé sighed. "I could eat him up," she lamented with a wink.

Marina smiled. "Behave yourself! He is younger than we are."

Salomé shrugged with a wicked smile and opened her mouth to answer. Marina quickly covered her mouth with a hand, and brought a finger to her lips with the other, as she jerked her head towards the boy, Salomé nodded, forcing herself to stop laughing at her sister. They giggled quietly a couple more times, and finally settled down. They finished their trek in silence.

Caribe walked across the clearing with a sure step. Everybody in the village was still sleeping, endlessly lulled by the falling rain. He went up the steps unto his mother's front porch, absentmindedly swinging the empty hammock in front of the window, as he rapped once on the front door. "*Mamá,*" he whispered urgently.

Leila opened her door wide, ushering them into her candlelit abode. "Come in, ladies," she welcomed in a husky voice. Letting the door fall shut, she walked past them to her rocking chair. "Before we begin, let me introduce myself. I am Leila. This is my son, Caribe."

Marina looked at the boy in silence. *Something is going on.* She met and held Salomé's gaze steadily, causing a frown to flicker on the other girl's brow. "I am Marina."

Leila nodded. "Child of the ocean," she replied softly. Caribe's breath caught in his throat. His mother turned her attention to Salomé. "And your name," she said with a smile and a wink, "can be found in the Bible." She turned to look at her son, mischief dancing in her eyes.

Caribe choked on a laugh, dreadlocks rioting around his head as he coughed. "Sorry, ladies. Private mother and son joke," he explained finally. He chuckled silently. The language, as well as the girl's faces as he had sketched them, had all come to him in a dream. A sort of tool to gain the advantage, so that the visitors were not immediately suspicious when contacted. This instance was extraordinary, however, he groaned to himself. These visitors were going to change things for them, in a big way. They just didn't know it yet.

Leila shushed her son. "Never mind, boy, where are your manners? Why don't you get us some coffee, baby? It is nice and hot, just right for a morning like this."

Caribe served them in wooden cups, grateful for the opportunity to keep his hands busy. "It looks like more rain, today," he finally said into the silence.

"Yes, it will," agreed his mother.

Salomé cleared her throat. "What exactly are we doing here?"

"Well, right now, we are having hot coffee to get our morning started," Leila answered. "How did you ladies like our storm last night?"

Marina relaxed a little, her breath escaping softly. "I have never seen anything like it," she admitted. "Does it always storm like that? I mean, is this a regular occurence here? And where are we, anyway?"

Leila laughed. "No, it does not always storm like that. Just on occasions are we blessed with what happened last night," she looked at both girls in turn, "and the things it leaves us."

"Good things?" asked Salomé.

"Sometimes." She smiled at Marina. "You are in *Encantada*. Welcome."

Caribe stepped in, interrupting gently. "Mamá, please let me show the girls around. I'll be back in a while, and I'm sure they'll have plenty of questions by then."

Leila laughed. "Go on, you. Let an old woman start her morning in peace. I will need all my energy to answer your questions when you get back."

The girls graciously thanked their hostess and followed the boy outside. Before they could say anything, he turned to them and held his hands up. "Okay. Here's the deal. I have something to show you. Just pretend you are in a..." he stopped for a moment, struggling to find the words. Although he had been given this blessed tool in his dreams, Caribe knew that the only way he could do it is if he didn't think too hard on what he had to say, and just let the words flow. But there were some things he didn't understand himself, and he felt he needed to be sure. "...movie set." There. He said it. He didn't know what it meant, but judging from the girls' excitement, it couldn't be anything bad.

"A movie set!" exclaimed Salomé. "What kind of movie?"

This, he was playing safe. "You'll see," he smiled mysteriously. Marina didn't say anything.

It had stopped raining, finally, but the jungle was drenched. Everything was dripping. Water fell from the higher leaves to the lower leaves, and to the ground. They walked in silence, taking a different path than what they had come in on. It was a friendly silence, however. The kind young people can fall into, even though they don't know each other very well. Caribe stopped suddenly. "Did you girls take history in school?"

The girls stopped and looked at him. "Sure," answered Salomé. "Does this have something to do with the movie set you are going to show us?"

He began walking away. "Everything." The girls followed.

"It must be a tropical setting," commented Marina, finally breaking her silence. "Is it an action movie, or romance, or maybe even a thriller?" she asked hopefully.

Caribe groaned to himself. "All of the above." Whatever that meant.

Salomé laughed. "Oooohh, I love thrillers. So, who's in it? Kiefer Sutherland? Robert De Niro?"

"Actually," Caribe cut in, "you don't know the people." He flashed her a smile. "But you will," he finished with a wink.

Salomé smiled and grabbed his arm, hugging it to her chest impulsively. "Caribe, you all right, baby."

Marina grabbed his other arm and smiled into his eyes. "Yes, you are."

And so, arm in arm, the improbable trio headed through the wet jungle into town, in the early morning hours.

Everything in town was still closed. The wooden buildings were dark from the rain, and water rushed in the gutters. Trash must have been collected recently, because the streets were relatively clean. Signs hung from chains on wooden posts, outside of businesses. They walked from a commercial area to a more residential one. The streets were wide, and the houses grand and mysterious behind towering walls and wrought iron gates. Plantations, almost. They reached the top of the hill, and stopped to catch their breaths. Caribe turned to the girls. "So, what do you think, so far?"

"Pretty elaborate set, mister," Salomé answered.

"Yes," Marina agreed. "Not many people around, is there?"

"Not yet," he answered. Next to them, was a small arch with a heavy wooden door. It was almost completely hidden from view by the most splendid bougainvilleas, growing wild on each side. The rain had shown no mercy on them and some of the small colorful flowers lay plastered on the now muddy, dirt road, while the rest swayed in the breeze, under the weight of the raindrops. "I have a surprise for you," he told them. Without waiting for an answer, he turned and opened the door in the arch.

The girls followed him through it, and stopped. They gasped. The view was absolutely breathtaking. The ocean was spread out before them, bordering the town they had just crossed. It was the color of polished steel, much calmer than the day before. Pale sunlight reflected off the water, the morning gathering up its strength. They couldn't believe their eyes. Before them, lay a harbor. An actual, working harbor. The real thing. Vessels bobbed in the water, as men bustled back and forth, like ants working hard, determined to beat the approaching heat. They were majestic. Ships like the girls had never seen before, or even knew existed. Their sails were folded, and the crow's nests seemed to be miles high. They had figureheads. Beautiful, detailed, carved works of art, painted in bright colors. New, as opposed to the faded, splintering antique ones they ever saw pictures of. One of the ships even had a skull and crossbones. Marina elbowed Caribe. "*Mano*, this is too creepy. It looks too real."

"It does, doesn't it?" agreed Salomé. "If I didn't know any better, I'd say it *is* the real thing."

Marina tugged at his hand. "Take us back to your Mamá, baby. Now I have a few questions for her."

Caribe bit the inside of his cheeks, keeping in the sigh of relief. He bowed, ushering them back the way they came. "As you wish..."

Jackson's eyes flew open, and his hand slammed on the snooze button. The alarm clock had just blared music, the blue LED screaming that it was 6:00 a.m. He closed his eyes again, with a sigh. He needed time to regroup. Dozing off, he chanted the girl's names in his head. *Salomé, Marina, Marina, Salomé... Salomé, Marina, Marina, Salomé...* The alarm clock screamed again, and this time he turned it off. Flinging his feet out of bed with a groan, he lay there like that for a moment, flat on his back, knees bent, feet firmly on the floor, eyes staring at the ceiling. *Please, God, guide me on this mission.* He sat up and got out of bed, slipping into the bathroom for a shower. He came out, clean and damp, head a little clearer. He slipped on a plain white T-shirt, and a pair of cut-off jeans. Dropping to his knees by the side of his hotel room bed, he continued his prayer. *I need help. I can't go home without them. Show me the way, please.* He crossed himself swiftly and got to his feet. Stopping to fill a backpack, he took one final look around the room. The girls' stuff was right where they had left them the day before. Tears came to his eyes. He shut the door behind him without looking back.

Out on the ocean, the men were silent. Quentin's heart throbbed heavily in his chest. His conscience was clear, as far as that in truth, he didn't kill the girls. But just the fact that they hadn't even been able to search for them sooner, felt each time, like freezing water icing over his heart. It didn't matter that it had been absolutely impossible to, because of the weather. The storm out over the ocean had been real. He felt like he had betrayed the girls because he had told them he would be back, and it had taken him almost twenty-four hours to do it. It burned in his chest, and stung the back of his eyes. He didn't want to cry in front of Jackson, but he may have to. He shook his head. Up ahead, a silhouette appeared over the horizon. "There it is, man. We're almost there."

Jackson didn't move. Actually, other than that he was in a vertical position with eyes open, he showed absolutely no signs of life. He was still as a statue, the outer body containing the tempest of his thoughts.

Quentin came in as far as he could safely go, and cut the motor. He knew exactly where he was going. Jackson observed him as he hastily anchored the small boat, and swam ashore. He beckoned from the beach, beginning to pace excitedly. Jackson followed him. He waded unto the sand, the waterproof backpack barely wet. "Right here, man, I swear to God, they were right here last time I saw them." He fell to his knees, sinking his fist in to the sand. His shoulders started heaving, and he gasped for air.

"Yo, man," Jackson said, falling to his knees beside him. "Don't freak out on me, baby. Just tell me what happened," he soothed, his voice rumbling. "Slowly."

Quentin looked up at him, tears trapped behind his eyes. He owed it to Jackson, he knew. Besides, he had the truth to back him. He shook his head and sighed. Sitting down on the sand with a thump, he began to relive the day before. He told Jackson what happened.

"I'm really sorry, man. Who knew this storm was going to happen?"

"Ever heard of the Weather Channel?" the older brother asked.

"Dude, I'm sorry!" Quentin implored. "It was a judgement call, you know? I didn't trust Todd to get back to civilization and tell anybody about what went down and where they could find us, and especially not you. But I know where we left them, and here we are now. Look at the driftwood behind you," he said, getting to his feet.

Jackson watched as Quentin hoisted two large sticks, one in each hand, and shook them at him, like they were proof. "Driftwood," Jackson shrugged. "What about it?"

Quentin threw them down in disgust. "Bullshit!" he exclaimed. "To you, it may be driftwood. And so it was, to me, also. But to the two butt-kicking mamas we ended up here with yesterday, they are fucking weapons!" he screamed. "That is why Todd left them!" His shoulders slumped suddenly, and he shook his head mournfully. "They actually threatened us with them." He looked straight into Jackson's eyes and straightened his back, chin going up with restored energy. "I swear to God, Jackson, we didn't harm them. Think about it, man. Just the fact that we didn't just fucking bail and not say anything. We faced you, man. That's got to count for something."

Jackson held up his hands. "Hey, chill, dude, I believe you, Quentin, man. Now just help me fix this. They're here, right? You left them alive, right?"

Quentin nodded his head rapidly. "Yeah, man."

"Well, Quentin..." Jackson clapped a hand on his shoulder and grabbed the other young man's right hand with his, pumping it briefly. "I am going to find them." He pushed Quentin towards the boat. "Now get the hell out of here, and keep your mouth shut."

Quentin stumbled in the water, not believing his ears. "What?"

"You heard me! Keep your fucking mouth shut. And the same to Todd. I don't want any gossip or rumors flying around about my girls. Nothing! The last thing we need is the cops to get involved in this before we know what's going on. You got all that? Now get the hell out of here!"

Quentin stared at him for a moment, and he released the breath from his body with a big sigh. He knew Jackson well enough to know that he meant every word. "What can I do for you, man?"

"Well, actually, dude, I brought my cell phone," Jackson laughed, holding it up for the other to see. He put it in his backpack once more, turning serious. "Truth, man, come check on me in a few days. We won't be missed for a while, but if you are true to your soul and sorry for real, come check on me in a few days." With that, he shouldered his backpack and walked down the shore.

Quentin looked after him. Feelings mixed and blended, and fought each other, inside him. Relief flooded him, that the matter was now out of his hands. Jackson was taking care of it. He felt guilty that this had happened to begin with, and God knew he would do anything to make it better. Fear teased his stomach, stilling his thoughts for a moment. He was afraid for them, but he knew they were survivors, their parents having trained them since they were children. Quentin swam out to the boat and headed back. He stole one last look at Jackson over his shoulder. All he could see was a black speck on the beach. *God, help us,* he thought. He would be back in a few days.

"So, girls," crooned Leila. "How did you like our little town?"

Salomé laughed. "Everybody was still sleeping, but it seemed quiet. It's probably not, is it?"

Caribe's lips twitched. "Not exactly."

Marina moved to stand in front of Leila. She went down on her haunches, her skirt bunched between her legs, until they were eye level. Leila pretended not to notice. Marina softly put her hands over hers, stilling them, making the older woman's eyes meet hers. "Talk to me," she said softly.

Leila sighed, excited and joyful. *This is the one*, she thought in amazement. "You better sit down, then," she chuckled, and waited for Salomé to join the other girl in front of her. They sat back and crossed their legs, not really understanding. "The things I am going to tell you are not for the faint of heart," she began, her hands moving in an invisible dance. "But you, ladies, are strong and brave. You have come far, to fulfill a plan, not of our own making." She paused, looking at each girl in turn, meeting their eyes and holding their gaze. "What did you feel when Caribe showed you the ships in our harbor?"

"Weird," answered Salomé. "I thought it was strange, how real everything seemed."

Leila nodded slowly. "That's what you thought, *bebé*, but what did you feel?"

Salomé thought for a moment. "That it was real." She glanced at the young man next to her. "But Caribe said it was a movie set."

Caribe shrugged. "That is the only thing you would understand."

Salomé frowned and tossed her head. "I'm not an idiot."

"No, you are just a female, in for a big surprise."

Leila clapped her hands, scowling at her son. "Now, children," she scolded. "This behavior is not making things any easier."

"I felt it was real, too." Marina looked at the woman in the rocking chair. "But how could that be possible?"

Leila smiled, rocking back and forth gently, again. "You come from an age and time where you see wonderful things. There are advances in all different fields that seem miraculous. You are witness to phenomenoms on a daily basis." She looked at Marina. "And it is because of all of this, that your mind would enable itself to open up to the possibilities of the unknown, the unexplored, the unheard of, even. Movie set," she added, "was just a term given to Caribe, to say to you, so the transition would be easier. Your instructions are to pretend. Just pretend you are in a movie set..."

"*What?*" demanded Salomé.

"You are now here, right in this place, and you have come to contribute something. You have skills, and talents, and knowledge we have no concept of. Therefore, your arrival here, being you two young ladies of excellent health and upbringing, must have a reason. Are you with me so far?", she looked up to see the girls nodding. "So, let us all pretend that you are here to share your wealth of wisdom. What have you got to contribute, girl?" she asked Salomé.

Salomé blinked her eyes. "Me?" she said, glancing at Marina. Looking back at Leila, her fingers absentmindedly plucked at her skirt. "Like what have I got to contribute to this place?"

Caribe leaned towards her, his voice low and friendly in her ear. "Pretend it's a job interview," he whispered. "Show her what you've got."

Salomé nodded. "Okay." She looked straight into Leila's eyes. "I'm a biology major. My concentration is botanical plants that can cure certain ailments, therefore making us rely less on pharmaceuticals. I haven't finished, though, but I'm familiar with the basic stuff you can obtain and use at home. I took a few classes in business administration, and in the future I would like to start my own business."

"What kind?" Leila asked gently.

Salomé shrugged. "Something in the fashion or beauty industry."

Marina rolled her eyes playfully. "She's a fashion model," she explained and stopped herself.

"Like her mother," interrupted Salomé with a laugh.

Leila widened her eyes at her. "Really? Is she very beautiful?"

Marina smiled. "My mother," she answered proudly, "is stunning!"

"Oh, my God!" Salomé agreed. "Marina's mom is teaching me everything I need to know, and she is so gorgeous, I can only hope to be as incredible as she is."

Marina shook her head with a smile at Leila. "Salomé is a model. Actually, a very talented and successful one, so basically, she can do whatever she wants."

Leila's bangles jingled on her arms as she reached out to brush Salomé's hair away from her face. "Marina is right. You have got it in you to do whatever and be whoever you want. What about your own mother?"

Salomé smiled, melting into the woman's caress. "My mom is a woman of medicine. She isn't thin like a model, but she is an exceptional woman with the kind of body," she said, as her hands floated over her breasts and hips, "that men kill for."

"You two sound very close. Are you related, or something?" asked Caribe.

"We were raised together," explained Marina.

He nodded. "That explains it."

"Anyway," continued Salomé, "I think I want to be a midwife, some day. I really love the botanical studies, though."

Leila nodded, the smile lighting up her eyes. "That's what you have gone to school for, and that is what you do. What do you like, though? What are you good at? Do you have any skills?"

"I play the piano, and I sing," Salomé answered. "I design clothes. I make potions at home for common ailments. I love children," she sighed, "and I love Tae Kwon Do."

Leila raised her eyebrows, but didn't ask any more questions. Instead, she turned to Marina. "What about you, *bebé*?"

Marina sighed. "I, too, love Tae Kwon Do. And children." She glanced at Salomé with a teasing smile. "Actually, now that I think about it, children like me better." They laughed. She looked back at Leila. "I am good at math, but that's only a basic necessity for daily life. I am good at organizing things, although truth be told, I'd rather be alone. I'm into astrology and I think that this universe is much more vast than we give it credit for. I love color, and I'm good at making plain things beautiful. I can't sing like Salomé, but I can paint and I can write. I am not afraid of hard labor, as long as it's honest. I believe in doing random acts of kindness. I would love to be a wife and a mother someday, because I would like to pass on the values I have been taught. I believe in God the Father, the Son, and the Holy Spirit." She looked at each of their faces in turn, before turning back to Leila. "Now, what's the deal?"

Leila looked straight at her. "A time warp."

Salomé shook her head, not understanding. "A what?"

"A time warp," she repeated, frowning. "I believe that is the term." She looked at Caribe for help. He nodded. "You remember that storm, last night?"

Salomé's eyes stung with tears, beginning to understand. "That wasn't an ordinary storm, was it?"

Leila shook her head with a smile. "No, it wasn't." She reached out with her hands and took one of the girls' in each of hers. "That storm is the equivalent of transportation to where you are, right now. When Nature exposes herself the way it did last night, it switches planes, so to speak. So you are in the same place you ended up yesterday, but at another time."

Marina gasped. "How do you know all this?"

Leila chuckled. "I am much older than I look, *bebé*," she teased. "I have lived here my whole life. I have seen many, as you."

"Well, where are they?" Salomé demanded.

Leila shook her head. "They are all gone. Some made it, some didn't, and others just left, on the verge of madness. This is not for everybody. Some people were just in the wrong place at the wrong time."

"Did they have destinies to fulfill?"

The answer was slow and thoughtful. "Yes, they did. Some of their destinies were not here, however."

"How do we know you are telling the truth?" Marina asked. "You know I am."

"What about our families?" Marina insisted. "They are going to die over this!"

"Oh, don't you fret, now," soothed Leila. "God has no intention of keeping you here, baby. He is just borrowing you for a moment."

"So how do we get home?" asked Salomé. "You just wait for the next storm?"

"When is that?" Marina demanded.

Leila shrugged. "You will know when the time comes."

"How do we know about all this? How can we believe you?" Salomé challenged.

Leila chuckled again. "Caribe, son, please get these young ladies a nice hot drink, will you, baby?" She kept rocking gently. "They need a little time to think things over."

Caribe did as he was told, and came back with two cups of hot herb tea. These cups were not wood, however, but shiny tin. The girls drank slowly and thoughtfully. Leila waited until they were finished. Caribe took the cups from them with a smile. "All done, ladies?"

The girls nodded their heads. "Yes." They felt miserable.

Leila took the cup Salomé had been drinking out of. She looked inside at the leaves in the bottom and smiled. "Look here! You are incredibly smart, but you hide it from people. I see a trail of men behind you, falling like flies." She grinned at Salomé. "And like flies you swat at them." She tipped the cup this way and that, the smile never leaving her face. "Everything you touch, you turn to gold. Success follows you everywhere you go, and it will do so here, also." She continued. "You will meet many people, and you will change the lives of most of them. But there are also other people, who love you passionately, that will conquer any obstacle to save you." She hid her expression as she caught sight of the beautiful tall black man with cornrows, in the bottom of the cup. Plenty of time for that. She turned to Marina. "You are meant to be here. There are people waiting for you here."

"For me?" Marina asked, surprised. She was shocked. How did she ever end up in a place, where people she didn't even think she knew were actually waiting for her?

"Yes, baby," answered Leila. "You will find here, everything you have ever dreamed of. You will know peace in your soul, like you have never before. Your spirit will evolve here, making you the woman you are meant to be."

Tears stung Marina's eyes, and her voice came out shaky. "Now, tell me how I am going to meet a tall, dark stranger."

The sarcasm wasn't lost on Leila, but she pretended not to notice. Caribe flinched and Salomé stared at her sister, never having known her to be rude. "You are hurt, and confused. You need time to think," Leila suggested. She looked at each girl in turn. "There's a lot of work to be done. I am sure you are absolutely overwhelmed, but know this. You are chosen. You have done nothing wrong, and you shouldn't feel as if you are being punished, or that only bad will come out of this," she paused. "Instead, think of this as the adventure of your lives." She held up her hand, as Salomé was about to interrupt her. "As far as your parents are concerned, do not fret over them. This is time travel," she winked at them. "You may go back just in time to have never been missed."

Salomé grabbed the old woman's hand, tears streaming down her eyes. "Are we going back for real?"

Leila stroked her face, catching tears on her fingertips. She answered slowly, making sure she was understood. "Eventually, it will be possible for you to go back. Eventually," she paused, "you may not want to…"

Caribe thought it was as good a time as any for him to jump in, and he did. "There are a few things you need to do. After you get organized and settle down, you need to go out and search for what you are meant to do here." He explained himself. "I don't really mean, actively search. Just keep your eyes open. There are no coincidences. There's a reason why you ended up here, and when the meaning is clear to you, you will know what to do. But you will have to go out and meet people, know your way around. For now, we have a place where you can live, just while you get used to Encantada. "

Marina's tears fell down her face, and she blindly grasped for Salomé's hand. "Were you waiting for us? How did you know we were coming?"

"I have been dreaming about you for a year, now," Caribe answered.

Salomé turned her face to him, shocked. "A year?"

He nodded. "Ever since they took Don Manuel."

The question was inevitable. "Who is Don Manuel?"

"My father." Caribe slipped an arm around each of the girl's shoulders and squeezed them tight.

"They took him? And who the hell is *they?*" Salomé demanded.

Leila squeezed her hand. "All in good time, *bebé*. For now, you need to rest. Absorb all of this, and make peace in your minds."

"But how did you know it was us?" Salomé insisted.

Caribe loosened his hold on the girls and looked at his mother. Leila pressed her lips together and nodded her head. Caribe reached into the pocket of his pants. He pulled out two sheets of papers and smoothed them lovingly. "I saw you."

The girls peered down at the drawings. Each paper held a bold, accurate portrait of each one of them. The girls screamed.

Jackson sat back and stared at the ocean. He felt he was in for a long wait. So far, there had been absolutely no sign of the girls, but he was never going to give up. He knew Quentin was telling the truth. The boy was too scared to do otherwise. And he especially believed the part about the driftwood. That sounded exactly like something they would do. He knew the girls could kick ass. Their parents had made sure they raised strong, active, assertive women, and not whimpering, defenseless females. Their parents had also made sure all their children learned survival skills. Out in nature, as in the street. It had been like a second school for the three children. Jackson paused to reflect on their families.

Their dads had known each other all their lives. Grew up together, spent time at each other's houses, their families visiting often. They had gone to school together, and even graduated from college together. Life had thrown them a curveball earlier on, and together, while they were still in school, they had ended up raising Joe's newly orphaned twin nephews, Deveraux Azure and Catamaran St. Jacques, better known as the *blue cat*. They were both, active sports men. Basketball, surfing, and Tae Kwon Do, they did everything together. They had even met their future wives about the same time. Joe Banks was a taller, heavier, more mature version of Jackson. He was a master black belt in Tae Kwon Do, running his own school in the evenings. In the daytime, he was a basketball coach for the local high school. And ever since his children had grown, he volunteered his time, reading stories to small children at the library in town, every other Saturday morning. The Saturday mornings he was home, he spent in bed with his wife, Shayla. Pablo Aguilar was his latin counterpart. Dark skin, black-as-night hair, he was good looking as only a latin lover can be. The children had heard stories all their lives of the inseparable two. Pablo was CEO of his own company, a manufacturer of computers and accessories. Business had been successful quickly, and he had treated his whole family to a better life. Joe had been included. To balance out his high-tech professional life, Pablo had pursued sports and extra-curricular activities with a passion. He got himself the best hobbies money could buy, and settled down to a good life. He bought a nice piece of land, and proceeded to build, made to order, two houses. His and Joe's. The houses had a little distance between them, giving each man the privacy they required, but secretly connecting the two houses, was a tunnel. The men settled down in their respective dwellings, immersing themselves in jobs and homes, and a nice bachelor lifestyle, even as they took good care of growing rambunctious twin boys, when they met their future wives.

As luck would have it, the women were best friends. A blessing in disguise. The one was curvy and voluptuous, her body belying her brains. Shayla had skin the color of mocha, and eyes like drops of honey. Her smile could melt your insides, and her scowl could send grown men running. She was a doctor. A woman's doctor, delivering babies for most of her day. Devoted to her family, she was a strong, generous woman, overcoming the handicap of her race, in a world that still shunned color. Her hands were soft and comforting, her voice soothing. Her hair a black cloud around her head, straight and long, her grandmother's Native American blood running strongly in her veins. Sloane, on the other hand was a fashion model and consultant. Raised in Hawaii, she was the all American dream girl next door. Thin as a reed, gracefully elegant, she was an avid surfer and looked it. Her skin was tanned, and her hair, also long and straight, hung to her waist in a rich, sun -drenched blond mass. Her eyes sparkled like two turquoises in her face, teeth always flashing white in a constant smile. Pablo had announced to his family and Joe's, the day after meeting her that he had finally found the mother of his children. She ran a talent agency in the daytime, making enough money to help keep them in a comfortable style, and when the sun went down, she was more than happy and willing to let her hair down, so to speak, and dedicate herself to her family. The women happily accepted the men and their twins. And so the men married the ladies, and proceeded to have a good life.

Then, came the kids. God blessed Joe and Shayla with two, first Jackson and then Salomé, while Pablo and Sloane had the one girl, Marina. But it was a comfortable arrangement. The connected houses, the parents' life-long friendships, and the unconditional support of four loving families; it all contributed for all the children to be raised together, a set of adored twins, and three kids with two sets of parents. Later on, an extraordinary set of circumstances brought a third girl into their lives, a young Oriental girl named Xaira Chang. She was received by the twins and by the Aguilar-Banks crew with unconditional love and fierce joy. The number of children, grown and teenage, at that point reached the half dozen. They all shared alike, and felt comfortable with each other. Parenting was shared equally among the four adults, and they were respected alike by all six children. Love was multiplied.

It was a good life. They didn't lack for anything. Physically, emotionally, or spiritually. They had been taught to take advantage of school and treat it as a friend, not an enemy. All three children were now in college together, each pursuing an interest or a career that would provide them with a future, and keep their way of life. They studied together, played together, and lived together. Throughout their growing-up years, the families had gone camping together, taken trips with each other. The parents had resourcefully pooled all their talents and skills, and passed them on to their children. They had been taught to be of social value; kind, respectful human beings, compassionate and considerate. They were grateful for all they had been blessed with and praised God constantly. They had also been taught to do without, to be humble, and to learn to make the best of what they had. To never lament whatever Life threw at them, but to make the most of each experience and trust God to take care of them. Actually, it was a fantastic life. And now this.

Jackson sighed. *I guess I have a lot of explaining to do*, he thought. He pulled out his cell phone from his bag, and fingered it. His arms lay on his raised knees and he held the phone in his hand loosely, rubbing the buttons with his thumb. He took a deep breath. The phone on the other end of the line rang a couple of times, before it was answered.

The familiar voice boomed at him, joyful and exuberant. "*Yo!*" Jackson closed his eyes, his heart beginning to race. "Yo!"

"*Jackson!*" His father exclaimed. In the background, rubber squealed on a court, while boys panted and grunted from exertion. "How's my baby boy?"

"Hey, man, just chillin'," Jackson forced a smile into his voice. "Just checking up with you, like I promised."

"Staying out of trouble, man?"

"You know it!"

"How're the girls?"

"They's chillin' too, man. This Spring Break deal is actually kind of cool."

"Can I talk to them?"

"Naw, they are unavailable, right now. You know females. One has to go to the bathroom and the other has to go to talk to her."

"I see," Joe chuckled.

"Hey, Dad, just one thing. We got invited to go camping on this small island, a bunch of us, and we really want to go. It's for a few days. The only thing I'm not quite sure of is the reception on the cell phone. There might be a lot of roaming. But I promise I'll get in touch, Dad. You cool with that?"

"Cool as a cat, baby. Just remember to call."

"Thanks, man. Give Mom and Mami a kiss. Tell Papi he owes me a game of one-on-one. I can't wait to come home and kick his ass." He could picture his father's beautiful face, head thrown back, as he roared with laughter.

"You got it, baby"

Jackson smiled. "'Bye, baby"

"Love you, Jax."

"Love you, Joe." Jackson stared at the phone in his hand as the call ended. He took a deep breath and looked up at the gray sky, the words screaming in his mind. *I just lied to my own father! Now, help me! Let me bring them home! Please, Lord, give me a sign...* He got to his feet with a deep sigh, and trudged on down the beach. To his right, lay the jungle, thick and menacing. Up ahead, were cliffs of rock. To his left lay the ocean, slightly agitated, disguising the ferocious power it had displayed the night before. Behind him, was pure beach, ending in the tiny cove Quentin had brought him to. He searched his instincts. Shelter. He looked in front of him again, feeling drawn to the cliffs. With a sigh, Jackson headed towards them.

The sun was shining a little bit stronger, a visible white ball in the silver sky, white and black wisps of clouds passing each other. The jungle seemed a little bit brighter, and the day was slowly getting warmer. It was beginning to steam as the sand stretched out, pockmarked from the recent bubbles that fossilized in the heat. Jackson stopped to change clothes. He automatically looked around him to see if anybody was watching, at first, but then he shrugged his shoulders as he remembered he was alone. First, he peeled off his white T- shirt and tossed it carelessly into his backpack. Then he took off his jeans, and stepped into surfer's baggies. The jeans safely tucked away, he looked around him one more time before continuing his trek. He was happy to discover that the cliffs were actually closer than they appeared to be. Stopping at the bottom, he craned his neck up. Halfway up, he could see a cave. His breath caught in his throat. Looking wildly at the rocks in front of him, he found it. Sunlight glinted on the trail that seemed to disappear into the jungle. He caught glimpses of it, as his eyes traced what he believed to be a path up the mountain. It was. He shook his head, and took a deep breath.

"Ready or not," he whispered.

The trail did end at the cave, and Jackson stopped outside. The morning sun over the ocean shone right into it. There was obviously nobody there, but he hesitated anyway, trying to organize his thoughts. What was he looking for? Any sign that they've been here, came the prompt answer. He strode inside the cave with determination. Looking around, he saw the same things the girls had seen, sensed the same things they felt. There were the candles and the matches, and evidence of people having slept there. An empty bottle of wine, water bottles, a matchbox with a burnt piece of paper inside. He smiled and shook his head slowly. Turning around, Jackson saw their bags. He sat down on the blankets and began rummaging in each one. Nothing out of the ordinary, really. Just your basic girl stuff like hairbrush, mirror, beach towel, lip balm, conditioner. Putting the bags aside, he twisted on the blankets he was sitting on. Standing up, he looked at them closely. They definitely looked slept in. Grabbing one in both hands, he bunched the fabric in his fists and buried his nose in it, taking a deep breath. The familiarity of the fragrance pounded on his senses. "I can still smell you!" he shouted at the walls. Throwing the blanket to the floor, he ran back outside hands cupping his mouth. "*Salomé! Marina!*"

"*What?! What's wrong?!*" Caribe asked, alarmed.

Leila chuckled to herself, and reassured her son. "It's all right, baby. They are just surprised and a little frightened to see proof of what we say. They will be fine."

Caribe sighed, shoulders slumping, head shaking mournfully. The girls were shaking, eyes wide, trembling fingers over their mouths. He smoothed the papers gently and gave them to his mother. "Here, Mamá, you better keep these." He stood up and took one of each girl's hands. Tugging at them gently, he pulled them to their feet. "Come with me, ladies. You need some time alone. We have a place all ready for you."

Leila stopped them as the girls turned away. "Marina!" She smiled into her hazel eyes, as she stopped to look at her. "You are going to meet a tall... dark... stranger..."

The girls followed him out silently, misery clear on their faces. Caribe led them to a couple of huts, just on the outskirts of the small village itself. People were already wandering about, just beginning their early morning chores. Some openly stared at the girls as they walked by with their tear-streaked faces, others barely gave them a glance. The trio went in a small, wooden gate, not strong enough to keep anyone out, really, but it gave the semblance of privacy. Caribe led them into the first hut. The girls looked around them sadly. There were a couple of hammocks and a rocking chair, a small table but no chairs to sit in, just mats on the floor along the wall. In a corner, was a stack of brightly colored fabrics. They turned to look at him. He smiled, holding up his hands. "Relax, ladies, just relax. Take some time to think about what is going on, and to accept it, basically. You are, after all, on a trip of sorts, and you have things to do." He hooked his arms around their necks and hugged them gently, before letting them go and looking at them once more. "You don't have all the time in the world, though. You have places to go, and people to meet. I suggest you take some time out to collect yourselves, and then, just go out. Either my mother or I will be more than happy to show you around and explain to you anything you need to know. Grieve now," he added. "You might soon be liking it here." He shrugged. "Who knows?" Turning around, he walked away. "I am right nearby," he reassured. "I will come back and check on you a little later. Things might look quite different by then."

The girls looked at each other, as they were left alone. Resigned, they began exploring. Their surroundings were quite primitive compared to what they were used to, but there was enough to keep them comfortable at a time where there were no modern appliances, no electricity, no internet. The utensils they found were made of wood and metal, a lone, beautiful silver fork among them. Dishes and cups were made of wood. They found a well in the back, in the middle of the lushest, most beautiful backyard they had ever seen. It was graced with banana, and lemon trees in the middle, while the borders were marked with more majestic mango and avocado trees. Back inside, they were more aware of their surroundings. Wispy lace curtains hung on the windows. The wood of the hut itself, was painted in bright colors, inside and out. On closer look, the colorful fabrics were breathtaking. The details were those of making the place feel comfortable and friendly. Single bamboo sticks hung from the eaves of the house, close together so they clicked as they swayed in the breeze, just like a windchime. In front of the door there was a mat of woven palm fronds, so fresh it was still green. On the walls hung assorted hats and baskets made of the same material, as the bowls on the table, in which the girls found fruit. A lot of love had gone into the place. Birds sang outside, and the bamboos creaked softly in the grove next to the hut. They could hear the faint gurgle of a brook running behind it. With a sigh, they each sank into a hammock and stared up at the ceiling, watching the shadows on the walls that appeared as the sun gathered strength outside.

"What are we supposed to do, Marina?" Salomé asked. "I don't know. This is overwhelming."

"Yeah, it is. Good thing we're not hysterical females" Marina chuckled. "Not really."

"Seriously, though. This time warp thing is kind of weird."

"I agree, but what's the option?"

"Well, how about, it's all a hoax. These boys planned all this, like it's some kind of reality TV show, or Candid Camera or something."

"You think?"

"Maybe, they got our pictures, and that's how Caribe got those sketches. They're going to string us along until the very end, and then they are going to surprise the hell out of us with TV cameras, some money, friends and relatives being in on it, and a grand prize for us being good sports."

"That sounds nice."

"You think so?"

"Nope."

Salomé sighed. "Me neither." She fell silent for a moment. "I guess this is the real thing, isn't it?"

"I guess so."

"So, what should we do first?"

"I don't want to just sit around here and mope. I don't even want to think about it. This is the situation we're finding ourselves in at the moment, so let's just go with it. We'll mourn later. For now, maybe we should just go exploring to begin with."

"Go back into town, now that there must be people around?"

"No, I'm not ready for that, yet. But let's find out more about this place.

Check out the surroundings. Let's get Caribe to show us around."

"Okay. I agree with you all the way. I don't want to think about it, either. I can't handle it right now. Let's go, I guess."

The girls swung their feet out of the hammocks and looked around them one more time in wonder. Just as they headed to the door, a shadow crossed their threshold. "Ready, ladies?" asked Caribe.

They explored. All day, that's what they did. Explore. Caribe showed them the jungle around the village, as he knew it. Trails led to mountains. and clearings. Highlights included an abandoned stone temple with a majestic waterfall close by. They stopped there to rest, before continuing towards the ocean. There, they marched along the shore and past the cliffs where the cave was, and back towards the village. Once in front of their huts again, Caribe smiled at them. "I hope you enjoyed yourselves, ladies."

Salomé smiled at him. "Very much, sir, why, thank you."

Marina pulled at a dreadlock, her eyes looking into his. "Thank you, Caribe. Maybe we should go out and get to know some people on our own, now."

His face lit up. "There you go. You are brave. I thank God for your visit." With that, he left them once again, and the girls were on their own.

They looked at each other, smiling as they started wandering. Except for the clothes and the primitive dwellings, it seemed to be a normal, regular day for the inhabitants. There were dogs in yards, yawning lazily and scratching in the sun. Little children stared at them wide-eyed, barefoot and naked from doorways, thumbs in their mouths, dark skin dusty in the afternoon sun. There was a gang of boys hanging out under a breadfruit tree. The light filtering through the splayed leaves, danced on their faces. They remained sitting on the ground, feet stretched out in front of them, the banter growing louder as they caught sight of the girls, their laughter leaving no doubt to the subject of their conversation. The girls ignored them, their carriage straight and regal, as they approached, straw sandals on their feet, flowers in their hair. The boys got to their feet as the girls reached them. They were the equivalent of teenage hoodlums in modern time that much was obvious, and the girls stopped in their tracks, as they proceeded to step out into their path, coming to stand in front of them. The girls looked at each other, eyes connecting as they transmitted messages to each other, smiles never leaving their faces.

The leader stepped forward, a huge grin splitting his face. "My name is Francois," he announced. "These are Kiko and Manuel," he continued jerking his head at each boy, over his shoulder. His eyes seemed to devour the sisters. "You ladies must be new in our village."

Salomé laughed, her feet unconsciously falling into fighting stance. "No, just visiting."

Marina moved, distracting them. "You have a lovely village. Do you live here?"

"Yes!" answered Francois, while in the background, Kiko and Manuel nodded their heads eagerly. "I was born here! " he exclaimed proudly,. "I would be more than happy to show you around."

"No, that is not necessary," replied, Salomé. "We already have someone here that is taking care of us."

Francois' eyebrows went up, making him look sinister, for a moment. He was shirtless and barefoot, as were his associates. His hair was nappy, short dreads standing up on end, sprouting from the top of his head. His eyes were pale gray, like the very first light of dawn, and the very last of dusk. Full lips pouted from under a generous nose, skin taut over high cheekbones, black skin shiny. "This village is quite small, compared to the town," he said smoothly, his hand motioning to the tiny buildings below them, visible among the banana and yagrumo leaves. Everything swayed in the warm breeze, so only glimpses were had. The girls followed his hand, and then looked back at him.

Marina smiled to herself. *He's a player.*

"It must be someone I know," said Francois, while the guys behind him looked at them expectantly.

"Could be," answered Salomé evasively. Marina looked at her, meeting her eyes. The girls mentally high-fived each other and looked back at Francois.

Annoyance crossed his face. "Does this mystery acquaintance have a name?"

"Do you always interrogate your visitors?" asked Marina in feigned surprise, Salomé's warm chuckle in her ear. "It seems quite rude, since I was under the impression that I was a guest in your village." She turned to Salomé. "What about you, my friend?"

"Oh, certainly, I thought I was a guest, also, what a shame. We really must speak to this lady and find out what is going on in this village, and why guests are treated this way."

Francois frowned, confused. "I didn't mean ---" he began.

Salomé cut him off. "As a matter of fact, Francois, you must know who we are staying with. It is the mother and son over there, "she said, pointing behind them. She grabbed Marina's hand and squeezed, biting her cheeks to keep from laughing in the poor boy's face.

"Goodbye, Francois," Marina gasped as Salomé jerked her along. She stopped a moment to put her hands on her hips and looked at the other two boys. She smiled at them "Goodbye, Kiko, Manuel..."

Francois suddenly grabbed Marina by the waist, jerking her towards him, tearing her away from Salomé's grasp. Salomé skidded to a stop and looked back, bewildered, hair flying around her face. Marina felt strong arms encircle her, and a hot breath on her neck. "Soon, it will be hello," he murmured.

That feels like a threat.

Suddenly, he rammed his hips against hers, crotch straining to rub. Marina felt her life-long training kick in, as she put her left hand agaist his chest. Her right foot moved out behind her, and with a swinging motion, her right hand came up in a blur, connecting forcefully with Francois' face. It all happened in a moment. Surprise had made Francois turn to follow Marina's foot with his eyes, so, because of the angle his face was in, her hand had connected with the corner of his mouth. She jumped out of his arms, out of his reach, and now watched him lick the blood from his lip, his eyes glowing. "I like this," he finally said.

Marina shook her head in disgust and turned to walk back the way they had come, her hand in the air, blocking her view of the three hoodlums. Talk to the hand.

Salomé reached her side and grabbed her other arm, hugging it to her, laughing delightedly at the outcome of their first encounter by themselves. "Damn, baby, you kicked butt, back there! Papi and Daddy are going to be so proud of you!"

Quick tears stung both their eyes, but they were determined to get this strange experience over with. "I sure did," Marina laughed. "Nobody's gonna mess with Thelma and Louise!"

The girls made their way back slowly. Following the line of the bamboo grove, they found the small river running behind it. There, they were amazed at what they saw. The bamboos had hidden the running water from view, and it was like a whole other world. There was a clearing that ended at the foot of the mountains. The afternoon sun sparkled on the glistening rocks in the river. There were women down by the water. Women all ages and sizes, around a dozen of them. It seemed like they had just finished doing their chores, mainly washing clothes, and were now beginning to head back to the village. There was laughter and singing. Teeth flashed white in dark faces, and beautiful cloths encased their bodies. The girls took a place on some rocks and watched as the women paraded past them, bundles on their heads or in their arms. Marina and Salomé smiled and nodded at each one of them in turn. The women nodded and smiled back without slowing down, some of them even waved. Their eyes were curious, but polite, being careful not to stare. The last one went by, and their laughter and songs faded as they continued into the village. The girls looked back at the river. There was one female left.

Actually, she seemed kind of in distress, now that they thought about it, as they looked closely. The lone girl must have been fifteen, if that. Strapped to her back was a baby, and incredibly, she was holding another in one arm. The other arm was busy with a pile of clothes draped on some rocks, at her feet. Next to her, skipping happily in a circle pattern, among some other rocks, was an energetic three-year old girl.

Salomé stared. "Is that their mother or their sister?"

Marina grabbed her hand and headed towards the girl. "Only one way to find out. Girlfriend needs help."

They reached the girl, greeting her softly, so as not to startle her. "Hello. May we help you?" asked Salomé.

The girl looked around surprised, and threw them a weak smile, turning back quickly to the little girl, who had now stood still to stare at the visitors. "No, thank you," the girl answered, shaking her head. Her hand shot out towards the little girl, who was now walking backwards into the river, her eyes never leaving the two beautiful strangers. "Ali! Come here, baby!"

Marina moved, circling the little girl, so as to stand between her and the river. The girl moved closer to the older one, who shot Marina a grateful look. Salomé put her hand on her arm. Teasing, she repeated, "Hello. May we help you?"

The young girl bit her lip and tears came to her eyes. She began shaking her head, but Salomé raised her chin and widened her eyes at her. The girl caught her head in mid shake and started nodding slowly, Salomé encouraging her. "Yes. I need help," she admitted, her voice trembling. She glanced over her shoulder at the setting sun, and a wail escaped her throat. "*Ay!*"

"What's the matter, baby, are you late?" soothed Salomé. "Is that it, *mami*?"

The girl tugged at the little one so she stood in front of her, and she then started beating the rocks frantically with one of the pieces of clothing at her feet. "I am late!" she wailed softly, trying not to sob.

"Aw, baby, don't cry, we'll help you," Salomé said, reaching out her arms. "Here. Give me the baby. My name, by the way, is Salomé. And that's Marina," she said, her voice soothing.

Marina reached her side and took the baby in her arms, while holding the little girl's hand. "Come here, babies," she sing-sang as she went back up to the trail. "I need to show you the most beautiful butterfly I have ever seen in my entire life!" she exclaimed, widening her hazel eyes at the little girl. The baby in her arms pushed back against her chest, looking at her as if he wasn't sure he saw what he just thought he saw. The little girl slapped her free hand against her mouth, hunching her shoulders as she stifled a giggle. The baby chuckled as Marina turned her widened eyes on him.

Salomé picked up a piece of fabric and held it up. She smiled apologetically at the girl, and shrugged her shoulders. "I don't know how to do this. Will you show me?"

The girl nodded, tears shimmering behind her eyes. "I will show you." She gave Salomé a shy smile. "I am Leilani."

So, while Marina entertained two out of three young ones, the other girls washed the clothes quickly, and came to join them on the trail. They headed back to the village, laughing and chattering. They reached what was obviously Leilani's house, and they quickly went to the backyard to hang the clothes to dry, on thick strands of ship's rope. Once that was done, everybody ran to the front porch, now awash with pink and orange from the setting sun, pretending it was a race against time, and they just won. They all fell on the floor, panting and giggling, the babies screaming with laughter, the little girl holding her stomach and rolling on the floor.

As they were still catching their breaths, a lone figure of a man caught their attention as it seemed to be headed straight at them. Everybody fell quiet as he came closer, stopping in front of them, his face stern and foreboding. He grunted, as his eyes skimmed all the children in turn, lingering a little longer on Marina and Salomé, before stopping to look at Leilani. "Is everything done?"

She raised her chin at him, her eyes challenging. "Yes, it is." She stopped him as he seemed about to say something. "You can check for yourself."

The man scowled. "I will." He strode past them into the house, staying inside long enough to see that everything was in order, and that there were clothes hung out to dry in the backyard. He came back out and walked past them without giving them another glance. Everybody stared after him, his graying, wooly head, catching pink lights from the evening sky.

The energy shifted as he seemed to disappear into the dusk. Nobody said anything as crickets started chirping and frogs began singing, in the quickly darkening jungle. The breeze flowed in, caressing their hot skins. Salomé spoke first. "Who was that?" she asked softly.

The voice was sad as it answered, "Our grandfather."

That answers one question, thought Marina. Out loud, she said, "Leilani, can we help you with anything, tomorrow?" She winked at her as she tousled all of the children's heads. "It looks like you are kind of busy."

Leilani laughed. "Maybe," she conceded.

The girls stood up to leave. "That settles it," Salomé smiled. "We will see you later."

They parted with smiles and hugs, and went back to where the hut where Caribe had taken them to, in the morning. As they approached, he appeared in front of them. "You must be hungry!" he exclaimed, laughing as the girls nodded eagerly. "Come with me. My mother is inviting you for your first evening meal in Encantada."

The young women eagerly followed him back to his mother's house. Leila received them with open arms, her shells clicking as she hugged them to her chest. "Hello, *bebés*, how was your day, today? How do you feel?"

"Wonderful!" exclaimed Salomé. "We actually met some people!"

"Who?" asked Caribe, genuinely curious.

Marina laughed. "Moe, Larry and Curly!"

Caribe frowned, confused. "Who?"

"Marina!" scolded Salomé. "Never mind her, she's silly. Their real names were Francois---"

"Kiko and Manuel," chorused mother and son, the older one shaking her head, the younger one scowling.

"Bad news," said Leila, setting a plate, heaping with fried fish, on her small table. "Who else did you meet?"

"Leilani, and some children she had with her," answered Marina, helping the older woman with a pot full of boiled roots.

"Those are her brothers and sister," said Caribe, picking up the wooden plates and passing them to the girls.

"No parents?" asked Salomé, as Caribe shook his head. "How sad! They are so young!"

Marina filled the tin cups with the cool water from the porcelain pitcher on the table. "So, who's the man with the attitude, who came by making sure all the chores were done?"

Leila stopped in her tracks. "You saw him?" she demanded. "You saw Jeremiah?"

Marina glanced at Salomé, and looked back at Leila. This lady is serious. "If you mean the scary man with the attitude, yes, we saw him." Marina handed her the cup. "Who is he?"

Leila pressed her lips together, looking at each girl in turn. "The grandfather," she said sadly.

The fish was exquisite. Fresh caught mahi-mahi at its best, flaky white meat, steaming still from the fire it had just been cooking in. The root mashed into a creamy substance. Leila proudly produced a small lead crystal decanter, with a yellowish liquid inside. She unstopped it, dribbling drops of the liquid on each of their plates. "Here is how you eat this," she smiled, swirling the liquid into the root, with her fork, until it was absorbed, like melted butter. She took some in her fork and tasted it, her eyes rolling with appreciation. The girls imitated her. As they had their first taste of their meal, they closed their eyes in bliss. Olive oil.

Dessert was fresh mangoes, and the cleaning up afterwards. was shared. Caribe approached them as they dried their hands on their skirts, just having washed their dishes. "Are you up to a little more excitement?"

"Yes!" shouted Marina, dancing around him.

Salomé grabbed his hands and pulled him out the door. "Lead the way, baby!" she laughed.

Caribe stopped at his hut as they walked by. The girls followed him. Just inside the door, was a candle on a table, which he lit with the matches sitting next to it. The room came to life warmly. The place glowed with a beautiful display of artwork. Colors and themes abounded as the walls held pictures of places, and animals, and people, and things in Caribe's life. The girls looked at them, in awe of being in the presence of such magnificent pieces of art.

"Caribe, *papi*, did you do all this?" Salomé asked.

He nodded, grunting as he looked around his abode. Finally finding what he was searching for, he pulled out three tiki torches on short sticks. "Let's go, ladies."

"Wait," pleaded Marina, drifting to a wall with a display of portraits that seemed to be different from everything else in the hut. She moved his hammock aside and ducked under it, to get a closer look at the wall. Salomé came up behind her, intent on the drawings in front of them. They stood silent for a moment, transfixed by the beautiful sea of faces, sketched in bold strokes, the spirit seeming to come through the portraits. Marina gasped. "Caribe!" she whispered. "Are all these people visitors ?"

Caribe towered behind them. "Yes."

"Have you met all these people?" asked Salomé.

"No. But my mother has."

"My God," laughed Salomé, "how often do these time warps come along, anyway?"

"These visitors," explained Caribe, patiently, "are from my mother's whole lifetime, and some from her mother's before her." He waved his hand in front of the papers, his hands casting funny shadows on the silent faces. "I have never met any of these people." He smiled at them. "You are my first visitors."

The girls smiled back.

They ended up at the beach. It was dark, and the line where the jungle began was completely black, even as the stars twinkled over the ocean. At their backs, the mountains were silhouetted with a line of fiery coral, from the blazing setting sun behind it. The three young people stuck their tiki torches in the sand and sat down. Caribe clapped his hands to get their attention. "I have brought you here, to share a secret I have," he grinned playfully. "It is a secret that has made me a better man, able to handle whatever, I personally consider, injustice Life throws at me."

"What's your secret, baby?" laughed Salomé.

"Tell us your secret, papi," urged Marina.

Caribe played along. "I will share with you my secret, ladies," he teased, "about how to make myself feel better." He stopped, while the girls clapped and cheered. "First," he finally continued, "you think of everything you are not going to have for a while. Things or people you are getting out of your lives. Things you may have to do without." The girls held his gaze, even as they squirmed inside. "And when you know for sure, what those things are," he finished, "you burn them."

"Burn them," echoed Salomé.

Caribe nodded. "For example, ladies," he said, brandishing with a flourish, a dried out palm frond. It was brittle to the touch, as he tore off a piece, holding it over his tiki torch. He held it there for a moment, in suspense, until the girls finally tore their eyes away from his hand, and looked at him. Flames flickered, and shadows danced on their faces. "I have here, my chance at school. Something very dear to me, that I cannot do at the moment." He shrugged. "I cannot feel sorry for myself every day of my life, because I cannot go to school right now." He waved the piece of brown leaf hypnotically over his torch. "So, knowing that it will happen when God wants it to happen," he said, prolonging the suspense, "I burn it!" He put the leaf to the fire, and watched it start to smoke, its edges rapidly curling, and finally catch one flame, before he dropped it to the sand, where it went out, tiny dots of red embers crackling along the out-line. "My friendship with Francois," he said suddenly, ominously, "has been poison in my soul. I need to say no more," he said, looking at them, as he dropped another piece of leaf on his torch. Without saying another word, he handed them palm fronds of their own.

Forewarned is forearmed. Marina tore off a piece of hers, and looked at Salomé as she waved it mysteriously over her tiki torch. "Ben & Jerry's Light Chocolate Chip Cookie Dough Ice Cream," she intoned mournfully, dropping the leaf on her torch.

Salomé laughed, holding a piece over her own torch. "Internet!" And so, they went back and forth. "Johnny Depp!"

"Air conditioner!"

"Hair detangler and conditioner!"

"Red lipstick!"

"Margarita on the rocks with Jose Cuervo Gold and Grand Marnier, salt on the rim!"

"Usher, crooning in my ear!"

"Mad TV!"

"Hot water!"

"Nike Air walking shoes!"

"George Carlin and Chris Rock!"

"Xaira Chang, Jesse Coltrane, and Catamaran St. Jacques!"

"Derek and Tyler Butler, Rashawn Blackmon, and Deveraux St. Jacques!"

And after a while, they were done, understanding, and grateful that Caribe had provided them with an outlet that they could use when necessary. They headed back; home, for now, you could say. Caribe said goodbye to them on their front porch. "There are two tubs of water by your back door. They have been in the sun all day, so the water is warm. We thought you might like to clean up a little, before going to bed," he smiled, as they squealed with joy. "Candles and matches are right there, by the entrance. I live close enough to hear you scream," he teased. "Seriously, just call out my name if you need anything. I will hear you."

They exchanged hugs, and goodnights. The jungle seemed explosive with a symphony of night life, never heard in the modern world of headphones they usually lived in. It was soul cleansing. The girls grinned, as they found towels and bars of soap. They washed quickly, and wrapped some fabric around themselves, in the fashion of a sarong. Climbing into their respective hammocks, they lay in the dark, laughing at the racket around them, swinging gently in the dark, a warm breeze blowing softly through a lone, open window.

"Today, wasn't too bad," Salomé commented.

"You are in shock," teased Marina.

"No, really!"

"You don't know what you are saying!" They laughed.

"Do you know what I mean, though?" asked Salomé.

"Absolutely," Marina agreed softly. "Tomorrow..."

"We are going into town, baby!"

Shadows flickered on the cave walls, as Jackson stared at his cell phone. It had started roaming earlier in the afternoon, and he couldn't get a signal. He threw it in his backpack, grumbling, pulling out a bottle of water. He had enough provisions for days. Training with his dads, he had known to bring along the basic necessities. Anything extra he needed, he could find in the girls' backpacks. He glanced down, at what he knew was his sister's. Picking it up lovingly, he placed it on the blanket next to it, guessing that it was there where she had slept. Using Marina's bag as a pillow, he made himself comfortable in her bed. He sighed shakily, as a gust of wind blew out the candles and the cave went completely dark. Of another shade of black lay the entrance to the cave itself, through which Jackson could barely make out the shadow of the ocean, but could easily hear the pounding surf below. He closed his eyes and fell asleep, dreaming of the day ahead, and what he had to do to try to find the two main girls in his life.

The next day, the young women went into town. Caribe had decided to stay back, claiming he had things to do. Leila took them there, instead, looking regal and beautiful in one of the nicer, brighter fabrics she had. Her dreadlocks glistened with some lotion she had put in them, giving off a nice fragrance. Off had come the shells and feathers, and instead, she wore a single gold chain, around her neck. The young women followed her eagerly, loving the freedom of their new clothing. They had only each other, to tell them how they looked, but Leila had confirmed that they looked beautiful.

"Are you excited? You are certainly going to turn heads, today."

Salomé nodded, eagerly. "Very excited."

"A little scared," admitted Marina.

"Not to worry, ladies, this is part of your mission. It cannot be fulfilled, if you do not go out and meet the very people you are meant to help."

"Is there a story we are going to tell people, about how we came to be here, out of nowhere?" asked Salomé.

"You are staying with me," answered Leila. "You are family that have come to visit with me, for a while. You got here a couple of nights ago, by a boat that brought you to the cove, but had to leave immediately to continue its voyage."

"Got it," said Marina.

They ascended the path into town, the same way they had the day before. This time, it was bustling with activity. There were people walking along the boarded walkways, along both sides of the street. Men, women and children. The girls gasped, suddenly overwhelmed by the sights and sounds. Women sauntered by the storefronts, in long dresses with high collars, parasols in their hands. Some of them walked alone, some of them had children hanging to their skirts, still others were escorted by men. These men wore white tropical linen shirts, with tight pants ending at shiny boots. There were yells as people passed each other, crossing the lanes where horse and buggies tread, along with riders on horseback. Amongst these people were others, wearing the bright colored sarongs, and white cotton cut-off pants, as worn by those from the village. These people hurried about, some with bundles on their heads, others with bags on their backs. They walked alone, or in groups, happily greeting each other as they passed by.

The first establishments they passed were a type of farmer's market, where people had tables spread out under old almond trees, singing out to passersby, trying to sell their merchandise. It ranged from fruits and vegetables, to grains, and already prepared breads and specialties. Among other items, were stacks of the beautiful fabrics, and artisan crafts, such as jewelry, tools and weapons, hand-crafted by the people of the village. The girls observed that although, everything was fantastic, very few dressed up people stopped at these tables. The people mostly attracted were loud, noisy sailors, and working girls. Past the almond trees, lay stables, and different shops, like a blacksmith, a tailor, a candle maker, beautiful signs announcing their different businesses.

Leila led the girls into the general store on the strip. The girls felt the men outside stare at them, as they entered the building. Being accustomed to admiration from males, where they came from, the girls looked at each other, before dazzling the men with their smiles as they stepped through the doorway. Tinkling bells announced their arrival. Inside, it was cooler in the shade. The girls looked around. Around them, stacks of shelves held bolts of cloths and fabrics, ribbons, boxes of exotic buttons, and colorful threads. Housewares sat side by side with exquisite scrimshaw carvings of whales and ships. Books adorned a whole shelf, right below a display of saddles and blankets on the wall above it. Behind the main counter, stood a young man, patiently listening to the rantings of an old lady.

"You are right, Mrs. Calloway, it is preposterous that the ship hasn't arrived, yet, but you know, after that terrible storm the other night, they are bound to run a few days behind. I promise," he continued, "that the moment the ship comes in, and your order reaches this store, I will ride out to your home and bring you here myself, madam," he offered graciously, as he quickly rolled his eyes at the newcomers, while he bent to kiss the old lady's hand.

Predictably, the woman melted under his flattering attention, and batted her eyelashes at him, as she swatted at him playfully with the fan in her hand. "Oh, Mr. Kline, you are such a rascal," she laughed at him, old blue eyes crinkling at the corners, shoulders shaking with mirth beneath a beautifully embroidered, cream colored shawl. Her hair was so white, it shone as if with its own light, piled high on top of her head. Her skin was wrinkled and lined with age, her eyes sharp behind glasses. She turned to look closely at the new arrivals. "Leila," she muttered, eyes raking over the woman dismissively. "Who are these young ladies with you, this morning? I believe, I have never seen them before."

Leila's laugh tinkled, as she joined the pair at the counter. Her voice was happy and melodic, as she addressed the old woman. "Why, hello to you, Mrs. Calloway, how are you feeling this fine morning?" She held out her hands to the young women behind her. "These are my relatives, coming to visit from Cayo Largo."

"Relatives?" Mrs. Calloway snorted, letting her eyes go up and down Marina's frame, lingering on the girl's bronzed face. "I see no resemblance," she added. She turned to Salomé. "This one looks more like you."

Leila laughed, genuinely delighted. "This one, Mrs. Calloway," she scolded gently, "has a name. Meet Salomé, and this other young lady, with all the sunlight in her hair, is Marina. They come from my husband's village."

Mrs. Calloway turned her still piercing blue eyes on the older woman. "Your husband, I see. Have you ever heard from Don Manuel again, Leila?"

Leila's smile never left her face. "No, ma'am, but my heart tells me, it will not be long." She held the old woman's gaze for a moment, before dismissing her, and turning to the storekeeper. "Good morning to you, Mr. Kline, how have you been?"

"Why, Leila!" he answered, obviously delighted. "What have I done lately to be so lucky, to have you grace my humble store?"

The girls studied the man, as he came around the counter, to hold Leila in his arms. He was tall and formidable. Bright blond hair graced his head, and brighter blue eyes closed, as he hugged her tight, smile soft as he whispered in her ear. Leila chuckled in his arms, seemingly tickled by his words. His shirt strained against his broad chest, sleeves rolled up his arms. Bright red suspenders held up dark pants, cuffs falling on a pair of worn, very old boots, His arms were massive, as they enclosed Leila, making her look like a bright jewel trapped between them. She caught his face between her hands, looking into his eyes before kissing his cheeks. "You never change, do you, boy?"

He agreed, looking sheepish. "No, ma'am." He turned to look at the girls, curiously. "I heard your names and that you are from Cayo Largo." He smiled. "Welcome to Encantada. I am John Kline, proprietor." He shook each of their hands in turn. "Please feel free to look around. I will be glad to be of any help."

"Thank you, John," Salomé grinned at him.

Marina nodded her head. "Thank you, very much, sir."

"Where is that ravishing young wife of yours?" demanded Leila. "You are not running her ragged as you usu ally do, are you?"

"Oh, no, ma'am, you have got it all wrong," he laughed. "My wife puts me to work."

As if on cue, a muffled voice called out from behind the immense wall of shelves in back of the counter. "John Kline, you better not be telling any stories," it warned. They all turned to look at the apparition behind the voice, as she joined them. The young woman was as small and delicate, as the man was big and tall. She was wearing an old, faded dress, faint flowers sprinkled over the fabric. Her skin was as pale as the moon, and her hair as black as night. Sharp green eyes glittered at them, in a friendly smile. Perspiration clung to her skin, and there was a dark smudge on her nose, from when she brushed her hair away with the back of her hand. On her hip was a beautiful baby boy, face scowling as he looked at the strangers from under thunderous eyebrows. His green eyes were fierce, and his ebony hair confirmed he was his mother's son. "Hello," she greeted, shyly joining her husband's side. His arm went around her automatically, holding her and his son next to his side with a grin. "I am Larissa Kline." The girls smiled back at her, delighted to meet this female, closer to their own age. "This is Max."

Leila stroked the baby's cheek. "Why, hello, Maxie, precious boy of Mamá that you are. How you have grown!" she exclaimed, coaxing a smile from him. "Hello, lovely lady," she continued, embracing the younger woman and kissing her on the cheek. "These are my friends, Salomé and Marina," she introduced. "They are visiting Caribe and myself for a while. How have you been feeling lately, baby?"

Larissa shrugged, shifting the baby from one hip to the other. "All right, all right. We are preparing ourselves to be real busy as soon as the ship comes in. We need to make space for our inventory, and there are just so many things to be done, there don't seem to be enough hours in the day!" The females around her all nodded their heads in agreement. "And then, there is this one," she said, rolling her eyes over the baby's head. "It will be a miracle if I ever get anything done."

John agreed, still smiling, but his eyes growing serious. "It is true, Leila. Success has its price," he said, also shrugging. "We cannot afford employees at the moment, and little Max is a hurricane in here, tearing the place apart, while Larissa helps me run things. She cannot do both things at the same time," he sighed.

"Oh, everybody hush now," Leila scolded, holding her arms out to the baby. "Why don't you just hand him over, and we will be absolutely thrilled to take him with us for a little while, so that you two can get some work done in peace." Taking the baby from Larissa, she crooned in his ear. "Come here, Max. bebé, we are going for a walk, so Mamá can help your Papá and get some work done, while we go out and play."

Larissa nearly jumped for joy. "Really, Leila? You do not mind? Are you busy?" she asked worriedly.

"Not at all. These young ladies have experience taking care of children, don't you girls?" she asked them.

Salomé nodded. "Yes, we do. We love children."

Marina cooed at Max over Leila's shoulder. "Can I hold him?" Before Leila could reply, the baby stretched his arms out to her, practically flinging himself from the older lady's arms. "I guess so," she answered herself, laughing.

"Are you sure?" insisted Larissa, a frown creasing her brow.

John laughed. "Woman," he rumbled, pulling his wife away from the females leaving his store. "Let them take the child, why don't you?" He embraced her from behind, burying his face in her neck, before leering at her. "We have work to do, in back," he added, wiggling his eyebrows at her, his huge hands slipping down to her hips, drawing them to his.

"John!" she exclaimed, scandalized, but thrilled to pieces, as she melted into her husband's embrace, a blush creeping up her neck to her cheeks.

The women laughed as they reached the door. "Do not worry," laughed Leila.

Salomé smiled at them as she followed the older woman out. "It was a pleasure meeting you."

Marina hesitated at the doorway, coaxing Max to wave to his parents. This wasn't a shy child, and although he glanced at them, he was mesmerized by Marina's face, his chubby fists already grabbing handfuls of her hair. "Thank you so much, for letting me take care of your baby. Enjoy yourselves." As she walked out, she heard the laughter explode behind her.

"We will!," John Kline boomed through the closed door, making her smile.

The group kept walking, even happier now with the baby's presence, keeping mainly to one side of the street. The other side seemed to be mostly of houses and apartments. As they walked, they began to attract a little attention, from males and females alike. Marina nibbled on one of the baby's ears, as he pressed his face against her chest, in delight. We must make quite a sight. And oh, what a sight they made. Women literally stopped in their tracks, and turned to look. Men, balancing on the back two legs of their seats, let their chairs fall with a thump, as they walked by. The women smiled and acknowledged the nice, admiring, respectful looks they received.

They completely ignored the negative, scathing looks of jealousy, and the naked lust in leering eyes. They kept walking, hips swinging with their happy gait, baby cooing uncontrollably. The day was even brighter, after the time they had spent at the Klines' store.

Leila stopped in front of another door. She hooked her arm through Salomé's, looking at her happily. The shiny black dreadlocks shook around her beautiful shoulders as she spoke. "You, my friend, are going to love this place."

"What is it?" asked Salomé, eagerly peering at the storefront.

'You will see. Come inside, follow me," answered Leila mysteriously. The girls followed her inside.

The place was splendid. High ceiling, from wich the most magnificent chandelier hung. Carpeted stairs curved along a mirrored wall, up to a dark second floor, gas lights intermittently glimpsed behind huge potted plants. Marina gasped, cradling the baby's head gently, against her. The baby, also in awe of where he was, was momentarily silent. He rested his head on Marina's shoulder, sucking the thumb of his left hand, his other hand around her neck, a fistful of hair still clenched in it. Max sucked faster, his bright green eyes looking around him. In front of them, beyond the chandelier, lay one of the most elegant rooms they had ever been in. The walls hung with decadent, beautifully framed mirrors, fit for a palace. Marina thought her eyes would overload from the majesty of the room. Those must cost a fortune. She kissed the top of the baby's head absentmindedly, and glanced at Salomé. "You're drooling," she whispered.

Leila chuckled. "Come, look closer," she invited.

Salomé went in like a zombie, stopping to stare at the walls. Between the mirrors, hung swatches of the most incredible fabrics she had ever seen in one place. In the corners of the room were wax dummies, the equivalent of mannequins, dressed with beautiful period gowns. "I've died, and gone to Heaven," whispered Salomé, beginning to move quicker, more excited. In the middle of the room was a round piece of furniture, back high, so that people could sit in a circle side by side, with their backs to each other. It was covered in the most delicious coral velvet, a trim of black fringe at the bottom.

Marina spun around, laughing, Max squealing suddenly, head thrown back to glance at her for a moment. He smiled at her, not relinquishing his thumb. As she ended her pivot, his head fell back on her shoulder. "This place is absolutely awesome! I wonder what it is?" She glided to the seat, and sat down, cooing at Max.

Suddenly, from behind one of the pieces of fabric, came out two ladies. The one in front took no notice of them. The other one frowned briefly as she glanced at them, but then rewarded them with a smile when she saw Leila. The first lady swung to stand in front of a mirror, eyeing herself critically. "I am not sure, Miss Swan, I am just not sure," she declared, exasperated.

Miss Swan went to put her arms around the other woman's shoulders, but not before an exasperated look fleetingly crossed her face. She was a gorgeous platinum blonde with sleek straight hair, framing an angelic face, blue eyes dark and deep, like the middle of the ocean. Her body was that of a stripper's, voluptuous and generous, even under her long skirt and long sleeves. The collar of her dress was moderate, and her breasts strained aggresively against the fabric that encased them, wanting to be free of the material.

Marina studied her closely. This woman wears full coverage as if she were exposing her cleavage! How does she do it?

"Now, now, Mrs. Seymour," crooned the blonde. "Give yourself a chance!" she exclaimed, putting her hands on the other woman's shoulders and looking at her in the mirror.

"I know! I know!" the other woman wailed. "It is only that the ship is going to come in any day now, and I so wanted to look my best for William, and I just wish Liana hadn't fallen sick, because she is the only one that understands my body ---"

"Mrs. Seymour! Please!" Miss Swan looked like she wanted to shake her. "Take a deep breath, now, darling," she coaxed the image in the mirror. "There you go, sugar, breathe, breathe." She squeezed the other woman's shoulders with a kind smile. "Excuse me a moment, while I greet my friend." She hurried over to the waiting women. "Leila!" she exclaimed happily, bending down a bit to hug the older woman. "How have you been, old woman?"

Leila laughed. "Fine, bebé, just fine. How about you? What is this I hear about Liana falling sick? I have not heard this."

Miss Swan waved a graceful hand in the air. "Oh, it is nothing. Just happened yesterday. I sent her home --- well, actually, Dr. Richardson did," she smiled, rolling her eyes, "with a fever. Poor thing is exhausted," she explained.

"So, business is good?" asked Leila.

"Very. It seems like I do a little bit better each time. Right now, we almost have more business than we can handle. I really could use an angel fallen from Heaven."

Leila laughed, and pulled Salomé closer to the young woman. "Dominique, meet your angel."

Dominique Swan stared from one to the other, until her eyes finally came to rest on Salomé. "My angel?" she murmured.

Leila nodded. "Salomé is a fashion designer. She comes from Cayo Largo and is staying with me for a while."

"Really?" asked Dominique, her eyes momentarily smoldering as they caressed the Salomé's face. Then her expression changed, a bright smile suddenly lighting up her face. "Welcome to Encantada, Salomé," she said, nodding towards Mrs. Seymour, still fretting in front of the mirror. "Show me what you can do."

Salomé turned to look at Marina, their eyes connecting. High five. She stepped up to the challenge. Smiling at Dominique Swan, she went to the other woman. "What seems to be the problem, Mrs. Seymour? Maybe I can help you."

Mrs. Seymour tore her eyes away from her image long enough to glance at Salomé in the mirror. "It's all wrong," she wailed, tears spilling from her eyes.

"Why, of course it is," agreed Salomé, making the woman start in surprise. "First of all," she explained gently, "black is not your color. Your skin is too rich and creamy, to be obscured by something so serious. What you need," she continued, drawing the woman's hair back from her face, baring her beautiful neck, and showing off her high cheekbones, "is something in a deep, rich, creamy, chocolate brown, that will make your husband want to eat you up."

The woman's tears stopped. Her eyes widened, at the possibilities, and a smile was born on her face. "That's exactly what I want!" she whispered. "But what about the style?"

"That's not right, either," Salomé declared, waving a hand in the air as she tossed her head. "Here, let me show you," she said, stepping closer to the other woman. Her hands hovering over her figure, their eyes met in the mirror. "May I?"

Mrs. Seymour waved her on. "All right. First of all, th is dress is cut way too high for you. You have a beautiful figure, and I'll bet you have a stunning cleavage. Why do you want to hide it? You want to look sexy, don't you?"

Mrs. Seymour gasped. "Sexy?"

Dominique turned her back to the pair, facing Leila and Marina with a hand to her forehead, her eyes closed in prayer. Marina buried her face in the baby's neck. Leila chuckled. Salomé ignored them all. "Yes, sexy. So what you do, is, you have your gown cut a little lower, and a little tighter, the better to show what God blessed you with, in a tasteful way, mind you, never to be mistaken for a shameless, streetwalking hussy..."

Mrs. Seymour watched, mesmerized, as Salomé's hands tugged at the front of the black gown she was wearing. When it was low enough, Salomé gently cupped her breasts on the sides, lifting them and pressing them a bit closer together. Mrs. Seymour smiled, as cleavage appeared where before, there had been none. She nodded her head firmly. "That is exactly what I want!" Salomé let her go with a grin. "Now, about the rest of the dress." She turned to Miss Swan, an innocent expression on her face. "Would you happen to have anything I can draw with?"

Dominique didn't miss a beat. "Why, of course, Salomé! I shall be right back," and with a twirl of her skirt, she disappeared back the way she came from. Marina met Salomé's eyes. High five. They turned, as Dominique reappeared, holding out a pad of paper, and a charcoal pencil. She handed them to Salomé, without saying a word.

Salomé turned back to Mrs. Seymour, eyes on the pad in her hand, as she scribbled furiously. "The style of the dress has to work with the shape of the model," she announced. "You, madam, are a beautiful woman with amazing curves." Mrs. Seymour blushed at her image in the mirror. "And you happen to be a little bit heavier than the current fashion allows, am I right?" Salomé asked, glancing at her. "I mean no offense," she smiled.

Mrs. Seymour smiled back, proudly. "None taken."

Salomé continued scribbling and finally, held up the pad in front of her face, studying it closely. She seemed satisfied with the result, and a smile lit her face. "So, you make your own fashion." She presented her sketch to the woman. The others rushed to look over her shoulder. On the paper, was a beautiful gown, with a low cut bodice, and an empire waist. The hem seemed to brush the floor, and only straps were there to hold it up. It was simple in design, and pleasant to the eye. Salomé pointed at the sash she had drawn on the empire waist. "This is to cover this," she tapped the woman's sides a little, with her wrists. "And this," she continued, pointing at the neckline of the dress, "is meant to draw the eye away from that little problem area, and up to where it counts." She relinquished the pad to Mrs. Seymour, and stepped towards the mirror. Next to it, hung the richest, coffee colored velvet they had ever seen. "Now, imagine that," said Salomé, fingering the fabric lovingly, "in this."

Mrs. Seymour nodded, pointing at the sketch in the pad. She beamed at the women around her. "That is exactly what I want!" Turning to the blonde woman, she rewarded her with a dazzling smile. "I will be the envy of my friends and enemies," she laughed mischievously. Tears shone in her eyes. "Thank you. You have my measurements. I will be back in a couple of days." And she disappeared back the way she had come from, to remove the tormenting gown, and change back into her own clothes.

Dominique Swan stared at Salomé. "You are hired!"

Outside, people stared as they shouted with happiness. "I have a job, girl!" cried Salomé.

Marina held her hand out in front of her. Salomé slapped it. "Way to go, mami!"

Leila put her arm around Salomé's shoulders. "I am proud of you!" Max sucked on his thumb in his sleep.

A little further down, the town seemed to open up into a sort of plaza. In the middle of it, stood a very small building made of wood, a little bigger than a hut. It was alone, nothing next to it. The cross in front of it, made sure everybody knew what it was. "A church!" whispered Marina. "Can we go inside?"

Leila smiled at her eagerness. "We can, and we are."

The women reached the church, just as a couple of cowboys rode up on their horses. The two men dismounted, and turned to smile at Leila. "Mamá!" they laughed.

"Oh, stop, you are such boys, the both of you!" she laughed. Turning to the girls, she made the introductions. "Ladies, these are the two single, most important men of Encantada. This, is Pedro Barbosa," she said, pointing to the taller of the two men. "He is the law." She beamed at him. "These are, Marina, and Salomé. They came to visit from Don Manuel's village in Cayo Largo."

Pedro Barbosa was tall and muscular. He was younger than you would expect a lawman to be, but he exuded authority, like nobody his age, that they had ever met. Black hair hung straight, from under his cowboy hat. His brown eyes were shaded by the brim, as they smiled at the young women. He actually touched his hat and nodded his head at them.

Marina raised her eyebrows, as she cradled the baby in her arms, and smiled. *No way! This is awesome!*

"Ladies... Pedro Barbosa, *a la orden.*" He smiled at them, from behind an attractive stubble on his rugged face. "Welcome to Encantada. I hope your stay here is pleasant and memorable."

The girls murmured their appreciation, and tore their eyes away from the lawman, to look at the other man, standing next to him. This one was a little bit shorter, but just as powerfully built. Beneath his cowboy hat, his hair hung also, straight, so he strongly resembled Pedro Barbosa. He also had an attractive stubble, but his features were softer, as if he were more at peace with himself. His brown eyes shone kindly.

Leila squeezed his arm. "This is, Padre Ignacio," she announced happily. The priest snatched the hat off his head and beamed at them, the smile brightening his whole appearance, dusty as it was from his recent ride. He bowed over each of their hands, kissing them respectfully. "Ladies…"

"Padre Ignacio!" Leila hissed into his face.

The padre, startled, frowned at her. "Leila?"

"My friends here, arrived in the storm, the other night."

The men seemed to freeze. They stared at the girls. Salomé shot a glance at Marina. They took a step backward. *They're looking at us, like we are aliens.* The men still didn't move. The girls took another step backward. Leila looked from one to the other. Another step. Pedro Barbosa was the first one to react. He grabbed hold of one of the girls' wrists in each of his hands, and hauled them behind him, into the church. The girls stumbled after him, as Leila and Padre Ignacio followed. The priest slammed the door behind them, shutting them away from the rest of the world.

"What is going on?" demanded Salomé, as the priest lit a candle. To her surprise, there were tears in his eyes, and a beatific smile illuminated his face.

"I have prayed for so long, to be blessed with the experience of meeting a visitor," he told them, voice trembling. "I will always be Your Servant, Lord," he continued, directing his voice to the altar, "thank you for blessing me in this hour of need." He looked at the girls. "Come, please, let me bless you." The girls followed him to the altar. There, he quickly lit incense. Holding a silver vessel in his hand, he sprinkled holy water on the girls, making the sign of the cross over their heads. "In the name of the Father, the Son, and the Holy Spirit," he intoned. "Thank you, Father Almighty, for bringing these women to us, that they may help us, Lord, that they may assist us, Lord, and that they may show us the way. Please, let their stay here be safe and happy, as they too, travel the path that brings them closer to You, oh, Lord. We thank you in the name of your Son, Jesus Christ, who with You, reigns in the kingdom of the heavens, forever and ever, Amen."

"Amen," they all chorused in response. Salomé and Marina smiled at each other, a sense of peace washing over them as they accepted the blessing.

Padre Ignacio cleared his throat. "Ladies, your secret is safe with us. Enjoy your visit in Encantada," he said, hurrying to blow out the candle and open the door to the church, once more, before any curious passerby stepped in, looking for either of the owners of the horses outside.

Leila laughed as they stepped back outside. "Thank you, Padre Ignacio.

Please come by and visit for a cup of coffee, some time."

The padre winked at the girls. "I will! I am anxious to get to know our visitors better, and maybe exchange ideas about our different cultures?" he asked hopefully.

Salomé laughed. "Think you can handle it, Padre?"

"Salo!" Marina apologized. "She is a joker."

"Let us see how it goes," said Leila.

"Anything you ladies may need," said Pedro Barbosa, "please feel free to ask."

"We will," they promised. And away, they went, on their merry way, leaving the men staring, behind them.

They stopped for lunch at a vendor, buying fresh fried fish, along with chunks of bread. After making their purchases, they stopped to eat at a tiny park in the residential area Caribe had taken them to, the day before. They sat on some marble benches facing the harbor, where men seemed to be busier than they had been, prior to that. The ladies munched contentedly, quietly. Max slept on. Once they had finished and disposed of greasy paper bags and napkins, they continued with their outing.

Next up, were the docks. Leila took them right next to the ships they had seen yesterday. The girls craned their necks, in awe of the majesty of the vessels. The crow's nest looked tiny from where they stood, as the mast pole disappeared into the sky. The timbers creaked, and water lapped against the sides, where small sea animals clung to the green slimy moss draped over the wood. That they were impressive, was to say the least. Nothing in their modern twenty-first century world, had personally exposed them to something like this. In their time of Universal Studios' thrilling themes, nothing had ever quite looked like this. Men bustled all over them, like working ants. There seemed to be a sense of urgency, as arms wiped off the sweat from shiny faces. Bare-chested men grunted, bulging muscles straining, doing hard labor. As it happened anywhere they ever went to, some men stopped what they were doing to leer and shout out sexual innuendos, while the more responsible ones smiled at them appreciatively, and continued working. After a while, the girls shook their heads and joined Leila, who was waiting for them at the end of the dock. They kept walking, slowly, looking at the businesses in the area. They were obviously in the middle of what seemed to be an important seaport. Around them, people of different nationalities chattered in all kinds of languages. It wasn't an extremely large seaport, of course, being on an island, but from what they could see, from the men and women milling about, it seemed to be a somewhat wealthy one.

Their next stop was unmistakable. It was a two-storied building, faded paint peeling in the wind. The balcony upstairs was dripping with females draped over the railing, their costumes leaving no doubt as to their trade. Salomé and Marina looked at each other, and rolled their eyes. The women in the balcony squealed as they caught sight of Leila. Actually, they made such a racket, that the men sitting below the balcony left their chairs to crane their necks up and see what all the noise was.

"Girls!" scolded Leila. "I just came by to tell you, that I will have your orders ready by next week," she called to them, stopping in front of the entrance. The women expressed their disappointment, and continued with what they were doing.

The ground floor announced itself as a tavern. The entrance consisted of elaborately carved swinging doors, flanked by a pair of formidable, tobacco shop wooden indians. Panes of glass adorned the windows, where the name of the establishment read in exquisite lettering, done by hand in gold paint:

The Siren's Lair

"Kudos to the commercial artist," murmured Marina. Receiving no reply, she turned to Salomé. Seeing her friend stand so still, she stepped closer, shifting the sleeping baby from one shoulder to the other. Max sucked at his thumb rapidly, for a moment, before settling down again.

Salomé stood transfixed, as if struck by lightning. The wind blew her hair around her shoulders, but she still did not move, her eyes never wavering from the scene in front of her. To the left side of the entrance, was a row of chairs against the wall. They were each occupied by a male, all apparently coming from different walks of life. In the middle, sat an Indian, not unlike the wooden ones guarding the establishment, but one of flesh and bone. He was impressive, to say the least. His blacker than black hair hung in a single braid down his back. Intense black eyes, peered back at Salomé, from beneath a black cowboy hat with a lone feather tucked into the band. He seemed to be just as shocked as she was. His skin was a beautiful, rich copper, leather armbands accentuating his muscles, his sleeveless shirt gaping open against a massive chest, beaded with sweat. A thick leather cord encircled one wrist, and a string of turquoise beads graced the other. His hands had been working on a piece of wood he was whittling on his lap, but they had slowed down with the group's arrival, and were now still. Cotton pants, such as those worn in the village, hugged his massive thighs. Salomé let her eyes travel over the man, roaming, taking their time, almost rude in her persistent observation. When their eyes finally met, it seemed as if they both held their breaths. Marina's skin tingled, as she watched everything unfold, her heart connected to her sister's, as never before. She murmured in the baby's ear as he fretted in her arms, dreaming.

Salomé finally smiled at the man, dazzling him with her beauty, as all who were present witnessed. He smiled back slowly, intimately, his eyes never leaving hers. Salomé felt herself grow warm in familiar places. "Hey, baby..." she drawled.

"Hey..." the deep voice answered, making her feel as if he had just coated her with honey.

Salomé took a step toward him, and he stood from his chair, towering over them. His hands fell to his sides, useless, knife in one, wood in the other.

Leila laughed softly, easing the moment, calling attention to herself. "Indio, how you have grown, *bebé*," she teased.

The young man tore his eyes away from the beautiful girl in front of him, and turned to Leila, his eyes crinkling at the corners, as he laughed. "Leila!" he exclaimed, bending down to hug and kiss her. "You barely come to town anymore. We don't see you enough," he said.

Leila peered into his eyes anxiously, seeming to search for something.

"That is right, baby, things are not the same anymore." She took his ravishing face between her hands, and kissed his forehead. Changing the subject, she smiled brightly and gestured at the girls. "These," she announced, "are my family from Cayo Largo. They come from my husband's village, and will be staying with me for a while." Playfully, she pulled Marina in front of him. "You know Master Maximillian Kline, don't you?" she asked, presenting the sleeping baby.

Indio walked around Marina, bending down to peer at the baby, until he was eye-level with him. His voice was hushed, and awed. "Good afternoon, Master Max," he whispered, caressing one tiny hand with his finger, the sun kissed digit contrasting darkly against the baby's white skin. "It is a beautiful day, and your companions are lovely," he added. The baby sucked on his thumb contentedly, snuggling deeper into Marina's shoulder, at the sound of the brave's soft, rumbling voice. Indio looked at Marina, and both pairs of eyes crinkled at the corners, in shared amusement.

"Marina," said Leila, providing her name.

"Marina," repeated Indio in a whisper, backing away from the sleeping baby, and giving her a bow, the smile never leaving his eyes.

"Indio," Marina whispered back, with a nod. She moved to the side, leaving her sister standing by herself.

Leila drew out the suspense. "Salomé," she finally smiled.

The couple approached each other, until they were as close as they could get, without actually invading each other's space. Indio looked into Salomé's eyes, mesmerized for a moment.

The men he had been sitting with snickered. One of them called out encouragement. "Say something, man! Cat got your tongue?" Loud laughter followed.

Indio didn't seem to notice, as he absently put what he was holding on the ground beside him, never taking his eyes off the girl. He took her hand in one of his and brought it to his lips, while the other one touched his heart, their eyes still connected. His lips clung to her hand, before raising his head. "Salomé..."

The smile they shared lit up her face, gracing her mouth. "Indio..."

It was an awkward moment suddenly, where anything beyond that could become clumsy or embarassing, so Leila stepped in. "We are on our way back home, right now. Since morning we have been here, visiting with people. But now, we must head back."

Indio looked at Leila, eagerly, the words stumbling out. "They are staying with you?"

The women did all they could to not laugh in his face at his expression. As sophisticated women that they were, they managed not to. "Yes, baby," Leila answered, "they are staying with Caribe and I." Indio glanced at Salomé, a fire beginning to smolder in his eyes. Leila caught his chin in her hand, and gently turned his face so his eyes met hers. "Does this mean I can expect a visit from you, soon?"

Indio blushed, embarassed at the gentle teasing. "Maybe," he admitted.

Leila raised her eyebrows and rolled her eyes at him. They laughed, and the women began to slowly move away. "Indio," Leila said at last. "When is Carlitos coming home?"

Indio answered absently, his eyes, once more, all over Salomé. "Any day..."

On the way back, Dominique Swan stepped out of her store, as they passed by. "Salomé!" The group stopped in front of the woman. She was smiling, anxious to speak to them, before they walked off. "How soon will you be able to work? Could you possibly start tomorrow?"

Salomé nodded, pleased. "Why, of course, Miss Swan, I will be delighted to join your team, and contribute my ideas and experience to your business." She held out her hand, professionally.

Dominique shook it with a smile, secretly impressed at the young woman's presentation of herself. "Excellent, Salomé, I will expect you in the morning."

They said their goodbyes, and the women made their way slowly, going back the way they had come. It was still early, and the sun still shone strong on the Klines' front window. The bells tinkled against the door when they entered, just as they had, hours before. The place seemed deceptively calm, as there were signs of customers having been there. "Hello," called Leila.

John Kline grinned from behind the counter. "Hello," he laughed. "How was your day?"

"Fine, fine," smiled Leila. "How was yours?"

With a big grin on his face, John put his finger to his lips to silence them. When he got their attention, he rolled his eyes, hands over his heart, and smacked his lips. The women laughed, as the beautiful Larissa made a sudden appearance, from the back of the store. Not having to see her husband, to guess what he was up to, she playfully shook a fist at him. "John," she warned. "You are not saying anything you shouldn't to our visitors, are you?"

He grinned at her. "No, darling, I haven't said a word."

Everybody laughed. Sleeping Max exchanged arms, and settled down, finally, in his mother's. Larissa looked at the women. "I do not know how to thank you!" she exclaimed softly. "Besides, a little time for husband and wife," she admitted shyly, "we actually got a lot of work done. Cleaned shelves and displays, rotated the inventory, and made room for the new merchandise we ordered. Gaitano should be here any day now," she explained, "and we are finally ready. How can I ever thank you?" she asked them. Turning to Marina, she squeezed the young woman's hand. "I appreciate this, from the bottom of my heart."

Salomé stepped in. "Actually," she said to John Kline, confidentially, "we really could use some pants, like the boys wear in the village." She explained, as she caught sight of the frown on his face. "Where we come from, women wear them all the time."

The store owner shook his head, the smile never leaving his face. He bent down, reaching beneath the counter, coming up with half a dozen of the garments, clean, new, and neatly folded. "Here you go, ladies, on us."

"Is there anything else?" Larissa insisted.

Marina shook her head, smiling at the woman's sincerity. "Hush," she whispered, winking at the glowing, young mother, "you will wake up Max."

The trip back to the village was pleasant, silent for the most part, as each woman was lost in her own thoughts. Once they reached the village and reached the path that led to the river, the girls parted ways with Leila. They went down the trail, to where the women were laughing and singing, in the middle of their chores. Suddenly, behind them, came Leilani, stumbling as she balanced babies and bundles, all at one time. Little Ali ran next to her, bravely trying to keep up. Leilani stopped short as she caught sight of her new friends. Without a word, Marina took one of the babies and Ali, while Salomé took the clothes from Leilani, leaving the girl to follow her, with the other baby on her back. The women welcomed Salomé with laughter and banter. Marina smiled as she listened to the voices calling to each other at the riverside. *I guess we have just been accepted.* She kissed the nappy head on the baby against her chest, and grinned at the little girl looking curiously up at her. Their routine that day, only varied in that, when it was time to leave, the group left with the rest of the singing, laughing women. Once again, they helped Leilani tend clothes on the ship's ropes in the backyard, and went to sit on the front porch.

Marina smiled as she watched the babies crawl towards each other, stop, gurgle at one another, and keep going their separate ways. They were twin one-year old boys, the only thing distinguishing them, similar birthmarks in different places. Juan had his on the nape of his neck, while Jaime had his on the side of his face. Small beauty spots, nothing major, but clear marks, to tell them apart.

They are adorable.

"Incoming," announced Salomé suddenly. Everybody turned to look at the man approaching with slow determination. The white wool covering his head was unmistakable. It was much earlier than the day before, the sun higher in the sky, but here he was, coming down the narrow lane, like it was nobody's business.

"I knew it!" Leilani hissed quietly, her eyes defiant. "I did good, yesterday, having everything done when he came by," she explained in a hushed tone. "That was too much for him."

They fell silent, as the man came up to them. This time, no words were exchanged. The grandfather marched up the rickety steps to the balcony, and strode into the house. Once again, he was inside, long enough to check everything carefully, and take a look at the backyard. When he came back outside, he seemed uptight. The expression on his face was stern, his eyes raking over Marina and Salomé rudely. Without saying another word, he left. Like the day before, nobody said anything, right away. The babies climbed into laps, Leilani brushing back her little sister's hair. When the breeze finally blew the man's negative energy away, they all looked at each other with a sigh of relief, and smiled.

"We," announced Salomé with a smile, stroking the younger girl's face, "will be back tomorrow."

The girl nodded. They said their goodbyes, and parted ways.

Later that afternoon, the beach beckoned to them. Changing from their beautiful sarongs into the pants the Klines had just given them, and camisoles Leila had thoughtfully provided for them, they followed Caribe through a back way, out of the village, and into the jungle. "What I am about to show you, is a special place," he had announced mysteriously. "It is a secret place I will share with you, where you can be alone." And so, they marched quietly through the jungle, until they came to a small clearing, the nicest they had encountered so far. They weren't far from the ocean. They could hear it, and actually catch glimpses of the waves at a distance, among the thick foliage. But what caught their attention, what made them cry in delight was the small pool in front of them. And a pool it was. The bottom was sandy, and the water was crystal clear, sparkling turquoise, rimmed by rocks and logs, stone ledges and fallen trees. There was slight movement to the water, but not enough to disturb its tranquility. The girls watched Caribe as he shimmied up a tree, feet planted firmly where there was no moss, hauling himself up with a vine. When he got to where he wanted, he swung from a branch, letting himself drop into the water, like a cannonball. The girls screamed with laughter, immediately joining him. The water was delicious, warm from the sun, with faint threads of cold currents teasing their skin as they wrapped themselves around their ankles and calves. Soon, the trio was swimming laps, back and forth, slowly, synchronized, side by side. Exhausted, they finally hauled themselves out of the water, and stumbled back to the village. The girls thanked their chosen guide, before parting ways, and getting ready for the evening.

"You know, I can get used to this," Salomé said, shaking her wet hair, as she sat on the steps of their balcony. The breeze had died down earlier, making the whole afternoon still, but there was a new evening wind, beginning to announce itself, gently. The bamboo whispered in their grove. Over by the breadfruit trees, a small cloud of lazy mosquitoes, hung suspended in the fading light. Down the path, a dog fight broke out, vicious snarling ending, as yells broke the afternoon silence.

Marina smiled. "You?" she teased. "Naaww…"

Salomé laughed. "Hey!" She tossed her head back, closing her eyes to the fading sun. "Do you know what I mean?"

"Yes, *mami*, I know exactly what you mean."

They fell silent for a moment, each one engrossed in her thoughts. "What do you miss the most?"

The answer came back instantly. "Our parents, and Jackson. In light that we are in a situation too incredible, beyond anybody's wildest imagination, nothing else matters."

Salomé looked at her sister, nodding solemnly. "Right…"

"But that guy we met today, was really cute," Marina teased. Salomé laughed. "Boy definitely's got it going on!"

"I think he liked you."

"I hope he did."

Later that evening, after a light meal of assorted fruits, the young women found themselves, once more, in Leila's cabin, asking questions.

"Leila," Marina began, "can you tell us some things? We have been here two days already, and the only thing that is working for us is not thinking about it."

"That works," agreed Leila, winking at her, as her hands busied themselves with the shells and strings on her lap. "What kind of things would you like to know?"

"I," declared Salomé, "want to know all about that beautiful indian boy we saw in town, today."

"Wait!" laughed Marina. "Ask about him, later." She turned to the older woman again. "What is Leilani's story?"

Leila sighed, rocking rhythmically. "Leilani must be around fifteen years of age. She is the oldest of four children, born to a young couple, named Joaquin and Reina."

"And what about the grandfather?" asked Salomé.

"Jeremiah," answered Leila, pressing her lips together. "He is Reina's father." She looked at the girls helplessly, at loss for words.

Marina frowned. "Is he in charge of them, or something? He comes by in the afternoons, to make sure all the work is done, but I get the impression, however, that the children are on their own."

"They are."

They thought in silence for a moment. "So, where are Joaquin and Reina?" asked Salomé, finally.

"Gone," came the quiet answer.

"Gone?" Salomé echoed, frowning. "Did they just get up and leave their own children?!"

Leila laughed sadly. "Oh, no, baby, they did not get up and leave," she said, shaking her head. "They were taken."

"Taken?!" The girls chorused, shock clearly evident in their voices. "But how?" demanded Salomé. "Who would just take some children's parents, and why?"

Leila thought a moment, before answering slowly, and carefully. "You have come to a place, bebés, where men may not be as civilized, compared to what you must be accustomed to." She hesitated. "There are men," she continued slowly, "vicious, savage men, lawless, soulless..." Her hands fluttered absently in her lap. "Some of these men have come to this island on occasions, and when they leave," she stared absently out the door, the setting sun dying slowly in the reflection of her green eyes, "they take some of us with them..."

"Did these... men, take Joaquin and Reina?" Salomé asked.

"Yes," Leila nodded slowly. "Last time they came, they took many people from this village. Leilani's parents, Francois' parents, others lost sons, brothers..."

Salomé's eyes widened, shock clear in her face. "What about the females?"

Leila shook her head sadly. "Only half of the women in the village are left."

"When did this happen?" Marina asked.

Leila's laugh was short and desperate. "Last time?" A fierce look crossed her brow, as she handled the shells in her lap. "It has been almost a year."

"Leila," Salomé said gently. "Did they take a loved one of yours?"

Tears sparkled quietly in her eyes, her mouth beginning to tremble slightly. She seemed to be in extreme pain, as she looked at each girl in turn. "Of course they did. How could these men come, like thieves in the night, raid and rape in our village, and not take at least one beloved, from every family here?" she asked bitterly. The girls waited in silence, not knowing how to respond. "They took from me, my most valued treasure," she continued. "The night they came... they came, they threatened me, and our son. He defended us, until they hurt him so bad, he could not even help himself. So, in order to save us, he had to go. And they took him."

Tears stung the girls' eyes, as the realization hit them. Marina stood up, suddenly overwhelmed by the information thrown at them. She paced quickly, like a caged animal, shock clear in her face. "Caribe's dad?!"

Leila looked at her, confirming the saddest part of the story. "Yes," she answered mournfully. "They took Don Manuel."

That night, the girls lay in their hammocks silently, wide awake, swinging slowly in the dark. The day had been exciting, and the sun had set a while ago, but they were not sleepy. Two days had gone by, already, and still, they couldn't bring themselves to speak about the implications of their situation. They swung gently, listening to the nocturnal symphony around them. The wind had picked up a little, blowing away all traces of the day's heat. In the dark of the night, they heard the faint sounds of drums. Steady, beating drums, accompanied by chanting. They couldn't quite tell where the sounds came from, not having heard them the night before, so they just lay there, listening in the dark.

Suddenly, out of the dark, came a familiar voice, calling them in a stage whisper. "Marina! Salomé! Are you sleeping?" It was Leilani.

Salomé laughed. "Who can sleep with all this racket?"

Marina called out. "Girl, get your butt over here, where we can see you!" The females converged on the stairs, their forms silhouetted against the night sky.

Marina stroked the younger girl's hair. "What in the world, are you doing running around in the dark like this, and who is taking care of those babies?"

Leilaini jumped around in excitement. "My aunt," she said rapidly, "my aunt is taking care of the babies."

"So, what are you doing?" Salomé asked.

Leilani looked at each of them, her smile wide and bright in the dark. "Would you like to dance?"

The jungle seemed to have a heart of its own, as it pulsated to the beating of the drums. The young women moved closer, wondering at the scene that unfolded before their eyes. In a small clearing, on the beachside of the village, a perimeter was laid out by tiki torches, stuck in the sand. To one side, was a group of men, young and old, all playing an assortment of drums. Those that didn't seem to own one, were content with banging on tin cups, or rattling a necklace of shells. The result was a rhythmic pulse, that overpowered the senses, until their whole beings were throbbing as one. To the other side of the clearing were, what in any modern music presentation, would be known as the chorus. This assortment of natives were chanting, as they swayed to the drums, laughing and cheering on the dancers.

The dancers were in the middle of the clearing. At first they seemed to be moving independently, each one intent on his or her own moves. But as the drumming progressed, the girls realized that the dancers fell into subtle patterns. Yes, subtle at first. A male and a female would come face to face for a moment, and after mirroring each other's movements for a few steps, they would each spin around and find another partner. This evolved into a line, where everybody was doing it at the same time, stomping, jumping, spinning and twirling; until it seemed as if they all moved in perfect synchronization. Not very subtle anymore, but progressively agressive. Bright colors stood out against dark skin, as the torches brought life to the dancing itself.

Leilani parted the leaves they were standing behind, and stepped out into the firelight, leaving the girls no choice but to follow. Everybody turned and smiled at the women, without stopping what they were doing. The women looked at them with a little less interest than the men, since they had already met by the river.

"I guess this is the party," Salomé joked, laughing as she looked around her in delight.

Marina nodded. "I hope we're not crashing."

The noise was endless. They swayed, dancing where they stood. The villagers smiled, beckoning at them, teeth flashing white in the dark. Leilani joined the dancers. Without missing a step, the fifteen-year old jumped right into formation, dancing with all her heart and soul. It was beautiful to watch, as the rhythm took over her, transforming her face into sheer joy. Marina and Salomé, too shy to join them, danced where they stood. The villagers laughed and called at them, but respected their shyness towards them. The young women thrilled at the sights and sounds, as they danced around the perimeter, staying in the sidelines, happily sharing with these people, with whom they were now living.

From a distance, two figures watched the proceedings in silence. Their horses munched contentedly in the dark, as they sat on their saddles, observing the villagers at their festivities. They weren't evil men, out to harm anyone. They were just local islanders, who enjoyed the colorful traditions of the natives. And the beautiful women. As the men watched, they caught sight of Leilani jumping into the group of dancers.

The old sailor smacked his lips, before sighing with regret. "If only the prettiest ones weren't the youngest ones," he lamented softly.

His partner chuckled. They had been coming up here for years, watching the natives from a distance, dancing their hearts out in frenzied abandonment. The drums made them feel rejuvenated, they decided. The younger man patted the old sailor's back reassuringly. "We are here just looking, old man, remember? Just looking," he laughed softly. He was Asian. His head was bald, and brown almond eyes peered out from a clean shaven face. He was middle- aged, but physically formidable, like a samurai.

The sailor grunted, shrugging his hand off, a smile playing around his mouth, as he pretended to whine softly. "And what about those two, Jimmy?" he asked, pointing out the newcomers, as they entertained the villagers themselves, dancing away from the impressive group of dancers.

Jimmy had to look twice, because he didn't believe it the first time. His eyes widened, as he recognized them. "Silas! Those strangers! Aren't those the females we saw ---"

Silas cut him off, a huge grin splitting his face. "Yep. They sure are." He cackled under his breath, old blue eyes squinting, white mustache shaking with laughter. "Those are the same women we saw today, while we were sitting out, in front of the Lair."

Jimmy chuckled, smiling at their antics, admiring their young bodies as they moved in the firelight. "They are quite beautiful," he whispered.

Silas smiled in the dark. "Yes," he agreed softly. "They are. Especially the darker one." He sighed. "She must be quite special."

"How do you know?" Jimmy asked, turning to look at him.

Silas answered, without taking his eyes off the women. "Because I know one big, bad Indian, who would give anything, to be where we are right now."

Jimmy shouted with laughter. "What are we waiting for?"

"Let's go!" urged Silas, turning his horse around and taking off at a gallop, Jimmy close behind him.

The town was quiet when they first rode up, very few people milling about with candles or lanterns. But as they found themselves on the other side of the plaza and church, the closer they found themselves to the docks, and the more people there were out on the streets. Closing businesses, rushing home, or just walking on the boarded sidewalks, people scurried about, doing one thing or another.

The main attraction on the whole strip was, of course, the Siren's Lair.

Across the street from it, men wandered around in circles, exchanging lewd comments with the girls in the balconies. These were waving their handkerchiefs at them, some blowing kisses, others displaying their breasts. The men groaned or cheered, depending on what the exchange of words was, at the moment. Downstairs, people passed by its glass plate windows, where inside, you could catch glimpses of the bar patrons, as they consorted with the women.

Silas and Jimmy jumped off their horse, tying them up front. The pair was as odd as possible, turning heads as they walked into the bar. The two men were almost equal in size and build, the major difference between them being their age, rather than their backgrounds. They approached the bar, and sat down in adjoining bar stools, grins threatening to split their faces. Behind the bar, the brave in question, polished the bar top with a rag, as he cleaned up after his patrons. He caught sight of the two men in his mirror, and made his way towards them. He looked at them, suspiciously, aware that the men were about ready to burst. "You two look like the cat that swallowed the canary," he rumbled. He was wearing a white shirt with garters at the sleeves, his black cotton pants long, falling to the toes of his cowboy boots. His hair was in a neater braid, this time a feather stuck in it, and no hat. "What are you up to?" he asked.

Silas couldn't stand it. "Oh, nothing," he drawled. "Me and Jimmy just went out for a ride in the jungle, you know..."

"Yes, sir!" Jimmy said. "We heard those drums, and we just had to go up there, you know..."

Indio looked from one to the other. "Right, right," he agreed carefully. "You go up there to look at the dancers."

"Exactly!" cried Silas.

Indio grunted. "Do they make you feel young, old man?"

"I do!" laughed Jimmy. "I feel young!"

Silas caught Indio's eyes in the mirror, as he turned to serve them a couple of drinks. "You would feel young too, son, if you saw what I just did..."

Indio turned around with the drinks in his hands, the swift movement making his braid fly over his shoulder, resting over his heart. He set the drinks in front of his friends firmly, and brushed his hair back in exasperation. He didn't have time to play games. "And what would that be, Silas?"

Jimmy jumped up, not being able to resist teasing the brave behind the bar. "Wait! Wait!" he cried. "I just remembered something, old man!"

Silas ignored him, not taking his old blue eyes from the younger man's piercing black ones. "Well, it occurred to me, as I was watching tonight, that Jimmy and I have been doing this for some years," he began, determined to draw it out for as long as he could. "And because of that, we have been watching the same people more or less, for all that time." He stopped, as the young man with the feather in his hair, turned to serve a patron. Indio returned, apologetic, saying nothing, waiting for him to continue. Silas continued. "Then, suddenly, I noticed, as we sat there watching these dancers, Jimmy and I," he looked at Indio, prolonging the suspense, "that there were a couple of women there that I hadn't seen before."

Indio shrugged and laughed, shining the bar around their glasses. "So what, old man? Maybe you missed a ceremony or two."

Silas pretended to think about it. "No," he drawled slowly. "I'm sure we have never missed one," he said, turning to the Asian man next to him. "Have we, Jimmy?" he asked, his eyes giving away his amusement.

Jimmy took a swig of his drink, almost choking on his laughter. "No, old man, we haven't missed one," he said. "But I will tell you something," he told Indio. "These women were really nice."

Indio wasn't convinced. "Really?" he asked suspiciously.

Silas smacked his lips. "If only I were younger," he began, "but now, I can only content myself by watching." He laughed. "They were beautiful," he said, "just like two angels. But one of them, my friend was special," he announced.

"What makes her so special?" Indio asked.

"Wait! Wait!" Jimmy cried for the second time. "Old man, I forgot to tell you!"

This time, Silas let him speak. "What?" he prompted.

"Those two new females we saw tonight?" Jimmy said, a smile on his face. The other two men just looked at him, waiting for him to finish what h e was saying. "We have seen them before, Silas! Don't you remember?"

Indio grunted. "So, you are getting old, sailor, if you can't remember meeting two beautiful women."

Silas ignored him, the smile fixed on his face. "Where?"

"Right here! We saw them right here!"

Indio threw back his head in laughter. "One of the girls upstairs get lost in the jungle and had to dance her way back?"

Jimmy and Silas exchanged glances, before turning back to Indio.

"Actually, not from the girls upstairs."

Indio shrugged, picking up a glass and shining it, before placing it carefully on top of a pyramid of glasses behind the bar. "Sometimes, it feels as if this whole island is full of women," he grumbled.

Silas laughed at him. "I remember," he said. "They were quite exceptional, too." He pointed at the Indian's chest. "You, my friend, must remember them, too."

Indio rolled his eyes. "Gentlemen," he sighed patiently. "I talk with women all day." He grinned, suddenly. "For as long as I am waiting my turn to go back to sea, that is what I do. Talk with women."

"Yes," Jimmy agree, "but these women, you met today."

Indio froze, his eyes going from one man to the other. "Today?" he repeated.

Silas finally let him off the hook. "Leila brought them."

The men watched as a range of emotions played over the Indian's face. There was surprise, and confusion, but most of all, there was genuine interest. He moved closer to the men, elbows on the bar, his eyes intent on each of them. "Salomé," he said softly. The men nodded.

"And the other one," Jimmy offered.

Indio nodded his head. "Marina." He stared at his hands for a moment, before looking back at the men. "And Salomé? Dancing?"

Jimmy glanced at the ceiling, a look of pleasure washing over his smooth face. "Dancing, my friend," he answered. And before Indio could ask again, he nodded his head, confirming, "Salomé."

Indio shook his head, dazed, seeing the beautiful black girl in his mind's eye, as she stood before him this afternoon, hair dancing around her face, bright colors encasing her body. "Salomé," he repeated.

Silas stood up suddenly, as did Jimmy. They both downed the rest of their drinks and slammed their glasses down on the dark wood bar. "I suggest, my friend," the sailor announced, "that the next time you hear those jungle drums calling, you get your ass out there." He clapped his hand on Indio's shoulder. "You just don't know what those drums will do to you."

Back in the jungle, the dancing ended, and the villagers marched back home, still laughing, swaying and chanting. Leilani was dropped off at her hut, and Marina and Salomé proceeded on their way home, sharing a lone tiki torch that one of the women from the river, had so thoughtfully provided them with. Halfway home, they were stopped in their tracks by three figures. They recognized Francois and his crew.

The young man stepped out to meet them, a huge smile on his face, as if nothing had ever happened between them. "Ladies!" he cried in a low voice. "Such a pleasure to meet with you, again"

The girls stopped for a moment, measuring their options. They weren't scared of him. Years of Tae Kwon Do training had taught them to not be afraid of any man. They had also been taught, however, that to show all they knew, would place them at a disadvantage, while in an encounter with a foe, or an attacker. On the other hand, the idea of Francois learning where they lived was not appetizing to them. So they stood there, for a moment, measuring their options.

Salomé stepped up to bat. "Francois!" she replied, letting delight creep into her voice. Marina looked at her sharply, detecting the tone of amusement. Salomé glanced at her, reassuring her with her eyes. "Where were you?" she demanded. "You missed the party, boy!"

Francois laughed. "You mean, the dancing?" he scoffed, with a wave of dismissal. "That is children's game," he said, silver eyes glittering in his beautiful face.

Salomé put her hands on her hips. "Really?" she asked. She turned to Marina with mischief in her eyes. "You hear that, Louise? Francois here says that the dancing is for children."

Marina nodded her head, never taking her eyes off the young man. "I heard, Thelma."

Salomé sighed. "Well, that is just too bad, Francois, you missed it, but I guess we will see you another day," she said, grabbing Marina by the hand and jerking her behind her, this time giving Francois a wide berth. "These children have got to sleep. Goodnight."

"Wait! Pretty lady!" Francois pleaded, as they began to walk away. The girls stopped and looked at him. He was looking right at Marina, eyes boring into her, doing with her body as they pleased. She stood as still as she could, not letting him see her shiver under his repulsive gaze. "I need you to do my other side now," he called, pointing to the side of his face, opposite from his swollen lip. His free hand went to his crotch. "I liked it," he said.

The girls turned away in disgust, leaving the three young men laughing, behind them. Once they got to their hut, they cooled their skin with some fresh water that Caribe had, once again, provided for them. Putting on some clean pants and tops, they toppled into their respective hammocks, swinging happily as they wound down from their exciting night. They talked softly for a while, shared their impressions of the day's events, and said their prayers. Soon, they were fast asleep, dreaming of the third millennium from which they came, where they had homes, parents, and a brother, who would brave Hell or high water, to come to their rescue.

In the cave, Jackson paced slowly, sleep evading him. He had spent a good enough day. The island was a little bigger than it seemed, but he had gone as far as he could in one direction, today, putting in practice everything he had ever been taught about Nature, and surviving outdoors. He called on the girls occasionally, but not really knowing what to expect in this place, he mostly laid out trail indicators for them, and left out signs that they could read, among the brush and foliage. So far, nothing. But he wasn't ready to give up. Tomorrow he would do the exact same thing, walking in the opposite direction.

It was a lonely task, he admitted, and not one for just anybody. You had to have a special core, and the heart to do what he had set out to do. He felt responsible for the girls. After all, they had gone on this vacation together. It wasn't that he was their keeper. They were old enough to take responsibility for their own mistakes. It was just that, even after having spent their whole lives together, growing up and practically living with one another, the three of them really enjoyed each other's company, in a way in which only true friends can. They just genuinely liked each other, even when they already loved and adored one another. They were a team. A good team that was only completed with their parents.

Jackson sighed. The parents. No use thinking about them, right now. He only had a few days left, before he had to report back with his dad. He had to handle it by then. He walked to the mouth of the cave, and looked out over the ocean. The breeze caressed his warm skin, the jungle rustling as it blew around it. On the horizon, he could make out the faint lights of a cruise ship. He smiled, as he envisioned the people laughing and dancing aboard, having left their cares on shore. Up above, a lone plane droned in the starry night sky. And then, it was quiet again. He had never felt so humble.

Going back inside, he lit half the candles, suddenly needing light. He reached into his backpack, pulling out a sketch pad, and some pencils. Flipping through the pages until he came to a blank piece of paper, he stopped, his hand frozen over it, pencil held loosely between his fingers. With eyes staring blankly at the pad in front of him, he began to see in his mind. His hand started moving, slowly, at first. His fingers were hesitant, as they moved the pencil around the paper, lines becoming shapes. His strokes became bolder, stronger, the images clearer. He couldn't stop. His hand flew over the paper, drawing, smudging, shading and contouring. And after a few minutes, he was done.

Jackson held it up, looking at the results. Not bad, he thought proudly. Sadly. He laughed at himself. I can make a living at this. He wanted to cry. Drawing his knees up, he held the piece of paper loosely in one hand, while the other ran over his cornrows, smoothing his hair, seeking some comfort from the familiar gesture. He would glance at the picture, and away from it. He began rocking, humming, and nonsense going through his mind.

Lord, he prayed. *I need some help. Please.*

And he left it at that, knowing that God didn't need a constant reminder of a person's troubles. The paper fluttered in his hand, as he continued rocking. He rubbed his eyes with his other hand, pinching the bridge of his nose between thumb and forefinger. Exhaustion fell on him like a cloak, the energy draining slowly from his body. This must be the hardest trial of his lifetime. Expelling his breath from his body suddenly, he got to his feet, paper firmly in his hand. Blowing out the candles one by one, the cave became darker, until there was only one left. Crouching down next to that one, he studied the paper in his hands one more time.

Laughing out from the paper were his girls. One tied by blood, and the other tied by the grace of God. Tears came to his eyes, as they lovingly traced their faces. The drawing was exquisite in the expressions it had captured. In it, the girls were laughing, as if at a joke. They were half turned away from each other, like they just couldn't stand it. The drawing was flawless. He had captured the movement of their hair around their faces, and the crinkles of laughter around their eyes, mouths open, faces glowing. Closing his eyes for a moment, he thought he could hear them. The chant began in his head. *Salomé, Marina; Marina, Salomé...* He opened his eyes again, looking at the paper one more time, before putting it away lovingly, in his backpack. He blew out the candle.

The cave plunged into darkness once more, and he turned to where he had laid down the night before. The fragrance was becoming faint on the blankets, but he could still smell them. He sighed, and closed his eyes. The picture branded in his mind, Jackson finally fell asleep.

"Good morning, ladies."

The women opened their eyes slowly, squinting against the morning light. It was still in their hut, dust particles caught suspended in the rays of sunlight, filtering in the window. The night creatures were silent, and different birds sang to each other, going about their day. It was a hazy day, the sun shining hot against a pale blue sky.

Marina stretched in her hammock, letting her hand drop to the floor, her knuckles brushing the wooden boards. She squinted against the sunlight, and smiled at him. "Good morning, Caribe."

"I am to accompany you into town, where you begin to work today, I understand," he told Salomé, who was rubbing her eyes with the backs of her hands, as she yawned.

Salomé sprang out of her hammock at the words, remembering, her face breaking out into a huge smile. "Oh, my God!" She rummaged among the beautiful fabrics that Leila had provided for them, and chose one with a bright red background, the designs on it done in tones of khaki and sand. She held it up for her friends' approval, and they both nodded their heads. "I have to go to work!" she beamed.

Some time later, after washing off the night's perspiration, and eating hastily a breakfast that consisted of more fruits, the trio headed into town. Their first stop was the establishment of one, Miss Dominique Swan. The door was locked when they got there, so they rang the bell outside, and waited. A curtain moved at a window upstairs, and shortly after, the door opened.

"Salomé!" exclaimed Dominique delighted. "You are early!"

Salomé's smile faded, as her brow creased in a frown. "Am I too early?" she asked worried. "I will be happy to go and come back whenever you are ready."

Dominique laughed happily, her hand already around the dark girl's wrist, pulling her inside. "Don't be silly! It is wonderful that you are here, now. It will give me time to begin showing you some of the things you need to know, before the first client gets here." She flashed a dazzling smile at her companions, as she pulled Salomé inside. "You two have a wonderful day."

The two girls hugged goodbye. "Good luck," whispered Marina, smilin g into her sister's eyes.

The town was even busier than the day before. There seemed to be an urgency as the inhabitants of Encantada hurried about. Caribe and Marina sat on a lone bench at the plaza, and watched everybody go by for a moment.

"How are you doing?" Caribe asked, genuinely concerned. His eyes looked a bit worried as he turned his head towards her, his thick black dreadlocks framing his beautiful face.

Marina smiled at him, sliding the back of her hand gently down the side of his face. "I am fine, baby." She passed her thumb over his top lip, rubbing away the beads of perspiration that had gathered there.

He grinned, and caught her hand, pretending to gnaw on it, as a puppy with a bone. They both laughed as she shrieked, causing the people hurrying by to turn their heads momentarily towards them. "Mamá tells me that you have been somewhat busy," he said.

Marina shrugged. "That is only because you take off, most of the time." He nodded. "Are you enjoying yourselves so far?"

Marina stared deep into his eyes, realizing that, apart from the affectionate hugs they exchanged on occasion, she had never been this close to him before. His eyes were a warm brown, with golden flecks in it. They reminded her of the stone named tigereye. They were just like her cousin Deveraux's. "So far?" she murmured.

Pain flashed in his eyes, casting shadows in its depths. "Marina..." he murmured apologetically. "I did not mean to imply..." he trailed off, suddenly looking miserable.

She shook her head, smiling at him. "Of course not," she reassured. "Considering that Salomé and I cannot even begin to fathom
the magnitude of our predicament, and absolutely cannot grasp the
implications of what that storm has brought to our lives ---" Tears
threatened to spill over, and she took a deep breath, blinking them
away. "Yes, Caribe, we are enjoying ourselves as best as we can."

This time, it was he who caressed her face, erasing the tears
from her cheeks. "Marina..." And he had no words. They stared at
each other, isolated as they were, sitting on their bench, while the rest
of Encantada hurried by.

Marina's lip trembled. "I miss Jackson," she confessed shakily.
Caribe didn't ask who Jackson was. He thought he knew. Instead, he
put his arm around the older girl, drawing her head down towards
him in comfort, his dreadlocks brushed back from his shoulder.
Marina let herself melt into him as they fell into a pleasant silence.
Caribe draped his other arm behind the back of their bench, and
stretched his long legs in front of him. They didn't say anything for a
while. So caught up were they in their own thoughts, that they were
unaware of being watched.

Under the eaves of the building across the street, the two men
smiled at the sight of the couple sitting on the bench. As they leaned
against the barber shop, they waited for an indication that the two
were intimate, somewhat, but there was none. Just two friends sitting
together, one seemingly consoling the other.

Jimmy poked the old sailor with his elbow, and nodded towards
them. "There is the other one," he smiled.

Silas grinned. "What are we waiting for?"

They pulled themselves away from the store front, and walked
away, their steps taking them towards the docks. As they approached
the Siren's Lair, the streets were so congested with people on foot
and on horseback, they had to stop a few times, just to get moving
again. The Lair wasn't open yet, of course, but inside, they could see
their friend getting ready to start the day. They looked at each other
before going in, smiles huge in their faces. The men were enjoying
themselves immensely. "Good morning!" called Jimmy, even as the
blast of noise from the street announced their presence.

Indio's head shot up from behind the bar. They noticed he was shirtless, as he seemed to suddenly appear in front of the wall mirror. He smiled at them, as the door fell closed, muting the outside noise. "Well," he laughed. "What are you two troublemakers up to?"

Silas pretended to be hurt. "Troublemakers? Oh, come on now, cowboy, why would you even say that to us? We're your friends," he cried, almost pouting. He tugged at the white beard on his chin, in seeming distress.

"Friends," repeated Indio with a laugh.

Jimmy put a hand over his heart. "You hurt my feelings, hombre," he said. "When have we ever betrayed you?" he asked, almond eyes squinting at the brave.

"You are right," conceded Indio, cutting him off. "Never." He tossed aside the rag he was holding, and like last night, put his elbows on the bar and leaned towards them. "All right, gentlemen, what is it this time?"

Silas grinned. "Well, Jimmy and I were just back over by the barber shop ---"

"Yes," interrupted Jimmy. "They have a new girl there that actually cuts hair." He preened at himself in the mirror. "Makes me wish I had some, just so I could go and get it cut," he said as an afterthought.

The men laughed. "Well, we were just over there," continued Silas, "minding our own business..."

"As usual," chuckled Indio.

Jimmy nodded his head as if it were a compliment. "As usual," he repeated.

"And suddenly," Silas went on with his story, "we see a pair of young people sitting on the bench right at the plaza, over there by the padre's place." He put his hand over the Indian's before he lost interest. "The boy was Caribe."

"Yes," confirmed Jimmy. "No confusing that young one. Spitting image of his daddy."

"But the girl..." Silas looked at him expectantly.

Indio stood up straight, looking down at both men. He held his breath. "The girl..." he repeated slowly.

"Why, it was the other one," Silas said, shrugging his shoulders, feighing indifference, but never taking his eyes off the young man's face.

Jimmy nodded, as he turned to look at him. He nodded, confirmi ng his thoughts. "From yesterday."

The men had to leap out of the way, as the Indian jumped over the bar, reaching for a shirt as he dashed out the door, leaving them looking after him. They burst into laughter, as the doors swung shut.

The Klines' General Store felt comfortably familiar, as the pair went inside. "Hello!" cried John, even before the bells had stopped tinkling against the door. "Caribe! How are you, young man? Not getting any taller, are you? I will be looking up at you, if you keep this up," the storeowner rambled on, coming around his counter to hug the young man.

Caribe answered his embrace, a huge smile on his face. "Mr. Kline."

John laughed heartily. "When are you coming over to do portraits of my boy and my wife?"

The younger man ducked his head, embarrassed. He was overwhelmed, whenever his artwork was complimented, being that his talent came natural to him, a genuine gift of God. He thought he was good. No, he knew he was. It still humbled him, however, whenever anyone made a fuss about his art. "Whenever you say, Mr. Kline," he laughed.

"Do I hear familiar voices?" asked Larissa, stepping out from the back. The women embraced warmly, and the small, black-haired beauty stared up at Caribe, a naughty look crossing her face. She hooked her arm through his, and batted her eyelashes at him, making them all smile. "Why, hello, there. You seem remarkably familiar," she flirted, smoothing the young man's shirt over his chest. "I'm afraid I must be mistaken, though. You look so much like a sweet young boy I know from the village. He was my special friend, when he was little, but then he grew up some, and suddenly had no time for me." She dazzled him with a smile. "I'm afraid I must apologize, however, for being so confused. There is no comparison between the little boy I am thinking of, and such a tall, handsome, strong young man, as you."

Caribe rolled his eyes for a moment, before suddenly sweeping her off her feet and spinning her around. To their delight, Larissa shrieked, clinging to Caribe as he set her down, suddenly. "Madam, I am no boy, and you are not mistaken," he announced, his face alight with laughter. "It is I, Caribe, son of the marvelous Leila, and the honourable Don Manuel, now, a man."

Before anybody could dwell on the mention of Caribe's father, Larissa took control of the conversation. "Yes, you are, Caribe, and a fine man, at that." She turned to look at Marina, eyes sparkling. "What are you up to, today?"

Marina shrugged, returning the other woman's smile. "Nothing much. We are still getting used to Encantada. You know how it is, when you find yourself in a new place..."

"Yes," interrupted Larissa, rolling her eyes. "Everything seems so new for so long, and it takes a while to get accustomed to every-thing." She smiled. "I know exactly what you mean. It happened to me when I first got here." She took Marina's hand, walking her qui-etly past the sleeping baby, who lay on a cot in a corner. "It seemed as if I were on vacation forever, and then, one day," she threw her husband a loving look, "I felt like I was home."

John smiled and returned her look with a passionate one of his own. "You were always home, darling. You just didn't know it yet."

Larissa seemed to thrill at her husband's attention, even as she waved her hand at him playfully. She turned back to Marina. "Anyway," she said, pulling the other girl behind her, "come with me to the back, and tell me what you think of this idea John and I have of making this place function better..." The women's voices trailed off as they disappeared.

From the corner, came a sudden cry. The two men looked at each other. John's eyebrows raised, as he looked knowingly at Caribe. "Baby's awake," he announced.

Caribe smiled. "Yes, he is." He crossed to the cot, picking Max up and holding him up to his chest, bouncing him gently as he did so. "Come here, baby, baby," he crooned. "No tears, man, no tears..."

Max stopped crying, the voice obviously familiar to him, and well loved. He snuggled against the young man's chest, dreadlocks held fast in his tiny hands.

John Kline came up next to him, patting the young man on the back, and stooping to kiss his son's head. He smiled warmly into Caribe's eyes. "You are very good with children, Caribe," he remarked. "Ever thought of having any of your own?"

Caribe nodded. "Thought. Yes."

"Well?" prodded John. "I know you are young, but not that young. What I mean is, some boys younger than you already have children. What are you waiting for?"

Caribe laughed. "A couple of things, actually." John raised his eyebrows. "First?"

"The right one," answered Caribe automatically.

John grunted, and walked away, going back to his place behind the counter. "I would say," he conceded, "that would be the most important aspect of all. The right one. Very important." He looked at the boy curiously. "What is the other?"

Caribe looked straight into his eyes, his voice dropping. "I am waiting for the day when there will be no more men, women and children taken from my village." John felt his breath catch in his throat at the young man's words. Caribe's eyes never wavered from his. "I will not bring a child to this world to lose it, as my father lost his."

Just then, the door announced another customer. The two men looked as the large shadow stepped over the threshold, seeming to loom over them momentarily. The man stood with his face in shadows, silhouetted by the sunlight at his back. He stepped inside, unmistakable now. John held Caribe's eyes, sealing the moment, respecting the confidence shared by the boy, before looking at the newcomer. "Indio!" he exclaimed happily. "What brings you here, to our side of town, man?" The two men shook hands heartily, warm smiles on their faces. "I thought you were extremely busy with your bar, what with Gaitano coming soon and everything."

"I am, John," admitted the Indian. "I just thought I would take a break before I opened today." He turned to Caribe. They exchanged greetings, hands clasping warmly, smiles on their faces. "When are you coming to work for me, man?"

Caribe laughed. "When you change jobs," came the prompt reply.

"What can I help you with, Indio?" John asked, genuinely curious. "Is there something I can do for you? Any of the girls at your place need anything?" Indio shook his head with a smile on his face. "No, sir, whatever they need, they can get for themselves. That's why they are working women, right?" He paused, as the men laughed. "Truth is, I came here to speak to one of you, about something very important." He walked around Caribe, peering at the baby, who was now jumping in the boy's arms. "I came to speak to Max."

"Max?" The baby's father laughed. "I am sorry, hombre, but I'm afraid the baby hasn't been saying much of anything lately, and you know, we just can't figure it out..,."

Indio threw him a smile, before taking the baby from Caribe. "Max!" he laughed. "Just the man I wanted to see!" The other two men watched as he proceeded to cradle the baby, making him giggle, before lifting him high over his head, making him squeal. By the time Indio swung him back into his arms, Max was in love. "Max, I've been looking for you, man," Indio continued, bouncing the baby high on his chest, as he paced in a short circle. "I am sorry you were asleep when I saw you yesterday," he continued softly, crooning at the baby, "but I need you to tell me where I can find," he sing-sang, "the beautiful girls you were with."

Caribe stiffened suddenly. He had been half paying attention to the Indian, his eyes on the delighted baby. Now their eyes met. He stood up straight. "No."

Indio stared straight at him. "Yes," he said softly.

Caribe stepped towards him, causing the storeowner to hurry from behind the counter and step between them, keeping an eye on his son. "No!"

Indio held out a hand, suddenly understanding the young boy's reaction. "Caribe," he said. "Not for that, man! What are you thinking of?"

At that moment, the women came back out, stopping short at the scene unfolding in front of them. Max took one look at Marina and screamed, delight evident in every cell of his little body. Marina rushed toward him, keeping a wary eye on the tall brave. "Max!"

Indio was just as delighted. "Marina!" He stopped himself from rushing her, and decided to gently hand over the baby, instead. As she took him from his arms, he kissed the top of his head, stopping to whisper in the baby's ear, tickling him with his breath. "Thank you, Max, baby!"

Marina smiled at the baby as he hunched his shoulder and squirmed, his little eyes squinted shut, peals of laughter coming from him. "Hello, Indio," Marina said, turning the smile on him.

"Hello." And then, he couldn't say any more. He stood looking at the girl in front of him, and he felt almost as nervous as he had yesterday, when he stood before her friend. This one is very beautiful, he thought to himself. They both are. He looked at her. She didn't know him, he realized. She wouldn't know what his intentions were. And he didn't know how to explain. So, he just looked at her, questions screaming in his eyes, while his hands still played with the baby, now in her arms. He smiled, thought of something to say, and then smiled some more. But no words came out. Once, he looked around him, only to find he had an audience, as the Klines and Caribe, as Marina, stood silently, waiting for him to say something.

Marina smiled to herself. Cat got your tongue, baby? She had never seen any man act like that because of her friend. Sure, there had been many guys interested. But this one was different. Deciding to let him off the hook, she smiled at him. "Salomé is working."

The sigh of relief seemed to explode from his chest, his face transformed by his grateful smile. "*Gracias*," he said sincerely, the word rumbling deep in his chest. And with a grunt, he waved good-bye to everyone and walked out. Salomé is working. It wasn't until he spotted the bench in the plaza, that he realized, he didn't ask where.

Back inside the store, everybody looked at each other. Larissa gasped. "What was that all about?"

Marina winked at her. "Love at first sight."

"My, my, of all people..." murmured Larissa.

Marina frowned, suddenly alarmed. "What is wrong with him? Is he not a good man?"

Larissa rapidly comforted her. "Oh, no, honey, there is nothing wrong with Indio, why, he is a perfect gentleman. Please, do not let his rough appearance fool you, he is an absolute pussycat."

John snorted. "Pussycat!" Caribe smiled.

"Indio is one of the nicest, kindest, generous men this island has to offer," Larissa continued, completely ignoring the men. "Honestly, you couldn't do much better than him, and," she added with a wink, "he is extremely nice to look at."

"Woman!" her husband thundered, eyes crinkling with laughter. "You have gone too far!"

Marina laughed. "Well, what does he do?"

"Indio is Gaitano's right hand," Larissa answered. "At the moment, he is keeping an eye on the Siren's Lair. He bartends downstairs, and watches the girls upstairs," she said, rolling her eyes.

Marina frowned. A pimp? She chose her words carefully. "Does he own the business," she hesitated, "with the girls upstairs? Does he run it?"

Larissa shook her head rapidly. "Oh, no, honey! No, he is only keeping an eye on it for the owner."

"Where is he or she?" asked Marina.

Caribe and John Kline looked at each other, eyebrows raised. *She*, they mouthed at each other.

Larissa smiled gratefully as she looked into Marina's eyes. She sighed to herself. *She*. "*He* is away at sea with Gaitano, at the moment, soon to be back."

Marina smiled. *I don't think I want to know who Gaitano is.* "Well, I guess it's all right, then. Salomé is a big girl."

"Lucky Indio," John said, smacking his lips. Larissa pretended to smack him. Caribe grunted.

Marina widened her eyes suddenly, and shaking her head with a huge grin on her face, she brought it closer to Max's until their foreheads were touching. Max roared. He had never seen anything funnier. The grownups chuckled. Marina pressed her lips against his coal curls as she switched him from one hip to the other. She smiled at Larissa, tearing herself away from green, cat eyes. "Do you need help with Max today?"

Larissa automatically shook her head. "Oh, no, really, " she began, unaware of her husband signaling over her head and behind her back.

Marina tried to catch what he was saying, without letting Larissa know. John was wildly crisscrossing his arms in a negative gesture, while moving his head up and down in a single, exaggerated nod.

"Awww, come on, please," cajoled Marina, "I really need a baby fix." She shook her head vigorously. "I mean, time with a baby. You know..." she smiled at Larissa. "It makes me feel like a mommy."

Larissa smiled. "Well, to be honest," she glanced at her husband. "Yes. Thank you very much. I could get a lot done, if I had someone watch over the baby for a few hours. I do twice the work," she explained.

Marina kissed the baby. She began speaking to him, her words musical as they came out in a tone meant for babies alone. "You mean if you had a friend to watch over the baby, while you worked with your husband in the business you are building together." The other woman smiled, nodding. "It is a joint venture, and it is worth having someone help with the caring of the child, because at the end, there will be a profit, and the business will be a success!" Max began jumping up and down on her hip, like a bucking bronco, squealing at her speech. Marina chuckled and continued in the same tone. "Which of course, will mean a better way of life and a secure future for said child."

"Enough!" laughed Larissa, while behind her, her husband gave Marina the thumbs up sign, blue eyes sparkling. Businesslike, she continued. "I will need around four hours. It is still quite early, so we are actually talking about half a day." She smiled, walking her visitors to the door. She kissed her son. "Be back in the early afternoon. That should be enough. That way you can get your own things done."

"Deal," Marina agreed. "We will see you soon."

And they left. The man, the woman, and the baby. The bells tinkled as the door closed behind them.

"Where to?" asked Marina.

Caribe held out his arms, taking the baby from her. "Have you been to church, yet?"

"Kind of," Marina answered. "Well, we met Padre Ignacio. And he blessed us. So, yeah, we were in church, but we didn't go to mass or anything."

"Would you like to?"

"Yes!"

So they paid a visit to the little church, in the middle of the little plaza, and caught the morning mass.

Once Marina was done admiring all the scrimshaw work, evident in the sunlit church, they continued on their way. First a mandatory detour to Salomé's workplace. Both Salomé and her new boss were ecstatic at the baby's surprise visit. After kisses and tickles, they left for a change of scene.

"You know what would be really cool?" Marina asked Caribe.

They were walking slowly. He was holding the baby in one arm, and showed him, people and buildings and things, with his free hand. Each and every time, Max followed the boy's pointing finger with his eyes, until he saw what he was being shown. "What?"

"If I could check out every single place in this strip."

Caribe nodded. "Where do you want to start?" Marina smiled. *I love this guy.*

They took their time. They stopped to speak to people, and to stare at buildings. They entered businesses, to observe daily life on an island. When the sun was at its highest, they took a break. The baby was getting fussy, and they felt hot and drained, from the scorching sun. Without looking where they were going, they entered the next available place. It was cooler than the street they had just escaped. Blinking while their eyes adjusted, they didn't move, at first.

"Max!" a delighted voice reached their ears.

Caribe looked at Marina apologetically, before shooting an unhappy look at the grinning brave. "I'm sorry, I wasn't looking where we were going. We don't have to stay here."

Marina looked around her quickly, passing a glance at the ridiculously happy young man behind the bar. *How silly! He looks like he just won the lottery!* Marina headed towards the nearest barstool. "Yes," she disagreed happily. "We do."

Caribe hung his head, his forehead touching Max's. "Not good, *papi*," he sighed.

They sat down, and faced the bartender. Indio was almost at a loss for words, there were so many things he wanted to ask. His excellent training kicked in. "May I get you something to drink?" he offered.

Marina shook her head and smiled. "No, thank you. Do you serve food here?"

Indio looked at her, surprised. "No..." he answered slowly.

Marina took Max from Caribe, and turned him towards the mirror hanging on the wall in front of them. Max looked at her and back, a couple of times, before losing interest. He kept a wary eye on himself, however, as he stuck his thumb in his mouth, intent on the grownups' conversation. "Wouldn't it be nice if you did?" she asked.

Indio smiled. Calling two men over, he spoke in a low voice to them, causing them to look over at the boy, and the girl, and the baby. The men took his place behind the bar, and he disappeared suddenly. Marina and Caribe entertained themselves with Max, as they waited. A few minutes later, Indio was back. In his hand, was a brown paper bag. Marina smiled to herself, as she pretended not to notice. He busied himself opening the bag, and laying out everything on top of the bar, in front of them. Marina looked, from the corner of her eye, and hid her face in the baby's neck, shaking her head. More fish, more fruit, more bread. *I'm on a diet, and I didn't even know it.* "Enjoy yourselves," he told them, before going back to work.

They did. First, they fed Max. The little guy was so grateful to be fed by his caretakers, that he made the most valiant effort, of trying to feed himself. A quite messy endeavor, but one that brought laughter to everybody watching. As the fish on their plates suddenly found themselves wrapped up in bread, drinks magically appeared in front of them. Non-alcoholic drinks, so they could share with the baby. Without saying a word, Indio served them, paying them much more attention than he was, to the rest of the customers. Taking a nice long drink from her glass, Marina winked at him over the rim. Visibly relaxing, his features settled into a secret smile.

Marina turned suddenly to Caribe. "Guess what I did last night!"

Caribe held Max on his lap once more, the baby's back firmly against his chest. Marina tried to wipe the baby's face with one hand, while keeping his hands from stopping her, with the other. Max just squirmed, laughter evident in his face, as he gave them a hard time. Caribe grunted. "What?"

Marina didn't notice as Jimmy and Silas moved closer to them, catching every word they said. "We went dancing!" she said, excitement in her eyes. Caribe just raised his eyebrows at her. Indio didn't even pretend he wasn't listening. He put his rag away, and leaned on the bar, in front of them. Behind them, Jimmy and Silas quietly slapped hands and shot Indio an I-told-you-so look. They were ignored. "Leilani came last night," Marina continued, "and next thing we knew, we were dancing with the natives." She held her arms out for Max, who seemed to be fading fast.

Caribe stood and held her chair, as she followed. "How did you like it?" he asked, smiling, stopping to pay for their meal. One look at her face told him, as she stopped to smile into his eyes.

"Absolutely loved it! We can't wait to go again!" She stopped to say goodbye to their host. "Thank you for everything," she said shyly, holding out her hand.

Indio squeezed it warmly. "My pleasure," he reassured her.

The couple and the baby headed towards the door. "Do you know when there will be drums again?" she was asking the dread-locked boy eagerly.

"I am pretty sure tonight," they heard him say, as the door closed behind them, and they got lost in the crowd in the street.

The old sailor and the chinaman took up the seats that had just been occupied by the incongruous pair. "You know, Jimmy," drawled Silas, "it feels real good to know that although some people," he glanced at Indio, "don't appreciate you trying to help them, the truth always manages to come out."

"I know exactly what you mean, old man," sighed Jimmy, rubbing his smooth head as he looked at himself in the mirror.

Indio was silent, as he prepared a couple of drinks. Setting them on the bar in front of his friends, he looked at each man. "Gentlemen, your information has been most valuable, to say the least. I thank you." He pushed the drinks towards them., with an apologetic smile. "On me." He poured one for himself and held it up. His friends held up their glasses, joining him. *"¡Salud!"*

The sidewalk was now in partial shade. The sun had moved lazily, continuing its relaxed journey towards the western horizon. The smell of salt was sharp in the air, and tiny drops of moisture coated everyone and everything. Marina stepped out to the street, after looking carefully down both directions, making sure no buggy, nor horse, nor human being on foot was coming. Caribe leaned against one of the posts supporting a strip of roof over the sidewalk. Crossing his arms, and one foot over one ankle, he smiled with a big sigh. *She is like a child!* Marina lifted the sleeping baby higher on her shoulder, and raised her freckled face towards the sun, closing her eyes, and taking a deep breath. The sun sparked blue lights off Max's head with the raven wing's hair. Above it, Marina exhaled with a huge smile on her face. She looked at Caribe, and joined him. He put an arm around her shoulders with a laugh, guiding her among the ever increasing sea of men.

Up ahead, there was a break between buildings, on the apartment side of the street. Right in the middle, between a couple of two-story boarding houses, was something Marina hadn't seen yet. Yesterday, she had been so overwhelmed, that she had walked down this street on auto-pilot, trying not to overload. Today, there was an incongruous building, set back a few yards from the sidewalk, with a path leading to its entrance. Somebody had taken great pains to give it some semblance of beauty and serenity to it, and they had done a good job. It was a straight path with nice, smooth river stones paving it. Bordering it were rows of glorious conch shells, their white spiny peaks pointing towards the sky, and their blushing insides, sleek and glassy to the touch, all in single file. On either side of this spectacular paths, were beautiful gardens of cacti. The building itself was made of white stucco, its windows round, with two bars of iron, making a cross in the middle of them. The entrance was arched, and to one side was a massive wooden door, with black iron trim. Marina had the impression it wasn't closed very often. At the top of the building, massive wooden logs jutted out, spaced out evenly. There was no sign, no name, no address. "What's this?" Marina asked finally. The landscaping is beautiful.

Caribe steered her down the path, towards the entrance. "Come and see," he invited.

Inside, a man rose from behind a desk, at their entrance. Marina laughed. "Oficial Barbosa! "

"Pedro!" he smiled.

"Pedro," she repeated, looking around her. "So this is it, huh? This is where this town's law is taken care of?"

Pedro Barbosa nodded at the young man with her first, "Caribe." He turned back to Marina. "Yes, ma'am. This is the place."

She glanced mischievously behind him. "An ybody in jail at the moment?"

"Just a local bum. Disorderly conduct. He gets obnoxious when he gets drunk," he explained.

Marina nodded in understanding. "Is there much crime, here in Encantada?" She missed the glances exchanged by the men.

Caribe's eyes went cold. The lawman shot him a warning look. "Some," he answered evasively.

Marina pretended not to notice, playing the flighty female part expertly. "Well, *oficial*," she said, glancing down at his desk, "it seems like you are extremely busy, just like the rest of the town." Gently, she turned Max in her` arms, until she was cradling him, his cheek pressed firmly against her breast. "We are out playing, so we should leave now, and not take up more of your time."

She glanced at the baby as he sucked vigorously at his thumb, in his sleep. "Besides, we need to deliver this one back to his Mamá."

Pedro Barbosa nodded, the smile never leaving his eyes. "*Buenas tardes*, Marina," he said.

Marina nodded back at him. "*A usted, caballero*," she smiled.

"Gracias."

At the door, she turned back to look at him, and met his eyes. She smiled.

You're hiding something, but that's okay. I'll find out.

Their walk back to the Klines' was uneventful. Shade crept over the street, cooling it down some. Larissa took her sleeping son, gratitude on her face. She cooed at the baby as he woke up, delighted to find himself once more in his mother's arms. Struggling to get up in an upright position, Max once again looked around him with glee. John cleared his throat. "We know you are only visiting, but if you are available, and if there is any way possible, we would like to pay you for watching over Max, a few mornings a week"

Marina began to protest. "Oh, no, please, it is no big deal! He's a sweetheart!"

They ignored her. "We are preparing ourselves, because soon we will be extremely busy, and every spare minute we can put into this place will be rewarded," Larissa explained.

John nodded. "Yes. As soon as Gaitano arrives..."

Again!

"...we will be flying high, so best get our wings ready."

Marina agreed. And so, they talked about it, coming to an agreement, in which Max would be taken to Marina's hut in the village, where she would watch him carefully at home, half of the time. The other half, she would come into town and entertain him there. Everybody happy, Marina and Caribe took their leave.

The rest of the day went without incident, as Marina spent quiet time with Leila, on her front porch. Soon, Salomé would be home, and they would go to Leilani's, and do it all over again. Marina sighed contentedly. Then she giggled. *Oh, my God! We've actually got a routine!* And then she thought of something else, quickly. Before she remembered.

Salomé stepped out on the shady sidewalk and stretched luxuriously. She felt energized. The morning was spectacular. *If only I could put this job experience down on my resumee when I get home, I'll be set!*

And with that happy thought, she decided to go for a walk before she went home. Walking slowly, lost in her thoughts, she was unaware of anyone around her. She just stared at the buildings, looking at each one as she walked by, focusing on the stationary among all the movement. And, as Marina, she noticed the small white abode, with the river pebble path, and the cactus garden.

Shaking her head, she focused. "That's beautiful," she said softly, aloud. And before she knew it, she was checking both ways, crossing the street, and walking up the conch bordered walk. Finding herself, standing just inside the door, she saw two dark heads huddled together in conference, over some documents spread out on the desk. The heads looked up.

Her heart stopped at the sight of the younger one. She was frozen to the spot, smile glued to her face. Twenty-first century upbringing kicked in, and she saved herself, turning to the older man. "Oficial Barbosa!"

The lawman couldn't help but smile. He had heard his name exclaimed in that happy sing-song tone, only once before in his whole life. That morning. "Pedro."

"Pedro." The same smile. He went to introduce her to the man next to him, but she stopped him. "We've met." She turned to Indio. "Hey, baby..."

Indio felt ghost fingers glide over the back of his neck, and it was all he could do to keep her from seeing him shudder. "Hey..." he smiled back.

Pedro Barbosa looked from one to the other, and sighed. "What are you up to, today?" he asked her.

"I was working. Now I'm going home," she answered, her eyes caressing Indio's face.

The object of her attention let his eyes slide down her hips. He looked up, embarrassed, trying not to blush. "Would you like to be walked home?" he offered suddenly.

"Yes," she said softly. "Please."

And as they left together, laughing, Pedro Barbosa was left, sitting at his desk, talking to nobody there. "As I was saying, Indio, before we were so pleasantly interrupted, this matter needs to be taken care of, immediately." He shuffled the papers in front of him, together, until he had them stacked neatly. "Carlitos is going to have some heads over this." He scraped back his chair and stood up, walking to his doorway, looking after the couple. "Gaitano will want revenge," he said softly after his friend, "and it is up to us, *hombre*, to make sure he gets it."

Salomé looked at the young man walking next to her, from under her eyelashes. She was stoked. They had barely spoken. She did most of it, but he remained happy and quiet. Too soon, they were there. In the village.

They parted ways with a smile. "I will see you soon," he said. "Sure, baby." And then he was gone.

Marina was already waiting for her at Leilani's. "You look like the cat that ate the canary, but tell me about it later. Right now, why don't you just go and help Leilani with the river thing, and I'll hang out here with the kids, and help picking up."

Salomé held up her hand. High five. "You got it, baby. See you later."

"Alligator." And Marina stood at the doorway with the children, looking after the other girls, until they couldn't see them any more. She turned to Ali. "You, and me, we are going to help Lani, okay?" The little girl, predictably, nodded her head eagerly, eyes wide, hands clapping.

There really wasn't that much to do, Leilani, obviously, being an excellent housekeeper. Even with three small children at home. Marina put the twins facing each other in one corner of the room, chubby legs spread apart, bright white nappies on their little bottoms. They screamed with laughter, absorbed at what was in front of them. Marina had just shown them a baby version of catch. Juan and Jaime were now intent on rolling a beautiful, ripe grapefruit, back and forth at each other. So, Marina and Ali swept, picked up toys, folded clothes, fed the babies, and washed the dishes. Then, they went to lie on the hammocks outside. Ali with her dolls. Marina with a sleeping twin cradled in each arm. They swung lazily, waiting for the others to get back. But when they were finally settled down, for some naptime, the porch stairs creaked.

Jeremiah didn't say a word, didn't even look at them, as he helped himself into the house. Nobody moved. When he came back, he deigned to acknowledge them with a glance. Raking his eyes over Marina, stretched out on the hammock, his eyes lingered on his grandsons, insultingly. Each baby had his head on Marina's breast, as she held them close together. She unconsciously tightened her arms softly. The old man's nappy head looked even whiter, in the early afternoon sun. More so than usual. And then, he was gone. And then, it was like he had never been there.

"Caribe!" Salomé called, her clothes still damp from the river.

He looked at her, his hands becoming still over his sketchbook, trying not to frown. He was working on something, and he had a feeling it was important. "What?"

Salomé sighed, hands on her hips. "I need to work out, man. This is cool and all, but there is a lot of bread in your diet. I don't want to get fat," she winked at him.

"So, what would you like to do?"

"Would you go with us, if we went running on a trail? I t would help." Marina shot to her feet, excited. "Cool!"

Caribe shrugged. He was past wondering about anything they asked of him. "Are you going running dressed like that?" he asked, pointing at the fabric that clung to her slender frame.

Salomé pretended to huff at him. "Of course not! I'm going to change and put on a pair of those," she informed him, pointing at his cotton pants, white against his shiny dark skin.

That got his attention. Caribe looked down at himself, and then up again, from one girl to the other. A grin spread slowly on his face. "I am very interested." Laughing, they kicked him out of their hut, and made him wait outside while they changed. Then, the three of them hit the trail.

They ran. Hard. The boy keeping up like a bodyguard. But in fact, that was his job. No harm was to come to these visitors. They were under his care, so to speak, and he was not about to fail. The girls just ran. Like the wind. Like their lives depended on it. Toward answers. Away from questions. They just ran. And their bodies, gratefully, did not let them down.

Caribe led them in a loop, private, quiet. Only the wind whispering in the afternoon, and the birds and small animals around them, accompanied them in their desperate race. Deep in the jungle, the trail was of sand, and their feet hit hard, rhythmically, leaving deep prints where there were usually none. As they approached the small, hidden pool they had played in the day before, they stopped for a swim, cooling down. When it was time to continue, Marina begged to stay, pleading she needed time alone. The village was only ten more minutes away, and Caribe knew she was perfectly safe. So they left her alone, and Marina did laps, to complete her workout, relishing just being by herself. After a few minutes, she glided to a stop on one side of the pool. Pushing off with her feet, she drifted off on her back, towards the other end of the pool. Lines spread out in an inverted V, from the top of her head, as her hair floated around her.

I am a mermaid.

And with that thought, she glided to the side, so that she was in the middle. With her back to the ocean, she couldn't see the water behind her. Spreading each of her arms to either side of the ledge she was leaning on, she let her head fall back, catching the rays of the setting sun. Eyes closed, she smiled to herself. Knees and ankles together, she swirled her legs around luxuriously, in elliptical movements.

I have scales, and I have a tail.

Finally, laughing at herself, she let her legs float naturally apart, and ended up doing more exercises. Scissors. She grinned, and did a couple of more laps. The wind swooped down suddenly, parting some leaves.

Marina never saw it. Out on the horizon, a massive ship appeared, slowly getting larger. It was headed towards the harbor of Encantada.

"Encantada!"

The young man smiled, as the men below him roared. Up above, in the crow's nest, the blond sailor lifted his face to the sky, joyful at seeing land for the first time in so many days. He sighed. Home. But where was home? He didn't know. It seemed to him, like lately, home was wherever he wasn't at the moment. The last couple of years, had been progressively bad for him, as restlessness threatened to overpower him, and make him lose everything he had achieved and struggled for. He looked at his men. They respected him, he recognized with pride. Most admired him, and some even loved him. He looked around. The majority of them were an assorted group of men, some good, and some bad, others, just plain mean. But there was one thing he knew for sure, and that was that they were all faithful to him. He cast his eyes over them slowly. Despite their faults or shortcomings, they were loyal to him and his family. In the end, it was all that mattered. A selected few were outright friends. Joshua, up in the crow's nest had been sailing with him since he first started, some years ago. The boy had barely been thirteen. He had somebody of confidence in every area of his ship. Sails, ropes, galley, hold, everywhere. He had his very own private, secret, anonymous army, known to each other and to himself. Everybody else was paid labor. Privileged, loyal, paid labor.

"Encantada! That whore!" snarled the old sailor next to him. One of his army, he was the entertainment. His name was Marcus, and his specialty was dirty limericks, and bawdy songs. The crew loved him.

"Easy, old man," he laughed. "There are those who consider Encantada a precious princess."

"Princess," the man scoffed. "Princess of Hell!"

"Hell is what we make it," he goaded.

"Then we must have made Encantada," he snarled.

Over Marcus' shoulder, he spotted the owner of the Lair, headed straight towards him. The Italian was tall and lean, sculpted like a Roman god. His white shirt billowed, and his black hair tossed in the wind. The smile on his face was stark white, genuinely happy, in his sun darkened face. "Encantada!" he cried. "Captain! Home!"

He laughed. "Encantada, Giancarlo!" Their hands met and they embraced, heart to heart. Stepping back, they looked at each other. Giancarlo was one of the two men closest to him. A good friend of the family, the young man trusted him with his ships, and all his business and personal affairs. A perfect private, secret, anonymous soldier. The third musketeer was back in Encantada, taking care of Giancarlo's business, watching over the Lair. That one, he trusted with his life.

After kissing the top of Marcus' bandana head, Giancarlo looked at his friend. "How do you feel?" he asked, genuine worry looking out through his eyes. The young man shrugged, his eyes wandering to the ever-growing island.

"Looking forward to a little fun, for a little while."

Giancarlo laughed. "Be careful what you wish for, my friend." It sounded like a premonition, as his Captain looked at him. "Be careful what you wish for."

Caribe sat on the floor at his doorway, frowning at the paper in his lap. Candlelight flickered, morphing his shadow on the balcony's ceiling. The paper held an outline in charcoal pencil, the silhouette of a man. There was nothing else. He was resisting knowing. Putting the paper and pencil aside with a big sigh, he shook the dreadlocks out of his face. Drawing up his knees, and folding his hands over them, he stared off into the darkness. Nothing moved. The bamboo was quiet in its grove, tired from all the whispering and swaying. Frogs were conspicuous because of their absence, while the crickets went off, taking advantage of the situation. Birds called, and insects chirped. Then, he heard something else, amongst the familiar night-time symphony. Drums.

"Caribe!" He turned his head, to look at Leila, leaning over the balcony railing on her front porch, across the way. "Go out, bebé," she urged. "Do not stay home. Go out and distract yourself, Caribe. You deserve some time for fun, papi."

Caribe sighed, getting to his feet, and waved at her. He knew she was only going to stay there, until he left. He put away his pad and pencil, and blew out the candle. Closing the door behind him, he headed out. Caribe heard the giggles before he saw the girls. *I don't want to know.* He began whistling as he got nearer, making his presence known. He didn't want to scare them, when he came out of the dark. "Ladies," he said, smiling.

Marina's voice rang out happily. "Papi!"

Salomé laughed. "Hey, baby! What are you up to? Come over here, and talk to us for a while."

Caribe shook his head, dreadlocks swinging around his head. "No, my friend. You come over here, and go out with me for a while."

"What's up?" asked Salomé.

"Swimming in the dark, papi?" teased Marina.

He held out his hands to them, his eyes glittering. "Would you ladies like to dance?"

And that's when they heard the drums.

This time was different. This time, they were convinced to join the dancers in the middle of the clearing. Except for their straight hair, and the absence of extra body adornments, the girls blended right in with the natives. Their brightly colored sarongs were just like those worn by the dancers, so they knew they would give them freedom of movement. They were much earlier than last night, and there wasn't that many people yet, making it easier to learn the steps as they went. By the time everybody was there, the girls were dancing like their hosts.

The Siren's Lair was jumping. There were rumors that Gaitano's ship had been spotted. Everybody in the bar was boisterous, excited.

The girls upstairs had a waiting list that would keep them busy all night.

Indio couldn't wait to see his brother. This was the first time Gaitano had ever left him. Times were not good. There were whispers of treachery. They needed to take care of business. He was busy cleaning the bar, when he heard a familiar voice above him.

"Hombre." Indio looked up at Silas' smiling face. "It's kind of loud in here, isn't it?" The old man said, paying for the drink put in front of hi m.

Indio shrugged. "No," he rumbled, looking at him suspiciously. He put a second drink in front of the Chinaman.

"It must be," Silas insisted.

He sighed. "Why?"

Jimmy waved his fingers over his ears. "It must be," he said, squinting one eye, and cocking his head to one side. Suddenly not playing, he downed his drink and put the glass down on the bar top. He smacked his lips, and looked at his bartending friend. "You can't hear the drums."

Without saying another word, the two men turned around, and headed out towards the door. For the second time today, Indio jumped over the bar.

The drums were thunderous, their beat taking over their hearts. As they watched, Indio understood why the old sailor and the chinaman had been witnessing these dances, for so many years. To say the least, it was wonderful.

The colors, the sounds, the synchronization. It all raced inside his veins, in a oneness with what he was witnessing. On either side of him, Silas and Jimmy sighed contentedly, swaying to the rhythm. They were the soldiers at home, and this was one of their perks, for being good sports, and staying behind. Indio's eyes devoured the magnificent spectacle before him. Dark skin glistened, and bare feet stomped, shells jingling on ankles and wrists. Half naked males spun in the air, before landing on their feet, dancing. Women lifted bare arms above their heads and undulated colorfully draped hips, in return.

Silas nudged him, and still, he couldn't tear his eyes away. "Look," the old man whispered, pointing to the middle of the the group of dancers. "Right, over there," he crooned in a hushed voice, finger pointing.

"Can you see them?" asked Jimmy quietly, bald head reflecting the ray of moonlight that filtered between the leaves. His face was in half shadows, giving him the appearance of a warrior. He was.

Indio went still, as he caught sight of them. Among the darkness of the native's skins, stood out the lighter, bronzed one of Marina. The firelight from the tiki torches just accentuated the golden highlights in her sun lightened hair. The curls danced around her shoulders, strands clinging to her wet back. The knot that held her sarong taut, lay soaked, between her breasts. Her legs were strong. Thighs, thick, from Tae Kwon Do; calves, cut, from running. Her skin glistened with a sheen of moisture, catching the firelight, casting shadows. He was mesmerized.

"Got nothing to say, now, do you?" the old man laughed softly, slapping a hand on his shoulder.

Indio slowly shook his head. He couldn't speak. Dancing next to Marina was Salomé. The young woman was aware of nothing but herself. He watched her as she twisted, and stood with legs apart. She bent her knees, the skirt creeping up her body, as she slapped both hands on her thighs, and shook her head from side to side, her long hair whipping around her face. The bartender groaned. He leaned over his horse's neck, as if he were in pain, to the amusement of his companions. Salomé had straightened up, and was now stomping and chanting, with the rest of the natives. He took a raggedy breath.

The chinaman patted him on the back. "Had about enough, cowboy?"

Indio shook his head, his skin crawling and tightening on his arms, his thighs. "No." His voice came out, little more than a croak.

"Well," said Silas, eyeing the clearing. They were now finishing, the drumming, having reached a frenzied peak. Everybody looked exhausted, and joyful, as if they had shared a mystical experience. They were all smiling, complimenting one another, especially their new visitors from Cayo Largo. The men backed their horses quietly, away from their hiding place. "Jimmy and I are going to head back into town, see what's going on." They turned their horses around, and walked them slowly, away from the villagers. "You'd better take a detour, and indulge yourself in that waterfall over yonder, for a little while."

Indio grunted. "Why?"

Jimmy answered, "Cold water,"

In town, people rushed to the docks. Gaitano's ship had just entered the harbor.

Salomé groaned, her forearm flung over her eyes, blocking out the morning sun. She crawled out of her bed, and readied herself for work. When she was about to leave, she woke Marina. "Max'll be here any minute," she murmured, kissing her sister on the forehead.

Marina sighed, hauling herself out of her hammock, and stood in a spot of sunlight, stretching her aching back. When John Kline finally arrived, she was waiting for him with a list of toiletries and necessities that she and Salomé needed urgently, if they were going to spend any more time, going back to basics. The storeowner was somewhat puzzled by some of the more stranger requests, but he admitted to her that it was within his power to get all of what the girls wanted, exotic as some of them may seem. He wrote down and drew pictures of the items in a small pad he carried with him. When he was finished, he handed Max over to her with a big smile. The baby promptly took over the floor, crawling through rays of sunlight, gurgling in pockets of shade. The father knew in his heart, his son was in good hands. God had answered their prayers.

"We don't know how to thank you, Marina," he began.

"Nothing to it," she smiled, raising both hands in the air, pointing towards Max with her head. "It's called supply and demand. You need a service, and I provide it for you. I am not doing anything these days," she smiled, rolling her eyes, "and you need someone, a friend, to watch Max for a few hours, while you remodel your store."

John nodded. She wasn't the usual, simpering, hesitant female that abounded in Encantada. "I couldn't have put it better, myself," he teased, getting back on the horse that had brought his baby and himself to the village.

Marina shrugged, framed in the doorway, Max draped around her feet. "It's called daycare."

The day unfolded like any other, and Max was an angel. Marina had such a good time, in fact, that she had Caribe sent word to Leilani. The younger girl came by with her siblings, and dropped them off, leaving to do her chores by the river unbelievably early. Jeremiah was in for a shock, today. The children's house was one of the cleanest, best kept huts in the village. The household ran tight and disciplined, under the loving care of the older sister. But Leilani was still a little girl herself, and more than playing mommy all the time, she needed to do girl things. And that's why Marina took care of the babies. They spent the morning playing games on the sundrenched floorboards of the hut, while village life went on around them.

Indio stirred, his eyes still closed. He could feel the warmth of the sun on his face, and it felt good. He had been dreaming of the new girl, Salomé. They were at the waterfall, spending some time together at the pool. It wan't an erotic dream, not yet. Just a nice, pleasant dream, where he was in the company of one of the most amazing women he had ever seen in his whole life. The lagoon was quiet, and they were alone in the jungle. The mist of the waterfall was so real, that he thought he could feel wet drops on his face. He frowned. There were more drops. Opening his eyes slowly, he looked up at the laughing face of his Captain. His brother. He closed his eyes again, and smiled, with a sigh. "Carlitos."

The young man laughed. "Indio! Is this the way you've been handling business while I've been gone, man?" He put the porcelain pitcher he had been holding, on the bedside table, shaking the water off his hand.

Indio sat up and got out of bed, bare feet flexing on the cool stone floor, sunlight washing his naked chest. They embraced, patting each other on the back, ending with one solid kiss on the cheek. They then pulled back, smiling into each other's eyes, relieved to be together again. "Carlitos," he repeated, shaking his head. "What did you do, man, come in like a thief in the night?"

The man he called Carlitos chuckled, and threw himself in a chair in the corner of the room. "No, man, not at all. Actually, we were docked and unloading by ten o'clock last night." He paused. His legs were stretched out in front of him, feet encased in fine, leather boots, crossed at the ankles. His arms were on the chair's armrests, and he was making a tent with his fingers, over which he peered at his best friend, with piercing turquoise eyes. "The Lair was my first stop. Even before I go to the comfort of my own home, I think of you." Now, his eyes were laughing, as they followed Indio around the room, as he got ready. "I must have just missed you. One of the girls told me you jumped over the bar, and tore out of there like a bat out of hell." Now, his eyes were curious. "Nobody knows where you went."

Indio pointed a finger at his chest. "Good." He reached for a shirt, throwing it on. His thick fingers braided his hair expertly, and he was ready to go. Carlitos just looked at him, a smile on his face. Hauling himself to his feet, he joined him at the door. "They did mention, however, that when you finally came back, you were wet. Like you had been swimming."

Indio grunted.

Outside, the street thronged with people, doing things and going places. It seemed as if the population had doubled overnight. There was a markedly abundance of sailors, that had not been evident before. And on everybody's lips, like an answer to a prayer, was his name. Gaitano.

Carlos braced himself, as they came out of the Siren's Lair. He was never very comfortable with the amount of attention he got, immediately following one of his successful voyages. He preferred when he had been on the island for a while, and nobody paid any attention to him, until it was time for him to leave, again. Walking slowly up the street, away from the docks, he felt he was home. But his heart told him there was something better. They walked side by side, the two grown men, relaxed in each other's space. They had been raised together, and their strong bond was evident in the way they, at moments, seemed to move as one. That they looked good, no doubt. They both seemed to be in uniform. Black pants, tight on their legs, and white billowing shirts, no wide red sashes at their waists. Where one had a pair of the blackest boots anybody had ever seen, the other's feet were encased in moccasins. One wore a hat and coat, the stubble on his face, leaving no doubt as to his profession. Gold hoops hung at his ears. The other wore feathers in his hair, and beads around his neck. His unlined face, clean and hard, like a statue's.

Carlos smiled. With every step he heard his name. On some lips, a prayer; on others, a curse. *Gaitano.* He sighed to himself, even as he walked directly into the sea of faces, eyes not meeting anyone's. It wasn't that he was aloof. He just had an image to maintain. He'd been gone a long time, and they had missed him. They needed him. It was his island.

Not missing a step, the men turned down the conch bordered path.

Inside, the lawman was waiting for them, sitting on his desk, facing the doorway. They exchanged greetings.

"Carlos," Pedro Barbosa said warmly. "How was your trip?"

"Fine, Pedro, just fine. We made contacts with some of the minor islands along the way. It seems that the raids have been happening everywhere."

The lawman slammed his fist on his desk, visibly shaken. His voice trembled with outrage. *"This has got to stop!"* he roared.

Indio's face never changed, his expression never wavered. He didn't even blink. But at the corner of his eye, a muscle twitched. He looked at Carlos. "This has got to stop," he echoed.

"Giancarlo and I have been discussing it at length. We suspect that there is someone amongst us, leaking information." When he looked at the men in front of him, his eyes were deadly. "I am calling a meeting, tonight, usual time, usual place. I expect everybody to be there, no excuses. Let them know," he told Pedro, his voice dripping ice. The lawman felt the hair stand up on end, all over his body. It was at times like this, that he recognized that, next to Carlos Gaitano's immense name and power, his badge was just that. A piece of metal to hang on his shirt. Indio's skin tingled. In his mind, he let out a war yell, like those of his ancestors in the Southwest desert. He was ready. "This matter will be taken care of, once and for all."

And without another word, the pair left, leaving the lawman looking after them, with gratitude in his eyes, and a prayer of thanks on his lips.

They kept walking, their steps leading them to the General Store. Mrs. Calloway was standing at the counter, her back to them as they entered, and from the amount of eye-rolling John Kline was doing, she was obviously, giving him a hard time. They all looked up at the sound of the bells. Mrs. Calloway's hand flew to her chest, and she gasped, eyes fearful behind her glasses. She backed herself into the counter, and John Kline's hand shot out to steady her.

"*Gaitano*," she murmured, her lips trembling.

Carlos sighed inwardly, as he frowned fiercely at the old woman. On the inside, Indio rolled on the floor with laughter. It never ceased to amuse him, the people that were scared of Carlitos.

John went around the counter, and steadied the quivering woman. "There, there, Mrs. Calloway, stop this nonsense. Why, if I didn't know any better, I'd say you'd just seen a ghost."

"I dreamt he was dead," whispered Mrs. Calloway, her eyes never leaving the man's face.

Larissa stepped in at that moment, from around the back. She was muttering to herself as she peered at a notebook with numbers on it. Absently, she brushed back the black hair from her face. Looking up, she saw the two men, and froze. *They are formidable!* She didn't say anything for a moment, just observing them in silence. The men felt like squirming.

"You are scaring my customers," she finally accused. "Did you not see the NO PIRATES ALLOWED sign outside?" She screamed with laughter, as Carlos rushed her, faster than lightning, and threw her over his shoulder. Mrs. Calloway's jaw dropped open, expecting him to just walk out the door with Mrs. Kline. Instead, he deposited her on the counter, next to her husband. Larissa giggled, her eyes sparkling at him. "Nice to see you, Gaitano," she said tenderly. "Larissa," he answered, his voice making her name sound like a poem.

She sighed, and John Kline playfully glowered at all of them. "We have much business to discuss. This voyage was a complete success. Also, when you come by the warehouse, I have some things for you and the baby." Reaching into one of his coat pockets, he pulled out a small kaleidoscope. It was beautifully made out of brass, and glass, and wood. Shiny, it looked like a telescope on the outside, but on the inside, it held a magic kingdom of swirling colors and patterns. "This is for Max." He looked around him, as Larissa gasped, gently taking the fine instrument from him. Putting her eye to it, she held it up to the light. She gasped again. "Where is he, by the way?" Carlos asked, looking around them. Caught up in the exchange of words, Mrs. Calloway also frowned, and looked around.

Larissa put down the kaleidoscope, delighted. "Max?" she asked happily. "He's in daycare!"

Carlos and Indio walked away chuckling. They turned back the way they had come, walking slowly. "How have things been here?" Gaitano asked.

"Damn quiet," came the immediate reply.

Carlos raised his eyebrows. "No excitement? Not even at the Lair?"

Indio shook his head, just a slight movement. His eyes were firmly ahead of him, warily watching the faces. "There is nothing exciting about the Lair, anymore," he mourned softly.

Carlos laughed. "Do not tell me you are tired of women!"

"Not women. Just those."

Carlos nodded, understanding. He never frequented the Lair himself, unless he was out drinking with his friends. "I know exactly what you mean." As they approached a storefront, Carlos stopped. "Let us go in here. I need to talk some business for a moment."

They stepped inside, and were immediately greeted by their reflections in different mirror, hung up around the large room. Indio rolled his eyes, catching sight of the swatches of cloth draped on the walls like art hangings, and the wax dummies in the corners. Suddenly bored, he stood right under the outrageous chandelier, and looked up at it, his eyes reflecting the twinklin g lights. A voice behind them greeted them warmly. *"Gaitano!"*

Carlos turned, and stared at the beautiful pale blonde beauty headed his way. "Dominique," he bowed.

"Gaitano," she smiled, nodding at him. "How nice to have you back."

"How's business?"

"Wonderful. I cannot keep up with the demand! I even had to hire a new girl."

"Liana's not working for you, anymore?" Gaitano asked, genuinely curious.

Things were bound to change while he was away on a voyage.

"Yes, she is. She has just been sick, and not able to come to work."

Carlos glanced at Indio, still entranced by the chandelier above him. "I will expect you at the docks, this afternoon." He laughed at her expression. "Yes," he answered before she asked, "I got what you ordered."

Dominique clasped her hands and spun around, the fabric swirling around her legs. "Thank you! Thank you!" She stopped, hugging him briefly, before stepping away to look at him. "I knew I could count on you."

At that moment, Salomé stepped out from the back. Rich fabric lay draped over her arm, as she studied a piece of paper in her hand. She looked up, noticing the men. Her eyes found the brave under the chandelier. Without making a sound, she sidled next to him. "Hey, baby," she said softly.

Indio froze, and his heart skipped a beat, his eyes dropping immediately to meet her laughing ones. "Hey," he answered softly.

They stared at each other. Salomé looked up at him, forgetting everything. "This is where I work," she offered. "Did you need something?"

Indio thrilled at her teasing, shaking his head slowly. "Gaitano had business with Miss Swan. Come," he said, taking her hand, and leading her to his brother. "Salomé," he introduced, his voice caressing her name, making his brother look at him.

Salomé looked up at one of the scariest men she had ever seen. His energy was evident, in every inch of his tall, powerful frame. The black shadow on his face was thick, hiding the ravishing good looks under it. His eyes were just like Mami's. When they were growing up as children, they had teased Sloane for being the only one with blue eyes in their family. This man's eyes were just like her second mother's. She smiled into them. "Nice to meet you."

The man swept the hat off his head, revealing thick, curly black hair. His voice rumbled deep in his chest. He took her hand and bowed over it, pressing his lips to it without breaking contact with Salomé's green eyes. "Salomé"

Indio finished the introduction. "Gaitano."

Salomé raised her eyebrows, having heard the name incessantly, almost since they ended up in this place. "Gaitano," she repeated softly.

Dominique broke the moment. "Salomé is my new employee. She is staying in the village with Leila and Caribe, for a while, and has agreed to help me. Now that you are back, I will be swamped with new customers and new orders.

"That is a bad thing?" asked Gaitano.

"No," she conceded. "But it can be overwhelming."

Indio stood next to Salomé. He held her eyes. "Would you like to have lunch with me?" he asked suddenly.

Everybody stopped and stared. Oblivious, he waited for Salomé's answer. She nodded, smiling into his eyes. "I would like that very much. Thank you for asking me." She glanced at Dominique, who nodded encouragingly at her, her blue eyes wide behind Gaitano's back, smile splitting her face.

Dominique stopped the brave, as he looked as if he were just about to walk out with her new employee. "Indio? I need her for another couple of hours, but you can come and get her later, if you want, is that all right?"

Indio nodded. His eyes never left the girl. "I will come pick you up later," he told her.

Salomé nodded. "Sure, baby. Ill see you in a little while."

Indio smiled and left. Gaitano stared after his friend, and with an apologetic smile at the women, he followed him outside. "Indio!" he called at the brave's back. He caught up to him, and they fell into step, moving comfortably together, nodding absently as people greeted them. "Beautiful girl," he murmured aloud.

Indio smiled.

"Marina!"

Marina looked about at the sound of Caribe's voice. "What?!"

"Would you like to go into town with me, this afternoon?" He stood in her doorway, arms at shoulder level, propped against the doorframe, hands hanging. He was making faces at the baby on the floor.

"Sure," she smiled. And she didn't ask any questions. So far, any and every outing with Caribe had been educational, fun, and inspiring. He was their guide in this impossible journey. "Why don't you bring me Ali and the twins, and have Leilani go do her thing before John gets here to pick up Max. That way, I'll be able to go with you and come back to be at Leilani's, when Jeremiah shows up to do his inspection."

Caribe smiled, and winked at her. "Done" Marina blew him a kiss, and he was gone.

And that is how it came to be, that when John Kline came to pick up his only son, instead of one baby, he found three. The babies were all sitting on the floor, little heads huddled together, intent on sharing a toy Caribe had rapidly made them. Two nappy heads flanked the sleek one, all with jet black hair, as they intently studied the figures made out of bamboo sticks. Languishing in one of the hammocks, Ali swung, little feet pushing off the wall, while her head hung upside down, fingers brushing the floor, as she watched her brothers, and their brand new best friend.

John chuckled, and winked at Marina, as they exchanged a look. "They multiply!" he laughed.

"God forbid!" she answered, rolling her eyes.

Max looked up at his father's voice, and babbling at the other two boys, he stopped what he was doing. Running, as only babies who just learned to walk, can, he threw himself at his dad, flinging both little arms around his legs, and craning his head up at him, gurgling excitedly. John scooped up his son, kissing him soundly. Max, turned around in his arms, and pointed to the two other little boys. John walked him back over there, and squatted down, smiling as they turned to look at him. "I am pleased to meet you, gentlemen," he told them softly. "I am Max's dad."

Marina laughed. "Meet the local twins. Jaime is on your left, and Juan has the distinguishing birthmark by the side of his jaw."

John took both their hands, shaking them gently. "Jaime, Juan," he crooned to each of them, "John Kline, at your service." The twins laughed at him, loving the attention. "If you ever need anything, please feel free to ask."

"I'm Ali!"

John turned his head to laugh at the little, upside-down voice, coming from the hammock. He gently took one of her little hands and brought it to his lips, tickling her with his whiskers. "Enchanted, madam. You are quite beautiful, Miss Ali,". Ali giggled, covering her mouth with her hands, and turned to look at Marina. Marina covered her mouth with her own hands, and widened her eyes at the little girl, in complicity. John smiled and straightened up, Max wildly gesturing at the babies. "I brought you what you asked for." He made a funny face. "Larissa wants to talk to you about a certain contraption you have in there. She is dying to know what it is for."

Marina hid a secret smile. "I shall tell her when I see her," she teased, catching the fleeting look of disappointment in his eyes.

They chatted back and forth for another minute or so, and the men left. Next, came Leilani. Her face broke out into a beautiful smile, the peace she felt, evident in the way she walked, and the manner in which she held herself. She had changed a lot in the last couple of days, looking more relaxed. Once Marina found herself alone, Caribe showed up.

They took the trail into town in silence. The boy seemed unusually thoughtful. Marina respected his privacy, and kept her questions to herself. When they reached town, they found themselves caught up in a tide of people, like Marina had still to experience. It was scary, and she suddenly feared getting lost. Caribe winked at her in reassurance, when he caught sight of the distress in her face. Taking her hand, he squeezed. Locking her fingers with his, Marina felt herself relax. Caribe won't let anything happen to me. He navigated expertly among the crowd. They headed towards the docks.

Salomé put her elbows on the bar, and rested her chin on her hands. This works, she thought, happily. The brave had appeared at her workplace, to take her to lunch. He was definitely the big, strong, silent type, and she soon discovered that he was extremely quiet, content to just look at her. Her small talk had just filled in the awkward silences, and he was educated, and polite enough to keep up his end of the conversation. Now, he was busy behind the bar, helping the girl he had left tending, while he treated Salomé to lunch. She sighed, catching sight of the fabric straining against his behind, as he bent over to retrieve a bottle the girl dropped. At one end of the bar, sat Jimmy and Silas, happily watching her, watching him. They were enjoying themselves immensely. But they weren't laughing any longer. Before their eyes, they saw the beginnings of a beautiful relationship. They watched Indio visibly relax, and become more loose, while talking to the girl. She laughed often, and teased the brave. But the truth was she was just as thunderstruck as he was.

"I am off, already," she said to his back.

Indio turned around, his lone braid whipping around his torso. "Lucky you."

"I suppose you have a lot of work to do," she smiled, as he grunted. "Would I be in your way if I tagged along?"

Indio turned to look at her carefully, his eyes gliding along the fabric that hugged her curves. Her long hair cascaded around her, and her eyes beckoned. "Salomé," he explained softly, "if I let you tag along, I will not get any work done, and neither will anybody else around me."

Salomé smiled. "Then I better not."

Indio smiled back. "Better not." He walked around the bar, and accompanied her to the door. Behind them, the old sailor and the chinaman slapped hands, happy for their friend. Outside on the sidewalk, they stood, just looking at each other. "I will walk you back," Indio offered.

"Indio!" They both turned to see Gaitano coming out from the alley next to the Lair. "Let's go!"

"You have to go," Salomé told him.

Indio hesitated. It seemed that the whole street was moving towards the docks. He didn't like the idea of leaving her to go alone, navigating the mob, in the opposite direction. At that moment, two familiar faces appeared. His eyes met Caribe's. The boy's look held his steadily, coldly.

Marina greeted them happily. "Hey, Indio!" He nodded at her. "Salo!" she cried excitedly. "Let's go, *mami*, we're helping Caribe today." Indio watched the boy's eyes change, challenging him.

Salomé nodded. "Cool!" She tossed him a sassy look over her shoulder. "Indio can't play, today."

They both blew him kisses and crossed the street, laughing, their arms around each other's shoulders, promising Caribe they wouldn't be long, they just wanted to look at something. He nodded his goodbyes at them, and disappeared down the alley.

Caribe sighed. He was getting used to them. They were both like children, when they were together. He started pacing, keeping an eye on them. Across the street, they were standing in front of a store window, laughing at some display. Distractedly, Caribe stepped off the sidewalk, and stumbled into the alley. Suddenly, he felt himself hauled roughly back, a strong arm going around his neck, choking him, as fingers grabbed his dreadlocks, hauling his head back. His eyes widened, until he recognized the voice in his ear. "There seems to be a misunderstanding," Indio said softly.

Caribe put his hands on the arm around his neck, giving himself room to breathe, as his fear turned into anger. "You are the only misunderstood here," he retorted bravely.

Indio held him firmly, and turned him so that they were facing the girls. Totally unaware, the girls were turned in their direction, clueless as to what was going on. They seemed to be looking for the village boy. Indio felt jealousy creep over him. "You have become bold, boy," he taunted.

"I am the man of my house!"

"You thought I wanted them for the Lair," Indio accused softly, hissing in his ear.

Caribe struggled. The arm around his throat tightened once again, and pain shot through his scalp. He stopped. "They are not sirens!"

"No," agreed Indio. "They are not." He shook the boy in his hold. "Look at them!" he instructed. "They are beautiful. They are ladies. They will never be sirens." His breath cooled the boy's ear with his words. "You see the one?" he murmured. "The one who takes care of the baby? See her? Her hair looks like the sun got caught in it, doesn't it? And look at those thighs, almost as big as a man's. That one makes my breath catch." He felt Caribe stop struggling in his arms, as he understood. "See her friend, now?" he instructed. "The beautiful working woman, staying with your family? She looks like an Egyptian princess, doesn't she? It makes you wonder, if her skin is as silky as it looks," he rasped. He squeezed Caribe one more time. "That one..." he continued in the boy's ear, his words, almost threatening. "That one makes my heart stop."

Caribe broke loose, and turned to look at the Indian. They faced off. For a moment, Caribe realized the magnitude of being the travelers' caretaker. Without a word, he turned his back on the brave, and crossed the street towards the girls. They laughed when they finally caught sight of him. Indio watched as the boy laughed back at them, and proceeded to put an arm around each of their shoulders. The girls happily slipped their arms around his waist, and away they went, down towards the dock.

Indio stared after them, his feelings raging deep inside. He felt Carlos come up to stand next to him. Gaitano had caught the end of his exchange with Caribe, but had missed out on what was going on. Now, all he saw was the village boys' dreadlocked head disappearing into the crowd, his arms around a couple of females, with beautiful sarongs. Indio grunted at him and moved. "Let us go."

The docks were loud and packed. People screamed at each other. There were throngs of workers, as they unloaded the ship that had just come in. "What are we doing here?" yelled Salomé at Caribe.

"We help get everybody's merchandise in order," he yelled back, pointing to something ahead of them. The girls looked. Along the nearest warehouse, there were crates turned over, serving as tables, spaced at intervals. At each crate sat a man, with a load of papers, checking things out, and barking out orders. Accompanying these gentlemen were more men, following out their orders. Stretching in front of these crates were lines of people, waiting.

Salomé looked aghast, at the lines. "Oh, God! These must be the unemployment, food stamps, driver's license, and Medic Aid lines!" she said in Marina's ear.

Marina shook her head, with a smile. She pointed out the longest one. "You forgot that one,"

"What is that one for?" Salomé asked.

"That one," Marina teased, "is for a reggaeton concert." Salomé giggled. "Who's playing?"

"Daddy Yankee."

Caribe shook his head as they high-fived, heads thrown back in laughter. He steered them to the last crate. A familiar voice boomed out at them. "Caribe!"

The girls looked up as they recognized it. "John!"

"Exciting isn't it?" he laughed.

"Very," agreed Salomé.

"Scary," admitted Marina.

The girls watched, as Caribe set out to work. There was merchandise and wares, behind the crates. Apparently, these were all categorized and numbered, labeled with the name of the recipients. The problem was that there were many recipients. Their system was lacking. A person would go to the man at the crate, and give them their name, address, and a description of what they were there to receive. The man would then look them up by last name or by the category of the merchandise, find a number, and give it to one of his helpers. This person, in turn, would run the number, to where there were other men waiting to dispatch the merchandise itself. The problem lay in the time it took for the articles to be found, and brought back to the persons claiming them. Meanwhile, people stood sweating in the sun, awaiting their turn.

Salomé grabbed Caribe's arm, as he passed by. "You've got to be kidding me!" she exclaimed, gesturing to the crowds stretching out behind them. "How long does all of this take?"

Caribe looked at her, aghast. "How long do you think it takes?" he asked, crossly. "At least a couple of days!"

Marina's jaw dropped. "No way!"

Upset now, Caribe pulled his arm away from Salomé, and took a step backwards. He glared at each of them. "You are silly girls, and you are wasting my time!"

"Oh, no, baby!" Salomé pleaded, taking hold of his arm, once more. "Let us help." She turned to John Kline. "Would you trust Marina and I to help you, and maybe make some suggestions for moving this along a little bit?" she asked glancing at the crowd once more. "We can cut your time in half," she winked at him.

The storeowner stepped back, gesturing to the crate. "Oh, please, be my guest!"

Salomé thanked him with a smile, and swung her hips, as she stood behind the crate. She took the charcoal pencil that was in John's hand, and turned over the top paper in front of her. "We are going to start from scratch," she announced, to the now curious males. "Marina is going out with a blank piece of paper, and will get from each single person in this line, their name, and what they came to get." She looked at Marina. "You get this paper back to me, with no less than ten names at a time. I will find their number and write it next to their information. Then, it gets taken back there," she said, gesturing to the mounds of crates and boxes, behind her." They all looked. Caribe cringed. Marina shuddered. John Kline shook his head with a sigh. "By the time everything on that paper is dispatched, I should have at least twenty more names, ready to go."

Caribe nodded. "Yes"

Salomé continued. "Here's the deal, though." She turned to John. "How would you like that time cut in half?" He raised his eyebrows. "You need runners. Just by looking at all this, I dare say your boss can afford to pay for a little extra help. You need runners. Look around you," she said, gesturing at the people milling around, not standing in lines. There were groups of teenagers, laughing, egging each other on as they harassed the girls. Bunches of little boys ran around in packs, bare feet thundering on the wharf, like wild mustangs. Older people stood around, silver hair glinting in the sun, leaning on canes or hobbling about. "Here is how this could work so much better. You get the little boys to take back there, the pieces of paper with the information. Half the teenagers have muscle, so they would help carry the stuff over here. The other half can help locate the merchandise by area. Then, we will have the older gentlemen, dispatch the items to the people." She had their full atten tion. "The children will work for candy, and coins. The teenagers, you offer some money, and those old enough to drink, you buy a round at the bar where Indio works. The older people, you offer money, and housecleaning for a week, for free. You make it a social event and bring them all together. Everybody wins."

Marina nodded, reaching for a pencil and a piece of paper. "Let's do it!" Turning to the first person in line, she flashed them her brightest smile. "Hello! My name is Marina, and my sister and I are working for," she paused, and then suddenly remembered. "Gaitano! At the moment, we are assigned to John Kline, the owner of the general store in Downtown Encantada. We are here to make this thing go faster. I just need your name, address, and what you are expecting. Would you happen to have a number of reference? No? Not to worry. My associate has it at the desk." By the time she had finished, she had a small crowd around her, nodding their heads.

"About damn time!" snarled the third person in line.

Caribe nodded. "I will go get the recruits," he announced, heading to the groups of wandering males.

Salomé raised her eyebrow at John Kline. "Well?"

John kissed the top of her head, and laughed. Slapping his hands together, he rubbed them vigorously. "Let's do it!"

It was a hit. After the initial wait, while the system got going, everything ran on smooth wheels. The line seemed to flow, without stopping. Children would surround Salomé, waiting for her numbers, and would then scatter, racing each other to be the first ones to deliver the papers. Teenagers yelled at each other, as they got a rhythm going. People turned from cranky and ornery, to happy and patient. The success was such, that during a break, Caribe helped establish the system for the other lines.

"That's amazing," murmured Gaitano. They were standing side by side, at a second-floor window of the warehouse behind the crates. Undetected, they watched in awe. The spectacle before them was without precedent. The lines, the blessed lines, part of their lives, as sea merchants, were actually moving! They pressed their foreheads against the glass, the better to look at the two young women that stood out from the rest of the crowd. The one, sitting down; the other, all over the place.

Indio sighed, as his eyes caressed the top of Salomé's head. She moved sideways in the seat someone had so thoughtfully provided for her, the better to cross her legs. From his vantage point, he could see the fabric of her colorful sarong, ride up her thighs. He groaned to himself, as he felt the material of his pants grow tighter in the front. Every time she moved, he could see her cleavage. "I like that woman," he finally admitted.

Gaitano chuckled. "Excellent taste, my friend," he conceded. But his eyes kept going back to Marina. "What about the other one?" he asked, following her every move. As they watched, they saw Caribe and Marina begin to pass one another, then stop, and go back towards each other. Marina said something apparently funny. With a big smile on her face, she took hold of his dreadlocks and pulled his face to hers, giving him a kiss on the cheek. They watched as he held her for a moment. She turned her face up towards the sun, eyes closed, laughing wildly. He kissed her face, and they parted ways again, each one to do their job.

Indio glanced sideways at his brother. "That is Marina."

Gaitano nodded. "Marina..."

Marina never saw him.

Later that day, a very happy trio reached the village, exuberant over their success at the docks. The whole town was talking about the two women from Cayo Largo. Although they had had a full day already, they still went for their run.

The loop seemed shorter today, than it did yesterday. They ran past trees, and rocks, and clearings. They sprinted over fallen logs, and ducked under hanging vines, detoured around suspended spider webs. And all they could think of was the trail, and the motion of their bodies. When they finally arrived at the pool, they made it a race to the edge, and dove in headfirst. The laps they swam were automatic, just like their running, as muscles screamed in protest. Once again, Marina stayed behind, and once more, she pretended to be a mermaid. Finally, before she was too relaxed to move, she did one final lap and got out of the pool. Wringing the water out of her hair, she looked back at the turquoise water with longing. Heaving a big sigh, she left.

Gaitano smiled. While the matter at the docks had been taken care of, by their Cayo Largo guests, he had gone to the Lair, where one of the girls had gladly trimmed his hair, and shaved his face. She had made sure to let him know, that she was more than happy to include more for his money. He graciously declined. I refuse to risk catching anything, thank you very much, love, he thought to himself. He shook his head at her with a smile, not committing to anything else. Finally changing his outfit, he sneaked through some back allies, to the beckoning beach. Nobody recognized him, thankfully, looking as he was, like his real self. When he finally reached the shore, he raised his face to the sky, and let out a shout. Seagulls screamed at him, as they scolded him for ruining their concentration. He flexed his toes in the sand, reveling in the massage his feet received. He began walking.

The sun felt warm on the side of his face, as it headed towards the mountains. The wind felt good through his shorter hair, and he felt lighter without the beard. He looked younger, too, and he enjoyed that. It helped keep the attention off him, and most people didn't even recognize him. He knew where he was going. It had been his getaway since he was a child. Now he used it to stay in shape, and as therapy. As he approached the pool, he heard feet pounding on the trail up ahead. Curious, he kept himself hidden in the shadows. As he watched, he saw the couple come into view. It was Leila's son, Caribe, and that new girl... the visitor from Cayo Largo, that so impressed his friend. Salomé. They didn't look like they were running from anything, he decided as they went by. Continuing on his way, he stopped short at the edge of the natural pool, when he heard splashing. Hiding again, he dropped to the ground. Crawling on his stomach, he parted some leaves, to take a better look. What he saw made time stand still for him.

Marina. The other one. She was there, right now, in his pool, the one he had claimed as his own, precisely because nobody ever went there. He watched her at play. She did laps, at first, coming dangerously close to spotting him. He stood still, as he saw her take a breath with a stroke. She dove, turned, and kicked off, heading in the opposite direction. Then, she glided to the middle, where she lifted her face to the sun, facing the mountains. There, he watched as she seemed to exercise her legs, swirling them in the water as she held them close together. He heard her laugh and get out of the pool, twisting her hair with her hands. He saw the water drip to the ground. Satisfied, she tossed her head and gave one last look around. Then she headed towards the trail, and disappeared. He could hear her pounding feet go in the same direction of her friends. He sighed. She never saw him.

That night, the drums played violently, the celebration intense, relief for the safe homecoming of Gaitano and his crew, overwhelming. The dancing was at a frenzy. And when the girls gyrated and twirled, feet pounding, senses pulsating, they were not alone. When they closed their eyes, bodies glistening from sweat, faces turned up, mouths parted, he was there. Indio. And next to him, the pirate, Carlos Gaitano.

The candle flickered on the table. The men looked at each other, and back at their Captain. They had already congratulated each other profusely on the success of their voyage, and it was time now, to take care of business. Gaitano looked at each one in turn.

His men. Not his crew, but his soldiers. Those, sworn fidelity to him, and his family.

Indio stood shoulder to shoulder with him, arms crossed, face stern. His hair was loose, covering his shoulders like a blanket. He wore a simple suede vest, trimmed with shells. A feather hung from one ear, and turquoises screamed against his dark wrists. Indio was his Quartermaster. When they weren't on the ocean, it was he, who was in charge of the men. For this particular voyage he had stayed behind, being needed more at home, in Encantada, than he was on the ocean. Giancarlo had taken his place instead, and at the same time he fulfilled his own duties. The Italian was the Ship's Master. In other words, without him, they weren't going anywhere. The handsome rogue was also the legitimate owner of the only brothel in town, the Siren's Lair, which also made him filthy rich, by pirate's standards. Money did have its privileges, however. In his case, it allowed him to leave his business in trusted hands, while he went out and played with the boys, in the high seas. The women of Encantada were devastated, that they could not entice him into leaving his bachelor ways. Padre Ignacio was the priest with the pistolas. He had a higher interest in being one of Gaitano's soldiers in Encantada. Besides being committed to saving lives, he was dedicated to saving souls. Pedro Barbosa half-sat on his desk, one foot on the floor, the other, swinging. He was cleaning his pistol. Sitting on the desk, next to his thigh, lay a dirk in its scabbard. He had been pledged to his father, Don Carlos Gaitano, and ended up here in Encantada, under his command. Finally, was a massive black man, standing in shadows. His head was shaved, and he sported gold earrings. The lack of a shirt accentuated his huge muscles, and his pants looked like they had to be made especially for him. The rescued African had been baptized with the name of Solomon. He was his Boatswain.

"What did you find out, Carlitos?" asked Padre Ignacio, concern written all over his face.

Gaitano moved closer to them, his voice hushed in the adobe building. "We heard rumors about an extremely bloodthirsty captain that is brutalizing the natives, along a string of islands, just to the north of here."

The padre crossed himself. "Does he show quarter? Is there any pattern to his madness?" He looked around the room, trying not to panic. Giancarlo shook his head sadly, in silence. The other three didn't move.

"We need to stay one step in front of them," Carlos continued. "Already, we have the advantage, by just knowing about him."

"That is not enough, Carlitos!" cried Padre Ignacio.

"Could we even hope to stand a chance, if he makes it to Encantada?" asked Pedro Barbosa without looking up from what he was doing. He did his best thinking, when his hands were occupied.

"Solomon learned some information about the ship, if not the captain himself. Every single target has been loaded. Every single one!" He looked around at each of them. In the last week alone, he hit five ships off the coast of Jamaica. Successfully."

Padre Ignacio shrugged, confused. "You target ships. That is what you do ---"

Gaitano cut him off. "Pirate ships."

The room fell silent. The punishment for a pirate raiding other pirate ships, was death. Solomon's voice rumbled from the corner. "He seems to know exactly when another ship has been successful."

"But is there a common denominator we should be looking for?" insisted Padre Ignacio.

Carlos looked straight at him. "They are all Gaitano ships."

The next day, life went on as usual. Actually, it was unusual. The day before had been such a success, that most of the businesses were actually closed in town, while their owners re-stocked and took care of the merchandise they just received. Sort of like a holiday. Village life, however, remained the same.

Marina stretched luxuriously, rolling in her hammock. For a moment, she hung with her head upside down, like Ali had, the day before. Pushing herself off the wall gently, she sighed. It was her day off. Straightening up and exiting the hammock, she shook her head with a smile. Standing at the doorway, she surveyed her surroundings. Usually, she was going somewhere, or doing something, or talking to someone. It seemed like there was always people around her.

Today was cloudy again. Salomé had gone on to Dominique Swan's store. She could see Leila walk down the path, a bundle on her head, on her way home already, from the river. Marina began to go to help her, but the woman waved her away, with a mock scowl. "A day off is a day off, missy," she called happily. "Tomorrow it will be gone." Marina chuckled.

Turning back inside, she pulled out the bag John Kline had brought her the day before. In it, was a special made razor. She held it up in front of her, and smiled in bliss. Standing up, she made sure there was nobody around. They had put up coverings on the windows, and these hung still in the morning air. Marina stepped out the back door, where there were always tubs of water, thanks to the attentions of Leila's loving son. So, looking around again, Marina convinced herself that she was alone. And that is how, in the privacy of her backyard, while sitting on the steps, with her skirt hiked up, Marina shaved herself smooth.

Finally, she left the house. Walking past Caribe's hut, she spied him on his front porch. He was scowling at a piece of paper in his hand. Marina looked at him for a moment, and decided to leave him alone. He had been preoccupied lately, more so than usual. She noticed him talking to himself. *What is wrong with that boy? I hope he's okay.* He sensed her looking at him, and raised his head, his eyes meeting hers. From the path, she blew him a kiss, waving happily at him. Caribe's smile reached his eyes. He blew her one back. And then he went back to his paper. Marina sighed, and kept on walking.

It turned out to be a Nature walk. The jungle was darker than usual, since the sun didn't seem to have energy to shine. She walked slowly, taking her time. Her feet took her in the loop they usually ran in the afternoons. Walking, as she was, she could actually appreciate everything. The jungle seemed to embrace her. She felt humbled. The variety of things to see was what kept her from thinking. She kept walking, slowly.

Unknown to her, a distance away, someone was using her swimming place.

Gaitano cut the water like a knife. The cold water washed over him, waking him up. He needed a clear mind to go to work. This last voyage, successful as it had been, may be just that, his last voyage, if he didn't do something quickly. To top it all off, yesterday he had discovered some discrepancies in his books. The man he had left in charge of his books was not his usual accountant, and there was bound to be differences. However, just because he was out at sea, did not mean he wouldn't find out if anything was amiss. He shook his head and continued his laps, letting go of his thoughts. As he turned, he detected movement out of the corner of his eye. Among the leaves, he could see patches of white. It was her. The other girl. He chuckled to himself. This could prove interesting. He knew the exact moment she saw him. She didn't take another step.

Marina stood, and held her breath. In her pool, was a man. She frowned. Of course, she had never been here this early before. But she had been under the impression that nobody ever came here. Where did he come from? But right now, it didn't matter. She watched him. His strokes were strong and sure, his breathing beautifully synchronized. She smiled. This was an athlete. She could relate. Dropping to the ground, she made herself comfortable, glad she was wearing a skirt today. The man looked good.

"I know you are here."

Marina froze. She shook her head quickly, fearing her mind was playing games on her. She strained her ears, trying to pick up any noise over the thundering of her heart. She watched as he swam away and reached the far side of the hidden pool.

He turned and flung his head back in a boyish laugh. "I know you are here!" he called out, before disappearing underwater.

Marina blinked. She did a quick mental scan of her surroundings and perceived no danger. But she couldn't move. She just held her breath and waited for him to swim back. Water churned from his kicking feet and his whole body glistened in the struggling sun, as he headed straight towards her. Marina gave herself credit for not being too surprised, when he came to a gliding stop in front of her. Turquoise eyes held hers, as she gasped. Tears stung the back of her eyes. *Mami.*

The man, unaware, stared at her, his eyes boring into hers. "I know you are here," he repeated, softly. He reached up, and began parting the foliage framing her face.

Marina shrank back in a sudden panic attack. His eyes held hers as he reached out tentatively. "Please," she gasped. The man before her cocked his head to one side. "If you touch me, I will pass out from fright," she whispered.

He chuckled. "Well, we can't have that, can we?" Just as suddenly, he let go of the leaves in his hand, letting them fall back into place. "What is your name?" he asked, softly.

Marina caught her breath and let it out shakily. She licked her lips, and her answer was barely audible. "Marina."

He was silent for a moment. "Carlos," he finally said. And with that, he dove underwater, came up a distance away, and swam across the pool.

Marina watched him for a moment. A gust of wind caressed her. Deep in the sky, thunder rumbled. When she had him near again, she dared to speak to him first. "Did you come in on Gaitano's ship, or do you live in town? I have never seen you before."

He chuckled, once more coming to a stop in front of her. "Nor I, you," he answered. He didn't want to scare her so instead, he turned his back to her and leaned on that side of the pool, the back of his head close to her face. " Are you new here?" he asked curiously, his voice gentle.

Marina relaxed. "No, we are just visiting." He nodded. "I don't know how long we'll be staying, though," she added softly.

At this, he was glad she couldn't see his expression. His friend was a little bit too interested in her friend. It would be sad, if Indio didn't get a chance to explore his feelings for the divine Salomé. "How do you like it, so far?" he asked casually.

She shrugged. "It's not home."

"Where is home?" He was genuinely curious about this woman.

Her voice was sad. "Far away."

"Do you want to go back?"

For a moment, Marina thought she couldn't speak. She managed to choke out her answer. "Yes."

Gaitano turned around, to peer at her through the leaves. He saw tears in her eyes. "Maybe I can help you," he offered.

"Maybe." Then, she graciously changed the subject. "What do you do?"

He chuckled. "I, madam, am nothing but a humble seaman."

"Did you come in on Gaitano's ship?" she repeated.

He nodded, wondering how many people she knew in Encantada. "Yes."

"So you are a sailor."

His eyes crinkled into a smile. "You could say that."

"What do you do?" she asked, genuinely curious.

He didn't think about what he was doing. The conversation came naturally, flowing freely. The only person that made him feel this relaxed was Indio. "Right now, I am working on some books."

"Accounts?"

He nodded. "Some things have been happening while we were gone."

She frowned. "I thought Gaitano was successful in this voyage."

Carlos smiled. *She doesn't know.* "He was, some," he replied modestly.

"So what is the problem?" Marina was mesmerized by his eyes. Their bright color brought warm memories.

"He left some people in charge to handle his affairs while he was gone. Some things ran smoothly. Others, not so." He looked straight into her eyes. "The numbers do not match up."

"So, find where the problem is," she suggested.

He cocked his head to the side, genuinely curious. "Do you know anything about numbers?

Marina choked on her laugh. "Yes, as a matter of fact," she managed to say. "I am an educated woman," she continued, carefully. "Maybe I can help."

"Maybe," he conceded.

Marina shook her head. She saw the skepticism on his face, and the only thing she could think of was because of her gender. She rolled her eyes with a laugh. *Whatever!* She stood up, brushing the seat of her skirt. He craned up, catching sight of bits and pieces of her. "Well, I must go." And although she didn't want to; even if she would have rather stayed talking to the friendly stranger, nodding her head, she left him looking after her. "Carlos..."

Gaitano smiled to himself. "Marina..."

The day grew progressively heavier. Thunder rumbled regularly, but it wasn't any closer than it had been this morning. Leilani's aunt had been by earlier, with a huge smile on her round face. "You stay today, girl," she crooned. "Take the whole day off. I will take care of the babies for you," and she left, leaving her a bunch of red hibiscus, stuck in a wide bottomed bottle of black glass.

Marina thanked her with a kiss on the cheek. "Please tell Leilani I will be there for Jeremiah's inspection." The woman chuckled and widened her eyes at her with a nod of complicity. She left, laughing and waving, her ample body swaying down the lane, a bundle of bright colors on a beautiful, dark skinned canvas. And Marina was left alone.

Throwing open the windows of the hut, she set about tidying it up. In ten minutes, she was done. Dishes, washed and clean. Clothes and fabrics stacked neatly in corners. The bright red flowers were in a place of honor, in the middle of a window frame, standing out vividly against the lead sky. I wish I had something to read. She took one last quick glance around, making sure the tubs of water were outside, soaking up the sun's heat. With a big sigh, she laid in the hammock. And she slept. All day, that's what she did. Sleep. And dream.

They were on a road trip. The one they had taken on her twenty-first birthday, just Salomé and herself. They had wanted to take the Mustang convertible her mother had surprised her with, with the approval of her father. It was a beautiful, black, sleek, cruising machine. When she first spied it that morning, it was nothing more than a dark stain on her driveway, as she looked out the kitchen window with a cup of hot chocolate in her hand. Salomé stood next to her, even then. They were both wearing oversized football jerseys, a habit left over from their high school days. As was also a habit, that Salomé sleep over at Marina's on the eve of her birthday, almost since they were born. Now, they were standing side by side, steaming cups in their hands, shock on their faces. Framed by the high hedge on both sides of their double, stone paved driveway, stood the car of their dreams. The black vehicle was so shiny, that they could see the sun's reflection. Its top was up, and from that distance, it looked to them, like black velvet. Tied all the way around it, holding the doors shut, was a huge silver silk rope with a loose knot tied on top, its oversized tassels hanging over the windshield. The vanity license plate was framed in chrome chain that sparkled, like an ID bracelet. It read, Sloane's Baby. The girls screamed. They ran out, and took their first spin in it around the neighborhood, still in their football jerseys. They were sure that the car had been there so that they could embark on their trip that had been scheduled for later that day. But fate intervened in the guise of Pablo Aguilar. After the four grownups and the three children participated of a small, intimate birthday lunch, the girls were told the devastating news. They were not to take the Mustang. Instead, they were to go in Pablo's silver F150, with extended cab. There were tears. That's not fair, they wailed. It's for your safety, the fathers argued. It will be all right, the mothers consoled. Jackson said nothing. And then the fathers left, in the brand new car, to go shopping for the mothers. They were looking forward to a weekend alone with their wives. Jackson took off for parts unknown. The girls were left with the mothers, whom after a kiss and a hug, waved them goodbye, as they drove off in Pablo's pickup truck. Destination: Ocean City.

The lights, the sounds, the people! After a salty drive up the coast, the girls hit the main strip. They grinned at each other. The parents had pitched in with a little extra, just so they could have fun at the slotmachines and the tables. And here they were, driving to their hotel, not knowing where to look first. The sights, the music, it was all overwhelming. Especially the lights.

The girls had showered, changed, and had a bite to eat, all in under an hour. Their room had a spectacular view of the avenue below. Right now it was a mess, what with duffel bags open with clothes hanging out, and backpacks thrown in the chairs. But the girls looked beautiful, in their dresses and jewelry. The only thing in the room that rivaled their beauty, was the crystal vase sitting on the middle of the table. It was already awaiting them when they got there. Birds of paradise. They had been sent anonymously, but Marina knew.

They had the best time of their lives. Careful with not getting caught up in the gambling frenzy, they spent most of their time walking around, people watching. It was at one of the tables, that Marina felt arms go around her waist, familiar arms that held her warmly against a hard chest. His breath blew warm in her ear. "Happy birthday, mamita," and he kissed her cheek. He held out a flat, square, brightly wrapped gift in front of her face. "For your eyes only," he whispered, moving his head to kiss her other cheek. Marina felt him stumble against her slightly, as Salomé threw herself against him. She sighed. "Jackson." Taking the package from him, she turned around in his arms and looked up with a sigh. **I love having an older brother.** *His tiger eyes glittered at her. Their lips met in a soft fraternal kiss. The three of them had the best time of their lives. And that is how Marina remembered her twenty-first birthday. Having a blast, with her sister, and suddenly, the night getting better with the arrival of her brother. Jackson.*

"Marina, baby, wake up." Marina rubbed her eyes and yawned, looking up at Salomé. "Want to run with us?" she invited.

They ran. The jungle seemed unusually quiet, as its shadows grew. It still didn't rain, even though the thunder was coming with more frequency. Nobody spoke as they finished their laps in the pool, and Caribe and Salomé continued, leaving Marina by herself. She finished her routine, and got out. Shaking her head, she had just begun running again, when she heard a noise behind her. Peering through a screen of leaves, Marina saw him. The flash of his body as it hit the water reached her, before the sound of the splash it made. He began his own routine in silence. After a couple of laps, he finally came to a gliding stop, right in front of where she was standing.

"Are you married?" he asked suddenly.

Marina almost choked on her surprise. "No!"

"Good." He floated on his back for a moment, before swimming back.

"Are you?" she asked.

His laugh was genuine. "No, no, not me."

"Good," she answered. "See you next time." And she began turning away.

"Wait!" She turned back to look at him. "Do you think I could see you?"

He held his breath. Marina stepped out of the foliage. She was even more beautiful than he imagined. Her skin was burnt to a nice bronze, her hair was streaked with sun lights. The pants she was wearing were riding low on her hips, molding themselves to her wet skin. He could clearly see her panties underneath. Letting his eyes travel up, he let them caress her smooth belly, to her top. It was nothing more than a piece of fabric, tied at her breasts. He smiled. "I brought some books. Would you mind taking a look at them for me?" Marina smiled back.

They spent the next couple of hours sitting side by side, heads together, going through numbers. He explained each and every step of his business. The system was primitive in its simplicity. It was all based on the goods they brought over from a voyage, and its eventual distribution. Marina finally found a discrepancy. It seemed that every time he was importing arms and ammunition, something strange happened. There would be an inventory, reported at the port from where they were anchored. That inventory would match with the numbers that were taken down at the moment of unloading. However, there were papers missing, where there should have been evidence of the people receiving the weapons.

Marina finally looked up, rotating her shoulders to relieve a cramp. She smiled, as his eyes met hers. *He has Mami's eyes.* "You are being scammed."

He frowned. "What does that mean?"

She sighed. *I have to be more careful.* "All these papers are in excellent order. Your business is thriving. But for some reason," she continued carefully, "there are shipments just disappearing. Look here," she said, pointing to a paper. "All this is in perfect order. You have descriptions, dates, destinations, and even the signatures of the people in charge. Then you come here," she held up a piece of paper. "And they don't match. It seems like there is stuff just not making it to Encantada. Tell your boss..."

Carlos frowned for a moment. "My boss?"

"Gaitano," Marina answered impatiently, flashing her eyes at him.

He noticed they were hazel. "Of course," he amended rapidly. "My boss, Gaitano." He smiled. "He will be very interested in what you have to say about what is happening to his business."

Marina rolled her eyes at him with a smile. "Tell him that everybody is doing their job at the ports of call where he does business."

"So what is the problem?"

Marina stood up and stretched, eyes closed, head thrown back, arms flung out and up in the air. From his vantage point, where she had left him still sitting, he could see the fabric tighten over her breasts. Her nipples pressed against the material, and inside his head, he groaned. Marina stamped her feet to get her circulation back, and stepped back smiling, as he stood up to join her. "Gaitano may have to clean house." She pointed at the papers in his hand. "It looks like an inside job." At his look, she explained. "That means that whatever is going wrong, has its roots at home. Somebody is paying, or God knows what, something to someone else, to make things disappear like magic."

A stillness settled over him at her words. It makes sense! "What is the common denominator?"

She shook her head sadly. "I need more time to figure that out. The only way I can let you know, is if I have a little more time with the books."

He didn't think. "Please." He put them in her arms, squeezing her shoulders in gratitude. "How long would it take you?" he asked. "My boss," he hesitated. "He would be grateful."

Marina sighed, hugging his ledgers to her chest. "Tell him, anything I can do to help..." She looked at him. "I'll take them home. Could I get them to you tomorrow, or are you in a big hurry to get these back?"

He shook his head. "Is there anybody whom you would trust---"

"Caribe," came her automatic reply.

"--- from town that I could send to retrieve them?"

She thought for a moment. A secret smile crossed her lips suddenly, and a saucy look came over her face. "Indio."

Carlos nodded, happy for his brother, relieved at her choice. It was also his choice. He agreed. "Indio."

She looked up into his eyes, one last time. "*Adios, Carlos.*"

Carlos took her hand. Without taking his eyes off hers, he brought it to his lips. He winked at her. "*Adios, Marina...*"

Out on the ocean, the boat came closer. The young man looked steadily, his eyes fixed on the craft, even as he heard the motor. Jackson closed his eyes. There was only one person in the whole world, who knew where he was. He waited while the person in the boat cut the motor, threw anchor, and swam ashore.

Quentin met his eyes, sad. "You didn't find them?" he asked, when he finally reached him.

Jackson shook his head. "Not yet." He waited, as Quentin just looked at him. He had spent the last two days, doing some of the most extraneous physical activity he had ever done, in his whole life. It showed. Jackson had spent his days climbing mountains, and charging through waterfalls. He had swum in lagoons, and dashed across small valleys, sprinting over brooks. He had been bitten by mosquitoes, flown at by fruit bats, and visited by assorted insects and reptiles. He had worked out like an Olympian. What he hadn't done was, find his sisters. He looked at the other young man steadily. "You are sure you left them here."

Quentin nodded, panic gripping him. "Yes, man! Alive! You must have found something of theirs!"

Jackson let him off the hook. "Yeah, man, I found their bags. Signs, of them being in a cave. Over there," he gestured at the clif fs that loomed in the distance, over his shoulder.

Quentin looked terrified for a moment. "So, what happened to them?"

Jackson shrugged his gaze fierce as it swept over the ocean. He had lost weight, and his eyes were different. He looked leaner, meaner. "For all I know, we are playing a game of hide-n-seek." He glanced at Quentin. "Relax, man. I know they are alive." Before the other boy could say anything, he drew out his cell phone from the pocket of his T-shirt, and punched some numbers, before holding it to his ear. "Where's Todd?"

"Todd disappeared, man. He's just nowhere to be found."

"Good." Then he turned his attention to his cell phone. "Hey, Mom, sorry I missed you. We are having a great time, and we want to take advantage of every last minute, so we'll be camping for another week. Tell Dad, Papi and Mami we send them our love. Talk to you later." And he hung up. He turned to Quentin. "Check on me in a couple more days."

Quentin just stared at him, before shaking his head. He turned to leave, shoulders slumped, head down, when he looked back at Jackson, one last time. "I am praying for you, man."

Jackson forced a smile. "Thank you, man. So am I." Quentin left.

Jackson went back to the cave. For a moment, he stood outside, at the edge of the cliff. The ocean churned, spread out before him. He had kept a steady vigil, every night that he had been there. It had been for him, a time of prayer and meditation. He had communed with Nature, as he had never had a chance to, before. He felt good. And he knew, way deep down inside, where his soul was connected with the oneness of the universe, he knew his sisters were alive.

Sighing shakily, he took one last look at the ocean. It was going to storm soon. Very soon. And it looked bad. He went inside the cave.

"Hey, baby."

Salomé turned around at the now, familiar rumble. Her eyes crinkled with laughter, as she smiled at him. "Hey..." They exchanged looks.

Marina smiled as she looked from one to the other. "Hey, Indio."

Indio returned her smile and approached her. She was sitting at the table, ledgers open, candlelight flickering. A charcoal pencil was clutched in one hand, and in the other she held a single piece of paper, with scribbles on both sides. Her nose was smudged, where she had scratched, but she looked radiant. "Marina," he rumbled softly. "My..." he caught himself in time. "...boss is interested in your assessment of his books."

Marina raised her eyebrows, teasing. "Well, I am quite flattered, considering that your boss doesn't even know me." Indio coughed. "Seriously, I think I found where the problem might be." She looked into his eyes. "There are a lot of stops at a place named Carey." She watched as the brave went absolutely still. "If I were Gaitano, I would check up myself on why, every time a certain group of dockworkers sign, things don't match up."

"Do you have any names?"

Marina hesitated. His voice had lowered even more, and it was just hitting her, the magnitude of this favor she was doing. She had some important seaman's ledgers in her hands, where she had finally discovered evidence of some serious tampering. She had only found it because she was a twenty-first century college educated woman, and numbers were her strength. Only Gaitano would know how bad this whole thing was. *I don't think I want to get involved.* Marina lowered her voice also, acknowledging his seriousness. "Indio, I cannot rightfully point any fingers at anyone. If Gaitano is as serious as I think, he needs to take care of business." She looked at him sadly. "Do you understand these books?" He nodded. "Come here," she said softly. "Closer." He stood up and peered at what she was pointing at. By the candlelight, she was spreading some papers in front of him. She didn't speak. Instead, her fingers floated silently over columns, lines, paragraphs. They went back and forth over the papers, stopping to point out dates and places. She waved her hands over the papers and stopped. Outside, the frogs were tuning up, preparing to begin their nighttime symphony. A cricket chirped from right outside their window, loud and shrill. Thunder rumbled. It sounded closer than it had, all day. She still didn't speak. With all his attention on her, Marina let her fingers glide again. She pointed at one item on each of the papers. Indio froze. Suddenly he saw it. Marina hadn't needed to say the names.

Indio straightened up, his face grim, his expression ferocious. He heard Salomé gasp beside him, saw her throw her friend a scared look. "Thank you," he said to Marina, forcing the lines of his face to relax, into the semblance of a smile. He kissed the top of her head. "My boss thanks you."

Salomé walked him to the door. "Is everything all right, baby?"

Indio turned to look at her, in the dark. The candle on their table flickered behind her, making her silhouette glow, framed in the doorway. He smiled, the shadows playing on his face. He took her hand, and turning it over, pressed his lips against her wrist. She felt a slight suction from his mouth that made electricity shoot through her veins. Pulling away, he stepped backwards, not trusting himself to leave her alone. "Salomé..."

That night, Caribe went to his mother's house. There, he sat at her feet, while she lovingly cleaned and dressed his locks. He paced, sat, and paced some more. Her table was littered with papers and charcoal pencils. After going for a short run, chasing thunder, he came back, steadier, calmer. He sat down one last time. And under his mother's loving eyes, he finished his drawing.

"Soon, bebé," she crooned. "The storm will be here soon."

Caribe sat thoughtful, for a moment. Finally, he shook his head. "Mamá, there must be a reason why these storms are so close together." He looked at her. "Is it the end of the world?" he asked.

Leila threw her head back, in genuine, joyful laughter. "Caribe!' she finally gasped. "No, mi bebé." She shook her head at him. "Don't forget, our visitors come from another time. Do you think, my son, they came from the past?"

Caribe shook his head, suddenly embarassed. "Of course not." He grinned, bashful. "What are we in for, Mamá?"

Leila returned his smile. She stretched out her hand, fingers waving, asking for the piece of paper he had just finished. "It can only be good."

Caribe studied the portrait of the man he had just drawn. "I hope God hears you," he said, handing over the paper with a sigh.

Leila smiled, and said nothing. She looked at the man on the paper in front of her. A sense of peace came over her heart. Relief and compassion for their visitors. This man would help matters enormously. She studied his face, thinking how handsome he looked. Like her husband, like her son. Even through the charcoal she could see the lights in his eyes. She leaned her head back and began rocking, lovingly tracing something in the portrait, her smile growing. Caribe went around her, to see what she was looking at. His mother's fingers were tracing the man's hair. It was in cornrows.

Indio walked past the Lair, ledgers in hand, without looking inside. He went down the alley on the side, to the back. Right behind the building was a tall fence, surrounding a small lot. The garden and small house in it seemed to be done by the same person that had designed Pedro Barbosa's office. The elements used were the same, but in a smaller scale. Indio strode down the path, mocassins silent on the river pebbles. He opened the door to the apartment. Two men looked up, as he entered.

Carlos Gaitano started to say something, but thought better of it, at his friend's expression. Whatever it was, it didn't look good. He glanced at his Ship's Master, Giancarlo watched the brave warily. Nobody spoke. Indio dropped the ledgers heavily on the table the men were sitting around. Without a word, he stood between them, and proceeded to open the books. Pulling out the telltale papers, he silently translated Marina's scribblings, doing the same hand dances she did, The men watched, intrigued, as his finger went back and forth on the papers, just as hers had. Shock settled over their features, as they suddenly saw it. Giancarlo stood up suddenly, knocking his chair over. His features were transformed, by a quiet rage nobody but his associates, had ever seen before. Carlos slapped both his hands on the table with all his might and roared.

That night, nobody had to invite the girls to the clearing. They arrived there by themselves, and took their places among the villagers. They were welcomed naturally, as if they had always been a part of their lives. Settling down to where they had been watching from in secret, for the last couple of nights. the four riders, got off their horses. The old sailor, the chinaman, the brave, and the pirate sat side by side, in silence. The drums took over their spirits. Jimmy and Silas nodded their heads in rhythm to the beat, happy smiles on their faces. Indio looked on, entranced by Salomé, fascinated. And Gaitano... he shook his head as his heart seemed to skip a beat, at the sight of a sudden movement of a hip swiveling, accompanied by a flash of thigh. From where he sat, he could see drops of perspiration, catching the light of the tiki torches, slide down bronzed skin, disappearing into a cleavage. He groaned, just like Indio had done, the very first night. Carlos Gaitano's eyes never left Marina.

Marina never saw him. Later that night, it stormed.

It dawned, the gloomy day showing the ravages of the night before. To Marina's surprise, when John Kline came, he had Leilani with him. "I just ran into her on the way here," he explained, shrugging. He laughed, as the children all clamored for her attention. Two nappy heads and a sleek ebony one, all crowding around her legs, little arms stretched out. He laughed. "I th ink you got something here." Marina looked at him questioningly. "The other day, when Gaitano came into the store, Mrs. Calloway was there. He asked for Max, and Larissa informed him that he was in daycare." He chuckled. "The woman went into shock, to say the least. It was too much for her. The combination of Gaitano, that close to her, and Larissa's happiness at not having Max around, in the store, well..." he shook his head. "Let me just say this. There have been more women than usual coming to the store, pretending to buy." He chuckled again, turning to leave. "They are driving Larissa crazy." He stopped, blowing kisses at the babies, and stroking Ali's head. "They want to know about daycare." And he left.

Marina, thus, began her day. After setting the babies up with their toys, she shook her sister, who still slept in her hammock. "Salomé!" she called softly. "Salomé, wake up, mami, you're going to be late for work." She watched her stir, and then stretch back to life, shaking the hair out of her face. There were dark circles under her eyes. "Are you okay, Salo?"

Salomé smiled as she stretched, but her voice came out a croak. "No." She frowned, and cleared her throat. "I had a nightmare." She swung one leg out of the hammock, steadying it. Sitting up slowly, she put her other foot on the floor, and stood up. She winked at

Marina, but her eyes were haunted. "I must be hoarse from all the screaming I was doing in my dreams."

Tears came to Marina's eyes, but she could only shake her head. She hugged her sister, and whispered in her ear. "I got a surprise for you."

Salomé whispered back barely audible. "What?"

"I got John Kline to make some things for us. I think they'll make our stay here, a little more pleasant." She held the bag out to Salomé.

Salomé peered inside, frowning. Finally, emptying the bag on the table, she began to smile. There were custom made razors, a perfumed bar of soap, and another, made out of beeswax. There were two beautiful glass bottles with stoppers. The contents looked suspiciously like a homemade version of shampoo and conditioner. "How do you do it?" Salomé asked, admiration in her eyes.

Marina shrugged, smiling. "I got connections."

Salomé happily took a razor and a bar of soap. She went out the back steps and sat down to wash the sleep away, in the privacy of their backyard. When she came back in, her legs were silky, and her underarms smooth. Marina laughed. Her sister was grinning like a fool. "Thank you, *mami*, my quality of life just went up.

Marina watched as her sister slipped on some pants, and wrapped a flower print fabric around herself. Back home, in the twenty-first century, it said runway. Here, it said, required. Salomé braided her hair in a single one, falling down her back. She slipped on straw sandals. "You look like Indio," Marina pointed out.

Salomé winked at her. "That's kind of the idea."

"You are going to make the townspeople have heart attacks when they get a look at you in that outfit!" accused Marina, laughing. "You slut!" she hissed. They high-fived. Marina smiled gently. "You must be really depressed, if you are going into town dressed like that."

Salomé nodded. "I am. I'm just going to try and stay in back, all day today." And with that, she smiled and waved goodbye to them, and she was gone.

They held another meeting. This time, in the second-floor of the warehouse, from which the Captain and his Quartermaster, had first spied on the visitors from Cayo Largo. They sat around a table, Gaitano and his soldiers. Only Solomon stood, at the window, watching for anyone coming. The success of their meetings lay on the secrecy of their meeting places.

Gaitano looked around, taking in his men's faces. "I have to go and report to Don Carlos," he said gravely. "This is a direct attack on the Gaitanos."

Pedro Barbosa raised his eyebrows, and rubbed his hands over his face. "How soon are you leaving?"

Gaitano didn't hesitate. "As soon as they can get La Gitana ready."

Padre Ignacio stared at him. La Gitana was a Merchant Carrier that had been sitting in the harbor, for weeks, now. He quickly calculated the time it would take for it to be ready to go. "That could be less than a fortnight."

Gaitano nodded. "Yes."

"I am going this time," announced Indio.

"That means," Giancarlo told the lawman, "that the Siren's Lair will be taken care of by Silas and Jimmy."

Barbosa nodded. The pair were Gaitano's soldiers on land. "That makes my job easier," he admitted.

"Then, it's decided, gentlemen. This meeting is now, over," announced Gaitano.

They left.

Leila sat up, startled. Although the day was gloomy, it felt a little bit warmer than usual. She gasped, when she realized how high, the invisible sun was, up in the metallic sky. "Caribe," she whispered, holding her head between her hands, trying to grasp the last wisps of her dream. Getting out of bed, she went out to her front porch and cupped her hands around her mouth. *"Caribe!"*

Caribe lurched out of his hammock, stumbling to the window. The panic in his mother's voice had woken him up. She was frantically waving at him. He quickly ran outside, crossing the sandy path, and took her in his arms. Her eyes were wide, in her beautiful dark face. "What, Mamá? What?"

"You have to go into town, *bebé*, run as fast as you can! Go find her, quick!" She pushed him back towards his hut, her words rushing to get out.

He stopped in his tracks. "Who?" he asked crossly, shaking his dreadlocks out of his face, as he pushed her hands away.

"Salomé! Before he finds her!"

Caribe's eyes widened, understanding what she was saying. Around them, drops fell from leaves, remnants of the night's storm. "Mamá!" He didn't know whether to laugh or cry. The joy he felt for his friends was that immense.

Leila nodded, smiling at him, her eyes still wide, now filling with tears. "He is here, Caribe."

Caribe ran.

Dominique Swan looked up, startled, as Leila's son burst in, as she was measuring a client. A little scream escaped her throat at the sight of him, before she actually recognized him. When she noticed who he was, she let out a sigh of relief. She murmured apologies to her customer, and turned to scold him. *"Caribe!"* Then she saw the wild look in his eyes. Growing alarmed, all of a sudden, she took a step towards him. "Is everything all right, honey?"

Caribe could only shake his head, craning his neck to look behind her. "Salomé?"

"She is not here, baby. Gaitano's brave came and took her to lunch." She pointed at the door behind him. "You just missed them, as a matter of fact. They just left."

Caribe thanked her and rushed out.

A few streets ahead of him, the couple in question walked side by side, making people turn and stare at them. They looked alike, both in pants, both in braids. But that's where it ended. The swing of the hips and the flowered top were unmistakably female. She matched his stride, however. Something he noticed with pride. When they got to the Lair, he held the door for her, while still standing in the door-way. She smiled at him, and had to walk past him sideways, he took up so much space. Her breasts brushed against his ribcage. Over her head, silently, he let out a shaky breath.

Sitting quietly, at the corner of the bar, were the Captain and the Ship's Master. They caught the exchange between the couple. The look on the Quartermaster's face made them laugh. They watched in silence as the girl sat at the bar, while Indio ran behind it, to take care of her. From their gestures and their body language, they understood she wasn't hungry. So they talked. As they did so, the brave casually took off a leather band he was wearing and slipped it around her wrist. It was too big for her, and he pushed it up her forearm, until it wouldn't go any higher. The men smiled as she reached up and stroked his face, while casually keeping up their conversation. The importance of the exchange was kept in their knowing looks at each other. Other than that, it was as if nothing had happened.

Caribe burst in suddenly, squinting as his eyes adjusted to the gloom. He spotted Salomé right away, and made a beeline for her. The men at the corner watched with even more interest. Silas and Jimmy sidled up to the bar, keeping a wary eye on the boy, and another on the bartender. *"Salomé!"*

Salomé spun around in her stool, as she caught sight of him in the mirror hanging behind Indio. "Hi, *papi*, what are you up to?" She frowned, taking a good look at him. His eyes were wide, and he looked like he was running.

Caribe just looked at her. He turned his head towards the bar for a moment, bending at the waist, hands on knees, taking huge gulps of air. As he came up, he noticed that Indio held one of Salomé's hand in his, on top of the bar. He straightened up, taking her free hand. Looking into her eyes, he couldn't explain, he could only plead. "Come with me."

Salomé shook her head, not understanding. "What?"

"Caribe..." The name, as it came out of the brave's throat, was a warning growl. itself.

"Indio..." That name, coming out of Gaitano's throat, was a soft warning.

"Just come, Salomé." He pulled at her hand. "Please, come with me." Giancarlo showed up magically, beside Indio. Putting a hand on his shoulder, he squeezed in warning. The brave shook him off. "No," he said, having eyes for none, but the village boy.

Salomé looked from one to the other. She felt fear slip under her skin and fill her senses. She didn't know why, but she wanted to cry. "You're scaring me," she accused suddenly, squeezing Caribe's hand. "I am not going anywhere, until you tell me what is going on." A sudden thought gripped her in panic. *"Marina?"*

Caribe shook his head wildly. Reaching into his pocket, he reached for a piece of paper. "Please, Salomé. You must come now." He offered it to her.

"No!" The brave trembled from emotion.

Salomé slipped her hands out of each of theirs, and took the paper. She jumped off the barstool, giving herself room. She walked away a few steps, and turned towards the bar, her back to the entrance. The men all watched her. Her hands trembled as she began opening the piece of paper slowly. Tears shone in her eyes, even before she finished unfolding it. Salomé had caught sight of the cornrows. Her hands began shaking violently. Her mouth moved, but no words came out. Gaitano came to his feet as her face crumpled, ready to catch her if she fell. The men were dumbfounded by her reaction. She had eyes, only for the paper, and the boy who had given it to her. Her hand reached out to him. "Caribe?"

Caribe took her hand. "He's here," he whispered, looking into her eyes.

"Does Marina know?" Salomé didn't see him shake his head. She was slowly going into shock. Her eyes were beginning to get glassy, and she felt a distant buzzing in her body, as if she had taken drugs. A wail escaped her throat. Indio lunged, over the bar. Out of nowhere, six hands were holding him back.

Caribe shook his head. "Come," he repeated, pulling on her. He put an arm around her shoulders, and steered her towards the door. They didn't look back, as the brave growled.

"No!" Indio roared.

"Let's run," they heard Salomé sob, as they reached the door. "Let's run." They never heard the thrashing behind them.

Indio roared again. It took him a few minutes to get them off him, but he did it. By the time he ran out to the street, Caribe and Salomé were long gone.

Gaitano looked after his brother and sighed, shaking his head. It must be serious. He turned back to the other men, when something caught his attention. Salomé had dropped the piece of paper. Gaitano bent to pick it up. She had dropped everything over this. He studied it. It was the portrait of a young man. The drawing was excellent, since great care had gone into it. The man in question was extremely handsome, making Gaitano frown. Who could this be, that made her run away like a bat out of hell? He noticed that the man appeared to have light-colored eyes, and his hair was styled in tight braids against his scalp. Earrings hung from his ears. Except for his hairstyle, he looked like any other young man who had progressed from village life, to adventure at sea. Thoughtfully, he put the paper away, before Indio saw it. As his brother came back inside, he spoke to him, softly. "Keep your eyes open," he warned quietly, "but don't be rash. You met her, a grown woman, with a full life already."

Indio met his eyes. "I want to know *everything* about that woman," he rasped quietly.

Gaitano nodded. He knew things would work out for his brother, no matter what. "You will, *papi*," he chuckled.

Jackson was awake. He kept his eyes closed, not really wanting to get up. This was his fourth day on this forsaken island, and he dreaded it. He didn't know how long he could keep this up, and more importantly, how long he could keep it from their parents. Opening his eyes, he rolled over to look at the cave's entrance. The day was dark, thunder still rumbling in the distance. He had passed out last night, lulled by the raging storm. He sighed. It wasn't that he dreaded going out, looking for the girls. He just didn't want to go out, and not find them. Again. *It's not over, till it's over*, he thought. Half an hour later, he was on the beach.

Things seemed different, somehow, but he couldn't precisely put his finger on it. Jackson looked around him, as if he were seeing things for the first time. The storm had passed, but rain still fell in a mist. He began walking along the shore. The tide was high, and the surf pounded on the beach. The sand was spongy from the excess of water, bubbling in his footsteps. Jackson looked up. Up ahead in the distance, he saw what seemed to be a big piece of driftwood in the sand. Big enough to be a log. But as he kept walking, he noticed that it wasn't a whole unit, but consisted of two different parts. The harder he stared, the more he was convinced they were moving. Incredulously, he recognized what it was. They were human. He stared hard. As he looked down the shore, there were two people, running his way.

Salomé felt the blood beat in her head, to the rhythm of her pounding feet. Caribe ran next to her, a silent shadow. They hit the beach, and kept going. They were never going to stop. Sandpipers scattered out of their way, and seagulls screeched overhead. Crabs scurried into their holes, their whole world shaking as the pair thundered by. The gentle drizzle beaded on their hair and eyelashes. Salomé blinked. Up ahead, a lone figure headed towards them. She would recognize that walk until the day she died. She screamed.

"*Jackson!*"

Jackson stopped, his heart threatening to pound its way out of his chest. The hairs stood up on his arms. His fingertips tingled. He had a moment of deja vu, as he recognized the smaller figure sprinting towards him. Then he heard her scream. Jackson took off running, to meet her. The relief that washed over his body, threatened to overwhelm him. Her name escaped his throat in a yell. "*Salomé!*"

They didn't fall into each other's arms, as much as they collided. And when they did, he realized with sadness, the state she was in.

"*Jackson!*" she screamed, mouth gasping, tears pouring from her eyes. She alternately pushed him, swinging her arms at him, trying desperately to connect, and would then, pull at him, wrapping both arms around him, and clinging like a little girl. "*What took you so long?!*" she screamed at him. Her sobs overpowered her. "*We've been so scared! You didn't come! What took you so long, Jackson?*" She clawed at his shirt, head thrown back as she howled to the sky. "*Where were you?!*"

Caribe stood frozen to the spot, before dropping heavily to the sand. He was frightened out of his mind. Although he knew that the visitors were handling their situation magnificently, he was aware that they didn't let their true feelings out. But, this... His eyes watered, as he watched. This was beyond anything he had prepared himself for. Seeing them together, the resemblance was striking. They complemented each other, like only a brother and a sister could. Before his eyes, they performed a dance of intense emotion, rage dueling with compassion and relief. He watched the man back away from her swinging arms, as she hysterically screamed at him, pursuing him as she cried. The other man grabbed her suddenly, immobilizing her, as he spoke in her ear. Caribe's chest tightened as he watched his friend struggle until overcome by exhaustion. She had stopped screaming, and was now sobbing softly against the taller boy's chest. The young man's face was streaked with tears, as he dropped to the sand and sat his sister on his lap, rocking her in consolation. She shuddered in his arms. As the village boy watched, his friend calmed down, finally at peace. Turning his head to look at the ocean, as the pair rocked gently, a short distance away from him, Caribe sighed shakily. Putting his hands to his face, he brushed away his own tears.

The trio stayed on the beach for most of the day. Caribe stayed in the shadows, letting the siblings rejoice in each other. Once Salomé had calmed down, although her emotions still raged, there were more smiles than tears. Looking around her, she spotted Caribe sitting to the side. She smiled through her tears, and stretched out her hand towards him. Caribe took it, without taking his eyes off the other man.

Jackson nodded and stretched out his hand. "How're you doing, man? I'm Jackson."

The other young man put his in it, and shook it. "Caribe."

They looked at each other, for a moment, their eyes connecting. Salomé spoke softly. "Caribe and his mother have been taking care of us."

Jackson looked at her. "What is the deal with this place? How big is it anyway? I've gone out every day, looking for you."

Salomé shook her head. "You are not going to believe this," she began, hesitating when he raised his eyebrows at her. "We have been here all along." She hooked her arm through his, as they sat side by side, and leaned her head against his shoulder.

Jackson glanced at Caribe, who shook his head, and looked down at his feet. Looking back at Salomé, he let his eyes travel over her. Feeling a knot in his throat, he pressed his lips against the top of her head. "Tell me, Salo."

Salomé pointed at the ocean, where there were still storm signs, evident. "You see that?" she asked.

Jackson followed her gaze. "The ocean?"

Salomé shook her head quickly. "The storm," she began, her eyes wide in her face. And then she couldn't say any more. She looked at him, her eyes caressing his face, his hair. "It causes a time warp."

Jackson stared at her. First, he wasn't sure he heard right. But she wasn't laughing. He couldn't believe it. "You are serious."

Salomé bit her lip, miserable. There were very few people she admired and respected more than her older brother. "I know, it sounds like Twilight Zone." Fresh tears flooded her eyes, and her voice broke. "But that's what happened. The storm causes a change in the air, or provokes a shift in time, or something!", she finished with a wail, beginning to cry all over again.

Jackson couldn't speak. He couldn't accuse her of lying, or even playing with him. She wasn't, he was sure. Never before, had he seen his sister, Salomé, in this state of emotional distress. That he was the cause of it was almost more than he could handle. "So what time is it?" he asked. "I mean, what's the year?"

Salomé shook her head, her eyes brimming with fresh tears. "I don't know."

"You don't know?" he asked, shocked. She started sobbing again.

Holding her in his arms once more, he closed his eyes as she wailed. "I'm sorry, Salo, I'm sorry, *mami*. It was my fault that you got into this mess. I just want to understand." He looked over her head at Caribe. The boy looked as miserable as she sounded. "Has she been staying with you?" Caribe pressed his lips together and nodded his head. "Is there somewhere she can lay down? I need to take care of her, right now." He shook his sister gently. "Come on, baby, you've got to help me now, I can't carry you," he urged gently.

Salomé nodded her head, standing up, with one last sniff. She looked ravaged. Raking her fingers through her hair, she felt the leather band slip down to her wrist. Absentmindedly, she began pushing it up her arm, when suddenly, she remembered. She froze, a shocked expression on her face. New tears, as she looked at Caribe. Her voice was a silent wail. *"Indio!"*

The two young men looked at each other, as the girl between them started crying all over again.

Marina's day was going smoothly. The babies had been perfect angels, and Ali had actually helped her with them. John Kline had come by to pick up Max, and Leilani had showed up for her family, soon afterwards. Marina was left alone suddenly, and she looked around her. It seemed to her, that every time the children were gone, it left a vacuum. The scary part was, she admitted to herself, she missed them. *I could get used to this.* As soon as the words appeared in her head, she blocked them out. The only reason why Salomé and she could even function, at any level, was because they put all their effort and energy into not dwelling on their situation. The only thing was, if something didn't happen soon, they would end up making new lives for themselves --- Marina shook her head hard, rubbing her face as if she could erase her thoughts.

The rest of the day passed without incident. She spent the afternoon, keeping busy. Leila seemed overly mysterious today, so Marina avoided her. She went down to the river and socialized a bit with the women. They were all her dancing companions at night. The women laughed when they saw her, and invited her to join them at the river. Marina obliged. As gray as the day was, they made a colorful sight at the water's edge. Marina, dressed in a white gauzy skirt, with a matching strappy top, stood out among the colorful, chattering natives. Women were the same, Marina discovered, no matter what age in time, how old they were, their race, or nationality. They all laughed and talked about the same things, wherever they were. Men, children and sex. Marina laughed as she caught some of the local gossip, having been among them long enough now, to match faces with names. The result was that she was caught up on the latest event that occurred.

Once the women left the river for home, Marina was on her own again. She waited for Caribe and Salomé to show up for their daily run, but they were late. Shrugging, she went for a walk, instead. Her feet naturally led her down where they had been before. Before she knew it, she was at her little lagoon. Instead of going in, however, she contented herself by sitting on the ledge on the side, and putting her feet in. She didn't do laps, or scissors; she didn't even pretend she was a mermaid. She just sat there, relaxing. All of a sudden she jumped as a splash startled her, and she looked, to see a familiar body knifing through the water, at her. She smiled, at the sight of a head of black hair, being propelled by powerful, bronzed arms.

Carlos Gaitano glided to her, eyes dancing. He treaded water in front of her. They didn't say a word for a moment. He finally smiled. "Marina..." he began, her name feeling like precious wine on his tongue. "My boss," his mouth twitched at the corner as he said the words, "thanks you." They stared at each other for a moment, losing themselves in each other's eyes. Suddenly, words that he had not planned on, that he had never dreamed of, rushed out of his mouth. "He would be very interested to know, if you would work for him."

Marina was shocked. Laughing, she splashed him. "I don't believe you!" She shushed him away, shaking her head. "Go on! Go finish your laps, and then come and talk to me," she urged.

Carlos inclined his head. "Why, thank you, I will." Without another word, he took off, swimming with a sure, steady stroke. Finally, he was back. "I have never seen you around, before. You are not from here."

"No. I am not." She felt him stare at her, but wouldn't say more. They would have time. Her look on him was curious. "What about you?" she finally asked.

Carlos thought for a moment. "This island is what I now call home." He paused. "Have, for a while."

"What do you do?" she asked, genuinely curious.

He turned serious at that and frowned. "I run things for someone." Marina waited for him to continue. Carlos didn't say anything else, either.

She smiled to herself as she squirmed, making herself a little bit more comfortable, on the rock she was sitting. "You don't look too happy about that," she finally commented.

"I am not." A silence fell over them, following the admission, his words echoing in their heads. Suddenly, his hand shot out and grabbed her ankle. He tugged playfully.

Marina jumped at the current that shot through her at his touch. Her mind screamed fire, as she laughed and tried to get loose. "So, get another job," she panted, praying he wouldn't tickle her and reduce her to a mass of screaming nerve ends.

Carlos casually grabbed her other ankle, slowly scissoring her legs. "Maybe, some day," he conceded. They both stared fascinated, at his hands. He grinned sheepishly and stopped. She laughed again. He looked like a schoolboy, caught indulging in a private pleasure. Embarrassed, that he had let his guard down, he released her ankles, eyes twinkling as she smiled into his face. "My boss is going to want to know whether you will work for him or not."

Marina looked at him. She shook her head. "I don't know," she admitted. "Do I have to work with him?" she asked.

Carlos frowned, turquoise eyes clouding. "Do you have a problem with that?"

Marina was nodding her head, even before he finished asking the question. "Yes! I don't even know who he is, and he scares me!"

He couldn't hide the shock in his face. "Why?"

Marina did a theatrical sigh, and rolled her eyes at him. If you have to ask, you wouldn't understand. "Why does he want me to work for him? I'm sure he doesn't have a single female working directly for him!"

Carlos frowned at her words. She was right, he didn't. "Let us just say that he was very impressed over your talent with the books."

Marina shrugged. To her, it was nothing, but she realized that in his man's world, there just weren't any women like her and Salomé. The barrier wasn't just the differences in centuries. It was also about education, upbringing, values, knowledge, and self-worth. She shook her head softly, her hair swinging around her shoulders. "I don't want to work for Gaitano," she said in a low voice.

This time, his look was puzzled. "Why?"

"Actually, I already have a job," she said suddenly, grasping at straws. "I take care of some children."

Carlos watched as her face settled into a smile, directed at something that only she could see. "You don't do that all day long," he pointed out.

"I would rather work for you," she said unexpectedly, her eyes meeting his squarely.

Carlos just smiled at her. His reaction was to throw his head back and roar with laughter, but he was smart enough to realize, that would probably be the wrong thing to do. He had to be careful. Instead, he took her hands in his, and kissed them, one at a time, while his eyes kept twinkling into hers. He chuckled as she smiled back. "You now work for me." He saw a quick look of worry cross her face. "I will send Indio," he paused, "of your complete trust," he continued, winking at her, "two or three times a week, to your home with the books. It will depend on the amount of business." His eyes wouldn't stop smiling into hers. "That way, you keep your babies..."

Marina's eyes widened, and she gasped. "Thank you!" She laughed. "That will work!" Happily, she held a hand out, in front of his face. He looked at it, and back at her. She shook her head as if with a child. Taking his hand, she spoke to him softly. "Where I come from, when people make a deal," she said slowly, lifting his hand so that it was facing her, "their hands come together in agreement. Like this," she continued, slapping his hand in a high-five. "Deal."

Carlos smiled. She looked at him expectantly. She held up her hand again. "I would be more than happy to work on your books for you, Carlos."

He nodded his head and high-fived her. "Deal."

Marina laughed and tousled his wet hair. "We'll talk about the details later." She stood up and brushed herself off, stretching from sitting down for so long. "Just send Indio," she said, with a wink.

Carlos splashed her. He shook his head with a smile, as he heard her laughter echo away from him, down the trail.

Leila looked up as the three young people cast a shadow on her threshold.

"Come in! Come in!" she greeted excitedly, ushering them in. Caribe and Salomé stood to one side, letting Jackson stand by himself, in front of her. "There you are!" she exclaimed softly. "I have been waiting a long time for you, and now you are finally here..."

Jackson glanced at his sister. They had spoken all afternoon, and Salomé had clued him in on the visitors' receiving committee. He looked back at the beautiful woman in the rocking chair. She didn't look much older than his own mother, Shayla. Until you looked into her eyes. He nodded his head. "Ma'am..."

Leila practically radiated her happiness at this new visitor. "I am sure you have had a few questions answered.

Jackson nodded. "Yes, they have." He cleared his throat, not knowing what to say. "Salomé tells me, something happens with the storms."

Leila nodded. "Something," she said vaguely. She laughed at his look. "There are things that are better left unknown, bebé. Better that we content ourselves with just knowing that they happen for a reason."

He frowned. "What reason could we possibly have, for being here?"

Leila's eyes twinkled at that. "That is for you to discover."

They stayed with her for a little while. Leila insisted on feeding them, before letting them go. Together, the three of them made their way to the girls' hut.

Caribe stopped suddenly, a worried expression on his face. He looked at his brand new visitor. "Marina," he began.

Jackson's face rivaled the sun, breaking through clouds. "Marina…" he repeated.

"Will she react the same way?"

Salomé and Jackson stopped in their tracks and stared at him. They looked at each other. Jackson looked down, and started shaking his head. "Oh, man…"

If it weren't for the fact that he didn't even know what year it was, he would die laughing. He exchanged a look with his sister, once more, and turned back to the village boy. They nodded their heads.

Caribe sighed. By the time this night was over, he would be completely drained. "Let me go in, first," he offered. They were already standing in front of the hut. Without waiting for an answer, he went up the porch steps, and stood at the doorway. The siblings saw him pause, and then enter.

Marina grinned at him. Except for the little bit of socializing she did with the villagers today, and her encounter with Carlos, Marina had been by herself, since the children got picked up and taken home. "Caribe!" she cried, relieved to see him. "My God!" she exclaimed happily, standing to hug him. She put her arms around him and rested her chin on his chest, craning her neck to look at him. "Where have you been all day? I've been dying here, and I haven't seen Salomé since she left." She laughed. "Did you see her? She wore pants into town today. I hope she didn't get into trouble." She giggled. "I wonder what Indio had to say when he saw her."

"Marina," interrupted Caribe worriedly.

Marina frowned, pulling back to look at him better. Her hand automatically reached out to stroke his dreadlocks. "What's the matter, baby? Is something wrong?"

"I am jealous."

Marina froze. Whipping around to look, tears were already in her eyes, because she knew. A gasp escaped her throat when she saw him. She started sobbing. "Jackson?" And then she could say no more. Stunned, she gazed at him. Quietly, she choked on her sobs. Caribe looked away as he saw his other friend fall into the new stranger's arms, sobbing hysterically. His name tore out of her throat in one scream after another. *Jackson! Jackson! "*

Jackson closed his eyes, tears streaming down his face. He caught the out-of-control girl, and locked her in his arms, his breath in her ear. "Marina, Marina, *mami,*" he crooned. "It's okay, baby, it's okay. I'm right here, boo." He covered her face in kisses, finally burying his face in her hair. "I got you, baby," he promised. "I got you..."

That night, when the drums played, the riders were there. It was like therapy to them. Something that took them out from their daily routine, and got their senses racing. Jimmy and Silas sat back as usual, heads nodding, feet tapping, distant smiles on their faces. Indio and Gaitano, were another story. They had only been coming up here for one thing, and one thing only. Tonight, they weren't getting it, for as hard as they looked, and as long as they stayed, the objects of their admiration were just not there.

Down the trail, the village lay quiet. Everybody slept. The jungle noises seemed magnified, as the man crept up the hut's stairs. He winced, as a board creaked, and froze momentarily. Moving again, he approached the open window. Looking in, he frowned, as he saw what he was looking for. He watched for a moment, and then, silently retraced his steps. As he jumped off the balcony, something fell out of his hair and floated to the ground, where it lay, gleaming against the dark earth. It was a single, white feather.

Inside the hut, the three young people slept soundly, huddled together like puppies.

Jackson threw his arm around Marina and grinned. They had just spent the morning sightseeing, as best as they could. Max had been picked up at his parent's general store, first. The baby had made a commotion over Marina, and had fallen in love with Jackson at first sight. After that, they had dropped Salomé at Dominique Swan's shop. Miss Swan herself had been left speechless by the newcomer's good looks. Padre Ignacio had blessed him, and Pedro Barbosa had shaken his hand gravely, while welcoming him to Encantada. Now, they were standing in the middle of the street, looking at the front of the Siren's Lair. He looked up at the balcony, from where kisses were being blown his way. He laughed, shaking his head. "You've got to be kidding me!"

Marina grinned back. "Nope."

Jackson laughed again. "But this is a whorehouse!"

"Yep."

"And this is where that guy that likes Salomé works?"

Marina nodded her head, shifting Max from one hip to the other. Today, she was the one wearing pants into town, only to discover that although people stared, it actually wasn't that big of a deal. Of course, she didn't hear the groans, as she walked by. "Yeah," she answered. "But he's actually kind of a nice guy, big and mean-looking as he is."

Jackson nodded, taking one last look at the girls in the balcony. He took a deep breath. "Well, let's do it, then."

Inside, were the usual customers.

"Max!" Marina laughed as Max jumped in her arms, at the sound of his welcoming committee. She led the way to the bar, and sat down.

Silas finished wiping the spot in front of her and grinned. "Well, well," he said. "Nobody has introduced us, yet, but they call me Silas, whenever they're not calling me names." His eyes twinkled.

"You see that chinaman?" he asked, pointing at Jimmy. Marina and Jackson both turned to look, and were met by the other man's smile. They waved and he waved back. "That there is Jimmy. We take care of this place, when both the owner and that savage are away at sea," he explained.

Marina was delighted. "Marina," she said, introducing herself. "And this is Jackson." The men shook hands and she asked the old sailor if they could have lunch. Silas nodded his head with a big smile and nodded at Jimmy. The chinaman left.

Jackson looked around. "This is just a bar," he said.

She nodded. "The girls are upstairs."

He laughed. "I'm loving this."

Silent, as a shadow, Carlos Gaitano watched, from the other side of the bar. It was the man in the sketch. His eyes caressed the girl next to him. He felt bold enough to approach her in public. His soldiers had already been warned that Marina from Cayo Largo was unaware of his true identity. Standing up, he walked towards them. "Max!" he exclaimed, reaching for the baby. He bent his head and kissed Marina warmly on the cheek, lips lingering.

Surprised, Marina returned the greeting, and gratefully, relinquished Max, he of the black hair, and the green eyes. The infant went willingly, immediately hugging the man, babbling the whole time. She looked at him in the mirror. Carlos was bouncing the baby in his arms, his dark head next to Max's as he kissed him. Their eyes met. Her heart began to melt. Marina smiled secretly. He smiled back. Taking a deep breath, she put a hand on each man's arm.

"This is the only time I'm going to explain this," she began, smiling at Carlos. "My father, Pablo Aguilar, and Jackson's father," she said, glancing at her brother, "Joe Banks, grew up together. Since they were little boys. When they became men, they ended up marrying best friends. Shayla," she continued, glancing at Jackson again, "and Sloane," she touched her own chest. Joe and Shayla, had Jackson and Salomé. Pablo and Sloane, had Marina. The best friends ended up living next to each other, in a private piece of property, and the children grew up together." Marina grinned at Carlos through the mirror. He smiled back, and turned to Jackson, shaking his hand warmly. She introduced them. "Carlos, Jackson."

Jackson smiled back at him. "Nice to meet you." He looked around him, politely. "Nice place you got here."

"Thank you," Gaitano smiled. He returned the baby to Marina, as Jimmy appeared in front of them, paper bag in hand. Silas gave the bar one last wipe, and helped his buddy lay out their meal. Jackson was in for a treat of bread, fish and fruit. The pirate reached into the scabbard at his hip and pulled out a folded piece of paper. He casually tucked it into the waist of her pants, and patted it. "Look at it when you are outside," he said softly. "Nice to meet you," Carlos told Jackson. "Enjoy your meal, and welcome to Encantada." He tousled Marina's head, and winked at her in the mirror. "See you later." She blew him a kiss, and he left. At the door, he met Indio going inside. They stopped and had a few words, and he was gone.

Jackson caught sight of the brave in the mirror, at the same time Marina did. He chuckled, as Indio stopped to stare at them. "Let me guess," he said softly. "That must be the savage Silas just mentioned." He began pushing himself away from the bar.

Marina's eyes widened, clutching the baby to her chest, as she tried to stop him. *"Jax!"* she hissed. Silas and Jimmy watched with interest.

Jackson stood up, raising both hands in the air. "I'm cool, baby, it's okay," he laughed, pulling away from her. "I just want to go and introduce myself." Marina covered her eyes with her hand and bowed her head, shaking it. Max squealed with laughter, his hands holding her head. Jackson sauntered over to the last barstool, and draped himself over it. He folded his hands on the bar, and looked up at the Quartermaster, waiting. Indio met his eyes, suspiciously. Jackson just smiled. "You must be the boyfriend," he finally said, holding out his hand. Indio looked down at it, and back at the tiger eyes in front of him. Jackson kept smiling at him. "I'm the brother."

Indio froze. He glanced at Marina. She nodded, smiling. He looked back at the newcomer in front of him and felt himself relax. The resemblance was unmistakable. Suddenly, he felt ashamed. He reached out and smiled into Jackson's eyes, shaking his hand warmly. "Indio."

"Jackson." He reached into his pants, and pulled something out, placing it on top of the bar. Covering it with his hand, he waited as his sister's love interest looked down, and back at him. "I'm really glad to meet you. My sister thinks a lot of you. Be glad she didn't see this." And winking at Indio, he clapped his new friend on the shoulder with one hand, even as he uncovered what was lying on the bar with the other. He walked away, to join Marina and the baby.

Indio looked down. It was the white feather. He met Jackson's eyes, in shock. Jackson winked at him. And then, Indio laughed. At himself, at his narrow escape, at his new friend. "Thank you!"

"This is incredible!" Jackson exclaimed, craning his neck to look up the mast of Gaitano's ship. Max's head fell back on his shoulder, green eyes spying the crow's nest. He gurgled softly. Jackson kissed the baby's forehead, and looked up again. His eyes traced the ropes, the cannons, the decks. He shook his head and laughed at the young woman next to him. "How in the world did you guys end up here?"

Marina laughed softly. Her face was in shadow, while the sun behind her, outlined her figure in fire. The wind blew her hair back, throwing streaks of light into the blue sky. "We didn't choose this. But it only makes sense, that if we're on an island, of all places to be, when a time warp occurs..." she choked for a moment, and laughed, tears streaming out of her eyes. She wiped them away quickly, before Max saw her. "I feel like I'm on Treasure Island." Shrugging, she rolled her eyes, smiling shakily. Her voice was soft. "Natives, and Indians, and pirates, oh, my..."

Jackson stared at her for a moment. He saw her lip start to quiver again, and tears pool in her eyes. He mouthed the words at her, beckoning with his head. "Come here." His arm went around her, as she collapsed against him, sobbing quietly. Blinking his own tears away, he brought them into a group hug. Rocking softly, he held the woman and the baby. He whispered, pressing his face against her hair. "I got you."

Gaitano watched from the warehouse window, as Marina's shoulders shook under Jackson's arm. His heart went out to her, and he realized he felt exactly as his brother did. *Carlos Gaitano wanted to know everything about Marina Aguilar!*

Carlos looked at the woman keeping pace with him. He felt like teasing her, all of a sudden. He had made sure he was at the pool first, today, and when she got there, he casually offered that they swim together. "Want to race?" he asked.

"No." She didn't miss a beat.

"Why not?"

"Can't win," she gasped. "No point."

"How do you know if you don't try?"

Marina rolled her eyes.

Carlos grinned. They glided to a stop together, and looked at each other. He moved towards her, putting an arm on either side of her head, on the ledge behind them, trapping her between them. She put her hands on his arms, and looked straight into his eyes. They held each other's gaze. Hard. He drifted closer, until their noses were almost touching. It seemed to Carlos, like things started happening. To him. No. To them.

Marina drew in a ragged breath, and let it out shakily. She felt like she could drown in his eyes. They were absolutely devouring her. She licked her lips. *Carlos...*

He grinned again. "Nervous, my friend?"

She giggled. "Of you?" She smiled. "Well..."

Carlos brought his face closer, until their breaths were mingling. Their noses finally touched. He smiled against her lips. "Good girl," he murmured. "You haven't fainted yet."

She smiled back. "I don't want to drown"

Without warning, he pressed his mouth against hers. Marina clung to him, returning the pressure of his mouth. All of a sudden, he let go. "I would never do that."

Marina looked at him, dazed. "What's that?"

He cocked an eyebrow at her, not being able to stop his grin. "Let you drown."

Marina laughed. She looked down, embarrassed, at the small waves between their bodies. Looking into his eyes again, she laughed harder. Carlos joined her. "You know what?" she finally gasped.

He nodded. "You forgot, didn't you?"

She grinned. "Completely."

Carlos reached down and deliberately put her arms around his neck, as he nuzzled hers. Scooping her in his arms, he lifted her so that their chests were touching. "Think about this," he whispered, kissing her face. "If that is what happens from just this..." he pressed his mouth against hers, again. "What would happen..."

Marina held him tight, and smiled. "If..." she whispered.

Carlos drew back and comically rolled his eyes, imitating one of her more humorous gestures. Rubbing his nose against hers, he corrected her. "*When...*" His arms tightened around her, crushing her breasts against his chest. "I really kiss you..." He kissed her again. And again.

Marina smiled, looking dreamily into his eyes. "I shall forget my name," she admitted.

He laughed. Then, he dunked her. Marina kicked away from him, and came up to hear him laughing as he swam away. What she didn't know, was that he didn't want to scare her away. She climbed out and wiped the water off her arms and face. She shook her head, water flying out of her hair. She laughed, as he stopped, treading water.

"Your name is Marina," he announced to her, blowing her a kiss as she waved goodbye to him with a smile. "*Marina, divina, muñeca preciosa...*" Rolling her eyes at him, she blew him a kiss. Silly man.

Carlos watched her disappear into the jungle, hair dripping, the fabric of her pants, plastered to her backside. The leaves fell back into place, once she passed, hiding her swinging hips. "*Mia...*" he added to himself. "You are mine," he said to no one in particular. Then he sighed. "My what?" He shook his head and swam away. Then, he too got out of the water, and disappeared, forcing himself to not follow her. Instead, he took the scenic route home. Carlos walked along the beach. Alone.

Later that evening, Indio showed up with the books. Dropping them off, he took Salomé for a walk. Marina was left alone, forcing herself to focus on the numbers. Imprinted in her mind were turquoise eyes, bronzed face, and midnight black curls. She smiled, and concentrated.

Caribe stood by quietly, as Jackson studied his drawings. He had discovered that they had that talent in common. He felt flattered at the young man's compliments. Finally, Jackson reached the portrait of his sisters. He whistled. "Dude! This is almost like a photograph!"

Caribe smiled. He didn't know what a photograph was, but he understood by Jackson's reaction, that it must be something impressive. "The dreams don't leave me alone until I finish the drawings."

Jackson grinned at him, holding the paper to his chest. "Can I keep this?" Caribe shook his head, and returned the grin, holding out his hand.

"Maybe." Jackson returned the girls' portrait.

"So, where am *I*?" Jackson asked, looking around.

Caribe drew a piece of paper out of his pocket and handed it to him. "Salomé dropped it yesterday, when I went to find her at the Lair," he explained. "Gai--" he shook his head, remembering that Marina didn't know. "Carlos found it on the floor, and kept it from Indio." He caught Jackson's frown, and sighed. "Indio really likes Salomé," he explained. "He got a little upset when I showed up, and Salomé just left without explanation." He frowned, shaking his head. "Very upset."

Jackson chuckled. "Boy's got it bad, huh?" He unfolded the paper in his hand.

Caribe had to repeat the words in his mind. Understanding, he nodded and rolled his eyes. "Very bad." They laughed. "Carlos gave it to Marina, and Marina gave it to me."

Jackson looked down and couldn't speak. It was almost like looking in the mirror. He shook his head. "Caribe, this is awesome. They both are." He laughed happily. "Our parents would kill for these."

He returned the portraits to the artist, and clapped him warmly on the shoulder. "One thing I'm curious about, though."

"What?"

Jackson pointed at the walls of portraits. "This is what you could call a hall of records of the visitors, as you call us, that come through, just like we did, on that freak storm that you got going, out over the ocean." Caribe nodded, as they walked outside, and made themselves comfortable on the front porch. "So, is there a record somewhere of the dates of these visits?"

Caribe frowned, shook his head, stopped. He thought for a moment. "I do not know," he finally admitted. "Mamá can tell you about many visitors that have come through over the years, but dates?" he shrugged. "You would have to ask her. Why are you interested in the other visitors?"

"Oh, no," he shook his head. "I'm not that interested in the other visitors." He paused, choosing his words carefully. "Nature is cyclical. That means," he explained, "that it repeats most of the things it does, in patterns." He turned to Caribe. "Have you ever thought that there might be control to be had, over this time warp thing? Didn't Leila tell the girls that they could go back?" He began pacing restlessly. "Do you think they want to stay here?"

"I know they do not," Caribe answered. "But they have something to do here, and I believe they accept that."

Jackson turned on him, his eyes shooting sparks. The passion in his voice left no doubt, as to his feelings for his sisters. "Dude! Our parents are going to die over this! We are all they've got in this planet!" He slapped his hands down hard on the railing, and looked up at the stars. Over the mountains, the last light of the day was melting into the landscape. "I came all the way here to get them." He faced the villager.

Caribe shook his head solemnly. "It is not time, yet. They have just arrived. Besides, there are other people involved now."

"I know, I know," Jackson cut him off. "The Indian, the pirate..."

"The babies."

Jackson nodded. "The babies," he agreed softly. He looked at Caribe. "How can I go back without them?"

Marina looked up as Salomé and Indio came in. She was practically howling with laughter, and he was chuckling. "You two look happy! What's up?"

Salomé shook her head at her. "This guy cracks me up!" She looked at him. "You wouldn't know by looking at him, either," she said, admiration creeping into her voice.

Indio just smiled, as he took the books from Marina, kissing her warmly on the cheek. "How are they looking?" he asked.

Marina shrugged. "It's all about Carey, Indio." She looked straight into his eyes. "Tell your boss, that he better get his butt down there."

He frowned. "Is it that bad?"

She nodded, sympathy in her eyes, as she chose her words carefully. "Gaitano stands to lose everything."

Silence fell between them. He kissed her again, and turned to Salomé. She put her arms around him, stroking his hair, and whispering in his ear. Marina watched as he nodded at Salomé's words, and kissed her tenderly, before leaving. Salomé turned to her friend, a dazed look in her eyes. "I'm in trouble, Marina. I'm not going anywhere until I get together with this guy and give it a chance." Tears filled her eyes. "I've never felt like this before."

Marina hugged her. "I know, *mami*. Just follow your heart."

The drums that night sounded different to the riders. They sat quietly, mesmerized, eyes flickering with torchlight. Tonight, the energy was unleashed. Gaitano and Indio smiled at each other. As they watched, Marina and Salomé danced with reckless abandon. Next to their girls, were two young men. One dreadlocked, the other cornrowed. The four of them manifested that night, the passions raging in them, all.

"Gaitano."

The men looked at Solomon, as he materialized from the shadows. They had heard him coming, so they weren't surprised. Carlos didn't take his eyes off Marina, as he greeted his Boatswain. "Solomon," he said softly. "Come join us, son. What brings you, all the way out here?"

"Captain. There is a ship spotted. It has been coming steadily nearer all afternoon. The boy at the crow's nest cannot see it any longer. He thinks it doused its lights."

The four men all looked at each other at the young African's words. Jumping to their feet, they quickly mounted their horses. Carlos took one longing look back at Marina, catching her spin around, hair flying around her laughing, upturned face. Turning his horse around, the pirate rode after his soldiers.

"Larissa!" Marina exclaimed happily, as she caught sight of the beautiful raven's hair and cat's eyes at her doorway. "Max!" she smiled, holding her arms out for the baby.

Larissa laughed. "Honey, you are a godsend!" She kissed her baby goodbye and smiled at Marina. "I came today," she explained hastily, "because I am dragging Caribe into town, come high or hell water, so he can help me out a little bit at the store."

Marina laughed. "Good luck! You might have to take Jackson along. They have become inseparable."

Larissa raised her eyebrows. "I'll take Jackson," she smiled, batting her eyelashes. They laughed. "Actually, Jackson is good for business," she winked at Marina. "So, I guess, I will take him." And with another laugh, she was gone. It wasn't long, before Leilani came along with the children. They visited a while, although they saw each other every day. Leilani looked more like a teenager should, with each passing day. Marina coddled the younger girl, to that one's delight, making a fuss about how pretty she looked, stroking her hair, and making her laugh. "You look beautiful, mami." She squint her eyes suspiciously. "Is there a boy in the picture that I don't know about?"

Leilani laughed, embarassed. She bowed her head, shaking it. "No." Her eyes shot to Marina's, face beaming with the whitest smile. "Yes."

"Do I know him?"

The girl shrugged. "Maybe."

"What does he look like?"

"His eyes are like the sky when the storm comes."

Marina froze, her hand going up. "Hold it." She looked aghast, at her friend. "Not Francois!"

Leilani nodded eagerly, her voice dreamy. "Yes, Francois!"
Marina stared at her. "Leilani, do you trust me?"

Leilani frowned. "Of course ---"

"No Francois, baby," Marina said softly. "He's a player. Listen. I have something to tell you about Francois." And she did. And Leilani listened about cheaters and players, and she understood.

Finally, she wiped her last tears away, and sniffed. She smiled at Marina. "I thank you." She shook her head solemnly. "No Francois. No games."

They hugged, and Leilani left. Marina turned to the babies. "All right, you guys. What type of bug are we going to torture today?"

They laughed, clapping. Marina bowed. They roared. Ali pretended to throw fairy dust, waving an invisible magic wand. And that's how their day began. Marina and the babies.

Gaitano stared through the spyglass, at the ship. It was just sitting there. Not a good sign. She wasn't flying any flags, but her cannons were visible. "You know, Indio, I'm beginning to think Marina is right. Somebody is giving out information. And it has to be from here."

"Carlitos," Indio interrupted, falling back on his childhood nickname, whenever they were alone. "The problem is at Carey. She has mentioned it twice."

All of a sudden, the door burst open behind them. They turned around, startled, only to discover Solomon himself. His eyes were wide in his face, and he was out of breath. *"Captain!"* he panted. "Kid spotted a longboat, about three miles down the shore!"

Gaitano and his Quartermaster looked at each other. In an instant, they were gone.

Indio ran all the way to Dominique Swan's shop. He burst in, looking wildly around him. Miss Swan herself was standing by a mirror, taking care of a preferred customer. *"Indio!"* she scolded.

Salomé walked out, a stunning gown in peridot green silk, held against her body. Indio stared. Then, he shook his head. His voice was a low rumble to her ears. "Salomé, come." He took her wrist gently, pulling her firmly.

Dominique stepped in front of them, hands on hips. Her white blond hair reflected the chandelier lights. She was frowning. "And where do you think you are taking her, young man? Salomé works for me, and she is working right now!" Indio looked straight at her. After a moment, he saw Dominique back off, in her eyes. "I need Salomé today. I am sure your customers will understand. She will be back tomorrow." And without another word, he put the jewel-toned dress in Dominique Swan's startled arms, and whisked Salomé off.

Indio took her to his cottage. She had been outraged at his silence, all the way home. He didn't blame her, but she could wait. Pulling her behind him, he entered his home. The bed was neat and clean, as he'd left it this morning. Afternoon light filtered through a piece of stained glass over his door. Salomé spun around, eyes spitting fire. "Hey, baby," she said coolly. "What's going on?" she demanded, hands on hips. His eyes dropped to those hands, on those hips. Salomé decided not to let him see her squirm. "You're acting like a boyfriend. What gives?"

Indio just stared at her, mesmerized, at seeing her in such familiar surroundings. She looked like she belonged. He took her in his arms, and kissed her face desperately. "Trust me," he rasped. And then, for a moment, he couldn't let her go.

Salomé stroked his face. She made him look at her. "I trust you, baby."

"Then, wait for me." He pressed his lips against hers. Then, he was gone.

Salomé stood, shaking her head, hand to her mouth. She grinned. There was nobody there to hear her words. "I'm not going anywhere, baby."

Gaitano ran like the wind. He had already organized and dispatched his soldiers. Padre Ignacio and Pedro Barbosa had men of their own, people from the village that they trusted, patroling its borders. Solomon and Giancarlo were actively searching for the crew of the longboat. And he, well, he just had to get to the village. He was unaware of the jungle racing by him, vines reaching for him, thorns and branches grasping at him. As he approached the village, he thought everything looked normal. His heart still pounding, he went straight for Marina's hut. The villagers had caught word about his interest in the young woman, and thought it amusing to keep his identity a secret. That way, when he showed up in the middle of the day, striding down their main path, nobody thought anything of it. Outside the dwelling, he hesitated. There were no signs of life. Making a decision, he went up the stairs. Standing in the doorway, his heart skipped a beat, as he caught sight of her.

Marina was in the middle of the floor, amidst a tangle of blankets. Her hair was tied up in a loose braid, and she was laying on her side, knees drawn up slightly. One arm pillowed her head, and the other arm seemed to contain the three sleeping babies, next to her. On the other side of the babies, as if keeping them in, was little Ali. They were all fast asleep. Gaitano let out a breath, as he watched. Dust danced in the ray of light coming in through the window. Outside, the bamboo creaked and sighed, swaying in the breeze. Down the path, a dog barked, and then stopped. From the backyard, he heard the song of an unhappy cricket, caught in the dark of an overturned bucket. As he looked, one of the babies fussed in his sleep, and Marina's hand moved in hers, to quiet him. The baby gave a deep sigh, and snuggled closer. Then they all settled down again. Gaitano smiled, tracing Marina's outline, his eyes lingering on her face, and her body, curved around the children. He let out a shaky sigh. Going back outside, he made himself comfortable on the front porch, standing watch. As he waited, he pulled out a dirk from its scabbard on his hip, and began polishing it.

From his vantage point, it seemed that he could see everything. The hut was high, on a small hill, and it actually overlooked the rest of the village. People walking by, waved at him without calling out his name. He smiled, and waved back. Only a trio of young men didn't acknowledge him. They stood in front of the hut and stared at him insolently. The boy in front had clear eyes, and he didn't look very happy at his presence there. Gaitano stilled his hands and stared him down. The boy said something to his friends and threw back his head with laughter. The friends tittered, but kept a wary eye on the pirate. They continued on their way. He glanced inside to see if anybody had heard the boys laughing, but the hut remained quiet.

Gaitano began to pace, restless. He stepped softly, so as not to make too much noise on the porch. Hearing a sound, he looked towards the front. Coming down the path, never taking his eyes from him, was Jackson. Gaitano stopped pacing, and squared his shoulders, waiting for him. As Jackson climbed the steps to join him, he put a finger to his lips.

Jackson nodded, still not taking his eyes away. "Hey, man, how're you doing?" he asked, hand outstretched.

Carlos took his hand, and their chests met, as their hands pressed on each other's back. "Jackson," he responded warmly, sincerity in his eyes. "I am fine. How about yourself, man?"

The two black-haired men stepped back, the better to look at each other.

Jackson smiled, his eyes taking in the situation. The dirk in the pirate's hand, the stillness of the hut, the stealth of the man in front of him. He cocked his head to one side, tiger eyes gleaming. "What's going on, man? Everything all right?" Gaitano hesitated. "Don't lie to me," Jackson warned him. "I come home to find Marina asleep inside with the babies, and you are out here, like a bodyguard," he moved his head, making his earrings glint in the sun. "Something is going on."

Carlos nodded, and shrugged. He decided to tell the truth and test the brother's reaction. "There's a ship a few miles out. It's been there since yesterday, and they are not coming any closer."

Jackson froze. A puzzled frown crossed his face. "Are they in trouble?" he asked hopefully.

Gaitano shook his head. "No."

"So, what's the deal?"

"We don't know yet. My men are searching for whoever left a longboat on the beach."

Jackson looked at him in alarm. "Is there danger?" He glanced anxiously at the girl inside.

Gaitano held his eyes. "We won't know until we find them."

"What if you don't find them---" He shook his head, anger in his eyes. "Who the fuck are *they*, anyway?"

Gaitano shook his head. "No telling without a flag." He looked at Jackson. "Do you trust me?"

Jackson stared at him in silence for a moment. "I don't know," he admitted. "All I know about you is that you can make things happen around here. I don't know if you're the boss, or the boss' son, or what the deal is..." He glanced at Marina again, and sighed. "My sisters like you. Both of them. But Marina..." he shrugged. Tiger eyes stared into turquoise. "She trusts you. Or at least, she's not afraid of you." He nodded. "That's good enough for me." He locked eyes with the pirate one more time. "Yes. I trust you."

Gaitano nodded. "Good. Now, know this." He turned, and pointed at different spots around the village, that disappeared into the jungle. "I have men posted in all those places." He turned back to Jackson. "If the people that got off the ship were to mean us harm, they wouldn't get far at all. As a matter of fact, they will never make it near this place."

"So, why are you here, personally?"

"I'm making sure."

Jackson nodded. Inside, a baby whimpered. "Does Marina know you are here?"

Gaitano mouthed the word, as he backed off. "No." He held Jackson's eyes.

Jackson grinned. "I'm cool, dog, go do what you gotta do. I won't tell."

Carlos Gaitano smiled at his friend, and then he was gone.

That night, candlelight flickered in the warehouse on the docks. Inside, Gaitano and his men, held court. Before them, were the owners of the longboat. Ten men in all, they had been surprised by Pedro Barbosa, and company. The fight was over, before it began. Pedro had intercepted the leader as he was getting ready to enter the village. The man had in his possession, a pistol and a knife. But at the sight of a group of village men waiting for him at the trail leading to their homes, he had given up. In a matter of minutes, he had been detained, soon followed by three more that were following him. The other six men had been ambushed by Solomon and Giancarlo, along with the help of Jimmy and Silas. Now, they stood before the pirate and his soldiers, all waiting for answers. Carlos Gaitano stood in the shadows, waiting for the detained men to shuffle in. His face seemed to be carved from stone, as he watched. They now stood before him, side by side, chained to each other. A meaner looking bunch he hadn't seen in a very long time. Unless you counted his own. These men, however seemed vaguely familiar. "Who is your captain?" he asked. Silence followed. Stepping out of the shadows, he stood before them. "What is your ship's name? Who sent you here?"

The men looked at each other, and back at him. One of them coughed, at the end of the line. Everyone turned to look at him, but the boy hung his head. Indio turned to Gaitano. They exchanged a look. Pedro Barbosa stepped up. "Men, welcome to Encantada. Seeing as how you belong to no one, you are now ours. Have a nice stay."

The ten men began grumbling, some in anger, others, in fear. Solomon glanced at his Captain. Gaitano jerked his head towards the door. The men were escorted out, Pedro Escobar in front, leading the way, and Solomon, taking up the rear. Giancarlo sighed, shaking his head. He looked at Gaitano. "Somebody is interested in you."

"Yes."

"The ship is gone."

"Yes."

"Do you think this is all tied up?"

"Of course."

Giancarlo glanced at Indio and sighed. Then he smiled, eyes twinkling. "La Gitana is ready."

When the drums started and the natives danced, that night, there were no riders. Instead, Indio took Salomé home, where he hugged her fiercely before kissing her goodnight. Then, he went to join his brother in preparation for the voyage ahead of them. Part of him was humming with the excitement at the thought of being out on the ocean again. But the rest of him was screaming at the injustice of bad timing. For the first time in his life, Indio did not want to go.

It was Marina's day off again. Jackson, Marina and Salomé were at the beach. In all these days, since the girls had gone missing, they had neglected their forms. Tae Kwon Do is not just a martial art; it is also, a discipline. Caribe watched fascinated at their synchronization, as they practiced kicks and punches, blocks and turns. After a while of just looking at them, he decided to try it. Caribe laughed happily, as he matched, step by step, his friends. The early morning sun left beads of perspiration on his face. He might not have been as tight as they were, but he could keep up.

Since Jackson had arrived, they each had their own hut, next to each other. These were, where they went to, after their morning run. Salomé left for work, and Caribe took off to do whatever it is native island boys do, first thing in the morning. Marina sat on the steps overlooking the backyard. She was wearing a pair of pants, and one of the fabrics, around her chest. Her hair was mussed up, around her face, still damp from the bath after her run. Jackson sat between her legs, his elbows resting on her thighs, head fallen to one side. Marina had her fingers, in his hair, and a comb lay next to them. She was tackling his cornrows. That is how Carlos Gaitano found them.

"Jackson!" The pirate called out in a low voice, as he approached them, his eyes caressing Marina's face, just as the clilmbing sun was.

"Hey, man!" They slapped hands, and smiled at each other.

"Thank you for your concern yesterday," Carlos told the young man, as he bent his head to kiss Marina's cheek. He smiled a good morning into her eyes, as he turned back to Jackson. "The matter we were talking about has been taken care of," he said, winking at him.

"What matter?" Suddenly remembering, Jackson raised his eyebrows, and smiled. "Right, right." He held out his hand again. "Good job, man."

"Whatever," mumbled Marina, turning his head a little more.

Carlos watched in silence as they finished. He waited as Marina assured her brother he looked fantastic, while providing a small piece of shiny tin for Jackson to look at himself. Once satisfied, the brother left. And finally, they were alone. He glanced at Marina, loving the smile on her face. "I heard from Max..."

Marina arched her eyebrow at him. "Max..." she murmured. "And what has that silly boy been saying to you? I thought babies told no tales."

He stood in front of her, and looked longingly at the spot Jackson had just vacated. "May I?" he asked, looking into her eyes.

"Please," Marina said, scooting back to fit his larger frame.

Carlos turned his back on her and sat down, making himself comfortable between her legs. He pressed his back against her breasts, and draped his arms on her thighs, hands caressing her bare legs. Marina bit her lip, and smiled, over his head. *Thank God, I insisted with John Kline, for the razor!* She laughed silently. Carlos sighed contentedly. Marina raked her fingers through his hair, massaging his scalp gently. Carlos closed his eyes. "Max told me..."

"Yes, Max..." she whispered in his ear, blowing softly. Carlos caught her head and brought it down next to his. He didn't kiss her, though. Instead, he rubbed his head against her, like a black panther to its mate. Marina felt her blood rush through her veins, and her world spin. "What did Max say, Carlos?" she murmured, rubbing her nose softly against his scratchy cheek.

Carlos turned his head until their mouths were a breath apart. "Max told me he wouldn't see you until tomorrow."

Marina opened her eyes and looked straight into his, and smiled against his mouth. "Max is a traitor."

Carlos kissed her. "Come on." He stood up, and helped her to her feet. "You have the day off, I am not doing anything..." He smiled and shrugged. "I want to know you better," he admitted.

"And I, you," she told him.

He took her hand and led her back through the house, closing the doors, as they left. "I want to show you *my* Encantada." He pulled her along the path, into the trail that led to the mountains. "The one I was raised in." He locked his fingers with hers, and winked at her.

Marina thought she was going to die.

Carlos looked at the woman next to him and grinned. He had decided to test her, so to speak. So far, she had practically matched him step for step, as he led her up a mountain trail. When they got to the top, he stood back in silence, and watched Marina take in the view. He smiled, as she gasped. In fact, it was breathtaking. Undetected, they could see the whole village and town, below them. The natives were barely more than brightly colored stains in the landscape. In town, they looked like ants scurrying about. And at the docks, the ships seemed majestic, even from this distance. Marina turned to look at him, and she laughed. He smiled, and they took a seat on a grassy spot, in the sun, the jungle at their backs. Their eyes lingered more on the ships, than on anything else. Carlos plucked a blade of grass, and ran it slowly down Marina's arm. "Would you like to sail on a ship like that?"

Marina shook her head. "No."

"No?" He frowned.

She shook her head again. "Never."

Carlos kept silent for a moment, but curiosity got the best of him. "Why not?"

Wrinkling her nose, she shrugged. "Rats. Ships are nothing but floating rat hotels."

Wanting to laugh, he settled for just raising an eyebrow. "Is that a fact?"

She nodded now, smiling. "Absolutely. I refuse to put myself in a place where humans are outnumbered by rodents."

"Rodents, huh?"

"Yes, rodents. Besides, why would I ever want to go on a ship? Pirates, as far as I know, are mean, nasty, and smelly. Being out on the ocean, under God knows what circumstances, I am sure cleanliness is not one of your priorities. So, why am I going to submit myself to the company of the likes of that? And, I'm sure you don't take care of yourselves, or each other, so why would I go anywhere that nobody is going to care about me?" She glanced at him, reassured that he was listening to every word. "Throughout all this, I haven't even mentioned scurvy, which I'm sure you are familiar with. Well, that is caused by a deficiency in vitamin C. Maybe you could bring yourself to mention to your boss, Gaitano, that he can control that by providing you, men, with fruits for your voyages."

Carlos nodded thoughtfully. "You have strong opinions about the subject."

She turned back to the view of the harbor, her eyes sad. "I don't want to sail on a ship." *I may never find my way back here, to go home again.*

From there, they went back down the mountain, but this time on the other side of town, from where the village lay. Along the shore, was an abandoned lighthouse Marina had never seen before. Carlos took her inside. Nobody had been there for a very long time, and it showed.

"Was this ever working?" she asked her guide.

He nodded. "Many years ago. I was a little boy."

They were at the top, looking out over the ocean. "I like the view," she told him. "But even more, I love the solitude."

From there, they walked down the beach, past their private pool, and around the far side of the village, to the waterfall. There, they swam in the small lagoon, and played under the cascading water. They were now, all wet, and slippery, their skin feeling slick to the touch. Embracing, they let their hands slide all over each other. Finally, ducking under the beautiful cascade, they sat on a ledge of rock, behind it. Marina with her back against the wall, Carlos' head in her lap. She finger-combed his wet hair, hypnotized by the water falling before her eyes. He looked up at her, mesmerized by the wet material clinging to her breasts. Sighing, he took one of her hands and brought it to his lips, taking a finger into his mouth. Her eyes met his, with a smile. "I've been thinking," he said.

Marina couldn't resist teasing him. "You have, huh?"

His eyes devoured her, as he brushed the hair away from her face. "I've been thinking," he repeated. "That I am ready to take this one step further." Marina searched his eyes, her smile, slowly fading. He sat up to face her, stretching a leg on either side of her, as he did so. Taking her face between her hands, he gazed deep into her eyes. His thumb rubbed her lower lip. "Sometimes," he murmured. "I look at you and wonder if you have come from a different world." Marina held her breath. "Or if you stepped in, out of my dreams." He buried his fingers in her hair, rubbing her head softly. He shook his head. "You are my good friend, right?" She nodded slowly. " That will not change," he promised, kissing her forehead. "I would just like a woman in my arms, once in a while."

Marina was drowning in the pools of his eyes. *Sloane's Baby ain't no fool.* She reached up with a hand, her fingers tracing his mouth. She frowned, her hazel eyes searching his face. "Surely you are not lacking in that department." He cupped her face, erasing the lines she was creating. "I am sure women throw themselves at your feet," she said softly, staring at her fingers on his mouth.

Carlos caught her hand, and turned it over, tracing the delicate lines on the inside of her wrist, with his tongue. "Yes," he admitted. "They do." He rolled his eyes, making her smile. "Quite inconvenient for me, actually."

She put her forehead against his, her breath on his lips. "Poor baby." Sliding her face against his, she whispered in his ear. "What is it exactly what you want from a woman?"

"Right now?"

Marina grinned and pulled away, leaning back on her hands, his hands still on her face. "Sure, baby."

He sighed. "I want to be able to hold and kiss a woman, sometimes." He looked away from her eyes, entering foreign territory. "Hug and touch, without it necessarily having to be anything more than that."

Marina's eyes widened. "Why, Carlos ---"

He cut her off with a look. "Sex, I can get." He stared her down, and she nodded.

"I have no doubt. Being a woman, I know what other women do around the likes of you."

He chuckled. "Actually, the only thing wrong is that it gets boring."

"And meaningless."

He nodded. "And meaningless, after a while. Affection does not equal sex."

"Sex should equal affection, as opposed to rage or control."

"Agreed." He brought her face closer to his, making her lean towards him once more, as his legs drew her closer to him. "So, with that in mind, I am just expressing an emotional need I have for affection without the sex."

She laughed. "Why, Carlos! You just need a makeout partner!" He just looked at her, waiting for an explanation. "Kissing, touching, caressing, without sexual intercourse," she elaborated.

"All right, I will take it."

"Just like that, papi?"

"Kiss, touch, caress... yes. Just like that. I will take it," he repeated. "Marina," he breathed against her mouth, "will you be my makeout partner?"

She thought about it. "How would you kiss me ---" She didn't get to finish.

His mouth was too busy ravaging hers. Marina felt a shift inside her. She had never experienced losing her mind before.

Carlos devoured her. The relief he felt, overwhelmed him, sweeping over him in waves. How often did one achieve such a mental state of fulfillment? He hadn't even realized, he was looking for something. No kiss had ever touched his soul before. Marina let herself fall back under the assault, the pirate leaning over her. Her head started spinning, and she began pushing him away. Carlos changed his intensity, but he did not take his mouth off hers. They looked into each other's eyes, mouths still glued together. Marina licked his lip. He tried to say something, but shook his head instead. He frowned to himself. Marina gazed at him. He tried once again. "I ---"

"Sshh," she hushed him, putting a finger over his mouth. She passed her thumb over his lower lip, staring deep into his eyes. Carlos took her thumb and sucked it into his mouth, scraping it with his teeth, making her smile. He gently touched the burn marks around her face. She smiled and shrugged. "That happens." Throwing her arms around him, she held him close, her lips against his ear. "Now, it is my turn." She licked his earlobe. "Help me up." Carlos obeyed, swinging her unto his lap. "Mmmm," she murmured, holding his face between her hands. "Let me show you how this girl likes to make out." She looked into his eyes and pressed her mouth against his. Before he could get into it, though, she drew back. A look of dismay crossed over his features, but she began kissing his face softly, making sure he felt the pressure of her lips. "I believe," she whispered, "that there are certain things..." she grazed the shadow on his face with her teeth. "... that shouldn't be hurried."

His lips parted as her tongue danced across them. Carlos felt tension building up. He clenched his fists, not wanting to interrupt her. He was just aching to hold her tighter. She licked along the outline of his lips, stopping long enough to dart her tongue in his mouth, flicking it against his own tongue. He drew in a shaky breath, and she was raining kisses all over his face again, their breaths mingling. Carlos adjusted her on his lap. Marina cautiously shifted, more than aware of his hardness against her bottom. She raked her fingers through his thick hair, distracting him. He shot her a quick look. She smiled, bringing her mouth to his again, slowly adjusting their lips for a kiss, heads tilting slowly. They held each other's gaze. Marina felt a prick of tears, behind her eyes. *I adore you!* The scream tore through her mind. She closed her eyes, and kissed him.

Carlos felt himself relax. No woman had ever kissed him like this, before. Like they were home, inside him. He had been around the world. Had met some of the most beautiful women in creation. All sizes, all colors, every age imaginable. He had been seduced by geishas, and courtesans; had shared intimate moments with mistresses, wives, a few teenage girls, and some older beauties that had taught him a trick or two. He had even shared quarters with a wild gypsy woman for a short time. But nothing, in all his vast experience, had prepared him for the shock waves that coursed through his body at Marina's kiss. The finest wine in the world couldn't compare to the taste of Marina's mouth. He felt chills run down his spine as her nails grazed the back of his neck. Time seemed to stop. The world, as he knew it, ceased to exist. His senses drowned in her kiss. He groaned.

Marina ended the kiss, sucking his lower lip gently, into her mouth. Their eyes met. She let go and sighed, shakily. Then, she grinned. "That, my friend, is how you make out." she gently loosened his grasp on her, and looked down at his arms. All the hairs were standing on end, goose bumps distinctive, in spite of his dark tan. He followed her gaze and met her eyes again. They got to their feet slowly, never breaking eye contact. Marina smiled, senses screaming. They ducked back under the waterfall, and crossed the pool, to leave, and got out of the water.

Carlos stole one last kiss, gazing into her eyes. "*Bruja*," he whispered raggedly. "You are a witch…" He took her hand, and led her back, locking his fingers with hers. Marina's smile, when it came, was private.

The village was quiet, when they got back. Leilani waved happily from her front porch, the twins and Ali, happily climbing all over her, as they played in the afternoon light. They waved back, walking slowly, finally making it to her hut. There, they embraced. He whispered in her ear. "When can we make out again?"

She grinned. "You want more?"

He nodded. "Most definitely." Fire burned in his eyes. She hugged him, stroking his back. "Eventually, maybe."

He nodded again, and with one last kiss, he was gone. Marina hugged herself, thrilled to pieces, as she found herself alone.

The docks were bustling with people, helping getting Gaitano's ship ready. The pirate sent for Solomon. The young African listened solemnly at his captain's request. Nodding, he walked away, chuckling to himself, as he shook his head. Gaitano must have it bad. The man's orders couldn't be clearer. Solomon was to gather up as many able-bodied men, as he could. Their presence was required on La Gitana. Their purpose, to catch rats, until there wasn't one left on the ship. Pedro Barbosa had already spoken with him, as soon as he got back into town, from his day with Marina. Apparently, the men had been kept overnight in one of the warehouses, where they had been submitted to Jimmy's interrogation skills. The man could charm a priest into confessing his wet dreams. And, as a result, now they had a destination. Still no names, yet. These men in particular were at the very bottom of the pecking order. They responded to commands, but were granted no information. They just did as they were told. However, one word kept popping up consistently. *Carey.*

Gaitano sighed, as he entered the Lair, his eyes immediately adjusting to the gloom. Indio was behind the bar, talking to Salomé, as they gazed into each other's eyes. Her hand was in his, as he absently fingered the leather band he had given her. Jimmy and Silas were working. In one corner of the room. Jackson sat, surrounded by some of the girls. He was joking with them, and they were laughing at his antics. The girls were relaxed, and... natural, he realized. None of them were working, so to speak, and instead, were just sitting around, having fun, enjoying themselves with the newcomer in their midst. Jackson saw him enter and raised his hand, calling him. "Yo! Gaitano!"

The girls chorused, "Gaitano!" They dissolved into giggles.

Carlos smiled at them, and looked at Jackson warily. The two men met in the middle of the room, and greeted. Shake, hug, step back. Their eyes met. "You know," Carlos said, leading him to the bar. He met Indio's eyes, and two drinks were put before them. They touched glasses, and drank, eyes on each other.

Jackson nodded. "I guessed."

"How?"

Jackson shrugged, leaning until his back touched his sister's. "I guessed."

He felt the reassuring pressure of Salomé behind him, giving him support as she listened. Carlos nodded slowly, the question in his eyes. Jackson shook his head. "No, Marina does not know."

Not pretending any longer, Salomé turned around and wrapped her arms around her brother's chest, her chin resting on his shoulder, as she looked at the pirate. "I knew. We won't tell," she said. "That is up to you, or she is going to have to find that out, all by herself."

Carlos took another drink, thoughtful. He frowned. His eyes met Indio's.

The brave's gesture was almost invisible, but Carlos understood he was on his own, on this one. "I have my reasons." He watched as the siblings reacted. Salomé just smiled.

Jackson just chuckled. "I hope they are good enough to stand on their own, when Marina finds out."

Carlos nodded. He could still feel her mouth on his. Shaking his head, he glanced at Indio. "How is La Gitana coming along?"

Indio grunted. "Almost done."

Carlos nodded again. "Good." He looked back at Jackson, leaning back in his sister's arms. "I see you've been keeping the ladies entertained."

Jackson waved a hand in the air. "You know, how it is...", he laughed, glancing at the girls, where he had left them, and blowing them a kiss. They giggled, returning the gesture. Jackson looked back at Gaitano. "I need to know one thing, though, man." Carlos sat next to him, sipping from the glass Indio put in front of him. He looked at the man with the cornrows. "I want to know," Jackson said slowly. "How do you practice safe sex here?"

Gaitano and Indio looked at each other, the exchange in their eyes, silent. "Safe sex?" Carlos asked.

Jackson nodded, smiling at the other man's discomfort. "Yeah, man, safe sex."

Salomé's eyes bore into him, before glancing at Indio. "Yeah," she chimed in. "I want to know, too." She glanced at Indio again. The men seemed to be at a loss for words.

Jackson chuckled, enjoying their discomfort. "You know!" He looked at both men, now. "These are my sisters," he announced to them, taking Salomé's hand up to his face and kissing it. "This one is my flesh and blood. Marina," he looked at Carlos, "is my heart and soul."

"And mine," Salomé murmured.

The men waited for him to continue. "You guys are obviously, extremely attracted to them." He nodded, in approval. "They are big girls. I taught them how to take care of themselves, " he continued, "from men like us." Jackson winked at Salomé in the mirror. He turned back to the men. He had their absolute attention. "Now," he glanced from one to the other, "what measures do you gentlemen take, to ensure that a female does not get pregnant, or catch anything?" The men were at a loss for words.

Salomé glanced from one to the other, also, seeming to find comfort from the proximity to her brother. "Yeah," she drawled. "Enquiring minds want to know."

"Catch anything?" Carlos repeated slowly, frowning.

"You know," Jackson urged him. "Catch something. As in disease, from being with multiple sex partners, without protection, who in turn, have sex with multiple partners, themselves."

Carlos caught Indio's smile, as he attempted to hide it. He met Jackson's eyes. "That is a personal question."

Jackson shrugged. "These are my personal sisters." For a moment, they all fell silent.

"Skins." Everybody turned to look at Indio. He met each of their eyes in turn, finally looking at Salomé. His gaze softened as he took in her features. "Skins," he repeated softly.

Carlos nodded. "We use animal skins." Catching Jackson's stare, he turned to him. "Our father taught us well, also. We are clean. Your sisters are safe."

Jackson felt silent for a moment, staring at them. Nothing inside him indicated that they were lying, or making it up. "All right, then." Taking both of Salomé's hands in his, and kissing them one after the other, he pulled away from her embrace. "Now, that that's settled, I, personally, feel better." He looked at Carlos again. "It is nice to know that the men my sisters crave are responsible adults, who know how to handle their business." He slapped hands with each man, and went back to sit with the girls. Delighted at his return to them, the sirens surrounded him once more.

Later, as the sun began setting, Jackson and Salomé, met with Caribe and Marina, for their daily routine. The four of them pounded the trail, each lost in their own thoughts. Marina parted company with them at the natural swimming pool, as usual. She dove in head first. Cutting the water like a knife, she began her laps, her mind churning, just as the water was, under her feet. So intent was she on her own thoughts, she never heard Carlos until he was swimming next to her. She stopped at the edge of the pool, and smiled at him, as he kissed her. "Did you finish whatever it was that you had to do?" she asked, eyes smiling.

Carlos gazed at her. He finally nodded. "Yes, I did. Thank you for asking."

Marina frowned. "What's up?" She reached out and stroked his face. "What is the matter, papi? You look like something is bothering you."

"I am sailing tomorrow." They both looked at each other in shock, at his words. He didn't mean to say it like that, and he wanted to kick himself, as he caught sight at the hurt that flickered in her eyes. "Come with me."

Marina stared. *Go with you? Where?!* "No."

"Yes."

Marina shook her head, backing away from him. "No." She felt a chill, lick along her spine. She shuddered. "Why?"

"I need to take care of some business." His eyes caressed her face, sliding over her nose, lingering on her mouth.

"Your business. Not mine." She turned her back on him, wrapping her arms around herself.

"You *are* my business."

"No."

He turned her around to look at him. "I am going on a trip," he explained, voice low, "to take care of that matter with the books. *You* are in charge of Gaitano's books. *You* are the one who found where the problem was. *He* needs to report this."

Her eyes flashed. "That is *his* problem!" She pushed away from him. "I thought you were my friend!"

"I am!"

"Well, I don't want to go!"

"What about me?"

"What about you?"

"I need you there, Marina," he pleaded, holding his hand out towards her.

Her eyes watered, but she shook her head. "I get seasick."

"I will get you something to ease your discomfort."

Marina didn't answer. She didn't trust herself. Instead, she pushed off, swimming away from him. He followed her, keeping pace with her, as they did a couple of laps. She stopped again. "Gaitano doesn't need me!"

Carlos' hand reached out to stroke her face, but she pushed it away. "Yes, he does."

She shook her head, beginning to tremble. "You can't make me."

Turquoise clashed with hazel. "Yes, I can."

Marina felt she was dying inside. She held on to the rock ledge, and panted. Water churned behind Carlos as he swam away from her. She shot daggers at the flashes of skin, glinting in the sun. *I can't do this anymore, today. I just can't.* She sighed and buried her face in her arms. *I don't have to.* A tear slid down her cheek. *I won't.* Marina took a deep breath and hauled herself out of the water. She squeezed excess water out of her hair and looked around for her skirt. She yanked it from the rock it was laying on, and flicked it free of sand with a couple of movements of her wrist. She stepped into it. The gauzy material proceeded to immediately cling to her wet skin, outlining the smooth, curved columns of her thighs. She flipped her wet hair over her shoulder and stalked off into the jungle.

"Marina!"

She pressed her lips together, blinking furiously at her tears. He didn't yell her name again. She didn't expect him to.

Marina felt herself get sucked into the jungle. The setting sun had slipped behind the clouds, plunging the scenery into a deep shade, earlier than usual. High above her, beyond the treetops, thunder whispered. It wasn't relaxing, at this moment, although it had stopped being scary, for some time, now. There was a rustling noise and, all of a sudden, he was next to her. She glanced over at him. Carlos met her eyes, but didn't say anything. She looked ahead, and made her way with determination.

I don't know if I can do this, any longer. God, help me, I'm crazy about this man!

Tears began falling. Overhead, lightning split the sky. Marina braced herself for the thunder that followed. Rain, just dropped from the sky, pouring, washing her tears away. She felt herself relax. And then, she sensed Carlos move closer to her. He matched his stride to hers. Their hands touched fleetingly, in rhythm with their pace. Carlos reached over, lacing his fingers with hers. Marina felt tears well up, again. She shook her head. Carlos lifted her hand and pressed his mouth to it. *Oh, God, oh, God, oh, God...* He searched her eyes hungrily. *Oh, God...* She saw resignation pass over his eyes. But it wasn't a giving up resignation. It was more like, when you put something on hold. The pirate wanted to lick her fingers, to fasten his mouth on the pulse at her wrist, and suck, as if he were a vampire. He grazed her knuckles with his teeth, he couldn't resist. Her smile touched her eyes, but wasn't strong enough to make it to her lips. They kept walking in silence, their fingers interlocked.

The rain fell steadily on their heads. There was a spot lighter than the jungle, up ahead, as they approached a clearing.

Marina looked over at him. "What are your plans? Right now. I need to know."

Carlos searched her eyes. They indicated imminent panic. "I am going to spend some time with you, tonight."

Her eyes widened, and she lost her breath. She gasped, and shook her head, finally meeting his gaze, fiercely. "I need you to know, sir," she declared, "that I am on the brink of overload. So, if you think you are going to spend any time with me, tonight, you will wait right here, while I go and take care of some business." She whirled around, to stomp off. He grabbed her by the arm. Marina swore under her breath. She made a big show of deliberately looking down at his dark hand on her arm, before lifting her eyes, to meet his. *Oh, no! He suspects something!*

Carlos' eyes smoldered at their center, like rays of sunlight caught in their lagoon. "What is going on?"

I can't lie to him. "Just give me a few minutes. The house is a mess." He frowned. *He doesn't believe me.* Carlos let go of her arm, and nodded.

Marina ran. The jungle flashed past her in wet angry streaks of black and green. She was careful to not get off the path, so as not to shred her feet.

When she reached the front of her hut, sure enough, there they were. As they had been for the past few nights, that she had noticed, although they had not been aware of it. The boys were huddled under the tree in front of her steps, huge grins splitting their faces. Inside her head, she screamed as she forced her face to go blank.

God! You idiots!

Francois stepped up, eyes shining outrageously. "Louise!" he exclaimed, with the delight of a child.

"Get the hell away from my house! Don't ever come here again! I am sick and tired of you guys!" Tears came to her eyes, and she looked even more beautiful. Vulnerable. Darkness was creeping up on them, as the last vestiges of light clung to her. Rain fell steadily, making her wet skin draw their eyes to the curves under the clinging material. Francois groaned, as his teeth flashed white against his skin, taunting her. His steel eyes smoldered in his beautiful ebony face, with the most cruel intention. Marina's stomach dropped and her skin began to crawl.

He laughed wickedly, betraying the evil in his mind. "I will have you. Now." He cocked his head to one side mockingly, and his voice was sweet as he sing-sang. "Louise," he crooned. All of a sudden, everything seemed to happen at once.

Marina screamed. *"I will not be raped by you!"*

Francois' hand shot out, her wrist suddenly in it. Marina stumbled as he pulled her savagely against himself. Carlos stepped out of the jungle. Everyone froze. The whole scene played out, in a matter of seconds. Carlos was suddenly beside them. "Is there trouble here?"

Marina gasped. His tone sounded relaxed, but being his brand new best friend, she knew. *He will do anything for me.*

Never again, would another opportunity come by, in order for her to play the damsel in distress. When, ever again, would she have the chance to throw herself against her man, wrap her arms around him, and bat her eyelashes, where tears cling as she wails. *Oh, Carlos! He wants to rape me! Help!* He was sure to come to her rescue. But, she was so angry, that instead, she made eye contact with him for a second. Carlos' fists clenched. He needed to see how she would handle it.

Marina turned back, her full attention on Francois. Whipping her wrist away from his grasp, she repeated herself, but this time, her words were low, as she picked up where she left off, when Carlos made his appearance. Her fists came up. *"I will not be raped by you!"* Her hand shot out in a blur, retribution in motion. Francois' head snapped back, and he stumbled. Marina dropped her fist and shook it gently, knuckles screaming.

Carlos stepped in between them. He laughed. "Ow! That must have hurt, huh, Francois?"

Marina moved in a blur, her mind shutting out everything but a steady, relaxing, empowering chant echoing inside her head. *Don't fuck with me!* Her foot connected with the place where the black boy's future children lay.

Carlos grabbed her by the waist and spun her around, out of the way. "Oh! Hey! Lady!"

Francois dropped to his knees, eyes rolling, breath gasping. Kiko and Manuel turned tail and ran. Marina screamed after them. "Oh! Now you run! Some fine friends you are!" She turned and twisted in Carlos' arms, until he dropped her.

His arms kept her cradled within them without touching her. He laughed again, a deep, sexy, throaty laugh that caught her attention. He nuzzled her neck. "Hey, baby," he crooned. "I will give you your prize, later."

Marina's chant rose to her lips, but she caught it before it spilled, and she said it out loud. *I am a lady.* Looking deep in his eyes, she pushed him away from her, even as he laughed softly. "Don't mess with me," she told him. Her eyes flickered angrily at him.

His smile faded and he sighed. "I won't, baby." Pulling her towards him, he pressed his lips against her forehead. He spun her around suddenly, sending her away with a pat on the butt. Marina melted. Striding towards her front door, she swung her hips at him, leaving the two men alone. Carlos grinned. A groan behind him, made him turn. "Hey! Francois! How are you feeling, son?" Holding out his hand, he helped the young man to his feet.

Francois forced a smile, white teeth glinting in his face, even as pain shot out of his eyes, like sparks. "She got me good, boss," he groaned, hands cradling his rapidly swelling sex through the thin material of his pants.

Carlos shook his head and put his arm around the younger man, steering him away from Marina's home. He chuckled, for a moment enjoying Francois' discomfort. Stopping suddenly, he spun the boy around to face him. " Francois." The young man's eyes widened, fear trickling down his spine, now overpowering the pain between his legs. Carlos looked deep into his eyes. "I have a pretty good idea of what it was I just walked up on, Francois. Although, the truth is, I don't want to know," he shrugged, in the exaggerated way required of actors on stage, so as to be well seen by the audience. "There is one thing, and one thing only, I need to say to you." Carlos' voice dropped to a snarl. "Leave the lady alone. She is with me." His face relaxed, grinning again, belying the fire smoldering in his turquoise eyes. "I know who you are, Francois." His voice dropped even lower. "I know where your mother lives, after your father got taken. I know who your sister secretly meets with; also, when and where. I know all about your uncle's mistress and your grandfather's children. I know where your grandmother goes to church." His eyes never left the young man. "I even know, about you harassing Leilani, whenever you catch her alone." The young man's eyes filled with tears, sheer panic making a whimper escape his throat. "As of this moment, you are leaving this lady, the hell alone." Carlos smiled as the boy flinched. "Don't you ever let me catch you over here again. Ever." Then he turned around, and as darkness dropped on him, making him almost invisible, he let himself be swallowed by the jungle.

Marina walked around her hut, pacing in circles, in the dark, hands rubbing her arms, trying to ward off the shivers. Carlos walked in, relaxed. *As if he owns the place.* Marina smiled. He caught her by the waist and hugged her. She had changed out of her wet clothes, and was now wearing a pair of, a little too big, cutoffs, with a rope around the waist, and an oversized shirt. Her hair was curling around her face and shoulders, and she smelled good. He buried his face in her hair with a smile. "Here, let me help you." Walking Marina around the house, he began shutting windows and doors. When they got to the front porch, they stood there for a moment, leaning against the posts in the dark. His arm was thrown casually around her shoulder, as he surveyed the scene, natives scurrying in the dark, trying to get out of the rain. Marina's arms were wrapped around his torso, her head against his shoulder. They both watched as Caribe and Jackson came down the path, straight at them, chattering and laughing, soaking wet. The two young men stopped suddenly, as they caught sight of the couple. They looked at each other and smiled, slyly, hands sliding against each other. They looked back at the couple. Carlos smiled mischievously, and drew Marina closer, kissing her soundly. He looked back at them, and chuckled, as the pair backed away, smiling and apologizing. The couple went back inside, closing the door behind them.

Carlos walked her towards the hammock, strung up in the middle of her living space. Without letting go of Marina, he dropped down into it, bringing her down with him. Making himself comfortable, he adjusted her between his legs. Marina began shivering. His arms squeezed her for a moment, and then his hands rubbed her arms. Marina shivered harder. Carlos' hands rubbed more intensely, relishing on the heat emanating from her skin. Marina's heart rate dropped a couple of beats. He smiled to himself, and brought his lips to her ear. "I took care of it." Marina nodded. She didn't want to talk about it. Carlos knew. Finally. Now she was safe. A shaky sigh escaped her throat. Carlos chuckled, and pushing with one foot against the wall, he began to rock them. "What is that noise?"

Marina's home seemed to reverberate as the sky opened up, pushing the rain down, harder. She snuggled against him, purring, as his hands caressed her gently, smoothly gliding over her skin. Marina closed her eyes. *I'm melting.* "It's raining harder, papi," she murmured.

"Yes," he agreed, with a laugh. "But what is that noise?"

Marina's eyes opened, searching his, ears straining. Carlos felt her body tense in concentration, and relax again, at discovery. "I had the boys put a tin roof on this place." She sat up, swiveling between his legs, turning to get a better look at him, in the darkness.

Carlos reached over, to where he had spotted a candle and some matches, when he first came in. He lit the candle silently, and held it up, to peer into her eyes. "Explain."

Marina smiled. "So I could hear the rain."

Carlos smiled. He blew out the candle. "Sleep, Marina," he urged. Marina stiffened. Carlos caressed her. "Sleep, mami, *tranquila*."

Marina melted into him. They passed out.

"Dude, tell me more about these storms."

Caribe looked up at Jackson. They were in his hut, talking about art, drinking wine, laughing together. "What do you want to know?"

"You can go back, right? Willingly?" Caribe nodded. "Yes."

"Do you know this for a fact?" Jackson shook his head, as Caribe just looked at him. "Okay, how about this. Has any visitor that ever come through, gone back home, and then come back here again?"

"No," Caribe answered, shaking his head. "But it *is* possible."

"Yes."

"Exactly! So, basically, if one were to figure out the timetable on these freak storms, they could gain control over the time warp."

Caribe's dreadlocks bounced gently, as he chuckled. "Let me guess. You are going home."

Jackson just smiled at him, streaks of candlelight sparking off the cornrows covering his beautiful head. "Now, tell me. What kind of stuff comes through and what doesn't?"

Caribe took a sip of wine from the bottle and smacked his lips, wiping the back of his hand over his mouth. "What do you mean? Personal stuff?"

"Right. For example, when the girls went into the cave, the very first time, they had some personal belongings, that didn't come through, after the storm. Personal belongings with modern items of the twenty-first century." He had Caribe's full attention. "What they found, on the other side of the time warp, were some clothes and some other items, like candles and matches, and papers that were already in the cave when they first got there."

"Of course. Nothing to identify the moment in time."

"So, if I were to go out to the cave, let's say, with some supplies from here. Papers, clothes." His eyes betrayed his inner excitement. "They are bound to be there, the next day, after the storm."

Caribe nodded, smiling slowly. "Yes. So there are some things from here that you could take with you."

"Exactly." He laughed. "My sisters also noticed that some silly dated stuff they were wearing disappeared, but their jewelry stayed. The earrings they were wearing are classic designs." He paused. "Did you, as visitor caretaker, observe anything else on, or about the girls, that you know is not from now, but came through anyway?"

"Their marks."

Jackson looked at him. Caribe's dreadlocks were bouncing again. "What marks?"

The young man shrugged. "The marks," he insisted.

"Freckles? Beauty spots? Birthmarks?" Caribe shook his head at each one. "What the hell are you talking about?"

Caribe's hands floated over his back, waving around his left shoulder. At Jackson's puzzled look, he took a piece of paper from the table, and a charcoal pencil. He sketched furiously, and showed Jackson what he had drawn.

Jackson froze. It was a symbol. And then he had a flashback. It was his eighteenth birthday, and the whole family celebrated, with a trip to a local tattoo parlor. The dads had rented the artist for the evening, who happened to be family. Snake Coltrane, or Uncle Jesse as they called him, was married to his father's younger sister Rain. He had been more than happy to please them, and they all got the same thing. A tattoo behind their left shoulder. It symbolized their family group, in a tribal form. Shaking his head, Jackson came back to the present. He smiled at Caribe. "The tattoos came through." Turning around, he loosened his shirt and showed Caribe where his own was.

Caribe held up the paper, next to Jackson's tattoo. It was a perfect match. Jackson adjusted his shirt again, and it was his turn to drink some wine. "Why do you want to go?" Caribe asked him.

"Something is going down."

"What?"

"I don't know, for sure, but something is definitely going down. The town has been scrambling for the last couple of days, getting this ship ready, at the harbor. Somebody is sailing."

Caribe nodded. "Gaitano."

"Exactly." He looked at Caribe meaningfully. "We just saw him. Does he look like somebody that is getting ready to leave?"

"No."

"But he is, right?"

"I believe so."

"So, why do I get the impression that Marina is going with him, and she doesn't know it yet?"

Caribe slapped a hand on his forehead, his eyes wide. "He is taking her!"

"Looks like it, doesn't it?"

"And if he takes her, somehow, Salomé will end up going."

"You got it, now."

"But they will be safe," Caribe protested. "These men ---"

"Are thinking with the heads they got below their waists, and not with the ones sitting on their shoulders." They chuckled. Being men, they understood.

"But your sisters will be safe," insisted Caribe. "These men will protect them with their lives."

"Oh! Don't get me wrong, dog, I trust them. Even if they are trying to get into their pants, I trust them. These men obviously care for my girls, very much. But that's not what worries me."

"What is?"

"What if they leave Encantada, out over the ocean, to a world where there is no time warp? What if they can never make their way back?"

"You think the storms are going to disappear just because they go on a trip and come back?"

Jackson shrugged his shoulders. "You tell me."

"No. That is not going to happen."

"Good enough. Either way, there is trouble brewing in Encantada, and you need help. Bad."

"What are you going to do?"

"I am going to try to go home, and bring back my crew." Caribe's face lit up. "You have men?"

Jackson smiled wryly. "Yeah, man. I got two men. And two women."

The earth shook. Marina's eyes flew open, flashes of light splitting the sky. *Oh, my God!* She sat up suddenly, making the hammock rock.

Carlos' hands slid around her shoulders, and eased her back against his chest. "Storm," he whispered in her ear. She nodded, melting against him. Carlos kissed her face gently as his hands moved down to cup her breasts. Marina froze. Carlos whispered again. "Relax." His thumbs brushed her nipples, through the fabric. Marina jumped, as a jolt of pleasure shot through her crotch. "You are dreaming," he murmured in her ear, tongue gliding down the slope of her neck. His hands slipped inside her shirt, hands expertly molding her bare breasts, fingers alternating, pressing into her hot skin, in time to music only he could hear. Marina moaned softly. "You want more?" he asked.

She sighed, and nodded, head thrown back, her hands on top of his. "A little bit more," she said, voice low and sexy.

It was all Carlos could do to keep himself from ravishing her in the rocking net cradling them. "I will make you feel good," he promised. Holding her away from himself, he slipped out from under her and climbed out of the hammock carefully. He held out his hand and helped her out. They walked to a pile of blankets under a window, and sat on it, facing each other, knees drawn up, cradling each other. Marina felt the heat rising out of their bodies' proximity. She hesitated. He read her mind. "I won't do anything you don't want me to," he whispered against her mouth, burying his fingers in her hair. Marina fell back under his gentle assault, leaning back on her hands. His hands cupped her face as he ate her mouth. Her world began to spin. She could feel the cool night air against her breasts. His fingers trailed down her neck, his tongue tasting the hollow at the base of her throat. She gasped, tears springing to her eyes, from emotion. His hands pushed her shirt open, capturing her breasts, molding them once again. Marina's arms weakened, and she fell back. Carlos followed her, his mouth burning a trail down the middle of her chest. She felt the pressure of his manhood on her, hesitant. She reached for his hips and pulled him down against her. Wrapping her legs around his waist, she molded herself to him. She held him so tight he could feel her heat through the material of their pants. He groaned, chuckled, and snarled, grinding himself against her, his mouth clamping down on a breast. Marina gasped as he sucked her into his mouth. It felt as if her heart was going to leave her chest, through her skin. His tongue swirled around her nipple. She wanted to scream. Instead, she took handfuls of his hair, and pressed his head tighter to her breast. He ravaged her, sucking hard, biting soft, licking slow. Her legs began to shake, making her lose her hold on his waist. They dropped to either side of him, knees bent, trembling. She gasped for breath, as Carlos' hand moved lower. He stopped for a moment, as she grasped his wrist. His mouth abandoned her breast, to move to the other one. She moaned softly, as she felt her whole body tingling. The rope around her waist had disappeared, and suddenly his hand was there. She felt him seek entrance, his finger rubbing gently. Her loins yielded gladly. Carlos sucked hard, as he felt her wet heat envelop his finger. They both moaned. Marina squeezed. Carlos caught her nipple between his teeth and licked furiously, pulling desperately. Marina contracted around his finger, holding him inside, as hard as she could. Carlos went deeper and moved, the palm of his hand pressed against the source of all her pleasure. Tears came to Marina's eyes, as she whimpered and sighed. The drumming of the rain on her roof was surreal. The only thing of any substance right now, was Carlos' hands and mouth. He pressed harder with his hand, and searched deeper with his finger, as her contractions became stronger. She bucked her hips, as he explored. The world around her dissolved, her only reality, the pirate on top of her. Finally, hooking his finger upward, he encountered a small, smooth area, deep inside her. He rubbed it gently, curious. Marina didn't know whether to scream or sob. First, she did neither. He kept rubbing. Then she did both. He had found her spot. And as she let go with her voice, her body released all her pent-up longing, in an intense climax. Carlos felt the rush of wetness on his hand, and groaned, his mouth full of breast, smiling around her nipple. He eased the pressure and rubbed his face against it, scratching her screaming skin, before kissing his way down her belly, until his tongue reached her navel. It traced a slow, wet circle around it, dipping inside before moving back up to her chest. He rubbed his face against her other breast. As her contractions eased, he moved his hand, slipping his finger out of her, sliding it over the center of her being, making Marina jump. He laughed softly. "*Suave, mami.*" Drawing his hand out of her pants, he put his finger in his mouth, tasting her.

Marina stretched luxuriously as he massaged her breasts gently, bringing her down slowly from her climax. She felt like purring, a slow smile spreading on her face. *This will work.*

Carlos kissed each breast before buttoning her shirt up, again. The rope magically appeared in his hand, and he tied it loosely around her waist again. He couldn't resist one last caress of her sex. He laughed as her hips bucked. Finally, lying down, he gathered her into his arms, pressing her back against his chest. He turned her head and kissed her passionately. Breaking away finally, he smiled, stroking her hair. "You are an excellent makeout partner."

"What about you?" she asked softly.

"Next time." He pressed her buttocks against his groin, and cupped her breast, as he nuzzled her neck. "Sleep, Marina," he murmured.

She brought one of his hands to her mouth and kissed it. "I'm not going anywhere," she warned softly.

His voice was just as soft, but firm. "Yes, you are."

Marina wiggled her butt, burrowing against him, pressing his hand harder against her breast. "You can't make me."

He laughed softly, moving quickly, so that Marina was on her back, holding his full weight. "We can do this all night, if you want." He kissed her deeply, his tongue on a quest of her mouth. Lying down beside her again, they resumed their position. His mouth was next to her ear. "Yes, I can."

Marina closed her eyes, snuggling against him. *You can't make me.*

Marina looked at Larissa, as she hurried towards her, Max in her arms. "I am so sorry, honey, I didn't mean to keep you standing there, but the baby has been a little bit restles, today, what with missing you yesterday, and all." She looked at Marina suspiciously. "Are you all right, honey? You seem... different, somehow," she trailed off.

Marina smiled reassuringly, taking the baby. "I'm all right, mami. Just a lot of things going on, lately." She lifted Max over her head for a moment, cooing at him as she brought him down again, next to her face, for a kiss. Max was loving it. He put his hands on her head and smooched her, his wet, little mouth on hers. Then, he pressed his cheek against hers, gurgling contentedly.

His mother smiled, tears in the back of her eyes, from pride and joy. "You have brought such happiness into our lives, Marina, I only pray, someday we'll be able to do the same for you."

Marina gasped, tears stinging her own eyes. "You lie," she hissed, laughing quietly. "I have not brought you happiness! I only provided you with time alone, so you could enjoy what you already have." They giggled.

Larissa blew them a kiss, as they left. "See you later, darlings."

Salomé looked up, startled, as a shadow crossed her threshold. Today was her first day off, since she began working with Dominique Swan. She certainly wasn't expecting anyone. Indio stood there, looking down at her. "Well, hey, baby, come on in." She swept the fabric she was working on, off her lap, and stood up, offering him the rocking chair.

"Salomé," he rumbled, deep in his chest, his eyes shining. He took the seat she offered, and followed her with his eyes, as she went through the motions of picking up.

Salomé glanced at him and winked. "Good thing, I like the strong, silent type."

Indio began rocking softly, his mind churning. *Do or die*, he thought.

Grabbing her wrist as she walked by, he pulled her unto his lap, cuddling her. "I have something to ask," he murmured.

She snuggled deeper into his lap, her body naturally adjusting to the shape of his. He held her closer. Salomé wrapped her arms around his neck, kissing him softly on the face, before drawing back to look deep into his eyes. "Sure, baby," she smiled. "What's on your mind, handsome?"

Indio grinned. "You." He ran a hand along her side, so it rested just beneath her breast. His fingers traced the round outline, tentatively. Salomé grinned and held his hand against her, so he could feel the heat he inspired.

"What about me, baby? You want to get together with me?" He nodded. "Just you."

Salomé stared at him, her voice a whisper. "*Just* me, baby?" He nodded, capturing her face in his hands, and kissing her forcefully. Inside her head, she screamed. *Oh, my God! Oh, my God! Oh, my God!* She wrapped her arms around him, responding to his kiss, letting him know how she felt. She chanted in her head. *He wants to kiss me, and take me away...* She held on tighter. *He really wants me...* She sighed. Then she drew back and looked at him. "Are you sure, Indio? We are just getting to know each other, papi. Do you know what you're saying?" She widened her eyes at him, smiling. "Don't mess with me."

Indio's smile was slow to come, and his look was of the bedroom eyes variety. His eyes were half closed, and he licked his lips. He let her eyes linger on his mouth, before dropping his own to her cleavage. He let his thumb graze her nipple. Salomé held her breath, not wanting him to hear her moan. "I am sure." Indio put his arms around her again, kissing her once more. "Salomé," he murmured, almost gasping, "I ---"

Salomé was startled, for the second time that day, as another shadow crossed her threshold.

Carlos stepped in, his face unreadable. Salomé stared at him, entranced by his appearance. Here was the pirate, personified. His boots were polished to the highest shine, the cuffs folded, where his tight pants could be seen. His shirt was snow white, open at the chest. He didn't wear a sash, the shirt hung over the pants. There was a scabbard with a dirk at one hip, a pistol at his other. A black bandana covered his ebony hair. Turquoise eyes blazed out of his dark face, like twin sunlit pools. Carlos Gaitano looked impressive. She let out a shaky breath. He took another step forward, his face unreadable. "Good afternoon," he said formally. "I am sorry to interrupt." He looked around until his eyes landed on the curtain in the opposite corner of the room. "As you were," he said absentmindedly.

Indio and Salomé didn't reply. They watched curiously, as he drew the curtain back, and began to inspect Salomé's clothes. He spotted a canvas bag in the corner, and bent down to retrieve it. Turning to them, he tossed it to the girl on his Quartermaster's lap. Finally, Salomé spoke up. "What's going on, Gaitano? What do you think you're doing?"

Carlos glanced at her. "You are packing."

They watched again, as he paced around the hut. He stopped short in his tracks, as he finally took a good look at them. Dismay seemed to cross his features, as he took in the scene. Indio was in the rocking chair, his legs spread comfortably, feet bare, pants cut off at the thighs, shirt open at the chest. Salomé was cradled in his lap, their arms wrapped tightly around each other. There were traces of kissing, around her mouth. His hand was on her breast. Carlos sighed deeply, meeting Indio's eyes. "Sorry, papi," he murmured.

Indio held his eyes and nodded, except that it wasn't really a nod. It was more like the thought of a nod. A shift of air between the two men as they held eye contact. A vague vibration in space, where two minds --- no, two souls, meet in pure love and total understanding, the source of which was the beating of two hearts. The two hearts of lifelong friends. No. Brothers. Unwittingly, Indio's body began to thrum in anticipation.

Salomé felt her heart sink as she sensed something pass between the two men.

Carlos turned towards her. "We are sailing." He hesitated. "I am taking Marina." He spread his hands, helplessly. "I thought you would want to be with her." He scowled suddenly, making Indio tense.

Salomé bolted upright. *"No way! Marina would never agree to sail off this island!"*

"Bad timing, *amigo*," Indio grumbled.

Salomé's eyes clashed with Carlos'. "Where is she, by the way?" She stood in front of him, glaring up into his face.

"On her way to my ship," he said, softly, controlling his anger. "In which we will be sailing, in half an hour." He glanced at Indio. *"Nos vamos."* He looked back at Salomé. "With you, or without you," he said softly.

Salomé just stared at him, as if he'd gone crazy. "Oh, hell, no! Uh -uh. No way! *Hell, NO!* You are *not* going anywhere with Marina!" She stepped back, chest heaving, so as not to start beating him with her fists. Her breath came fast and hard, almost panting, hysteria threatening to take over. She gasped, tears coming to her eyes. She screamed inside her head. *Oh, my God!*

Carlos looked at her, seeming to search, deep in her soul. She was obviously terrified, just as he expected Marina to be. Something about the ship, or about sailing, was scaring them to pieces. Or was it the fact that they'd be off the island? But why? Carlos shrugged. No time, now. He pointed at Salomé's bag. "Suit yourself." He turned to leave, and stopped at the doorway, to look at her. Their eyes clashed. Hers, angry and hurt, with disbelief and fear. His, steady, hard, a little sad. *"I am taking Marina."* And he was gone.

Salomé gasped. Indio stood up quickly, to hold her. He searched her eyes, feeling her fear, as the tears overflowed. "I will be there," he reminded her.

She nodded, making the tears fall. "Baby, I need you to cover your ears for a moment, while I go say something very unladylike."

Without waiting for his answer, she turned and strode across the hut, flinging open the back door. She screamed. Indio's lips twitched as the f word reverberated in the afternoon stillness, echoing in the jungle.

Marina walked slowly, taking her time, looking in the windows. She smiled to herself, recalling the night before. Carlos had left at dawn, kissing her soundly, his hands all over her, making her squirm. He had lowered his weight on her outstretched body, looking deep into her eyes, in the early morning light. After kissing her some more, and whispering in her ear, he was gone. She sighed. The whole thing scared her. The man was taking over her every moment, sleeping and awake. She shook her head as if to clear cobwebs, and switched Max to her other hip. He squealed. She laughed. Suddenly, someone loomed in front of her. She stopped in her tracks, startled.

Padre Ignacio looked at her, apologetically. "*Buenos dias, Marina.*" She smiled, sighing in relief. "*Buenos dias, Padre Ignacio.*"

"Have you been to mass lately?" he asked.

"Why, no, actually, I have not." She grinned as he held out his arm, for her to take.

"May I?" he asked, winking at her.

Accepting graciously, Marina laughed. "*Gracias, Padre.*"

They reached the small church, isolated, in the middle of the small plaza. Leaning against the run-down post in front of it, was Pedro Barbosa. He touched his hat, smiling at Marina. "*Buenos dias, Marina.*"

Marina nodded, releasing Padre Ignacio's arm, and shifting the baby's weight. "*Buenos dias, oficial.*"

The three of them stepped inside, Padre Ignacio leading Marina to the very front. She sat down, settling Max on her lap. She looked around her, noticing she was not alone. Besides Pedro Barbosa, there were a few other men, she had seen around town.

"*En nombre del Padre, del Hijo, del Espiritu Santo...*" Padre Ignacio put a hand over his chest, and raised the other, making the sign of the cross over the small congregation, in blessing. The mass had begun.

The church door opened quietly. A shadow slithered in, letting the door fall silently behind him. He slipped into the last seat in the church. Kneeling in the shadows, his eyes riveted on the curly haired female in front. And in this fashion, Carlos Gaitano attended mass, before he had to sail, leaving before it was over. Marina never saw him.

After the final blessing, Marina turned around to find herself face to face with John Kline. She smiled. "John! Hi! I must have just missed you. We haven't been out long, at all."

The storeowner chuckled, holding his hands out to his baby son. Max willingly went to his father, gurgling and squealing with delight. Marina laughed. She looked at the tall, blond man. "I have never seen you here, before. I wasn't even aware you went to church."

A shadow crossed over his face, sadness creeping into his eyes. "I usually don't. I just came to get Max."

Marina frowned, confused. "Max?" She smiled at the baby, her eyes preoccupied. "I thought yesterday was my day off..."

"It was," he interrupted. "Marina."

Marina whirled around, to face Pedro Barbosa. Her stomach dropped at the expression on his face. She knew. "What is going on, oficial?" She watched in mounting horror, as Silas and Jimmy flanked him.

Pedro Barbosa held out his hand. She looked down at it, and back into his eyes. He took a step forward, as she began to shake her head. "You need to come with us, Marina."

She gasped. "No." Backing up now, her hair swinging about her face as she looked around her. "Where is Carlos?"

Pedro Barbosa kept coming after her. "Carlos is busy at the moment. He will see you later." He stopped. "Come with us, Marina. You need to."

"*No!*"

"*Marina!*" Padre Ignacio hurried towards her.

Marina began crying. "*Padre! This is the house of God!*" she screamed. "*You would have them take me away from here? You brought me here, yourself!*"

"Marina..." Padre Ignacio pleaded.

"No!" she screamed in horror, sobbing openly, now. *"This is the house of God! How dare you!"* Max started screaming, howling in sympathy, squinted eyes swimming in tears as he clawed at his father with one little hand, the other stretched out to Marina, tiny fist clenching and unclenching frantically, beseeching. Marina cried harder. The men split up, going around the pews, towards the door. The candles flickered as they passed by. Marina turned around and made a dash for the door. Gasping for air, she yanked the door open. Standing before her, was Solomon. She screamed, the terror in her voice, bouncing off the walls. He reached for her, and she ducked, pushing past him. Solomon lunged and grabbed her easily by the waist, keeping her from escaping. Marina twisted in his hands and punched him in the face, making him stumble. Instinctively, he tightened his hold on her, as he rocked to one side, from the force of the blow. He looked at her, through squinted eyes, a muscle twitching on his cheek. Marina screamed. She couldn't stop. Solomon calmly grabbed her and threw her over his shoulder. He turned and headed to the main street. Marina cried, pummeling his bare back, and flailing with her legs. She was wearing pants today, and the material stretched over her butt, as he smacked her on her behind. She howled, and renewed her efforts, snarling like a she -cat. Solomon spanked her again, making her stop her squirming. She would fall, if she didn't stop.

Jackson heard the commotion, as people passed the Lair's front window, running towards the docks, pointing at something behind them. He crossed the floor, and opened the door. Standing in front of the building, he looked to see what everybody was fussing about. Coming down the street, was a big, black sailor. He had a bandanna around his head, and he was wearing no shirt. His pants were cut-off to right below his knees, and on his feet were scuffed up boots. Flung over his shoulder, was a female. A screaming, wailing, howling, female.

Jackson ran towards the figure. He would've recognized Marina's cry, anywhere. *"Yo, man! Leave my sister alone! Put her down, right now!"*

Solomon's eyes met his, but he kept moving. He grunted, pushing Jackson aside. "Out of my way."

Jackson reached out to grab Marina, when suddenly he was held back by a pair of hands. "What the ---" he exclaimed, looking up into Pedro Barbosa's eyes.

"Jackson..."

Jackson turned his head, momentarily distracted by Marina's wail. He lunged after Solomon, growling at the lawman. "This is *kidnapping!*"

"She will be brought back," the Pedro answered calmly, leading him to his office.

"Jackson..."

Jackson looked back at his sister. Her eyes were flooded with cascading tears, and her arms reached out towards him, beseechingly. She kept getting smaller, as he looked. He roared, lunging again, trying to free himself from Pedro Barbosa's hold. To no avail. He was marched steadily, to the small adobe building. And then he couldn't see Marina anymore.

La Gitana rocked, proud and regal, eager to depart. Men scurried all over her, putting the finishing touches for her journey. Only the most basic crew would be going on this trip. Everybody else would stay on Encantada, preparing for their return. Gaitano watched from the window in his warehouse, as Solomon strode into view. Over his shoulder, was Marina from Cayo Largo. She didn't look too happy, from where he was. He couldn't see her face, but her movements spoke volumes. He turned away. There will be time to deal with that, later.

Giancarlo stood up from the table he was sitting at, shuffling the papers together, before handing them to Gaitano. "We are almost ready, Captain."

"What about Indio and Salomé?"

"They will be boarding in a few minutes."

"All right, then." He handed the ship's Sailing Master the ledger. "Please see that Marina gets this."

Giancarlo raised his eyebrows. "Do you think she will want to do your books, after all this?"

"No." He shook his head. "But she will." He winked at the Italian.

His friend looked at him, thoughtfully. "This one is different, Captain," he finally said. "What is it?"

"I don't know," Gaitano admitted. "This one doesn't know who I am, and yet, she likes me."

"You haven't given her much choice," his Sailing Master pointed out.

The pirate shrugged. "Maybe." His eyes sparkled.

"What about her sister?"

He shrugged again. "If she comes, it'll be of her own accord."

"Taking Marina by force does not give Salomé much choice, now, does it?"

"No matter how you put it, I need Marina, so I can make my presentation before the council, complete."

"What about her brother? Jackson?"

"Jackson trusts me. He will get over it."

Giancarlo shook his head, clapping a hand on his shoulder. "Good luck, man."

"Thank you." They walked out of the office. "Get ready to sail." Encantada seemed to cheer, as the ship left its moorings. A Merchant Carrier was designed for speed, needing only the minimum crew necessary. La Gitana's barely numbered fifteen. It would be a quick voyage, their destiny clear. Carey. And Don Carlos Gaitano.

Carlos stood on the deck thoughtfully, smiling absently at the people waving from the docks. They were quickly getting smaller. Behind the mountain, a tired sun sank, no energy left to shine. The sky was getting rapidly darker, and thunder rumbled straight above. He breathed a sigh of relief, smelling the rain in the air. Whitecaps broke out on the leaden ocean. Drops of salt blew in the air, coating everything it came in contact with. His men sang and shouted from the ropes, the crow's nest, decks, everywhere! The joy of being reunited with their beloved ocean evident in their strong, laughing voices. Gaitano looked around him, satisfied everything was in order. Now, to more important matters. Turning around, he headed down below, to administer some damage control.

"Caribe!" Jackson burst into his friend's hut. His words were met with silence. There was no one there. He dashed out, and ran to the middle of the path. Both Marina's and Salomé's huts were dark. He stood there, bewildered, wondering what to do next. Thunder rolled down from the mountains, and the natives were walking around, laughing and chattering, hurrying home before the rain fell.

"Jackson!" He turned around to see Leila calling him from her front porch. She beckoned at him, the tiki torch in front of her house, lighting up the huge smile on her face. He sprinted over to her. *"Jackson!"* she exclaimed happily. "Come in, come in, bebé. I have something for you." Leila hugged him, kissed him on the cheek, stroked his hair, looked into his eyes. "First we talk," she said, pulling him by the hand. Making herself comfortable in her favorite chair, she began rocking back and forth, smiling happily at him. Jackson couldn't help but smile back, as he sat down on the floor in front of her. "How is it going, bebé?" she asked. "How has it been working out for you here?"

"Fine, until today."

She nodded, waving her hand in the air. "We will talk about today in a moment. Tell me how you like Encantada."

Jackson grinned, relaxing. "I like Encantada a lot, actually. I mean, it doesn't have any of the things we are accustomed to. It has been a nice break from the real world, as we know it."

"Yes. One always needs something different. It helps put our own lives into perspective."

"Right. So, this has been a fantastic experience, but I'm not sure if I want to stay."

Leila raised her eyebrows at him. "If you stay?"

"The girls, I think, are in love," he said, rolling his eyes. Then, he laughed mischievously. "At least, in lust!"

Leila laughed with him. "What is that expression you young people like to use so much?" She shrugged. "Whatever..."

Jackson smiled at the twinkle in her eye. "Whatever. Right..."

"They are good men, Jackson."

"They are."

"What is bothering you so much?"

"Our parents."

"They must be worried."

"No. By now, they are quietly going crazy, terrified out of their minds."

Leila rocked quietly for a moment, allowing Jackson time, for his own words to sink in. "What are you going to do about it, Jackson?" she challenged softly.

Jackson looked at her. Held out in front of his face were some papers. He took them from her, smoothing them on his thigh. He looked at the first one. It was the portrait of the girls, as drawn by a dream-inspired Caribe. The girls looked natural, and happy. It was a perfect match to the real live ones. The next paper, held the portrait of himself. You could practically see the gold shine in his earrings. His cornrows were perfectly detailed, as were the shadows in his eyes. Jackson shook his head at the mastery his friend possessed. It was a God-given talent, as yet, unknown. He looked at the third paper, and frowned. In it were numbers. He stared. In chronological order, there was a list of dates, from the 1400's onward. He turned the paper around, and found the last date. He didn't notice the year as much, as the month and day. It was March 25. Today, by his calculations. The date before that was March 21. Four days earlier. Jackson felt his stomach freeze, and excitement start to crawl on his skin. "Why, Leila, how nice of you to ask." He stood up slowly, and kissed her on both cheeks. "I am going to take care of business." He kissed her hand, winking at her, over it. "I got a storm to catch." And then, papers in hand, he was gone.

Flashes of lightning illuminated the path that led up the cliff, to the cave. Jackson ran the last few steps, shielding his papers from the fat drops of warm rain that were beginning to fall. He hesitated at the entrance for a moment, waiting for the next flash of lightning, so he could locate the things inside the cave. Remembering where the candles and matches lay, he went straight for them. His hands fumbled, as he clumsily lit a candle. The cave seemed to come to life, flickering softly. Everything looked exactly the same as he had left it. Nobody had been there in the last four days.

Crossing eagerly to the far wall, he surveyed the pile of blankets. He nodded, satisfied. Exactly as he had left them. Dropping on them, he rolled on his back, the papers clutched in one hand. He just lay there for a moment, legs in the air, knees bent. Grabbing his legs, he did a few crunches, and a couple of side twists. Groaning, he stretched out, letting his legs fall to the ground. Flinging an arm over his eyes, he groaned again. Then he prayed.

I came and stayed here. Looked for them until I found them. Not with some jocks. But in the middle of pirates. They are safe. They are reasonably happy. And now these guys just took them, to only You know where... but as safe as they'll be, it's not just about the girls anymore, is it? Something is going down, and these people need help. And it looks like I'm the only one that can get it for them, doesn't it? 'Cause that's why I got this passport to get out of here, isn't it? Well, if that's the case, Papá, let me do it. Let me go home and bring back reinforcements, the only way I know how. Let me reunite my family, and help the people of Encantada. Please... PLEASE, GOD! I beg that you allow me to do this, give me strength of body and mind, heart and soul, please, Papá, guide me, that I may do this in the name of Your Son, Jesus Christ, who with you, rules, now and forever. AMEN...

Marina looked up startled, at the knock on the door. It had been the third one, in a matter of minutes. First, Solomon had come back right after he brought her here, dropping off a bag, with what she assumed were her bare necessities. The second person to visit had been the Sailing Master. She recognized Giancarlo, as the owner of the Siren's Lair. It made her realize that most of the other men she had been seeing regularly, frequently, must all be Gaitano's sailors. Giancarlo had dropped off the ledger she usually worked on, leaving it on the table. His expression had been understanding when he looked at her, and he had even tried to cheer her up, but had ended up leaving, instead, murmuring words of comfort. Since then, the ship had been sailing. She was doing fine, thanks to some pills Solomon had made her take before he left her alone. And now, there was someone else.

The door opened, and Indio peered in. He stopped in his tracks at the sight of her. She was sitting in the middle of the bed, arms hugging her knees, face buried out of sight. She looked up at him, as he came inside. In a moment, he was next to her. Her face was streaked by tears, and there were dark shadows under her eyes, from all her crying. As their eyes met, he saw tears pool up again. She was obviously, far from done. His heart wrenched, and he held her face between his huge hands, gently. Her lower lip trembled. "Marina," he rumbled, deep in his chest. "Marina, look at me." Tears spilled as she looked into his eyes. "I will be here," he assured her, caressing her face gently, wiping her tears away. "I will be here, and I promise, nothing will happen to you." He swore to himself as she nodded, visibly shaking, making more tears fall.

Marina watched through her tears, as dismay crossed the brave's features. She put her shaking hands over his wrists, keeping her face cradled in his hands. She looked into his eyes. "Indio," she whispered raggedly. "I am so scared..." she broke off, shaking her head and pushing his hands away, Her hair whipped about her face as she looked around her, frantically. She looked back up at him. *I am so scared..."*

Indio nodded, his heart tight in his chest, for her. He held her face in his hands again, making her look at him. "Marina," he rumbled again. "Do you trust me, mami?" He smiled at her nod. "I will be here. To defend and protect you." He kissed her forehead, and peered into her eyes. "From anything and anyone that threatens you." He kissed her face gently. "Do not be afraid, Marina..." And he was gone. Outside the cabin door, he turned to those, waiting for him. He held the door open for Salomé. "She needs you." Salomé nodded and went inside. He closed the door behind her, and faced his brother. Carlos' eyes met his. "I would stay out of her way, right now." He chuckled. "You are going to have to fix this one. Fast." Carlos' eyes followed him, as he went off to do his duties. He turned back to his closed cabin door, wondering what was going on inside.

Marina shuddered, her eyes wild in her face, as she looked at her sister. "Please, Salo, please help me," she rasped. Lunging for her best friend, she threw her arms around her and pulled her closer, pressing her mouth to her ear. "I'm freaking out, mami, I'm losing it! Please don't let him see me like this!"

Salomé embraced Marina, alternately crooning and hissing at her. "Hush! Chill, baby, just chill!" They switched positions on the bed. Salomé pressed her back to the headboard and rocked Marina, knowing that nobody would see her face if they came in, suddenly. "I got you, boo," she whispered in her ear. Salomé buried her face in her neck for an instant, squeezing her eyes shut tightly, trying to hold back her own tears, as a range of emotions tore through her. She looked up, straight into the eyes of the man who so terrified and fascinated Marina. "You've got to go."

Carlos shook his head, his eyes glued to the girl in her arms. "What---?"

"You heard me, you've got to go." Salomé glanced pointedly at the door. "No screaming, no crying, no show," she added under her breath.

Carlos stepped closer. "What is wrong? What is the matter?" he asked, genuine concern in his voice. "Is she all right?" He took another step.

Salomé's hand shot out, halting him in his tracks. She glared at him, signaling for him to wait. Marina began sobbing in her arms, a wail forming in the back of her throat. "It's okay, baby," Salomé whispered, stroking her hair and rubbing her back. "I'll be right back. He won't hurt you, I promise," she added. *He won't leave*, she reasoned to herself, *at least he can stay put*. She glanced at the man in question once more, as she slowly but firmly extricated herself from Marina's grasp. "Here, boo, hold on to that," she murmured, handing her a pillow. "I will be right back." Once she got out of bed, she moved quickly to the door. She opened it and looked back at the man, jerking her head for him to follow her.

Carlos looked back at Marina, where she lay curled up in the middle of his bed, her face buried in the pillow between her arms, her body racked by sobs. His bed, for God's sake! He took a step towards her, but Salomé's voice stopped him in his tracks. *"Carlos!"* she hissed.

Carlos' hands balled into fists at his sides, until he felt his fingernails digging into his palms. His heart was pounding. A fear like he had never known before, began creeping into his soul. He had never felt anything like this. *I cannot lose her!* Taking a deep breath, he followed Salomé outside, softly pulling the door closed behind him. He opened his mouth to speak, but Salomé put both her hands on his shoulders, and looked deep into his eyes. She slowly shook her head, pushing him back against the wall. Leaning against the opposite one, she crossed her arms and just stared at him. From inside, they heard Marina cry. Her wails rose and fell, her sobs heart wrenching. Carlos looked at the door, and back at Salomé. Tears were spilling from her own eyes, as she kept looking at him, silently accusing. He struggled to find the correct words. He held out his hand to her. "I did not mean to cause this."

Salomé nodded, making the tears fall. She just stared at his hand, before taking it in both of hers. She raised it, rubbing her face against it. "I know," she answered sadly. "But you did." Kissing his hand, she let it fall back again. Shadows danced around them, from the ship's rocking motion. Elsewhere, men shouted to each other, voices ringing with laughter.

Carlos raked his fingers through his hair, swearing at himself. He dragged his hands down his face, his breath ragged. He looked at Salomé, startling her with his intensity. "How can I fix this?"

Salomé nodded, seeing the truth in his eyes. "Very carefully."

He nodded. Closing his eyes, he let his head fall back against the wall, with a thump. Quiet rage crossed his features. "I never meant to frighten her," he murmured.

Salomé's eyes blazed green fire at him. Her voice came out in a startled whisper. "Papi, you *abducted* her!" She rolled her eyes. "How did you *think* she was going to react?"

"I didn't think," he admitted. They were speaking in angry whispers.

Salomé tore into him. "That's the problem, right there. You didn't think! You just *took* her, like those heathens that hit the village last year!" And then, her stomach dropped. *Oh, my God, I went too far...* Her eyes watered.

Carlos' turquoise pools seemed to freeze before her eyes, turning into twin glaciers. His eyes roared at her, as his voice remained a whisper. "Do not say that," he replied with calm control, "it is one of the reasons she is here." At her vacant stare, he elaborated. "It has to do with the books she is working on."

Salomé shook her head. "So, let her know! Don't let her be frightened of you!"

"I did not bring her here to ravage her, or sell her into slavery---"

"*Let her know,*" Salomé repeated slowly.

"I care for her."

"She should know *that*, too."

"What do you do? In Cayo Largo?"

Salomé shook her head slowly, not remembering. "What do you mean?"

"What do you do back home, when Marina gets like this?"

Salomé rolled her eyes again, letting out an exasperated breath. "Marina has never *gotten* like this!" she hissed at him, reproachfully. "*Nobody has ever treated her like this!*"

Carlos' eyes smoldered as he looked at her. He could see what Indio saw in her. She was stunning. Chest heaving, eyes flashing as she stood before him, he had to admit, here was one of the most beautiful women he had ever known in his life. Salomé was unlike anything he had ever seen before. *Good job, Indio!* "What would you have done," he repeated slowly, not as angry, anymore, "if Marina had ever gotten like this."

"Family meeting."

He frowned at her swift reply. She couldn't be lying. "Family meeting?"

"Yeah, family meeting. By the way, where is Jackson?"

Carlos shrugged, not fooled by the momentary distraction. "Jackson got detained."

Salomé licked her lips, and nodded, her hair shaking about her head. "Uh-huh. *Detained.* That's what *you* call it." Her eyes shot more green fire at him. She looked beautiful to him, and his heart reached out with joy for his brother's. Said brother materialized suddenly, leaning on the wall next to Salomé, and listened quietly to their exchange. She took comfort from his presence next to her. "Let me guess. Detained, involuntarily, however ---"

"How do you know he didn't go with Pedro Barbosa willingly---"

"*Because!* Boy was screaming the town down, when Indio and I walked by!" She threw her hands up in the air, as Carlos shrugged. Indio's lips twitched and his eyes crinkled at the corners. "Pedro Barbosa wouldn't let him go to Marina," she accused. *"He told us!"*

Carlos looked at Indio, who confirmed with a nod. Another shrug. "Jackson was going to stop Solomon from bringing her here."

"*Solomon* was *taking* her!" Salomé stamped her foot quietly. "*Jackson* is her *brother!*"

Carlos' icebergs roared at her again. "I'm her ---" he caught himself, frowning.

Salomé widened her eyes at him. She stepped up to him, as close as she could, hands on her hips, moving her head from side to side. Indio hid a grin behind his hand, his eyes sliding away from his brother's frowning ones. *"What?"* Her voice was soft, but Carlos sensed it menacing. *"You,"* she whispered slowly, "are her *what?*" She raised her hands to his face, and slapped her hand on the leather band around her opposite wrist. "You are her *nada!* As far as Marina is concerned, you are some *guy,* whom she kept running into, who is really awesome, and she likes *a lot.* So, she *likes* this guy, who ends up hooking her up with a really cool job, doing the books for Gaitano, and it seems, like *he* likes *her,* also, except," she took a deep breath. "What she really *doesn't* know is that this incredible *guy,* she likes *so much,* is actually, Gaitano *himself,* whom she would rather have *nothing* to do with, because she is *afraid* of him!" She stepped back, panting. "And now, the poor girl is on this *pirate ship,* and she is scared to pieces," she said softly, "and *you,*" she pointed a finger at his chest, "are directly responsible." Salomé held his eyes, as they clashed with hers. *"Now, fix it!"*

Carlos nodded. "What is this family meeting about?"

Salomé swept the hair out of her face with a sigh, and rubbed the back of her neck. She was emotionally exhausted, and it wasn't over, yet. "When a family member is in distress, they need support from the rest of the family." She sighed, surrendering. "You call a meeting, you talk it over, everybody together. You reassure the person, show them love, and the problem gets absorbed by everybody, so it's not so big, or so bad, anymore. Help, understanding, affection, unconditional love..."

"Your family is not here," he pointed out.

She rolled her eyes at him. "Obviously. But neither is yours," she shot back at him. "Who do you have here? Indio..."

Indio finally spoke up. "Solomon and Giancarlo."

Carlos nodded. "Get them"

Indio nodded and he was gone. Carlos Gaitano and Salomé waited in silence, their eyes never leaving each other, as the cries subsided in the cabin behind the closed door between them. Suddenly, the narrow hallway filled with Indio and the rest of the men. Salomé nodded at them, and looked pointedly back at Carlos, jerking her head towards the door. "Let's do it."

Marina looked up through beaded eyelashes, as the door opened, after one knock. They poured in, single file, one after the other. Carlos, Salomé, Indio, the owner of the Lair, and the African they called Solomon. She sat up slowly, as they spread around the room, shutting the door behind them. They all stood looking at her, no one saying a word. Carlos moved to the center of the room, the rest staying behind him. She watched wordlessly as his hand raised for a moment, before he let it fall helplessly at his side. He cleared his throat.

"Marina Aguilar," he began, his eyes searching hers, hungrily. He looked behind him, his eyes asking for help, getting none. He looked back at her, not being able to help his eyes from sliding down her softly heaving chest. "We, the crew of La Gitana, are calling a family meeting," he continued softly. Marina widened her eyes at him, and he hesitated, as she met Salomé's eyes, behind him, before turning back to him. Her mouth twisted, and her hazel eyes burned with fury. He braced himself. "Your sister has indicated that when a person is in pain, or grief," he took a deep breath, "as you," and all of a sudden he couldn't look into the pain in her eyes. He half-turned towards his men. "A family meeting is called, to help ease the person. So, we have come, to help you. We can talk about it, there is nothing to hide."

Marina arched an eyebrow at him, and pointed at the group behind him, with her chin. "So, who is your family, Carlos?" She got out of bed, slowly.

Carlos gladly turned to stand sideways, the better to introduce them. "You know Indio." He touched the brave, smiling into his eyes. "I was raised with him, just as you have been, with Jackson. The difference is, Indio's parents are not in the picture, just mine. Still alive," he added, answering the question in her eyes. "Indio is to me," he continued, "as Jackson is to you, my brother, and my best friend. The one who knows me best. So far," he added with a wink that nobody else saw. Marina relaxed. She wiped at her face, not wanting him to see the effect he had on her. He continued. "Giancarlo is the owner of The Siren's Lair, as you well know. We are business partners, and we sail together, so you can see, there has to be trust there. Also, we met when we were teenagers, and have been extremely good friends, ever since." He shook hands with Giancarlo, and finally turned to Solomon. "Solomon, I have not known as long. Long enough, however. I owe him my life. That is good enough for me." He met her eyes.

Marina nodded, tears still in her eyes, looking at each one in turn. "What are your jobs? What do you do?"

Indio stepped up. "I am the Quartermaster," he rumbled.

Marina looked at him, mesmerized, as the candlelight licked at the planes of his face, the hollows of his eyes. In her mind, she sighed. *You go, Salo...*

"I am First Mate. That means," he explained, carefully not looking at Carlos, "if the Captain gets killed or cannot perform his duties anymore, I take over. I am also the Quartermaster," he continued. "I keep order at sea, and on land. On the ship, I am Pedro Barbosa." He smiled, as Marina's mouth twitched, and she rolled her eyes. "In town, I am responsible for the crew. A lot of decisions fall on my shoulders, and for my efforts, I get a bigger share than most." Marina smiled to herself, as behind him, Salomé clasped her hands together and brought them to her cheek, batting her eyelashes. She had to frown slightly at the silly woman, to make her stop.

Marina turned to Giancarlo. "I thought you just ran a stable," she said, her tone softening the rudeness. It was Carlos' turn to hide a grin.

Giancarlo couldn't hide his. "I plead guilty, Marina Aguilar of Cayo Largo," he said, graciously reaching over to kiss her hand. "My name is Giancarlo Ilarazza, and I do, in fact, own the brothel known as The Siren's Lair. That is in Encantada," he said with a shrug, his eyes twinkling outrageously in his perfect face. "At sea, I am the Sailing Master." He watched her move her lips, repeating his title, silently. "I am in charge of the navigation and the sailing of the ship. I direct the course."

"So, you know where we are going," Marina interrupted.

Giancarlo inclined his head. "Absolutely."

She nodded. "Good. Maybe we can talk, later." Ignoring Carlos' look, she turned to Solomon. "*You*," she accused softly, "put your hands on me." She stared at him, cocking her head to one side. "Did you know," she asked, "I could kick your ass all over this ship, before you ever catch me again?" She glanced at Salomé, as the other woman gasped, and clamped her hands over her mouth, her laughing eyes wide, over her fingers. She looked back at the handsome young African. "Solomon..."

Solomon outright laughed in Marina's face. Not at her, but with her. "I love a challenge," he smiled. "I may just give you a chance to do as you promise."

Marina's eyes burned into his. "You are on!"

Sobering, he stood up straight, pride in his face. "I am the Boatswain. I am responsible for the maintenance and the supplies of La Gitana. I inspect the sails, and I am in charge of all deck activities. I report to my Captain."

Marina nodded, and began to pace in front of Carlos, looking him up and down. Everybody else stepped back, as she walked around him, measuring him. He closed his eyes, with a sigh. She wasn't making it easy for him. "I have one more family member."

Marina stopped in front of him. "Where?"

He reached behind him, pulling at the other girl, to stand beside him. "Salomé."

Marina just stared. "No. Salomé is *my* family."

"Exactly. But now, she is Indio's love interest, and *he* is *my* family."

Salomé waved her hands in the air, between them. "Okay, okay, that is enough! You can keep this up all night, at the rate you two are going." She pushed Carlos. "Tell her the real reason you are here."

Carlos glowered at her. "I am."

Salomé shook her head at him. "No, you are not. Now, repeat after me. I am sorry, Marina," she urged.

If looks could kill, Salomé would have dropped dead. "I am sorry, Marina," he said, looking right at her, ignoring the woman next to him. "It was never my intention to terrorize you. You were brought here, because your knowledge about our books is required, in order for us to make a presentation to a council that sponsors us." He spread his hands helplessly. "Let's just say, that I believe, you can help us solve this. We do, truly, need your help."

"And who are *you?*" Marina asked suddenly.

Carlos stood straight, lifting his head, without breaking eye contact with her. "I am the Captain," he answered. "My men follow my orders. I have made the right decisions, so far," he explained, "and they have gained wealth, while no one has been hurt. They respect me. I cannot ask for more."

"So, what are you called, Captain Carlos?" Marina asked, pacing before him once more. "I thought Gaitano was the Captain."

Carlos nodded, not daring to look away. "I am."

"Who *are* you?" she repeated raggedly.

"Marina, I admit," he glanced behind him, "I have led you to believe otherwise..."

"Who?" she insisted, fire in her eyes now.

"Carlos Gaitano."

Marina froze. She felt for a moment, as if everything were in slow motion. Shaking herself, she got herself together enough to arch an eyebrow at him. "Oh, I get it. You are a liar."

Carlos' anger blazed, for an instant, matching hers. "You would not have had anything to do with me, otherwise."

She nodded. "True."

"I wanted a chance to get to know you. When the numbers and the books came up, I had one."

"Right. But there's one thing you failed to mention."

He sighed. "What?"

"That *you* are the *boss*."

He nodded. "I am."

"So, what does that make me?" Marina said softly, fresh tears stinging the back of her eyes. "The boss' *bitch*?"

The moment froze in time, as everybody reacted at one time. Giancarlo and Solomon grinned at each other. Indio covered his eyes with his hands, shaking his head. Salomé gasped, rising on tiptoes, olive eyes wide over her left hand covering her mouth, her right hand snapping in the air behind and above Carlos Gaitano's head. Said pirate glared at Marina, not amused. "You didn't know I was the boss," he growled, "so that just makes you, *my* bitch."

Marina gasped, tears spilling out of her eyes. She lowered them, ashamed. Her head came up, then, her intention clear in her eyes.

Salomé gasped. *"No!"*

Carlos caught her hand easily, long before she got a chance to raise it. Swinging her around, he trapped her in his arms, spinning her to face his men. "Marina," he said slowly, for her ears only, "let us respect the crew. We can talk about this later. For now, they need not be part of our personal affairs," he said, rolling his eyes at his men, over her head, before lowering his head to kiss her cheek.

Marina struggled in his arms. "You called the family meeting!"

Salomé nudged Carlos, whispering in his ear. "I promise you, Marina," she urged, "not to ravage you, or make you a slave..."

He nodded, impatiently. Resting his chin on top of her head, he repeated, to her, as well as to his friends, "I promise you, Marina, not to ravage you, or make you a slave."

Marina stopped squirming. "Oh, really?" she asked softly. He let go of her, as she savagely pushed herself away from his arms. "Well, I, apologize to you, *Capitán Carlos Gaitano*, in front of your crew, and my friend, if I just disrespected you. I know better," she confessed, glancing at him. "I was raised to respect men, because they may just hit back. I know this, and I am sorry."

Carlos nodded, puzzled. "I accept your apology."

"You know what, though?" Marina asked softly. "I will do your books because that is my job, but personally, you need to leave me alone."

"I will sleep in the hammock," he offered.

Marina smiled. "Yes," her eyes flashed at him. "You will."

"What more can I do, Marina, *divina*..."

She stopped him, before he went any further. *"Leave me alone!"*

"I cannot!"

"Well, papi," she smiled, lifting her left hand in front of his eyes, and rippling her fingers. "I don't see any ring," she said huskily, stroking his face, before snapping her fingers in the air. Turning her back on him, she crawled back into bed.

Once again, everybody froze, for a moment. Then, all hell broke loose. Giancarlo and Solomon, fell against each other, doubled over, hiding their laughs behind their hands, in genuine macho camaraderie. Indio threw his head back, looking up at the ceiling, his hands over his face, shoulders shaking with silent laughter. Salomé began dancing around, smile splitting her face, hips swinging, hand snapping in the air, as she jumped in silent laughter of her own.

Carlos Gaitano raged. "What does that mean?"

Salomé was the only one who dared to laugh out loud. She went to him, putting an arm around his shoulders. She was still shaking from laughter, and he looked at her suspiciously. "Well, baby," she drawled in his ear, "it means, that as far as Marina is concerned," she smiled, enjoying herself immensely, "you are just a *guy* she met, that she happens to *really* like. *Nothing more*," her voice dropped to a huskier note. Putting her other arm around him, she rubbed the leather band around her arm, in front of his face. She watched him, following her hand, with his eyes. "So, you don't have any claim on her," she gave the leather one last caress, before pushing him away from her. Holding her wrist in the air, she pointed at the armband, lips smacking, nodding her head. "*This* is what really counts, papi. How bad do you want to be with her?" Indio grabbed her by the waist, and pulled her back, against him, his smiling mouth next to her ear, scolding her softly.

Carlos frowned, and looked back at Marina. As they all watched, she curled into herself, pillow tucked between her legs, and between her arms, hair spread out behind her. In front of their eyes, she fell asleep.

They all filed out. Giancarlo and Solomon parted ways, laughing at their Captain, off to do their duties, under the leaden night sky. Carlos mumbled, as he passed by. Indio guided Salomé to his own cabin. It was smaller than Gaitano's, but just as nice. He playfully pressed her back against the door, pinning her wrists above her head. He nuzzled her neck, for a moment, breathing in her fragrance, making her squirm. Slowly, he brushed his lips against hers, running his tongue slowly over them. He smiled against her mouth. "*I* never said anything about not ravishing *you*," he teased with a growl.

Salomé laughed, even as she melted. She met his hips with hers, rubbing against him. "How about making me a slave?" she asked in a husky voice.

Indio groaned. "*My* slave," he conceded.

"Right now?" she pressed her mouth against his, in invitation.

Indio slipped her arms around his neck, his hands sliding to her butt, pressing her against him. "I have to go to work, right now," he breathed. He squeezed her, kissing her roughly. "I will be back." He pressed his forehead against hers, holding her face between his big hands, kissing her again.

Salomé pulled her head back, her chest rising rapidly. "I will wait for you," she assured him, looking into his eyes. She lunged at him, pressing her lips against his again, hungrily. She staggered when he released her, his mouth searing hers, before he left. The door closed behind him.

Hours later, the men went to their cabins, to sleep.

Carlos crawled on the bed towards Marina, nuzzling her neck affectionately, when he reached her. She turned over, murmured his name, put a hand behind his head, bringing it down towards hers, and pressed her lips against his, before pushing him away from her. All of this, in her sleep. Carlos hung his head and sighed. He kissed her cheek softly, crawling backwards until he was off the bed. Sighing again, he stripped off his shirt, and boots, letting them fall on the floor by his table. Dropping heavily on the hammock, he pushed off with one foot against the desk, rocking gently. He studied her. Before he knew it, he was asleep, himself.

Indio let himself into the room quietly. His eyes adjusting, he could see a shape in his bed, under the covers. Silently reaching for a bucket of water in the corner, he rinsed quietly, trying not to splash. When he was finally clean, he approached his bed, and drew the covers back slowly. Lighting a candle next to the bed, he stared. The sight brought a slow smile to his lips, and fire to his loins. Salomé stretched luxuriously, like a cat, her hooded green eyes, shining at him. Her lips parted and she licked them, holding her arms out to him. Indio thanked his spirits and fell on her, hungry, desperately kissing her. Ravishing her. She laughed softly in his ear, holding his head, accommodating him between her legs, her body yielding to his. Indio groaned, as his skin felt hers. Salomé was wearing nothing, but his leather arm band.

Jackson groaned, turning his head slowly. He opened his eyes, blinking at the light outside the cave entrance. The storm last night had been majestic in its splendor. He had fallen asleep, right in the middle of it. He didn't know if the time warp had occurred yet, but something had definitely woken him up. Stretching, he got to his feet painfully, shuffling to the mouth of the cave. He looked out-side. It looked exactly like it did, when he was practically living here. The ocean was gray, thunder still rumbled, the beach was deserted. Something had woken him up, though, and he couldn't quite place it. He squinted his eyes at the white ball of fire, struggling its way up, out of the horizon. Scrubbing his face with his hands, he wiped the last vestiges of sleep away, and smoothed back his cornrows. Jackson listened carefully. There was something different. Then he saw it. Flying towards him, passing overhead, was an airplane. He froze, his eyes registering, but not believing what they were seeing. Then he whooped with laughter, jumping high in the air, punching the sky with his fist. He dropped to his knees, slapping the earth with his hands, tears of joy streaming out of his tiger eyes. Looking up at the sky, he raised his arms to Heaven, in praise. The words tore from his throat in a shout. *"Gracias, Papá!"*

Jumping to his feet, Jackson raced inside, skidding to a halt, in front of the pile of blankets. Placed neatly on top of the pile he hadn't slept on, was Salomé's bag. He looked at the pile next to it. At the head, was Marina's bag, sitting next to his. He laughed happily, shaking his head, his shouts echoing around the cave, bouncing off the walls. He reached into his sister's bag, and pulled out a bottle of water he had refilled on the last day he had spent here. Drinking thirstily, he shook his head. "Leila, I thank you," he said into the emptiness around him. Looking around him, he spotted the papers on an overturned crate, where the candles were. He picked them up, suddenly afraid. One look made him let out air from his lungs in a gust. He relaxed, relief flooding him. There were the portraits of the girls, and the paper with the dates. "Thank you, Lord," he murmured, tucking them carefully into his backpack. Reaching into the front pocket, he reached for his cell phone. He held it in his hand tightly, for a moment, eyes closed, lips moving in more prayer. It hadn't failed him so far. Taking the cell phone out of his backpack, he walked outside, punching in a number. A sleepy voice answered on the other end.

"Quentin." Jackson smiled, at his friend's reaction.

"Dude!" Quentin screamed into the phone. Jackson could see him in his mind, bolting upright, springing out of bed, stumbling, fumbling. *"Where have you been?"* He sounded terrified.

"Quentin," soothed Jackson in a low rumble. "Chill, baby. Come get me."

Quentin was already pulling on his jeans. "Dude, I'm there."

"Marina..." The voice sounded so real. She was dreaming of being caught in the rain, with Caribe, during one of their runs. In her dream, she lifted her face to the sky, feeling the raindrops. "Marina..." This was no dream, however. She struggled out of her sleep, and rubbed her eyes before opening them. Hovering over her, grin splitting his face, as drops of water clung to his fingertips above her, was her beautiful dreadlocked friend.

Marina gasped and sat up quickly, her arms immediately reaching for the boy, hands waving frantically to embrace him. "Caribe," she cried softly. "I am so glad you are here," she whispered, holding him tight.

Caribe laughed softly, returning the hug, and kissing her face, as she kissed his. They drew back to look at each other. "I am here on a mission," he explained in a whisper. "I am to keep record of this voyage, with my drawings."

She high-fived him, eyes sparkling with pride, for him. "Awesome!"

Caribe nodded, and tore himself gently out of her arms. "Come." She nodded eagerly, jumping out of bed. "Where?"

"Sunrise."

"Wait for me outside."

They embraced again, and Caribe turned to leave, so she could get ready. He froze. In front of him, was the hammock, with the Captain, still stretched out in it. The pirate's ankles were crossed, and a hand lay on his bare stomach, while the other cushioned his head, his elbow bent, above him. His eyes gleamed at him behind slits. Caribe didn't know what to do. He had to assume the man was awake. Believing this was so, he looked straight into the man's eyes, and smiled, shrugging. He wasn't surprised when Carlos moved nothing but a finger at him. He seemed to glance at Marina for a moment, making sure she wasn't watching. Then, the pirate smiled and winked at him. Caribe let out a sigh of relief, his dreadlocks dancing around his face. He quietly slid his hand against the pirate's on his way out. Shutting the door behind him, he leaned against it, waiting for Marina to finish getting ready.

Carlos followed Marina with her eyes, as she washed her mouth, her face, and stripped. Finding a small towel, she wiped her body down. He held his breath, swallowing a groan, so she wouldn't hear him. She slipped on underwear, and a pair of pants, tying them around her waist with a piece of rope. She topped that off with a piece of flowered fabric tied at her breasts. He watched her frown, and look around her. Her eyes fell on his shirt. She picked it up, bringing it to her face to breath his fragrance. His heart softened, as he saw her close her eyes and smile. She slipped the shirt on, but it was too big. Not caring, she rolled up the sleeves, and buttoned up, only where her midriff showed. He saw her frown slightly, as she looked down at herself, smoothing her hands over the fabric. Then she shrugged, suddenly turning towards him. Carlos closed his eyes, before she caught him. He felt her move towards him, and stop in front of him. Her hand softly stroked back his hair, and she bent down to press her lips to his. Keeping his eyes closed, he returned the pressure as if in sleep, and sighed deeply. She laughed softly, her fingers slipping in his hair to tousle it. Showing utmost restraint, he didn't breathe. Then the door clicked, as she let it fall shut behind her. Carlos opened his eyes slowly and smiled, his hands going down to rub the front of his pants.

Caribe looked at her, and smiled. "Hi, mami," he murmured, hugging her again. He pointed at the cabin next door, raising his eyebrows. "I'm not going in there. Indio is not sleeping in the hammock, I am sure. He will kill me, if I go in there. You go."

Marina grinned at him, and knocked on the door softly. She heard Indio's voice rumble. Opening the door slowly, she peeked her head in. The couple was already up and dressed, finishing getting ready, to leave the cabin. Indio was studying some maps by candlelight, at his tiny desk, and Salomé was snapping a blanket in the air, letting it float down gently, as she made their bed. She looked over her shoulder, and smiled softly. Marina raised her eyebrows, glancing at Indio, teasingly. Salomé looked radiant. Walking towards the door, she caught sight of the young man behind her sister. "Caribe!"

Caribe shook his head quickly, waving his hands in the air, wildly, in a negative gesture. He looked genuinely worried for a moment, and then left them, in disgust, after catching the mischief in Salomé's eyes. "I will be on deck."

Salomé laughed. "What is wrong with that boy?" Marina rolled her eyes.

Indio joined them. He slipped a possessive hand around Salomé's hip, his eyes, amused. "Why is it," he drawled, "that every time you and I are spending time together, Caribe shows up, and you drop everything ---"

Salomé reached up, putting her fingers over his mouth. She pretended to scold him. "Hush, child! If I didn't know better, I would think you were jealous of that boy!" She smiled, and reaching up on tiptoes, brushed her lips against his.

Indio growled at her, even as his hand remained solid on her hip, not letting her go. "I *am* jealous."

Salomé pried his hand away, and turned it palm up, burying her mouth in it, making him smile. She let go of his hand and backed away, slowly. "No. You are just *silly*."

Indio grunted. He reached with one hand behind Marina's head, drawing her towards him for a kiss. She lifted her face to him, with a smile, returning his affection. Smiling back, he stroked her hair, and let her go. He turned back to Salomé. "No."

"Yes," she laughed, waving at him.

"No," he repeated, trying not to laugh, himself. He called after them, as they began climbing the steps to get on deck. "I am the *boyfriend*!" He chuckled, as he heard their peals of laughter.

Up on deck, Caribe was waiting for them, by the main mast. The girls joined him. The three of them stood, shoulder to shoulder, the dreadlocked man between the two long-haired women. They watched in silence, as the white sun did a push-up on the edge of the world. It stayed in the air. They smiled. Thunder rumbled overhead, the sky dark. With the light of day, they could see whitecaps forming on the ocean. The did full circles where they stood, looking all around them There wasn't any land in sight. They looked back at the sun. It seemed to struggle, trying to do another push -up. Marina laughed. "Cool sunrise, Caribe!" She waved her hand at the horizon. "Monochrome!"

"It's different," agreed Salomé. They looked around them, again. This time, they were more aware of their immediate surroundings. Already, half the crew was at work. There were men at the lines, at the ropes, at the sails, even at a few cannons. They were mostly laughing and singing. The breeze blew steadily, giving movement to everything on deck. It was exhilarating. The girls turned to Caribe, excitement on their faces. "What now?" Salomé asked happily, green eyes flashing in her dark face.

Caribe just smiled at them for a moment. They feel safe with me, he realized, proudly. "Forms." He laughed, as they turned to each other, mouths open, eyes wide.

They chorused whispers. "Forms?"

He nodded. "Forms. You don't want to lose touch, do you?" he taunted, assuming the position.

They stared at him, and looked around them self-consciously. Marina didn't know whether to shake or nod her head. Salomé waved her hand at the sailors around them. "Won't we be in somebody's way?"

Caribe grinned, shaking his head. "Everybody is busy," he rolled his eyes.

Placing one foot forward, he bent his knees, bouncing slightly. His dreadlocks looked like springs around his head. His fists went up. He beckoned the girls with one hand. "Come on," he coaxed, as if they were the babies. "You can do it," he laughed, as he saw them weaken. He beckoned them again. "You want a piece of me?"

The girls howled with laughter, falling over each other, pointing at him. Caribe bounced higher, a grin splitting his face. Salomé looked at him, accusingly. "Jackson taught you that!"

He shrugged, dancing around them. "Of course." They stopped him. "Okay. Let's do it."

The sun had done another push-up, and it was warmer. The friends made a triangle on deck, and began the ancient forms of Tae-Kwon-Do. Before long, they were flowing with the ancient movements. It was a while, before they realized they had an audience. Most of the men stood around them, staring, laughing at them. It almost looked as if they were dancing, the way they moved together, their clothes billowing in the breeze. Finally, they heard the laughter. Ignoring it, they finished what they were doing, and stopped.

It seemed to them, like everybody was there. They had been absorbed, not realizing that the crew of La Gitana was facing them. And they were quite amused. Giancarlo chuckled behind his hand, while Solomon shook his bald head, his earrings glinting in the pale sunlight. Indio had eyes only for Salomé, while Carlos smiled at them as if they were children. Only Joshua, the boy that had come down from the crow's nest, had shown genuine interest in his shining eyes.

Gaitano stepped forward, his laughing face beautiful, to their eyes. The woman's, her friend's, and the artist's. "Ladies!" he called into the wind. "Caribe! My men are quite intrigued by your movements." He paused, waiting for the laughter to die down, behind him. "Is it steps to a sort of, violent dance?" The men roared.

Marina and Salomé dropped their stances, laughing as they high-fived and rolled their eyes. "Tae-Kwon-Do," Salomé explained, after the teasing had subsided, "is more than an oriental martial art." She looked at the men, as they began to listen. "It is a discipline. A way of life." She stood with her feet apart and knees bent, showing them. "What you see is *this*." She began the form all over again, Marina and Caribe quickly catching up. The three friends smiled, as the crew whistled and hooted, quite entertained. "What you *don't* see is *this*." She turned to Marina, and winked at her. "Assume the position."

The men stared, eyes glazed over, as the women fought. They twisted around each other, hands up, legs striking out, fists flashing. Nobody laughed then. They just watched, mesmerized, as the two women moved, punching and kicking, in a synchronized dance. Not violent, but strong, and forceful, connecting and evading. Finally breaking from their reverie, the men roared, screaming encouragement, cheering them on. The girls stopped suddenly, and faced each other. They bowed and turned back to the men. The sun had climbed even higher, and perspiration shone in their faces. The men clapped, happy smiles on their faces.

Gaitano looked around him, in wonder. He had never seen a happier crew. He turned towards the women once more. "You have proved your point, ladies ---" he stopped, at sudden laughter behind him.

Solomon stepped forward, standing beside them. He was grinning. "*That* is why, Captain."

Gaitano frowned. "What?"

"At the family meeting last night, Marina said she could kick my ass."

The pirate laughed, remembering. His eyes slid to Marina, quickly taking in the wind whipping her hair around her face, and his shirt billowing around her, as she came down from her workout. "She probably can, Solomon."

Giancarlo and Indio stepped up next to them, smiling in anticipation. Giancarlo rubbed his hands, a wicked look on his laughing face. "I smell the prospect of making some money."

Indio slapped Solomon on the back, and lowered his voice in conspiracy. "Mine is on the girl." Giancarlo burst into laughter. Gaitano glanced at Marina again.

Solomon grunted. Pulling up his pants, he ignored his laughing comrades and approached the woman. "Marina. I will give you a chance. Just one." He laughed.

"*Aguilar!*" Gaitano called her over. "Come here." She rolled her eyes at Solomon, as she walked by him, and went to the pirate. He turned her around, and gathered her hair, quickly braiding it, in spite of the wind. Indio offered a piece of leather, and it was done. Marina turned around, the question in her eyes. Gaitano shrugged, caressing her face. "I have done his hair," he explained, pointing at Indio. She nodded, smiling. Then she looked back at Solomon. "Give me the shirt," Gaitano said suddenly.

Marina laughed, happy to be rid of the extra fabric, bound to hinder her movements. "I hope your men don't freak," she teased.

He shook his head, taking the shirt from her. "They know better." He looked into her eyes. "Now, show me what you've got."

Marina bowed to him, and turned around, facing Solomon. She began dancing around him, just as Caribe had done with them, earlier. "Solomon..." she taunted in a sing-song voice, "come out and play..."

Solomon laughed, shaking his head at her. "You really think---"

Marina stopped him, blowing him a kiss. "I *know*." She danced closer to him, taunting him harder. "Solomon..." She bent at the waist and stretched out her arms, eyes on his, her fingers beckoning, her shoulders shaking at him. "Come out and play..."

Solomon stood up straight, as the men laughed, around him. He looked at the pirate. "Captain."

Gaitano shrugged. "You are alone on this one, son."

"I do not wish to hurt the lady, sir," he taunted, looking at Marina.

The Captain chuckled. "I am afraid the lady has designs on hurting you, sailor."

Indio rolled his eyes, and laughed at Marina, even as he slipped Giancarlo some coins. The Sailing Master took them with a smile, writing his name down on a piece of paper. *"Aguilar!"* Indio cried. "Please do not hurt my Boatswain!"

Marina laughed, her braid swinging as she tossed her head, eyes glowing. "Your Boatswain hurt *me*, my friend." She laughed wickedly. "He will pay!" She blew Solomon another kiss, wiggling her hips at him. She glanced at Gaitano. "Captain!"

He inclined his head towards her, playing with her. "Aguilar..."

"Permission to kick Solomon's butt! Sir!" More laughter.

Gaitano looked at the Boatswain. "I am glad it's not me, man." He turned to Marina. "Granted."

Marina flashed him a smile, and went back to her song. "Solomon..."

The young African walked towards her and stepped into her space. He eyed her warily. Marina started slapping him. He blocked her hand, after a couple of stings. "Had enough?" he mocked Marina.

Marina moved in with a combination kick and punch. She bounced out of reach as Solomon doubled over first, then snapped his head back. Their eyes met. She widened her eyes at him. "Have you?"

Solomon wasn't laughing anymore. He charged her, getting in a few slaps. Indio stepped forward, and Gaitano detained him. He shook his head slowly, a smile on his face. Solomon slapped Marina again, making her braid whip about her face. "Not yet, little girl," he laughed.

Marina nodded, smiling. "Good!" And she attacked. Solomon backed away, hands up, not blocking fast enough. She looked like a windmill on him, connecting a kick or a punch from every side, until she finally drew back. She faced off with him, panting heavily, wiping the sweat off her brow. Her fist was up, aimed at the Boatswain's face, her knuckles screaming, cut and bleeding. "How about now?"

Solomon lifted his hand, for a moment, death in his eyes. He hurt all over. He licked his lips and tasted salt, wondering if it was sweat or blood. The men screamed. He hesitated. His fist was aimed right at her face. "How about you?" he asked ominously. It was Indio's turn to hold the pirate back.

Marina concentrated, achieving tunnel vision, focusing on Solomon. She clenched her fists tighter, her body thrumming with the challenge. She laughed at him. "Of course not. But there is something you must know." She smiled at his expression. *I will hurt you.*

Solomon lunged at her, quick as lightning. Marina was faster. She knocked him flat, and danced away from his reach. She sucked in her breath and looked down at Solomon. The young man was now, finally, on his knees, struggling to his feet. He looked at her, his face bleeding from a cut at the corner of his eye. There was reluctant admiration there. Holding on to his aching ribs, he winced, and threw the word at her, laughing. *"Bitch!"*

Marina blew him a kiss. "I'm the *Captain's* bitch," she said with a wink, patting him on the butt as she walked by. Salomé met her and they high-fived.

"Marina!" laughed the pirate, a pleased look on his face. "Salomé! Caribe! Would you please be so kind as to show us, the crew of La Gitana, th e ancient forms of Tae-Kwon-Do? From what I have seen, we could all benefit from it, and we would have advantage over our opponents." A murmur rippled among the men, as they agreed.

The trio looked at each other and nodded. Assuming position again, they began their forms once more. When they turned around, they realized that the whole crew was following their movements.

And that is how, the divine Salomé Banks and Marina Aguilar, introduced the pirate crew of La Gitana, to the ancient art, taught to them by their fathers.

Once they were done, Salomé and Marina retired to the cabins down below, while Caribe remained on deck, showing a very interested audience of very mean men, different techniques.

Jackson smiled, feeling Quentin's stare. "You still don't believe that my sisters are all right, huh?"

Quentin laughed. "God! Yes! Of course, I believe you! Where are they?"

"With friends."

"What did they say?"

Jackson looked at him in silence for a moment. "The same thing you did. Thanks for not lying to me, man."

Quentin shot him a look of relief. "Sure, man. This has been one of the experiences of my life, I'll tell you that," he confessed.

"Good. You need to know who your friends are, and what they are capable of." Jackson pat his back.

The other man looked away, embarrassed. "You're right, of course. Now, I would just like a chance to apologize to your sisters."

Jackson nodded. "Cool, man. Don't stress it."

They finished the boat ride in silence. Once on the mainland, the men took care of the boat, and shaking hands, parted ways.

Jackson sat in the parking lot for a moment, head on the steering wheel, taking deep breaths. He was getting ready to do, one of the most difficult things he had ever done in his life. He sighed, and banged his head softly a couple of times on the wheel beneath his hands. Once again, he prayed. *You've come with me this far... Please, take me home.* Sitting straight again, he looked into his eyes, in the rearview mirror. In them, he saw his sisters. Shaking his head, he started his black SUV. Air conditioner blazing, he cranked his stereo, as he left the parking lot, and joined the traffic. Finally, making it to his Exit ramp, he got on the highway and headed home. He had a couple of hours to think about what he was going to say. Sighing again, Jackson focused, relaxing, as Bob Marley wailed.

Marina groaned, as she carefully stripped the clothes she was wearing, and washed off. Dressing again, in a simple dress, she sat at the table. Salomé washed up, herself, and threw on another dress. She joined Marina. The ledger lay open in the middle of the table, larger than life. Salomé peered at it. "What is so special about this thing? Why is everybody so uptight? Can you even talk about it?"

Marina nodded. "Gaitano, apparently, has an empire. There are records of his legitimate businesses, like trading he does with some islands off Encantada, and trips he makes regularly to Carey. There are other records, of ships they take. Names of the vessels, the captains, the crew. Genuine, detailed accounts of pillage and plunder."

Salomé gasped. "You are kidding me!"

Marina shook her head. "No. It talks about what they captured, casualties, how the spoils are divided, all that good stuff."

"Amazing."

"Yes. So, there are these other records, of the legal merchandise that makes it to the harbor at Encantada. Well, every so often, certain items don't make it. Mainly, weapons obtained during the pillaging and plundering."

Salomé looked thoughtfully at the ledger. "What is the common denominator?"

"Come. Look." Marina invited her to read the numbers. "Gaitano's ship, goes out on the ocean, does its stuff. You know. A pirate's gotta do, what a pirate's gotta do. They fly the Jolly Roger, and make contact with an unsuspecting victim. So, they pillage and plunder, maybe someone gets killed, maybe someone else gets marooned. They keep anything of value, food, and weapons." She tapped the book. "That is all here. Detailed down to how everything gets distributed among the crew."

"Where do they go from there?"

"Carey."

Salomé frowned. "Isn't that where we are going?"

Marina shrugged. "Is it?"

Salomé nodded. "Yeah," she said sadly. Just then, Indio walked in on them. Sitting down quietly, he joined them, flushed and sweating from the workout he just went through with Caribe.

Marina continued. "So, they go to Carey, and..." she drifted off, turning to Indio. "What is it? Is it a company, an organization? Do you report to someone else? Are you just somebody's employees?"

Indio shook his head. "There is a comittee that monitors activity, so that nobody calls too much attention upon us."

"Okay, so you check in with these guys, and you leave, with the weapons, to go back to Encantada."

Indio nodded. "Correct."

"So, why is it that every time you get back to Encantada, there is a fraction of your inventory missing?"

Indio just looked at her. "So, how can anything be missing, if it is all recorded at Carey, as point of departure?"

Marina shook her head sadly. "I don't know, but here is the sheet from Carey, and here is the one from Encantada. This is the page that is missing. It says here, that on March twenty-third, some of these weapons were to go to," she peered at the page. "McClintock, Gaynes, Smith ---" she stopped, and stared at her sister.

Salomé was nodding her head, at each name. "... Smith, Dowling, Jameson, Baker ---"

Marina gasped. "Salo! How did you know?"

Salomé shrugged, waving her hand at the book. "I saw that list," she began.

"When?"

"Well, on March twenty-third, I guess."

"What happened?"

"That was the day we got the latest merchandise at the shop. The bolts of cloths came in crates, instead of cases."

Marina stared at her, wide-eyed. "So, where did you see the list?"

Salomé thought quietly for a moment. "It came with one of the cases. I only memorized it, because when I saw it, Dominique tried to hide it from me, and it just sparked my curiosity, so I read it, when she wasn't looking. I memorized them, chanting." She showed them, drumming a beat on the table, and closing her eyes, reading the list from her mind.

Marina gasped, and covered her mouth, her eyes twinkling over her hand. Indio stared at them, looking from one to the other. He slapped his hands down on the table, and pointed a finger at his girl-friend. "Say no more. Not another word. The Captain needs to hear this." And he was gone. Marina and Salomé just stared at each other in shock, until he returned. Indio came back in, Gaitano at his heels. He sat down between the girls, once more. "Now, please repeat."

They did. Gaitano sat, stunned, as he read the names from the list in his hand, while Salomé drummed, her head swaying back and forth, chanting. When she was done, she smiled at him sadly. "I can't explain," Salomé said, shaking her head, "how a dress shop ends with a packing list for weapons obtained during a raid or something. On our records, these recipients are *Mrs.* McClintock, *Miss* Gaynes, *Old Widow* Smith."

"Why are they packed in crates?" Marina asked. "They are bolts of fabric!"

Gaitano nodded. "That would explain how the weapons disappear. They are being smuggled."

"Into Dominique Swan's shop?" Salomé asked, startled. "But why?"

Marina laughed, slapping her hands on the table, and rocking in her chair. "Oh, we have *got* to find a connection! There has got to be one!" Her eyes blazed.

Salomé's eyes sparkled, as she looked at the pirate. "Gaitano, I would be more than happy to spy for you!"

Gaitano looked at her. "Thank you. I accept your offer. We will discuss the details, later. Of course that means you are also, now, working for me." He smiled when she nodded, and turned to Marina. "What else have you found?"

"Well, these papers," she said, pointing to another page, "are detailed accounts of the goings on in the islands, what with the abductions and all. The descriptions are pretty gory and graphic. The island natives call this Captain, the *White Devil.* They say he is made of moonlight." Marina looked sadly at her friends, around her. "This monster is a senseless, vicious, psychopath. He needs to be stopped." She pulled out a map from under the stack of papers. Putting some marks on it, she turned to the pirate. "Gaitano," she said softly, "every single time you are either here, or here," she drew a soft charcoal X on Carey and on Encantada, on the map. "This creature is always, right around here." She traced a small circle, right in between the two Xs. "You need to figure out, who knows ahead of time, wether you are coming or going, on this ocean. This guy hits the water before you do. Do you run into anybody you know, out here?"

Gaitano frowned, his eyes merely turquoise slits, as his mind raced. "We run into many people out here," he shrugged, still frowning. Something was clicking.

Marina looked at him. "Yes, but taking a look at this guy's activities, the thing with the weapons going missing, ties up with the abductions, almost to the day. This guy would weird you out, papi, his energy must be so negative and dark."

Carlos nodded, and smiled at her, distracting her momentarily. "*Gracias, Marina,*" he said, turning to leave. He bent down and kissed the top of her head. "Your insight is most appreciated. Now," he looked right into Indio's eyes, "we have work to do."

Indio nodded, and stood up. He kissed them both, and smiled. "Have a nice day, ladies."

They smiled at his back, just before the door closed.

Up on deck, Indio caught up with Gaitano. "What are you thinking?"

Gaitano smiled. "I think that before this is over, Marina is going to deliver this monster to us, on a silver platter."

Indio laughed. He agreed.

Sloane Aguilar looked up at the ceiling of her spacious kitchen. It was her day off, and she had slept in, taken care of the mail, and caught up with the news. She was relishing being alone in the house, a luxury she was rarely granted. At this moment, however, all the growups were at work, while the children were enjoying themselves on Spring Break. They hadn't heard from said children for a few days, however. It was Jackson's room she was trying to peer into, and he might have come home early --- She shook her head. He wouldn't leave the girls alone. There should be nobody home.

There was another noise, as if somebody had dropped something heavy, on the floor above her head. Sloane jumped, her heart beating a little faster. She brushed her golden hair out of her face, and peered out the kitchen window. There, sitting on the driveway, was Jackson's SUV. She breathed a sigh of relief, and closed her eyes for a moment, heart pounding. Looking at the clock, she saw the time. Almost noon. Crossing to the refrigerator, she reached in and pulled out an assortment of fruits. Quickly cutting them in pieces and making an impromptu fruit salad, dividing it into a couple of bowls. She went back to the refrigerator and grabbed a glass bottle with homemade lemonade. A couple of cups of ice, forks, napkins, and she was ready to go. Juggling everything like the most seasoned waitress, she exited the kitchen, and crossed the vast foyer. Flanked by arches leading to an amazing courtyard, was a curving Spanish tiled stairway, leading to the living quarters. Going up the stairs, she went down the wide hallway, and knocked on the solid wooden door, leading to the apartment over the kitchen.

"Come in." The voice was muffled, as it floated to her, through the door. She opened it, and was met by loud music. Stretched out in an armchair, in front of his entertainment center was Jackson. She smiled. He was slouched down, long legs straight out in front of him. There was a remote control in his hand, a bowl of popcorn in his lap, and a twenty-ounce plastic bottle of Coca-Cola, hanging from his other hand. She frowned at him, and waited for him to lower the volume. Then, she smiled again. He put the bowl of popcorn aside, and set the soda next to it. Standing up, he smiled at his other mom. *"Mami!"* He embraced her, kissing her on the cheek.

Sloane just smiled at him. "Jax! I didn't expect you back so soon. I thought I had the house all to myself, today. How're you doing, baby?" She kissed his cheek, and set her offerings on the coffee table next to her. "Dad tells us you spoke, a few days ago, and you were all having too much fun."

Inside his head, Jackson rolled his eyes. In front of this lady, who helped raised him, he showed respect, and just smiled. "Something like that."

"Well, never mind, eat first, talk later." Sloane took the vacant seat next to his, passed him a bowl of fruit, and proceeded to have a nice lunch with her son. Once they were done, they kicked back for a little while. Finally, Sloane turned to him, a million questions in her eyes. Jackson sighed, rubbing his hands over his face. *"Mami,"* he started, and cleared his throat. Sloane did not move. It was his tone of voice. She did not know why, but she was scared. He began again. "Mami. The whole drive here, I kept hoping you would be the one in the house. I prayed that of the four of you, I would find you first." He looked at her.

"I need help, Mami."

Sloane frowned, never having seen the haunted look in his eyes before. "You are scaring me, Jackson. Speak."

He sighed. Taking a sip of lemonade, he peered at her over the rim of the glass. Putting it down slowly, he licked his lips. "Okay, Mami. Just listen, please, okay?" He waited for her to nod. "A few days ago, Salomé and Marina went on a field trip, to a little island. I was supposed to go, but I got held up, and didn't make it." He shook his head in self-disgust. "They ended up going with a couple of guys from school, but they found themselves alone. Well, these geniuses figured out that it would be a good idea to have sex with them." He sighed, and rubbed the back of his neck.

Sloane laughed. "Don't tell me they sent the boys to the hospital!" she joked.

Jackson closed his eyes, grimacing. "Not exactly," he said. Standing up, he began pacing in front of his window. From here, he had a clear view of the driveway, and the sprawling yard next to it. "One of the guys lost it."

Sloane gasped. "Did they get raped?"

Jackson turned to her, horrified to see the expression in her face, and quickly reassured her. "No, Mami, no, chill. They didn't get to touch them. But this psycho just left them on the island."

Sloane felt her heart drop. Standing quickly, she bent to pick up their dishes. "Come with me downstairs. Help me clean up." Without waiting for him to answer, she turned around and left the room. Jackson bowed his head, and followed her. Downstairs, Sloane quickly washed the dishes, and poured herself a glass of chardonnay. Pouring Jackson one, she sat down at the small bar, in a corner of the immense kitchen. "Go on," she said, finally. "I'm listening."

"Mami. I swear this is the truth, you've got to believe me. I didn't find out about it till that night, and it was storming, and too late to go get them. First thing the next morning, I had one of the guys, Quentin, take me." He frowned, feeling he had to explain a little bit. "Quentin is the non-psycho guy who was with them. He told the girls he would get them help, and he came and told me what happened." He sighed, and passed his hands over his cornrows, pacing again. Sloane followed him with her eyes, and took another sip of wine. "I had this guy fucking drop me off, so I could get them. I couldn't find them." Not looking at her, he began talking faster. "I couldn't find them. They weren't there! I had their bags, and where they slept that first night, and all, but they had just disappeared! I spent my nights, in this cave they had found shelter in, and my days, I would pound the beach, the mountain, the jungle, just looking for them. It was as if the island had swallowed them." He stopped, finally and looked at her, without seeing her. She realized he was looking at a memory. "And one night, it stormed again. Just like that first night they spent there. And when I woke up the next morning, there was Salomé. Just running down the beach towards me."

Sloane gasped. "What happened, Jackson? Where were they?" Her voice broke. "What about Marina?"

Jackson went to her, and crouched down, so that his tiger eyes were looking into her turquoise ones. "Marina's fine, Mami, just fine. They both are. But they are not here anymore. Not right now."

"What do you mean?"

"Those storms, out over that little island, just offshore." His eyes were pleading, as he held her elegant hands between his. "They do this weird trick with the ocean, and they create a time warp." He watched, as his words sank in. Sloane stared at him, shocked, and moved to stand up. He stopped her. "It's freaky Bermuda Triangle stuff, Mami, but you wake up, at another time." Suddenly, he was on his butt, as Sloane pushed him away from her, and stood up, walking away from him, and putting her wine glass down.

Spinning around suddenly, she faced him, golden hair whipping around her face, hands on hips, chest heaving under her faded, Grateful Dead T-shirt. Tears shone in her eyes. *"Jackson Banks!"* Her accusing voice broke on his name. She took a deep breath. "You haven't lied to me, since you were three years old!"

Jackson just looked into her eyes, until he saw the realization of the truth of his words. *"Exactly!"* Standing up, he walked over to the kitchen sink, and grabbed the phone on the wall next to it. Coming back, he offered it to her.

Sloane just looked at it, shaking her head. "Well, where are Marina and Salomé right now?"

Jackson laughed. "You don't want to know," he assured her. "But actually, they are stuck over there for the moment. I figured out a way to go back and forth."

"Jackson, stop! What are you saying to me? Where are they? What year is it?"

He laughed again. "I don't know the exact year, Mami. But I know one thing, though. Marina and Salomé managed to land themselves in the middle of the *Golden Age of Piracy*." Jackson lunged as Sloane's knees buckled. Her tan faded, as she looked at him, her eyes silently begging for him to laugh and say he was playing. But she could see he was not, and her heart felt like it was going to leave her chest. He offered the phone to her once again. "I'm calling a family meeting. I need help."

Sloane nodded, numb, tears in her eyes. Taking the phone, she punched in a number. Putting the person on hold, she punched another. Then, she did it again. The Aguilars and the Banks were now on a four-way conference call. Sloane took a deep breath. "Everybody there?" she asked.

Her husband, and Marina's father, Pablo Aguilar, was the first one to answer. "Hey, *Mami, que pasa?*"

Dr. Shayla Banks' voice sounded worried. "Sloane, are you all right, *mami?*

Joe rumbled over the sounds of a basketball game. "What's wrong, baby?"

"Jackson's home. The girls are not. He is calling a family meeting. Right now." The phone went dead in her hand.

While they waited, they hit the Internet. Sloane felt as if she were having an out-of-body experience. Jackson was pointing out ships, and clothes, scenes of harbor activities, weapons and maps. She asked him to stop, she was on the brink of overload. But by the time, she was calm again... By the time, she was downstairs in the kitchen, greeting her husband and her best friends, with a pitcher of Margaritas... she believed him. Sloane believed Jackson, and his tale of Encantada. Taking a deep breath, she faced her family. Ever the hostess, she poured them each a Margarita, making sure they were comfortably seated around the bar. They touched glasses, and drank. Then they looked at her. Sloane took a deep breath. "You have all been called here, because Jackson," her voice broke. Before they could react, she recovered, shaking her hair back, and smiling, in spite of her husband's frown. "Jackson has a story to tell. It is not an easy story to listen to," she continued, all eyes glued on her. "But you must decide for yourselves. Before he begins, I want to add that the only reason I know about it before you, is," she gasped for air, "because he needed to be backed on this. Well," she threw Jackson a smile. "I just want Jax, and you," she looked at each of them, "to know, that I do. I believe him." And she said no more.

All eyes turned to Jackson. He looked at Sloane. She nodded. Taking a deep breath, he began his story, all over again. No one said a word, throughout the whole time it took him to tell it. And then, he began describing details that Sloane hadn't heard yet. When he got to the part about Solomon taking Marina away to La Gitana, and Pedro Barbosa detaining him, Sloane excused herself. Jackson fell silent, waiting for her return. He started, as he heard a noise overhead. It sounded like Sloane was trashing his room. Excusing himself, he sprinted up the stairs, and opened the door to his apartment. His beautiful blonde mom turned to him, with tears in her big blue eyes. "Jackson," she whispered. "Where's your stash? I can't do this, straight." Jackson shook his head. He quickly provided her with what she wanted, and watched her relax before his eyes, after a few seconds. She thanked him, visibly feeling better. "I just needed to open my mind a little bit. Come on." Hooking her arm through his, they went back downstairs.

Pablo Aguilar looked suspiciously at his wife. She just smiled at him, sweetly. He shook his dark head, and turned to the young man he had helped raise. "So, you mean to tell us, that Marina is on this pirate's ship?"

Jackson nodded his head. "Yeah. She is. And I know that Salomé is with her. It's like this. Marina met this guy, and Salomé met another one. The guys turned out to be bosom buddies. Kind of like you guys," he told his dads. " No, more. They are brothers, somehow. These guys, actually, are like the Hollywood version of what I guess was the real thing. They're young, and extremely successful at everything they do." He laughed. "And," he added, looking around the group, "they really like your daughters."

They fell silent again, as Shayla stood up and fixed the second pitcher of Margaritas. They all held out their glasses, for her to pour. She sat back down again, tears in her eyes, her expression one of shock. Her husband reached out and took her hand in his, raising it to his lips for a kiss. Their son continued.

"Here's the deal. The pirate kind of hired Marina to do his books for him. I guess it was just an excuse to hang out with her, though. The thing is, Marina discovered that this guy was being ripped off, big time, and," he looked around at his parents again, "all hell broke loose."

Pablo scrubbed his face with his hands. "That's my girl," he sighed sadly.

"Well, the pirate had to go take care of business. He reports to someone on an island not too far away, I guess. It's not like they're going to be gone months," he shook his head. "But he needs her, because she's the one that can explain what is going on."

Joe frowned at his son. "So, he just *took* her?" Jackson nodded his head. "But aren't they *friends*?"

"Yes. As in, very close." Jackson sighed. "Gaitano only did it, because there was no way in hell she was getting on that ship, otherwise."

"Why's that?" asked Shayla, finally.

"Because she's scared to be stuck out in their world, and lose the opportunity to catch a time warp storm, back home."

Sloane began to cry softly. "Is that possible? That they could never come back?"

Jackson quickly shook his head. "No. But the girls don't know that, yet. So, I guess it must be a little dramatic."

Pablo raised his hand, interrupting. "Wait. What about this pirate fellow? Is he going to *rape* Marina?" He started rising out of his seat.

Jackson bit his lip, his eyes twinkling. "Papi. With all due respect." He took a deep breath. "When Gaitano finally gets together with Marina, it won't be rape."

Shayla gasped. *"Jackson!"* she scolded. Joe frowned at his son, even as the younger man shrugged.

"It's true!" he laughed. "And *you!*" he pointed at his parents happily. "*Your* daughter is the one with the *boyfriend!*"

"That is *not* funny, mister!" warned his birth mother.

Jackson held up his hands. "I know, I know, and I'm sorry. But these guys are really nice people, no matter what their day job is. The

thing is, there have been raids on other islands, they got hit themselves last year, and people are taken against their will, as slaves." He
sobered. "That's when they're not being slaughtered." The grownups
seemed to freeze. "That is why Gaitano took Marina. He wasn't going
to leave her on Encantada, while he was away at sea, and he couldn't
protect her, I guess. It looks to me, like the guy is crazy about her."

"Or just crazy!" shouted Pablo, banging the table with his fist. *"I
don't care that he's a pirate! He's a grownup male that should know better
than to scare a girl to pieces!"*

"Papi," soothed Jackson. "I'm sure he will work it out with her."

Pablo stared him down. "You trust this guy?"

Jackson didn't hesitate. "Yes." Pablo slowly settled down.

Joe looked at his son, thoughtfully. "So, how do you, from the
twenty-first century, establish initial contact with these people?"

Jackson answered eagerly. "That village guy I was telling you
about? His name is Caribe. He dreams about the people that come
through in the storms. And he sketches them. He's much better than
I am," he admitted. Reaching into the backpack he had brought
down to the kitchen, he pulled out the papers. Keeping them rolled
for a moment, he explained to the parents. "First, he dreamed of
Marina and Salomé. He recognized them because of this." He pulled
out the first paper and handed it to them. They all circled around it,
admiring the sketch of their daughters.

Shayla gasped. "This is excellent! Why, you can almost hear
them laughing!"

"He's incredible!" agreed Jackson. "And the night I came
through, he did this." He showed them the second paper. "Caribe
showed this to Salomé, and she lost it. It sent her running down the
beach, to get me." He shook his head at his parents. "By the time
she got to me, she was hysterical. I have never seen her like that. She
totally freaked out on me, Dad," he confessed, looking at his father
with tears in his eyes. Joe Banks swallowed, blinking back his own.
"But, this guy that's with her? It's like he's her boyfriend. I'm sure he's
that serious about her."

"But that's *impossible!*" cried Shayla. "They can't just *stay* there!
They *have* to come back!"

Jackson laughed bitterly. "Well, you better go and convince them, before they don't want to come back!"

"Jackson!" scolded his father.

"Dad! Life there is relaxed! There is no stress! As long as the pirates are in town, and they are protecting the island, there is nothing to worry about, except these damn freak storms!" he shouted.

Joe Banks stood up, eye level with his son, and shouted back. *"So, what the hell do we do now?!"*

Jackson looked down, lowered his voice, apologetic. "Dad, come with me." He looked at them. "Mom, Papi, Mami. Please. All of you. Come with me. Check this place out. Let's help them, help these people. There is a reason why all this happening. There is a higher power pulling some strings. Salomé and Marina have a purpose in Encantada right now. There is no coincidence. Let's just all go, and be there for them. Please."

The grownups just looked at him. They were in collective shock. Pablo cleared his throat. "How do you get to this Encantada?" Sloane stared at her husband, mouth trembling.

Jackson pulled out the third paper. He handed it to his other dad. "Papi. Enter this in your computer. It should come up with a pattern, and possible dates for other time warps." He pointed at it, encouraging Pablo. "Go on. It'll tell you when we can catch the next storm out of here."

Pablo looked at the paper suspiciously and back at his son. He stood up, and strode to a computer in the corner. With his back to them, he sat, and began working. They waited in silence. In a few minutes, he came back with a printout in his hand. He shook his head, raw admiration in his face. He looked at Jackson with pride. "Oye, *papito*, if this is correct, there is another storm in three days."

Jackson closed his eyes. *Gracias, Papá!* "So, what are you going to do?"

Shayla stroked her son's face. "Jax, baby, leave us alone for a few minutes. Let us talk about this. It's no game. This is real, and we need to treat this with all the seriousness it deserves. Just go upstairs, and we'll call you in a little bit, okay, baby?" Without waiting for an answer, she turned to her husband, and began sobbing against his chest. Joe's arm went around her, as he murmured in her ear. Jackson's heart broke. Head down, he turned, and left the parents alone.

He stared at the big screen in his room, without really being able to see anything. His mind was hundreds of years away. He had no notion of how much time had gone by, when there was a knock on his door. Jumping to his feet, he opened it. His dads were standing there, standing by opposite sides of the door frame. They came in, and greeted him in the usual style. Hands meet, pull, chests touch, hug, head on shoulder, release. The three males of the family stood around, looking at each other. His father spoke. "We're with you, Jax. Let's plan this. We'll go catch a storm with you, baby."

Jackson froze. He stared at them. First, his eyes started stinging, and then his heart began pounding. His face crumbled, and he gasped for air. His mouth opened, and a keening sound came out. Joe rushed to catch him, as he collapsed. Pablo helped lower him to the floor. There, the three of them rocked in each other's arms, as Jackson, finally, cried.

That night, Shane Butler joined them. He was the parents' lawyer, and close friend. Shane had gone to school, and college, with Pablo and Joe. His wife, Heather, was good friends with Sloane and Shayla. Their grown sons, Tyler and Derek, were older than Marina and the Banks duo, but were still good friends, and actually shared living quarters in an old abandoned warehouse building downtown, which Pablo, Joe and Shane had bought together for the children. The Butler men practiced Tae Kwon Do at Pablo and Joe's school. In other words, they were close. And that is why, when the Banks, and the Aguilars, sparing Jackson the telling of the tale for the third time, consulted their lawyer, and told him about their daughters and Encantada, Shane Butler, Esquire, believed them. As a matter of fact, he didn't even blink. Instead, his eyes twinkled from behind his glasses, as he looked at Jackson. "Jax! Always your sisters' keeper, I see." He chuckled, shaking his blond head, and held out his hand. There was respect and admiration in his eyes. "Let me shake your hand, son." Jackson complied, studying the family lawyer, suspiciously. "I have never met a time traveler before." He laughed. "I'll tell you one thing," he confided with a wink. "You've got more balls than I do." The men sat around a table in the kitchen. Sloane and Shayla had disappeared, to comfort one another. Shane Butler took off his glasses for a moment, rubbing his eyes, pinching the bridge of his nose. "I have to apologize," he told his friends. "But if it weren't for the fact that the girls may be in danger, I would die laughing." Putting his glasses back on, he spread his hands out, helplessly. "The thing is, that you don't have a choice," he told the dads. "You have to go over there, and, either pull them out," he looked around at all of them, "or make sure for yourselves, that they are fine." He shook his head, thoughtfully. "From what Jax says, the men they are keeping company with, seem to be fine fellows. They are obviously, hard working men, with feelings for the girls, hopefully running deep. But Salomé and Marina are legally adults. You can't *make* them do anything. You can only assist them and support them in their choices." He looked around, as the men nodded their heads in reluctant agreement. He noticed that Jackson just sat, slightly apart, silent, watching his dads closely. The young man looked as if he had gone through hell and come back. "Now. Time for what you pay me for."

The men sat forward eagerly, as the lawyer brushed his hair back with his hands, pale blue eyes studying them from behind his glasses. Joe frowned at him. "What would *you* do?" he asked suddenly.

Shane laughed, pointing at his chest. "*Me?* I sure wouldn't be wasting my time, like you are." He laughed again. "I'd be out on that island, camping already, looking up at the sky, praying for rain." He smiled, as the men relaxed, smiling reluctantly.

Pablo shook his head. "So, you suggest we just go."

Shane frowned at him, for a moment. "You didn't call me here to ask me what I think, Pablo. The only reason I am even here, is because you need someone to water your plants while you are gone," he said, eyes twinkling all over again.

Pablo looked as if he had just gotten caught. "Busted. You know me too well," he chuckled.

"Okay, okay," interrupted Joe. "So, how do we do this?"

Shane smiled and rubbed his hands together. "I thought you'd never ask." He turned to Jackson. "First thing you do, is eliminate Todd and Quentin from the picture. Swear them into secrecy, threaten them with bodily harm, I don't care. The thing is, you don't want anybody else, outside of this house, to know about this. If the boys ask, the girls are well, and happy, and they are forgiven. End of story." He looked around at them. "As far as transportation for you, and getting you out on the ocean, and dropping you off on the island, I will take care of that myself." He spread his hands on the table, drumming his fingers. "Now," his voice dropped lower, "let's get down to the logistics of this." He turned to Jackson. "How do these storms work?"

Jackson shrugged. "They come in, do a weird dance with the ocean, and they go. When you wake up, you are on their island. Because of the time thing, none of your personal stuff comes through. When I got to the cave, I found Marina and Salomé's bags, but obviously, they weren't there. The cave had candles, matches, blankets, some clothes... It's as if it were an in-between place, or something."

"So, nothing from our time goes through to theirs," commented Shane.

"Exactly. Nothing that would identify where we come from. It would probably turn their world upside down." The men nodded, in silent agreement.

"So, how did you stay in touch, again?" asked Shane.

Jackson shrugged. "My backpack had my cell phone." He rubbed his head. "First, I called Dad, not knowing how long I was going to be gone." He glanced at the older Banks. "Sorry I lied to you, Dad." Joe shook his head at him, and he continued. "Then, when I came back, this morning, I called Quentin to pick me up." He pushed the papers he had brought back, over the table, to the lawyer. "I managed to bring these back, because I needed proof to back me up. These people have lived with visitors like us, for many years. It's just not known by the whole island. The privilege is granted to a couple of people only. No one else on the island knows."

Shane studied the portraits silently. "You didn't do these," he said, looking at Jackson over the rim of his glasses.

Jackson shook his head. "No, I'm not that good. I wish," he added.

"And, this is the time table, you are talking about." He waved the dates Jackson had brought over from Encantada, and the computer printout Pablo had obtained. At their silent nods, he studied the papers for a moment. "Well," he finally said to them, giving the papers back. "Joe, you got some vacation time coming, don't you? Shayla needs to get time off from her office. Sloane needs to leave her shop..." he drifted off, scribbling furiously. "Heather would love to take care of it for her, while you are gone." He smiled, shaking his head. "Which only means, it'll be hell, trying to get Tyler and Derek away from there." The men laughed. Sloane's shop was notorious, for always being full of half naked models, trying on clothes for upcoming fashion shows. Shane scribbled some more. Finally, he turned to Pablo Aguilar. "Pablito," he smiled at his buddy. "You, my friend, can afford to retire, and just drop out of sight. Your business runs on its own. Call your boys, and have your reports sent to me. By the time you get back," he stopped, as they all stared at each other. Shane studied the time table again. They had only been talking about going to Encantada. Nobody had mentioned coming back. "Let's see. This says, three days, and then the next date isn't for another month." He shrugged. "That's not too bad. By the time you get back, things should be running smoothly. Going back to basics should be a good way of keeping it real." He winked at the men around him. "About your place, I can get Tyler and Derek to help me. You know, come around, put your mail and your newspapers inside the house, so it's not so obvious, you are gone."

"Drive my cars around, once and twice, for me. Keep them up." Pablo suggested.

Joe laughed. "While you are at it, make sure you do water the plants, and you can help yourselves to our refrigerator and our pool."

Shane nodded. "Done deal. What about the blue cat?" he asked, referring to the twins the men had raised from birth, ever since they were young teenagers.

Joe laughed. "Blue and Cat are just goint to have to sit tight." He shook his head ruefully. "Ignore them. You don't know anything."

Shane cocked an eyebrow. "What about Xaira?" Xaira Chang was a stray, so to speak, that Marina had come home with one day. The girl had attached herself to Marina, and they now shared a floor at the old warehouse building.

Pablo grinned. "That may be a little harder, but you still don't know anything," he offered, making Shane chuckle. They settled down, for a moment, turning serious.

The lawyer looked at his clients and friends, once more, a distant smile on his face, worry hiding behind his eyes. "*Muchachos*, I wish you luck. I will pray for you. Go see to your daughters. Check them out, help them. Make sure they are safe. I will be back in a couple of days. Anything else you need, just call me." Standing up, he shook hands with the three men, and he was gone. Pablo Aguilar and the two Banks males stayed around the kitchen table, each lost in his own thoughts.

Upstairs, the two mothers faced each other. They were in Jackson's apartment, gaining comfort from his presence in the house. They were too distraught to enter either of their daughter's old quarters, unsure of what was awaiting them. They paced in opposite directions, turned, walked towards each other, passed, and turned again. It was their own private dance, one they had established from their school days, whenever they had a dilemma that they needed to work out. Now, it was serving them well, as they, too, were each lost in her own thoughts. The women stopped again, and faced each other once more. Looking at each other again, they sighed, and with tears in their eyes, fell into each other's arms. They stood there like that, heads together, as different as night from day, gathering strength and comfort from one another.

Shayla was the first one to draw back. She had changed out of her doctor's uniform, and into workout clothes. Stripes ran down the sides of her nylon pants, as they hugged her strong legs, and a white T-shirt strained across her ample chest. She looked like her daughter's sister, hair braided out of the way, eyes big in her face. "Sloane," her voice wavered, and tears came to her eyes. "Are you ready for this?"

Sloane shook her head sadly, tears in her own eyes. Her blond hair fell over her face, even as she swept it back, savagely. "No!" she exclaimed softly. "Of course I am not ready for this!" she hissed. "But I am doing it. I am going to that cave, and God help me..." she trailed off, her distress evident in her eyes. "Shayla, Jackson isn't making this up!"

Shayla squeezed her, whispering fiercely in her ear. "Of course not, mami! He would never put us through this. He loves those girls, more than he loves himself."

"They are women!" wailed Sloane, tears spilling.

Shayla laughed shakily. "Yes, they are, baby." Taking Sloane's perfect face between her hands, she looked into the beloved turquoise eyes. "We just got to go and check out those men, they are hanging out with."

Sloane smiled in spite of herself. "I hope we are doing the right thing."

Shayla stroked her hair gently, brushing out of her face. "Could you live with yourself, if we didn't go?" She raised her eyebrows, as Sloane quickly shook her head. "Could you just give up on them, never see them again, never?"

"No! Of course not!" Sloane stared at her, aghast.

Shayla smiled again. "Well, mami, it looks like we are going on a trip." Sloane nodded, smiling through her tears. "We certainly are," she agreed.

"We are going to see our babies."

They held each other's gaze for a moment. Then, sobbing quietly, they fell into each other's arms, once more.

The women looked at each other. They were sitting around a table, Indio and Gaitano with them. The men were resting, before they had to go on watch. In front of them, on the table, were maps, where they had proceeded to point out to the females, the route they were taking. After a while, they had fallen into a comfortable silence, listening to the ship make its noises, as it rocked on the waves.

Carlos suddenly turned to Salomé. "Do you like your job?" he asked with male curiosity. "What is it exactly that you do?"

Salomé smiled lazily at him, elbow on the table, hand propping up her head. She was doodling lazily on a blank piece of paper. "I design garments for women that make them look better, than their options usually do. Dominique already has a seamstress, Liana, I believe is going out with the town doctor," she added mischievously, pretending to gossip.

The men nodded. Indio gathered her hair in his big hands, braiding it gently. His voice rumbled out of his chest. "Dr. Kyle Richardson."

Salomé winked at Marina. "He's a cutie," she mouthed at her. Marina rolled her eyes and hid a smile. "Well, Liana creates the actual garment. I just draw it for her on paper." She closed her eyes for a moment, relishing Indio's touch. "This allows me to have only direct contact with the client, and nothing else, really. So, once I'm done with my designs, I actually have quite some time on my hands, so..." she let her voice drift off, as her eyes sparkled. "I snoop around."

They all looked at her in shock. Marina felt shame wash over her. "Salomé! How could you? You know better!" she said, in a mortified whisper.

Salomé shrugged, unconcerned. She kept doodling idly, her braid hanging down her back now, Indio's hands to himself. "I would never have done this, but," she stopped her hands, and sat up straight, looking at them, "the lady's a little weird."

Gaitano and Indio exchanged looks. "Weird in what way?" asked the pirate, having learned quickly, the meaning of the slang term.

She laughed. "Actually, queer."

Marina's mouth dropped. Clasping a hand over it, she stared at her.

"No..."

Salomé thought in silence for a moment, her hands clasped, elbows on the table, lips pressed together. She frowned, looking inward. Then her brow relaxed, and her eyes focused on them. "Dominique Swan's shop," she said slowly, "I believe, is nothing more than a front, to provide some ladies with," she frowned again, looking for a word, "certain services." Finished, she looked around at them. They weren't sure how to react.

Gaitano sighed. "All right. I will ask. What kind of services?"

Salomé's smile became mysterious, as she looked at them through slit eyes. "Dominique Swan," she licked her lips, "likes women."

Marina gasped, her eyes as wide as they would open. She covered her mouth again, struggling to hide the laugh trying to escape her. "Salomé! No!"

Salomé nodded her head at her sister, and rolled her eyes. The men were interested, she could see, but nothing had prepared them for this. "How do I know?" she asked, teasing them. "Because, when I first got there, she looked at me," she turned to the brave, "like *you* look at me." He blinked. She laughed. "When I first got there," she turned to the pirate, seductively smoothing the shirt over his chest, "she wanted to help me try some clothes on, so she could," she looked straight into his eyes, "*fit* me." Gaitano swallowed.

"You never told me," accused Marina, when she finally could speak. "Does she come on to you?" She knew that being a model, like Sloane, Salomé was an expert at fending off unwanted female advances. Their beautiful mother had taught her to defend herself.

Salomé shrugged, leaning back again, drumming her hands on the table once more. "We have been busy, away from each other. Besides, I let her know right away that she was approaching the wrong female. Then one day, Indio discovered where I work, and now she just looks at me with lust, from across the room."

The pirate threw back his head with laughter. He glanced at his Quartermaster, shaking his head. Looking back at Salomé, he gazed at her with genuine affection. "Now, explain to me, mami, how Dominique Swan's," he hesitated, searching for the right words, "sexual preferences, translate into any services she may be providing."

Salomé smiled at him, nodding. "You think this is funny, don't you?"

"Quite," he admitted.

"Okay, Captain," she turned her full attention on him. "Check this out." She waited a moment, gathering her thoughts. "There are rooms, upstairs, where the ladies change, and try out their new clothes. These rooms," her eyes crinkled at the corners, at the memory, "not only have mirrors, but they are full boudoirs, with beautiful velvet reclining furniture, where a lady can lay down," she stared straight at him, "while another lady... makes her feel better..."

Gaitano just looked at her, stunned. Then, a slow smile spread on his lips, at the visual.

Indio chuckled. "Can I watch sometime?"

Salomé laughed and slapped her hands on the table. "I don't want to hear about it!" She pointed at them. "I am not giving you any details on this one, you guys are just nasty!" she laughed again. "Just let it be known, that every time you guys set sail, there are some women in Encantada, loving it!" She glanced at Marina with a wink. "And each other..."

They laughed, comfortable together. The years of friendship between them and their strong mutual attraction creating a warm safety net around them. Carlos shook his head. "Enough. We have to go back to work. Thank you for entertaining us, ladies. Salomé," he smiled at her. Turning to her friend, his eyes softened. "Marina, would you mind walking out with me for a moment?"

Marina nodded, surprised. It was obvious that she had forgiven him, but it still hung between them, that he had just taken her. She followed him outside. Closing the door behind her, Gaitano pinned her suddenly, against it. Her wrists over her head, he held them there as he pressed his body against hers. His breath was hot on her cheek, as his mouth left a wet trail from her cheek to her ear. "I miss you," he rasped, breathing heavily. She knew exactly what he meant. Marina struggled against his grasp, wanting to touch him. Instead, he held her tighter. His mouth finally descended on hers. Marina opened her mouth, hungrily welcoming his. She was just letting him know how much she missed him, also, when he was gone. She felt herself start sliding down the door. Catching herself, she managed to stand, as Indio opened it. Smiling at her, he tousled her head happily, and he, too, was gone. Marina sighed, and went back inside. Joining Salomé on Gaitano's bed, the two settled down, for some serious catching up. The pow-wow lasted until they fell asleep, heads together, hair spread out on the pirate's berth. When the men's shift ended, Indio took Salomé into his cabin, and Gaitano, quietly, laid down next to Marina. Resting a hand on her hip, he fell asleep, a prayer on his lips.

"Marina..." Caribe only had to call her the one time, the following morning. She squinted up at him and smiled, rubbing her eyes. She went to get out of bed, but Gaitano's arm snaked out and caught her playfully. Caribe smiled and left them waking up, and getting out of bed. On the way out, he boldly knocked on Indio's door. At the brave's grunt, he dared to peek his head in. " Salomé..." She turned to him with a smile, nodding, and waved for him to go ahead. Indio nodded politely. And then, Caribe went on deck, to wait.

A few minutes later, the two women, and the Carptain and his Quartermaster came up. Caribe moved into position with the girls, and the forms began. In a matter of seconds, they were joined by the rest of the crew. The ship sailed on, in the morning sun, its decks sprinkled with martial arts movements, as the wind helped them along. This day, the women did not go below deck to spend the day in the comfort of their cabins. Instead, they stood by the men, assisting the different crew members in their different chores, learning a little bit about every aspect of the ship.

Gaitano frowned, as he watched Marina. She seemed to be trying to outdo herself. From where he stood, he could see the drops of sweat sliding down her chest, to disappear inside her, no, his shirt. She seemed desperate. "Aguilar!" She whipped around, turning to look at him. He jerked his head, softening the command to come over, with a smile. His eyes caressed her as she put down what she was doing, making a comment that put a smile on the sailor's face. Then, she made her way over to him. Finally reaching his side, she smiled up at him, but couldn't hide her sad eyes. He frowned.

"Capitán..."

"Marina," he began, trying to not look at her, keeping his eyes on the horizon. "It seems to me, that you are working extremely hard. There's no need to push yourself until you drop ---"

"Gaitano," she interrupted him, shaking her head. "I need to. If I don't..." she bit her lip, as tears filled her eyes.

The pirate gripped the wheel beneath his hands, and glanced at her. "Marina, don't you forgive me?"

"Yes," she answered miserably. "But I still need to deal with it. If I work, I don't think about it." She started walking away.

"Marina!" Playfully, she spun around, stamping her foot and tapping it, her arms crossed over her chest. She widened her eyes at him and pointedly looked at the wheel in his hands, flinging an arm out at it. She pointed at him and mimicked steering. Then she grinned and winked at him, letting her arms fall and walking away. He laughed and nodded, and went back to steering his ship. He had finally found a woman that understood, that he had a job. He chanted under his breath, joy in his heart. "Marina, *divina*..."

By sundown, the women had put in a whole day's work. To their delight, and embarassment, the crew cheered them. Thanking them, they went down below, leaving them to Lucas and his nasty songs. They parted ways, in front of their cabin doors, embracing, wishing each other a good night. Once alone, in their own cabins, they each cleaned up, and immediately passed out on their respective beds.

Marina opened her eyes, trying to get her bearings. Candlelight flickered around the cabin, and the ship was rocking a little bit harder. Squinting, she focused on the figure in the chair, in front of her. She studied him, in the quiet candleglow. He had kicked off his boots, and his long legs were stretched out in front of him, the smooth fabric of his pants, clinging to his muscular thighs. His shirt was untucked and open. His chest was bare, dark hair lightly covering it, trailing down the middle, around his navel, and into his waistband. Marina licked her lips, and stirred. His shoulders were big, rounded, his arms massive, as they rested on the chair's arms. From one hand, a brandy snifter hung carelessly. His other hand was busy, twirling a knife around, threading it through his fingers. Marina let her eyes go back up, caressing his arms, along his throat, to his face. There, they dwelled on his strong chin, before straying to his mouth. She stared. The pirate licked his lips, and she felt a rush of familiar warmth. She looked up. Their eyes met. And locked.

Gaitano couldn't move. He had been there for a while, studying the dark curves, draped on his sheets. He had let his eyes roam over every single inch of her, having his way with her in his mind, until she woke up. Now, he couldn't move. She was sitting up, leaning back on her hands. Her chest was moving a little bit faster, and he simply couldn't break away from her hazel eyes. Her lips parted. He couldn't speak. She just studied him, and there was nothing he could do about it. His fingers involuntarily tightened on the snifter. The knife fell out of his other hand, bouncing on the floor once, before clattering as it slid under the table.

Marina felt herself lose control slowly. She had little sexual experience, feeling she had never encountered a partner she wanted to indulge herself with. Nobody had inspired her that way. As far as knowing what to do, however, Jackson had hooked her up, on her twenty-first birthday. His private gift to her had been a very graphic, sexually explicit, porn movie. He supported her choice of not having sex with just anyone, but was worried about her knowing how to please a man, when the time came. The movie was his way of giving her a lesson in theory. Marina had been indebted to him. And now, here she had a chance to do something she had never done before, personally. Something she absolutely craved to do to this man, who made her feel so helpless, but that made her come alive like no one ever had before. *This is what I want.* She smiled slowly.

Gaitano froze. His heart skipped a beat, and then, began to pound faster.

He watched, helplessly, as Marina rolled over until she was on her stomach, eyes glowing, still looking at him. She raised her backside slowly, stretching like a cat, and, hair in her face, began to crawl towards him. His lips parted, his breath coming, silently, faster. Stopping at the edge, she swung one long leg unto the floor. Gracefully, she slid out of bed, and approached him, a pillow in her hand. A bead of sweat slid down his face. With a wicked look in her eye, she bent over and caught it on her tongue. Gaitano could not move. She threw the pillow on the floor, licking her lips. Gaitano could not breathe. Smiling, she went down on her knees, in front of him. Taking the glass out of his hand, she set it on the floor next to the chair. He held his breath as she turned to him. Their eyes locked once more. He wanted to say something, but no words came to him. So he kept quiet. Marina took his face between her hands, and caressed him, rubbing her thumbs over his lips, slipping her fingers into his hair, stroking and pulling. Her voice was a whisper in his ear. "You are dreaming." Bringing her face close to his, she kissed him. He responded, hungrily. His arms went to wrap around her, but she pushed him back. The smile on her face intrigued him. He sat back again, watching quietly. She licked the hollow of his throat, just as he had done to her, a few days ago. He sighed. She massaged his chest with splayed hands, fingers digging into his muscles, loosening them. He felt himself slip lower into the seat. Marina ran her tongue down his chest, slowly, taking her time, circling his navel when she reached it. Her hands encircled his hips, her fingers crawling into his waistband, opening his pants. Gaitano gasped, as he felt her hair brush his midriff. Marina laughed softly, reaching in, and drawing him out, pleased to notice he was circumcised. She hadn't seen many male organs, personally, but loving art, she thought this way, they were more beautiful in an aesthetic sense. He groaned, ready for whatever she wanted to do to him. Marina smiled into his eyes, holding him in her hands, squeezing gently, rubbing, making him harder. In his mind, he sprang up, yanked her to her feet, and threw her on the bed, sinking gratefully between her legs, into her flesh. Marina laughed softly once more as she saw all this in his eyes. Giving him a squeeze, she lowered her head, and without breaking eye contact, proceeded to finally put into practice, one of the most important lessons she had received in how to please a man. Gaitano buried his fingers in her hair and held her head, as his hips rose to meet her. Her tongue snaked out and did a thorough exploration of his shaft, swirling around its head. He groaned. Marina smiled to herself as she took him into her mouth, not breaking eye contact, determined to make him feel just as good as he had her. If not better. He sucked in his breath, as she completed the first movement. Closing his eyes, he leaned his head back. A smile slowly spreading on his face, Gaitano groaned again. He couldn't even breathe by now, his only reality, the gently bobbing head under his hands. High on the power of it, Marina moaned softly, as she pleased him. Carlos' hands guided her. They held her head, his heated whispered instructions, hoarse in the night. She did everything he asked. Loving every minute of it, she brought him to a climax. Then she swallowed it all. Smiling mischievously as she finally raised her head, she smacked her lips, making him grin.

Gaitano chuckled. He was spent. Sweat was dripping down his chest, and his breath was labored, while he recovered. He didn't move, as Marina proceeded to wash his private parts, rinsing him off and patting him dry. She washed her face and rinsed her mouth, before turning back. As she walked by him, he yanked her by the wrist, holding her on his lap. His mouth hovered over hers, when he realized that she hadn't shown any revulsion in pleasing him. His eyes were full of wonder, as he pressed his mouth against hers, faintly tasting himself. He felt his manhood stirring again. Mentally shaking himself, he just looked into her eyes, as their mouths teased each other. "Thank you," he finally managed.

Marina winked at him and gave him one last kiss, hugging him tight before letting him go. She put the snifter back in his hand, and picked up the pillow. He watched as she crawled back into bed, and curled up, once more, dark curves on his white sheets. He finished his brandy, his body slowly floating down from its high. Breathing a deep sigh, he stood from the chair and flung himself into the hammock, not trusting himself, not to make love to her in the middle of the night. He was no fool. Closing his eyes, he smiled into the dark, still feeling the suction of Marina's incredible mouth on him.

Their third day out on sea was the same as the other two. Caribe woke them up to do forms on deck, and then, everybody went back to work. This time, however, Marina vanished below deck. Feeling herself sinking into a depression, she climbed into bed and shut out the world. She couldn't move. Up on deck, Gaitano frowned at his closed cabin door. He wanted to go to her, but Salomé had stopped him, shaking her head. She explained to him that Marina needed to be alone. It was all he could do to keep himself from joining her in his cabin.

"Why is she sleeping at this hour?" he asked curiously. "Yesterday, you couldn't get her to rest."

Salomé nodded sadly, and shrugged her shoulders. "Marina is just so sad, right now, she can't handle it. Sleep is nothing more than a defense mechanism. The body protects the mind, giving it the rest it needs. She'll be okay," she reassured him, "but truthfully, Gaitano, this is just getting scary. I don't blame her," she added, before flipping her hair over her shoulder, and stalking off, hips swinging.

Gaitano pressed his lips together, and called for his Sailing Master. "Giancarlo!"

The Italian sailor promptly reached his side. "Captain..."

The pirate looked at him. "Let us make a small detour," he suggested thoughtfully. "Let us stop at Arrecife for a couple of hours. We can make up for the time we take, with the evening wind."

Giancarlo stared at him, a look of amusement on his face. "*Arrecife?* Capitán, Arrecife is nothing more than a sandbar, in the middle of the ocean."

Gaitano smiled. "True. It is. But Arrecife happens to have the best beach on the whole ocean. Maybe everybody would just like to go for a little swim."

Giancarlo nodded slowly, a look of enlightenment on his face. "I will get on it, right away."

Word spread quickly, and the crew got excited. Half an hour later, Joshua called down from the crow's nest. *"Arrecife!"* The yells echoed among them, the crew bursting into cheers. A few minutes later, it seemed to Gaitano that nobody was on board. It was as if everybody had jumped ship. The shouts of joy and screams of laughter were contagious, as the whole population of La Gitana splashed in the warm coastal waters of the sandbar, Arrecife.

Quickly counting heads in the water, Gaitano made sure there was nobody left on his ship. Finally, he was able to go to Marina. Standing in front of his cabin door, he hesitated. Opening it quietly, he peered in. The soft sunlight was coming in the only window, outlining Marina on his bed. He went to her, determined to help her.

"Marina," he called softly. *"Divina..."* She stirred. Brushing her hair away gently, he whispered in her ear. "Let us go swimming." Marina opened her eyes, and rolled on her back to look at him. He nodded. "Let us go swimming." Pulling on her hand, he helped her sit up, and get to her feet. "I will race you," he grinned.

Marina grinned back. Dashing to a large porcelain bowl full of water, she splashed water on her face and rinsed her mouth quickly, with some paste John Kline had provided her with. Next to her, laughing, Gaitano did the same. They both grabbed the same towel at the same time. Marina stepped out of her skirt and into some pants, as the pirate pulled off his boots. He chased her out of the cabin and up the steps to the deck. When they got there, Marina stumbled to a halt, as she heard the shouts of laughter on the beach. Turning around, she located them, and watched. Everybody was playing in the water. Gaitano stood by her, still grinning. "Capitán! A beach!" she cried happily.

Gaitano laughed, and climbed on to the side of the ship, holding on to a rope for balance. The breeze whipped his hair around his head, as he swayed gently. Looking back at Marina, his eyes challenged her. "Can you dive?" He extended a slow hand out towards her. Marina smiled and took it, climbing to stand next to him. There, they stood for a moment.

On shore, Salomé held Indio tight, as he spun her around in the water, weightless. Over his shoulder, she caught sight of the two figures. She tensed in the Quartermaster's arms, making him stop. "Indio, look, baby," she whispered urgently. He turned around. From where they were, they could see the ship rock under the other couple's feet. Gaitano stood holding the ropes, shirtless, pants cropped to his knees. Next to him, Marina balanced herself, holding his hand, the other stretched out to her side. A single braid hung over her shoulder. As they watched, they saw the couple straighten, as the pirate let go of the rope. They waited a beat, and dove in together. Salomé clapped. "Bravo! Bravo! I give them a ten!" At Indio's puzzled look, she just shrugged and grinned. Draping her arms over his head, she proceeded to try dunking him. She failed. Laughing, he embraced her, dragging her underwater with him. By the time they came up for air, Gaitano and Marina were closer, their features distinguishable. Indio and Salomé watched as the other couple reached them.

Marina glided to them and began swimming around them in circles, changing strokes as she went, alternating between back, front, and side. "Hey, baby," she laughed at Indio.

Indio laughed back. "Hey!"

Gaitano began swimming in circles behind Marina, in the opposite direction. They smiled when they passed each other. "How do you like Arrecife?" he finally asked Salomé.

Salomé laughed as she tried to dunk Indio again. "I am loving it!"

Marina treaded water, waiting for him to catch up. "How big is this island, anyway?"

He thought for a moment. "About a mile long, and half a mile wide."

"Is it sandy all the way around?"

"Yes."

She smiled. "Thank you."

"Why?" he asked, but she didn't answer. Instead, she began swimming away.

"Salo!" she called to the other girl. "Let's run!"

Salomé kissed the top of Indio's head and kicked away, swimming after her sister, leaving the men looking at each other. Feeling someone next to her, she turned her head and saw Caribe swimming at her side. "Papi!"

Caribe grinned. "I know where you girls are going!"

They hit the shore running. It seemed to them as if they had been aboard La Gitana, for ages. Setting a pace, the trio pounded the sand side by side, muscles thankful.

Gaitano and Indio treaded water, watching after the friends. The runners got smaller, until finally, they rounded a corner, and ran out of sight. Indio chuckled. "Permission to kill that boy, Captain, sir!"

The pirate laughed. "Jealous, my friend?" He shrugged. "Caribe is to them, like Jackson."

The brave grunted. "Exactly. And Jackson still has more power over her than me."

Gaitano frowned, trying not to laugh. "You have a point, there."

Indio finally smiled, and turned to his brother, mischief in his eye. "Or he did..." he said mysteriously, beginning to swim. "...until this trip..."

Gaitano let go, finally, and both men laughed. They swam to shore, and there, they stretched out, quietly talking business, while the women finished running. After the third lap, the three young people stopped, breathing heavily, exhilaration in their faces.

Indio grumbled. "Maybe I should run like they do."

Gaitano agreed, smiling. "She will kill me, before I am forty." They laughed again. Turning to the women, they stood up, brushing the sand off the seat of their pants. "Ready, ladies?" They nodded. With a sharp whistle, the Captain gained the attention of his crew. Cupping his hands, he yelled into the sky, *La Gitana!* The girls watched, astounded, as everybody ceased their activities, and began swimming to the ship. Gaitano smiled at them. "Let us go." They joined the exodus, excitement building up again, as they climbed rope ladders, to get on board.

The crew set to work immediately, tending to their different tasks, as if orchestrated by one magic hand. Within minutes, they were moving again, the sails catching the wind, and picking up speed.

Marina gazed in awe at Gaitano. "Your men must love you."

He winked at her. "I will settle for their respect." Turning her around, he sent her on her way, with a pat on the butt. Marina smiled over her shoulder at him one last time, and tossed her head, swinging her hips. As expected, he watched, mesmerized. So lost in thought was he, that Giancarlo crept up on him undetected.

"Lucky for you, I was not an enemy." The Italian gazed after Marina's backside. He sighed. "I will tell you something, Carlitos," he said softly. "If these women had been sirens, they would have ruined me."

Gaitano laughed at his friend. "Why is that, Giancarlo?"

Giancarlo rolled his eyes, making a mock sound of disgust. "Look at them," he hissed. "I do not know a single man who could keep up with their stamina. They would be killing the clients." He winked at his Captain, and walked away, with a pat on the shoulder.

Carlos Gaitano smiled to himself, shaking his head.

Many hours later, in the still of the first moments of the morning, when it is still dark, right before dawn, they crept into a harbor. The docks were quiet, the town dark. Overhead, a lonely seagull scolded them. Throwing anchor quietly, the crew of La Gitana brought down their sails. They arrived. With sighs of relief, they watched the dark outline of their destination. Happy, they would rest now for a couple of days. It would be a nice stay. It always was, whenever they reached this particular island. That was why it was known as a haven, for sailors like them. And this was where the council would be held. Carey.

The next day, it was a quiet crew who did their forms, aboard La Gitana. Happy as they were to have reached Carey, as usual, they were aware of the importance of this trip. The outcome of the meeting they were attending would determine their personal future, as individuals, as pirates, and of Encantada. Once they finished their morning exercises, they quickly did their chores, and prepared to go ashore.

Gaitano called a quick meeting, just before they left. He looked around at his men, and women, giving last minute instructions. "We are to go directly to *El Callejon*. They will be expecting us." He turned to Marcus. "Old man, you, Joshua, and the rest, go enjoy yourselves. Keep your eyes and ears open, and we will meet later, this afternoon." He turned back to Indio. "Indio, Giancarlo, Solomon, you, of course, come with me." Now, he looked at the women. "Salomé." He smiled, as she cocked her head at him. "For your own safety, I invite you to join us. It is an important meeting. All men, but for one," he shrugged apologetically. "I suppose, as long as you stay quiet, you will not attract too much attention," he winked at her. Then, he looked at Marina. "You, will be by my side. You are my accountant, and you have found evidence of tampering with the Gaitanos. I will need you to present your findings."

Marina looked down at herself, aghast. "I am not going dressed like this!" she wailed softly. Salomé quickly nodded, agreeing. The girl looked around at the men. Finally, she spotted the boy that worked the crow's nest. "Joshua! Lend us some pants!" At the boy's shocked expression, she smiled. "Please. Yours are the only ones that will fit us." Joshua glanced at Gaitano, who nodded. Smiling shyly at the women, he led them away. Marina tousled his hair. "Good boy," she teased, "we won't bite!" A few minutes later, they were back on deck, Joshua's pants snug and tight, clinging to their hips and thighs, shirts, long and hanging. "Ready," she announced, smiling.

Gaitano frowned, wondering what effects their look would have in a room full of pirates. "That will have to do." He glowered at her. "You stay by my side." She smiled, and nodded. "Caribe, you come with us." With one last look at each other, the crew of La Gitana boarded the longboat, and rowed ashore.

Shane Butler looked around at his friends. It had been a silent ride to the island. Shayla and Sloane looked as if they had cried themselves to sleep in their husbands' arms every night, since he last left them. Joe and Pablo didn't look much better and Jackson... The haunted look in his eyes tore at his heart. The young man obviously felt directly responsible, even as he understood that he couldn't control a freak whim of Nature. He pressed his lips together, and waited, as the family regrouped. They were all staring at the island, but as of yet, they couldn't move. He sighed. It hadn't been easy, the last few days. His friends had been in a state of perpetual shock. He had found himself more active than he had expected to be, orchestrating their affairs. From calling Quentin, and reassuring him that everything was back to normal, to getting last minute instructions about Sloane's shop, he had been there, every step of the way, holding their hands, so to speak. This morning had been the worst, what with collecting their assorted keys for house, vehicles, and offices. He sighed again. Clearing his throat, he broke the ice. "Okay. Everybody listen. This isn't a funeral. It's more of a vacation." He turned serious, as they all turned vacant stares on him. "Actually, it's neither, and I realize this. But you can not go in there in defeat. Salomé and Marina would die to see you the way you are right now." They nodded their heads sadly at him. "Go. Explore the island, check it out, have a nice day." He looked around him. The sky was heavy with rain, and the ocean was churning whitecaps. "It looks like it's going to storm." He winked at them. "Please, just make sure you remember everything. I would like a detailed account of your experiences when you come back."

Jackson was the first one to snap out of it. "You're right, man." He looked at his parents. "Let's go." Standing on the edge of the boat, he slipped into the water, keeping his backpack aloft.

The rest of the family moved. They all embraced the lawyer, in turn, and followed Jackson. Shane Butler stayed where he was, until he made sure they all went on shore. Grabbing his cell phone on a whim, he punched some buttons. He watched through binoculars, as Pablo Aguilar reached for his back pack. When he picked up, he smiled. "Just making sure this thing works, Pablito. Good luck and God bless. I will come back tomorrow, to make sure you made it through the storm. We'll see you in a month." He saw Pablo Aguilar nod, and turn to wave at him. Turning the boat around, Shane Butler left. He couldn't wait to confirm that the Banks, and the Aguilars, had, in effect, achieved time travel.

Marina silently reached over. Salomé quietly grasped her hand, locking fingers with her, squeezing. They couldn't move, they couldn 't even breathe. But most of all, they couldn't believer they were there.

El Callejon had turned out to be just that. An alley. But at the end of the alley, was something, reminiscent of *Romancing the Stone*. Behind an extremely thick and heavy wooden door with huge iron fixtures in an arch in a wall at a dead end. There, lay the most splendid courtyard the women had ever seen, even in their time. Bougainvillea sprouted from enormous clay pots in a cobblestone yard, the fragile fuchsia petals making a carpet around each one. The fountains were graced with Old World fish, and sea dragons. There were mermaids, dolphins, and even Poseidon. The arches were adorned with elaborately scrolled grill work in iron. The hallways off the courtyard were tiled, with beautiful mosaics, like those from the time of the ancient Greeks. At the end of one such hallway, they had come upon double doors, flanked by huge, mean looking pirates. They had nodded to Gaitano, as they had approached, looking after the women curiously. Now, they stood facing the committee.

The room they found themselves in was large enough to hold a banquet table at one side. Facing the crew of La Gitana were six chairs, somewhat like thrones, and in each was a pirate. Five men and one woman. They smiled a greeting at the crew, before addressing their captain. "I hope you bring good news, Gaitano." This, from a formidable looking Asian fellow, even larger than Jimmy.

Gaitano nodded. "Jai-Ling!" he exclaimed softly. "Greetings. I present to you, my accountant, Miss Marina Aguilar of Cayo Largo, and her sister, Miss Salomé Banks. Marina has been recently employed by me, to take care of my books, and she has discovered some interesting events." He took her hand, and pulled her forward to stand by him, with a reassuring smile. Marina gripped Salomé's tighter, making her move up, next to her. "Marina," said Gaitano, looking into her eyes, "would you please report to the council what you have found?"

Marina just stared at him for a moment, and swallowed. He squeezed her hand, and let it go, stepping back. Marina grasped Salomé's hand tighter, as she attempted to do the same. She closed her eyes, for a moment. *God, help me.* Then she turned to the council. Recalling every instruction ever given to her by her parents, she cleared her throat, and began, introducing herself, once more. "*Buenos dias.* My name is Marina Aguilar, and I have been working for the last few days as accountant of *Capitán Carlos Gaitano*, leader of *La Gitana*, out of Encantada." She stopped, swallowing. She had their full attention. "While working on his books, I have discovered discrepancies, regarding the transport of arms and ammunition obtained during raids done to other ships, between the months of November and March. These arms and ammunitions have been catalogued and inventoried, at their arrival here, at Carey. There is even evidence of the merchandise being shipped on Gaitano ships headed to Encantada. However, once the ships arrive over there, the inventory doesn't match." She stopped for a moment, unsure. Salomé quickly squeezed her hand, not letting go. Marina looked back at the crew of La Gitana. They all met her eyes, encouragement in their own. *My God, their futures depend on this!* She turned back to the pirates in front of her. They too nodded at her, encouragement in their eyes, also. Marina smiled, gratefully. She continued. "After extensive studying of the books, I have come to the conclusion that the hits on these particular shipments, coincide with the raids on the islands, and the kidnappings." There was a gasp. All turned to look at the lady pyrate. She had her hand clamped to her mouth, and tears shimmered in her brown eyes. Her curly red hair framed her face, making her look like a wild woman, even as her clothes hugged her curves. She was stunning.

"Are you all right?" asked Jai-Ling, voicing everyone's immediate concern.

She shook her head sadly. Taking her hand away from her mouth, she stood up, smiling apologetically at the women before her. "I am Rouge. My ship is the *Sea Gypsy*, and my crew is composed of all women." She smiled ruefully at Marina and Salomé's expressions. "Some of us are ladies, true women, and others are men at heart with the bodies of girls, but we are all females." She stood sideways, so she could address everybody present. "On January sixth of this year, my ship stopped at *Las Joyas*. We were crippled from a storm the night before. When we approached the first island, there was nobody there," she said, her voice breaking. She bowed her head for a moment, her hair falling over her face. Then she shook it back, and looked at them, eyes staring. "*Alive*," she said softly. The men all stared at her, transfixed by the tale. "It was a massacre." Tears slid down her face. "Their village was full of dead bodies." She began shaking. "We see plenty of bloodshed, but this was beyond any battle I have experienced at sea, beyond anything I have ever heard you," she waved her hand at them, "talk about." Her breath came heavy. "This was senseless and vicious. The villagers didn't have a chance." Her hands went to her chest, as if her heart were causing her pain. "We got out of there and went to the next little island. The same."

"*No!*" This from Giancarlo, his eyes wide with shock.

"*And the next!*" she screamed. "And as we approached the last one," her eyes blazed at the memory, anger and horror battling together, "as we round the tiny cove, there, in front of us, heading away from us was a ship..."

The pirate next to Jai-Ling rose from his chair, fists clenched, vein throbbing at his temple. As he did, a surge of energy seemed to spill into the room. He was formidable looking, in that he was exactly, as you would expect, a pirate to look. The long coat, the hat, the polished boots, and the gleaming sword at his side were all most impressive. He was older than the rest of them, and had an air of authority about him, that made him stand out from the rest. His dark hair was flecked with silver, and the wrinkles around his amber eyes pronounced, from the years in the sun. His handsome face was marred by a scar that ran from one ear, across the cheek diagonally, to the chin. "*What flag was it flying?*" he roared.

Rogue shook her head sadly. "It wasn't." She looked at each of them. "We had to hide. Ever since then, I have been trying to be as far away from this monster, as possible." She glanced at the women. They were both staring at her with identical expressions, their hearts in their eyes with compassion. "This is the first time I have been able to make it back here, since last year."

Silence followed Rogue's revelation, and there was quiet for a moment. Marina stepped in, sadly. "This individual is referred to by the islanders, as the White Devil. The magnitude of his viciousness is horrific." She lifted the ledgers to her chest, while still clasping Salomé's hand. "I believe that this person stalks Gaitano ships, following them or running from them. The person responsible for these crimes, has prior knowledge of the comings and goings of the Gaitanos, because," she took a deep breath, "he manages to be away from them, at the same time he remains in the area. So, the events occur, on the wake of Gaitano's ships passing."

Another pirate stood up, this one dressed in a robe and turban. His earrings reflected the candles around them, as did the vicious looking crescent sword at his hip. He stepped forward and bowed to the women. "I am Suleiman, and I sail, usually, the Mediterranean Sea. I have come all this way, in hopes of establishing trade with the Caribbean. However, this matter with this heathen, has affected us all. My men, the crew of *Chymera* are uncertain about our prospects here. Also, I am concerned about the disappearance of arms and ammunition, when I, too, as all of you, have that as part of our inventory, after our raids." Behind him, the other pirates nodded.

Marina just looked at them. Salomé squeezed her hand again. "When these ships are making the voyage back and forth between Carey and Encantada, the smaller islands are struck. Encantada itself was hit last year, natives taken, their present whereabouts unknown. This event devastated the community, and the people live in unnecessary pain and fear."

"What do you make of it?" asked another pirate curiously. This one was very young, with bright curly red hair, and pale blue eyes. He had the bored look of a teenager, as he sat slouched in his throne, one leg thrown over a chair arm. His tanned face was sprinkled with freckles, and in spite of his looks, there was authority in his presence. "I am Jack, Captain of the *Black Mermaid*."

Marina closed her eyes for a moment. "What do I make of it?" She turned to look at Gaitano, her eyes haunted. He frowned. "Permission to speak freely, Captain, sir," she said softly. He hesitated. Looking in her eyes, he finally nodded. Marina straightened up once more and met their patient looks. "This," she began, "I can only see as a hostile takeover." Salomé squeezed her fingers in surprise, at the modern term. The pirates, indeed, looked confused. "That means," she explained quickly, "that someone has designs on the Gaitano empire. I would look closely at the people you run into out on the ocean. This person, or group of individuals, is here, present in Carey, when you embark on your voyage, or at least, when you stop here with the merchandise. There must be someone getting paid to directly supervise the handling of the merchandise. There must be someone else in Encantada. As a matter of fact," she said, remembering, "my sister, friend, and associate, Miss Salomé Banks," she squeezed her hand, "found evidence of some tampering with some lists of customers who were to receive said arms and ammunitions, at her place of employment, Miss Dominique Swan's dress shop." She stopped, and took a deep breath. "I suggest that you look into the implications of a connection between Miss Dominique Swan herself, her dress shop, or both, with the activities here at Carey. Also, what could be the possible reason for her to receive such merchandise?" She looked at them each in turn, setting their minds on fire. "Is it simple theft? Robbing from the Gaitanos for their own profit? Revenge?" She glanced at Gaitano. "Maybe you messed with the wrong pirate, at one time or another. Jealousy? Is there anyone among you who is craving the power of the Gaitanos? Did somebody here kill somebody's relative, or stole their wife, or kidnapped their child? Has anybody here heard about anyone, among you, who might be a little bit crazier than the rest of you?" She glanced at Salomé. "My Captain, Carlos Gaitano, suggested that Dominique Swan's may be a way of smuggling the missing weapons." She shrugged. "What for? Could she be selling them and keeping the money? Could she be smuggling them on to elsewhere? Or could she be providing the monster with a means to achieve his goals?" She looked back at her pirate. "At Gaitano's expense? What do you stand to lose, Capitán, if your merchandise keeps disappearing, and this monster is not caught?"

Gaitano met her eyes, squarely. "Encantada."

Marina's eyes watered. Her heart had whispered the suspicion at her, but her mind didn't want to hear it. Now, he confirmed it. Pressing her lips together, she faced the committee once more. "If this monster isn't any of you," she said boldly, "you should find him. Because at the end, the way he operates will affect you. If Gaitano is his goal right now, and he achieves success, what makes any of you think, you won't be next? At this rate, it would be a matter of time, before this demon leaves you with no islands to work with. Organize yourselves, look into your own books, check and see if there is anything going on with your companies. Eliminate possibilities, and with patience, you will find your man."

A different pirate stood from his throne, and approached her. This one was black, and big, like an older version of Solomon. His head was shaven, also, and the mandatory earring in his ears, spoke of his trade. His face was jovial, handsome, easy to smile, even as his eyes remained cold as stone. "I come from Africa," he introduced himself. "They call me Sultan. I, too, as Suleiman, have come here in search of trade." He stretched out a hand to Marina. "Miss Marina Aguilar of La Gitana de Gaitano." She put hers in it, and he bowed over it, kissing it swiftly, before releasing it. "Would you be so kind as to check my books?"

Marina looked at him in shock. She glanced at Gaitano, but his eyes betrayed nothing. She looked at the rest of them, suspiciously. "Do you all need your books looked into?" They nodded, and she shook her head, suddenly shy. "Do you trust me to do your books?"

The pirate with the scar laughed. This one, was sitting in the middle, and except for his outburst, had remained quiet and pensive, throughout the whole presentation. He, as much as the others, was recognizable, as the stereotype. But this particular pirate's energy field was immense. It seemed to Marina, that it touched her, just from his movement. It would explain why he had stayed so still until now. *Gaitano!* he cried. "Do you support your accountant on her findings and her theories? Do you trust this female at your side to be true? Does she have at heart the best interests of you and your men?" At Gaitano's nod, he laughed again. "Do you back her?" he asked slowly.

Without a word, Gaitano stepped up to stand by Marina again. Indio followed. As Marina watched, the entire crew of La Gitana stood side by side, next to her, facing the council. In a dark corner, Caribe sketched furiously, catching everything he could, as fast as he was able.

Indio took one more step forward, addressing the council. "Yes. We, the crew of La Gitana, under our Captain, Carlos Gaitano, back Marina Aguilar, in her assessment of our most serious situation."

The man smiled again, and sat back, his energy withdrawing, as a pet keeping close to its master. "Well, then, Marina Aguilar, proceed."

Marina looked in surprise as the pirates in their thrones, all produced their books. She sighed. "This will take a little time." She turned to her team. "There are six of them, and six of us. We should each take a book and do this. Does everybody know what they are looking for?" Gaitano and Indio nodded, but Solomon and Giancarlo did not. Marina quickly produced papers to show them. "If you see anything like this, it's wrong. If all the papers match, we're good. If anything is missing, we," she shook her head, "I mean, *they*, are in trouble." They nodded at her. "Let's do this. And while we do, please show them what to look for, so they can do their own books, and not rely on anyone who may screw them over." She smiled at them. "Let's go."

In a matter of minutes, each pirate in his or her throne, had one crew member of La Gitana next to them, going through their personal books. After half an hour, Marina looked up, from the Sea Gypsy's books, brushing loose strands of hair back from her eyes. She looked tired, and sad. "Okay! Everybody done?"

Pirates dragged their eyes away from their books, glassy from concentrating on dates, names, and numbers. Gaitano nodded at her. "Done."

"Okay. I have a feeling about this," she wondered out loud. She turned to the two pirates from across the Atlantic. "I would like to hear about your books first." She turned to Gaitano's crew. "Giancarlo, would you please begin?"

He nodded, and looked around at the group. "I have looked into the books for the *Chymera*, of Captain Suleiman, from the Mediterranean." He smiled. "Everything is in order. There are no discrepancies, no merchandise missing."

Solomon spoke up. "I checked the books of Sultan's *Kalahari*. Everything is in order here, also."

It was Salomé's turn. "My book was for Jai-Ling's *Ocean Wind*. His books are perfect."

Indio spoke up. "Jack's *Black Mermaid's* books are also perfect."

Everybody turned to look at Marina. She sighed, hating to be the bearer of bad news. "My book was for the *Sea Gypsy*, sailed by Captain Rouge." She looked square into the other woman's brown eyes. "She has whole pages of merchandise missing, dated back to January. Not big quantities at a time, but instead, a little bit taken every time. Her dates coincide with Gaitano's for being out on the ocean, when the raids on the islands take place." She frowned thoughtfully. "This guy must know you!" she blurted out. Everybody stared at her. Feeling self-conscious, she shook her head and shrugged, apologizing.

Gaitano was next. "The books I looked into also have serious discrepancies, between the months of January and March, also a little every time." He glanced at the pirate with the scar, before meeting Marina's eyes. " *La Gaviota*, captained by Don Miguel Gaitano." He watched her body shudder, and he put his arm around her, holding her close to his side, as she controlled herself.

Marina looked straight at the scarred pirate. "Don Miguel," she said in a low voice. "This is an inside job. By that, I mean, that the man responsible for all of this walks among you. He may not be in this room, but he comes to Carey. In order for him to have access to the information he does, he needs to be here, at the same time you are." She glanced at Carlos and back. "Who do you know, wants to be you, or have what is yours, so bad, that they are killing and robbing to do it?" Tears welled up in her eyes, as the men looked at her silently.

Don Miguel Gaitano finally spoke. "Carlitos, your father could not make it here this morning, but his decision is final. You have one month to take care of this matter. You are to find, bring back, and execute the person responsible for this." The younger pirate held Marina tighter, as he felt her slip down his side. "If you are successful, you shall continue to rule Encantada, and it shall be given to you. On the contrary, if you fail, Encantada will fall into the hands of the highest bidder."

Marina felt him tremble with self control. "*Sí, Tío.*" She stared at Carlos, as he pressed his lips together, his eyes fixed on the older pirate's. Her eyes flewback and forth between them. Uncle? And then she saw it. The resemblance was there. Carlos addressed the group in general. "I will do whatever is in my power to put an end to this madness." He shrugged. "I am not losing Encantada."

They nodded. Don Miguel Gaitano stood up slowly, and approached them. "That will be all. I expect to see you all tonight at *El Baile del Luto.*" He turned his vast energy on Marina and Salomé. "Miss Banks, have a pleasant stay at Carey. Anything you need, please feel free to ask." Looking at Marina, his eyes twinkled between her and his nephew. "It has been a pleasure meeting you, Marina Aguilar, accountant of La Gitana de Carlos Gaitano. Your talent and assessment has been invaluable. Enjoy yourself." He opened his arms to embrace her boss. "Carlitos. Long time, papi. Your parents will catch up with you tonight, at El Luto." He hugged and kissed his nephew, and stood back to look at him, pride in your eyes. He raised his eyebrows, teasing. "This must be it, huh, papi?"

Gaitano laughed at his uncle. "Maybe, old man. See you tonight." Marina and Salomé stopped Rouge, as she made to leave quietly.

Salomé spoke first. "We are really sorry for your experience on the ocean, this past winter."

Marina reached out a hand to the young woman. "We hope that we have been of some help." Spontaneously, she opened her arms to Rogue, and did not move.

Rogue looked from one girl to the other. Salomé opened her arms, also. A long distant memory tickled the back of her mind. The affection of a woman. Being the captain of a ship full of women pyrates, there was not much chance of receiving any affection from her crew, without being misunderstood. The women she led were for the most part, sex driven, wild women. The ones that liked men, as herself, just didn't bother with the rest. Tears stung her eyes, as she stepped into the embrace of these strangers. She had had a hard time, and she deserved some sympathy. The women hugged. "Thank you," she whispered. Stepping back, she noticed that the men were looking at them. Meeting their eyes, she realized no one was making fun. They were all watching with respect. She smiled at her new friends. "See you tonight." And she was gone.

Little by little, they all left, to do whatever it is that pirates do, whenever they are in town together. The crew of La Gitana left the room, crossed the courtyard, and exited El Callejon, in search of a good time.

Carey. The women looked around them, as they stepped out of El Callejon, and into the main street. The morning sun was still climbing in the sky, and people were beginning to come out. The streets were starting to fill with pirates. Gaitano turned to the group. "You are free to do whatever you please," he informed them, even as he grabbed Marina's hand. "We will meet again, later." He pulled her closer to his side, absently raising her hand to his mouth.

Giancarlo smiled at the open show of affection. It hadn't been a romantic trip for the couple, and it was good to see them together off the ship, and away from the men. "Captain, if you please," he glanced at Solomon, "we have no plans. We would be delighted to help you show the ladies around."

Solomon nodded. "If you please, Captain."

Gaitano shrugged. "Suit yourselves." And they set off.

Marina and Salomé linked arms, as they walked, with the men on either side of them. It was clear that they were not lady pyrates, and the looks that followed them were of curiosity and interest. Any smoldering looks of lust or desire were quickly discouraged by the company they kept. It seemed to them, that in minutes, the streets were teeming with pirates. The more they walked, the louder, the more crowded, the crazier the streets got. And then, at the end of one particular street, they could see a marketplace.

Salomé turned eagerly to Indio. "Oh, please, baby, say we can stop there. I have money from the shop. Please?" She stopped to throw her arms around his neck and rubbed noses with him, murmuring against his mouth.

Indio kissed her and laughed. "Anything you say, baby." He slipped his arm around her shoulders, as they kept walking.

Gaitano looked at Marina, as she stood by, silent. "Do you have money?" he asked, knowing the answer. He smiled as she shook her head. "I haven't paid you, yet," he teased. "Come on. I will take care of you."

And suddenly they were there. The girls gasped. The tables were tended by pirates themselves, but the merchandise was like nothing they had ever seen in their time. There were silks and fabrics from the Orient, as well as incenses and brass adornments from India. There were different tools from other countries. One table flanked by a whole group of men, had an assortment of beautiful weapons, all with inlaid handles, and elaborately scrolled blades. Marina and Salomé stood at this table, mesmerized. They would look at each other, and back at the assortment.

Gaitano chuckled at them. "Do you ladies know how to handle any of these?" he asked curiously.

Salomé shook her head, regretfully. "No, not yet." She glanced at Gaitano as he frowned. "Our fathers are teaching us. These would be excellent for them." And she looked at Marina. The men watched curiously, as the girls held a silent conversation with their eyes. Suddenly, it seemed like they agreed on something.

Marina turned to Gaitano shyly. "If it is all right with you, Capitán, and if it is not too much," she looked up into his eyes and smiled, "I would like to get one of these for my father."

Gaitano smiled into her eyes, nodding happily. "Carlos."

Marina frowned for a moment, shaking her head. "What?"

"Carlos." His hand caressed her face. "We are off the ship, and you are not my accountant right now. You are my..." he hesitated, smiling into her eyes. "Friend," he finished softly. Behind him, Salomé rolled her eyes, and Indio shook his head, chuckling to himself.

Marina looked away from his eyes, not wanting him to see the disillusion in hers. "Carlos." She pulled her face away from his hand, and stroked the blade on the table before her. "If you would be so kind, my father would cherish this gift." Her choice shone in the sun, deep, rich, lapis lazuli stones sprinkled throughout the handle.

Gaitano frowned to himself, not sure he liked that she had pulled away from his touch. He wondered what had caused it. To her, he just turned on a smile, searching her eyes, even as she avoided them. "It would be an honor, Marina Aguilar." He made a gesture at the silent men tending the tables. In a moment, the sword was wrapped up and put away. He turned to Salomé. "Please put your money away. It would please me to purchase your father's also." He laughed as she nodded eagerly, and touched one with jade embedded in it. "New weapons for the masters, courtesy of their devoted daughters." The second sword was rapidly taken care of, and put away with the other. Money exchanged hands, and the deal was done. They walked away.

They lost Solomon at the next table, where beautiful African girls were selling colorful beads. The girls were eagerly surrounding him, as they walked off. They passed more weapons, more fabrics, tools, house wares, sails, ropes, supplies. It was endless. They began passing a table attended by some Arabs. The men wore loose pants, turbans, and swords, making them look more like Aladdin's forty thieves, than the businessmen they had seen images of, in the twenty-first century. The table was draped with black velvet, the better to display the jewelry.

Indio stopped, putting a hand on Salomé's shoulder, and gesturing at the table. "How about something for your mothers?" he offered. "My treat," he added, winking at them.

Salomé and Marina looked at each other and laughed, their eyes filled with excitement. Salomé turned to Indio, mischief in her face. "Oh, yeah? What can you afford?"

Gaitano hid a smile, as the brave laughed. He looked at his woman, his voice quiet and sexy. "Everything."

Salomé and Marina looked at each other again. Their eyes said it all. Without a word, they slid their hands against each other. Salomé wrapped her arms around the brave's waist and squeezed him. "Thank you, baby." Marina watched as his eyes filled with love, and he bent his head to kiss her. She turned her head, and met Gaitano's eyes, watching her. They were smoldering. She looked away. The table before them beckoned.

The selection wasn't large, but it was unique. The pieces were handcrafted, obviously, and breathtaking in their value. In their time, they were antique, museum quality items. Here, in this marketplace in Carey, they were being presented as baubles for wives and sweethearts, mothers and daughters. Salomé quickly decided on a set of pearls. Multicolored pearls strung together in an amazing bracelet. It consisted of seven strands, gathered at a clasp made of gold, rectangular in shape and inlaid with rows of tiny, miniature white pearls, in a long, narrow grid. The earrings were drops with a pearl of each color, graduating in size, from the largest one closer to the earlobe, to the smallest one, hanging close to the shoulder. Indio smiled. "Would that be Shayla Banks' style?"

Salomé nodded. "Absolutely." Tears formed behind her eyes.

Indio looked at Marina. "How about Sloane Aguilar?" he asked softly.

Marina hesitated. Then she made up her mind. Only one item would do for her beautiful mother. She picked up a pair of earrings and showed them to Indio. They were simple in their design, long drops of lapis lazuli set in silver. The raindrop design had a frame of tiny silver beads around it, giving it texture. The stones were smooth, and rich in color, deep and alluring, like the middle of the ocean. She smiled at him, as he gestured at one of the men behind the table. "Lapis lazuli, to match Papi's sword," she explained. The items magically disappeared, as had the swords. They continued.

The sun had been climbing steadily, and it was now hanging right above them. There were even more pirates out and about, and the women were glad of the company they were in. At a table full of art pieces, they had run into the Black Mermaid's Jack. The young pirate immediately spied Caribe's drawings, and expressed genuine admiration. He ended up offering to show Caribe around. By the same token, they had found Rouge at a table filled with beautiful glass lamps, and had picked her up, to Giancarlo's delight. Salomé and Indio explored as a couple, and Gaitano stayed close to Marina. Now, they were looking around for somewhere to eat. The men went to hunt for a place to buy food for them, leaving the women huddled together in front of a table loaded with carpets from the Orient. All of a sudden, Marina caught sight of Caribe. He had his back to them, standing around with another man and a couple.

"Caribe!" He ignored her. Marina frowned. It wasn't like him. She nudged Salomé, and pointed him out to her. *"Caribe!"* she called again. The man turned around, directing a frown at her. Marina gasped. Grabbing Salomé's hand, she pulled her along as she approached the man who was staring her down. "I am sorry," she smiled, apologizing, riveted by the man's dreadlocks. "I mistook you, or so I thought..." she trailed off. The man next to him turned to her. His head was shaved, and smooth. His shirt hung in tatters on him, his feet bare and dirty. His handsome dark face was full of scars. His eyes were the color of silver coins. Marina gasped again, her world beginning to tilt. Salomé clutched her hand, beginning to shake. At that moment, the young black couple with them turned to look at them also. Marina thought she was going to fall, and turned wide eyes on Salomé. Her friend was as surprised as she was. Rouge joined them quietly. Marina turned back, thinking fast. She chose her words carefully. "You look like somebody I know. We just came in on La Gitana with Captain Gaitano ---" she stopped. The people looked thunderstruck.

"From Encantada?" the woman asked anxiously. Marina hesitated. She looked at her sister again.

Salomé looked at her, a smile beginning to lighten her face. "Oh, mami," she murmured. "This is too good."

Marina nodded, looking back at the people in front of her. "Who are you here with? Are you with someone?"

They seemed to withdraw. The woman began crying against her mate's shoulders, and the other men shook their heads. The light-eyed one spat on the ground. "No." His voice was musical, like the natives. "We were taken a year ago, and made slaves. We were separated from our families!"

Marina looked around her again. "But who are you with now?"

The man comforting the woman spoke up. "Nobody. We were put on a boat, tied and blindfolded, out on the ocean, left to die." He swallowed, mixed emotions flitting on his face. "We got picked up by one of the pirates headed this way." He stroked his wife's head. "We are trying to find Gaitano, but at the same time we do not want to call attention to ourselves. The monster may be here."

Salomé laughed. *"No way!"* She grabbed her sister, and turned her to look into her eyes, her own jewel green diving into the hazel depths. "Marina!" she said excitedly in a low voice. "Remember what she said about there being a reason for us being here? Think! Quick! If this were a Hollywood movie, who would these people be?" she whispered urgently.

Marina nodded, shocked. She turned back to the group. "You don't know me, but I know who you are. We," she pointed at Salomé and herself, "are going to get you out of here. But we have to take care of something first. *Do not move.*" Grabbing both Salomé's and Rouge's hands, she towed them behind her. When she was a distance away from the villagers, she turned to Rouge.

"We just met, and I know you don't know us, but please believe that we are sure of this. These people got taken from Encantada, probably by that same guy you hid from for so long. Help us. Let's go back, and you tell Gaitano that you want to show us the Sea Gypsy, and we'll be back soon."

Rouge was stunned. "Why, of course! I ---"

"We will explain later," said Salomé, spinning her around, as the crewmembers of La Gitana came into view.

Rouge stepped up. *"Gentlemen!"* she cried happily. "While you search for a good place for us to eat, I will be showing the ladies around the Sea Gypsy." She laughed, rolling her eyes. "They are not convinced that it is a ship, just like any other." The men laughed, and waved them away. They kept going, and disappeared.

Once out of sight, the women went back to the group they had left waiting for them. Marina called to them, waving at them urgently. *"Come with us!"* she hissed at them. Casually strolling away, she led them back through the crowd, in the direction they had come from. Finally finding what she was looking for, she stopped at the table with the African girls. *"Solomon!"* She could barely see his smooth shaved head, as it was being fondled by many female hands. *"Solomon!"*

The Boatswain seemed to dive out of a sea of beautiful black skin, and scowled at them. Marina waved at him urgently to come over. Reluctantly, he left the women with many whispers and many smiles. Facing the women again, he approached them, his scowl growing deeper. "This better be good, Aguilar."

"Solomon! I know we are not the best of friends, but I do respect you." She glanced at the people behind her. "I am asking you, please. You have to do something for me, right now."

Solomon crossed his arms and laughed, shaking his head. "Oh, no! I do not *have* to do anything!"

Marina stamped her foot at him. *"Yes! You do!"*

Salomé reached a hand out to him. *"Please, Solomon!"*

He laughed again, ignoring Salomé. "Why? I do not answer to *you!"*

"No! But you answer to *Captain Gaitano*, and *I* am his *pet!"* Marina stopped to take a deep breath, as she heard the women gasp behind her. She didn't dare look at Salomé. "I am asking you please, Solomon, *please*, you've *got* to do this for us! I *promise* I will *never* ask anything of you again."

Solomon looked curiously at the people behind them. He frowned. "If I do whatever it is you are asking me..."

Marina looked into his eyes. "A favor shouldn't require anything in return."

He made a sound of disgust. "You are wasting my time!"

Marina grabbed his arm as he began turning away. "No! You are wasting ours!" she cried, glancing at the people behind her. She spun him around. "Solomon! If you don't do this for me, I swear to you," she said, tears in her eyes, "I will call you out and challenge you right here, right now, and proceed to kick your ass all over the pirates' playground, where they can all see!"

Solomon yanked his arm away from her grasp with a roar. *"I have been doing forms!"*

"You can't take me!" she screamed softly at him. Some people passing stopped to look. Everybody froze and remained silent until they moved on. Marina glared at Solomon. *"You are not ready!"* she hissed at him. "But if you do this, you can call me out, challenge me, and redeem yourself in front of your crew mates."

Solomon trembled with anger. He actually really liked her, but having been cast into the role of the bad guy with her from the beginning, they were having a hard time. *"Bitch!"*

"Fine! If you don't help me, somebody else will."

"Why *me?*"

"Because I trust you!" She watched the anger recede in his eyes. *"Please."* She waved a hand behind her. "All you've got to do is get us with these people, on La Gitana. *Right now.* I'll explain later." Her voice fell to a whisper. *"Please."*

Solomon felt himself deflate on the inside. He nodded. Leading the women and the strangers through the crowd, they all began running. Into the pirates, through the pirates, away from the pirates, towards the docks. In a few minutes, they were on the longboat, headed towards the ship. They did the short ride in silence, only the sound of the water against the boat. Soon, they found themselves on deck of La Gitana.

Marina stood facing the natives, the others at her back. "I am Marina. I am Carlos Gaitano's accountant. This is Salomé, my sister. Solomon is La Gitana's Boatswain, and Rouge is Captain of the Sea Gypsy." She looked at each of them, her eyes caressing their faces. "We don't have much time right now, but I want to prove to you that I am whom I say I am." She turned to the couple. "You must be Joaquin and Reina." She rushed to explain, at their shocked expression. "I know Leilani. Live close to her in Encantada. I take care of your babies." She rubbed the girl's arm as she began crying again.

Turning to the silver-eyed man, she looked at him through slit eyes. "You must be Francois' father." He nodded. "Francois got fresh with me," she informed him. "I took care of it. You might want to have a talk with him."

The man threw back his head and laughed. "I will punish him myself!" he cried happily.

Marina finally turned back to the dreadlocked man. She studied him silently for a moment. He did look like Caribe. An exact, older, more mature version of Caribe. She blinked back tears. Drawing Salomé to stand next to her, she addressed him. "We are visitors." They saw recognition in the older man's eyes. "You must be Don Manuel."

The man bowed deeply, taking each of their hands and kissing them.

When he straightened again, tears shimmered in his eyes. "At your service."

Salomé laughed. "Caribe came with us in this trip. He is on shore right now, but he will be back later with the others."

Don Manuel nodded, his tears falling. "It will be a pleasure to reunite with my son."

"We will surprise him," offered Marina, hugging him briefly. "For now, we have to go back before all hell breaks loose." She looked at the Boatswain helplessly. "Solomon..."

The young man had been standing to one side quietly, observing the exchange. He shook his head in admiration. Taking over, he gave instructions. "Don Manuel, the men I have aboard will be more than happy to see that you and your companions are made comfortable for your return trip back to Encantada. I will row the ladies back ashore, before they are missed. You will be in good hands, and we will see you later. Eat, get some rest, and keep out of sight." The natives nodded. With a shrill whistle, Solomon called over one of the crew members that was back already, from shore. He spoke in the man's ear, and clapped him on the back. The man nodded and led the group of shocked islanders away. In a few minutes, Solomon and the women were back on shore. Once on land, they quickly raced back through the marketplace. Solomon stayed at the African girls' table.

As they parted, he looked into Marina's eyes, before shaking his head and turning away from her. The ladies continued on their way, until they were back where the men had left them. A few minutes later, they were reunited.

Giancarlo looked at their flushed faces. "Ladies! You look as if you have been running," he laughed.

Rouge tossed her head, distracting him. "It is so hot! We feel like we are dying here."

The men directed them to a small courtyard. It was not as nice as El Callejon, but it was quieter than the central marketplace. There, they found a table and had a late lunch, accompanied with a bottle of wine. After a nice meal, they stayed talking, enjoying the day. Being on dry land, and in good company, on a beautiful sunny day, made them all feel relaxed and happy.

"What is *El Baile del Luto*?" Salomé asked suddenly. "Isn't *luto*, mourning? You have a *mourning* dance?" She frowned.

Gaitano laughed. "Not quite. It is not a dance, and it is not of mourning." He turned sideway in the bench they were sitting in, his legs straddling it. Putting his arms around Marina's waist, he slid her over to him, until she rested between his legs. He just held there, not doing anything yet, aware of her discomfort. "It is an event where we get together and have a good time. We all wear black." His eyes caressed Marina's profile.

"So does everybody dress up?" Salomé asked curiously.

"If you wish," answered Giancarlo, studying Rouge. "As long as you wear black, you are dressed up."

Salomé, ever insistent, turned to the lady pyrate. "What do you wear to this thing?"

Rouge looked at Giancarlo, her lips twitching. "Black." They laughed.

Gaitano lowered his head to Marina's, his mouth close to her ear, so no one else could hear. "You are distant," he murmured.

Marina closed her eyes, reveling in the vibration of his voice. "You are in your turf," she answered quietly. "I feel out of place."

"Still scared?" he asked, rubbing his nose on the tender spot below her ear.

She smiled. "Not with you."

"I miss you."

"And I, you."

"Let's make out."

Marina's eyes flew open, and she pulled back to look at him. *"Right here?"* she asked, in a shocked voice.

"Yes." He laughed, and pulled her closer to him. "If you wish."

"No!" she whispered.

Gaitano wrapped his arms tight around her, nuzzling her again. "We are not aboard the ship. We are on shore, and we are having a good time."

"Yes," she agreed. "We also have company," she pointed out.

Gaitano chuckled. He caught her earlobe between his teeth and pulled gently. "Excuses, my friend."

Marina squirmed in his arms. "By the way, friends don't make out." Gaitano pulled back to look at her. His eyes searched hers. He could feel Marina's heart pound in her chest, under his arm. He smiled slowly. "Then, I guess we are not friends." He kissed her suddenly, swiftly, and looked at her again.

Marina gasped. "I thought you were my friend!" she whispered.

He shrugged. "I am trying. You can't make up your mind." He laughed as he caught the flash of anger in her eyes. He pressed his lips against her ear, once more. "Marina. You are my accountant, you are my friend, and you are my makeout partner."

Marina turned in his arms and put hers around him. She carefully pressed her left breast against his chest, until their hearts beat on top of one another. She couldn't see the pirate close his eyes with emotion over her head, as she laid her head on his shoulder. They shuddered. Behind them, their companions watched in silence. Marina held him tighter, and turned her head to whisper in his ear. "Carlos," she said softly, and her voice broke. She tried again. "Carlos, papi, have you ever thought that I may want to be *none* of those things to you?" She gasped, as he buried his face in her neck and took a deep breath, squeezing her tight. To their friends, it looked as if they were melting together. "That maybe I want to be more?" She put her hands on his shoulders and pushed him back from her, capturing his face between hands. "I'm scared out of my mind," she confessed quietly. Their eyes devoured everything they touched. They seemed to move in slow motion, finally closing their eyes when they were upon one another. Then their mouths pressed against each other. The other two couples stared, still silent. Slowly, the expressions on their faces became ones of laughter, joy, pride, and surprise. The couple didn't notice. Marina wanted to eat him up. And as she felt her mind leaving her body, she broke away. Carlos gasped. His eyes flew open. They searched hers, hungrily. Marina caressed his face. Tears stung her eyes.

"*Bruja*," he accused in a whisper.

Marina smiled to herself. Making herself snap out of it, she buried her fingers in his hair, and grabbing handfuls of it, pulled his head back so she could look at him better. "I want to go home. There is a party tonight, and I have nothing to wear."

Marina closed her eyes. They were in the longboat, Giancarlo and Caribe rowing across the water, to La Gitana. She sat in the back, with Indio and Salomé. Up in front, Solomon was speaking in Gaitano's ear. Salomé grasped her hand and locked fingers with her, in support. Indio watched, not understanding, not saying anything. Marina opened her eyes in time to see Carlos Gaitano look back, straight into them. Her heart skipped a beat, but he didn't say anything.

Once on deck, she sat by a pile of rope, not wanting to go below deck, until everything came out. As if in a daze, she listened as Gaitano called a quick meeting of the crew. He recounted what happened, omitting who the natives were. The guests were brought up. The crew welcomed them with cries of recognition. The young couple shuffled forward first, followed by Francois' father. By the time Don Manuel's dreadlocks made an appearance, Caribe was screaming.

"*Papá! Papá!*" He ran into his father's arms, no longer a young man, but a little boy, needing his daddy.

It seemed like La Gitana herself cheered, rocking in joy at the impossible reunion. Marina blinked away tears, and she felt Salomé nudge her. She looked up and realized, the men were cheering them.

Caribe came over and threw his arms around them, kissing them both passionately on the face. He couldn't speak. The girls hugged him, with all their might. When he drew back, tears were falling. He shook his head, and smiled apologetically at them. He went back to his father. Marina and Salomé smiled at each other, as they wiped their own tears. Indio came, and led Salomé downstairs. When Marina went to her own cabin, Gaitano was already there. His arms were behind his head, cushioning it, as he stretched out in the hammock, facing the bed. He looked at her through slit eyes. Marina looked at him. He still didn't say anything. She sighed and turned her back on him. Crawling into bed, she promptly shut out the world. And him with it.

Thunder crashed. Jackson turned around and grinned, as the women screamed. He went back inside and joined them, huddled around the candlelight. They had spent a good enough day. He had taken his parents to the cave, first, where they could see for themselves, where the events had occurred. Now, they were just hanging out, waiting for the storm. It hadn't been an easy day for them, but their determination to see this through had kept their spirits up as best as possible. They had gone exploring, first, in the directions Jackson knew lay certain places, like the town, the docks, the village. Of course there was nothing there, now, but Jackson insisted they knew where everything was.

Shayla called him over. "Jax, come here, baby."

She was sitting on one of the piles of blankets with Sloane. They had gone over the girls' belongings, gaining reassurance from the simple articles they had in their bags. They had found the sketch Jackson had made of his sisters, and had compared it to the ones done by Caribe. Actually, Jackson's wasn't that bad. He could be just as accomplished as Caribe, if he wanted. Jackson crouched down by his moms. "What's up?"

"What is it that Marina does again, baby? I know Salo works at a dress shop..."

Jackson grinned. "Marina takes care of babies."

The women laughed, delighted. Shayla beamed with pride, nodding. "Uh - huh. That's my girl! Taking care of babies, is what we do."

Sloane shook her white blond hair out of her face. "I thought you said she was doing the books for the head pirate?"

Jackson nodded. "She is. He wanted her to do them so bad, that he started sending them over to her place, so that she could do them at home." He smiled at Sloane. "Mami, this guy *really* likes Marina."

Sloane nodded at him, her eyes caressing his face, thoughtfully. "How do you feel about that, Jax?" She smiled. "Do *you* like *him*? Is this *boyfriend* material? Does *she* like him?"

Jackson rolled his eyes. "Yeah, she likes him. I thought he was stalking her at first, but then I realized that this man was truly attracted to her. I don't think he realizes just how much, yet." He thought for a moment. "I like him. I know he would never do anything to hurt her willingly. It would have to be one of those things, you know, if it didn't work out and he broke her heart or something." He frowned. "Although to tell you the truth, I think the heartbroken one will be him, if this doesn't work out for them." He grinned, suddenly. "Actually, the guy is crazy about her." He looked straight into his mom's blue eyes and nodded. "This guy is the real thing, Mami. I think they are excellent for each other."

Sloane nodded, her eyes watering. Shayla waved her hand in the air. "Oh, hush, now, don't be sad," she whispered to her friend. She turned to her son. "What about Salomé?"

Jackson laughed. "That is true love. This guy would kill and/or die for her." He shook his head. "They are great together. Look real good, too." Shayla laughed, tears shining in her eyes.

Jackson distracted them, then, and began talking to them about other things. He described in vivid details the village and the natives, the docks and the workers, the town and its pirates. He talked about the native dances, and about doing forms on the beach, early in the mornings. He recounted tales about the Siren's Lair, and about Silas and Jimmy behind the bar. He mentioned Pedro Barbosa, and Padre Ignacio. He told them about Max and Larissa, and John Kline's General Store. He talked about Leila and Caribe, the dreams and the visitors. By the time Jackson was done talking, they had a vivid picture of what was in store for them.

The men joined them. They had been off by themselves, mourning in their own way, just being next to each other, in silence. Now, they were ready to face whatever it is that lay before them. It had started raining now, and thunder rumbled more urgently. Joe Banks turned to his son. "Jackson. When these time warps occur, are you aware of them? Can you actually see them?"

Jackson frowned. "I don't know, really. I slept through both of mine."

Pablo nodded, and looked back over his shoulder at the cave entrance. "There must be some physical activity," his voice rumbled. His dark eyes looked haunted as he avoided eye contact with his family. He was doing everything humanly possible to stop his heart from breaking.

Joe stood up. "There is only one way to find out." Standing up, he went to the mouth of the cave. The rest followed him. They all looked out.

The wind was whipping the foliage around the entrance, rain falling steadily. Out over the ocean, lightning danced over the water, as if on a dare, lighting everything above and below it. Waves churned, and began a slow, circular movement. The family watched mesmerized, as the black clouds above, began their own movement, in the opposite direction. Everything began spinning faster. Suddenly, a funnel formed, linking sky to sea, sharing the same water. Everybody held their breath. They witnessed the frenzied water rush into the sky, and hang suspended for a moment. Suddenly, it was as if a shock wave came rushing at them, over the water, creating a ripple in the air that washed right over them. They gasped. Then, the sky opened, and dropped the water back into the ocean. The storm continued, slowly, painfully losing force.

Pablo Aguilar looked around at the rest of his family. They all had the same smiles on their faces. "That was it," he laughed.

Joe agreed. "That must have been it." He put his arm around his wife, kissing her forehead. "Tomorrow we look for Marina and Salomé."

El Baile del Luto. Marina leaned against the pillar and sighed. They had just arrived, a short while ago, and she felt as if she were in a dream. It had taken them a while getting ready, what with not knowing what to wear. But Gaitano had outdone himself. He had told her when he woke her up, that he had a surprise for her. It had turned out to be the clothes for the party. She smiled to herself, loving the way her outfit made her feel. Like a tramp. The way every woman should feel, with the object of her affection. Tonight, the clothes made the woman. Call it *Vintage Gypsy.* The bustier was a dream. Underwire, to make cleavage where there is usually none. Made of the most beautiful leather, down to the waist, soft and buttery, molding to her form. A wide strip of lace made it into a halter, gathered where it was attached to the leather, coming from the top of the bustier, slightly to the sides, and going around her neck. The skirt that came out of the bustier was lace, shimmery to the eye, liquid to the touch. All black. Black, as night. The better to show off her spectacular tan. To showcase her silver jewelry. Chandeliers made out of silver coins at her ears, cascades of the same at one wrist, and on the opposite ankle. She had gotten them as payment for services rendered as the accountant of La Gitana. The pirate had outdone himself. Her other arm was bare. She laughed to herself, because she jingled as she walked. Marina knew she looked good. No makeup, save for kohl around her eyes and stain on her lips, her tan could stand on its own. She had caught sight of herself in one of the huge mirrors that were placed around the room, and her reflection had made her gasp. She felt like a beautiful gypsy. The best part was, that Gaitano had dressed her himself. It had been an incredible sensual experience for both of them, charged with sexual tension that made their skin tingle, when they looked at each other. The only thing that had come out of it, had been a kiss, and in their eyes, the promise of more to come.

They had gone back to El Callejon and the courtyard. This time, to a different room. Cut right into the hill enclosing the town, it was a cavern. Torches were placed in strategic places, making shadows flicker and dance on the walls. All around her were pirates socializing. A few more ships had come in, during the day, and there were even more strange faces. It was an exclusive party. Apparently, only certain people were invited. Marina recognized the committee from this morning, as they milled about. It was amazing to her, how one color could have such variations. Jai-Ling wore a stunning silk kimono, with exquisite gold and silver threads making an awesome sea dragon design on the back. Suleiman's robe was made of a thin, gauzy material dyed black, as well as his turban, which was wrapped with a rope of black pearls. Both men wore wide legged flowing pants. Sultan wore no shirt over his black pants, and boots, a single lion's claw set in gold, hanging over his bare chest, his nipples pierced with small shiny gold hoops. Jack's bright red hair stood out among the crowd, as he sidled up to people, greeting them cheerfully, a wine glass in his hand. There were lady pyrates among the men, also. Some in dresses, actually, to her surprise, but most in the uniform of shirt and pants, all black for the party. Rouge had created a commotion at her entrance. She wouldn't have been recognized, if it wasn't for her spectacular fiery hair. Her outfit was formfitting, the fabric hugging every single inch of her phenomenal body. The beautiful black silk shirt was open at her chest, framing a stunning gold and pearl cross hanging over her cleavage. Elegant gold hoops graced her ears, a single large pearl hanging from the middle of them. Giancarlo glided to her as soon as she entered the room, and hadn't left her side since.

Indio and Salomé made a striking couple, as they quietly stood to one side, next to each other, silently surveying the scene. They were dressed as twins. Boots, pants and sleeveless leather vests. Where Indio's hung loose, Salomé's hugged her curves. They both had their hair braided down the middle of their backs. Indio wore the usual leather arm bands and strands of turquoises at his wrists. Feathers adorned his hair, and under his open shirt, strings of turquoises hung on his chest. Salomé wore her beloved leather band, and bangles on her other arm. Beautiful silver and turquoise earrings hung from her ears, and feathers also adorned her hair. They smiled at Marina, eyes twinkling, as she walked by them.

Marina glanced at the back of Carlos' head. His hair was black as night, and already curling around the collar of his shirt. Her eyes drifted down to the seat of his pants. Nice fit. She smiled to herself, as her eyes caressed him. He had actually been mysteriously gone for a while, and she was just now seeing him again. She had caught glimpses of him in an extra room off the cave, where there had been just men for a while, drinking, and passing what looked like a peace pipe. The whole crew of La Gitana had been in that room at one moment or another, and they had all come back, looking much happier and relaxed. Marina smiled to herself again, shaking her head, feeling relaxed herself. A few minutes ago, Caribe had called them over to a hidden corner, and had shared some of the peace pipe with Salomé and herself, when the men weren't watching. As a result, now everybody felt good.

Marina strolled casually, walking around the perimeter of the room. Everybody wanted to stare at her, and she met each look bravely, and with a smile. She shook hands with everyone, and introduced herself as the Gaitanos' accountant. She had borrowed some paper and a charcoal pencil from Caribe, and was now collecting names of pirates, crew members, and ships, quietly making inventory to work with, later. The meanest pirates would lose their frowns and smile back. Having done a circuit around the room, she gave Caribe the paper for safekeeping. Suddenly, she was opposite Gaitano, facing him. Her eyes caressed him. Carlos was stunning, all in black. The only thing he had of color, were the eyes in his face. He looked like a creature of the night. *God, I just want to eat him up.* Her heart fluttered, as he looked behind him, and turned back suddenly, a frown creasing his forehead. His head moved back and forth. *Looking for me?* He found her.

Marina caught her breath as Carlos' eyes devoured her. His smile was slow, seductive, his eyes never leaving hers. Over the space between them, he reached a hand out to her. She smiled, playful. Dramatically, she stretched out her hand, her fingers waving, until it seemed to both of them, that they touched his. They laughed silently at each other over the distance. Carlos blew her a kiss. Marina blew him one back. *I love you, baby*. He gestured with his head. She saw his lips move. *Come here*. She smiled. *Okay, okay*. She made her way around the rest of the circular room. Torches glowed brightly and the murmur grew louder as the musicians got ready, setting up to the side of the curved wall, strumming their guitars in preparation.

"Carlos!"

Marina froze. The voice was definitely female, and sounded a little too delighted, as if her acquaintance with the man were a little bit more. Marina decided that this was so, as she looked dumbfounded, at the woman standing in front of her guy.

Carlos looked as if he had been caught unawares. It was definitely a surprise for him, or at least he hadn't been ready. "Lola?" His frown came back, but his good breeding took over. "Lola!" He glanced over at where Marina had been standing, before looking back at the woman.

"Carlos, amado!"

Marina slinked her way closer, making it to his side, and turned to look at the woman, from a closer viewpoint. Black hair, so dark it was almost blue, was pulled back tightly in a bun. The cheeks were high, jaw line and chin, almost severe. But, oh, so beautiful! She could be a fashion model. Deep black eyes flickered over her and turned back to Gaitano. *Her eyes are dead*. Stuck in her hair was a beautifully carved peinilla made out of black wood, and inlaid with mother of pearl. It was holding a beautiful mantilla, worn and faded, almost a shame, against all that beauty. Her dress was black satin, whispering as she moved, tiers of faded black lace, cascading almost to the floor. It wasn't that she didn't look good. Lola was dazzling. There was one thing wrong, nonetheless. The woman obviously needed new clothes. But she still managed to stop the room. Her body was breathtaking.

Marina looked at the pirate, and raised her eyebrows when he glanced at her. *Splakow!* Gaitano looked away, frowning. A smile hovered around her mouth, but her eyes showed nothing of her true feelings. Not yet.

Lola put her hands on Gaitano's shoulders. She leaned towards him, her eyes eating him up, cleavage in his face, Victoria's Secret breasts straining to their fullest extent against the faded fabric.

Marina smiled. "*Papi*," she murmured, "magnificent as they are, her *tetas* are going to pop out." Gaitano scowled at her.

Lola ignored her. "It has been so long, *mi amor*." She moved in closer, lunging for a kiss. Carlos' hand shot up, catching her mouth. Lola drew back, looking at him, puzzled. Finally, she took a good look at Marina, her eyes insultingly raking her from her hair to her feet.

Marina smiled sweetly at her. *Not so sure of ourselves now, are we?*

Lola looked away. "Carlos," she purred, her eyes going from loathing to ardent lust, "let us get reacquainted, *querido*, for old time's sake."

Marina screamed inside her head. *Who the hell is this bitch?!*

Carlos coughed. They were beginning to draw attention. The people right next to them had already ceased their own conversation, to tune into theirs, with morbid curiosity. He felt his head buzzing, and everything slowing down. He caught Lola's wrist and pushed it away from him firmly, as she raised her hand to stroke his cheek. Lola's eyes went dead. He glanced at Marina. She stood frozen, almost in shock. Her fingernails were digging into her palms, and a scary stillness was settling over her. More people stopped what they were doing. Silence spread through the room in a rippling wave. From the single throne in the room, his uncle watched quietly, eyes sharp on the triangle of young people, hand idly caressing the sword at his side. Even the musicians, done with their fine tuning, were smirking as they looked on knowingly, hands poised on their guitars and drums. From across the room, Rouge made as if to go to them, her female intuition guiding her to stand by her new friend. Giancarlo slid an arm around her waist and pulled her close, his muscles tightening, as she strained against him. His other arm crossed over her chest, and drew her back to him, his mouth against her ear, whispering urgently. Rouge let her head fall back against his shoulder, and relaxed, her eyes alert, riveted on the pirate and the two women. Giancarlo stroked her arms absentmindedly, his heart beating faster, as he too, watched.

Gaitano's eyes burned blue ice, as he realized the extent of the predicament he was in. Most recent Golden Rule to follow: Never, *ever*, get caught by an *ex*-girlfriend, while out on a date with your *future* girlfriend. Inside his head, he groaned. He blinked slowly, as his fingers let go of the woman's wrist. Marina was barely aware of Indio and Salomé appearing magically, next to her. Carlos looked at the woman and smiled slowly, seductively, eyes smoldering beneath thick, long, black lashes that hid his true feelings. He was outraged. She was not going to mess this up for him. "Lola," he said clearly, his voice reaching out into the silence of friends and strangers caught in the middle of a drama. "I remember you fondly, and gratefully," he told her, rolling his eyes, as chuckles and giggles rippled around them. "But I have brought a companion here, tonight, that deserves all of my respect." He snaked a hand around Marina's waist, pulling her next to him, while his other hand seemed to ward Lola off. "This is Marina. She is my accountant." He squeezed her possessively, making a muscle twitch in Lola's cheek. He looked into Marina's eyes. "Marina is my best friend and my confidant." He turned back to Lola. "I brought her here with me, and I intend to leave with her." He absently brought Marina's hand to his lips. "She makes me happy." He winked at Lola as if confiding in her. "But I thank you for your attention. I am flattered that you consider me worth getting reacquainted with." Marina rolled her eyes. He smiled. "You look more beautiful than ever."

Salomé sidled up to him, smiling. "Nice catch, papi."

"Let me dance for you."

"No." Marina shook her head. Certainly, she hadn't heard right.

Carlos stiffened. "No."

Salomé laughed. "Girl, bitch wants to dance for your man!" Turning to Lola, she glared at her. "You are messing with my sister's man, bitch!"

Indio rumbled in warning. *"Salomé!"*

Marina pulled away from Carlos. He was *her* date. She glanced at him, furious at finding herself in the middle of this nightmare. "You brought me here." Her breath came out fast and hard, as she backed away from him, body thrumming with anticipation. "*Respect me*," she growled at him.

Carlos' heart dropped. He reached out a hand towards her. "Marina..."

"No!"

"*Divina...*"

"*No!*" She backed away from him, as he took a step towards her. Pirates seemed to surround her, creating a wall behind her. "Let her dance for you."

Carlos stared at her. He went to take one more step towards her, but caught himself in time. Over her head, he met the eyes of the members of his council. He looked back at her, again. He had never seen Marina so outraged before. Of course, it was his fault, once you got into all the details about how he should have expected something like this to happen once he was back in Carey, where he had lived for so many years. But he was a man. Why would he even think about something like that happening? There had never been any need to prepare for such a situation. Besides, he had not remembered Lola, because he had never loved her. There was a difference. Marina, he would have never forgotten. And with that realization, he could finally speak. "You are serious."

Marina looked down and shrugged. She turned her face to him again, focusing on a place right above his head. Carlos frowned, searching her evading eyes. "I can dance, papi," she taunted. Then, seeking distance, she circled Indio and Salomé, until the two stood between them. Carlos started towards her.

Indio moved. He slapped his hands down on Carlos' shoulders, stopping him in his tracks. "Look at you," he laughed. "You are making a scene." All the females in the room nodded, the lady pyrates murmuring in agreement. The crew of La Gitana looked at each other. Caribe moved closer, charcoal pencil flying over his paper. The musicians laughed softly. So did the rest of the guests, and just as suddenly, quieted down.

Energy shifted. The flames flickered from the torches around the room, casting shadows on the ceiling and walls. A new pirate stepped in. Some people stepped back. The man was dressed in all black, to end all. He looked stunning. Open necked shirt made of the most beautiful liquid silk, black as a starless night, showcasing the man's developed, scarred chest. Billowing sleeves suggested at the man's powerful arms. The pants were tight, of course, black as coal. The boots were to the calves and rolled over in a wide cuff, made of the finest, softest leather. His sword was sheathed in black leather at his hip, only the jeweled hilt visible, as it sparkled in the torch-light. His white blond hair was slicked back from his beautiful, clean-shaven face. Smile perfect. Black eyes laughing.

He looks like a black angel. Marina shuddered. *He looks like the Devil himself!*

The pirate laughed. "Hello, to all! Am I late?" His voice was rich, and seductive, his eyes sharp as they passed over the women in the room. "Or is this just beginning?" His eyes swept the room once more, and came to rest on the group. He walked towards them, stopping when he spotted the brave.

Indio moved, shielding Marina, and pulling Salomé to his side. "Xavier." Just that one word. It echoed around the room.

The pirate inclined his head. "Indio." The intruder's eyes turned to the woman next to him. He smiled. "Aaaahh. You must be the enchanting, Miss Salomé." He bowed slightly. "I have heard a lot about you."

Salomé smiled. "Not all good, I'm sure."

Xavier smiled with her. He sighed. "You assume correctly. Although, what is good, and what is not?" He took her hand and brought it to his lips, kissing it respectfully, before letting it go. "Is it not but a matter of perspective?" He laughed, and turned to Gaitano, giving Indio a wide berth. Marina observed this and filed it under: *I've got to ask about this, later.* The man moved on to Carlos. He bowed slightly. "Gaitano."

Carlos nodded. Inside, he felt as if he were going to explode at any moment. He couldn't believe any of this was happening. "Xavier."

"I have been hearing things about you, too. All good." He chuckled. "Too many, for my taste." A shrug. A sly look from behind hooded eyes. "I also heard about your companion. I am looking for an accountant, myself. Where is she?" Marina held her breath, not moving from behind Indio, as the pirate looked around. "I will employ her. Where is she?"

Carlos snarled at him. "She already has a job!"

Xavier cocked his head to one side, smiling infuriatingly. His eyebrows raised, slowly, betraying the man's amusement. "I will buy her."

The jolt was collective among everybody around them. Salomé gasped.

Indio moved the girls closer to him. Marina's stomach dropped. She looked up wildly, searching for help. Her eyes found the council. Their stone faces and still bodies reassured her, as they looked back at her. Jai-Ling's kimono hung open, his hands clenched at his sides. Rouge and Jack were on opposite corners, their fiery heads seeming to burn with light of their own. Suleiman's eyes seemed to be of glass, the firelight dancing on the wicked blade of his curved sword, the only indication of life in him. Sultan's chest flexed, the lion's claw rolling on it. And from his throne, Don Miguel Gaitano stared at her, the slightest frown on his face, in his eyes, a warning, stronger than any shake of his head. Marina pressed her lips together, and nodded. Quietly, she made the sign of the cross. She bowed her head for a moment and clenched her fists, her muscles rippling along her arms and back. "Not for sale," she murmured.

Xavier met her eyes, delighted. "She has spirit," he said with awe in his voice. He looked at Gaitano and laughed. "I will take her!"

Carlos roared.

"*Carlos! My son!* You look like you need some fresh air. It is quite intoxicating in here."

Everybody froze. Into their sanctuary strode Don Carlos Gaitano y Mendoza, the fabulous María Isabel Sandoval on his arm.

They were dressed to kill. His pirate outfit was head to toe, black silk and black leather. He too, carried a sword, but the jewels on his were blood-red rubies. The family resemblance was unmistakable. Carlos was nothing but a younger, even more beautiful version of his father. The older Gaitano was aging like fine wine, however. The lines his incredibly handsome face had settled into, over the years, as well as the silver streaking his jet black hair, added to his appeal. Eyes, the color of old silver, twinkled merrily. Marina turned her attention to the man, immediately attracted to him. *Carlos, thirty years from now.*

The woman reached for her son's face with both hands and a glorious smile on her red lips, as she drew him down for a kiss. Her skin was beautiful and milky, standing out against her black dress, making her look like a female vampyre. But she wasn't. She was Carlos' mother. Marina felt her heart melt, and tears burn her eyes. The woman was everyone's dream mom. Elegance personified, she reminded her of her own moms. Her hair was still pitch black, and her eyes were sea green, captivating. A small gold cross snuggled between her breasts, suspended from a thin gold chain. A wedding band and a diamond ring graced her left hand. Other than that, the rest of her jewelry matched her husband's outrageous rubies, framing her chest, dripping from her ears, sparkling like fire in the light of the cavern.

Carlos trembled in his mother's embrace. He felt as if he were losing control. María Isabel rubbed her hands up and down his back, soothing him, murmuring in his ear. After a while of this, the woman stretched her hand out towards Indio. Tears filled her eyes, as she looked up at the brave. *"Mi bebé!"* she laughed, holding Indio tight as he stepped into their embrace. Nobody moved or spoke as they stood there for a moment, the mother and the two brothers.

The music started softly. People moved back. All eyes were on Lola.

Don Carlos looked pointedly at his son. "I suppose you have provided entertainment for us, Carlitos." He glanced up at the ceiling, and back down at his boy, the smile dancing on his lips. "As usual."

Carlos shook his head, not trusting himself to speak. Xavier laughed. He bowed gracefully and walked away, his sailors flanking him, to go lean against a wall. The sound of castanets filled the room.

A whisper at first. A tease. Something at the back of your mind. Lola moved to the center of the room, commanding attention. Marina moved away, to watch, keeping as far from the pirate Xavier, as possible. Don Miguel Gaitano silently stood from his throne, crossing the room to greet his brother. They embraced, smiling into each other's eyes, as the music got stronger. More confident. Lola began moving, her arms lifting slowly, fingers curling into the air. She held a pose, and began dancing, lace whipping about her legs.

Don Carlos spoke, his eyes carefully scanning the guests present. "Am I wrong, or did we just walk in on two women fighting over Carlitos?"

Don Miguel chuckled. "Not quite. More like Carlitos fighting for one woman, as he tries to get rid of the other." María Isabel smiled to herself, enjoying the conversation between the two older Gaitanos.

"Who is he keeping and who is he getting rid of?" Don Carlos asked, amused, as he watched his son. Carlos crossed the room, all crackling energy, to the throne his uncle just vacated. He turned around and let himself fall into it heavily, his hand automatically reaching down to fondle his sword, just as the older pirate had done. Indio moved silently to stand next to him, his face like stone, only his eyes hinting at life. Don Carlos let his eyes caress the face of this other boy of his, and was met with a wink. He smiled.

Don Miguel coughed, choking on the laughter. "Guess." María Isabel rolled her eyes and bit the inside of her cheeks to keep from laughing.

Don Carlos pretended to be confused. He waved his hand at the dancing beauty. "Lola has always been there for him."

Don Miguel covered his eyes, shoulders shaking with silent laughter. "It is not Lola he is fighting for."

María Isabel couldn't stop herself anymore. She scolded them quietly, laughing almost as hard as they were. "Oh, stop, you two! You are quite impossible! Leave the poor boy alone. You have always amused yourselves with him, even when he was little." Her eyes met her son's over the distance. He looked away immediately, the older Gaitanos' amusement feeding his fire.

"What about Xavier?" Don Carlos asked, becoming serious.

Don Miguel grimaced. "I think he means trouble, *hermano*. A lot of trouble."

Don Carlos nodded thoughtfully, his eyes narrowing on the blond pirate leaning on the opposite wall. "Carlitos would never fight with one of his own, over any *woman*."

Don Miguel nodded in agreement. "Exactly, Carlos. Marina isn't just *any* woman." The men fell silent, watching the scene unfold. Meanwhile, Lola danced her heart out, to no avail.

Caribe slinked to Gaitano's other side, his face fierce, as he sketched, caught up in the moment. Rouge stirred in the cradle of Giancarlo's arms. She pressed her mouth to his ear. "Why is Gaitano so upset? What is it with him and Marina?"

Giancarlo's voice caressed her, his laugh soft. "I think we are about to find out." He buried his face in her neck, breathing deeply, making her laugh.

Salomé put an arm around Marina, as the music ended, and Lola went to stand in front of their pirate, chest heaving with exertion, beads of sweat running down her face. They watched him smile and thank her absently, his eyes going back to Marina.

Salomé pressed her head to Marina's. "Mami," she whispered. "You want me to take care of the music for you?" At Marina's nod, she gave her a squeeze and went to the musicians, swinging her hips. "*Buenas noches*," she began, dazzling them with a smile. The men grinned. "My sister is going to dance next, for Capitán Gaitano. I would appreciate it if you could make it special for them." She had their full attention. "*Caballeros*," she said, bending over and putting her hands on her knees, so that her cleavage was in their faces. She waited as they ogled her chest for a moment, and smiled when they finally met her sparkling green eyes. "I need you to play, as if you were making love to me." She slapped her hands on her hips, and moved them to her butt, and up around her front, casually over her breasts, hugging herself. She smiled, as their eyes flew to hers again. "With your instruments." They laughed, shaking their heads, enjoying the game. And the music started.

Marina closed her eyes for a moment, blocking everybody else out, but the man before her. She opened her eyes and looked at him.

He was slouching down, legs stretched out in front of him, a fierce scowl on his face. She licked her lips and smiled. Carlos watched her suspiciously, as she strained her ears, absorbing the music. She began moving slowly, hips undulating, as she got closer. He heard Indio catch his breath. Glancing at him, Carlos caught his brother staring at his girl. He chuckled. Indio shook his head and raised his eyebrows at him. Caribe shook the dreadlocks out of his face and laughed at them both. The music was like nothing they had ever heard before. The musicians were clear in the instructions they received. It had been to play as if they were making love to Salomé. Well, even as their eyes feasted on her, their fingers played the hell out of their instruments. It was musical lust. Everybody felt it. Carlos looked over at the corner where the music was coming from. Salomé had her hands over her head, the fabric of her shirt straining against her breasts, as she belly danced for the musicians, conducting them. He heard Indio take in a shaky breath as he, also, caught sight of Salomé. He turned his eyes back to the woman in front of him, no longer scowling, not yet smiling.

Dios mío... Marina trembled inside as she came nearer. *I am crazy about this man.* In the back of her mind, she was aware of every eye in the house, on her. But the only thing she cared about was the man in front of her. She swung her hips as she reached him. Swaying to the music, she reached out to stroke his face with one hand, while tapping time on her hip, with the other. The pirate froze. He only saw her. She took her hand away, and tossed her hair back, earrings tinkling in rhythm. Bending towards him, she cupped her breasts over the soft leather of the bustier, and squeezed them together, as if offering them to him. He watched for a moment, mesmerized, before his eyes flew to her face. She let go of her breasts, and straightened slowly, her hands gliding down her body, to stop at the top of her thighs. Indio groaned. Marina winked at him. Salomé threw him a loving glance. The pirates laughed softly, knowing smiles on their faces. Gaitano's eyes caressed her fingers, as she bunched the lace into her hands, slowly pulling her skirt up, fingers lingering sensually, before letting the fabric fall again. His eyes went to her face once more. She licked her lips. His heart skipped a beat. His pants began to get tighter. Caribe grinned, as he caught the pirate's soft moan. Marina turned around, tossing her hair, straddling his outstretched legs. Slowly, she lowered her backside on his lap, placing her hands on top of his. She began skimming her butt softly, from side to side, on his thighs. He began breathing heavier. Marina smiled, as she loosened his fingers from their grasp on the arms of the chair. She glanced at the pirates in front of her. They were all smiling. She winked at them and held up the pirate's hands in front of her chest. Closing her eyes, she licked her lips. Bending forward, she shook her breasts into the palms of his hands so that he was cupping them, and leaned back on his chest, her hands holding his tight against her. The pirates groaned. Marina laughed wickedly at them. The music tore through their senses, arousing them. She smiled, as she slid his hands down her ribs, over her belly, to her thighs. Pushing herself up, she got off his lap and faced him again. In the background, she could hear the pirates. They were cheering her on, and taunting him. Looking into his eyes, she put a knee on either side of him, on the seat. Marina straddled him, her hands, once again, on top of his. Carlos licked his lips, his eyes smoldering. She lowered herself, until his face was at her chest. To the delight of the guests, she held his head against her for a moment, stroking his thick hair. As she held his head, she stretched and arched her back slowly, so that his face was now at her belly. Her long hair brushed his legs and the top of his boots. The pirates stomped and cheered, catcalls and whistles echoing in the cavern. The couple didn't hear them. Marina returned slowly to her position, once again holding Carlos' head at her chest, before lifting his chin so he could look at her. Lowering her head, she licked his lips. Drawing back, her whole body rubbed against his. She dropped on his lap suddenly, pressing a kiss on his surprised mouth. His hands began to go up, but she held them down. Pushing herself up, she slid off his lap, her hand lingering on his face, the other one, once again beating a rhythm on her hip. Then she turned her back on him, and throwing him one last sultry look over her shoulder, she walked away from him, once more, undulating her hips, silver coins tinkling, as the music died down. The pirates all laughed, as Marina came back to them. Carlos couldn't move. Salomé high-fived her girl.

All of a sudden, Lola faced Marina. The woman was trembling from anger, her hands shaking, as she accused her. She spat out the word. *"Puta!"*

Marina shook her head, laughing inside. She couldn't believe it. Salomé stood by her, and faced the flamenco dancer. "Baby, did she just call you wh at I think she just called you?"

Marina smiled and nodded. "Yeah, she sure did." Turning back to Lola, she raised her eyebrows at her. *"Tu madre."*

The pirates laughed. Lola screeched as she lunged at her. Marina blocked her and slapped her soundly with her free hand. Rouge broke away from Giancarlo, going to stand behind her friends. Lola staggered, her face to her hand.

Salomé taunted her. "I told you he was my sister's man. He doesn't want you." Lola screamed again, throwing herself at Marina, claws out.

Marina slapped her again, her hair flying around her face with the movement. She was furious. Never in her life, had she fought before with another woman. She had been trained since she was a little girl, to always command respect, and maintain her place as a lady. A catfight was just too much beneath her. She would have never been caught dead in a situation like this, with just any guy. But this was different. It was all about him. *Carlos.* She found him. He followed her home. She was keeping him. He was hers. End of story. Marina slapped Lola again. *"Respect me!"*

Carlos sprung to his feet. *"Enough!"* he roared.

Marina turned cold eyes on him. *"Tell this bitch to back off!"*

María Isabel gasped softly, as she looked on from her place by her husband and his brother. "Who *is* that girl?"

The men chuckled, exchanging glances. Don Carlos nuzzled his wife. "I don't know, but I want you to dance for me like that," he murmured in her ear. She pushed him away, laughing, intrigue sparkling in her eyes. Don Carlos smacked his lips and winked at her, before turning to look at the older pirate next to them. Don Miguel nodded at the question in his brother's eyes. Don Carlos smiled at his wife. "If I am not mistaken, *querida,* that is the mother of your future grandchildren."

"She is?" she asked, a smile spreading on her face.

Don Miguel nodded. "Carlitos doesn't know it yet." They laughed softly.

Lola screamed again, and lunged at Marina once more. Before anybody else could do anything, she was pulled back by Solomon.

The Boatswain shook his head, eyes wide, laughing at the woman. "You don't want to do that."

Marina turned back to Lola. "Want more?" She met Solomon's eyes. He hesitated. Marina scowled at him. He let Lola go. The woman screeched again, and flew at her once more, face contorted with rage and jealousy. Marina slapped her again. And again. And one more time.

The flamenco dancer went down, screaming.

"Aguilar!"

Marina froze. Not out of fear, but out of respect. Turning away from Lola, she looked at Carlos. Smiling, she licked her lips, and parting them, she breathed, in true Marilyn Monroe fashion, *"Capitán..."* Marina's sultry tone made the word drip sex.

The room became silent, as the couple faced each other. The sexual tension between them hung invisibly in the air, those closest to them, being able to see the desire in each of their eyes. The screaming woman fell quiet, cowering on the floor, her eyes wide as she looked at Marina, a hand to her face. A couple of Xavier's sailors helped her up, leading her to lean against a wall, leaving her alone, out of the way. Carlos was standing in front of his throne, thunder in his face. Without a word, she lifted her left hand, turning it slowly so he could see the back, her fingers rippling. *Nothing here.*

Carlos felt his stomach sink. Before his eyes, he saw everything slipping away. Marina challenged him with her eyes. She hadn't said anything, but he knew. Beside her, a movement caught his eye. Salomé lifted her own left hand, and pointed at the arm band on her wrist. Pressing her lips together, she nodded her head slowly, eyes wide. Everybody watched, unaware of the silent communication between him and the two women, waiting for him to do something. Only Caribe, who was right next to him, could hear his words. Carlos turned to Indio, his voice soft. "Papi, help me out here. Give me something to put on Marina. Please." Indio nodded. Slipping a string of turquoise beads off his wrist, he handed it to his Captain. Taking the bracelet, Carlos crossed the floor to Marina. Standing in front of her, he took her left hand. Lifting it high in the air, he walked her around in a tight circle, for all to see. Looking into her eyes, he slipped the bracelet unto her wrist, pressing his lips to hers. Without saying a word to her, he dragged her behind him, back to the throne. Throwing himself into it, he yanked her down on his lap, pinning her hands so she couldn't do anything to him. They glared at each other. "How do you like being on my lap, now?" he taunted, his voice husky.

Marina struggled against him. "Let me go!" she whispered urgently, eyes blazing.

Carlos laughed, shaking his head. He had one thing on his mind, and there was no turning back. They were caught up in their own world, now, totally unaware of their surroundings. He held her against his chest, cradling her. "Why?" he tortured her. He pressed his mouth to her ear, his breath hot, as he whispered the words. "A couple of nights ago, you had me in your mouth, loving every minute," he scratched her face with the shadow on his, "and every inch of it."

Marina gasped. His words, nasty as they were, had caused her to tumble back in time, to the moment. She turned her head to look at him. Waves of pleasure rippled through her, as she sank into the depths of the blue pools of his eyes. Her voice came out husky. "Yes. I was, wasn't I?"

Carlos looked into her eyes, certain of one thing. She didn't feel offended by his words because she knew he didn't mean them as an insult. Marina understood him. It was as if she were like him. He groaned. What he saw in her eyes was excitement. He licked his lips. "Want more?" he murmured.

Marina turned her face and bit him on the shoulder. The pirates laughed. They hadn't heard what he said to her, but they understood her reaction. Carlos grabbed her by the hair with his free hand and yanked her head back softly, filling her open mouth with his tongue.

She pushed at him as well as she could, turning her head away, struggling against him. Tears formed in her eyes. "Get off me!"

Carlos laughed. Caught up in the moment, he wanted to hurt her for the chaos she was creating in his life. He felt himself losing control. Slipping his hand into her bustier, he cupped her breast. Looking into her eyes, he kissed her again, stopping her protests, his thumb brushing against her nipple. Fire blazed in her eyes. As he began drawing her breast out, he finally heard the pirates shouting. That was when he realized, he was ravishing her. In public.

"Carlos!"

"No!"

"Stop!"

"Gaitano!"

"Marina!"

All of a sudden, he felt a hand on his wrist, like a steel trap, making him let go of Marina's breast, as it pulled his hand slowly, out of her bustier. He looked up at Indio. The brave was standing in front of them, keeping them out of sight from the rest of the pirates.

Indio shook his head, laughing softly, black eyes wide with shock. "*Carlitos!* This is not the place!" he rumbled softly.

Marina jumped off his lap and turned to face him, eyes shimmering, even as her lips parted, and her chest rose and fell rapidly. "Carlos..."

"Bravo!" Everybody turned to look at Xavier. The blond pirate was smiling happily, clapping, as if he were at a show. "This has been quite entertaining, Gaitano, but it seems like she didn't appreciate that." He strode to them, long legs seeming to glide on the stone floor. Turning to the rest of the pirates, he announced. "I offer one of my ships, in exchange for the accountant of La Gitana."

Everything happened all at once. Marina gasped. Salomé screamed, terror striking her heart at the pirate's words. The crew of La Gitana shouted, moving forward. The women stayed by the walls, anticipating trouble. The council moved as one, to stand behind the crew. The older Gaitanos moved closer, away from María Isabel, shock in their faces. Everybody else got out of the way, including Xavier's sailors. Giancarlo grabbed Rouge, spinning her to one side, as everybody stepped back. The Gaitano men raced to Carlos' side, facing Xavier. Caribe straightened up from his crouched position, rage crossing his face. Indio held Carlos, as he moved to stand up. "No!"

Xavier smiled, his eyes mocking Carlos. He raised his eyebrows at him. "I raise my offer to two ships, one of them my very best." He raked his eyes insultingly over Marina. "I want her to dance for me."

Marina stepped back, hazel eyes wide in her tanned face. "No!"

Carlos tore away from Indio and stood up, looking him in the eye. Indio knew that look well. It meant that the pirate wouldn't hesitate, turning on him in a blind fury, and not even stop to think about what the outcome would be, from an encounter between them. Indio loved him too much, to put their relationship to that particular test. He knew Carlos wouldn't hurt Marina, and that was all that mattered. He stepped back. Carlos turned back to Xavier, death in his eye. "No." His voice was soft.

Xavier smiled, his voice tauntingly matching Gaitano's in softness. "Three ships."

Carlos smiled back, shaking his head. All of a sudden, he grabbed Marina's wrist and pulled her behind him with one hand, while the other pulled out his sword from its scabbard, in one swift movement. His voice was low and dangerous, although the smile never left his face. "Back off, Xavier. I am having a hard time, right now."

Xavier found himself looking at Carlos, across the length of the blade. He smiled. Stepping back, he drew his own. His mocking voice was a soft murmur. "Poor baby..."

The ringing of steel echoed in the cavern. In a moment, every pirate from the council, including the Gaitanos, as well as the crew from La Gitana, had their swords drawn on Xavier.

Marina's tears finally fell.

María Isabel's hand flew to her mouth, her eyes wide with fright, a horrified whisper escaping her lips, *"Carlitos!"*

The rest stood back against the walls, watching the events unfold. It wasn't their battle, and the Gaitanos were more than capable of taking care of themselves. They watched in silence, knowing that already, they had quite a story to tell. The crew of La Gitana moved silently, placing themselves strategically around the room. Marina began trembling.

Carlos glanced at her. His heart tore at the sight of her tears. On the inside, he raged. *You will pay for making my girlfriend cry.* "Now," he said softly, addressing the guests, "I am leaving with my accountant." His eyes fixed on the other pirate's. "Any problem with that?"

Salomé moaned, terror in her face. Rouge put her arm around her, protectively, while keeping her sword pointed at the blond troublemaker. Indio went to stand by Marina. Nobody spoke. Only Xavier, fearless, laughed. He looked Carlos up and down. "We can talk when you get tired of her," he said. He put his sword away, and watched with amusement the other pirates, waiting for them to lower theirs. Nobody did. Xavier shrugged, insolently, mocking them all. He looked back at Carlos. "For what I want her, it doesn't matter, if she has been with you or with anyone else." He winked at Marina. "Another time, perhaps." His eyes raked over her, lingering insultingly. His black eyes locked on hers. His voice was soft, making her skin crawl. *"I will have you."*

Marina didn't think. Yanking away from Gaitano, she strode straight towards him, rage in her eyes. *"Respect me!"* she screamed, the words leaving her mouth for the third time that night. Her hand shot out, a blur as she slapped him with force, hair whipping about her face, the coins hanging from her ears and wrist, ringing in the cavern.

Xavier stayed with his head looking down for a moment. When he straightened up again, she saw that she had caught the corner of his mouth, forcing the skin against his teeth. His lip was cut and bleeding. His tongue darted out, and he licked at the blood, his eyes on hers. He smiled, aroused, as if she had just done a sex act on him. "I liked that," he confessed, to her disgust. "May I do it to you?"

Marina met his eyes, trembling with rage. She stood there, as his eyes did whatever they wanted to her. And then she realized she was within arm's reach. His eyes met hers, his smile growing wider at the fear that flickered in her face. Just then, Marina felt herself being hauled back against a hard chest, at the same time that Xavier's hand shot out to grab her. The blond pirate's long fingers grazed her wrist. Indio's voice rumbled in her ear, his presence solid against her back, his arm crossed over her chest like a lifeguard. Xavier's laughter rang out in the cavern.

Carlos had not lowered his sword. Keeping his eyes on Xavier, he spoke to her, softly, reaching for her, once more. "Marina."

"I want to go home," she said, her voice low and husky, also keeping her eyes on the blond pirate, her hand reaching out blindly, to grasp his.

Don Carlos spoke up, finally stepping in, Don Miguel shadowing his steps, from the other side. The pirates around him stepped back, as he faced Xavier. "I am sorry, that this party has ended so soon, but as you can see, we are all done here." His eyes were as cold as ice, even as he smiled. "You have to go, Xavier."

Xavier nodded, polite, apparently no hard feelings. He threw Carlos a smile. "I will see you again. Remember what I said."

Carlos held the sword in front of his face. "*I will kill you*," he said softly. There were gasps all around him. "Remember what *I* said." Without looking at Marina, he turned to take her from Indio and picked her up in his arms, carrying her as if she were a child, never letting go of the sword. "Come on, mami," he whispered in her ear, as she wrapped herself around him. She wouldn't let herself cry, even as her legs went around his waist, locking at the ankles. Her arms held him tight, and she buried her face in his neck. Carlos squeezed her. "Let's go home, baby." He held her head against his shoulder, as if she were just that. His crew surrounded him, swords still drawn, pointed at Xavier and his men. Holding her tight against him, he gripped the sword as he walked across the floor. Nobody spoke as the crew of La Gitana all began to file out. Giancarlo winked at Rouge and caressed her face as he walked by her, his sword still pointed at the blond man that had ruined their party. She smiled at him, blowing him a silent kiss. The pirates made a path as the crew members left, a crying Salomé with them. Marina looked up through tear-filled eyes at the people she had shared the night with. Over Carlos' shoulder, she caught sight of Xavier and Lola, side by side, looking after them. Raising her chin, tears rolled down her face. Rage in her eyes, Marina lifted the middle finger of each hand.

Outside, it was raining. So intense had been the drama in the cavern that they had been totally unaware of the storm beginning outside. Carlos put Marina down gently, and grabbed her hand, dragging her behind him. Lightning lit up the sky.

"Carlitos!" The voice came up behind them.

The group stopped as one, vigilant of the cave entrance behind them.

Carlos sighed. "Papá."

Don Carlos came into view, accompanied by María Isabel and Don Miguel. He stood in front of his son, soft rain misting around him, by the torch light of the tavern next to them. "I am sorry you have to leave like this."

Carlos shook his head. Anxious to get going, he embraced him. "Do not worry, Papá."

His father laughed. "I wish to thank you for the entertainment. I am curious about one thing, however. Why did you stop the girls?" He glanced at Marina and back at his son.

Carlos jerked his head at his accountant. "She is a lethal weapon," he informed his father. "My accountant is highly skilled in a form of martial art. Marina would have killed Lola."

Marina smiled, wiping her tears away. "I am sorry, he usually isn't this rude." She held out her hand. "I am Marina Aguilar."

Don Carlos took it. "Aaahh. The accountant." He winked at her, and kissed her hand, making her laugh.

María Isabel stepped up, and pushed her husband away. "Go! Leave her alone, Carlos, you and your teasing." She hugged Marina, and kissed her on both cheeks, drawing back to look in her eyes. She smiled. "Marina Aguilar," she said softly. "My husband and I will be visiting Encantada next week. I know you leave tomorrow, and I am sorry we haven't been able to spend time together, but we will have time then." She caressed her face. "Have a nice voyage, Marina. We will see you soon." And turning, she stepped back to meet Salomé, as she waited for her men.

Don Carlos turned to her again. "Marina," he laughed. "I must thank you, for your excellent work on the Gaitanos' books. I would like to speak to you further, about your theories about the monster responsible for the attacks on the natives. We will be sailing to Encantada, around three days behind you. I shall be looking forward to speaking to you, then." Kissing her cheek, he smiled at her once more. Turning to his son, his eyes grew serious for a moment. "One month, Carlitos," he said softly, before winking at him. Carlos nodded. The two men embraced, and Don Carlos left to join his wife, saying goodbye to his adopted son and his mate.

Marina sighed, and looked up as Don Miguel approached them. He smiled. "Thank you for your help today, Marina. The Gaitanos needed fresh eyes to see better." He looked at Carlos. "Carlitos, have a safe trip. Take care of yourself. And your accountant," he added with a chuckle. Then, in a sudden impulse, he patted both their faces, looking from one to the other. "I have only one advice, for the both of you." They looked at him. "Do not let the other one get away." He laughed, and he too was gone.

"Come here." She looked at him. A small candle sputtered on his desk, offering enough light so they could see each other. Carlos was lying sprawled on the bed, the empty hammock swinging mockingly, next to him. He had discarded his shirt and boots, long ago. His sword lay thrown on the table. The pillows were propping his back, and his hand was behind his head. His other hand teased her, as it stroked the dark hairs on his belly, slipping under the waist of his pants. Her eyes followed his fingers. She licked her lips. Looking back at him, she met his eyes. She shook her head. He smiled. "Come here," he repeated.

Outside, lightning flashed, lighting up the sky, and everything inside the cabin. Marina rubbed her arms, as her hairs stood on end. "Why?" she asked huskily.

Carlos shrugged. "I want to talk to you."

"Talk."

His eyebrows rose, a smile spreading on his face. "Scared?"

Marina held his eyes, and pushed herself off the table she had been leaning on. She swayed towards him slowly. "Never."

His eyes flashed with approval, enjoying the game. "Your dance," he began.

She smiled to herself. "What about it?"

Carlos hesitated, for the moment at a loss for words. "It was..."

Marina came closer, licking her lips. "Did you like it?"

He sucked in his breath, and groaned. "Oh, yes..."

She laughed softly, coming even closer. "What about it?" Reaching the hammock, she stroked the rope that tied it to a beam.

Carlos swallowed. "Have you ever..."

Marina ducked under the rope and circled the bed, out of reach. "Danced for anyone..."

"Yes."

"No."

"No?"

She shook her head. "Just you." She gazed steadily at him.

"Would you dance for me again?"

Marina laughed huskily. "Maybe," she told him, "someday." She took a step closer, her eyes half closed. She licked her lips. "What's my motivation?"

Carlos looked at her. "You make me crazy," he said hoarsely, sitting up slowly. Desire invaded his body.

Marina backed up, as he swung his feet off the bed. "And you, me," she confessed, eyeing him warily as he stood and began approaching her.

He held out his hand. "Come here."

"Why?" They began circling each other.

"I want to talk to you," he repeated, smiling.

"Well, *I* want to talk to *you*."

He blinked, surprised. "Talk."

"Lola."

He stopped. "What about---"

"How serious?"

"Not at all."

This time, Marina stopped moving, and faced him. "You lie," she accused softly.

Carlos shrugged. Marina turned away, but not before he saw the hurt in her eyes. He reached out and took her hand. "Marina..."

"No." She snatched her hand back, her heart beating faster. "Lola," she repeated. "I'm just curious." Taking another step away, she turned and faced him.

Carlos let his hand drop. He sat on the table and studied her. "Why?"

She began pacing up and down, in front of him. "I want to know," she said casually, "why someone who doesn't even *know* me," she threw her head back, raking her fingers through her hair. Carlos moaned under his breath. She stopped in front of him, her hair cascading around her face, again. Her voice was husky as she continued, rage in her eyes, "would want to attack me, over something that wasn't serious at all."

Carlos flinched. "Marina, I wouldn't disrespect you."

"I know." She didn't care. "How serious, Carlos?"

"Only on her part, maybe," he conceded, frowning. "Not on mine."

"Big commitment?"

"Not at all." He smiled. *She is jealous.* "She was just someone I visited when I went to Carey."

"How frequent?"

He shrugged, happy now, loving her questions. "Twice, three times a year, maybe."

Marina began pacing again. "For how long?"

"Around a couple of years."

"How long ago?"

He chuckled. "Many years ago."

She frowned. "So, why is she like this, now?"

"I was very young. She met someone who could provide for her and preferred him over me. She stayed with him for all those years. She still managed to see me whenever I sailed in. I would never be with her again. The man lost his life, recently. Now, I'm a man..." he shrugged again.

Marina felt her blood run cold, as suddenly, a thought occurred to her. "Does she have a child by you?"

Carlos chuckled. "No, thank God." He explained. "I never gave her my seed."

She frowned. "How did you prevent a baby?"

He shrugged. Marina wanted to know everything about him, and he was loving it. "Skins. I never was with her, bare." His eyes caressed the woman in front of him. "I didn't stick around long enough for the relationship to evolve." He searched her eyes. "I understood one thing clearly, from the beginning. She liked my last name better than my first."

"I *love* your first name."

"I know you do."

Marina stopped and looked at him. "Did you love her?"

Carlos threw back his head and laughed. Jumping off the table, he approached her, fire in his eyes. "Does it look like I ever loved her?"

Marina backed up again. "I have nothing to compare with," she shot back at him.

Carlos lunged at her. "I will give you something, then." Throwing her on the bed, he held her down, looking down at her. "Let me just say this," he said finally.

Marina started breathing heavier. She struggled against him, getting more excited. "What?" she gasped.

He lowered his weight on her, placing his sex over hers. Marina's breath caught in her chest, as he pressed hard against her, molding her, through the fabric of their clothes, to him. "I never did to her, what I am about to do to you," he breathed in her ear.

Marina arched her back, trying to get more of him. "And what is that?" she moaned.

Just then, a clap of thunder split the sky. Carlos laughed, as she strained towards him. He rubbed his face hard against hers, scratching her again. He bucked his hips against her, making her gasp. "If you must know," he growled, "I am thankful for this storm."

"Why?"

Carlos released the pressure on her hands, and slipped them behind his neck, rubbing his chest against her breasts. His words filled her senses. "Nobody will hear you when I make you scream."

Marina slipped her fingers in his hair and pulled his head back to look at him. She had never been more excited, in her entire life.

His eyes smoldered, as lightning lit up the cabin, once more. Marina felt herself getting wet. He kissed her. Thunder rumbled across the sky. She yielded to him, her senses drowning in his kiss. Carlos' body moved in rhythm against her, his kiss growing deeper. Finally, he tore his mouth away from hers. Lifting himself off her, he began undressing her. The candle on his desk sputtered, and went out. Marina tried to stop him, but he just caught her wrists, laughing in the darkness. His low voice reassured her, as he stroked her, arousing her. Finally, flinging her dress to one side, he began kissing his way down her neck. Marina hugged him, tears stinging her eyes. Her heart felt as if it were going to pound its way out of her chest. Carlos traced a line between her breasts with his tongue. She shuddered. Detouring, he indulged himself with each breast, one at a time. A sob caught in her throat. Carlos moved lower. He stayed playing around her navel, as he slipped off her underwear. Marina held her breath. Her legs started trembling. Gently, Carlos rubbed his hands up and down her thighs. He nudged her legs apart with his head, blowing softly on her. Marina started shaking. Her hands grasped his hair. Carlos smiled. Placing his hands under her butt cheeks, he slipped his thumbs under and up towards him, in between. Marina moaned, as he spread her lower lips. Closing his eyes, Carlos lowered his head and flicked her with his tongue. Marina jerked against his mouth. He did it again. And again. Finally, he kept his tongue pressed against her clit, vibrating. She started shaking again. Carlos groaned, as he felt himself growing harder. It was her turn to be pleased. He had to make it count. He put his whole mouth on her. Marina grasped his head with both hands, and pressed herself against him, gorging herself on his tongue. Tears spilled from her eyes. The pirate feasted on her, first, making her buck, like the ship in the storm. Then, he devoured her, pouring his heart out through lips, mouth and tongue, his hands holding her against his face as he pleased her. A few moments later, he did it. Marina screamed.

Caribe opened the door, peering in. He had knocked, but had only been answered by a soft grunt. He glanced at the hammock, expecting the pirate to be in it. His eyes flew to the bed. Gaitano was propped against the headboard, rays of sunlight streaking his face and bare chest. There were dark circles under his eyes, and a heavy shadow on his face. He looked as if he hadn't slept much. His legs were stretched out in front of him, his white cutoff pants startling against his dark skin. Marina lay with her head in his lap, her arm thrown across his thighs in her sleep. Caribe noted the black pool, where her dress had been tossed carelessly on the floor. The sheet wrapped around her body practically glowed, against her sun darkened skin. She was still wearing her jewelry. The silver coins caught the sun light, as the ship rocked. Indio's turquoises made a splash of color on her wrist. Her body was curved towards the pirate, and his hands were on her head, his fingers combing her hair.

Caribe rushed to them, without thinking. Marina looked like she was okay, but the pirate holding her, didn't. He crouched down by the bed, his hand reaching to stroke her head, a frown creasing his brow. His eyes flew to Gaitano's face. "Are you all right?"

Carlos tried to smile, but his eyes were haunted, as he gazed at the dreadlocked young man. "I am." He could still feel Marina's terror, as she thrashed about during the hours before dawn, struggling through nightmares. He had wanted to kill, as he held her in his arms all throughout her ordeal, whispering in her ear that Lola was gone, and Xavier would never get her. "Marina had a very rough night, last night."

Caribe looked at him. "It looks like you both did," he said softly.

Gaitano nodded, his eyes locking on the boy's. This time, his smile was stronger. "No forms today."

Caribe nodded. Reaching over, he kissed the sleeping woman's bare shoulder, careful not to wake her. He crossed the cabin and stopped at the door, to look back. His heart went out to them. Exiting quietly, Caribe shut the door behind him, leaving the pirate staring off into space, his hands working in the girl's hair.

Jackson glanced over at his parents. They were all quiet, excitement in their eyes, as they absorbed everything. Dawn had been dingy and hazy, this morning, the jungle still dripping from the day before. Their personal things had disappeared, as expected, but they had found fresh clothes in the cave, when they woke up. After organizing themselves, and discussing what to do, they set off down the beach, towards town. Activity at the docks was minimal today, the only ship in port, the one Gaitano had sailed in. The warehouse seemed almost abandoned, compared to what it usually looked like. The parents kept silent, for the most part, keeping their questions to a minimum. Shayla and Sloane stopped, startled, at the sight of their first pirate. Their husbands stood protectively next to them, keeping a wary eye on the man. To their surprise, the nasty smelling giant grunted a greeting at Jackson with a nod of his head, sliding his hand against their son's as he walked by.

Shayla gasped, a smile playing around her mouth. "Why, Jackson Banks!" She pinched his cheek softly, just like when he was a little boy. "You have friends here!"

Jackson ducked his head, laughing. "Actually, they like me pretty well, around here."

His father chuckled. "My son, the public relations guy."

Jackson lifted his hands in the air, laughing. "Someone's gotta do it." Hurrying them along, he started their tour at the general store.

John Kline looked up as the bell tinkled. He watched in amazement as the newcomers poured in. Recognizing the young man in front, he dropped what he was doing and went around the counter, a smile splitting his face. "Jackson!" They greeted each other, in the fashion that Jackson had brought to the island.

"Mr. Kline! How is business?"

The storeowner rolled his eyes. "Slow, right now, but not for long, that's for sure." He smiled at him. "Where have you been, man? Last I heard was that Pedro had locked you up and you were yelling bloody murder until he had to let you go, just so he could hear himself think." They laughed.

"Yeah, well, it was his choice to lock me, so he had to put up with me." He waved a hand at his companions. "I left for a few days to get my parents. They have never been to Encantada." He made the introductions.

John shook the men's hands, and kissed the women's. "It is such a pleasure to be in the company of such beautiful women," he told them. "It is obvious," he told Jackson, "that your sisters are your mothers' daughters." They laughed again, falling into small talk. A little while later, they heard a baby's laugh.

Shayla turned to her son, excitement in her face. "Jax!" she said softly. "Is that the baby?"

Jackson nodded, pointing at Larissa, as she came into view, blowing hair out of her face, bouncing her son on her hip. She caught sight of him and screamed. *"Jackson!"* She went to him and embraced him with her free arm, kissing him soundly on the cheek. "I thought you left!"

He nodded, smiling at her. "Only for a few days. I went to get my parents," he explained. He made the introductions one more time.

Larissa looked at the four strangers. "It is such a pleasure to finally meet you! I can't begin to tell you what lifesavers your children have been. Especially Marina!" She laughed. Max jumped in her arms, making everybody stop and comment about him, as he turned on the charm. After a while, they bid their good-byes. As they reached the door, the baby began screaming. Everybody stopped and turned around.

Jackson frowned. The baby had tried to lunge out of his mother's arms, and was now half hanging, little arms stretched out, imploring. His tiny face was red, all scrunched up, tears streaming out of the green pools of his eyes. "Aw, Max," he soothed, going towards him. "What's up, buddy?"

The baby's father laughed. "He has been thrown off his routine, since Gaitano sailed." The Banks and the Aguilars looked at each other, at the mention of the name. "He misses Marina. She spoils him to death."

Jackson smiled, looking the baby in the eyes. "It's okay, man. She'll be back," he sing-sang.

Larissa laughed. "The truth is, he's been impossible since she left."

Jackson straightened up, rubbing Max's black head. "So, let *me* take him. I'll watch Max for Marina, until she gets back."

Sloane cut in as Larissa started shaking her head. "Oh, please, let us do this for you. Just let us know how long she keeps him out."

Shayla laughed. "Oh, come on, we need a tour guide. Besides, we love babies."

The Klines agreed. John thanked them. "Don't let Max get you lost," he laughed.

Jackson took the baby from Larissa. "Come on, baby. We're going for a stroll. Check out the girls, man." He kissed the top of his head, as the baby hiccupped, smiling through his tears. Joe and Pablo looked at each other.

"*Oye, papi,*" teased Pablo. "You look good with the baby."

Jackson winked at him. "Little bunny gets me the honeys..."

Joe laughed. "That's my boy." Waving goodbye to the Klines, they left, laughing.

Their next stop was Padre Ignacio's. The church was cool and quiet when they went in, the morning sun streaming through a piece of colored glass above the makeshift altar. There was no mass, at the moment, and the place was empty. Padre Ignacio sat at the front pew, head bowed in prayer. Max gurgled in Jackson's arms, happy to be where he was. Padre Ignacio spun around, swiftly getting to his feet and standing in the middle of the aisle. The women gasped. His hand was halfway to the pistol strapped to his robe. The men froze.

Jackson stepped forward, frowning. "What's up, Padre? It's Jackson."

Padre Ignacio stood paralyzed for a moment, and then his hand went to his heart, as a rush of air left his lungs. He wiped his brow and smiled, self-conscious. *"Jackson!"* He came towards them. "Where have you been? We've missed you."

Jackson laughed. "Yeah, I'll bet." Padre Ignacio stood in front of him.

Max turned his head to look at the man. His green eyes widened as tears pooled again, and his lower lip trembled. His tiny fingers clasped Jackson's shirt, with all their might. He squinted his eyes. Taking a deep breath, Max began screaming.

Jackson turned to look at the baby in his arms, trying bouncing him, but Max just clawed at him blindly. "Hey, Max, man, what is it, baby?" Sloane and Shayla swooped on him like mother birds, protecting him with their wings. They petted and stroked him. Max peered at Padre Ignacio and screamed louder. "I got you, boo," sang Jackson, moving him to his shoulder.

Padre Ignacio looked ashamed. "I am sorry. It's my fault. He was here. He saw."

Jackson focused his tiger eyes on him. "When?" He spoke slowly, his stomach tying in a knot. "What did Max see?"

Padre Ignacio hesitated. He glanced at the strangers, and back at Jackson. He shook his head, unsure of himself. "I don't know ---"

Jackson cut in, his voice cold. "These are our parents. I went and got them, and I brought them back." Padre Ignacio's eyes widened, as he stared at the couples. "Now, what did Max see?"

The priest bowed his head for a moment. When he looked up, there was resignation in his face. "Max saw when they took Marina."

Sloane stared at him. "What?"

Pablo stepped forward. "They took my daughter?" he asked, his voice ominously low.

"Oh, no, please, forgive me," cried Padre Ignacio quickly, holding up his hands. "I did not mean to imply she was in any danger. She is quite safe."

Joe glared at him. "Is that supposed to make us feel better?"

"What about Salomé?" asked Shayla. "Did they take her also?"

"No, no, no," sighed Padre Ignacio. "Salomé went of her own free will." He shook his head at himself. "Perhaps I should explain myself. Marina was not kidnapped, she was merely... tricked. The work she has been doing for the Gaitanos turned out to be more important than anybody expected. She discovered evidence of tampering. Thievery. Gaitano needed to report this to a council that monitors all the activities in these waters. It is not only piracy, here. We also have legal trade. What Marina found, is extremely important to the Gaitanos. She had already expressed that she would never get on a ship." His eyes twinkled. "She did not want to be outnumbered by rodents, I believe she said." The family relaxed a little, smiling. "The Captain had rat catchers on the ship for hours, before it passed his inspection. She had also mentioned something about scurvy being a result of a vitamin C deficiency. So..." he continued, mysteriously, "the Captain stocked up on fresh fruit." He shook his head, and turned serious again. "The Captain believed she would be fine, once she saw that she was safe. I believed it too." He met their eyes. "Our method may not have been the most conventional," he admitted, "but there are only so many things men can come up with..." he drifted off, staring into space, remembering.

Jackson glared at him. "What did Max see?"

Padre Ignacio searched Pablo's eyes. "I betrayed her. I brought her here for a mass. John came to take Max. When Solomon showed up to escort her---"

"Escort her, my ass!" shouted Jackson. "Damn African marched her through town, flung over his shoulder like a sack of potatoes, kicking and screaming!"

Joe and Pablo looked at each other. Jackson hadn't gone into details before. They turned back to the priest. Pablo stared at him, until the man shifted, uncomfortable, squirming under his gaze. "What did my daughter say," he asked slowly, "when she realized what you had done?"

Padre Ignacio sighed in defeat. Squaring his shoulders, he told them. Word for word. When he was done, the parents nodded.

Sloane tossed her head, blue fire flashing out of her eyes. "Good! I'm glad she said that. She is right. This is the house of God, and you," she said softly, "disrespected it. I pray nothing happens to her, Padre, or you won't be able to live with yourself." Tossing her hair, she marched out. Shayla took Max from Jackson, and followed her, leaving the men alone. They stared at each other.

Joe finally spoke. "I suppose you have already told yourself more than anybody could ever say to you."

Padre Ignacio had the decency to look ashamed. He grimaced. "Yes. But I assure you, gentlemen, that your daughters are as safe as they could possibly be."

"What's your guarantee, Padre?" asked Pablo.

"The men they are with love them deeply."

The men fell silent. A figure came in, walking towards the front, joining them.

"Jackson." It was Pedro Barbosa.

Jackson turned on him. "Oh, don't you Jackson me! What the hell were you doing, locking me up, man? Marina is my sister!"

Pedro Barbosa nodded, not saying anything, at first. Finally, he spoke. "You know she had to go, Jackson. Gaitano will not hurt her."

"That's not the point!"

Pedro Escobar turned to the two fathers. "I am sorry, let me introduce myself. I am Pedro Escobar," he said, holding out his hand. "I am, what is considered the law on this island." He looked from one to the other. "Gentlemen, I feel I need to explain."

Pablo nodded. "Of course."

"What is so incredibly important about Marina and the books?" Joe demanded. "What could happen?"

Pedro Escobar met his eyes. "If this matter isn't taken care of, we lose Encantada."

Outside, the sun was struggling to get warmer. Leaving the depressing atmosphere behind them, they headed down the street. Stopping in front of the Siren's Lair, Jackson shifted the baby from one hip to the other. He looked at his parents. "You remember that sitcom, *Cheers*?" They nodded. He grinned. "Check this out." Opening the door, he led them inside.

"Max!" The room seemed to burst with the greeting. The infant squealed with laughter. The parents all looked at each other.

Jackson laughed. "See what I mean?"

"Jackson!"

Jackson turned to the table in the corner, sauntering over, with the baby. As expected, the girls squealed and giggled, giving them both all their attention. "Ladies," said Jackson, "I have been out for a few days, but I am back." They began petting him. "However, today, I am out with my family, so if you'll excuse me, I'll be back later." He winked, and left them gossiping. Turning back to his parents, he joined them at the bar.

Shayla turned to her son, wonder in her face. She stroked the baby's head. "Jackson," she said softly. "Is this what I think it is?" The husbands chuckled. Joe winked at his son.

They all looked up as the old sailor approached them, a smile on his face. "Well, hello there, Max. Haven't seen you for a while, buddy," he said, taking the tiny hand and pretending to eat it. Max squealed. He turned to the strangers. "I'm Silas. I'm taking care of this place for the owner, while he's out playing at sea." He winked at them. Jimmy joined them, and Jackson made the introductions.

"Gentlemen," said the Oriental, looking fondly at Jackson, "you have quite a son, here."

Joe laughed. "Why, thank you. We think so, too."

"And your daughters are angels. Smart, hard-working, *and* beautiful."

"Yes, they are," smiled Pablo. "Would you happen to know when they'll be back?"

Jimmy grinned. "Actually, they are on their way back, as we speak."

Silas laughed. "Don't worry, Papá. You will see them in a couple of days." The Banks and the Aguilars looked at each other, relief in their eyes. The old sailor nodded at Jimmy, who quickly counted heads and left. He wiped the bar in front of them. "How long were you planning on staying?"

"We're not sure, yet. We just got here," said Joe.

Shayla smiled at the old man, her finger firmly in the baby's grasp, on the way to his mouth. "We would love to check out Encantada. Jackson has told us so many wonderful things about it."

Sloane nodded. "Our children really like it here, Silas. We just wanted to see for ourselves."

"Well," grinned the old man, eyes twinkling as he looked at them, his hands spread on the bar, "maybe you all end up staying." Just then, a customer called him from the other end of the bar, and he went to serve him. He missed the shock in all their faces. They hadn't thought about that. The implications were mind-boggling. By the time he got back, they had composed themselves once more. "I have never seen anybody adapt to a brand new place, the way these young people have. They are not children, granted, but still very young," he pretended to frown at Jackson.

Jackson laughed, bouncing Max on his knee. "You are just jealous, old man." Silas grinned at him. Jimmy came in at that moment, and put their lunch before them.

"The rest of our customers are the ones that are jealous," announced Jimmy.

Shayla frowned. "Why is that?"

Jackson laughed. "They don't serve lunch here. *We* get it, because the bartender is *Salomé's boyfriend*." The parents grinned at each other in the long mirror behind the bar.

"What's for lunch?" asked Joe.

Jackson jumped up. "Oh! Oh! Check this out, Dad." He started laughing. "No matter what! It's always going to be bread, fruit and fish." He broke off a small piece of bread and fed it to Max. "No matter where you go..." he chuckled.

"Oh, hush, Jackson," smiled his mother. "That's about all you need, anyway. And as good as this is," she rolled her eyes, smelling the steaming fish in front of her, "I can handle it."

They had a nice lunch, and finished it off with a round of beers from the bar. They sat, contented, looking around them, the clink of glasses familiar. They realized that bars were pretty much the same, no matter where or when they were.

"Silas!" Joe called the old sailor over. He smiled at him. "Where is a good place to stay in this town?"

Silas looked at him thoughtfully. Finally, he shook his head. "I can tell by just looking at all of you, that you are really fine folk." He confided in them. "I wouldn't put you up in this town. The best you can do is stay at your children's place. It will be far better than anything you can get down here. However, if you want, I'll put you up in the savage's room, the night before the ship comes in, so you'll be here early."

Shayla looked at him, startled. "The *savage?*"

Jimmy laughed. "Old man's just teasing, Mrs. Banks. The heathen is quite harmless." The men chuckled. She rolled her eyes at them.

Silas reassured her. "The truth is, I have never seen a neater man than he is." He smiled. "It is the nicest place in town."

"Don't worry, Mrs. Banks. We'll fix it up for you, so you can all stay, if you want," offered Jimmy.

"Thank you, Jimmy. That would be real nice of you. I am sorry we don't have any money---"

Silas cut her off. "Jackson can work it off." He grinned, then. "No, seriously, we owe him money for the help he does around here. Specializes in keeping the sirens in line. He just took off before payday, but we are good for it." The family thanked him and stood, smiling at the women as they walked by.

Next stop was Dominique Swan's shop. Jackson introduced them. They made small talk, as Miss Swan's eyes kept drifting to Sloane. The husbands looked at each other. Just then, a couple came in. The girl was exotic, almond shaped eyes, the color of the sky on a cloudy day. Her hair black, long and straight, like an oriental's, but the rest of her was pure native. Her skin was the color of cinnamon, her smile bright in her beautiful freckled face. The bright sarong she was wearing clung to her curves, as if it were hugging her. The man she was with was tall, muscularly built, and tanned, like everybody else on the island, as if he spent most of his time in the sun. Bright yellow hair peeked from under a worn, dusty cowboy hat. Intense blue eyes in a sunburnt face sparkled as he laughed at what the girl was saying. One arm was possessively around her waist, while his free hand grasped her hand, to bring it to his mouth. At that moment, they noticed the family in the shop.

The girl just stopped and stared, a big smile spreading on her face. She approached them quickly, excitement preceding her. She stopped, all of a sudden shy. "You must be Sloane Aguilar!" she exclaimed in a soft voice, coming to stand in front of the center of her attention.

Sloane swallowed her surprise, glancing at her husband for a moment. He shrugged, and she turned back to the girl with a smile on her own face. "Why, yes, I am. I'm afraid that I am at a disadvantage here..."

The girl laughed, suddenly self-conscious. "I'm sorry," she apologized, holding out her hand. "I am Liana. I have been working with Salomé for the last few days before she left. She has told me all about you, and your work. I am excited and pleased to meet you. Salomé has been showing me how to design..." she shrugged, embarrassed. Turning to Shayla, she laughed at the other woman. "And you must be Shayla Banks. Salomé explained that you are both her mothers."

Shayla laughed, taking the girl's hand. "Yes, we are. So, what do you do, Liana?" she asked after the girl greeted the men.

"Right now, Salomé is designing, and I just make the dresses." She glanced at her companion. "I hope to soon be designing, myself, and eventually buy my own dress shop." Taking his hand, she introduced him. "Kyle, this is Salomé's family. The Banks and the Aguilars." She grinned at Jackson. "I know who you are, just by Max." She squeezed the man's hand. "That is Salomé's brother, Jackson."

Kyle shook hands with the men, exchanging knowing smiles. "Jackson!" he exclaimed happily. "Pleased to finally meet you! Been hearing a lot about you, man," he laughed.

Jackson laughed, shaking his hand. "Any good?"

The man took off his hat, and ran a hand through his hair before putting it back on. "It's hard to tell, actually. The sirens are crazy about you," he winked at him.

Jackson shrugged, eyes dancing. "Well, I guess they know something good when they see it."

The cowboy turned to Shayla, a twinkle in his eye. "You must be the baby doctor."

Shayla nodded her head, shaking his hand. "Yes, I am. And you are..."

He grinned. "Well, I like to think of myself as this young lady's man..." he winked at the girl, making her blush, "but around here they know me as Dr. Richardson." He smiled at the men as they introduced themselves. "How long will you be staying?"

Joe put his arm around his wife and looked at her. "I don't know," he said slowly, turning to smile at the couple. "We just thought we'd surprise the girls, when they got back."

"We heard it would be a couple of more days, or so," Pablo smiled.

Dr. Richardon nodded. "That sounds about right."

"I am sure they'll be thrilled," laughed Liana. "Salomé talks about you all the time and I still have to meet Marina. I hear she's a dream with children."

Sloane laughed. "Thank you, she is. It has been a pleasure to meet you, Liana. It is so nice to see our daughters have made friends in Encantada."

They stood around talking a little bit longer, and they left.

Back at the general store, a sleepy Max held his arms out to his mother.

Larissa laughed. "I hope he wasn't too much trouble..."

Shayla laughed. "Not at all. We loved having him."

"He's quite the tour guide," joked Sloane.

Jackson sidled up to the storeowner at the counter. "Hey, Mr. Kline?"

John smiled at him. "Hey, Jackson!"

"Our folks decided to stay for a little while, but they didn't really come prepared. Do you think you could hook them up with some clothes, you know, some pants like the girls wear, for my moms, and some of those fabrics they use for everything..." he smiled as John chuckled, and got busy getting him what he was asking for. "Oh!

Some personal care items for all four of them, enough to last them a month or so..."

John finished with the items and wrapped them all up for him. With a wink, he put one more bag on top of the pile. "Here is an assortment of the strange tools Marina ordered. I am sure your mothers would appreciate them," he laughed. Sloane and Shayla looked at each other.

Jackson slid his hand against the storeowners. "Cool! Good job, man. Go ahead and put it on Gaitano's tab." At his parents' startled looks, he shrugged and smiled. "Tell him his brother-in-law charged it." With a laugh, he said good-bye and led his parents out.

His dad caught up with him. "Brother-in-law, huh?" asked Joe.

Jackson smiled. "Yeah, well, Gaitano's actually a good guy. I think you will all like him."

"Good," said Shayla. "Now, where is that village you rave about?"

"Marina, come here." Carlos Gaitano was sitting in a chair, in his cabin, in front of a beautiful, framed full-length mirror he had surprised her with. Her joy at the gift had been nearly overwhelming, and he had watched, amused, as she struggled to contain herself, tears of happiness streaming down her face. His heart had swollen with emotion at her gratitude. She had wanted to use it right away, and had sat him down in front of it. He hadn't realized he was in for a treat. He had never thought that a woman shaving a man could be such a sensual experience. Marina had taken her time and held his face softly, while using the blade carefully. She had whispered jokes and nonsense in his ear, making his eyes crinkle with laughter, as he struggled to keep his face still. Her hair on his arm had felt good to him, and he watched her in the mirror. He had never been this intimate with anyone before. She had just finished, and was now rinsing the blade in a porcelain bowl on the table. His eyes glowed as she flashed a smile at his reflection. Flinging water off her fingers, she came back, wiping her hands dry on her pants. Taking her by the hand, he sat her gently on his lap, cradling her. "I want to talk to you, some more."

Her eyebrows arched, and she laughed softly. "Why, Carlos! I thought they didn't exist! That they were myth!"

He played along. "What's that?"

Her smile became wicked as she flirted outrageously with him. "Men who like to talk afterwards," she murmured.

"Really? A myth, huh?" he asked, chuckling. "You, *mujer*, have been misinformed. We do exist. We are quite real."

Marina laughed softly. She loved playing with him. "So, what did you want to talk about?"

He brushed her hair back from her face, and looked into her eyes. "I loved doing what I did to you last night," he confessed, his voice hoarse with the memory.

Marina felt her face get hot. "Thank you. I loved you doing it."

He nodded. "Good. That means, I get to do it again," he smiled wickedly. Her eyes flew wide open. "Now?"

He shook his head, laughing. "Not unless you really need me to," he teased, making her laugh. "The truth is, I wanted to apologize," he continued. He watched the now familiar stillness come over her. "You were given a rough time, last night. I apologize for the way you were treated, spoken to, attacked, even," he hesitated, watching the memory flicker in her eyes.

"It wasn't your fault," she said sadly.

"No, but if it weren't for me, it would not have happened. These people are from my past. They should not be affecting our future." He watched with a smile, as her eyes widened with shock. "We make a good team, Aguilar."

"We do, don't we?"

"Yes," he murmured, "I intend to keep you." Taking her face in his hands, he pressed his mouth to hers, before she could reply. Closing his eyes, he didn't see the wild love flaring up in hers. He broke away, pressing his forehead against hers, his breathing ragged. He caught her hand and pressed his lips to the palm. Feeling the beads under his fingers, he grinned up at her. "By the way," he said slowly, gently playing with the turquoises, "you realize this means that we are more than friends. I recognized you last night, in public, as my makeout partner supreme." Marina burst out laughing. She couldn't help herself. He grinned. That's my girl. "You will never see Lola again."

She shook her head, smiling into his eyes. "Lola doesn't bother me."

"Xavier will never take you."

Marina went still and just looked into his eyes, quietly, for a moment. Finally, she spoke. "Lola doesn't bother me."

Carlos just stared, as she climbed off his lap and left the cabin. Swearing to himself, he followed her. Outside, the day was sunny.

They had planned to be two days in Carey, and never thought they
would be leaving early. Now, they had a whole day to spend however they liked. Carlos grinned, as he saw where they were. Already,
half the crew had abandoned ship. He called out happily to Marina.
"Arrecife!"

Marina was poised on the side, hanging to the ropes, just as he
had, the first time she came. She grinned. "Can you dive?"

He laughed, and climbed up beside her, taking her hand. Once
again, they dove off together. This time, when Marina joined her
friends and hit the beach, Carlos and Indio were right there with
them, running. The rest of the afternoon was spent with the crew
practicing what they had learned with their forms, fighting with
each other. The captain sparred with his accountant, to the delight
of their men. The intimacy between them, made their movements
into a dance.

Salomé shook her head as she watched. She turned to Indio.
"Does he realize how connected he is to her?"

Indio followed the couple with his eyes. "I think I have never
seen him like this."

Salomé grinned. "He put your bracelet on her."

Indio laughed. "Now, she is his, for the whole world to know."

Once the lessons were finished, it was playtime again. Some
frolicked in the water, while others lay down in the sun, or in the
shade, on the beach.

Gaitano and Marina went for a walk. A silent walk. Not saying anything, they held hands, fingers locked, and just glanced at
each other a few times. After a while, they found a secluded spot,
away from prying eyes. There, they stretched out on the sand and
looked at each other. Marina turned him on his belly and straddled
him, her hand brushing away the sand on his back. She proceeded
to give him a full body massage. She was sure he had never had one.
His groans told her she was right. So she gave him the best one she
could. Back and front. When she got to the front of his pants, she
pretended to ravage him, shaking her head and snarling, her hair
brushing all over his bare torso. He laughed, and pulled her head
up. She finished her massage with reflexology. The pirate felt as if he

had been broken down and made over. Then, he returned the favor. When he got to her front, he skimmed his hands over her private parts, already knowing those, intimately. Instead, he concentrated on kneading the muscles in her arms and legs, careful not to hurt her. When he got to her feet, he scrubbed them with sand, and rinsed them with ocean water. Then, he sucked her toes. Marina thought she would die, the pleasure was so intense. He sat her up, grinning into her eyes. Still, they didn't speak. They studied each other carefully, absorbing every line, every freckle, birthmark, studying every strand of hair. They caressed each other. They hugged and held each other in silence, rocking in the sun, the wind embracing them both. Their lips traveled over each other's faces. Their eyes remained locked together, as their bodies, in each other's arms. When the call for La Gitana reached them, in the afternoon air, they were ready. No words had been spoken between them, yet. But now, it was different. They had explored every inch of each other's bodies, and knew every single breath. They had stared into each other's eyes, until they walked the miles into one another's souls. Their hearts beat in rhythm, and their feet stepped in time. They weren't looking at each other now, as they reached the beach, and the sailors swimming towards the ship. But as they waded into the water, the pirate caught her face in his hand, one more time, turning her to look at him. Marina's hazel eyes locked on his. Shadows glided behind them, and he knew. Lowering his head, the pirate whispered against his girlfriend's mouth what he really thought of her. *"Bruja…"* Carlos Gaitano pressed his lips against Marina Aguilar's. *I'm crazy about you.* They didn't realize they each thought it at the same time, at the same heartbeat. Taking a deep breath, they smiled at each other, and swam back. They were going home to Encantada.

Their first stop in the village was Leilani's home. The girl was pacing up and down on her front porch, bouncing both babies in her arms at the same time. Ali shadowed her, a thumb stuck in her mouth, and the other one gripping her older sister's skirt. The girl quickly brushed her tears away, at the sight of the family, a big smile illuminating her face.

"*Jackson!*" she cried happily.

"Hey, baby! I've come to help you. The girls aren't back yet, and I'll bet you've been going crazy the past few days," he said, reaching her and kissing the top of her head, as he relieved her of the babies. He laughed as she quickly nodded her head. He introduced his parents, gently relinquishing one of the twins to each of his moms. "This one is Juan," he told Sloane, rubbing his cheek against the baby's fuzzy head. "And this one," he turned the baby's face towards Shayla, his thumb rubbing the baby's birthmark, "is Jaime."

The parents cooed over the babies and made a fuss over Ali, as Leilani watched on, fresh tears in her eyes. Jackson sent her inside to get the laundry. His father turned to him. "Is this where the old man comes?" he asked. Jackson had talked extensively about Encantada and its inhabitants, during the time he spent at home, waiting for the storm. The family felt comfortable, having heard all they could about everybody.

Jackson nodded. "Yeah, Dad." He looked at Pablo. "Papi, this guy is going to come for sure," he glanced at the setting sun, "like in an hour or so."

Sloane looked at him, cradling Juan against her chest. The baby looked, mesmerized, at the blond-white hair in his fist. "What can we do, Jax?"

"Just make sure the house is spanking. I'll help her at the river."
He grinned as Leilani came back out. Taking the basket from her, he
waved at his parents. "Hey, Leilani, I'll help you today. Tomorrow,
we'll be here earlier. I'm sorry if you've been having a rough time
lately, mami," he rambled on, all the way down the path, and to the
trail that led to the river.

Joe and Pablo looked at each other. They smiled. Joe chuckled.
"Our son, the good samaritan."

"Hey!" Pablo laughed, pointing a finger at him. "Don't be calling our boy any names!" They laughed.

Shayla scolded them, nibbling at the baby's hand. "Oh, stop,
you two! Go see what needs done, before the old man gets here!"

Sloane agreed. "We'll watch the babies, won't we?" she asked,
widening her eyes at Ali. The little girl giggled.

Joe sighed. "Yeah, yeah..."

Pablo clapped him on the back. "Let's do it, man." And they
disappeared inside.

They got to work. There were toys strewn around, and some
minor repairs to be done. The men located a box where some old,
rusty tools were, along with a machete, high on a shelf, away from
the smaller children's reach. With these, they hung back a few windows, tightened the gate at the end of the path, and steadied a wob-
bling chair. Finding a well, they brought water into the house, to
wash the walls and scrub the floors. With the machete, they cut back
the hedges around the shack, giving some semblance of order to the
back yard, revealing beautiful plants that had been hiding before.
When they were done, the men joined their wives on the front porch.
Throwing themselves down on the floor, they each took a baby, as
their wives went to inspect their labor.

"You should've seen it before," called Joe after them.

"Yeah," gasped Pablo.

The women laughed and continued their inspection. They
came back smiling. "Good job, you guys," complimented Shayla.

Sloane nodded. "We may not have seen it before, but it looks
really nice, now."

They sat down together, enjoying the late afternoon sun. The babies played on the men's chests, while Ali sat between the two women, heads together. This is how they were, when the gate banged on their walkway. Everybody looked. The men sat up, the babies cradled in their arms, protectively.

Jeremiah's eyes flicked from one to the other. They were all strangers to him. Joe and Pablo stood, as he came closer. They flanked the stairs, silently awaiting the man. The twins gazed at their grandfather in silence. Jeremiah walked right past them, without acknowledging them. Shayla and Sloane looked at each other. Quietly, they waited for the man to come back out. Jeremiah finally did, meeting the men's eyes. He grunted in acknowledgement, silent admiration in his eyes. Strangers were taking care of the children of his daughter, and doing a good job. He couldn't. Lowering his eyes, he walked past them, and went out the gate, never looking back. The setting sun dyed his head pink, as he grew smaller. Finally, they all let out a sigh.

"He always mad," said Ali in the stillness, shaking her head sadly.

"Oh, baby," crooned Sloane, stroking her hair.

"Why is that, darling?" asked Shayla, taking her tiny hand in hers.

"They took my mommy and daddy," she sniffed. Looking up at the two women, her eyes filled with tears, her bottom lip quivered, and she burst into tears. The women promptly scooped her up and walked her away, not wanting the twins to be affected. Joe and Pablo looked at each other. Behind the shack, the bamboo creaked in the grove, whispering as they prepared for the evening. The night birds began calling. A few minutes later, Jackson was back. The family gave back the babies, offered promises of visiting tomorrow, and continued on their way.

"This is amazing," whispered Shayla in awe, as they all crowded in Caribe's hut.

Leila beamed, nodding her dreadlocked head. "Isn't it?"

Candlelight flickered on the walls, illuminating the portraits of the visitors. The family stood staring at the wall, not believing their eyes. "These are all people that have come through like us?" asked Joe.

Jackson nodded. He smoothed the papers he had brought with him on the table, before adding them to the wall. They were the portraits of his sisters, and the one of himself. "This kid is awesome, guys. He dreams, and then he draws."

Sloane turned to Leila. "How many travelers have you personally met?"

"Personally?" Leila laughed. Her eyes went out of focus, as she looked inward. "A few, in my whole life. They have all been memorable in their own particular way." She sighed. "I met one when I was a little girl," she said softly, pointing to the portrait before the girls'. She shook her head at the memory. "I was just a little girl, and all I remember is that he left quickly. He was terrified."

Pablo chuckled. "I'll bet. It is very frightening to go through that storm and wake up in your time," he told her gently. His eyes caressed Jackson's face. "We were lucky. We were prepared, and we knew what we were in for."

Leila laughed, looking at Jackson fondly, herself. "You have a wonderful son. Our lives are better for it."

Jackson ducked his head. "Yeah, well, as it is, you guys need help. I just went and got some. Now that we are all here, I can't wait for the girls to get back."

The grownups nodded, and taking a last look at the wall of portraits, they blew out the candles, and quietly left.

That night, the drums sounded more exotic to Jackson, as he watched the dance, as seen through his parents' eyes. Laughing at the wonder in their faces, he jumped in, showing them how it was done. Before long, he was flanked by a set of parents on either side, joining in the festivities. The women danced around him, one as dark, as the other one was fair, smiles illuminating their faces. Seeming to contain the family, the men stomped and twirled, caught up in the frenzy of the night.

From their usual hiding place, the sailors watched in silence. They missed the girls, the dances were not the same without them.

But the women taking their place were just as beautiful to them, if not more.

"I wonder," drawled Silas softly in the night, "if those boys that left on that ship know, that their in-laws are in town."

Jimmy chuckled, shaking his head. "I don't know, old man, but I don't think they will mind. The mothers are even more beautiful than the daughters."

"Lucky fathers," laughed Silas.

Jimmy nodded, grinning. "It seems to me, like the savage and the boss are going to repeat history."

They laughed softly and turned their full attention back to the natives, the dancers, and the visitors.

"Encantada!"

The pirate looked up at Joshua in the crow's nest, as the cry echoed on the deck, among his men, shouts of laughter filling the air. He sighed, looking back in front of him. The last forty-eight hours had been hard on him. He had spent most of his time meeting with his immediate crew, formulating a game plan. They had to ensure the future of the Gaitano empire. The livelihood of many people depended on it. The responsibility was enormous, but they had no choice. The four friends had everything to lose. While all these meetings were going on, the women had absorbed themselves in assisting the rest of the sailors in their daily chores. At night, they had crawled into bed, muscles screaming, falling asleep before their cabins were entered by their respective sailors. This wasn't a romantic trip either, as the rest of the crew observed. The couples were intent on being professional and responsible with their duties. Admiration for them grew, with each passing day. The men contented themselves with having the women in their beds. They didn't see them long enough to hold a conversation with them, much less indulge in anything else. But now, they were almost home, and the pirate promised himself he would make it up to his girl.

The Banks and the Aguilars stood at the docks. They had spent the last couple of days sightseeing, so to speak. Jackson had taken them to all their favorite spots. They had gone exploring under waterfalls, and swum in hidden pools. They had climbed ancient ruins, and had eaten raw sugar cane, straight from the stalk. The villagers had been kind and friendly to them, patient with their questions, and seemingly childlike delight at their simple way of life. It had been relaxing and fun. And now, they were here, at the docks, La Gitana sailing in, getting increasingly larger, as they watched. Their hearts beating faster, the family anticipated the arrival of their daughters.

Marina looked up at Gaitano, as he sat on the side of the bed. She hadn't seen much of him lately, except at a distance, most of the time. The rest of the time, it seemed to her, they only caught each other, in passing. She smiled. "Hey, stranger." Looking into his eyes, she reached up to stroke his hair. He hadn't been this close, for a while.

Carlos caught her hand and kissed it, eyes smiling down at her. "We're home." He drew back as Marina sat up.

"We're home?" she asked, awake now. Her eyes were wide, as they searched his face. He nodded, and she grinned. "All right!" Sliding off the bed, she walked to the porcelain bowl on the table. Splashing her face, she laughed happily. "I'll be glad to be on dry land, Capitán," she murmured to herself.

Carlos hid his grin, pretending not to hear. "What are you doing later?" he teased.

Marina laughed, wiping her face. "When? Now, after the madness at the docks?" She shook her head, and combed her hair with her fingers. "Or maybe tomorrow after I get some rest?"

He just gazed at her. "You haven't kissed me in a few days."

She went up to him and pressed her lips against his. "I haven't seen you in a few days," she responded.

He nodded, patting her on the butt as she walked by him. "You've become a saucy wench!" he called after her.

"And you are acting like a boyfriend," she laughed over her shoulder. As she reached the deck, he heard him yell behind her.

"I *am* the boyfriend!" She laughed. Waiting for him, she scanned the docks. People were waving frantically, jumping up and down, shouting, pointing, laughing.

Salomé and Indio came to stand by her. "I've been dying to get home,"

Salomé confided in her ear. "That was scary."

Marina nodded, tears in her eyes. "Yes, it was," she whispered back. Indio looked at them both through slit eyes. He grunted.

Gaitano joined them. His eyes scanned the docks. "Something is different," he commented to his Quartermaster. "What is it?"

Indio pointed. "Over by the warehouse. It seems as if they are ready for us."

Gaitano looked, and a slow smile spread on his face. Marina glanced at him. He looked impressive. He was back in his pirate's uniform. His coat flapped in the breeze, and his hat cast a shade over his eyes. His sword at one hip, and his pistol at the other, caught the rays of the sun, as the ship rocked under their feet. She sighed. He was formidable. Just then, he glanced at her and caught her staring. He winked at her. Marina smiled and looked the other way. Standing with her sister and her friends, she too scanned the crowd.

"Look!" pointed Jackson. The four parents froze. The faces on the ship were now distinguishable. Most of the crew was busy with their chores, scrambling as they went about, preparing the ship for docking. But on the top deck, four figures stood out. As they watched, the females became their daughters. The moms gasped.

"There they are, thank you, Jesus!" exclaimed Shayla, tears in her eyes.

"There are our babies!" cried Sloane, her hands reaching out to them.

The men looked at each other, and turned back to their son. Joe embraced him. "Good job, Jax."

Pablo kissed his cheek. *"Gracias, papi."*

Jackson ducked his head and smiled at them. "I told you they'd be okay."

The four parents looked up again, the ship almost upon them, their eyes riveted on the men. *"Oye, papi,"* said Pablo, finally. "Which one is mine?"

Jackson snorted in disgust. He looked him in the eye. "You get the pirate," he said, and then turned to his father, "and you get the Indian."

The men looked at each other, and turned back to the ship, their eyes hungrily seeking their daughters'. Pablo's heart jumped, as, it seemed to him, Marina turned towards him. He held his breath. Her eyes scanned the crowd around him, and looked into his. They locked. His heart pounded. And then he saw the exact instant when she recognized him. The daughter of his heart. His *nena*. Marina's mouth dropped open, and her eyes stayed fixed on him. He smiled. Over the distance, before he heard his name, he saw her scream.

Marina scanned the crowd. The wind was at their backs, and it seemed as if they were gliding in. The people cheered, chanting her Captain's name. *Gai-ta-no*. She smiled to herself, proud of him, and happy to be associated with him. *I have never met anyone like this man*, she admitted to herself with a sigh. She wondered what would happen now. Concentrating on the faces in front of her, she thought she saw cornrows in the multitude. Sliding her eyes again over the area, a flash of white to the side caught her attention. Marina turned her head and froze. She had fallen into the familiar gaze of the most beloved eyes in the world, to her. She focused quickly, her mouth falling open. Marina Aguilar was looking right at Pablo Aguilar, her father. He smiled. She screamed.

"Papi!" Marina tore off running.

Salomé's heart stopped. *"Where?"* She scanned the crowd wildly, and then, she too screamed. *"Papi!"* Before either the Captain or the Quartermaster could react, she tore after her sister.

Carlos turned to look after them. "What the hell?" he growled. He started to follow.

Indio stopped him, and held him, pointing at the crowd. He rumbled in his ear, amused. "They didn't say *papi*," he chuckled. "They said *Papi*." He brought his head closer to his brother's. "See Jackson?"

The pirate sighted down the Quartermaster's arm, and saw Jackson. He seemed to be surrounded by people. Four, smiling strangers. And as he focused, he finally saw. *Papi*. The man seemed to be looking right at him, brown eyes searching his blue ones, assessing. He straightened up, and laughed into Indio's face. His eyebrows raised in amusement. "Ready to meet the in-laws?"

Indio chuckled. "I guess this means we are serious."

They walked slowly towards the ramp, the last ones off the boat. The pirate straightened his hat and smoothed his hands down his coat. He grinned. "I guess we are."

Marina and Salomé ran, racing past the people until they came to their family. They couldn't speak. Without a word, their parents embraced them, Jackson alternating between them. Then they switched, each girl in a different set of arms. When the tears had flowed for a while, and the shudders had died down, they all looked at each other. There were a million questions in their eyes, but not enough words to express them.

Jackson kissed his sisters. "I will explain. Let's go somewhere." He laughed as they threw themselves against him, smothering him with kisses. Just then, the men reached them. Jackson stilled the girls, to make the introductions.

Salomé winked at her mom and laughed, grabbing Indio's hand. "This here is the Quartermaster." She stood in front of him and rolled her eyes, making her parents smile. "He's my new boyfriend," she teased him, mugging at her parents. "So far, so good." The Banks and the Aguilars shook hands with Indio, and then turned to look at the pirate.

Sloane grasped her husband's arm as she looked up at the man. Marina smiled. "Carlos Gaitano is the Captain. I have been helping him with his books. He's my boss and my friend." She looked at her parents, the love for the man clear in her eyes. "We're kind of hanging." She nodded her head at their unspoken question. "It's going pretty good, actually. We're cool."

Pablo nodded and held out his hand. "Pleased to meet your acquaintance, sir. It will be a pleasure to speak to you. Right now, we would like some time to visit with our daughters."

Gaitano smiled and shook his hand. "Carlos Gaitano, at your service. Please, feel free," he gestured towards the town. "I hope your stay in Encantada is a pleasant one."

The moms smiled, and Joe shook his hand. "Thank you, Captain. We will see you later."

The two men looked after the family as they walked away. Instead of going into town, they began walking down the beach. As they watched, the family marched through the sand for a while, before they stopped. Melting into a group hug, the seven people stood in a circle, heads together. After a moment, they stepped away, and rubbed each other on the back. Then, they all sank down to sit on the sand, facing each other. From where they stood, they could see them start an animated discussion.

Jackson looked at his sisters. "I'm really sorry, you guys. There was nothing I could do ---"

Salomé interrupted him. "We know, Jackson." She smiled. "It was all right. They just went to a little island called Carey, a couple of days away."

Jackson frowned. "Yeah, well, what was so important that they had to kidnap Marina?" He scowled.

Marina shook her head. "It wasn't *kidnapping*, Jax! It was... *coercion*, I guess."

Jackson rolled his eyes at her. "You weren't going willingly, when *I* saw you."

Marina looked around. The parents waited expectantly. "No, you're right. I was kicking and screaming the whole way," she admitted. "I was freaking out, because I thought we would be stuck in this time." She shook the hair out of her face. "I didn't know what would happen, if we physically left this island."

Sloane took her in her arms and squeezed her, murmuring in her ear. Drawing back, she smiled at her daughter. "How did it go?"

Marina laughed. "The voyage? Half the time I was knocked out by something the doctor sent me, but other than that..." she shrugged.

"Jackson tells us there is trouble brewing on this island," Pablo told her, catching her chin to look into her eyes.

Marina felt herself sinking into the brown pools of chocolate, a warm fuzzy feeling coming over her. "Kind of. We don't know too much about it, except that when we got here, Gaitano realized there was something wrong with his books. I met him accidentally, and we got to talking," she rolled her eyes, making them all laugh, "and I ended up taking a look at his books." She turned to look at her father, the businessman. "Papi, this guy is being robbed blind, slowly. They are taking everything but the nails on the cross."

Pablo nodded at her, searching her eyes. They shared a passion for numbers, and worked well together. He was preparing his daughter to help run his own business. "Where do you think the problem is?"

Marina stretched and looked around at all of them, thinking. She finally looked back at her father. "He spends too much time on the ocean, I guess. Actually, he wasn't even here when we arrived, but sailed in a couple of days later. We experienced firsthand how his operation works, when he got here."

Salomé nodded. "It sucked. Their system was primitive when it came down to the distribution of the goods he brings back. The lines wrapped around the block, so to speak. Marina and I got them to do it a little bit more organized, and a little bit faster. Now the whole town loves us."

Joe stroked her hair. "So, your being here affects these people's lives."

Salomé nodded. "Tremendously."

"So," Shayla wondered out loud, "it is as Leila told us." The girls grinned at the mention of the woman's name. "You ended up here, because you have a mission." They nodded.

Sloane smiled. "So, did you do whatever it is you were supposed to? Are you ready to come home?"

Marina and Salomé looked at each other. Their exchange was private and quiet, as the rest of their family watched. Coming to an agreement, they shook their heads. "This isn't over," Marina said sadly.

"How did you guys get here?" Salomé asked.

Joe chuckled, rubbing his eyes at the memory. "Jackson came and got us."

She turned to stare at her brother. "You just went and *got* them?" She laughed, holding her hand up for a high-five. "Papi, you rock!"

Jackson slapped her hand with his, and shrugged. "Leila helped me. Papi did a computer printout. Now, we've actually got a timetable." He grinned. "We can ride that storm in and out of here," he said happily, his eyes sparkling.

Marina frowned. "So, when's the next one?"

Sloane put her arms around her, rubbing her arms. "In about a month," she said softly. "Jackson thought you might be in trouble, or you might need help. We took time off to be close to you girls, until the next storm comes along."

Marina put her arms around her mother and looked up into her turquoise eyes, tears forming in her own. For a moment, she felt like a little girl. "Thanks, Mami."

Sloane's hair covered them for a moment, like a beautiful silver blanket. She gazed into her daughter's eyes. "I love you, mamita."

Shayla gazed at Salomé. "We'll be here for this month. We have plenty of time to catch up."

Salomé nodded, her love for her family shining in her face. "Sure, Mom."

Joe stroked his daughter's head. "Now, isn't there work to do when a ship comes in?"

They laughed. "We better go." Standing up, they brushed the sand off their pants, and began walking back. Once they got back to the docks, there was a young African man waiting for them. The parents looked at each other, as the man smiled at them.

"If you would be so kind, as to follow me," Solomon said, smile bright in his face, earrings sparkling in the sun. "The Captain would like you to join us upstairs, in the warehouse," he pointed at the building behind him, "while we finish down here with the cargo. He thought you might like to sit down, out of the sun for a while."

Pablo and Joe looked at each other, as their daughters did. Joe shrugged. Pablo sighed and smiled at the young man. "Actually, that sounds like a plan. We would be happy to join him..."

"Solomon."

"...Solomon. Lead the way, son." The family smiled at each other, as they began following him.

Solomon turned and flashed a smile at the girls. "*You*, however, the Captain wants helping with the lines. He says *nobody* can run this better than you." He grinned at them.

Salomé put her hands on her hips and tossed her hair. "At least the man recognizes talent when he sees it!"

Marina just shook her head. She smiled at her parents as they turned once more, to follow the young man. "It's okay," she called after them. "Solomon *can't* hurt you." She laughed wickedly as the Boatswain flashed her a scowl over his shoulder. Turning back to her siblings, she smiled. "Let's do this."

Salomé looked around her. "We need Caribe."

As if by magic, the dreadlocked boy appeared next to them. He grinned. "Ready?"

The four young people high-fived. "Let's do it," Jackson said. "Show me." Heading towards the lines, they did.

The parents looked down on their children, their eyes on the activity below them. Shayla laughed and looked at the pirate. "Is this the way it gets every time you come back from a trip?"

Gaitano chuckled. "It used to be worse. It would take days to take care of everybody."

"What happened?" she asked.

Indio beamed with pride. "Salomé established a system to do everything faster, and better."

Joe laughed. "Causing you any trouble?"

Indio's eyes met his. "Not enough." Joe nodded.

Sloane sighed and leaned her head on Pablo's shoulder. "What do you think, Papi?" she murmured.

His eyes followed his daughter as she went from person to person, taking down names. "I think she looks like a wild woman," he muttered. She smiled. He embraced her, burying his face in her neck. "Just like her mother." They laughed.

The pirates looked up from the table where they were working at, distracted by the laughter. Seeing the couples relaxed and happy, they turned back to what they were doing. From the shadows, a man broke away from his companions, and strode over to the strangers. "They are your daughters."

The couples stopped at the sound of the deep voice. In front of them was a man they hadn't seen when they came in. He was big and muscular, his hands scarred from hard labor. The clothes he was wearing were obviously borrowed, and shoes hadn't made it to his bare feet. The pants stopped above the ankles, and the shirt strained against his chest. His skin was the color of rich, dark coffee. His face was that of an African king. His hair sprouted from his head in massive dreadlocks, reminiscent of Bob Marley. He smiled at them, kindness in his brown eyes.

The men looked at each other, and back at him. Joe cleared his throat.

"Yes, they are. Have you met them?"

The man laughed. "Yes, sir," he said happily. "I have." He waved a hand at the wall on the other side of the room. Standing against it were a couple, and a lone man. They were all looking at them. "Your daughters made it possible for us to be aboard La Gitana on her trip back home." He watched as the people waved at each other from across the room. "I know who you are," he said suddenly, his voice low.

Pablo gave a start, and quickly glanced at the pirates. They still had their heads down, peering at papers on the table. He looked the dreadlocked man up and down, measuring him. No warning bells were going off in his head, but still, you never knew. "Who are *you?*" he asked.

The man smiled and nodded at the young people down below, as they rushed from one place to another, helping the people of Encantada. "How did you get here?" he asked.

Sloane and Shayla glanced at each other. Going to stand in front of him, Sloane faced him, away from the pirates' eyes. "Our son, Jackson, came to us, thinking his sisters were in trouble. Who are you?"

The man chuckled softly, reaching for some papers in his pocket. He pointed out his son, among theirs. "Do you know Caribe?"

Shayla smiled, her eyes sparkling, as she looked up at the man. "We haven't met him yet," she said softly. "But we are looking forward to it. He has been extremely kind and generous with our children."

The man smiled and held out the papers to them. "I am Don Manuel. Caribe's father." He bowed to them. "Your daughters made it possible for me to reunite with my family. I thank you." He winked at them conspiratorially and smiled, walking back to join his friends.

The couples gathered around the papers, their eyes filled with wonder. Each paper had a drawing of a couple. In one of them, the Banks, and in the other, the Aguilars.

"Gaitano!" The woman looked startled, to find herself facing the pirate and his First Mate.

"Dominique."

The woman was visibly flustered. She turned to look at the two women behind her and forcing a smile, nodded her head. The women nodded back and turned to go up the stairs. The men watched them until they were out of sight. The shopowner turned to them once more, a new face on. "How was your trip?" she asked. "It was quite short this time."

The pirate nodded, observing her as he pretended not to. She seemed a little bit more excited than usual. "How is business?"

Dominique Swan visibly relaxed, distracted into small talk. "Fine, fine," she said, this time the smile, genuine. "I can't keep up, actually. Liana has work to keep her busy for the next couple of months. Right now, we are swamped, since Salomé took off," she glanced at Indio and swallowed. "I mean, now that she is back, I will be able to catch up."

"Actually," said Indio, distracting her some more. "That is why we are here. Salomé came home to find her parents in town. She will be back to work in a couple of days, if that is all right with you."

The woman frowned before she realized it. The men caught it before she turned her face back on. She tossed her platinum hair and flashed them a not- so-quick smile. "Why, of course that is all right, Indio. You are the boss, and she *is* your girl..."

Indio laughed, his eyes sharp. "Yes, she is."

She shook her head at him. "Well, don't you worry. Liana and I will do just fine for the next couple of days. We have, so far..." She turned to the pirate, excitement in her eyes. "Gaitano, did you get what I asked you for?"

Gaitano chuckled, the answer clear in his heart. "Yes, Dominique, I did. You can go down to the docks and get your merchandise." He laughed, as she clapped her hands with joy. Raising his eyebrows, he looked at Indio and turned to leave. "Don't worry, Dominique," he threw over his shoulder as they went out the door. When it banged shut behind him, he smiled at Indio. "You will be getting exactly what you asked for." The brave chuckled as they walked on.

The next stop was the general store. John Kline looked up as the bells tinkled. The shop seemed to be full of women at the moment, all chattering excitedly around Larissa. The pirate and the Indian looked at each other and smiled. The ladies had turned around at their entrance, and had grown quiet. Larissa looked around one of the women, and her face lit up with excitement. Remembering where she was, she pretended to scowl at them. "Did you need anything gentlemen?" she called, marching towards them. "Haven't I said something to you before, about scaring my customers?" She put her hands on Indio's chest and pretended to push him. The pirate caught her around the waist and spun her around, making her squeal. The women screamed, almost cowering together, their eyes wide with fright. Larissa surrendered, laughing as she was placed on the countertop, next to her husband. "Gaitano," she sighed, looking happily up at him. "I'm so glad you are back."

He grinned at her, kissing her on the cheek. "I am glad to be back," he said in a low voice. He turned to John and winked at him. "Came to take care of some business."

John nodded. "What can we do for you?"

The pirate hesitated. He licked his lips, searching for the right words. "I have a young lady down at the Lair, right now, visiting with her parents." He chuckled, as Larissa sat up straight on the counter and clasped her hands, excitement virtually shooting out of her eyes. "She hasn't seen a baby in a while, and I was just wondering ---"

"Say no more!" John laughed and disappeared behind some shelves.

"Here you go," he crooned, reappearing again, Max in his arms. The baby squealed at the sight of the men.

"Max!" exclaimed Indio, reaching out for him. The baby jumped up and down, laughing and clapping his hands. He lunged from his father's, into the brave's arms. Indio laughed happily, as he tickled the baby with a feather.

Gaitano smiled at the couple. "Thank you." He turned to walk away, Indio at his side.

"Tell her to take her time," Larissa called after them.

At the door, the men turned to wave good-bye and stopped to look at the women. Indio scowled at them, and they gasped. As soon as they left, the women swooped on Larissa, wanting to know how she could just give up her baby the way she did, to the savage and the pirate.

Larissa shrugged happily. "Max is in daycare," she announced with a laugh. "They are part of it." She winked at her husband.

John laughed and nodded. "That's right, ladies. Gaitano and his Quartermaster are just providing transportation for Max. Daycare is the best thing that ever happened to us. Now," he said, rubbing his hands vigorously, "how can we help you ladies, today?"

"Max!"

Marina's head shot up at the greeting. She looked into the mirror behind the bar, and her eyes met the pirate's. The baby was cradled in his arms, sitting comfortably with his back solid against the man's chest, laughing as people acclaimed him. She didn't move as he stopped behind her. He grinned, as the baby threw himself forward and climbed on her back. She laughed. "Is this for me?"

Gaitano chuckled, as he gently pulled her hair out of the way, while transferring the infant into her arms. Marina caught Max tight against her, breathing him, an expression of rapture in her face. Her family looked at each other in the mirror, as the pirate put both hands on the bar, on either side of her, trapping their daughter and the baby in his arms. His face softened as he gazed at them. "Just for you." He lowered his head to whisper in her ear, their eyes locked in the mirror. "You look good with a baby, mami."

Marina smiled and whispered back. "*Gracias, papi.*"

The pirate chuckled. He reached over her to press his lips to the baby's dark head, before kissing her on the cheek. With a last caress of her hair, he went and sat at his usual spot, at the end of the bar. Her family watched in silence for a moment, as the first man approached the pirate. Gaitano invited him to sit down, and proceeded to listen to the man.

Pablo and Sloane looked at each other, wonder in their faces. Their eyes met in the mirror, also, and they knew they had a lot to talk about. He turned to his daughter and teased. "*Oye, mami*, you look good with a baby."

Marina threw her head back and laughed. From his place by the bar, the pirate glanced over, his eyes quickly caressing her, before turning his attention back to the man in front of him. She looked at her father. "That, Papi, is just what the pirate said."

He smiled into her eyes without saying anything for a moment. "You like this pirate, huh, nena?" Marina nodded. She couldn't speak. Instead, she held Max tighter. Pablo nodded, and kissed her on the forehead. She blinked back tears, and buried her face in Max's belly.

They spent a nice time at the Lair, relaxed, catching up. Jimmy ran out for lunch for them, as usual, and they lost Jackson to the girls at a table, for a while. Pablo watched with interest, as Gaitano attended one man after another, until there were no more. Looking in the mirror, he gestured to Joe. Whistling softly, he caught Jackson's attention. The women of their family looked on, as the men stood together, talking softly. Finally coming to an agreement, they went in force, to the pirate sitting at the corner of the bar.

Gaitano looked up as the men approached him. If it weren't for who they were, he would be wary. Instead, he smiled and stood to shake each of their hands. "Sit down, gentlemen," he offered. "What can I do for you?" The men sat around him, relaxed.

Pablo smiled at him. "We would like to buy you a drink."

"It looks like they have been keeping you busy," said Joe.

"Thank you," the pirate smiled at them, signaling to Silas. "They have, actually." He waited until the old sailor brought back the beers.

"Put it on my tab, old man," Jackson said, as he thanked him. Silas nodded and left them alone.

Gaitano looked at each of them. "Now, what can I help you with?"

Pablo glanced at his men, before turning back to the pirate. "Well, maybe we can talk about what we can help you with."

Gaitano frowned. "I don't understand."

Joe smiled at him. "Jackson told us you were having trouble of some kind."

Gaitano looked at Jackson. "He did?"

Jackson raised his hands in the air. "Yo, man, just trying to help. I don't even know what your trouble is."

Gaitano nodded. He glanced at where Indio stood by Salomé, watching them. A flicker in his eyes, and the brave came to sit with them. "How would you know if I need help?" he asked, buying time.

Pablo looked straight into the eyes that were so like his wife's. "I understand Marina has been helping you with some books." At the pirate's nod, he continued. "And I guess she found something, or better yet, confirmed something for you, that is going on in your business."

"She did. I hired her as my accountant."

Joe nodded. "So, what did she find that was so crucial?"

Gaitano hesitated. "There were a few discrepancies," he said slowly.

Jackson shook his head. "No, man. What my dad means, is what was so important that you just took her?"

The pirates froze. Indio spoke up. "She wasn't in danger."

Pablo shook his head. "We are realizing it. The girls we have raised into women are not stupid." He turned back to Gaitano. "My daughter stumbled into something that was important enough for you to take her with you. I have been here for a few days. I have met Padre Ignacio and Pedro Escobar. And I know you are in trouble. How much?" He shrugged his shoulders. Gaitano still didn't answer, but Pablo Aguilar recognized a thinking man when he saw one. *"Que pasa, papi?"* he asked softly.

Gaitano sighed, and took a drink from his beer. His eyes wandered to Marina, where she was happily catching up with her mothers. He looked back at her men. "Marina calls it a hostile takeover." He hesitated, as Pablo and Joe looked at each other. "She suggested that we clean house." He fell silent.

Jackson grinned. "What you need is, to kick some ass." Indio grunted in agreement.

Pablo spread his hands. "So, clean house!"

Gaitano nodded. He looked at them thoughtfully. "Would you like to work for me?"

The men grinned. "You know what?" laughed Joe. "A paid vacation sounds fine, to me."

Pablo nodded. "Depends on what you want us to do. We're not pirates."

This time, Gaitano grinned. "No. On this, you are just men." He looked at each of them. "Family."

Jackson nodded, looking at him with pride "Anything we can do..." said Joe.

Pablo nodded. "Count us in, papi."

Gaitano nodded and smiled. Raising an eyebrow, he looked at the men. "What are you doing after you dance tonight?"

They looked at each other. Silent questions shot from their eyes, and then, slow smiles spread on their faces. They laughed softly.

Silently, the five men touched bottles, and drank.

The afternoon sun filtered through the leaves, the rays slanting on the dirt path. The group of people approached the village slowly.

Quino, Francois' father, stopped and looked at them. His eyes glistened like drops of silver, as he turned to smile at them. Taking Marina's and Salomé's hands, he kissed them one at a time. Tears shone in his eyes. His voice was low and soft, when he could finally speak. "I thank you." Smiling, he turned from them, and made his way home. They kept walking.

Leilani looked up as she felt the people coming up her walk. The babies crawled peacefully on the front porch, as she waited, the laundry basket at her side. She stared at the couple that approached her. Her mouth dropped open. A wail escaped her throat, rising in volume. Joaquin rushed to her and caught her, as she began falling. Leilani sobbed in her father's arms. Reina scooped up her babies as Ali wrapped her little arms around her legs. The reunion was charged with emotion as the family held each other, rocking on the front porch, the sun wrapping them in its last light. The strangers walked away, giving them privacy.

Leila looked up as a shadow crossed her threshold. A man stood in her doorway, the sun at his back, giving him a golden silhouette. She smiled, her heart constricting in her chest. Tears stung her eyes, and a knot formed in her throat. Putting her basket of beads to one side, she stood up slowly, a prayer escaping her lips. Tears ran down her face. The man stepped in, shutting the door behind him. Leila stumbled as she walked towards him, falling into his arms, trembling. The man caught her and held her against him, just feeling her emotion course through her body. A soft laugh rumbled deep in his chest. Laughing herself, she looked up into the beloved face, her hands gliding over his thick dreads. "Manuel," she whispered. His eyes locked on hers. Lowering his head, Don Manuel, finally, kissed his wife.

That night, the drums beat in a frenzy, the dancers almost out of control. The pirates sat, watching from their usual hiding place. This time, it seemed as if the natives were keeping to the background, all eyes focused on the families in front of them. The men were skilled as they spun and stomped, naked chests glistening by the light of the torches. Joe and Pablo circled their son, as Caribe and Don Manuel faced each other, stepping in rhythm, smiles wide in their dark faces. The women twirled and shimmied around them, hair flying, hips shaking, breasts heaving, as they expressed their joy and love for one another.

Silas and Jimmy smiled, as the pair beside them groaned. Silas turned to them, a chuckle escaping him. "If I didn't know any better," he drawled, "I would say you two were hurting for some females."

Indio grinned, a bead of sweat gliding down his face. "We are, old man."

"Yes," agreed Gaitano in a low voice, his eyes riveted on the woman with the sun caught in her hair.

Jimmy laughed. "You must have been dropped on your heads when you were babies! If it were me," he winked at them, "I wouldn't be hurting for mine, and she sure as hell wouldn't be dancing right now!" He smiled wickedly as Indio grunted. "At least not out here..." The men laughed. They sat back and enjoyed themselves, the drums beating in their heads, rushing through their veins.

Some time later, they came out of their hiding places as the dance concluded. The natives stood around laughing, some already making their way home. The families stood together, excited and breathless, complimenting and teasing one another. They looked up in surprise, as the riders came up on them.

Jackson laughed, face beaded with perspiration, eyes sparkling with excitement. "Yo, guys! You ought to try this some time! It's unreal, man."

The men smiled. They glanced over to the side, where Salomé and Marina still danced quietly, shaking their heads and their hips at each other. Joe cleared his throat, getting their attention. "What's the plan, men?"

The women looked at each other. Shayla frowned. "Plan?" She wiped the perspiration off her face, chest still heaving from the exertion.

Sloaned flipped her long platinum hair back. "Where are you going?"

Pablo swaggered to her. Catching her around the waist, he caught her against him and pressed his mouth to hers, passionately. "We are going to do, *man* stuff!" he announced to her, when he finally came up for air.

Sloane laughed, as he nuzzled her neck. She clung to him, smiling to the men over his shoulder. "Be careful," she whispered in his ear.

"I will, Mami," he whispered back.

Shayla hugged her husband. "You take care of yourself, baby." She looked at the pirates suspiciously.

Joe chuckled. "Go home, get some sleep. Dream of me," he murmured in her ear. She turned to look at him and grinned. He dropped a swift kiss on her mouth.

Gaitano watched, his heart tightening. Indio had left his side, to talk to Salomé, his big hand caressing her long hair as she hugged him. He searched for Marina. She was standing by herself, by one of the torches. One of the village boys was still playing a drum softly, just for her, and she was dancing for him. Without thinking, he got off his horse and went to her.

She smiled as he approached, eyes sparkling, her hair still whipping around her face, her hips still swinging. Finally, she stopped and threw her head back, laughing softly into the night sky. Her excited eyes met his. *"I love this!"* she whispered passionately. "I have never had a chance to express myself like this before, just my body and my feelings."

Gaitano groaned to himself, at the implications. He smiled at her, and stopped, riveted by the sparkle in her eyes. As he watched, her breathing slowed down, her chest rising softly. "You move very well," he complimented her.

"Thank you," she smiled, and stopped. She felt herself drown in his eyes.

He smiled, drawing closer. "You haven't kissed me in a while," he murmured.

Marina laughed, self-consciously, stepping back as she wiped the perspiration off her face and her arms. "I haven't seen you lately." He stopped, watching her, amused. Her eyes met his, not laughing anymore. "You are going to be real busy for a while, aren't you?"

The pirate nodded, not answering. She evaded his eyes, laughing softly. "Well, I am really glad to be home. It will be good for me to be back with the babies---"

"Marina." He stopped her. She looked up at him. He couldn't speak for a moment, as his feelings raged inside, his body exercising control over his sole impulse. Taking her hand, he gently pulled her to him. "I will send Indio with the books in a couple of days."

Marina swallowed and nodded. She shrugged and threw him a smile. "Sure." Pulling her hand away, she smiled at the boy with the drum again. Glancing at the pirate, she evaded his eyes. "I guess I will see you later, Capitán."

Gaitano swore under his breath and nodded. "Come here," he said softly.

Marina stepped back, shaking her head. "I'm going home. Later." Gaitano shook his head, catching her hand. "Come here," he repeated. Marina stopped, and let herself be drawn to him. She didn't want to look at him. She felt her face lifted towards his. "Gaitano..."

"Ssshhh." Lowering his head, he pressed his lips to hers. His heart rose in his chest, and a faint roar started in his head. He pulled back, looking at her. He couldn't do to her here, what his soul was commanding him to. He kissed her lips again, swiftly, and stepped back, letting her go. "I will see you later," he promised. And he was gone.

Marina looked after him, as he joined the men once more. There were four riders on horseback, waiting to leave. As she watched, her fathers, her brother, and Caribe, each climbed up behind one of the riders. Her father rode with her pirate. And in a moment, they were gone into the jungle, the sound of horses' hooves getting fainter in the night air.

"I want to thank you all for coming here." Gaitano looked around the room. They had decided on the Siren's Lair for their meeting, on this occasion, since it was the only place in town where a large group of men could be gathered, without being too conspicuous. "I know some of you are dying to go back to sea, but right now I need you here. There are some matters to be taken care of first." The men nodded, listening attentively. "We are going to start this with those closest to us." He turned to his Sailing Master. "Giancarlo. Go get your books. I am going to start this, right here and right now. Once you are done, go to Padre Ignacio's." He looked up, his eyes searching the lawman's. "Pedro, go get yours. Solomon will be in charge of going through it. Indio, you go with Pablo to the Klines'. And Joe, you come with me." He glanced at the boys. "Jackson and

Caribe, you wait here and keep an eye on things, until we get back." He looked around, one more time. "Everybody ready?" He smiled as they all nodded. "Let's do this."

Giancarlo walked over to the bar and laid his book out in front of Jackson.

The young man smiled at the Italian and got to work. Next to him, Pedro Escobar laid out his, as Solomon inspected it. Satisfied, the pirate and the brave left the bar, their in-laws close behind them.

The streets were deserted at this hour, their only lighting the torch they carried. Gaitano was still in full pirate costume, dressed to work. He clinked as he walked, the buttons of his coat hitting the sword at his side. Indio's sword was strapped to the middle of his back, and like the pirate, a pistol at his hip. Joe and Pablo looked at each other, excitement in their faces. They knew the weapons were there as a show of force, and not because any real trouble was expected.

They parted ways in front of the dress shop. Indio and Pablo kept going to the general store, and Gaitano stayed, pounding on the door.

"Coming! Coming!" They heard the voice through the door. A moment later, a latch was opened from the other side, and the door swung open. Dominique Swan stood before them, a candle in her hand. She blinked up at them, surprise registering in her face, as she caught sight of the pirate. *"Gaitano!"* she gasped, a hand going to her chest, shock in her eyes.

"Dominique." Gaitano smiled, eyes cold, as he pushed his way in, making the woman back up. Her eyes flew from his face to Salomé's father.

Joe observed closely. The woman looked a little like his friend's wife, with her fair coloring, but that was where the resemblance stopped. Sloane was a natural woman. Dominique Swan was... an *image* of a certain *type* of woman.

He nodded at her, serious. "Good evening." She couldn't answer, her eyes flying to Gaitano's face.

The pirate was all business. He went to a side table and began lighting candles. "I know this is inconvenient for you, Dominique, but we have been having some trouble with the merchandise we have been bringing over lately, and their final destination. If you would be so kind, I would like to inspect your books. Right now," he said looking at her. "From there, we will just go and take a look at your supply room."

Dominique gasped. *"Gaitano!"* They saw her scrambling desperately for words. "Couldn't this wait until the morning?"

Gaitano shook his head. "While you go do that, I will just take a look around, if you don't mind. Thank you." Dismissing her, with a wave of his hand, he wandered away from her, headed to the stairs.

Joe looked at her, as a cry escaped her throat and she blanched. Eyes wide with fear, she spun around quickly, and disappeared behind one of her wall hangings. He turned to the pirate and grinned. "Not too happy, is she?"

Gaitano shook his head. He looked up the stairs thoughtfully. Dominique appeared as he walked back to Joe. With trembling hands, she put the book down in front of him. He got to work.

"Who the hell is banging on my door, at this hour!" John Kline pulled the door opened and faced the men. He stepped back, blinking in surprise. "Indio!" He held the door open for them. "Come in, come in, man," he said, leading them to the counter. He put down the candle he was holding and looked at them, sudden alarm in his eyes. "Is everything all right?" He looked at Pablo. "Did anything happen to the girls?"

Pablo shook his head, smiling reassuringly. "No, no, the girls are fine."

Indio smiled at the storeowner, putting him at ease. "Gaitano sent us. We are to look at your books, make sure everything is in order." He looked into his eyes. "He's putting his hand in the fire, for you. We're just making sure everything is as it should be." He winked at the man. "We're cleaning house."

John Kline just gazed at him, the words sinking in. A smile spread slowly on his face. "Well, it's about damned time." Reaching under the counter, he drew out his book and set it down in front of them. "Gentlemen," he said, eyes shining with excitement. "Help yourselves."

Gaitano and Joe looked at each other. The pirate had brought some pages with him, from his own personal records, and a lot of things did not match. He had invited himself to the stock room and had proceeded to open crates and boxes. Laying between them, was an opened crate, bolts of cloth spilling out on the dusty wooden floor. In the middle, nesting among the brightly colored fabrics, were six pistols.

The pirate straightened up slowly, and turned to look at the woman. He didn't say anything. Her face looked as if it had aged ten years in the last twenty minutes. Tears were in her eyes, and her mouth was trembling, but she raised her chin defiantly. Gaitano cocked an eyebrow at her. "I don't recall these being part of your inventory, Dominique," he said, his voice dangerously low. "Who are these for?" She pressed her lips together, shaking her head. He stared at her.

"I will tear this place apart, and you know I will find everything."

She swallowed, holding a hand out to him. "Gaitano, please---"

He cut her off with a look. Joe looked from one to the other, glad he was on the pirate's side. Leaving them to their standoff, he got to work on a second crate. Digging down, he encountered metal. Gaitano looked at him expectantly. Joe pressed his lips together, a muscle twitching in his cheek. He went to a third crate, and a fourth. All of them had firearms. Finally, he shook his head and looked at Gaitano. "More of the same, Captain," he said softly.

Gaitano raised an eyebrow at Dominique. She turned from them suddenly, platinum hair whipping around her, arms holding herself, as if she were cold. She looked back at the pirate. Still, he didn't say anything. Joe shook his head with a sigh, and proceeded to open the rest of the crates.

Indio looked at John, a big smile on his face. They had just finished looking at his book, and going through his stockroom. Everything matched perfectly, Larissa's meticulous bookkeeping evident, in every aspect of their operation. The brave stretched out his hand to the storeowner. "Good job, man. Everything is perfect."

John grinned. "Has to be," he said happily, "when the boss is going to put his hand in the fire for you."

Pablo nodded in agreement. He, too, shook John Kline's hand. "Excellent business you got here."

John smiled, shaking his hand vigorously. "Thank you, Pablo. It is all that much better, since Marina has been taking care of Max."

Indio closed the book and handed it to him. "Gaitano will be by in the morning to talk to you."

John nodded, as he walked them to his door. "I will be looking forward to it." They bid each other goodnight, and Indio and Pablo left.

Silently, the two men moved together, their torch, bobbing in the dark, as they made their way down the street. In front of Dominique Swan's shop, they hesitated. Light shone around the edges of the door. Making up his mind, Indio put down his torch and entered the shop. The three people spun around at their entrance.

The pirate looked at his Quartermaster. "How did it go?" he asked.

Indio looked from one person to the other, feeling the tension in the air. "Perfectly. As expected. He will be waiting for you tomorrow."

Gaitano nodded. Indio looked at him, the question in his eyes. The Captain's eyes flickered at him. The brave froze. He turned his stony stare back to the woman. She stared back, eyes vacant and cold. The door opened again, and the room filled with men. In walked Pedro Escobar, followed by Jackson and Solomon. Giancarlo entered last, Caribe trailing behind him. The rest of the men stayed outside. Everybody looked at each other. Gaitano turned to Salomé's father. "Joe," he said softly. "Would you be so kind as to show Pedro what we found?"

"*No!*" Everyone turned to look at the woman. Her eyes were wild in her face, as she moved to block the way. "*Please, don't do this!*" she cried. The men exchanged looks. Solomon moved to stand by her, making her back up, until she had her back to the wall.

Pedro Escobar turned to Joe. The man sighed and beckoned him to follow. Pablo and Indio went after them. A few minutes later, they came back out. Pablo's eyes betrayed nothing, a scowl on his face, the only indication of his feelings. Pedro Escobar went past the men waiting for him, and flung open the outside door. They heard him say something to them, and he turned back, holding the door open for them. The men, all pirates, part of Gaitano's private, secret army, strode into the back and disappeared. A moment later, they started coming out, carrying the crates. The lawman turned to the woman, his eyes boring into her. "I need you to come with me, Dominique." He went to take her by the arm.

Dominique yanked her arm away from him, her chest heaving. *"I can walk!"* she snarled at him. Trying not to show how terrified she was, she straightened up and marched past the men, head high in the air. Pedro Escobar took a deep breath, and followed her out.

The men looked at each other. Gaitano turned to his men. "Follow me," he said softly. Not waiting for an answer, he started up the stairs, his Quartermaster, Sailing Master, and Boatswain at his heels. Joe and Pablo looked at each other for a moment. Turning to Jackson, they glanced upstairs. Not a word was said as they hurried up the stairs, catching up to the rest of the men. Caribe followed right behind them.

The hallway was spacious, carpeted in deep colors. Candles flickered on small tables along the walls, reflecting on the great mirrors put at intervals, between heavy doors with hangings over them. The men's shadows stretched and reached, crowding the hallway with eight giants. They stopped at the first door. Gaitano motioned with his hands and his head. They split up. Giancarlo and Solomon went to a different one, and Jackson and Caribe went to another door; Joe and Pablo went to yet another, while Indio stayed at his side. They ended up covering the four doors on one side of the hallway. Indio raised his arm in the air, getting their attention. On the count of three, a pair of men silently entered each room.

The pirate and the brave entered quietly, careful not to make any noise. They froze. Candlelight reflected endlessly into the mirrors that hung on the walls. The room smelled of burning incense and, a bit more. The men 's eyes scanned the room slowly, momentarily confused from all the reflections. Between the mirrors, rich drapes of deep red velvet hung, a rose pattern stamped on them. The carpet under their feet was softer than the one outside. It was exactly as Salomé had described. A *boudoir*. Against one wall was a lavish dressing table with brushes, and pots, and jars, bottles of perfume in beautiful colored cut glass. And then they saw. They held their breaths, as their eyes focused on the scene in front of them. In the middle of the room, was a beautiful piece of furniture, covered in a lavish leopardskin. In it, was a beautiful girl. She was on her back, her arms over her head, long fingers grasping the edges of the furniture, as her long blonde hair brushed the floor. Her eyes were closed and her lips were parted. Her expression was one of ecstasy. Her breasts were bare, moving up and down rapidly with her breathing. Her body was covered in a sheen of sweat, candlelight reflecting in the moisture. One leg was up on the seat, bent at the knee, while the other one was stretched out at a slant, foot on the floor. Between her legs, a brunette was busy, giving her pleasure. Looking up suddenly, she met their eyes. The men let out their breaths slowly. Without stopping what she was doing, the brunette reached up, cupping the blonde's breasts. Running her hands down, towards herself, she slipped them between the girl's thighs. Closing her eyes, she gave the girl one long lick. Looking back at the men, she winked at them. They began retreating, minds spinning. She blew them a kiss, as they backed out the door, and continued indulging herself. Once again in the hallway, the men looked at each other, eyes locking. Finally, Indio whistled under his breath, and shook his head, a smile on his lips. Gaitano looked down for a moment, and looked back at him, arching an eyebrow. He grinned. They groaned and high-fived, as they had seen the girls do.

Just then, they felt the other three doors opening behind them. Joe and Pablo looked dazed, as they approached them, identical grins on their faces. Giancarlo looked stunned. Solomon looked stoned. Caribe and Jackson reached them, and walked right by them, running down the stairs. The remaining men looked at each other and followed them. The cool night air hit them in the face as they gulped fresh air, away from the candles and the mirrors.

Jackson let out a war yell. "Whoah! Man! I can't believe that!" He passed his hands over his cornrows and started laughing. Caribe laughed with him, and they high-fived.

Giancarlo joined him. "How long has this been going on and why wasn't I told?" Tears of laughter streamed down his face. "I can do business with this!"

Solomon shook his head, dazed. "I have no words."

Jackson put his arm around the Italian's shoulders. "Yo, man, you don't even know! Let's talk business, Gian!" he said happily, walking the pirate away. "Did you know you can actually get people to pay you for letting them watch this stuff?"

"No!" The Sailing Master pulled back to look at the young black man. "Where do you come from, that there is a market for this kind of thing?"

The others looked after them, as the pair stopped a short distance away, talking earnestly.

Joe chuckled. "I'll tell you something," he said, smiling at his hosts. "I couldn't be staying up this late for anything better." They laughed. He smiled wickedly. "Unless my wife is staying up with me." More laughter.

Pablo turned to his potential son-in-law and just smiled at him. The pirate smiled back, eyes twinkling. Pablo chuckled, shoulders shaking, just looking at him. Finally, he stretched out his arms. "Carlitos," he said affectionately. "Come here," he beckoned, walking towards him. "I want to thank you," he said, putting his arms around him, in a warm embrace. Gaitano responded, rubbing the man's back. Pablo drew his head back to look at him. "This has been the best raiding party of my life!" And he kissed the pirate in the cheek. "When is the next one?"

Gaitano chuckled. "Tomorrow."

Pablo nodded, releasing his new friend. "Then we better get some rest." Laughing, the men went back to the Lair. Mounting their horses, the riders took the family home.

The pirates dropped off the men at the village. The two fathers went to join their wives. Jackson went to stay in one of Caribe's hammocks, while his sisters borrowed his hut. The night continued peacefully, the sky clear and full of stars. The jungle whispered restlessly, in the gentle breeze. A symphony of insects accompanied the night birds' calls. And as the village slept on, unaware of the night's excitement, the riders headed out to the waterfall. Where the water was cold.

Marina looked up at the sound of steps on their stairs. "Good morning," she called out, spying her visitors. Going to the door, she opened it wide for John Kline and the baby. "Max!" she exclaimed, holding out her arms to him. The baby went to her willingly, immediately nuzzling her, as he gurgled happily.

"Good morning," replied John, a twinkle in his eye.

Marina laughed, bouncing the baby gently. "How is business?" she asked. "I've been dying to visit with Larissa for a while."

"And she, with you," he replied. "She has been pretty busy lately. The women in town have been hounding her about the daycare."

Marina laughed. "She's going crazy, huh?" He nodded, widening his eyes. "Yes."

Just then, Salomé walked in, wringing excess water out of her hair. The backdoor was wide open, letting the morning sun flood the humble home. "Hey, John!" she greeted.

"Hey, Salomé! Guess who has today off?" he grinned.

"I know!" she cried happily. "Indio arranged for me to not have to go back for a couple of days."

John smiled. "Well, actually, Dominique Swan's shop is closed for a few days."

Salomé frowned. "Really? Is she sick?"

John laughed. "You could say that." And with a cheerful goodbye, he left them. The girls looked at each other and shrugged.

Midmorning saw the family wandering down to the beach. They walked slowly, taking their time, barely talking. They drew comfort, just from being together. They had brought blankets, to sit and lay on, and were now putting them down on the sand, anchoring them with assorted driftwood and shells. Max in the middle, they settled down for a nice talk.

"I need to tell him," Salomé announced suddenly. Everybody turned to look at her. Nobody asked what she was talking about.

Marina gasped, eyes wide. "Salo! Why?"

She shrugged, doodling on the sand with a stick of wood. Her green eyes looked out over the ocean for a moment, before turning back to her sister. "Indio's a really nice guy, you know?" she began, looking around at her family. "This whole experience of us ending up here, in this..." she waved her hand in the air, "...*place*, has been without precedent in my life. Nothing that has ever happened to me before, has prepared me for being here, at this place and moment in time." She hesitated, searching for words. "We didn't *ask* for this to happen," she said sadly, "it just *did*. And now we have to live with it." She searched their eyes. "I know Jackson got it down, so that we can go and come back. That's pretty cool, but..." she glanced up at the sky, and back down. "Why are we even here?" she wailed. "To help some pirate with some books?" She shook her head vigorously. "There's got to be more than that! We've come too far!" She stared out over the ocean again. "So much has happened in the last few days," she murmured.

Marina nodded her head and smiled sadly. "Natives, and Indians, and pirates, oh, my..." she murmured, winking at Jackson. He smiled back.

"And it's not just about that," said Salomé. "It's not just about Caribe, or Indio, or Gaitano. Nothing to do with the books, or the dress shop, or the babies." She looked around at each of them. "It's about *me*. It is *all* about me," she said slowly. *"Salomé Banks."*

Her family looked at her in silence, for a moment, her words sinking in.

Joe smiled at her. "And what does Salomé Banks want?" he asked softly.

Her head shot up, with a saucy grin. "Indio, for one." Marina smiled to herself and Jackson rolled his eyes. Salomé sighed. "I don't know all I want, yet, Dad," she answered. "I know some of the things I want. And right now, I want to stay here in Encantada."

"Encantada is a dangerous place, baby," her mother said softly.

Salomé shrugged. "I know, I'm living it. But, Mom, how will I ever know?" she asked. She turned to each of them, challenging. "Mami. For you to encounter the one thing that manages to blow your mind into a million pieces..." She looked at Pablo. "Papi. For real, man, would you just leave this place," she spread her arms out wide, "without exploring it to its limits?" She laughed up at the sky. "There are pirates here! We're living a damn history class! First hand, like nobody ever has before!" She looked at her parents. "Mom, you taught me to follow my heart. And you, Dad, taught me to be smart, take care of myself, and trust in God. That's exactly what I am doing. Jackson just made it easier for me to make a decision. He hooked us up with a way in and out of here. Well, I'm taking it. I want to stay, but..." she looked back over the ocean. "I need to tell Indio. He needs to know who I really am, and where I am from. If he can hang, I'm in. I want to stay and explore this further. I really like him, and I know it can develop into much more. If he can't hang, well..." she shrugged. "Then, I guess there is nothing to talk about."

Her family stayed quiet, everybody thinking on her words. Little by little, they all turned to look at Marina. She was sitting to the side with Max between her legs, busy playing with shells. She gazed back at them. "What?"

Sloane smiled at her daughter. "How about you, *mamita?*"

Marina knew everything she was referring to. She took a deep breath and shook her head. "No. Not me. I don't need to tell Indio *nada!*" Her family laughed. She sighed. "For real, I'm not telling that man anything right now." She scowled ferociously, her eyes raking over the waves coming in on shore. Her family smiled.

"Why not?" challenged Salomé. "He has a right to know."

Marina shook her head. "No."

Jackson laughed. "Marina, he has to know!"

"Why?" she shot back at him.

"What do you mean, why?" he laughed again. "That ain't right. You've got to tell him. He's interested in you ---"

"I'm his accountant!" she exclaimed, cutting him off. "He needed fresh eyes to see what was going on, and I happened to have them. I think my biggest value to him right now, is that I can help him fix this." She looked down at Max, rattling some shells in her hands for him. She missed the looks exchanged between her dads.

"You're more to him than that," protested Salomé.

"I'm his friend, if that's what you mean," she mumbled.

Salomé shook her head. "No, that's not what I mean."

Marina smiled. "Okay, I'm his makeout partner," she admitted. Her family laughed softly. "But that's not enough for me to believe that he would be receptive to some news of this magnitude."

Salomé gasped. "How do you know? Carlos Gaitano is just about the most awesome guy we have ever met!" She reached out and stroked her sister's back. "Come on, Marina, don't be like that. He's a great guy. I mean, they both are. Look at Indio ---"

"Indio," interrupted Marina, "is almost in love with you."

Salomé looked at her and smiled. She nodded at her family. "That's true. But Gaitano..." she began, turning back to Marina. She stopped. "You are scared to, aren't you?"

Marina shrugged. "Maybe." They waited. She said nothing else.

Pablo reached out a hand to her. "*Oye, mamita*, look at me." He caught her face in his hand and turned it towards him. "You want me to talk to this pirate of yours?"

Marina looked into his eyes, thinking about it. "Maybe," she finally said, softly. "But not yet, Papi, okay? Please?" Tears formed in her eyes, and she pulled away from him, looking back at the ocean.

He nodded. "Okay, baby. Whatever you say." Everybody fell silent.

Marina sighed, and glanced at them. She tousled Max's hair and rattled more shells for him. She scanned the ocean, and looked back at her family. She sighed again. "I am crazy about that man," she groaned. Nobody answered.

They stayed silent for a while, basking in the sun. The tide was going down, leaving strands of seaweed in a curvy line on the shore. Behind them, the palm trees shaded the entrance to the jungle, from the climbing sun. Sand pipers played with the bubbles in the sand, and seagulls patrolled the sky overhead. A lone alcatraz circled a certain spot in the water, before diving headfirst, only to appear a moment later, popping out like a cork, its catch flashing in the sunlight before it quickly disappeared.

Suddenly, they heard a faint noise, getting louder, as it came from the jungle. They turned towards the sound. To their amazement, out from the thick foliage, burst a pack of bare-chested men, all running together, Caribe leading them, with Indio and Gaitano behind him. The family watched, mesmerized. There must have been around twenty men. The whole crew of La Gitana, Don Manuel, and a few pirates from town. Slowly, they came to a stop, before them.

Caribe stepped forward, beaming. He spread his arms wide, shaking his dreadlocked head at them. "Good morning!"

"Good morning!" they chorused back, laughing.

"We are out, running, as taught by your daughters, gentlemen!"

Joe laughed. "Is that right?"

Marina laughed and looked at Shayla. "Mom, please watch the baby?" Already, Jackson and Salomé were on their feet, their fathers following slowly. Shayla nodded with a smile, waving her hand, and Marina leapt to her feet. "You guys, check this out." The men in her family looked at her. Cupping her hands over her mouth, she yelled up into the sky. *"La Gitana!"*

"Aguilar!" the men yelled back.

Marina laughed, as Joe and Pablo looked at each other. Pablo raised his eyebrows at her, his eyes dancing with laughter. *"Oye, nena,* you've been busy, ah?"

Jackson slid his hand against hers. "I'm impressed, yo!"

Salomé rolled her eyes. Laughing, she turned to both her fathers. "You guys, check *this* out." She repeated Marina's movements. *"La Gitana!"*

"Banks!" Their reply sounded like a shot in the morning stillness.

Salomé held up one finger, and raised her eyebrows at her family, indicating that she wasn't done. "If you please, show your Masters, what you have learned!" Standing before her men, she bowed. Then she turned to the shirtless men behind her. They bowed. Joe and Pablo looked at each other again. Then, they shared glances with Jackson. Facing the crew of men backing their daughters, they bowed. Salomé turned to the pirates, her face filled with joy. "Assume the position!"

The mothers sat with the baby, mesmerized by what was unfolding before them. The men watched with wonder, as the pirates performed in front of them. They executed their forms flawlessly. Their daughters blended with them, their cutoff pants being in uniform with the men. At the same time, they stood out, their brightly colored tops bringing splashes of life, amongst the men's bare skin. When they were done, they bowed to their Masters. Joe and Pablo bowed back, pride in their faces.

Joe called out to his daughters. "You've done real good, girls!"

Pablo laughed. *"Muy bien, muchachas!"*

Jackson clapped his hands. "Good job, ladies!"

The mothers laughed and cheered, blowing kisses at them, with cries for an encore. Salomé spoke to the men, and paired them off, placing herself with Indio.

Marina called again. *"La Gitana!"*

"Aguilar!"

"Assume the position!"

Once more, the family watched astounded, as the men began to fight. They danced around each other, displaying their ability with kicks, blocks, and punches. Their daughters were paired with their men.

Marina smiled at her pirate. "Ready?" He nodded, smiling wickedly. "Are you?"

She laughed. "I was born ready." And so, they began. They practiced, circling each other, concentrating on what they were doing. When they were done, they bowed to each other, and smiled.

This time, they got a standing ovation from the whole family. Even Max clapped his little hands happily, blowing bubbles as he laughed. The men formed a line, so they could bow to their Masters personally, and shake their hands. Joe and Pablo congratulated each man, complimenting them on their individual strengths, as observed by them.

When all that was done, the men grouped together to leave. Caribe in front, followed by the four commanding pirates, and the rest of the sailors at the end, with Don Manuel. Suddenly, a yell made them all look.

"Aguilar!"

Marina turned to look. She had already taken Max into her arms again, and she was watching Gaitano stand with her fathers, talking earnestly. It seemed to her, as if everybody were staring at her. She didn't yell back, however. Instead, she gave Max back to Shayla, and strode towards the men slowly. "Solomon," she sang, smiling slowly. Pablo and Joe looked on with interest. "Come out and play..."

Solomon strode slowly to the center of where they were standing. He looked at her mockingly, and beckoned her with his hands. "You owe me." Marina winked at him and blew him a kiss.

Slowly, the men backed away. Giancarlo called out to his friend.

"Jackson! Quick! Take down some names and numbers," he laughed. "Let's make some money!"

Joe looked at the pirate. "What's going on?"

Gaitano pressed his lips together and shook his head. "I think he's calling her out."

Pablo laughed and pointed a finger at himself. "My little girl? He's calling out my little girl?" He looked at Solomon, mischief in his face. *"Oye, Solomon!* You calling out my little girl?"

Gaitano cleared his throat. "Your little girl fights like a man, sir!"

Pablo grinned at him. "Good," he said softly. "That is how she is supposed to fight."

Indio and Salomé came over and joined them, as the pair circled each other. The brave turned to his Captain. "You realize, Solomon is intent on hurting your accountant."

Gaitano chuckled. "I am."

Joe frowned, not liking where this was going. "And why is that?"

Salomé laughed, her green eyes sparkling. "Aguilar," she announced to her family, "proceeded to kick Solomon's ass all over La Gitana, while we were out at sea."

Jackson laughed. "Way to go, mami!"

"Why did she do that?" asked his father.

"Solomon was the one who got her at Padre Ignacio's church, and carried her through town," explained Jackson.

Salomé laughed wickedly. "Then, while we were in Carey, she made him do a favor for her. Told him she would let him get back at her, and redeem himself in front of the men."

Indio looked at her and grunted. "When was this again?"

She smiled at the memory. "Carey."

"Where was I?" he asked.

Salomé stroked his face. "Finding us a place to eat." He looked at her suspiciously and grunted again.

Marina called out to them. "Masters!" They looked at her. "I need to lay down some ground rules, first." Her fathers nodded. She looked at Solomon. "If you embarrass me in front of my family, out of spite, I," she said slowly, "am going to kick your ass." She smiled as he grinned at her. "If you make the baby cry," she continued, "because you hurt me," she hesitated, licking her lips, "I," she looked him up and down, "will not hold back." She went to Gaitano and turned her back to him, holding out her hair. He quickly braided it for her. She walked back to the Boatswain. "Assume the position." Everybody held their breath, as they bowed to each other. They began.

Solomon knew better, this time. He had already had an encounter with her, and he was wary. He knew she hit hard, but he wasn't going to let her make a fool of him this time. He circled her slowly, as the men started betting on them. Marina laughed at him. He moved in. At first, they started sparring, going back and forth with their moves. Then, he got cocky. Moving in quickly, he got in a kick to her stomach she wasn't expecting. Marina doubled over, trying to catch her breath for a moment. She straightened up, and smiled, letting it pass. They circled each other again. Solomon laughed. He rushed her again. Marina defended herself, making him pursue her. Solomon had gotten much better since last time they fought, but he was still too green. Getting a little frustrated, he rushed her once more. A misstep, and his punch got her square in the face. Marina shook her head, a little dazed. Then, Max began wailing. Looking down at the sand, she pressed her lips together. Her face was throbbing, and her breathing was a little bit heavier. She lifted her head and raised her eyebrows at Solomon. She saw nothing but him. Then he laughed. And that is when Marina began giving him all she got. The men cheered, their yells as excited as any heard at some big game. Her family looked on. Marina was aware of her fathers observing her carefully. They were her Masters. And she showed them all she had learned from them. Solomon started backing up. He was strong and had a lot of force. He could punch hard, and kick fast. But when it came to keeping an opponent away from himself, he was a little bit too slow. At least, for Marina. He connected again, with another punch to the jaw. Marina looked at him square in the eye. And then proceeded to beat him. She saw an expression of dismay cross his features, as he realized she was giving no breaks anymore. She just came at him. He fought as best he could. Finally, once again, in front of the whole crew of La Gitana, Marina floored him. The men cheered, laughing at the entertainment they provided them. Solomon groaned.

Marina looked at him. "I told you not to make the baby cry." She bowed to him. Turning around slowly, she bowed to her Masters. Then, she walked away. Ignoring everybody else, she went over to her mothers and sat down. She groaned. The men started forming again, getting ready to leave them. Her fathers were still talking to Gaitano. Her mothers petted her. She took Max in her arms and held him, gathering strength from him. She raised her bruised face to the sun, letting the breeze cool her skin as it dried her perspiration. She hurt. She sighed.

"Good fight."

Marina's eyes flew open at the sound of her Captain's voice. "Thank you," she whispered, focusing on not thinking about the pain.

Gaitano's hand came up, his thumb rubbing gently over her cheekbone. He looked at the spot thoughtfully, before meeting her eyes. "What I would like to know is," he said softly, "how do I get you and Solomon away from each other?"

Behind her, her mothers laughed softly at his words. She pulled her face away from his hand. "Just tell your Boatswain to keep the hell away from me."

Gaitano sighed. He just looked at her for a moment, not saying anything. Then, he turned to her mothers, all charm. "Ladies," he said softly, getting their attention. "If you would be so kind…"

he searched for the words. "I am working on a little project that requires a female touch," he began slowly. Marina looked at him, but he wasn't talking to her.

"Do you need help, baby?" Shayla asked, laughing. He nodded.

Sloane smiled, as she rubbed her daughter's back. "We would love to."

The pirate breathed a sigh of relief. His smile was genuine, as he turned on his charm. "Thank you, ladies. I will arrange to get together with you later and discuss some details. I would like to invite you for lunch at the Lair, when your morning is done."

Shayla smiled. "Why, thank you, baby. We'll be there."

Gaitano turned to Marina again. "I will be sending Indio over with the books later." He turned her face to look at him, not saying anything, just looking into her eyes. Then, he smiled and straightened up to leave.

The women waited until he was out of earshot. Shayla took her hand. "Oh, baby..."

Marina shook her head. Tears formed in her eyes. *He didn't even kiss me.* She looked after the men as they ran down the beach, heading back to town. Her mothers looked at each other behind her back. Marina blinked back the tears, and buried her face in the baby in her arms.

"Max!" The baby jumped in Marina's arms at the greeting. He was a regular, now, and he was loving it. The girls in the corner table squealed for Jackson. He laughed, and went over to sit with them for a while. The family assembled at the bar. To their delight, Jimmy had been expecting them, and quickly went to get something to eat. Silas stretched his arms for the baby, and proceeded to take him behind the bar and show him the bottles, and glasses. He stopped at the mirror, and let Max talk to his reflection for a couple of minutes. Then, with a big smile on his face, he passed the baby back, over the bar into Marina's arms. From his place at the corner of the bar, the pirate quietly watched as Marina held the baby against her chest, pressing her lips on his head. She didn't see him.

"Ladies." The women looked up at the sound of the voice. The Lair's owner stood behind them, a smile on his lips. "If you would be so kind," he smiled, gesturing at the corner, "my Captain would have a few words with you."

Shayla and Sloane smiled at each other. They turned back to the Italian. "Certainly," said Shayla, as they slid off their barstools.

Marina watched them walk away towards where Gaitano usually held court. She rolled her eyes, muttering under her breath. "Whatever..."

Jimmy appeared suddenly, and spread their lunch out on the bar. Marina looked around her. Salomé and Indio were flirting outrageously with each other, at one end of the bar. Sloane and Shayla were talking to Gaitano, at the other end. Jackson was busy making the girls laugh at their usual table, and her dads were standing around, talking animatedly with Solomon and Giancarlo. She sighed. Looking down at Max, she stroked his black head and gazed into his green eyes. "Let's go, baby," she whispered. "Let us just go." She reached over, and helped herself to a piece of bread and some fruit. Wrapping it all up in a napkin, she grabbed a glass bottle filled with water that Silas had placed in front of her. Gently, she moved Max from one hip to the other, bouncing him gently. From his place behind the bar, Indio watched silently, as he listened to Salomé. He scanned the room and noticed that nobody else was watching. Without saying a word to anyone, Marina slid off her stool. A movement out of the corner of his eye caught Gaitano's attention. He watched quietly, as the two women in front of him talked animatedly to each other for a moment. Nobody noticed. Marina quietly left. He felt his heart sink a little as the door closed behind her. He glanced at Indio and met his eyes. The brave just looked at him as he took Salomé's hand and locked his fingers with hers, pressing it to his lips. His eyes flickered at him. Gaitano sighed and looked away, concentrating on the women in front of him.

Marina stepped outside and took a deep gulp of fresh air. She closed her eyes and lifted her face to the sun, basking in it for a moment. Max looked at her, and did the same. They stood there, for a moment, arms wrapped around each other, glowing in the bright daylight. Marina sighed and smiled at the baby. He turned his green eyes on her and smiled back. She nodded and without saying anything, started walking.

They walked. And walked. She took him past Pedro Escobar's, to show him the cactus garden, and the pathway bordered with conch shells. The baby gurgled softly, as she spoke gently to him, showing him the details in the landscaping. From there, she took him to the lookout where Caribe had taken them on their first day, on the finer side of town. Up there, through the arch and among the bougainvillea, they quietly had their lunch. Marina carefully fed the baby, tiny pieces of bread, and fruit. He would chew solemnly, and take sips of water. When they were done, they smiled at each other. Marina sat him on her lap and pointed out La Gitana. From their vantage point, they could see straight unto the top deck, where the sailors were busy at work. She murmured in Max's ear, telling him all about their trip to Carey. He liked the part about Arrecife best. From there, she carried the baby back into town, to the docks. Max craned his head back on her shoulder, as they got up close and personal with La Gitana, and looked up her mast to the crow's nest, and Joshua. From there, Marina hustled Max straight through town, without looking at anything or anybody. By the time she stood in front of the Klines' store, Max was asleep. She went in, and delivered a heavy baby to his smiling parents.

Larissa kept her for small talk for a little while, but finally gave up, when she noticed Marina's lack of energy. She smiled at the younger girl and rubbed her arm. "Honey, you better get yourself home, you can't even concentrate, you are so distracted. You are daydreaming, darling." She laughed softly, eyes twinkling. "Why don't you go and crawl into bed, and treat yourself to some really great dreams of your handsome pirate," she murmured.

Marina nodded. She smiled at the woman, and kissed Max. Ducking her head, she turned and left. The truth was, she was feeling depressed, suddenly. Sleep should ease it. So, she went home.

A figure lay in the hammock of her front porch. She could see him, as she approached the hut. The closer she got, the clearer he became. It was Indio. By the time she climbed on the front porch, she could see the book on his chest. She sighed. "Hey, baby."

"Hey." He searched her eyes. She evaded him. Walking past him, she went inside and sat down at the table. Indio came in and sat with her. He put the book in front of her.

Marina looked at him. "Please, wait for them." He nodded. Opening the book, she got to work. Indio watched her silently. He listened as she explained her method of work, teaching him how to do it. He nodded, and asked the right questions. When they were done, she closed the book and pushed it over. She smiled, even though her eyes were sad. "Looking good, baby."

Indio nodded. "Thanks to you," he rumbled. They looked at each other in silence. Indio took her hand and held it between his for a moment. "Solomon hurt you today."

"Yes."

"You've changed. Your parents are here, and you should be happy. You are, I can see that, but something is different."

Marina shook her head at him. "You are too clever for your own good." She sighed, and squeezed his hand. "I'm going through a hard time right now," she admitted. "The *Luto* at Carey messed with my mind a little bit. My parents being here force me to make a decision," she explained slowly, gazing at his hands. Slowly, she let her eyes drift up until they met his. "But I don't have enough information, and," she took a deep breath. "I don't want to make the wrong decision."

Indio stared at her, searching deep in her eyes. "That would be very sad for many people."

"I'm confused."

"Can I help?"

She dragged her eyes away from his, and looked back at their hands. "He didn't even kiss me today," she confessed, "has been the only thing that's been going through my mind all day."

Indio frowned. "Carlitos kisses you all the time."

Marina shook her head. "I know. But it bothered me that he didn't kiss me *today*, and that scares me."

"You've barely been with him today," he pointed out.

"He's busy," she mumbled.

Indio grinned. "He," he said softly, "has a name."

Marina rolled her eyes. "Whatever."

"Say it!"

Marina softly banged her hand down on the table, grinning back. "Carlos Gaitano."

"y Sandoval."

Her eyes sparkled at him. "y Sandoval…"

Indio laughed, patting her hand. "He's making you crazy, mami?"

Marina nodded and looked down, feeling herself blush. "Yeah," she admitted softly. She met his eyes again. "I've got to deal with this, on my own. I need to step back, for a little while, look hard and check out what I see."

Indio nodded. "Sometimes, we see more when we don't look," he said softly.

Marina thought about it for a moment, and nodded slowly. "Right now, I need to sleep this off for a while." She shrugged. "For as long as it takes." Suddenly, she grinned at him. "If you don't see me in a couple of days, just bring the book by." Standing up, she went to him and put her arms around him, kissing him on the cheek. Indio patted her face, as he held it against his for a moment, his mind churning. She laughed softly. "Would I offend you if I were to ask you to keep this between us?"

He chuckled. "Sleep, Marina," he rumbled, not committing to anything. "It will work out." Standing up, he picked up the book, to leave.

Marina held out her hand. He slid his against it. "Thanks, Indio." She turned and went to the pile of blankets on the floor. He watched her from the doorway. Spreading one out, she called out. "See you later." And right before his eyes, she lay down, latched on to a pillow and passed out.

Indio looked at her and sighed, shaking his head. He felt for Marina. And he felt for his brother. He had the feeling that something had to break soon, or it would all be lost. Taking a last look, his eyes caressed her hair as the sunbeams danced on it. His heart softened towards her, and his mind raced. Turning, he quietly left the house. His heart was decided. Carlos Gaitano would have to deal with this. He was the cause.

That night, the natives danced as usual. The men that watched, were there, as always. Gaitano looked and looked, but didn't see her. He frowned. He scanned the dancers again, but he still couldn't find her. He turned his head and met Indio's eyes.

Indio smiled, eyes sparkling wickedly. He leaned towards him, and spoke in his ear, his voice rumbling. "Not here."

Gaitano frowned again. "I thought you saw her today."

"I did."

"So, where is she?"

Indio chuckled softly. "She," he said slowly, "has a name."

The pirate laughed with him. "Marina."

"Sleeping." He paused, making sure every word sank in. "Marina doesn't feel too well, today."

Carlos drew back to look at him, but Indio would say no more. Finally, he sighed. "Why?"

Indio laughed softly. "Solomon hurt her."

"Bad?"

Indio shrugged. "Enough for her to want to sleep it off." He paused again. "She has a lot of things on her mind." And with that, he sat back and kept watching Salomé, whom, from across the distance, was seducing him without knowing it. Gaitano looked at him. Indio would say no more.

Later, Caribe and the male visitors rode into town, in the deep of the night. At the docks, Gaitano's army awaited their team leaders. Torches lit their faces, as they stood around, listening to their Captain's instructions. Then, they descended on the town. Knocking on windows, banging on doors, they went building by building, waking their occupants and invading their homes. Those that passed the surprise inspection were left with promises of restitution from Gaitano. Those that didn't, got marched down the main street, escorted by the men in charge of him, or her, to Pedro Escobar's. The raid was a success. And at the end, the men congratulated each other, and raced home, before dawn broke.

The next day, Marina got up and shook herself. Instead of staying, she got up early, and went to work out with Caribe. She passed on practicing her forms with the crew of La Gitana, and instead, went home to wait for Max. Leilani came by with Reina. They wanted to have a girls' day out with Ali, and would she please watch the twins, while Joaquin went to town, to work. So, Marina stayed home, and Juan and Jaime got reacquainted with Max. Once the babies were picked up by their respective fathers, she found herself alone again for a little while. Her mothers had been gone all morning, as well as Salomé. She was beginning to miss them, when they appeared. They hung out for a little while, and went to join the women at the river. There, they laughed, and danced, and sang, splashing as if they were children, enjoying being in the company of other females. They said goodbye to the women, and made their way home, to clean up and change. As they approached their cluster of huts, they found themselves facing two men.

Marina looked at Francois and his father. She stopped. The boy looked absolutely miserable, as if her were being unduly punished for something he didn't do. Behind him, Quino's amused eyes sparkled at Marina. She sighed.

Francois looked at her, sincerity in his eyes. "Louise," his voice broke and he cleared his throat. "Louise, I need to speak to you."

Marina pretended to scoff at him. "Ha! You already said all you had to say to me," she said snapping her fingers in the air and pretending to just walk right by him.

He caught her by the arm and twirled her around to face him, sheer desperation in his face. "Louise!"

Marina stopped again. Her mothers were watching her expectantly. "What?"

"Please, I want to say I am sorry," he pleaded. "I really am sorry, Louise!"

Shayla touched her arm. "Baby, why does he keep calling you Louise?"

Marina swallowed her laughter, as Salomé snickered behind her hand. "You were going to hurt me!" she snarled at Francois.

Francois bowed his head, nodding sadly. "I know. I was, I admit, but please," he looked at her again, "forgive me, Louise." He turned towards Salomé. "Thelma..."

Shayla's eyes widened and she smiled knowingly. "I see..."

Sloane laughed. "You girls are bad!" She looked at her daughter. "Please, Louise," she said, eyes twinkling, "forgive the boy and let's go home."

Marina looked at Francois. "Don't do it again," she told him. "And leave Leilani alone. She is a little girl still, and does not need the likes of you in her life!" She turned to wink at his father, and walked away.

Once home, Marina cleaned up, and changed. While her mothers and her sister were getting ready to dance, she crawled into bed. She needed more sleep. More time.

Later that night, Gaitano looked for her again. She still wasn't there. He turned to Indio and raised an eyebrow at him, the question in his eyes. Indio shrugged and shook his head. His eyes bore into the pirate's. Gaitano looked away.

This time, they headed out of town, into the more residential areas. Their raids were methodic, precise, and very well executed. The results were astounding. They found missing merchandise, and they uncovered traitors in their midst. The cover of night gave them anonymity in the dark. Nobody ever saw or heard them coming. Gaitano was taking back his island.

"Marina!"

Marina whirled around at the stage whisper. It was still early in the morning. John Kline had already come by with Max, and she was now bouncing him in her arms as she sang to him. She was expecting the twins, but they hadn't been brought by yet. Now, standing in his own doorway, calling her, was Jackson. "Hey, Jax!" she called softly. "What's going on?"

He crossed the floor to them, a smile on his face. "Hey, Max, how're you doing, baby?" he crooned, taking the baby from her. He bent his head to kiss Marina's face and looked at her, his eyes wide with excitement. "You've got to come with me." His eyes crinkled at the corners. "Right now."

Marina didn't ask. She looked at him and nodded, following him out. Jackson led the way to Caribe's hut. As they approaced, they saw Salomé coming out of Leila's house, leading Indio by the hand. The brave looked stunned, as he followed her. Marina gasped. "Oh, no!" she cried softly, grabbing Jackson's arm. "She told him!" Her eyes flew to her brother's face.

Jackson grinned. "Yeah, she sure did." He winked at Marina. "Now, let's see if he can handle it." Without saying another word, they climbed Caribe's front steps.

Inside, sunlight flooded the room. The hammock had been carefully hung against one of the walls, freeing up some space for them to walk around in. The table was littered with papers and charcoal pencils. Other than that, it was neat and tidy. Max gurgled at the sight of Indio. The brave turned around at the sound, and held his arms out for the baby, with a smile. Max went to him, immediately putting his little head on the bronzed shoulder. Indio's hand covered the little back, as he turned once more, to the wall with the portraits. Salomé stood to one side, giving him space. She glanced at Marina and winked at her. Caribe stood by the wall, ready for any question Indio may have. They waited, as Indio took his time, studying each face carefully. Then he came to their sketches. He rumbled softly, shaking his head. Eyes shining, he turned to Caribe. "You dream about these people?" he asked softly. "You actually see them in your mind first, and then just pass them on to paper, without ever having seen them in person, before."

Caribe nodded. "Actually, I am a sort of record keeper. It started a while back. I kept dreaming of these people, and the dreams wouldn't go away, until I sketched their faces. I couldn't figure out what was going on. Leila explained it all to me, after she saw the drawings." He waved his hand slowly over the papers. Then he came to the ones of the girls. "These," he smiled, winking at them, "were different. These, hadn't come yet."

Indio looked at him. "So, how did you find them? I thought they were from Cayo Largo."

Caribe shook his head at him. "Not from Cayo Largo." He shrugged. "What were we supposed to say?"

Indio grunted, studying the drawings. "You dreamed of Jackson?" he asked, coming to his portrait.

Caribe nodded. "I had to tell Salomé before he just came walking into town." He paused. "That was that day at the Lair..."

"I remember," Indio said. "It makes sense now." He turned to look at Salomé. "I know what you did when you saw this picture," he said, pointing to the paper on the wall, "but what was your reaction when you saw him for real?"

Salomé rolled her eyes and glanced at them. She pressed her lips together and shook her head at the memory. Her eyes filled with tears, at the thought. She looked back at Indio. "I freaked."

Indio turned his head to look at Jackson, for confirmation. Jackson nodded. Indio bounced the baby gently, pressing his lips to the black head, thoughtfully. He looked back at the wall. At the end of the gallery, were portraits of the Banks and the Aguilars. He glanced at Caribe. "You dreamt of their parents coming, also?"

Caribe nodded. "That was harder, because we were out at sea. By the time we got back, I knew they were already here. After the Luto, I didn't know how to tell them." He threw an apologetic glance at the girls. "Marina wasn't feeling too well, after what happened at El Callejon, and I wasn't comfortable with the idea of causing her more stress."

Jackson turned to look at Marina. "What happened on Carey, mami?"

Marina hesitated. She looked away from his eyes, seeking help. They just looked at her. She turned back to him. "Well, you know, it was nothing, really. Somebody had a misunderstanding, and I..." she drifted off, frantically searching for words. She shrugged. "Someone got confused and I set them straight," she said finally. Marina met his tiger eyes.

Jackson's eyes bore into hers. He didn't believe her. He grunted. "You know I'm going to find out." It had been their fathers' threat to get them to speak, their whole lives. Marina pressed her lips together, and nodded. They turned back to the Quartermaster.

Indio stood, thoughtful, in the middle of the room, bouncing the baby in his arms. "You say a storm causes this?" They nodded. He looked at Jackson. "And you just went and got your parents."

Jackson shrugged. "You know, man, my sisters go missing, I'm responsible. First, I go get them, and when I see what's going on, I'm smart enough to realize that this is bigger than anything we could've imagined." He looked straight into the brave's eyes. "You needed help. I got some."

Indio nodded. He kissed the baby absently, looking at Salomé. "What are you going to do?"

"Can you hang, baby?"

He looked at her, a slow smile spreading on his face. "Yeah, I can hang."

Salomé tossed her head and laughed. "What do you think I'm going to do?" She winked at him.

Indio laughed. "I don't know, Salomé, but I'm telling you right now," his eyes caressed her face, "you are going home with me."

Salomé smiled, her love for Indio shining in her green eyes, for all to see. "Sure, baby. Whatever you say."

Indio nodded. He handed the baby to Marina and looked at her thoughtfully. "You have to tell Carlitos," he said softly. Marina started shaking her head, but he stopped her with a look. "You have to tell him, Marina."

"I can't!" she exclaimed.

"You have to," Indio insisted, trying to reason with her. "You are his accountant, which means you are working for the Gaitanos. You are his friend, and that means, he trusts you. And then," he waved his hand in the air, glancing at Salomé, "you are his," he frowned for a moment, searching for the word, "makeout partner, he tells me."

Marina smiled. "Cool. Now he kisses and tells." Salomé and Jackson laughed.

Indio took a deep breath. "Gaitano has to know."

"I know. I just can't, right now."

"Why?" he challenged her. "I know you are not afraid of him. At least, not anymore. He has a right to know. What is holding you back?"

Marina bounced the baby, and began pacing in circles, her eyes seeking escape. "I'm not scared of him, but I'm afraid of how he is going to react."

"Why?" he asked again. "What do you expect?"

Marina shook her head sadly. "That's just it. I don't know what to expect."

Indio didn't say anything for a moment. "I can tell him, for you," he offered gently.

A laugh escaped her throat, and tears stung the back of her eyes. "Well, you better get together with Papi, on that one, 'cause he already offered."

"I will," he said suddenly. "The sooner, the better."

"I'm not ready!" she wailed. Nobody said anything for a moment. "I don't even know if he will care or not, or at least enough for it to matter to him, although, I know he cares for me, and I just don't know how to tell him, when I can't find the words, or the thoughts for that matter, to express something that means the world of difference to me, when he might just not give a damn, or care either way..." she gasped, filling her lungs with air. And then, she couldn't say any more.

Indio just looked at her. "I don't care how it happens," he said softly. "Carlitos needs to know." He held her gaze. Marina nodded miserably, and hid her face in the baby in her arms. Turning away, she left them and went home.

Juan and Jaime put in an appearance soon afterwards, giving her an excuse to keep busy and not think. The babies were good, and she kept them busy with paper and pencils. Marina found her mind wandering, and gathered them for a story, just to keep herself focused. They were picked up at their usual time, and she found herself alone again. Her moms had disappeared once more, and God knew where her dads were. They had become quite popular in town, shortly after their arrival, thus giving them an active social life in Encantada. Marina didn't go into town, and instead, once more, sank into sleep, seeking escape from what she knew she had to do.

"Marina!" Her eyes flew open, and she was looking up at Jackson's beautiful face. Behind him, Caribe smiled down at her. She smiled into the tiger eyes. He laughed softly. "Let's run."

The jungle embraced them. Their bare feet thumped on the sand trail. Birds called overhead. The sun felt warm on their faces. They explored, pushing vines out of their way, as they raced past. Their feet led them to the waterfall. There, they played like savages. Wild children on the loose. They found a vine that would hold their weight, and they swung out to the middle of the pool, dropping into the clear water, like a cannonball. Their war yells bounced from mountain to mountain. Some birds cheered them, and others scolded them, as they engaged in water battles, splashing each other ferociously. Exhausted, they took a break, floating on their backs, looking up at the sky. Then, they continued. The sun was beginning to hide behind the mountain. The jungle felt cooler, as they stampeded down their familiar trail. Once they got to the natural pool, they dove in. They did a few laps, before the men decided to continue.

Marina kept swimming.

Jackson looked around, as he heard a rustle in the leaves behind them.

He turned, as the pirate came out. "Hey, man," he said softly.

Gaitano met his eyes for a moment, before looking past him, to the woman in the pool. He was barefoot and bare-chested, his sword at his side. His eyes intense on the action in the water. When he finally spoke, his voice was soft, as he jerked his head towards the jungle. "Get out."

Jackson and Caribe looked at each other. Gaitano placed his sword on the ground softly, and crept to the side of the pool. Sliding soundlessly in the water, he began swimming behind Marina. They watched as she reached the far ledge, and turned. Her eyes glowed with pleasure, as she saw the pirate. The smile on her face said she had forgotten about them. Gaitano glided towards her, hands reaching out, a smile on his face. He drew her towards him, taking her in his arms. Marina wrapped her arms around his neck, pressing her smiling mouth to his. Jackson and Caribe looked at each other again. They smiled, and left the couple alone.

Gaitano drew back and smiled at the woman in his arms. She was raining kisses all over his face, murmuring to herself. He laughed, holding her tighter. Closing his eyes, he returned her kisses. "Marina..." He pulled back to gaze into her eyes. "Where have you been?" he murmured.

Marina laughed softly, her eyes caressing the lines of his face. "Missed me?"

The pirate pressed his lips together and nodded. His hands went down to cup her butt cheeks. Squeezing, he lifted her, weightless in the water. Marina wrapped her legs around his waist and sighed. He held her tight. "I haven't seen you around..."

She shrugged, laughing. "You've been busy..."

"True," he admitted.

She threaded her fingers through his hair, and drew back his head to gaze into his eyes. "Missed me?" she asked softly.

He groaned. "Yes. Want me to show you?" he murmured wickedly. Marina licked her lips, her eyes devouring his mouth. She kissed
him.

Gaitano groaned, as he adjusted her tighter against him, kissing
her back. He felt his whole body relaxing, flowing with the feeling
invading it, as he kissed her. She ended the kiss, drawing back to
smile into his eyes. "Not here," she whispered.

He nodded, licking his lips. His eyes searched hers, hungrily.
"Where have you been?"

"Around."

"I haven't seen you," he groaned, stealing a kiss.

She laughed. "What have you been up to?"

The pirate sighed, rubbing his face against hers. "I have been
busy. Your work on the books has been priceless." He kissed her neck
softly. "I have taken your advice."

Marina closed her eyes, her skin tingling where his lips left a
trail. "Advice?"

"I cleaned house."

She drew back to look at him, once more. "You cleaned house."

He nodded, smiling at her expression. "We have been conducting raids these past nights. Started with Dominique Swan's dress
shop." He chuckled, as she widened her eyes. "It was just as Salomé
said. We opened some crates, and..." his eyes grew hard at the memory, "there they were. Much more than we imagined." He shook his
head. "Upstairs was just as she described, also. The rooms, the boudoirs," his eyes sparkled, "the girls..." He raised his eyebrows and
smacked his lips.

Marina laughed. "Oh, you liked that, didn't you?"

Gaitano kissed her hard. Underwater, he molded her to him.
He pulled back to look at her, laughing at himself. "Actually, I did.
If you let me," he said, licking his lips, "I'll show you." He winked
at her.

She laughed again, catching his face between her hands. "Show
me what?" she murmured, rubbing her nose against his.

His hands squeezed her, before caressing her hips. "How much
I liked it," he whispered against her mouth.

Marina kissed him quickly, her answer in his eyes. "Go on," she whispered.

He took a deep breath. "We have had success," he informed her. "I was gone too long this last time I was away, before going to Carey, just now. Things got a little out of hand," he said, frowning at something only he could see. Marina kept silent, letting him sort his thoughts. "Now, we're back. We have gone through every inch of every building in town," he informed her, "and we have taken into custody every single person that had something that wasn't his or hers, and couldn't explain how they got it."

"What happens now?"

He focused on her and shrugged. "They get taken care of, and it never happens again."

"Were there a lot of people involved?"

He shook his head. "Not too many, fortunately. But enough for it to be a problem for the Gaitanos and Encantada."

Marina combed her fingers through his hair, thoughtfully. "You work fast," she said. "You're not going to need me anymore ---" she gasped, as he squeezed her tight, suddenly.

"I could not have done this without you," he muttered, his eyes boring into hers. "What makes you think ---"

"I showed Indio how to keep your books," she told him, grasping at straws.

Gaitano shrugged, his eyes twinkling. "I can't make out with Indio."

She smiled. "I see how you are. That's all you want me for, huh?"

"No," he said slowly, licking his lips as he looked at her mouth, "it's what I like best about you."

Marina laughed. "So, what happens now?" she asked, distracting him. He nodded, smiling into her eyes. "My father should be here any day now, to check up on things, himself. The council should be sailing in, soon. I need to present a thriving, economically stable Encantada, in order to keep it."

She frowned. "What happens if it's not?"

He kept silent for a moment, just gazing at her, his eyes caressing her face. "I lose Encantada. Anybody can bid on it."

Her eyes widened. "What are you going to do?"

The pirate laughed. "I am *not* going to lose Encantada."

Marina nodded. "What happens with the people and the businesses where you found something going on?"

He shrugged again. "Their businesses are given to people we trust implicitly. Everybody gets a chance. Padre Ignacio is in charge of that aspect of it." He smiled as he caught her frown at the priest's name. "It is done discreetly and quietly. No shame comes to the families of the people involved. Only the culprits are taken away, and then, somebody different opens their store the next morning, and that is all there is to it."

"Don't people wonder? Ask questions?"

He grinned at her. "Not to me."

Marina rolled her eyes at him and smiled. "Who got Dominique Swan's shop?"

He took a deep breath, making small waves between their chests. "That, I gave to Liana. She's the person that has been working there for the past couple of years. Now, she will finally be able to start a new life with the doctor."

Marina frowned. "What about the upstairs?"

Gaitano laughed. "That, Giancarlo took over." He laughed again. "Jackson has been helping him with some ideas on how to make money off the whole situation."

Marina laughed. "What does Jackson get out of it?"

The pirate smacked his lips again. "He gets to watch to his heart's content."

They laughed softly. Marina covered his face with kisses again. "Is there anything I can do to help?" she asked.

He closed his eyes, enjoying the woman in his arms. "I miss you," he whispered.

Marina pulled back from him, to look into his face. "Stay with me tonight," she said suddenly. "Just stay, Carlos, just tonight," she whispered. "Please..."

Gaitano's eyes flew open, searching hers. She meant it. He could see that. His body responded to her offer, tightening and rising, in all the right places. He wanted to stay. God knew he wanted nothing better. But not just for the night. And he knew, if he stayed, he wouldn't leave. He shook his head slowly, "I have to go out one more time," he began.

She laughed, looking away so he couldn't see the hurt in her eyes, not knowing that he already had. "That's right, you're raiding." She unwrapped her legs from around him, letting the water put distance between them. She felt ashamed at having asked, and mortified at being rejected. She didn't want to cry in front of him. "It's okay, I know you're busy." Her hands sought his, as she tried to free herself from his embrace. She laughed again. "Besides, I don't even have a place right now. I'm staying at Jackson's." She shook her head. "I'm sorry, I shouldn't have asked. I have nothing to offer you."

He frowned, reaching for her again, as she began drifting away. "Marina..." Catching her hand, he pulled her towards him once more.

Marina put her hands on his chest, keeping him from capturing her again. "Carlos..." She looked up into his eyes, hoping he didn't see the tears. " You want more, baby?" she whispered. The pirate pressed his lips together and nodded slowly. She brushed her lips against his mouth, looking into his eyes. His breath caught in his throat, as she began kissing him. He closed his eyes and responded. His hands captured her hips, pulling her towards him once more. She slanted her mouth against his, her fingers in his hair. He groaned, his world beginning to fade around him. He kissed her desperately, his lips claiming hers, his tongue invading her mouth and conquering. Gaitano felt as if he were drowning. He kissed her until they couldn't breathe anymore. She grabbed handfuls of his hair, and pulled his head back, gasping for air. His heart skipped a beat. There was pure, uncensored desire in her eyes. He groaned. Marina shook her head, chest rising and falling, hands trembling. He wanted to kiss her again. In her face, he saw she did, too. Marina pulled away. "So do I." In a moment, she was out of the water.

The pirate watched in frustration as the jungle swallowed her up. He hit the water in anger, at himself and at the circumstances that were keeping them apart right now. For the first time in his life, he had found a woman he actively wanted to pursue. Somebody that made him feel good all the time. He was old enough and smart enough to realize, they had known each other for a very short time. Things were bound to come up in their relationship. He felt they came from different worlds. But what he knew so far, what he thought and felt, was enough to assure him that whatever it was that he wasn't looking for, had come to him, in the form of a woman. *Marina.* Raising his face to the darkening sky, he roared.

That night, the riders found themselves, once more, watching the natives dance. The drums filled the night, as the light from the torches embraced the dancers. The visitors danced together, with each other, among the natives. The men yelled as they leaped about, feet stomping in the sand, bodies glistening as they passed each other. The women spun and shook, laughing and calling out, the two mothers dancing circles around their green-eyed daughter.

The pirate looked and looked, knowing she wasn't there. He was sitting down on the ground, leaning back, and knees drawn. Finally, he straightened up and gave a big sigh, dropping his head on his knees. Indio tore his eyes away from Salomé and looked at him. "I thought you saw her today."

Gaitano looked right at his brother and swore under his breath, shaking his head as he looked back at the dancers that were there. Indio hid a smile.

The raid was their last. They had successfully tracked down every person in Encantada who had thought they could take from the Gaitanos. The amount of items involved had been staggering, considering the time that the theft had been going on. Now, Carlos Gaitano and his army were facing the task of putting balance back in their lives, turning Encantada back into the thriving seaport it was meant to be. They owed their good fortune to the visitors. And as they finished this last raid on Encantada; as Pedro Escobar took away the last person to be imprisoned, the pirate and his crew celebrated with Caribe, Jackson, and his fathers, their unprecedented success. The men laughed, and cheered, enjoying the end of this particular phase of what needed to be done. And as they touched bottles and glasses, and drank to their good fortune, dawn crept up on them slowly, its long fingers reaching out to touch their port.

Out at sea, a ship sailed near, slowly coming closer, its inhabitants eagerly looking forward to the moment of their arrival. Their return to Encantada, and their reunion with their son. Finally, they had come. Don Carlos Gaitano y Mendoza and the fabulous María Isabel Sandoval.

"Marina…"

She froze at the sound of her name. She had been up since dawn, her mind in turmoil, from her raging feelings. The hut wasn't large enough to hold her and her thoughts, and she was now outside. The early morning sun flooded the backyard, bathing the foliage in bright colors. The bamboo creaked in the morning breeze, and birds called to each other, among the mango and avocado trees. She turned around slowly, to look back at the house. Leaning against the doorway, was the pirate, looking at her. She smiled. *"Capitán…"*

Gaitano smiled back. The sun had lightened her hair and darkened her skin, making her irresistibly exotic to him. He also liked that she wore pants like a boy, half the time, allowing her to keep up with the men. He watched as she approached him. It had been a long night, and she looked really good to him.

"Are you busy?" he asked.

Marina looked up at him. He looked as if he hadn't made it to bed yet.

She shook her head. "No, not at all. What's up?"

He sighed as she reached him. She looked really good to him. "I need your help down at the docks."

She frowned. "The docks?"

He nodded. "Don Carlos came in this morning."

Marina's face lit up. "He did? That's fantastic! My family will love meeting him."

He smiled. "I know. But right now, I need help at the docks. I have Salomé waiting for you. Caribe and Jackson are on their way, already." He took her hand and pressed his lips to it, as he looked into her eyes.

"What about the babies?"

He shook his head. "No babies today. I took care of that already." He pulled her towards him, slipping her arms around his neck. "Marina..."

She hushed him, shaking her head. "How was your raid? You look as if you haven't slept yet."

He grinned. "It was the last one, and it went well. I haven't made it home yet."

Marina's eyes sparkled. "Home..." she murmured.

"I'll take you there," he laughed. He looked at her for a moment, before pressing his lips to hers. "Good morning," he whispered.

"Good morning," she whispered back. She kissed him. Pulling away, they smiled at each other.

The pirate squeezed her, before leading her by the hand, back through the hut, and into the jungle, his fingers locked with hers.

"What can we do to make this ready for inspection?" asked Salomé. "There has to be something that will attract people here in order to do business."

Marina looked at her. "You mean, like tourists?"

Salomé nodded. "Exactly."

They looked at each other. It had been a long morning at the docks, and finally it was over. Now, they were all sitting at a table at the Sirens' Lair, brainstorming. Giancarlo had closed the bar to the general public, and a private party was going on. The crew of *La Sirena*, Don Carlos' ship, that of La Gitana, the Banks, the Aguilars, Caribe, and a select few of Gaitano's pirate army, were present. Noticeably absent were Gaitano, Indio, and their parents.

"So, why don't they make this into a tourist attraction?" asked Marina.

Jackson looked at her. "You mean, like back home?"

Marina shrugged. "At least a favorite pirate vacation spot. It should work. There are tons of pirates out there." She smiled. "You've got to start somewhere."

Salomé nodded in agreement. "You're right." She took a piece of paper and a charcoal pencil from Caribe. "Let's figure this out." She looked around the table. "When you go somewhere, what is one of the most important aspects of your vacation or trip:?"

"Where you stay," said Marina.

"What you do," added Jackson.

"You're both right," agreed Salomé. "So, first thing I would do, if it were me, would be to build a place where the crews of ships can stay whenever they're in town."

Caribe nodded. "That would help Encantada very much. Usually, they stay on their ship, or wander around town, looking for trouble."

"There you go," said Salomé, writing it down. "And then, once they're here, what do they do?"

"Come here," laughed Caribe. The women looked at each other, and rolled their eyes.

Salomé turned to her brother. "How is this place, anyway? The bar down here is nice and all, but what about upstairs?"

Jackson shrugged. "They are prostitutes. What do you expect? How is it supposed to be?"

Salomé sighed patiently. "What I mean, Jackson, is, are we talking about nice girls, or dirty hoes?"

Jackson laughed. "Actually, not too bad. Some are skanks, and some are just little sluts."

"And do they like this life? Don't they have any options?" she asked. Jackson narrowed his tiger eyes at her. "What are you thinking?"

Salomé smiled. "Make an escort service instead." They all stared at her. She smiled. "If you're going to make this place attractive for the other pirates out there, to come and spend their money," she paused, choosing her words carefully, "why don't you get them to pay for a service, where they get taken around and shown a good time?" Her eyes sparkled mischievously. "Like geishas, instead, maybe…"

Jackson laughed and stood up from his chair, calling to the owner of the bar. "Gian! Come over here, man, listen to this!"

"And," said Salomé, tugging at his shirt to sit him down, "you can charge for a tour of the upstairs of the dress shop…"

Jackson stood up again. "Gian!"

"Speaking of the dress shop," Salomé rambled on, "we should have a fashion show, for when the council shows up, so they can see what's done with the nice fabrics they import here." She scribbled furiously. "Now that Mami's here, she can organize it, and maybe Padre Ignacio should have a choir at church for Sunday mass." She stopped for a moment, staring into space. She began scribbling again. "The natives need to sell their stuff at that plaza in the middle of town."

"There should be special cabins on the beach, so Captains can keep an eye on their ships," offered Marina.

Salomé threw her a smile, writing it down. "Good girl!"

Marina laughed, and slid out of her chair. "You guys have fun. I'm out of here." She smiled, as Salomé waved at her absently, while she kept talking to the men. Marina turned and left, her feet leading her to the general store.

Larissa turned around as the bells tinkled on her door. Her face lit up. "Marina! I wasn't expecting you!" She laughed. "Gaitano came in early this morning, and said you couldn't take care of Max today."

Marina rolled her eyes. "He just needed help at the docks. I just want to see Max for a little while. It's crazy down at the Lair."

Larissa nodded. She went to the back, and returned, a smiling Max in her arms. She passed her son to her friend. "Here you go, honey."

Marina smiled into the baby's green eyes. "Hi, handsome," she whispered. She held him close, his ebony head on her shoulder. She stayed chatting with Larissa for a while, rocking Max gently as they talked. The bell over the door tinkled again, and both women turned around to look. It was Mrs. Calloway.

"Good afternoon," the woman called, spying Larissa.

Larissa rolled her eyes at Marina and smiled. "Good afternoon, Mrs. Calloway. What can I help you with today?" Marina smiled back and walked away, whispering to Max as she began wandering around the store.

Mrs. Calloway looked Marina up and down, disapproval written all over her face. "Savage," she muttered. Marina didn't bother pretending she didn't hear. She turned to Mrs. Calloway and laughed in her face.

Larissa took a deep breath, her smile glued to her own. "Now," she said softly, getting the old woman's attention, "what can I help you with, again?"

"The nerve of some people," mumbled the elderly woman. All three women turned, as the bell tinkled, yet again. A shadow crossed the threshold. It was the pirate.

Gaitano stepped in, smiling at the ladies. "Good afternoon."

Marina just stared at him, while Larissa smiled, and Mrs. Calloway cowered against the counter. "Good afternoon," chorused the younger women.

Gaitano turned his eyes to Marina. He laughed. "I said no babies."

Marina laughed with him, while a terrified Mrs. Calloway, and a delighted Larissa, looked on. "But I'm done. I did everything you asked me to." On a sudden impulse, she licked her lips and looked at the older lady. Mrs. Calloway's eyes widened with shock. Larissa clapped her hand over her mouth to not burst out laughing. "I just wanted to hold Max for a little while..."

Gaitano smiled, shaking his head. He reached for the baby, gently taking it away from her. Kissing the top of its head, he handed it gently to Larissa. "No babies," he repeated. "You need a break."

Marina sighed. "I need a baby fix," she smiled at him, "but you wouldn't understand." She waved goodbye to Larissa and went out the door.

Larissa stopped the pirate as he turned to follow her. Her bright green eyes smiled into his clear turquoise ones. "Honey, you should make a baby with that girl. I don't think anything else will make either of you happier..." she said softly.

Gaitano froze, searching her eyes. He could only see the truth of her words. He grunted. Scanning Larissa's face one last time, he nodded at her, and turned to catch up with Marina. Outside, he took her hand and locked his fingers with hers. Marina looked at him. *Public displays of affection, baby?* He glanced at her and smiled, squeezing her hand.

It seemed as if the Siren's Lair were even busier than it was when she left. They stopped outside, looking in for a moment. The pirate sighed. "I don't really want to do this, but I have to." He looked at her. "Stay by my side?"

Marina smiled, clinging to his hand. "Only if you promise not to leave mine." Gaitano nodded. Taking a deep breath, they went in.

Sitting at a couple of tables pushed together, was her family. With them, Indio, Giancarlo, Solomon and Caribe. They were avidly discussing the paper in Salomé's hand. Sitting at the bar with their backs to them, were Don Carlos and María Isabel, their laughing reflections in the mirror. The couple looked up as they approached.

Don Carlos' face lit up. "Marina!" He opened his arms and embraced her. Letting her go, he looked into her eyes. "I want to thank you," he rumbled in a low voice, "for everything you have done for my son and his island."

Marina smiled. "It has been my pleasure." She turned to his mother.

María Isabel smiled and kissed her on the cheek, hugging her for a moment. "I can't wait to know you better," she whispered in her ear.

Marina laughed softly. "Thank you. And I, you," she whispered back.

Don Carlos turned to his son. "Carlitos..." He held out his arms.

The pirate let go of her hand and embraced his father. He smiled, looking into the older pirate's eyes. "Papá..."

"Tio Juan is on his way."

Gaitano threw back his head and laughed. *Gracias!* He released his father and reached down to take Marina's hand again. "What about Tio Miguel?"

Don Carlos nodded. "On his way."

The pirate laughed again and turned to his mother. Another embrace. More whispered endearments. Marina's family stood to meet the Gaitanos, and there were introductions all around.

Don Carlos and Pablo looked at each other, smiling. "Your daughter has been of great assistance to my son," the pirate told her father, reaching out to shake his hand.

Pablo nodded, and motioned towards Joe. "We have been hearing nothing but good about both your sons."

Joe shook hands with the pirate. "Our daughters are quite taken with them." The men laughed.

Don Carlos motioned Marina over to them. "Marina," he said. "How would you like to work full time for our family?"

Marina stared, momentarily wordless. "Work?" she repeated, her mind spinning fast. "I don't know..." she trailed off, looking at her dads.

Pablo turned to the older pirate. "Marina has school to finish."

Don Carlos frowned. "School?" He searched Marina's eyes, wondering at her distress.

Joe put his hands on her shoulders, squeezing reassuringly. "Yes, school. The girls actually ended up here by accident, and there are some matters that need to be taken care of."

Carlos stared at Marina. "You are leaving?" She froze.

Pablo stepped up. "No, no," he laughed. "At least not at the moment." He turned to the younger pirate. "She just has things to do back home, Carlitos," he reassured him, "but we don't have to discuss any of this now." His eyes met Gaitano's squarely. His daughter was in distress, and he wasn't going to put her on the spot.

Gaitano nodded and turned to the girl. "We have to talk," he said. Marina nodded.

Joe massaged her shoulders gently, warningly. "Sure you do. But you don't want to talk here," he said, waving a hand at the crowded room. "There will be time to talk later, Captain."

Pablo stepped in, as the pirate looked at her suspiciously. "Right now, we are celebrating, no?" He met Gaitano's eyes. "Tonight, let's just have a good time, Carlitos."

Gaitano looked from Pablo, to Joe, his mind working quickly. He glanced at his own dad. Don Carlos warned him with his eyes. Sighing, he lifted Marina's hand to his mouth and kissed it, his eyes searching hers. "We have to talk," he said softly.

She nodded. "I know."

"Captain!" They all turned to look. Silas was beckoning, from the corner table by the end of the bar.

Gaitano grinned. "For now, let's enjoy ourselves for a little while."

Marina sighed. "Sure, baby." She smiled gratefully at her dads. Her family settled around the table, once again. She watched, feeling a little jealous as María Isabel sat with them, already getting along with her moms. Gaitano pulled her along behind him, to his table. There, Silas and Jimmy were shuffling dominoes. Marina picked one up, looking at the detailed carvings and the inlaid ebony on the beautiful ivory pieces. She looked at the old sailor, admiration on her face. "Did you make these? They are exquisite," she exclaimed softly.

Silas grinned at her. "Do you like them?"

She nodded. "Can I play?"

The pirates laughed. "Only if you are my partner," her Captain said. She agreed. And so, they played. Gaitano and herself against Silas and Jimmy. And they had a blast. All around them, there were sounds of celebration. The success of their raids had the Gaitanos in high spirits. They were enjoying themselves, together as a family, with their friends. But none was happier than the Captain of La Gitana, his face relaxed and laughing as he high-fived his girl across his table, the game of dominoes over, to begin again. Then, the door opened. The pirate strode in, reaching Don Carlos' side, before anyone realized who it was.

Salomé screamed. *"Rouge!"*

Marina's head jerked up, a genuine smile lighting her face. "Rouge!"

The pyrate looked up at Don Carlos. "You tricked me!" she accused, laughing.

Maria Isabel shook her head, looking on from the table, as Don Carlos laughed at the young woman in front of him. He shrugged. "You are a sore loser!"

Rouge shook her mane of beautiful red hair. "Sore loser? Me? Don Carlos!" She started laughing so hard, she couldn't speak for a moment. Don Carlos and María Isabel looked at each other, laughing with her. "Making a bet, and then keeping me busy, is just not fair!"

Don Carlos just shook his head. "Admit it, woman! *La Sirena* can beat the *Sea Gypsy* anytime, anywhere!" The pirates laughed around them, as the Banks and the Aguilars looked at each other.

Rouge reached out to embrace the older pirate, tears of laughter in her eyes. "You are so wrong," she cried, "it's not even worth it, straightening you out."

Don Carlos hugged her fondly, kissing her cheek as if she were his daughter. "How was your trip?"

She nodded, eyes shining. "Excellent!"

"I am jealous," said Giancarlo, striding up to them. Reaching for the pyrate, he picked her up, twirling her around. "I thought you would never get here!" He set her down, holding her close and nuzzling her neck.

Rouge laughed. "I almost didn't make it at all," she admitted. "It's kind of rough out there." She turned towards the entrance. There, lounging against the doorway, watching the scene unfold, was a lady pyrate. The woman was dressed as the rest of the pyrates from the Sea Gypsy, the same outfit as the men, but formfitting. This particular woman was tall, and athletic. Her hair was tied back, under a bandana. Her slanted eyes were the color of honey in sunlight, her skin bronzed like Indio's. She was drop-dead gorgeous. "Everybody," announced Rouge. "Meet my Quartermaster, Storm." The woman smiled and waved as everybody said hello to her. Marina exchanged glances with Salomé, as Jackson approached Giancarlo. Introductions were made all around, and the room settled again, happier this time.

The table kept brainstorming, the two lady pyrates with them. Don Carlos, Pablo and Joe stayed at the bar, surveying the scene. Indio finally left Salomé's side, to join them. Marina glanced up from her hand of dominoes, catching Jackson and Indio urgently speaking to the dads at the bar. They all turned to look at her, unseen from the pirate facing her. She bit her lip and quickly looked down, not wanting the Captain to see. At the table, Salomé was reading some ideas from the piece of paper in her hand, and taking a vote. Caribe sat quietly on top of the bar, sketching furiously, eyes hungry as they surveyed the scene. Marina caught him nodding his head, dreadlocks bouncing wildly, at something the men next to him, asked him. They all turned to look at her again. She looked down once more, her heart skipping a beat, as she played her last tile. Silas and Jimmy burst out laughing, as they showed her the remainder of theirs.

Gaitano stood up and came around, putting his hands on the table and trapping her between his arms. He lowered his head and whispered in her ear. "I have to talk to Rouge."

Marina wrapped her hands around his arms, throwing herself back against his chest. "I don't feel too well," she wailed softly.

He frowned. "What's wrong?"

"I'm getting a headache. I've got to go..."

"Wait for me..." He nudged her cheek with his nose before kissing it, and he was gone. Marina felt herself start trembling, as she looked at the men at the bar. They waited until Carlos passed them, before moving.

Indio broke away from them, and came quickly to Marina, occupying the space behind her, that his brother just vacated. Marina took a deep breath and braced herself, tears stinging her eyes. Indio lowered his head, his breath warm on her cheek. "Marina..."

She started shaking her head. "I'm not ready..."

"Marina," he said again, his tone soothing. "We are going to talk to Carlitos. Your dads, Jackson, and myself---"

A cry escaped her throat. "Not now!"

"No," he rumbled softly.

She winced as she felt severe pain slice through her head. "I've got a headache," she whimpered.

Indio rubbed his face against hers. "Ssshh. Don't worry. You will know when we do."

Marina's eyes pooled with tears. "I'm not ready..."

"He is..." He kissed her cheek and walked back to the men at the bar.

She shook her head again, mumbling to herself. "I don't feel too good."

Smiling at Silas and Jimmy, she got up from the table, and quietly slipped away, her men staring after her.

Outside, the sky was still light. Marina stopped to gulp fresh air into her lungs. Brushing her tears away, she began walking away from the Lair. *God, I can't deal with this, right now.* Breaking into a run, she quickly left the town behind her.

Back at the Lair, the pirate finally joined the men at the bar. A frown crossed his face, as he caught sight of the empty chair at his table.

Indio caught his arm as he spun around, looking for her. "Marina had to go. She couldn't wait for you."

The pirate narrowed his eyes as he looked suspiciously at the Quartermaster. Finally, he nodded. "All right. I just want to see her."

Pablo blocked his way, as he turned. "Oye, papi, at least wait for her headache to go away. Give her a little time to herself." Smiling into the pirate's eyes, he clapped him on the shoulder, and turned him around, facing the bar.

Gaitano sighed. *This is her father.* He felt he had the need to remind himself. "Of course. Can I get you a drink?"

Pablo shook his head. "How about, I get you one?" He went around the bar, and poured the young man a glass of wine. He smiled. "Talk to me. How are you getting along with our daughter?"

The pirate's face lit up. He laughed. "Marina is my best friend." He looked into Pablo's eyes. "I am very attracted to her as a woman." He grinned. "Not just how she looks, but how she acts, and thinks..." he trailed off, staring into space.

"When you are not with her, you miss her," smiled Pablo.

The pirate nodded. He looked again at the man in front of him. He sighed. "I guess we really have to talk."

Pablo nodded. "Yes, you do."

"Aguilar..."

Marina's eyes flew open. She felt a little better, after having slept most of the pain off. She caught a movement, and turned her head to look. Swinging in her hammock, with a smile on his face, was her pirate. She smiled back, relief flooding through her system. "Gaitano..."

He straightened up in the hammock, one leg on either side, feet on the floor. "How do you feel?"

She stretched, shaking her hair out of her face. The man in front of her watched, as the material stretched against her breasts. "A little better," she said finally, her muscles relaxing.

He stretched out a very small cobalt glass jar, with a cork stopper. A liquid swirled inside. "Dr. Richardson gave me this." He put it into her outstretched hand. "You have one dose there. It will make the pain go away, and you can sleep better. You will feel like new in the morning."

"Cool," Marina laughed. "Can I take this now?" She shook it in her hand, and held it up to the soft candlelight on the table.

Gaitano nodded. "Yes." He grinned. "Although I must warn you," he said, amused as she raised her eyebrows at him, "I have ulterior motives for providing you with relief."

Marina was speechless for a moment. *You're messing with me.* Finally, she found her tongue again. "Which would be..."

He laughed. "I need you at the docks tomorrow. Rouge came in on the *Sea Gypsy*, remember?"

Marina laughed with him. "Yeah..."

The pirate stood up, swinging one leg to join the other on the opposite side of the hammock. He joined her on the blankets, watching her as she tossed back the medicine and turned to him again. "Marina..." he began, reaching out with his hand. "*Divina...*" he murmured, stroking her face. He looked deep into her eyes. "Ask me to stay with you tonight..."

"No," she said, shaking her head. "Not tonight. Not here," she waved a hand around the hut. "This isn't where I want to be with you..." she trailed off, feeling as if she were going to drown in his eyes.

Gaitano stayed silent for a while, and then he nodded. "That's fair. At least let me stay with you until you fall asleep."

She nodded, slipping her arms around his neck. The pirate pressed his lips against hers, before easing her back down. Lying next to her, he stroked her hair until she fell asleep. Then, he left, one last destination in mind. The freezing cold waterfall.

"What are you thinking?"

María Isabel smiled, as her husband came up from behind, putting his arms around her. She leaned back against his chest and sighed, her eyes riveted on the scene below them. "I am thinking, I have never see Carlitos like this," she answered softly, wonder in her voice. Down on the ground, the docks were bustling with excitement, people rushing back and forth, happy, lines moving steadily. At the head of each, an assortment of people took care of the townsfolk. The crew of La Gitana, the Banks, the Aguilars and a few people from the village. All making what used to be an irate cacophony of stalled humans, into a harmonious joyful flow of energy.

Don Carlos rested his chin on top of her head. "Like what?" Their sons stood out among the rest of the crowd, tall, shirtless, swords shining at their hips, mingling with the people, as they wrote down information. He watched in amazement as they spoke personally to individuals, leaving everybody happy and smiling.

María Isabel's eyes followed their birth son, as he went down a line. "He has changed."

Don Carlos agreed. "Yes, he has." He laughed softly. "A few months ago, you wouldn't have caught him dead down there. He was up here, looking down on them, as if they were peasants and he was the..." he trailed off, as his wife started laughing. She shook in his arms.

"King?" She laughed harder. "That was your doing. Carlitos is your creation." She gasped, trying to catch her breath, tears escaping down her face. Above her head, her husband laughed with her. "You and your brothers. The three of you never let him forget who he was." She fell against him helpless with laughter. *"Carlos Juan Miguel*

Gaitano y Sandoval. The Pirate King." She giggled as her husband kissed her face, shoulders shaking with his own laughter. "And you told him over and over, since he was born, until he believed it. Now," her laughing subsided some, as her eyes caressed her son, "we see him, humble before us, actually speaking to those very same peasants." She sighed. "And to what do we owe this turnabout in our son?"

Don Carlos squeezed her, breathing in her fragrance. "To whom..." he murmured.

She squirmed, as he tickled her. "To whom..." she repeated, laughing softly. "Could it be..."

"Marina Aguilar," he breathed in her ear.

"The girl at *El Luto*..."

"His best friend."

"The accountant."

"His makeout partner."

"*Makeout partner*," María Isabel marveled at the word, not needing to ask what it meant. "You mean, the girl who takes care of his books."

"The girl who takes care of the babies."

"The one who exercises with the men?"

Don Carlos smacked his lips. "The one who messes with his mind."

María Isabel sighed happily, cradled in her husband's arms. "Carlitos likes that one?"

"Carlitos is crazy about her..."

"So, Miguel..."

"Was right."

"Marina Aguilar..."

"She is the one..."

"The mother of his children?"

"Carlitos does not know yet." He kissed the top of her head and let her go, his hands sliding down her arms. He left her for a moment, walking to the table against the warehouse wall, to pour some wine. He came back and offered her a glass.

María Isabel took it, and touched it to his. Smiling into his eyes, she sipped, and licked her lips. "Carlitos is losing control. He showed us at *El Luto*."

Don Carlos cocked his head to one side, nodding in agreement. "Yes." His eyes hardened, at the memory. "I confess, he took my breath away. For the briefest instance, I thought *El Luto* would finally meet its luck, and end in a bloodbath."

María Isabel shivered at her memory of the events. "Carlos!" Her eyes flew to her husband's face, now turned to stone. "Xavier will come after Carlitos!"

"No!" He cut her off. His eyes met hers, and he made his face relax. "No, Marisa, when he comes, it will be after Marina…"

María Isabel turned her back on him once more, drinking some more of her wine. "What are you going to do about it?" Her voice was deadly quiet.

"We are preparing for any and every possibility."

"Make sure you do." And she needed to say no more. They stood side by side, looking through the glass of the second story room. "Look at him," she whispered. As they watched, Carlitos caught Marina as she raced past him. He spun her around, stole a kiss, and sent her on her way with a pat on the butt. They smiled as she laughed, and swung her hips for him. "I have never seen him like this." Their son called after the woman, laughter making him shine in the pale sun.

Don Carlos sighed. "He can't keep away from her. It will be hard for him when he finds out they are visitors."

María Isabel's eyes once again, flew to her husband's face. She gasped. "They are? How do you know?" Don Carlos had told her about the visitors to Encantada, many years ago, after their child was born. The birth of their son had torn down the last barriers he had, holding him back from letting his true feelings out for the woman sharing his life. María Isabel had created life with him, from him, because of him. The result was an outpouring of deep unconditional love for the mother of his child. He had then proceeded to let her know every single thing about him. The visitors had come up, as part of his childhood lore, never having met one himself ever. Until now. María Isabel's heart began to pound. "But their parents..."

"I know, I know," he said, rubbing her arms, soothing her. "The girls came through first, and the brother followed them. When Carlitos took Marina to go to Carey, the brother went back to their own time, and came back with their parents in tow, to the rescue."

María Isabel gasped again, her mind racing at the implications. For a single moment, fear struck her heart. "So, people could just come through at will? Could we be invaded?"

"No, no, Marisa," he murmured. "Nobody knows." He pointed them out on their boxes, scribbling furiously as they tended to the public. "Look at them. Do they seem to you, as if they would bring on an invasion?"

María Isabel shook her head quickly. "No, no, of course not."

He cupped her face with his hands, rubbing his thumbs over her cheekbones. "There you go, Mamá."

"How did you know?"

"Indio told me."

"Indio knows?"

Don Carlos nodded. "Salomé decided to let him know, before they got any deeper. He took it like a champion." He sighed. "Now they are all on Marina to tell Carlitos. She told Indio she's not ready yet."

"So, don't rush her."

Don Carlos shook his head. "She doesn't know how to tell him. We are going to do it for her."

"When?"

He shrugged. "The sooner, the better."

María Isabel searched his face, her mind thinking rapidly. "How do you think Carlitos will take it?" She raised an eyebrow at him in mischief. "I think I know."

Don Carlos laughed. "After he kicks and screams?" He looked back at the throng of people, his eyes quickly finding their son. "He will take it like a man."

María Isabel nodded, agreeing with him. "He is intelligent..."

Don Carlos pressed his lips against hers. His wife closed her eyes, feeling as if she were melting. He broke away, looking deep into her eyes. "He will never let her go."

"Like you," she whispered.

He kissed her again, hugging her tight. "Just like me," he finally whispered. He held her close for a moment longer, and finally relaxed his arms.

María Isabel laughed softly. It seemed to her, that lately it was getting more and more difficult to let go of each other, whenever they found some time alone. She loved it. On a sudden impulse, she took his face between her hands, coddling him as if he were a child. Her passionate whisper warmed his heart. "Marina should be so lucky."

Don Carlos laughed with her, thrilled at her attention. They turned back to the scene before them, their eyes following their sons once again. Down below, Carlitos and Indio high-fived as they passed each other, laughing as they worked. "What about Indio?" he wondered out loud. "How do you see him?"

María Isabel sighed contentedly. "Indio has been a very good son..."

"We have been good parents to him."

"Yes, we have. It is strange how the boys seem to be repeating history. Aren't the girls' fathers best friends, growing up together, also?"

"Yes. The mothers were best friends, too. The children are so close, it's almost difficult to see where one ends and the other begins."

María Isabel laughed at his words. "That's true. It makes the boys crazy."

Don Carlos grinned. "It does, doesn't it? But they are like that, themselves. They have to understand."

She nodded. "They do. They just haven't had the opportunity to work it out, yet." She smiled as she caught sight of the green-eyed girl, busy giving instructions to the flock of little boys around her. "Salomé is stunning, isn't she?"

"Yes, she is. Lucky Indio. He tells me she is like that on the inside, also."

"Good. He deserves the best. I believe she is sincere about her feelings for him. Indio seems to have come alive, just from having met her."

"True love..."

"It is certainly heading in that direction."

Don Carlos thought for a moment. "You know, Marisa," he began softly, "there is a reason why these girls have appeared here, in Encantada, at this moment in time. I don't know what it is," he admitted, "and to tell you the truth, I don't really care what the reason may be. But the effect of their coming here, now, and not later, or before, is evident in just about every aspect of island life here." He took a deep breath. "I'm not just talking about Jimmy and Silas starting to serve lunch at the Lair, or about the Klines' store running more smoothly, since Marina has been taking care of Max. I see beyond that."

María Isabel nodded, excited, as she followed his train of thought. "Their ideas for Encantada, so Carlitos doesn't lose the island, are astounding. They want to present a sort of fair, for the meeting at the end of the month. They are calling it the *Pirates'*," she smiled as he nodded and said the words with her, "*Convention Expo...*" She laughed, eyes sparkling at him. "It sounds wonderful, doesn't it?"

He took a deep breath and rolled his eyes, before laughing into hers. "Intriguing, at least."

"Oh, stop, Carlos!" she scolded softly. "You love it!"

He sighed, nodding slowly. "Will it be elaborate?"

She waved her hand in the air, scoffing at the idea. "No, not at all! They are only going to present what the island already has to offer, in an attractive way for the visiting pirates."

Don Carlos nodded. "What about those huts they are busting their hides on?"

María Isabel laughed. "They are building a whole village, where the crew of the ships can stay when they come in, instead of taking a room in town. The sailors are making small houses by the docks, also. The huts on the beach are for the Captains to keep an eye on their ships, while they are here."

Don Carlos laughed. "I heard about that! My brothers will love that!" He shook his head, at something only he could see. "Imagine Juan and Miguel with their own places by the shore. They will never want to leave," he sighed.

María Isabel shrugged happily. "Carlitos would love having them live here. Besides, it is time they stop playing in the water," she laughed, eyes crinkling.

"I suppose you mean that for myself, also." She nodded. He sighed dramatically. "I thought so." His hand went to his heart, taking hers with the other one and bringing it to his lips. "You hurt me, querida," he murmured, looking into her eyes. His wife laughed softly, amused at his antics. He winked at her, squeezing her hand before letting it go. Her eyes spoke volumes. "What about the lighthouse?" he asked, when he could finally speak.

María Isabel widened her eyes, and nodded. "So, you have noticed..."

Don Carlos laughed. "How could I not? My son spirits my wife away, for hours at a time," he shrugged, "I get a little curious..."

She stopped him with a shake of her head. "You will know..."

He slipped his arm around her shoulders, stealing a kiss. He nodded, respecting the mother-son privacy he encountered on occasions. At having had a son, and raising a second one almost from birth, he had kept a strong hand on the upbringing of his children. By the time they were five, they were sailing with him on the open sea. María Isabel had been there for moral and emotional support. Other than that, they quickly entered a man's world, where they would grow up amidst privilege, excitement and danger. He knew his wife lamented that the sex of their children determined the amount of time she personally had with them. But as a family, they had managed to include her into their world, protected by them, and the two uncles. Any secret she had with her sons were precious spiritual jewels she cherished. He understood. He nodded. "Good enough..."

"What's this?" asked Pablo. Before him lay one of the most stunning weapons he had seen in his life. The blade shone like the sun itself, elaborate in its design, the hilt inlaid with precious lapis lazuli stones. A similar one, just as beautiful, lay in front of Joe. Instead of lapis, jade.

Indio laughed, flanked by their smiling girls. "A gift to the Masters, from their devoted daughters," he announced. The three of them slapped their hands to their sides, and bowed.

The table grew quiet, as they watched the men's reactions. Pablo shook his head, blinking back tears. His eyes flew to Marina's. They shone, as she nodded slightly. The value of the sword before him in their time was staggering. Joe ran his hands over his cornrows, glancing at his wife, before winking at his daughter. The men bowed. "We are honored," said Joe, "that our daughters think so highly of us..." The women hid smiles.

Indio leaned forward, between Sloane and Shayla. He presented them with their gifts. "These are for you," he rumbled, smiling at each of them, in turn.

The women gasped. They smiled as their daughters came around to hug them. The family embraced each other, and settled down again. The pirates seemed to disappear, and they were left alone with Rouge and Storm, from the Sea Gypsy.

Shayla turned to her daughters. "You girls are incredible!" she exclaimed, admiring her pearls. "How could you afford these?"

"Well, actually, we work pretty hard," said Salomé. "In Carey, they just took care of our expenses, so it works out."

Sloane looked at Marina. She smiled. "Can we take these with us?" she teased.

"Probably," Marina answered. "If Jackson took back the portraits and the time table for the storms, I don't see why these things wouldn't go through."

"Well, if they do, they'll be worth a fortune," sighed Sloane, holding up her earrings to admire them better.

Shayla agreed. "We could probably retire on these gifts alone." Salomé laughed. "That would be nice."

"*Max!*"

Everybody turned around at the familiar greeting. Striding through the front door, the baby in his arms, was Carlos Gaitano. He grinned, as Marina smiled at him. She stood to meet him at the bar. Her family watched as the man deposited the baby into her outstretched arms. The pirate proceeded to caress them both.

Shayla sighed. "Now, that makes a pretty picture."

Sloane smiled. "It does, doesn't it? Kind of makes me wish it works out for them," she murmured. Shayla squeezed her hand in understanding.

Rouge grinned. "Actually, the Captain is absolutely crazy about that lady." The moms turned to look at her.

"Is that a fact?" Shayla asked.

The lady pyrate nodded. "Carlos Gaitano has never openly expressed affection for any woman other than his mother, in his entire life," she confided. "In Carey, he recognized Marina as his companion, in front of the rest of the pirates."

Shayla frowned. "How did he do that?"

Rouge smiled at the memory. "He got jealous. Another pirate showed interest on Marina, and he went crazy. So..." she took a deep breath, "Gaitano wanted Marina to do something."

Storm laughed, her warm golden eyes, amused. Today, her hair hung in haphazard braids all around her head, swinging gently as she confirmed this with a nod. She looked very cute, as Jackson had already observed. "She went like this to him." Slowly, she lifted one slender hand, and turned it over. Showing the women the back, her long fingers rippled. "I'm not sure what it means, but he got incredibly upset..."

"How upset, baby?" Shayla wanted to know.

Rouge laughed, shaking her head. Her voice lowered to a conspiratorial whisper. "He backed down."

Sloane stared. "He backed down?" She pointed at herself, her face creasing into a smile. "From my daughter?" She laughed.

Storm laughed again. "Wait, wait!" she hurried to reassure them. "Marina didn't disrespect him or embarrass him in front of the other pirates, or anything. Gaitano backed down as someone who thinks they better stop before they ruin everything..."

The moms exchanged knowing glances. Shayla winked at the lady pyrate. "Gotcha..."

The women turned to look at the bar. The couple was sitting down now, their backs to the room, facing the mirror, holding the baby between them. As they watched, the pirate slipped an arm around her shoulders, threading his fingers in her hair. He bent his head and said something in her ear, making her throw her head back in laughter. Gaitano quickly kissed his way up her throat, before turning her head to capture her mouth. Their lips stayed pressed together until the baby threw himself at them, screaming happily.

Sloane laughed, her eyes caressing her daughter, as she looked up at the man before her with laughter in her eyes, the baby secure in her arms. "I understand that he just wants her at his side, most of the time."

Rouge nodded. "That night in Carey, he put a bracelet on her that Indio gave him."

Shayla nodded, understanding. "It must be those turquoises she's wearing. No wonder she doesn't take them off." Smiling, she turned to Storm, raising her hand and rippling her fingers. "This means, *I don't see a ring on my finger.*"

Rouge frowned for a moment, before her face cleared, enlightened. "Well, she just might get one." She sighed, glancing at the couple once again. "He can't stay away from her." Sloane and Shayla looked at each other. There was nothing more to add to that. The men approached their table, and they changed the subject.

Indio and Salomé joined Marina and Carlos at the bar. They were talking amongst themselves, when Jackson and Caribe approached them. "Ladies!" Jackson laughed at his sisters. "Let's run!"

Salomé slapped her hands on the bar, and jumped off her barstool. Indio lunged to grab her. "No!"

She danced out of his reach, laughing, green eyes glinting wickedly. "Yes!"

Jackson turned to leave, Caribe shadowing him. Passing his parents' table, he smiled at Storm and pulled on one of her braids. "See you later." He winked at her. She laughed and playfully slapped his hand away. He grinned as she nodded.

Marina slid off her own barstool, Max tight against her chest. She looked apologetically at the pirate. "I have to go. I'll drop Max off." Before he could say anything, she was halfway to the door.

The pirate stood up, dismay turning to anger. "No!" He began to follow her.

"Carlitos!" The laughing voice stopped him in his tracks. His father stepped in front of him, eyes flashing. "Let the poor girl breathe."

The younger Gaitano sighed, smiling at himself. He pressed his lips together and glanced at Indio, shaking his head. "You are right, *viejo*," he murmured for Don Carlos' ears only. Throwing an arm around his father, he steered him to the bar. "It's like I need her at my side, Papá!" he whispered fiercely.

Don Carlos looked deep into his son's eyes, seeing the truth of his words. He nodded slowly. "Let her breathe," he repeated softly.

"I feel Marina's crazy about me," he confided.

Don Carlos nodded again. "She is."

"I want all of her, *viejo*!"

His father laughed. "Let her breathe."

Carlos sighed. "She takes my breath away," he muttered.

Don Carlos grinned. "It seems to me, like it's time to make some decisions." He looked at his son's face in the mirror. "Is your accountant disrupting your life, *hijo*?" he asked.

He thought about it for a moment. Finally, he shook his head, sorrowfully. "What life?" he asked. "I am only alive when I am with her..."

"That is a pretty strong statement."

"It's the truth!"

"What about Marina?" he asked gently. "You know how she feels for you, but," he wondered, "does she have any idea of the extent of your true feelings?"

The young pirate shook his head, sadly. "No. She knows I feel comfortable with her, I trust her, and I desire her, but," he tightened the arm around his father's shoulders, looking into his eyes, "I don't know how to tell her what she does to me..."

His father laughed softly. "Think on this a couple of days, Carlitos. It will come to you. Meanwhile," he advised, "win her family over." He winked at his son. "It can't hurt."

Carlos laughed. "Is that how you got Mamá?"

Don Carlos shrugged. "Her brothers were crazy about me. She couldn't help herself." Father and son laughed, and headed back to the table to join the Banks and the Aguilars, as well as the two lady pyrates from the Sea Gypsy.

"Where are we going?"

"You'll see."

"How do I know you're not up to something?"

"Trust me."

"I want to."

A laugh. "You will."

"What's so important?"

A shrug. "Just something I wanted to share."

Suspicion. "Is this something going to cause me trouble?"

"Actually, it should cause you a thrill."

"I'm not seeing anything."

"Listen." The jungle nightlife rustled around them, as the light from the tiki torch preceded them. Birds called to each other from tree to tree, while assorted reptiles and amphibians scurried underfoot. Softly, drums began to play, rapidly increasing in volume until they were overpowering the senses. Their bodies throbbed to the rhythm. Coming out to a clearing, they came on the village celebrating. They watched for a while, as men and women gyrated and stomped, swayed and stepped, joyful expressions on their faces.

"I can't believe it!"

Jackson looked into the lioness eyes, and held out his hand. "Would you like to dance?"

Storm smiled into his tiger eyes, and put her hand in his. "I thought you would never ask." Smiling, they put out the tiki torch and leapt into the circle, dancing around each other, as if they were meant to do so.

A distance away, the riders watched from their usual place. A peace pipe had appeared on this occasion, and it had already made its rounds. Now, the crew of La Gitana and the Captain of the Sea Gypsy, were relaxed, enjoying the natives dancing to the drums.

Rouge laughed as she saw Storm. "I'm jealous..."

Giancarlo grinned. "Because she's with Jackson?" he teased.

The redhead shook her head. "Because she's *dancing*." She sighed, wondering if they would understand. "I feel all that passion inside me, I just don't know if I could express it as beautifully as that," she admitted.

The rest of the men looked at her. They had known Rouge since they were teenagers themselves. They had just never seen her as a woman before. Just as a pyrate. The fact that she had even confessed this to them made their hearts grow warmer towards her, their love for her as a friend, increasing. All hands reached out to stroke her, and she thanked them silently. They smiled, and turned their heads back to the scene in front of them.

Giancarlo whispered in her ear, his heart beating faster. "Maybe you haven't been motivated yet."

Rouge felt herself grow warm at his words. She looked at his stunning face, the tiki torch lights leaping in his dark eyes. He was more beautiful to her, than any Greek statue. The fact that they were good friends didn't hurt a bit. On the contrary, it gave them an edge. Their feelings had been developing for years, their mutual attraction destined to surge with all the respect and love they had for each other, since they were kids running together. Their hearts knew where they were headed. Their minds just had to accept it. He gave her a sexy smile. Rouge felt herself getting wet. "Maybe..." she murmured. Satisfied, Giancarlo kissed her cheek and they turned to watch the natives.

The pirate and the brave sighed, their eyes fastened on their women. Solomon groaned, as he caught sight of a group of teenage girls dancing together, to one side. Silas and Jimmy laughed. And then they heard the horse and rider approaching. They were still riveted on the celebration, when Don Carlos magically appeared out of the jungle, and joined them.

He laughed. "I knew I would find you over here!" He made eye contact with each of them, lingering on his sons. He cocked an eyebrow at them. "Is there a peace pipe around?" he teased, making them all laugh.

Carlos patted the ground next to him. "All gone, Papá."

Don Carlos shrugged. Hiking up his cutoff cotton pants, he sank to the ground with a soft groan. He watched with them, admiring Pablo's and Joe's women, mothers and daughters. He noticed that Rouge's Quartermaster was there, seeming to accompany Jackson. Everybody looked like they were having the time of their lives. When he finally spoke, his voice was clear, so they could all hear. "Tio Miguel is here. *La Gaviota* has arrived."

They all turned to stare at Don Carlos, even as he watched the dancers in the middle of the clearing, mesmerized. They turned back to the dancing. A few minutes later, they all got up and headed to town, to welcome the older Gaitano.

The brothers embraced, before pulling back to look at each other. They smiled, and sank down on barstools, facing the mirror. Two glasses of wine appeared magically in front of them. They took them, raised them, and touched rims before drinking.

Miguel Gaitano smacked his lips and laughed, his massive energy rolling warmly over those, present. "I must be getting old," he confessed. "I am very glad to be here."

His nephew laughed, as he leaned over the bar towards him, his eyes excited. "You will never be too old," he reassured.

"You are right, of course." He turned to smile at Indio. "How are you, papi? Did you get together with that beautiful Salomé?"

Indio laughed. "Of course, Tio Miguel. As we speak, she resides in my house with me."

The huge pirate laughed, his eyes shining with pride. "Excellent!" He turned back to his blue-eyed nephew. He cocked his head at him. "Carlitos..."

Carlos raised his hands, also laughing. "I am working on it..."

Miguel laughed. "Remember what I said." And he changed the subject. "How are things in Encantada?"

Giancarlo came around and joined them. "That, I can assure you, is the most incredible thing of all. Things have never been better." He rubbed his hands together. "Business is good."

"What about Marina and the books?"

"We have been busy the last couple of days, with Don Carlos and Rouge arriving one right after the other, it seems like all we've been doing has been unloading," explained Indio.

"What about when you first got back?"

Carlos smiled. It was his island, so it was his privilege to report to his uncle. "As soon as we got back from Carey, we took care of business. We conducted raids on all the people and places that the books indicated there were discrepancies with."

Don Miguel's eyes lit up with pleasure. "How did it go?" he asked.

Carlos laughed. "Our success was immeasurable."

"Did you take care of Dominique Swan?"

He nodded happily. "Oh, yes, we did. As a matter of fact, she is detained right now with the rest of the men we captured during the raids." He looked into his uncle's eyes. "At the moment, we are just waiting for Tio Juan to get here."

Don Miguel nodded. "He is on his way, papi. Should be here soon, if he doesn't run into bad weather." He looked around at the group of pirates surrounding him. "I took the liberty of asking the rest of the council to come. They should be here in another week or so."

"Excellent!" Giancarlo exclaimed. "It will only help to get this place ready for the *Expo*."

Don Miguel frowned. *"Expo?"*

Don Carlos smiled and rolled his eyes. "When Carlitos got back here from Carey, the girls were so concerned about the possibility of him losing his island, they dreamed up a plan of making Encantada for visiting pirates and pirates in general." He waved his hand in the air, as his brother listened attentively. "Nothing fancy or too extraordinary. They want to do a marketplace like we have in Carey, for the natives and the merchants."

The older Gaitano nodded, interested. "Sounds good. It would attract people here, that's a fact."

Rouge frowned thoughtfully, as she found herself listening intently to the conversation. "Aren't you afraid of attracting the wrong kind of attention?" she asked the crew of La Gitana.

The men looked at each other. Solomon shrugged. "It is a risk we all have to take." He looked the lady pyrate straight in the eye. "You are referring to the one they call the *White Devil*, don't you?"

She pressed her lips together and nodded, fear streaking across her eyes. "We don't know who he is!" she exclaimed softly.

"Any ideas?" asked Don Miguel. He looked around as he was greeted by silence. "I thought Marina had given you a clue as to how he operated."

Don Carlos looked at his sons. "Didn't your accountant say something about it being personal?" he frowned, trying to remember. "I wasn't there at your meeting, but that was in the report I received."

Carlos and Indio looked at each other, their faces setting like stone. "Marina did say something to the effect," Carlos admitted.

"She thinks it is someone that knows us. Someone that may have been wronged by us in the past," Indio added.

Giancarlo gave a harsh laugh. "What she said was, *who do you know, wants to be you, or have what is yours, so bad…*"

They all thought on the words. Solomon cleared his throat. "We all have enemies," he said, "but I don't know anyone who is that sick…"

"Or maybe we do know him, without realizing how sick he is," offered Indio.

"That makes more sense," said Carlos. "But we only stopped at Arrecife for half a day when we left Carey, and then came straight here. We didn't run into anyone at sea." He looked at his elders, and Rouge. "Did any of you?" The two men looked at each other, eyes speaking volumes. Rouge looked down, lost in thought. She pressed her lips together, and didn't speak.

Just then, the door was flung open and Joshua burst in, excitement all over his young, freckled face. His blond hair looked like straw in the candlelight, and his eyes sparkled with anticipation. "Captain! Captain!"

Carlos stood up, momentarily alarmed. He barely ever saw his young sailor out of his crow's nest. "Joshua! What's the matter, boy?"

"Captain! There is a ship out just over the horizon!"

"Slow down, boy! What are you talking about?"

Everybody looked on interestedly, as the boy stopped to gulp big breaths of air into his lungs. Straightening up, he looked at them, grinning. "There is a ship out over the horizon. If it keeps heading this way, it should be here by tomorrow, before noon."

Carlos laughed at the boy. "If they keep heading this way, you mean."

Joshua nodded. "They stopped. Must be waiting for morning."

"Any flags?" asked Indio.

Joshua shook his head. "I think they had a Spanish flag, but they took it down."

Giancarlo laughed. "At least we know they are smart."

Solomon came up behind the boy. "What kind of ship is it, Joshua?" He watched the boy hesitate. "Can you tell?"

Joshua nodded, and looked around them. He looked as if he was about to burst from excitement. *"Galleon."*

The pirates seemed to freeze, as they absorbed the news. Then the whole room burst into cheers and shouts of laughter. Don Carlos and Don Miguel looked at each other, smiles crinkling the corners of their eyes. They watched as the younger Captain commanded the attention of the room. "Is everybody ready to have some fun?"

They roared in response. Rouge smiled at Giancarlo. They had rarely sailed together, and now they might have a chance. He grinned. Solomon looked at Carlos, the son. "Permission to get everything ready, Captain, sir!"

Carlos nodded slowly, excitement coursing through his veins. He must have been getting soft, lately. It had been a long time since they chased anyone. Now, someone had come to them. "Permission granted. Get together the *Star Fish*, it is faster than the *Gypsy*. Go around the back way." Solomon nodded and disappeared, Joshua close at his heels. Carlos turned to Giancarlo and Rouge. "Gian, you guys take *Poseidon*, and wait in the cove." The couple grinned, hands blindly reaching for each other. "Indio and I will greet them in the morning with *Tiburon*." Everybody nodded and left, leaving the two brothers with their father and uncle. Carlos laughed happily. "Looks like we are going to have some fun, tomorrow."

Don Carlos grinned at his sons. "Are we invited?"

Indio laughed. "Why, of course, Papá! We couldn't do this, without you!" Carlos looked at his uncle. "About this monster..."

Don Miguel's energy rolled out, enveloping them once more, as he reassured them. "Let us wait until the rest of the council gets here, and we will compare notes, why don't we?" he asked, looking around, as they all nodded. "For now, I think we all need some sleep." The pirates nodded, and stood up, saying their respective goodbyes.

Carlos stopped Indio outside of the Lair. "Where are you going?" he asked.

Indio smiled. "I am going to get Salomé from the village, and bring her home. I don't want her to come through the jungle by herself after dark."

Carlos nodded thoughtfully, a pang of envy crossing his heart. "I will see you tomorrow, papi," he said absently, turning with a sigh and walking away, alone.

Indio called softly after him. *"Carlitos!"* His brother stopped to look at him. "We need to talk, papi."

Carlos nodded again, and forced a smile. "Tomorrow..."

Marina moaned. She had been having strange dreams all night, weird dreams of being chased, followed, pursued, and in which she had to run to save herself. She had been running all night, then, striving, with all her might, to keep ahead of her pursuer. Now, she had stopped running, and she couldn't breathe. Suddenly, she realized there was a weight on top of her. First, she froze, and then she opened her mouth to scream.

A hand clamped over her mouth, at the same time as a familiar voice whispered in her ear, soothing her out of her dreams. "It's okay," Carlos said softly. "It's Carlos, baby," he breathed against her cheek, holding her wrists down as she struggled. "Just Carlos," he crooned, brushing his lips against her face.

Marina struggled for a moment, before relaxing beneath him. He let go of her mouth, smiling into her eyes as she opened them. "Let me hold you," she murmured.

Carlos released her wrists, slipping her arms around his neck. "I miss you," he groaned, pressing his lips against hers.

"I miss you," she replied, responding to his kiss. Raising her knees, she balanced his weight between her legs, accommodating herself beneath him. "Don't move," she whispered, her mouth claiming his in a hungry kiss. Reaching down with one hand, she yanked out the sheet that had been covering her all night, so that the only thing between them was the fabric of her underwear and his pants. He felt her molding herself to him, until his sex lay snugly between the folds of hers. She squeezed her inside muscles, contracting around him, until he felt her damp heat. Marina held him closer and closer, until she felt as if she were going to fuse into him. Finally, giving him one last squeeze, her body released its hold on his, as a wave of pleasure washed over her, making her shudder in his arms. She ended the kiss, and sighing, smiled into his eyes. "Thank you..."

He grinned. *"Buenos dias, mami..."*

"Buenos dias," she laughed up at him, squirming under his weight. Smiling, he eased off her a little, arms on either side of her head. She stroked his face. The black sky outside her window was a few shades lighter, as the breeze announced the dawn that was creeping in from the ocean. "What brings you up here, so early, papi?" she asked, her voice still sleepy.

He laughed. "You."

She looked at him suspiciously, as soft shadows danced on his face, the room getting lighter gradually. "What about me?"

His turquoise eyes smoldered. "I need you today, to run things for me."

Marina frowned. *"For* you?" she repeated. "Where are *you* going?"

"Something came up last night," he explained, "and I have to take care of business."

Her heart began to pound. "You are *leaving*?" Tears stung her eyes. *"Don't leave me!"*

"Hush," he murmured, thrilled at her reaction. "I will *never* leave you, Marina," he promised, raining kisses on her face. His hips ground into hers, and his chest pressed against her breasts, making her gasp. "For as long as you want to be with me, I will never leave you."

"So where are you going, that you are leaving me in charge?"

He sighed, running his tongue slowly along her lips. Pulling his head back, he looked at her, his hand smoothing her hair back, the other one playing with her earring. "Joshua spotted a ship over the horizon last night." From her silence, he realized she was ignorant of the implications. Suddenly, he remembered that a few weeks ago, when they found the longboat and its occupants, he had kept the whole thing from her. "We need to sail out there, and check it out."

"What are you leaving me in charge of?"

"The docks." His thumb rubbed her frown away. "Tio Miguel's ship came in last night."

"*La Gaviota...*" she murmured. Then, she groaned. "I have seen her books. She is huge."

He smiled, and nodded. "That is why you have to get started earlier. Half its cargo was not ordered, so there will be more people than usual, to buy merchandise."

Marina groaned again. "And where are you going to be?"

"Out at sea," he laughed.

"Why do you get to have all the fun?" She held him close, easing him off his arms and holding all of his weight again, her breasts firmly pressed against his chest, her legs wrapped around his waist. Her crotch stroked his once, twice, three times, holding for a few beats, before relaxing again. "We haven't spent any time together, lately," she murmured, kissing his neck softly. "You haven't even brought me the books."

Carlos ground his hips against her, until he felt her sex clutching his. He groaned. "No, we haven't spent any time together." His breath caught in his chest, and he let go, his whole body relaxing on top of hers, as he made her melt under him. She whimpered in his ear. "I'll bring you the books after you do *La Gaviota*," he rumbled in the shadowy silence.

She laughed and squeezed him, kissing him on the cheek. "That's all you want me for," she teased, slapping her hands on his shoulders and pushing him off her. "My brains." She giggled.

He chuckled, amused, and pleased to see her happy. "You are my accountant, after all."

She shrugged. "That's just a part time thing." Her eyes glowed. "My real job is watching the babies."

He looked at her, thoughtfully. "You love babies, don't you?"

She nodded. "Crazy about them."

"Would you like a baby of your own?"

Her heart stopped for a moment, before racing off again. Her reply was slow to come, dreading the rest of the conversation. *Oh, God...* "Yes..."

"Would you like a baby with me?" he asked softly, making her look deep into his eyes.

Marina shuddered beneath him, fingernails digging into his shoulders. "Don't play with me, Carlos..."

He stilled her shaking head between his hands. "I would never play with you about something like that, mami," he muttered, his thumb rubbing her lips.

Marina saw the truth in his eyes. "We have to talk," she finally said.

He nodded. "We do." Sighing, he let her go and slowly got to his feet. Reaching down, he took both her hands in his, and helped her stand. He brushed the hair back from her face, as she stretched, her underwear glowing white in the soft morning light, the fabric tied around her breasts, colorful and bright against her sun kissed skin. "Go to the docks, you are in charge. Everybody knows," he said, giving her instructions. "Those you've never seen before, you just introduce yourself as Marina Aguilar, Gaitano's accountant. They'll know who you are," he assured her. "Pedro Escobar and Padre Ignacio will be there to help you, and Salomé, and your mothers, and mine."

She frowned. "Wait a moment. What about Caribe, Jackson, and the Masters?"

"They'll be going with me."

She nodded, in mock understanding. "Oh, I get it now. All the boys are going out to play in the water, while all the girls get to stay home and watch the fort."

He shrugged, his eyes dancing with laughter. "Something like that."

She shrugged, and then she grinned at him, hugging him tight. "Whatever," she laughed softly. "Have a good time. Please don't kill anybody," she teased.

He didn't answer, surprised at the request. "I'll see you later," he said, kissing her. "You'll report to me when I get back." He strode to the door, and looked back over his shoulder. "Marina, *divina*..."

Marina winked at him and blew him a kiss. His eyes devoured her where she stood, before he turned. He left. She sighed. Then she began to get ready to start her day.

"*Oye, papi*, what are you waiting for?"

The pirates looked at each other and chuckled. They had been out on the water for more than a couple of hours. The ship they had spied out over the horizon had approached stealthily, throughout the night, and they had woken up to find it much closer than imagined. Once it had spied them, however, it had proved to be a little skittish. Now, Gaitano raised an amused eyebrow at Pablo, as he looked away from the spyglass in his hand. "The right moment..."

"For what?" asked Marina's father, in a hushed tone. "Are you going to attack these people?"

The young pirate grinned. "Not unless they attack me first."

Joe cleared his throat, hands nervously smoothing his cornrows. His amber colored eyes were cloudy with worry. "What happens now?"

Indio put a hand on his shoulder, reassuringly. The man looked up at his daughter's companion, relaxing, as his voice rolled over him in a rumbling wave.

"We just chase them for a little while." He pointed up at the crow's nest, where Joshua was busy taking down the white flag they had been flying since they came near the strange ship. As Joe and Pablo looked on, the flag was quickly replaced with a Jolly Roger. Instead of a skull, an hourglass. Instead of crossbones, crossed swords. Gleaming white, on a pitch black background, its message was unmistakable as it snapped against the deep blue sky. The time travelers looked at each other, eyes searching into one another's souls. They shuddered. Indio smiled, understanding. "Now they know we mean business."

Pablo wasn't convinced. He waved a helpless hand at the fleeing ship a short distance away. "But what if they don't stop or if they fire at you?" His eyes kept going back to its cannons.

Gaitano laughed, and Indio shook his head at them. "Then," the brave announced dramatically, "we pull out one last flag..."

Suddenly, before them, a bright red piece of fabric was spread out on the deck, for them to see. The men peered at it, for a moment, their brains slowly absorbing what their eyes were transmitting. The flag was the color of fresh blood, unmistakable in its particular shade of red. At its center was an arm with a sword uplifted. Under the sword tip was the shape of a heart with what seemed to be drops of blood falling from it. On the opposite corner of the flag, behind the arm, was another hourglass, this one broken, on its side.

Joe and Pablo looked at each other again, seeming to draw strength and courage from one another. Finally, Pablo shook himself, and turned to the man whom he had begun considering his son -in-law. "*Oye, papi,*" he said again, jerking his head to the Jolly Roger waving against the sky, "that one is clear to us, but," he pointed in dismay at the red fabric stretched out between them, "what the hell does that one mean?"

The pirates all looked at each other, and laughed again. Indio waved his hand tauntingly, over the bright splash of color. "You are looking, but you are not seeing," he laughed at them. "The color alone should tell you."

Joe shrugged. "Danger?" he offered hopefully.

The pirates laughed louder. "Oh, no!" exclaimed Don Miguel, moving in closer. "You are not getting off that easy, my friend!" His eyes hooded suddenly, and before their eyes, he transformed, letting them have a glimpse of the pirate's soul. Lurking deep inside the rugged, scarred facade, a touch of evil caressed his heart. And it showed. The Masters looked at each other, their hearts sinking. It was not a Hollywood movie, there was no director shouting, no cameras, no soundtrack. This looked like the real thing, it smelled like the real thing, it felt like the real thing. This *was* the real thing. When they looked at Don Miguel again, the pirate's eyes were wide and laughing, and once again, he was their daughters' friend, the brother of one,

Don Carlos Gaitano y Mendoza, and the uncle of another, Carlos Gaitano y Sandoval. Don Miguel shook his head at them, reading the sudden fear in their hearts, his energy rolling out and enveloping them. "Do not be afraid of us," he warned, mock scowling at them. "We will protect you with our lives."

"Why?" Joe asked. "What is our guarantee? We are not pirates!"

Don Miguel shrugged. "We owe our lives to your daughters." He held out his hand out to Joe, raising a mocking eyebrow, as the corn rowed man looked at it for a moment, before putting his own hand into it.

"I accept that," Joe agreed. "I raised Jackson to be smart about his acquaintances," he raked a weary eye over them. "He trusts all of you, implicitly."

Indio bowed, before embracing his love's father. "And well he should," he laughed at the older man. "We have earned his trust. Implicitly."

Pablo laughed suddenly, as he remembered the topic of trust coming up, just today, right before they set sail on this wild mission. They had been preparing the ship they were on, and the Gaitano's crew had declared their loyalty towards Marina and Salomé, for their bringing such a change into their lives.

Solomon couldn't resist teasing Pablo. "I, however, have no loyalty towards your daugter," he laughed, bowing to his Master. "She has kicked my ass twice, so you mean nothing to me."

Pablo smiled to himself, as he caught the young African trying to hide a grin, his eyes twinkling deeply with mischief. He bowed back. "Be that as it may," he bantered with the boy, "you would have to beat me, before you hurt me, and by then, Marina's ass kicking would be mere love taps, compared to what I, shall do to you."

Solomon slapped his hands against his chest, as if containing his heart. The crew laughed as the Boatswain stumbled and fell to his knees, groaning as if in agony. He bowed deeply at Pablo's feet, going as far as to kissing his boots. "Forgive me, Master, for I have forgotten my place. It is madness, and will not happen again." He stood up slowly, and winked at the accountant's father. "You are the man."

Pablo laughed. "I see my son has taught you well." Solomon shrugged, and nodded, pleased at his first try at repeating a favorite phrase of his good friend, Jackson.

Coming back to the present, Pablo laughed again. "Both our daughters couldn't be so wrong at the same time." The pirates laughed with him.

Don Carlos put an arm around his son's accountant's father's shoulders. "Pablito," he laughed, "we may be pirates, and it may be overwhelming for someone who has never seen one up close, nevertheless a whole ship full of them." He waited for the roar of laughter that followed his words, to die down. "But, believe it or not, we are educated men." He raised a warning finger in a gesture for Pablo to wait until he was done talking. The other man had begun to shake his head in protest. "I grant you that pirates are not, as a rule. We don't get to be Captains from going to school. But we," he looked around him proudly, "these men you see here, in particular, are all educated men." He sighed. "Your daughters have been Heaven sent. They have given these fools a chance to exchange ideas with someone at their level. They don't usually get to meet any educated girls." Joe and Pablo looked at each other again, this time, a sense of relief in their eyes.

Carlos stepped in. "Things have changed," he said, as way of explanation. He gestured at the flag before them. "I am not the same anymore, and I would think twice, today, about having to use that flag." He turned to look at each man in turn. Taking a deep breath, he turned back to the piece of fabric. "Red means no quarter given," he explained hastily, pointing to each symbol in turn. "The arm with the sword means we are willing to kill, the hourglass is broken, so time has run out, and the bleeding heart means you will die a slow, and painful, death." He glanced at each of them again, taking in their shocked expressions.

Joe shook his head, dazed. He turned to his friend. "We asked, Pablito," he said softly.

Pablo shook his head back at him. "All this, because of a storm." Indio smiled at the reference, and Carlos frowned, not understanding. Marina's father turned back to him. "Have you ever used this flag?" He gestured in disgust at the young pirate's grin. "Let me say that in other words. Have you ever had to resort to fulfill all the things this flag promises?"

This time, the looks among the pirates were furtive, although the smiles were fixed in all their faces. Carlos raised his chin, and looked at Pablo straight in the eye. "Yes."

Joe frowned. "Did you enjoy it?"

Indio chuckled, his eyes momentarily wild. "We loved it."

"Stop!" Don Miguel scolded them, just as he did when they were boys, bent on mischief. "I apologize for my nephews, the savages," he glared at them. He turned back to the men. "They are playing with you, as they would with their father and myself," he explained.

The men turned to the father of the duo. Don Carlos nodded, confirming his brother's words. "It is true, they are playing with you. But it is also true, they did strike a ship once. It happened only once," he said, frowning at the memory. "It was bold and reckless. They were very, very young, and extremely, unforgivably stupid. It was their first time out, and," he turned to look at each of his sons, "they got high on the power. So they went crazy, thinking they were men, while everyone around them was amused with the boys."

Joe frowned, caught up in the story. He wanted to know everything about his daughter's man. "What happened?"

Don Carlos took a deep breath, and exhaled slowly, his eyes focusing again on the men in front of him. "They attacked a ship," he said slowly, "that attacked them back. Many people lost their lives. They managed to survive. But not before they did away with everyone on the ship." He paused, waiting for his words to sink in. Changing his tone, he continued briskly. "It happened the one time, and only on that one time, never to be repeated again. As soon as my boys realized what they had done, they were inconsolable. It was as if their souls were tortured," he said. Behind him, his sons turned away from his words, and occupied themselves with the running of their ship. Don Carlos smiled, knowing how his words affected his boys.

"And then what happened?" Joe demanded, fighting against a wave of overwhelming horror. This was the real thing. "They found religion or something?"

Don Miguel laughed. "You could say that," he said, tears forming at the corners of his eyes. "It was more like religion found them."

Joe and Pablo looked at each other before turning to Don
Carlos. "What does that mean?" Joe demanded.

Don Carlos laughed. "Their mother heard about their little
incident." He shook his head, his shoulders shaking at the memory.
He smacked his lips and widened his eyes, indicating the amount of
trouble their sons had gotten themselves into, not to mention their
compromising their souls. "María Isabel found them." He looked
into each of their eyes. At that moment, they were all fathers, connected by their children's love for one another.

Joe sighed, running his hands over his cornrows. "You need say
no more."

Suddenly, from above their heads, Joshua called. *"Star Fish!"*

The crew of *Tiburon* cheered. *"Star Fish!"*

Indio smiled at the men's puzzled looks. "Solomon." That was
all he needed to say. The men smiled, understanding. Before their
eyes, the ship they were pursuing seemed to hesitate, as if they, too,
had caught sight of the young African's ship. *Tiburon* sailed steadily
towards the runaway ship as it resumed its flight.

A few minutes later, Joshua called once again, from the crow's
nest.

"Poseidon!"

The crew of the *Tiburon* cheered once more. *"Poseidon!"*

Indio laughed. "Giancarlo and Rouge."

"Oye, papi," Pablo stopped Carlos as he swung by. "Do you have
to put that red flag up a lot?"

Carlos grinned. "Not really. People usually surrender." He
shrugged. "I have a bad reputation, so most of the time I don't have
to do much of anything."

Joe frowned. "Wait. I don't get it. You attacked a ship once, and
it was a bad idea. Is that the only time you have ever attacked a ship?
You mean every ship you have ever pursued since then, has surrendered to you?" he asked, suspiciously.

Indio laughed along with his brother, as he nodded. "Amazing,
isn't it?"

Pablo shook his head. "So, throughout your whole career, everyone has just *surrendered* to you..." He chuckled. "Some pirate *you* are!"

Carlos explained. "Oh, I *am* a pirate, alright! We have had our fair share of skirmishes, engaged in a couple of battles, here and there, definitely drawn blood..." He took a deep breath. "Just nothing like that first time, when we almost sent our souls to eternal damnation." His mouth twisted into a strange smile. "Every person we have killed since that one time has been in self defense." He caught the men looking at each other. His face settled into hard lines, and they could see the truth in the deep pools of his eyes. "I gain nothing by lying to the fathers of the woman who has given me my life back," he muttered.

Everybody fell silent for a moment. Joe looked down at the deck beneath his feet, lost in thought. Pablo finally stepped up and patted the young pirate on the shoulder. "*Oye, papi,*" he said, struggling to find the right words, "we are not judging you. This is your world. We have seen you, shared with you, worked next to you, played and laughed with you. You are an excellent person. Your profession may not be our choice, but your job does not make you an evil man. It's just not our world, but we accept it as yours. We respect you, Carlitos. You do whatever you have to do."

Carlos nodded, meeting Pablo's eyes. "*Gracias, Papi.*"

Pablo nodded back and went to stand with Joe, out of the pirates' way.

The pirates turned back to their spyglasses, while the ancient dance unfolded. The men looked on, in silent awe, as the *Star Fish* and *Poseidon* slowly corralled the immense ship looming before them. Soon, they were sideways, and firing their cannons. The girls' dads watched in mounting horror, as their hearts climbed a steep roller coaster in their chests. To their amazement, the pirates laughed, as if enjoying themselves, and were immediately at their own cannons. The Masters dove for cover. All three ships fired back at the same time. The hull of the unfortunate ship showed a hole, high up, almost on deck. The main mast snapped and keeled over. Soon, the ship was flying a white flag. The battle was over almost before it started. Quickly, the *Tiburon* overtook the now crawling ship, and the bloodthirsty crew proceeded to storm it. Joe and Pablo looked on, as their friends crawled on the immense vessel, as insects on a mission. They took up the discarded spyglasses.

Aboard ship, the crew of the *Tiburon* looked closely at the crew they had seized. The men were silent as the two Captains faced each other.

The captured man took a deep breath, making his massive chest expand. His sad gray eyes met the young pirate's laughing ones. "*Gaitano,*" the man finally said. "I can not say, in all honesty, that it is not a pleasure to meet you." His hands went up to his silver streaked black hair, smoothing it back from the wind. "I believed you were a legend of these waters."

Carlos laughed, delighted. "I am afraid you have me at a disadvantage, sir, for I, unlike you, do not know who I am facing." He stopped in front of the man, his hand fondling his sword.

The Captain nodded and introduced himself. "*Don Andres Segarra y Collazo, Capitán de La Diosa del Mar.*"

Gaitano nodded back. "*Carlos Gaitano y Sandoval, Capitán del Tiburon.*" He laughed, as the man glanced up at the dark gray sails on the ship along his, his eyes going to the Jolly Roger. "You recognized my flag," he said.

Don Andres' eyes flew back to his. "As I said, I thought the hourglass cradled by the crossed swords, was legend." He bowed. "Now that we have the formalities out of the way, may I ask you a question, *Capitán?*" He smiled as Gaitano cocked an eyebrow at him. "Out of mere curiosity of course, although your reputation precedes you." He laughed softly. "Which is true?" he continued. "That you are a wicked pirate, or a compassionate man?" He shrugged at the younger man's sudden look of interest. "I have heard both."

Carlos nodded, thoughtful, smiling to himself. "Interesting," he finally answered. "Which, do you think, is my reputation based on?"

The man laughed. "My mind confirms what my eyes see, and that is," he looked at all of them, "pirates, all around me." He waved a hand in the air, before turning back to the young man in front of him. "And before me stands a man, whose name is spoken of in hushed tones by those who believe in him, because be he wicked or compassionate, he is admired and respected by those who know him." He smiled, as he mused out loud. "Why would I fear such a man?"

Carlos chuckled. "You shouldn't. For there is truth to the rumor. But before we go into any of this, I need to know, what is *La Diosa* carrying?"

Don Andres drew himself up straight. "We come from Africa, sir." He glanced at the deck beneath his feet. "We carry slaves."

Indio stepped up next to his brother. "So you are headed to the Colonies."

Don Andres nodded. His eyes glinted as they raked over the brave. "You must be the one they call *Indio*." A puzzled look crossed his face. "How is it that you are brothers?"

Indio laughed. "Our fathers were best friends. Soon after I was born, my parents were tragically taken." He glanced at Carlos. "I was fortunate enough to be taken in by Don Carlos, as his son." He shrugged. "The crew knows me as the Quartermaster."

Don Andres raised his eyebrows, his mouth twisting into a painful smile. "I see. So it is you who will be, shall we say," he struggled to find the words, "relieving me of my cargo."

Indio laughed again. "Of course." Just as suddenly, he became still, drawing nearer to the Captain, the moccasins on his feet giving stealth to his steps. "But now, you are just wasting our time, Capitán." His voice rumbled, low and menacing in his chest. "As you can tell by our crew, we know a little bit about Africa." His lips twisted into a sarcastic smile. "Priceless as your slaves may be, they are not Africa's export of most value." His arms lifted, as if embracing the ship they had just invaded. "A vessel of this size," he laughed once more, his eyes skimming the cannons on either side, with the subdued sailors next to them, "must have a bounty much more valuable than just," his eyes turned back to the man in front of him, "slaves..."

Don Andres nodded, in acknowledgement of the young brave's words. "Agreed," he said in a low voice. "However," he added, a little worried, "our business would do well, if conducted in private."

The brothers looked at the man, searching his face for any deception, and finding none. Carlos spoke first. "Agreed. However," he added with a smile, "we would like to meet your man in charge of the slaves."

On the deck of the *Poseidon*, Jackson and Storm stood side by side, watching the events unfold on the ship before them. He was amused by, and attracted to her restless energy. "What's going on?" he asked quietly, eyes glued on his friends.

Her voice caressed him. "Just talk," she answered, as her slanted eyes flashed like molten sunlight at him. The attraction was mutual. "For now," she added wickedly.

Jackson glared at her, no longer amused. Her teasing didn't make him less afraid of what could happen. "You are nothing but a savage," he growled.

She shrugged, eyes twinkling merrily. "Like attracts like..."

Jackson turned back to look at the ship once more. "Lady, you don't know just how savage I can be," he muttered.

"Then I guess you will just have to show me, won't you?" she challenged.

Jackson held out his hand without looking at her. His voice growled at her once more. "You're on!" Storm smiled to herself, even as her eyes stayed riveted on the pirates on the other ship. Without answering, she slid her hand against his, the wind whipping her hair about her face.

Back on *La Diosa del Mar*, Don Andres' Quartermaster introduced himself. "I am *Don Luis Vega y Ramos*." This man was younger, but just as formidable as the Captain. A little bit taller, his hair tossed in the wind, the color of old brass, the sun sparking golden lights off it. His eyes were the color of mountains in the distance, sometimes green, sometimes blue, sometimes gray. He turned to Indio slowly, careful not to make any sudden moves. He realized that if Gaitano was a real man and not just a legend, there must be some truth to the stories they had been told about him. "Do you wish to conduct your business with us now, and here?" he inquired politely.

Indio's eyes raked over the tall figure, before locking on the man's face.

Don Luis met his gaze steadily, carefully. Indio liked what he saw. "No. Of course not, sir. We will gladly escort you back to Encantada, and we will do our business there."

Giancarlo and Solomon slowly circled the men, like sharks around a prey. The Boatswain laughed softly. "I, also, come from Africa. I am sure I know what some of *La Diosa's* precious cargo may be."

Don Andres pressed his lips together, and his shoulders slumped slightly in resignation. He met the young African's eyes. "And you would be correct, sir," he admitted. "Not all the men on this ship, however, are as educated as you are." He looked deep into Solomon's eyes, signaling him. "Don Luis and I made sure we wouldn't be victims of mutiny on board."

Solomon understood the man's warning, and backed away, bowing graciously. He laughed softly, his sword blade glinting wickedly in his hand. "It will be a pleasure doing business with you, gentlemen."

Relieved, Don Andres bowed back. He turned to his Quartermaster. "Don Luis, if you would be so kind as to fetch Mr. Williams for us," he said, his mouth twisting in distaste at the name.

Giancarlo stepped up, laughing. "Don Luis!" he exclaimed, as the Quartermaster was about to turn away. "I am Giancarlo Ilarraza, Capitán Carlos Gaitano's Sailing Master." The two men faced each other. "Permit me to escort you." At Don Luis' nod, they fell into step and walked away.

Don Andres turned back to the young pirates in front of him, when something caught his eye. Standing quietly, to one side, not moving, eyes fixed on the events unfolding in front of him, stood a pirate, older than the two young bucks standing in front of him. He looked hard, taking in every detail about the man. Finally, he smiled. Striding boldly towards him, he held out his hand. "You must be Don Carlos Gaitano."

Don Carlos shook his hand carefully, his other hand never leaving his sword, his eyes amused. "Did you think I was a legend, too?"

Don Andres laughed. "Why, of course!" He stepped back, chuckling to himself. "What else would I think, *caballero*, of someone as heroic as yourself?" He spread his arms out, indicating the ocean around them. "These waters are rich with stories of the Gaitano men. Am I safe to assume your brothers, Don Miguel and Don Juan, are real also?"

The pirates laughed, enjoying the man's mock dismay. Don Andres had already won their respect, and they were enjoying the Captain's attitude towards his current situation. Don Carlos chuckled, eyes twinkling in appreciation. He was surrounded by men all the time. But outside of his Council and his family, he rarely encountered anyone as educated as this one. He jerked his head towards *El Tiburon*. "Miguel will enjoy meeting you when we reach Encantada." He waited as Don Andres turned to look, his eyes going to the figures of the three men looking at him through spyglasses on the next ship. One of them was obviously much larger than the other two. He had heard enough stories about Don Miguel Gaitano's size and energy, to recognize him immediately, even from a distance. Aboard the ship, the pirate laughed as he realized he was the topic of conversation at the moment, and raised his hand in mock salute. Joe and Pablo watched in silence as the captured Captain waved back.

Don Andres turned thoughtfully back to the older pirate. "Is it true," he asked slowly, "that you have the authority to impart justice in these waters?"

The pirates looked at each other, before turning their gazes back to the Captain. The man's words weighed heavily in the air, even as the wind swept over them. Don Carlos finally spoke. "Have you been wronged, Don Andres?" he inquired, a slight frown creasing his forehead.

Don Andres shook his head hastily. "Oh, no, *caballero*." Then he looked around him, and looked back at Don Carlos, a sad smile creeping into his eyes. "Other than this, not I." He sighed deeply and shook his head mournfully. "Although in all honesty, the wrongdoing towards me and mine was not caused by you, but by those who sent me out here," he explained, his hands going back to smooth his hair again, "knowing I would encounter you."

The pirates laughed in appreciation at the man's ability to laugh at himself in the face of adversity. Don Carlos chuckled. "True," he agreed, "but your words give me reason to believe you have seen something that has troubled you."

Don Andres nodded, amusement fading to consternation, as he frowned, his eyes focusing on something only he could see. He weighed and measured his words carefully. "Your reputation and the stories told about you are far removed from what these old eyes have actually seen in these waters." He looked up, seeming to focus on them once again. "A man rumored to be as compassionate as you," he said, directing his gaze at the younger Gaitano, "could not have possibly committed the horrors I have encountered recently in this New World," he hissed suddenly. The men reacted as one. Hands on their swords, they froze, all eyes riveted on Don Andres.

Carlos was the first to speak, his tone low and controlled. "And what would those horrors be, Capitán?" he asked softly.

Don Andres began pacing restlessly, ignoring the sound of ringing steel, as swords were drawn out at his sudden movement. He tore at his coat, flinging it off and away from him, and loosening his shirt, as if having trouble breathing. He raked his fingers through his hair, no longer a Captain in control of his ship. "I have been to an island, not too far from here," he said shakily, "where the mountains seem to stretch to Heaven. Where the trees were so bountiful, that fruit lay on the ground, just rotting."

Carlos nodded slowly. "Most of these islands look alike."

"Waters as clear as those in the Garden of Eden, as blue as the eyes of an angel," Don Andres muttered.

"So far," Carlos said, impatience making him rude towards the older man, "you have described every island I know."

Don Andres ignored the interruption. "Where the men are tall and strong, as the slaves aboard this ship." He stopped pacing suddenly, his eyes wild as he scanned their faces. "Where the women are so beautiful, they make your heart ache, as they hold their babies." He gasped, his hands going to his chest as if trying to keep his own heart inside. "Where the natives all lay dead, in a pool of their own blood."

The pirates roared, pain and horror gripping their hearts. Rouge screamed up at the sky, her red hair whipping around her face, as if her head had caught on fire. She stumbled towards the captured Captain, her sword firm in her grasp, a wail tearing from her throat. Tears poured out of her eyes. "You saw?" she cried. "When was this? Where was this?" She began sobbing, her beautiful face transformed into a mask of pain. Her hand clutched at the man's shirt. "Don Andres..." she wailed once more.

The Captain grabbed her by the shoulders as her knees buckled, holding her up. "A few days ago," he said, his eyes wildly searching the beautiful pyrate's haunted eyes. "You have seen this also," he realized, not waiting to see her nod.

Rouge stumbled away from him and turned to the Gaitanos, gasping for air. Her eyes shimmered in pools, as tears kept streaming down her face. "I told you," she sobbed, her voice rising with emotion. *"I told you!"* she screamed. She stumbled away, as if dazed, only to come back and face Don Andres once again. "Any survivors?" she demanded, choking on her words.

"None!" he growled, fighting the shock that threatened to overwhelm him. He looked back at the Gaitanos. "The bodies were still warm..." his voice trailed off, his hand lifting towards them beseechingly, before falling helplessly to his side once more.

The pirates roared once more, each word a blow to their hearts. Bloodshed in a battle out at sea was one thing. The slaughter of innocent natives was another. They did trade with these people, and depended on them. They had friends on all these islands. Carlos grabbed Don Andres' arm and spun him around to face him. "Did you see any other ship? There must have been one close by, if it just happened."

Don Andres looked into the younger man's eyes, trying to regain his composure. "Why, of course, we saw a ship." He frowned at the memory. "It was just leaving the island, and we managed to hide before it saw us."

"A red ship," Rouge spoke up, from beside Don Carlos.

"The color of blood," Don Andres confirmed. "Very fast. It has three---"

"Three masts," she interrupted, sobbing. "The Jolly Roger---"

"Different," he agreed. "A dancing skeleton with a sword in one hand, and..." he sighed, looking at Rouge.

"And a bleeding heart held in the other," she wailed, her free hand going to her own heart.

Don Andres nodded abruptly, looking back at Carlos. He raised an eyebrow at him. "So, you have heard of this demon before."

Carlos nodded. "They call him the *White Ghost*."

"Ah, yes, of course," he said, nodding to himself. "I can see why."

Indio seemed to snap out of his shock. "You saw this person?"

Don Andres shrugged. "I looked through my spyglass, and saw the figure of a man at the wheel. His back was turned to me, however," he said thoughtfully, "but he must be older than we are," he added, looking at Don Carlos.

The older Gaitano frowned. "Why do you say that?"

"From where I was, I could see the sun shining straight down on the man. His hair is as white as snow." He turned to the brothers, giving them a slight nod. "That's how I know it wasn't you."

The brothers looked at each other with pain in their eyes. They turned to their friend, not knowing what to do or what to say to console her. Rouge just shook her head at them, angrily wiping the tears from her face, controlling herself as Giancarlo reappeared with Don Luis and two men in tow.

The Italian had been grinning at his friends as he approached, but sobered up as he caught their expressions. His eyes absorbed the shock in their faces. He knew something had happened while he was gone, when he took one look at Rouge's tear ravaged face. Next to her, Don Carlos shook his head in warning, making him bite his tongue to keep the questions from pouring out. He frowned to himself, but showed none of his consternation to the captive sailors. Instead, he pretended he didn't notice. He turned to the younger Gaitano. "Capitán," he said, laughing. "It seems as if Mr. Williams, here," he pointed at the man in question, "has a problem with *La Diosa del Mar* being taken over by pirates."

Carlos flashed his Sailing Master a look of appreciation. "And what would that problem be, Mr. Williams?" he asked, letting his voice fill with amusement.

The younger of the two men moved closer to Don Luis, his body language indicating that he had no problem whatsoever. The older one was just livid, however. The man was as dirty as he was smelly, his eyes flashing with barely controlled madness. He took a menacing step towards Carlos, stopping as the tip of his sword touched his chest. The pirates all held their breaths, their swords clutched tightly in their hands as they watched the scene unfold. Mr. Williams' yellowed eyes went wildly from face to face, before coming back to meet Carlos' steady gaze. He sneered, his face twisting into a mask of hate as it betrayed his disgust. "I have come a real long way, pirate," he said in a loud voice, making sure all those around him heard. "And I have seen many things no man was meant to see." He took one step back from the sword tip. "I have been to Hell and back, and I am almost home." His eyes became glassy as he became more deranged. "I have worked real hard to get these slaves, and keeping them alive until their final destination. Why," he asked, his lips twisting into an ugly grimace, "should I submit to the likes of you?" He spat at Carlos' feet, just missing him.

The pirates gasped collectively, and watched eagerly, as Carlos stepped closer, until the tip of his sword was pressed against the man's chest once again, this time, making a bead of blood appear. Had Mr. Williams heard about Carlos Gaitano, he would have known to back off. But lunacy has no reason. "You, sir," Carlos informed him in a dangerously low voice, "have no choice. As you can see," he pressed the tip of his sword a little harder, making the man's chest rise and fall faster, "you have been captured, and now, your precious cargo is mine." He laughed as the man's eyes blazed with pure hatred. He sensed, more than saw, Don Andres and Don Luis step back, aghast at the slave driver's boldness. "But today is your lucky day, Mr. Williams," he informed him, moving his sword up to the man's throat, and under his chin, making him tilt his head back. His turquoise eyes had frozen into icy pools of carefully controlled danger. "My accountant asked me this morning, to not kill anybody today."

He let his sword drag up along the man's jaw line towards his face, as if it were kissing him. "However, she didn't say anything about marking a man for his arrogance and stupidity." With one quick flick of his wrist, he slashed at the slave driver's face, making a deep crescent of blood appear on his cheek. Carlos laughed wickedly as the man's hand went to his face, his eyes filling with horror as he turned to look at his bloodstained fingers. "For the rest of your life, you will remember my name." He laughed again. "If anyone asks, tell them C is for Carlos."

Mr. Williams stumbled back, both hands to his face now, to keep the blood from flowing. *You bastard!* he shouted.

Carlos faced the man, head on, never taking his eyes away from him. The slave driver looked as if he were going to cry, while sheer undisguised hatred burned deep in his eyes. The pirate caressed his other cheek with the tip of his sword, making the man flinch and cower. Finally, the younger Gaitano turned away from him in disgust. "Let's go, men!" he barked. "Encantada!"

Indio turned to Don Andres and Don Luis. "Gentlemen," he said, eyes glinting like ebony, "if you would be so kind as to lead the way..." He gestured with his sword. The men looked at each other in resignation. They took Indio to the wheel of the ship.

Aboard *El Tiburon*, the men watched in shock as the scene before them unfolded through the magnified lenses of their spyglasses. Joe turned to Don Miguel, his heart pounding in his chest. "What just happened?"

Don Miguel's energy shifted, rolling out towards them, before he contained it and drew it back. "The idiot must have insulted the boy," he said softly, his eyes glued to the scene.

Side by side, the men watched as the pirates scrambled, occupying the ship. Behind it, the *Star Fish* and the *Poseidon*, were already backing away. Pablo kept his eye on the bleeding man left on deck. The injured slave driver seemed to be muttering to himself, hands going to his face, before wiping the blood off on his clothes. As Pablo looked on, a cry escaped him as the man reached into his coat. *No!* His heart rushed into his throat.

Everything seemed to happen in slow motion. They saw a glint of steel, as the man pulled out a pistol. The young pirate's name tore out of their throats at the same time, as they watched in horror as the man walked slowly towards the object of their affection, hiding the weapon as he went. *"Carlitos!"*

Blood called to blood, as Don Miguel whipped out his own pistol and fired into the air. *"Carlitos!"* The older pirate threw the pistol down and dashed to the cannon closest to him, loading it.

The startled pirates aboard *La Diosa*, looked back at the screaming men on *El Tiburon*. Don Carlos reached a blind hand towards his son, not taking his eyes off his brother. *"Que pasa?"* he muttered, as his son frowned.

Solomon frowned also, as he quickly looked around him, searching for the cause of alarm in his friends. He saw Mr. Williams' back, as he walked steadily towards his Captain. The slave driver was oblivious to everything around him as he approached the pirate slowly, the sun glinting off the pistol tucked at his side. Without thinking, the young African hurled himself after the disgusting wretch, his sword in front of him. Mr. Williams raised his hands, just as Solomon reached him. From their place at the wheel, Don Andres and Don Luis watched in horror as the scene unfolded. Indio stood as a statue between them, his heart gripped in cold terror as he watched his brother threatened by the barrel of a pistol. "Carlitos!" The Boatswain and Mr. Williams were steps away from the Gaitanos. Father and son turned in disbelief as they watched Solomon's sword slowly come out of the slave driver's chest.

The young African grinned, as if he had just pinned a butterfly. " *I*, however," he laughed, "was not asked to not kill a man today." He thrust his sword deeper into the man's back. More steel came out of the man's chest, making him drop his pistol unto the deck. Blood bubbled at his mouth, matching the blood on his face. Solomon thrust the sword again, until it was buried to the hilt. Laughing harder, he turned the still living man to the edge of the ship, facing the men aboard *El Tiburon*. "Our accountant will thank me." He began retrieving his weapon. The slave driver gasped. Solomon put his foot against the man's back, pulling out his sword and pushing the man overboard in one swift movement. There was a splash. It was over in a moment.

Aboard *La Diosa del Mar*, the pirates looked at each other in silence. The Captain's eyes met his Boatswain's. No words were needed.

Aboard *El Tiburon*, Joe Banks and Pablo Aguilar stood like statues, their minds churning, their hearts bursting. It was a love test. And they passed. Unconditionally, and irrevocably, Joe and Pablo loved Carlitos Gaitano with all their hearts. They finally looked at each other, their eyes betraying their feelings, as they reeled from shock. Respecting their need for privacy, Don Miguel turned and went to the wheel of his beloved nephew's ship.

A couple of hours later, a convoy of the four ships sailed into the port of Encantada.

Marina looked up sharply, as people around them started running towards the docks. Slowly, she turned around and began shuffling back the way they had come from. She groaned softly. "I just finished!"

Salomé swore under her breath. Slipping an arm around Marina's shoulders, she couldn't help but laugh. "Your boyfriend's timing sucks," she giggled, her tired body moving along with the masses.

"No," Marina shook her head and giggled back, "*yours* does. This is *his* gig. It's all Indio, baby!"

Exhausted as they were, they fell against each other, laughing helplessly. They found themselves, suddenly, standing right back where they had just been, only moments ago, in front of the Siren's Lair. Looking at each other, they laughed, saying the words at the same time. "I need a beer!"

Silas raised his eyebrows at them, as he saw the look in their eyes.

Shaking a finger at them, he scowled. "Oh, no, you don't!" he scolded. "You girls are going to eat something, first!" The girls growled at him.

Jimmy laughed. "I guess I better hurry!" He ran off to get them food, reappearing a few minutes later.

The girls were almost too tired to eat, but they were determined on having that beer. So they refueled with hot fish on warm bread, sweet mangoes and pure water, from the jungle. Silas and Jimmy watched over them with warm hearts, cleaning up after them, when they were done. Finally, they were served their beers. Their eyes met in the mirror behind the bar.

Salomé slipped her arm around her shoulders, once more, letting her rest her head on her shoulder, for a moment. The green -eyed girl lifted her bottle. Her voice was soft. *"Salud!"*

Marina lifted her own bottle, her eyes blazing pure love, right back at her sister. Her voice was just as soft. *"Salud!"* They touched bottles.

Suddenly, the door behind them burst open. They looked up as Indio strode in, straight towards them. They took one look at his face, and their hearts sank. They drank from their respective bottles, their eyes glued to the brave's.

Indio slowed down, and stood behind them, meeting their eyes in the mirror. His arm went around Salomé, automatically, making her fall against him, her back flat against his chest. He ducked his head for a moment, pressing his lips against hers. He smiled, as he looked up at them, again. "Ladies," his voice rumbled. His hand snaked out, wrapping around Marina's face. He tilted her head back on the crook of his arm, and gazed straight into her eyes.

Marina sighed and smiled up at him. This time, her voice came out hoarse. "No..."

Indio laughed with loving affection. "Yes." He kissed her forehead. "Please..." Then, her cheek. "I need you..."

Marina sighed, again. "Do I have a choice?"

Indio grinned and kissed her cheek again, laughing at her affectionately, as he pushed her gently with his arm, until she was sitting up, straight, again. Once more, their eyes met in the mirror. This time, he caressed Salomé's face with his hand. "Not really."

Marina sighed. She drank from her bottle. "Say no more." She let her head fall on her folded arms, for a moment, groaning to herself. Her eyes met Indio's again, as she drank from her beer once more.

Salomé laughed. "It'll cost you, though." Her eyes twinkled, as Indio looked at her, curiously. Salomé explained with a smile. "You let us finish our beers, first. Then, we go home, to drop me off," she winked at Marina, "and you treat my girl to something something from that peace pipe of yours, and then, we're good." She snuggled deeper into his chest. His eyes sparked with ardent desire. Salomé's laugh was husky this time. "The sooner you begin, the sooner you'll be done." She winked at him, slipping gently out of his embrace. "I'll be waiting for you, baby." She turned around suddenly, and kissed him hard on the lips, her eyes eating him up. "With bells on," she murmured.

The brave turned to the other girl, lifting his eyebrows at her in the mirror. He grinned like he just won the lottery. "You know she means just bells…"

Marina nodded at him and rolled her eyes with a sigh. "I know…"

Indio laughed, turned back to Salomé and stole another kiss. "Say no more."

Salomé and Marina finished their beers, and followed Indio to his house.

There, he hooked them up with his peace pipe, and joined them. Breathing deeply, they inhaled, relaxing finally. Indio closed his eyes, shutting out, to the best of his ability, the image of the slave driver advancing on his brother. A few minutes later, they smiled at each other. Indio kissed his girlfriend goodbye, and led Marina back to the docks.

Marina sighed, rubbing her eyes. They had been here for hours. Indio had hustled her to one of the warehouses, seemingly keeping her secluded. She hadn't seen anyone but Solomon and Giancarlo, since she had gotten here. Putting down her pencil, she glanced at the numbers on the page in front of her. The amount of merchandise on this ship was staggering to her.

La Diosa del Mar was a fine vessel, and the damage done to it by the men she knew, was minimal. Once the last of the goods were taken off, it would be sailed around the bay to a cove, where repairs would be done to it, immediately. The crew of the ship were now at a meeting with the Gaitanos and her fathers. The sailors were being advised by Pedro Escobar. The slaves... Tears sprang to her eyes and she shook her head. She had been spared the sight of the slaves in shackles, thanks to the kindness and consideration of her friends. Only Indio and Don Carlos understood that in her world, slavery had been abolished already, and was considered more than inhuman. Because of this, she had been put in a place where they were out of her sight and her hearing. However, the papers on the desk told the tale. Many had been taken, but not all of them had made it to Encantada. Some had perished during the voyage, and had been disposed of at sea. The rest were being taken care of by the kind, Dr. Kyle Richardson, accompanied by her own mom, Dr. Shayla Banks. Before her, was evidence of the goods that had been taken from and with them.

Marina sighed again. "Indio..."

The brave appeared at her side. "What's up? Do you need a break?" he asked anxiously, looking at her with concern in his eyes.

She shook her head and smiled. "No, no, we're almost finished." She shuffled some of the papers restlessly. "Once the inventory is taken care of..."

He grinned. "Are you done?"

She nodded slowly. "I think so..."

He laughed. "You see? That's what I'm talking about!" His braid brushed his bare back as he shook his head in amusement. "Anybody else would have me here at least until tomorrow."

She flashed him a smile. "Yeah, well, I just want to get out of here." She raked her fingers through her hair and leaned back in the chair. "Talk to me, baby. Tell me how this works. You go out and you capture a ship. Then..."

Indio took the other chair next to her and leaned back, studying her with interest. "We decide what is done with the crew, the passengers, and the merchandise."

"Okay, let's start with the crew. What happens with Don Andres and Don Luis? They are innocent victims..."

Indio nodded, smiling into her eyes. "And as such, they will be spared. As we speak, the Gaitanos are accommodating them, granting them the opportunity of a new life."

"What about their old life?"

Indio thought carefully before answering. He shrugged, his movements careful, and measured. "Sometimes, we find ourselves in certain places, due to circumstances beyond our control." He paused, as her eyes flew to his face and locked on his. "On these special occasions, we don't always have the means or the power to go back where we came from. Or maybe, where we came from, may not be the place we are intended to be at, but where we end up, instead." He watched closely, as she bit her lips, his words sinking in, his meaning flowing through her. "It is up to us, to make the best of what God puts in our path." He looked away from her for a moment, frowning at the stack of papers on the table in front of them. "Don Andres and Don Luis are very good men. Serious merchants, honorable navigators, professional sailors. They will miss their families, but their lives have been spared. They are grateful to us for this, but they understood that they were sent on a mission where they were not expected to succeed. Because of this, they hold no fondness for the men that sent them on this voyage. We," he continued, smiling at her again, "the pirates of Encantada, have given them the option to join us, and create a life for themselves here."

Marina smiled. "Let me guess. They get to live and stay, or stay and live."

Indio laughed. "They chose life over death." He scrubbed his hands over his face, exhaustion trying to claim him. "What about the sailors?"

"Encantada is their new home. They are now all pirates, with a new Captain." He shrugged. "They chose life."

Marina nodded. "What about the slaves? What are their choices?"

Indio met her eyes. "They cannot go back home. We do not sail to Africa, and we cannot guarantee them a safe voyage back." He watched helplessly as tears pooled in her eyes. "We give them their freedom. In exchange, they can become pirates and work for us, or they can settle in Encantada and make a living for themselves." He shook his head sadly. "We just can not send them home."

"What happens to the slave driver?"

Marina watched in amazement as a sheet of coldness settled over Indio's features, for a moment, making him appear as if he were carved from stone. "That particular individual does no longer breathe and talk."

She gasped. "Did he die?" She looked at the papers in front of her again, quickly looking for one where all incidents had been reported. "But there is no mention of that here." She looked at him suspiciously. "What happened?"

Indio looked deep into her eyes, waiting for her to connect with him. She finally did, and he could see shadows churning in their hazel depths. "The slave driver was going to kill Carlos, before anyone realized what was happening."

Marina's heart skipped a beat, before trying to pound its way out of her body. Her hands went up to her chest, trying to hold it in. "Father or son?" Her voice broke, a runaway tear sliding down her face.

Indio frowned, fighting the impulse of taking her in his arms and consoling her. When one was given bad news, the body and mind needed a little time to absorb the shock. "Son." His eyes didn't let her look away. "Solomon relieved the man of his life, sparing the Captain's." He watched her closely, as she gasped silently for air.

Exhaustion claimed her. "Indio..." she wailed. First, she squeezed her eyes shut, trying to hold back the tears. They won the battle, pouring down her face. Then she began sobbing, silently, her whole body heaving with emotion. Finally, she took a deep breath. Then, she let go. Marina cried. Indio let her. When she was done, the stress was gone as relief invaded her body. Her eyes, however, when they finally looked back into his, were still haunted. When she finally spoke, her voice was low, husky from the tears. "What happens to the merchandise?"

"It gets split between us." He leaned forward, suddenly, supporting his elbows on his knees. "What would you do?"

Marina shook her head, confused. Her mind switched to another mode, as she felt herself interested at his question. "What do you mean?" she asked carefully.

Indio grinned. "Just that, baby, what would you do..." His eyes flickered with the velocity of ideas going through his head. "What would you do if this were your ship that you just took? You are the one who gets to make all the decisions? It is up to you, who gets what..."

Marina's eyes lit up with the challenge. "Where do I start?" she asked, her hand reaching out to stroke the stack of papers on the table.

Indio leaned back, stretching his legs in front of him, crossing them at the ankles, his hands folded on his abdomen. His mouth twisted with humor, and his eyes sparkled, pleased with her response. "Wherever you want, baby..."

Marina held up her hand in front of his face. "You're on!" she whispered. Indio slid his hand against hers. She turned to the table. Shuffling through the papers, she divided them into three stacks. She looked at him. "There are three general types of merchandise here." Her hand hovered over each stack, as she spoke. "You have your basic currency, with your precious metal of the year, in this case, Spanish gold." She smiled to herself, as she continued. "Over here, you have your precious jewels, many diamonds, astounding jewelry, incredible dinnerware..." she trailed off, shaking her head. *If this is what they usually get, when they capture a ship, these guys must be millionaires!* "And finally, you have the merchandise obtained with the slaves." She sighed. "This is where I would begin." Indio stayed silent, letting her express herself. "The slaves' goods can be divided into two categories. The really great stuff that's really incredible, even for them." She looked at him, smiled, and said no more.

Indio chuckled, forced to break his silence, and become a participant. "And that would be..."

Marina lifted a piece of paper and read from it. "One leopard skin cape. One tiger skin cape. One male lion's hide, complete with full head and mane, reserved only for special ceremonies, worn by no other than the medicine man himself..." She took a deep breath, raising her eyebrows at him.

Indio laughed. "And who would get that particular inventory?"

Marina didn't hesitate. "Carlos, yourself, Giancarlo and Solomon. Don Carlos, Don Miguel, Rouge and Storm. Papi, Dad and Jackson. Basically, everybody that participated in taking this ship."

"In equal parts?" asked Indio, sincerely curious.

Marina laughed softly at him. "Of course not!" She smiled to herself, again. "In order of importance and direct participation."

Indio nodded, genuinely impressed. "What is the other category?"

Marina's smile faded. "The slaves' livelihood. All this ethnic jewelry, all these fabrics, these baskets, and utensils and stuff..." She shook her head sadly. "This category should not be divided by the crew." Lifting her head, she looked right into his eyes. "If *I* had taken *La Diosa del Mar*," she began, choosing her words carefully. "I would give these goods to the free men taken from Africa, so they can begin their lives here in Encantada." She shook the paper gently. "This is exactly what they need, to be motivated enough to make a new life for themselves. I don't mean to be cruel, but at some point they will have to think of it as a forced relocation. Besides, they get to be part of the *Expo*, and make some money of their own." She shrugged. "You've got to start somewhere. They are at the right place, at the right time."

Indio nodded in agreement, his eyes watchful and thoughtful. "What about the currency?" he rumbled softly.

Marina changed the papers in her hand. "You should split ten percent among you, and let the formerly slaves, newly freed men and women, split another ten percent among all of them. The children should have their fees separate. The remaining eighty percent I would give to the sailors, the deckhands, the mates." Her eyes flashed at him. "The important guys, like the one in charge of the gunpowder, the one in charge of the ammunition and weapons, the one in charge of the ropes..." she waved her hand in the air in a rolling gesture to indicate etcetera, etcetera. "I would give *them* a little bit more."

Indio nodded again, still keeping his eyes hooded. "What about the last category?"

Marina laughed softly. "That's all yours, baby." Her eyes searched his. "If *I* had captured *La Diosa del Mar*, only *Carlos* would get a bigger share than I did. After me, would come Giancarlo and Solomon equally, maybe a bonus to Solomon, out of my share, for saving my brother's life. *Again...*" she added softly, holding his gaze.

"Then I would work my way, from Rouge and Storm, all the way down to Jackson and my dads. There's a catch, though..."

Indio smiled, intrigued. "And that is?"

"I would not forget the women who watched your island, while you were out on the water." She smiled at him. "I would give gifts to everybody else, consisting of small trinkets of some value. I would bestow a percentage to the building of a beautiful church, in gratitude for my blessed good fortune. A percentage towards a new school for the children. *All* the children on the island, whether native or pirate, townsfolk, or newly freed slave. Education for *every* single small child and bigger ones, under eighteen." She laughed softly as the brave nodded in agreement. "Pedro Escobar needs some money, some deputies... You invest some of your wealth into what's going on, right now, making Encantada a unique pirate tourist attraction, vacation spot, escape plan, *whatever*!" They laughed together, feeling relaxed. "In short time, you will be richer than you ever imagined, whether you keep your investments, or turn around and sell at a neat profit." Indio's eyes flickered with interest at the proposal. "And trust me, baby, it *will* happen." She tossed the last papers back on the stack she had taken them from. Meeting his eyes again, he could see the truth in her words. "Once this thing gets off the ground and running, word will spread like wildfire. You'll have pirates dropping in on you, like they were long-lost relatives." She paused, waiting for him as he chuckled. "There will be pirates coming here, papi, begging you to sell to them."

"Who would you give the ship to?"

"For all my trouble, I would keep the ship for myself." To his amusement, she tossed her head and snapped her fingers in the air, wiggling her hips in the chair. Her laughter was contagious. "*La Diosa del Mar* would be *mine*, baby!" She stopped playing and leaned towards him, laughing softly. "That means I would give her to you."

"Who do you think *really* gets her?"

Marina knew the answer in her heart. "*You* do." She watched the smile on his face. "Who gets her for real?"

Leaning forward, he held his hand in front of her face. "*I* do."

Marina nodded, sliding her hand against his. "Cool."

Just then, the door behind them opened, Giancarlo and Solomon entering, carrying a large box between them. They set it down, heavily, among the rest of the boxes and barrels and crates. Giancarlo wiped his brow with the back of his arm, and grinned at them. "Done! This is the last one!"

Indio laughed, going to them, slapping their hands. "Good job! Thank you!" He waved a hand at Marina, behind him. "Marina's pretty tired, and I'm sure she wants nothing better than to go home."

Marina stood from her seat, nodded at Indio, waved at Giancarlo and beckoned at Solomon. *"Solomon!"*

Solomon wiped the sweat off his own face with his hands, and then wiping those on his pants. He smiled, as he approached her, until he stood in front of her. Suddenly, Marina threw herself against him, making him stumble. "Marina..."

She wrapped her arms around his back, holding him tight as they stepped together, as if in a dance. The men's eyes on her back felt like knives, as they wondered at her behavior. Shaking her hair out of her face, the accountant stared up into the African's eyes, holding him tighter. *"Solomon..."* Her voice broke on a sob that escaped her chest, and shadows danced in her eyes. Tears shimmered, lips quivered.

Solomon stared, fascinated by the play of raw emotions, rippling in her beautiful, beloved face. His heart lurched, as he realized the extent of his affection towards Marina Aguilar. Gently, he held her face against his chest, wrapping a protective arm around her back. Over her head, the Boatswain met the Quartermaster's eyes. His eyes were as sad as his soft, accusing voice. "You told her."

Indio grunted. "Marina has a right to know."

Solomon sighed, squeezing the woman in his arms, hushing her, his voice soft in her ear. "I agree," he told Indio. "The Captain is not going to like it, though."

Indio laughed. "The Captain doesn't need to know," he said mischievously. He indicated Marina with his hand. "Or do you think this girl is going to run out and tell him?"

Giancarlo laughed, shaking his head. "Not if that's what the news did to her..."

Solomon chuckled, the laughter rumbling deep in his chest. "You're right," he nodded at Indio. Stroking Marina's hair, he pressed his lips to the top of her head. "You are welcome, baby." He smiled into her eyes, as she drew her head back, to look up at him. "It's our secret, mami, if that's what you want." He hugged her tight, and kissed her on the cheek, before firmly releasing himself from her embrace.

Marina stepped back, laughing at herself. "Hell, yeah!" She sniffed, and wiped at her face again. "My crying doesn't leave this room. *Promise!*" she spun around, pointing at each of them.

They all promised. Giancarlo came over to her, hugging her before looking into her eyes. "I want to thank you on behalf of all the crew, for all the good work you have done for us, Marina Aguilar, Accountant of La Gitana." He bowed deeply, kissing her hand. His eyes smiled at her, as he straightened up again. "We are greatly indebted, and eternally grateful to you."

Marina smiled at him. "Thank you, Giancarlo. Your words make every minute worth it."

"Now," interrupted Indio, ushering them out. "Let us finish our job."

The men laughed as they went out the door, leaving them alone again.

Marina and Indio looked at each other again.

He grinned. "Ready?"

She grinned back. "Let's do it!"

Papers in their hands, they went to the last that had been brought in, eager to finish their task.

Once they were done, Indio and Marina looked at each other again, grinning like fools. She stretched, and groaned. He laughed as she let her body slump suddenly. "Ready to go home?"

She laughed. "Oh, my God, yes!" She waved a hand at the windows. "This is ridiculous, it must be very late." She looked back at him. "Did you decide how you are going to divide everything?"

Indio laughed. "Definitely." He ruffled her hair. "I am going to do it, just as you would."

Marina laughed, delighted. "I'm flattered."

"You are smart," he retorted. "And I am no fool."

Marina sighed. "Do you need help dividing everything?"

Indio shook his head. "No, not really. We do that together."

She laughed. "Cool. So, I'm free to go?"

He nodded. "Absolutely."

She winked at him. "Later, papi..." Turning around, she headed towards the door.

Indio matched her stride, laughing. "Later..."

Marina yanked the door open, blinking at the sudden daylight in her eyes. It was much earlier than she had thought, even though she felt incredibly tired. A movement caught her attention. Her eyes focused, landing on the men leaning against the wall of the warehouse. They were straightening up, as Indio stepped out, coming to stand next to her. Marina laughed softly, shaking her head at them. "Well, guys, have a good time." She held her hand out in front of her, and slowly walked past the men. Each of them slid his hand against hers as she walked by. Even Carlos. Her heart thudded in her chest as their eyes met. Her voice was a murmur. *"Hola, papi..."* And she walked on. She finished the line, which included her own men, and walked away. Suddenly, she felt herself being hauled back. In an instant, she found herself in Carlos' arms.

His turquoise eyes devoured her. He pressed his lips against hers, before drawing back with a sad sigh. He winked at her, as he let her go, a smile dancing on his lips. Eyes still blazing, he walked backwards, away from her, hands to his heart, as he blew her a kiss. *"Marina, divina, muñeca preciosa..."*

Marina laughed at him, taunting him gently. "Later, papi..."

Carlos stopped, his eyes raking over her, hungrily sliding over her hips. "Later, mami..." Smiling secretly, she whirled around again, and walked away. Rounding the corner of the building, she was gone. He sighed, and turned around, going to join the men in the warehouse.

"Leilani!" Marina laughed as she saw the young girl approach, holding a twin in each arm.

Leilani laughed back. "Marina!" She walked down the path, coming to stand in front of the porch, where Marina rocked in the hammock, a huge smile on her face. Leilani caught her breath, and smiled at her friend. "Are you done at the docks?" Relief flooded her as Marina nodded. "I need you today, mami."

Marina stopped rocking and put one foot on the floor, on either side of the fabric, now between her legs. She held out her arms for the babies, quickly nuzzling them, once they were deposited there. "Juan! Jaime!" she exclaimed softly, making the babies laugh. They embraced her, holding on tight. Marina smiled at Leilani. "I would love to! I am not doing anything today." She glanced over the girl's shoulder, as she spied her friend coming up the walk, behind her. "Well, I wasn't..."

Leilani turned around and laughed, at their visitor. "Another baby!"

Larissa gasped as she reached them, Max squirming in her arms. "I swear, honey, you should live closer to town. This is ridiculous." She smiled as Max crawled out of her arms, and unto Marina and the twins. "I hope you don't mind, honey. I promise it won't be all day."

Marina scoffed playfully. "Oh, please! What else am I going to do? It's not like I can go anywhere with the twins." She put her forehead against Max's, closing her eyes as he gaver her a big, wet kiss. "Besides, we all have a great time right here, in this very hut." She grinned at Larissa. "We go exploring. They think the backyard is an African jungle. Cool stuff."

Larissa's green eyes sparkled, as she gazed fondly at her friend. "You know, honey, maybe all these baby fixes you claim you need all the time... "She laughed softly, as she shook her ebony black hair out of her face. "It just may be your body trying to tell you something, sweetie." Her eyes shone with affection. "Have you ever thought of that? Of having your own baby?"

Leilani grinned at the turn the conversation had taken. "You would be the best Mamá in the world, Marina," she said shyly.

Marina winked at the young girl. "I think so too," she answered softly, making the girl blush, pleased at her friend's attention. Marina turned to look at Larissa, over her baby's head. "Yes, I have thought my body may be trying to tell me something," she confessed, "although, where I come from, I am still pretty young, for my body to be telling me anything, but take care and have fun, and I have some good years ahead of me." Hazel eyes went out of focus, as she kissed Max absently, at the same time she held the twins. "Yes, I have thought about having my own baby. It's part of my life plan. I don't see myself going through life without having a baby, sometime..." She closed her eyes and squeezed the three babies together gently, rubbing her cheeks on their soft heads. "Actually, a man I know just brought up this very same subject with me, not too long ago..."

Larissa's breath caught in her throat. "What did he say?"

Marina smiled to herself, her body growing warm at the memory. "He asked me if I would like a baby with him..."

Larissa gasped, her mouth dropping in shock, as suddenly, Marina opened her eyes and looked right into hers. "Who..."

"Carlos Gaitano."

Larissa's heart skipped a beat. "What did you say?"

Marina shook her head, tears shining deep in her eyes. "I couldn't say anything." She sighed, loosening her hold on the babies, a little. "We agreed we have to talk."

Larissa nodded slowly. After a while, she sighed. "Honey, do you want to have a baby with this man?"

Marina smiled at the question. "I want to *make love* with this man," she admitted with a grin, "*very much*, and *a lot*." Her friends laughed. "A baby?" She nodded slowly. "I want to be *everything* to this man. I feel like he is the love of my life, you know?" The three friends fell silent for a moment, each lost in her own thoughts.

Larissa finally shook her head. "Honey, all I can say is, something must be on *his* mind when he asked." She winked at Marina. "Keep him interested, baby. Make sure he *also* wants to make love to you, very much, and a lot." She laughed wickedly, making the other two girls grin.

Leilani squeezed her hand and smiled into her eyes. "He asked, mami." She threw her head back and laughed with the abandon of a child, her eyes gleaming with the knowing of a woman. "He *asked*, Marina!"

Marina frowned. "I know. I have to think about this." She smiled at her friends. "Go away, and leave me with my babies. You are both sworn to secrecy, by the way." She laughed as they crossed their hearts. Then she looked at them, her words serious and truthful, even as she smiled at them. "I would *love* to have that man's baby..." Larissa and Leilani looked at each other knowingly, and burst into laughter. The sound still rang in Marina's ears, even long after they were out of sight. Her heart sang.

Villa Azul means Blue Chateau. Usually, when a color is affixed to the name of a place, what it usually means is that it is the color of the building. But in this particular case, it referred to the color surrounding the building. Sky and ocean, ranging in tones and shades from the lightest baby blue, to rich turquoise, to deep indigo. The only break in the color was the line of palm trees in front of it, and the jungle at its back. It was paradise, and the house sat right in the middle of it.

The structure of the house itself was impressive, by Encantada standards. It was made out of stone, surrounded by a generous wooden balcony. Rounded arches indicated the doorways, and shuttered windows were flung back, letting the sea breeze cool down the interior. The entrance seemed shallow, consisting of a wall facing the front door. Hanging on the wall, was one, very large, beautifully framed mirror, giving the illusion of depth and space. Until you saw your own reflection. It was flanked by graceful, potted palms, on either side. Once you went around the wall, however, the whole house seemed to open up, the rooms mostly flowing into one another. Walls were almost inexistent inside the house, with exception of the exterior ones. There were stone staircases on opposite sides leading up to a second floor. Everything revolved around an open, sunny courtyard. Trees and potted plants were a very important aspect of the design of the house, for these were what gave the place some semblance of order, separating the different spaces from one another. The floor was alternately wooden, or tiled, or cobblestoned, depending on the space it was intended for. The walls were hung with mirrors, giving the space grander dimensions. The impression was of being inside a jungle.

Every window in the house was open at the moment, letting in all the blue of the ocean and the sky. There were beautiful different wind chimes, hung over the different seating arrangements. Plants in baskets hung suspended everywhere. It was not a formal place, by any standards, consisting mostly of beautifully carved rocking chairs, strategic hammocks, and huge, colorful, luscious cushions that people could use. Straight through the house, and out the back door, lay a beautiful yard, protected by the jungle and a bamboo grove, where at the moment, people were busy hustling about, preparing for a feast. It was a celebration. The guests of honor were not present at the moment, however. Neither were the wives and loved ones of the men present. But upstairs, in one of the larger rooms, designed for just such an occasion as this, were the crew of La Gitana, with the Gaitanos and the travelers. The room crackled with increasing energy, as Indio began.

Carlos Gaitano, Hijo, the son, looked suspiciously at Carlos Gaitano, Padre, and the rest of the men looking back at him. It was more than suspect to him, who the people in attendance were. He turned his head to look back at his brother. The brave met his gaze, head on, without flinching. They stared silently at each other for a moment, while the rest of the men waited patiently. Finally, Carlos broke the silence. "This looks like a family meeting." He smiled to himself. "Am I in some sort of trouble I am not aware of, yet?"

Indio smiled back. "Not yet."

"So, what's this about?"

"We want to talk to you about Marina."

The pirate froze. His eyes scanned the others, but he couldn't tell what was going on. His reply was slow and careful. "What about Marina?"

Indio just looked at him for a moment. "I want you to concentrate on how much you care about her."

"Why?"

Don Carlos cleared his throat and scooted forwards on his seat, leaning towards his son. "Carlitos, *hijo*," he began, "remember when you were a little boy, and I told you the stories about the visitors?"

He waited, as his son frowned thoughtfully. He could almost see the young man's mind racing.

Carlos glanced at Pablo before looking back at Indio. "The visitors?" he repeated.

Indio nodded. "The visitors. Don't you remember? Papá would tell us the stories, when we went to visit Leila, as children."

His brother nodded slowly, as he remembered. "Weren't they supposed to be time travelers?" he asked, searching his memory. "Some got to actually stay, but for the most part, the majority couldn't handle it." The pirate looked at his father, a cold, sinking feeling invading his heart. "I thought you never met any visitors..."

Don Carlos raked his fingers through his silver streaked hair, drawing in a shaky breath. "I hadn't until then, when I was telling you the stories." He shook his head ruefully, his eyes focusing on some distant scene, only he could see.

Don Miguel's energy rolled out gently, warm and comforting, his voice rumbling deep in his chest. "Neither had I, papi."

Carlos' eyes shot to his uncle, searching deep. He looked back at his father. "And now?"

Don Carlos laughed softly, his shoulders shaking in silent amusement. "Now?" he repeated, happily. "Now I have been blessed to know a whole family of them." He turned his head to wink at Joe and Pablo. The men smiled at the bewildered pirate.

Jackson sought to ease his discomfort. "When did you meet Marina? Were you here when she arrived?"

Carlos stood up restlessly, for a moment, dragging his fingers through his thick hair. His eyes were the color of a calm pool, caught in a storm. There were the beginnings of a shadow, already, on his face. "I wasn't here in Encantada, no. I was on my way back from Carey." He stopped his long stride suddenly, and turned to look at them. They all looked back in silence. Carlos sat down again, and faced them. "When I got home, she was just here." He gazed off into space, frowning slightly. "She was in my pool."

"They had already been here for a few days," Jackson urged.

Carlos nodded absently. "I heard she was from Cayo Largo."

Caribe cleared his throat. He stepped forward, gaining everybody's attention. "Leila decided to give them a place. Cayo Largo is far away enough, that it wouldn't be easy to check out, and since my father, Don Manuel, is originally from there, it gave her a reason to know them." He stopped talking for a moment, distracted by a faint tic in the young pirate's cheek. Not long ago, he would have been standing before these men, humbled, head down, meek and timid. If he were ever in their company at all. Since Marina and Salomé's arrival, it seemed to him as if his station in life had risen. Not only had he had the opportunity to hang out and spend some time with these men, but he had gained their trust and respect. Especially, since he had been commissioned to record some of their activities in drawings. His words right now, however, were not of an employee to his boss. Before anything else, he was these women's friend and protector. He spoke to the pirate as an equal. "I had been dreaming about them for a while. Marina and Salomé. My mother just told me who they were."

The pirate's face was foreboding, like thunder. It clearly indicated the storm raging inside. "How do they get here?"

Caribe laughed, his dreadlocks catching rays of sunlight as they danced around his face. "Storm." He nodded at the expression on the other man's face. "In their time, they get caught in a storm, and come out of it..." he laughed again, "in our time." Silently, he handed the pirate some select portraits he had retrieved from his wall, at home.

Carlos nodded slowly as he studied them. "You are very good," he said truthfully. "But these could have been drawn at any time..." He trailed off as the men in front of him chuckled, as if humoring a child. He squinted at them suspiciously.

"Could have," agreed Caribe happily, "but were not. I did these, days before they arrived." He reached out behind him to take Salomé's hand in his. Looking away from the pirate, he brought her hand to his lips for a warm kiss, and smiled into her eyes.

Salomé smiled back, tears shining. "I love you, baby."

Caribe nodded. "I know. And I, you." He turned back to the young pirate. "That's how I knew, when I went to get them, what they looked like."

Carlos glared at the men around him. "Did you all know about this?"

Laughter accompanied the shakes of their heads.

Don Carlos spoke up, first. "I found out when I got to Encantada. I visited Leila..." he shrugged his shoulders happily.

Don Miguel rumbled from his place in a corner. "Your father told me when I got here."

Giancarlo shook his head as his friend's eyes rested on him. "I am just hearing about this, Capitán..." He looked dazed, in a happy, unbelieving kind of way.

Solomon was next. He, too, shook his head. "I have never heard anything about this." He frowned, thoughtfully. "I am not sure I even know what is going on."

Jackson smiled at the African. "Don't sweat it, man, I'll explain later." Solomon nodded, and they all turned back to look at Carlos.

The young pirate's eyes fell on his brother. They searched long and hard, unable to read the answers he wanted. "What about you?" he finally asked. His voice was low and pained, filling the space around them. "How long have you known?"

Indio sighed, slipping an arm around Salomé. As Caribe before him, he brought her hand to his lips and kissed it. He never broke eye contact with his brother. "I have known for a few days. Not long at all." He glanced quickly at the woman next to him. "Salomé told me, because she wants to stay with me for a while, and see what happens..." He turned to his brother once more, love shining in his eyes. "...just in case it works out."

"What about the rest of you?" Carlos asked suddenly, changing the subject. His eyes raked over Pablo and Joe. The men looked at each other for a moment, and turned back to Caribe and Jackson.

The dreadlocked young man laughed. "Think!" he demanded. "You were there. You know exactly when Jackson came." He lowered his voice. "You gave my portrait of Jackson to Marina, so Indio wouldn't find it, remember?"

Carlos nodded slowly. "You tore out of the Lair, like a couple of bats out of Hell," he murmured. "You came in, looking for Salomé."

"The storm had been the night before," Caribe explained. "Leila didn't want him wandering into town and scaring the girls to death."

Carlos searched his eyes, silently for a moment. "Caribe," he finally said, "go get Marina for me."

Caribe nodded. "It may not be that easy. I think she's taking care of Max today."

Carlos gritted his teeth. "Larissa and John will be coming by later. Let them know the baby will spend the rest of its day here." He looked deep into the villager's eyes. "Tell Marina to bring Max."

Don Carlos stood up suddenly, putting an arm around Caribe. "Go get her, Caribe. Tell her *I* sent for her." He winked at the young man. "Show her the surprise I have for her. And then, bring her over. It will be fine." He looked over his shoulder at his glowering son. "Carlitos is just in shock."

Caribe smiled, and rolled his eyes playfully. "I'll be back, as soon as she lets me." The men laughed, and he was gone.

Carlos continued glaring at his companions. "What happens next?" he demanded, looking at Jackson.

Jackson chuckled. "Well," he drawled, stretching his legs in fron t of him, and smiling at the pirate, his hands clasped over his belly, " we meet, we like each other, we become friends..." The smile dropped from his eyes, leaving them as cool as glass. "I mean, from my perspective."

Salomé's voice broke softly into the tense air. "You already had Marina working for you."

Jackson agreed, his cornrows rippling sunlight, as he nodded his head. "Yeah, dude! My sister's been working for you, almost since the moment you met her!"

"I haven't forced her to do anything against her will..." his voice trailed off.

The energy shifted in the air, as all eyes bore into him.

Jackson shot to his feet. "Oh, yeah?!" he challenged, circling around him slowly. "So what was that little trip to Carey all about?"

"Carey..." Carlos shook his head, trying to shake off the cobwebs.

"You kidnapped her!" Jackson accused softly. He held up his hands as the pirate was about to speak up, and sat back down. "You took her, knowing she didn't want to go." He shook his head slowly. "It might be the way you do things around here, but where I come from it is a crime, punishable by law."

Carlos sought anger from deep inside him, for his defense. "I needed your sister!" he growled.

Jackson wouldn't back down. "Kicking and screaming, man!" He pointed at the young African. "Solomon carrying her like a sack of potatoes, while Pedro Barbosa puts me behind bars..." he snorted in scorn. "Some big man you are, huh?"

Carlos jumped to his feet. Jackson stood up just as quickly, in a moment, assuming the position. Everyone around them froze. Carlos' eyes shot blue fire, as he trembled with anger, facing off with his friend. "I did not hurt her!" he growled.

"Sit back down!" The two men froze, as Don Miguel's voice rolled over them, like thunder. Glaring at each other, they sank back to their seats. Don Miguel laughed, sending chills down both their spines. "Now, boys," he rumbled slowly, letting his energy sweep over them, before calling it back, "you may continue this conversation in a civilized manner."

Salomé stepped in, easing the moment. "Carlos, papi," she said soothingly, "think back to the day you took Marina on La Gitana. I followed, with Indio. Do you remember?"

Carlos nodded slowly. "What has that got to do with anything?"

Salomé slipped out from under Indio's arm and walked around Giancarlo, towards Carlos. Her movements were smooth and fluid, soothing to the senses. She stroked his hair affectionately as she reached him, trying to coax a response out of him. His stormy eyes bore into her green ones. She smiled sadly, and went to stand behind him, firmly putting her hands on his shoulders. Moving rhythmically, her hands began to slowly release his tension. "Think back to when Marina was in your cabin, that very first time..."

Pablo couldn't resist. "*Oye, papi*, Marina, *mi hija*, was in your cabin?"

Joe leaned forward with a sigh. "What are your intentions towards our daughter, son?"

Jackson laughed, shaking his head. "Fool's crazy about her," he muttered.

Salomé laughed softly. "Stop! You guys…" She shook her head at her family, and picked up again, with her singsong voice. "Gaitano," she called softly, over his head. "Think about what Marina looked like that very first time you saw her in your bed." She frowned warningly at her men, as they were getting ready to go off, again. Inside her head, she hissed at them. *No more jokes, right now! Please!* She waited until they nodded. The crew of La Gitana was greatly amused by the turn of events. Salomé had no time for them right now, either. "What was she doing? What did she look like?"

Carlos closed his eyes and frowned, remembering. He sighed, and looked at the men in front of him. His eyes went from Pablo, to Joe, to Jackson, and back. "Crying. Scared to death." His heart squeezed inside his chest. "I couldn't figure out why," he wondered out loud. His eyes sought his father's, his uncle's, and back to Marina's father's, her brother's. "Marina must have known, deep inside her heart, that I would never do anything to hurt her…"

"She did," agreed Salomé soothingly, her long black hair shining like a cape around her shoulders, as she squeezed rhythmically. "It wasn't you hurting her, she was worried about…"

Carlos frowned again. "Then, what?" His eyes shot to Indio's face. "

Marina believed that if she got off the island, something would happen, and she would never be able to go back to our time, at all," Salomé explained gently.

Carlos thought on her words, for a moment. Then he looked at Jackson, squinting his eyes suspiciously. "You," he began, in a soft accusing voice, " must have gone back. First, why? Then, how?"

Jackson rolled his eyes. "Papi, you took my sister." Turning serious, he leaned forward towards him. "Where we come from, we are students. We go to school. We have lives. Social. Family. Personal. We go to church. We have friends. We go out and party. We have jobs. I had a girlfriend…" Suddenly, he grinned. "Or I thought I had. Storm's looking pretty good these days." He raised his eyebrows and whistled under his breath. Soft laughter erupted around him.

Jackson had the floor, and he knew it. Everyone was enthralled, as he spoke. He worked it. "We go on vacation, and suddenly," he said slowly, "the girls... disappear..." He looked deep into the pirate's eyes. "They are just gone from my world, and... I... am... responsible..."

Carlos' heart lurched at the implications, imagining himself responsible for two females who suddenly disappear. "You came to get them."

Jackson nodded. "Exactly. Thing is," he explained, "I ended up hanging out for a while, because you need to catch one of those storms, in order to get back." Taking a deep breath, he looked into the twin icebergs. "I had to go back, when you took Marina. I believed the same thing myself, that they could never come back, until I spoke to Leila about it. She assured me that the storms were our way in and out of here. As soon as you sailed, I took the first one out." He looked over his shoulder at his dads. "We had been gone a long time, already. I just had to bring my parents back here." He smiled. "So far, it has been a good experience, I think..."

Joe chuckled. "It has been an incredible, amazing journey, papi," he murmured to the young pirate. "So far, it has been worth every minute."

Pablo nodded, gazing fondly at the young man in front of them. Carlos was visibly more relaxed, though no less angry. He sighed. "Marina is not of this world, Carlitos," he said slowly. "She is going to school, she has a job, she stands to inherit my company, and although she has no emotional attachments to anyone, at the moment, she has her whole future to look forward to." He held the young man's gaze. "Now, tell me," he shook his head, indicating everyone around him, "tell us, what are your intentions towards her?"

Carlos shook his head. "Why did she lie to me? Why didn't she tell me the truth?"

Indio raised his hand in a halting gesture. "This stops right now." His eyes clashed with his brother's as he pointed at him. "Wait until she gets here, and ask her yourself."

The room fell silent.

Marina's head shot up at the sound of the familiar voice. She smiled at her dreadlocked boy. "Hey, Caribe!" she called out, happily, as he drew nearer. Her eyes shone with affection as he finally stood in front of her. "Max and I are here chillin', catching up. Juan and Jaime just left, and it's the first time we've had a chance to be alone, all morning. Isn't that right, Max?" She nuzzled the baby, before looking back up at him. "What are you up to, papi, any good?"

Caribe laughed back at her, swooping to scoop the baby out of her arms and lifting him over his head. Max screamed with laughter, his eyes glassy, his face radiant. Caribe lowered his arms, holding the baby close to his bare chest, his head ducking to kiss him. Max gurgled contentedly, chortling to himself, fascinated at his fists full of dreads. Caribe grinned at Marina. "I have been sent to escort you."

Marina frowned, stroking Max's back, in front of her. "Escort me? I can't go anywhere with Max," she began protesting.

Caribe cut her off. "With Max. His parents will be where we are going." He smiled, reaching into the porch, swinging the door shut. "Come with me. They will meet us there."

Marina shrugged and smiled, being a good sport. "Where?"

Caribe smiled enigmatically. "Don Carlos sent for you. He has a surprise for you."

"Cool."

They walked silently on the trail, completely going around town. The walk was breathtaking. Being around noon, the sun shone straight down on the jungle that enveloped them. A soft breeze stirred the foliage around them, making patterns of light and dark on everything surrounding them, including themselves. Marina felt as if she were walking through a world of lace. It was calm and relaxing, soothing their senses. Finally, they came upon a part of the island Marina hadn't seen yet.

Caribe came out of the jungle unto a tiny, secluded beach, sprinkled with majestic palm trees. He led the way to the middle of the semi clearing. Built around the two tallest palm trees was a tent. But not just any ordinary tent. It was like the kind of thing a sheik would have in the middle of the desert, as he rested from the caravan. "How do you like it?" he asked her, laughing at her reaction.

She followed him, her eyes flying everywhere, trying to take it in, all at once. "Am I supposed to like it?"

He laughed again. "You sure are."

"Why?" Marina was now standing in front of the tent, her back to the ocean. The flaps of fabric were spread open, invitingly, letting the ocean breeze invade it. Marina stepped up to the doorway and peered inside. She gasped. "Whose place is this?"

To say it was beautiful inside the tent didn't begin to cover it. The sides were draped with lush, sheer fabrics from the Middle East. A beautifully carved, reclining piece held center stage, at a diagonal angle, with an unobstructed view of the ocean. It was upholstered in a breathtaking, rich, deep turquoise fabric, mimicking the shades of the water outside. Next to it was a beautifully rustic table, low to the sand, on short bamboo legs. The rest of the frame was woven with twine, and the top was a thick, heavily woven thatch, made of palm leaves. At the moment, it was holding baskets of fruits, and a small stack of reading material. Sprinkled randomly, all over the top were white seashells, and sun-bleached, dead coral. Draped from the top of the tent, was a black mosquito netting, designed for the recliner, to be used for sleeping. At least, resting, or taking a nap. A beautiful bamboo wind chime hung from the middle, clicking soothingly. Suspended between the two palm trees lay a hammock, beckoning invitingly. Of the most incredible shades of coral, complete with beautiful gold trim, it tempted, with fluffy, black pillows, made of different incredible fabrics, with gold details.

Caribe chuckled at her expression. "Yours." He shook his head as her eyes flew to his. His hands went up, crossed behind the baby's back. "Hey! Don't shoot the messenger!"

Marina frowned, concerned. "Stop teasing! What's up with this?"

Caribe smiled. "Actually, it's Don Carlos. He made this place himself, especially for you." He laughed softly, his dreadlocks dancing happily around his head. "Just a little motivation for you to stay and work for them."

Marina's heart beat faster. "But Papi already told him that I have to go back to school!" she hissed softly.

Caribe shrugged. "The message is, it is yours, regardless. If you stay, you keep it. If you go, you get to stay in it, until you leave."

Marina laughed happily. "Awesome! I'll take it." She stepped back outside, and looked around her.

In front of her, a ways away, a pile of rocks came from either side, almost meeting in the middle. They were not so high, that she couldn't see the deep blue ocean behind them, but they were close together enough, that they forced the surging ocean through a small canal they provided, making a nice natural pool, with enough movement to cause small waves on the shore. Marina was enchanted. It was, at least, five times as big as the one she shared with Carlos. The jungle lay around her on the other side, close enough to protect, far away enough to grant her privacy. The sky was cloudless at the moment, the sun shining white and hot on the sparkly sand, shimmering on the water, invitingly. Peace settled over them in waves. Even Max was subdued, sucking on his thumb softly. His eyes, a mix of peridot and emerald, glued on the horizon.

Marina looked at Caribe. "I'll definitely take it."

Caribe smiled and put his arm around her shoulders, leading her away. "Good. Don Carlos will be very happy to hear it." He walked her towards the rocks and around them, away from the way they had come.

Marina stopped and stared. They had just come into a similar cove much like her own, only larger. It was bordered by a line of palm trees, through which she could catch glimpses of a building. "What is this place?" she breathed into the quiet.

Caribe smiled, eyes twinkling. *"Villa Azul..."*

"Max!"

The baby squealed at the greeting. He began bouncing up and down excitedly in Marina's arm, gurgling happily at his audience. The men chuckled.

Marina looked around the room. They were all men. Except for the Quartermaster's girlfriend, they were all men. Her smile faded as she realized who they were. A murmur escaped her heart as it sank. She switched Max to her other hip, as her eyes met each man's, avoiding her sister's. Giancarlo and Solomon, Joe and Jackson, and in the middle of them, Carlos, with her father and his at each side. He was furious. His turquoise eyes had chilled into twin icebergs as they raked her from head to foot. Marina shuddered beneath the cold glare. Behind him stood Indio, Salomé at his side. Caribe left hers, to join Don Miguel in a corner, turning slowly to face her. Marina swallowed. She looked straight into Indio's eyes. Finally, she choked out the words. "Who called the family meeting?"

Indio held her gaze, and nodded slowly, not letting her break eye contact. "I did."

Marina nodded, just as slowly, back. "Okay..." She wrenched her eyes from his, sliding them down his chest, to finally meet Gaitano's. "So, now you know," she said huskily.

"Oh, I get it. You are a liar."

The retort struck home, making her flinch inside. Outside, she kept her features as composed, as she was able. The shadows crashing against each other, behind her hazel eyes, betrayed her feelings. "What did I lie about?" she asked, patiently. She had not been prepared for this. Now, she had to psych herself, on the spot. Her eyes searched for some break in the darkness of his, but found none. "What have I said, or done, that makes me a liar?'

"You represented yourself falsely, as someone and something you are not." All around him, the men grumbled softly.

Marina gasped as his words fell on her head like ice stones. "What are you talking about?" She bounced the baby gently, careful not to upset him. "I never represented myself in any way at all!" Her mind screamed softly.

"You said you were from Cayo Largo," was his first accusation.

Marina glared at him. Carlos was not going to give her any breaks. "Actually, *I* said no such thing." She looked up, distracted for a moment.

Joe moved from where he was, to stand by her. He held out his arms to her, his voice low and warm. "Give me the baby, *mamita*."

She shook her head, momentarily confused. "Dad?"

"I'll take Max, baby." He ducked his head to take the little boy from her, his voice a low whisper, for her ears only. "*Suave, mamita...*"

Marina pressed her lips together and nodded, her eyes going back to Carlos' angry pools. Shadows flickered behind them, like storm on the water. She sighed, gathering up all her courage and strength. "It seems to me, like... you, all... have been discussing this for a while." Her hand waved to include all of them. "Carlos..." her voice broke, but she kept her gaze steady on him. "I don't want to feel bad about something I didn't do, or had no control over." She glanced at Caribe. "You weren't even here when we arrived." She frowned, anger replacing her hurt. "How do you figure I was pretending something I wasn't, when we never, *ever*, discussed each other's families. Salomé got here with me, and then, Jackson showed up." She lowered her voice, as her pride took its rightful place in her mind. "Not once, did you ever ask me about where I came from or what my family was like..." Her voice broke again. "I just became your accountant. Then we were best friends. And then..."

"Why didn't you confide in me?"

Marina raked her fingers through her hair, in exasperation. "I'm just getting to know you, papi. Did you expect me to just come out, *Hey, baby, I just got here from the future. Can you show me around?*" She stared at him. "You haven't been perfectly honest yourself. It took one of these," she waved at their companions, "to get you to admit you were Carlos Gaitano, didn't it, baby?"

Carlos shrugged. His laugh was wicked. "I needed an accountant." His eyes raked over her body once more. "I did what I had to do."

Stunned silence fell over the room. Don Miguel's silent energy lashed out in admonition at his nephew.

Marina's eyes filled with unwanted tears. She took a step closer to him, making one run away, down her cheek. Her heart felt like a native's drum, the kind she danced to. She lifted her left arm slowly. The turquoises slid down her arm, towards her elbow. His eyes flew to hers. With her right hand, she hooked two fingers into the leather thong, where the beads were strung. She tugged softly. "Do you mean that?" she challenged, sustaining his gaze.

Carlos gazed back, looking for her heart, searching her soul. He was confused. "No," he admitted with a growl.

She lowered her arms. And, for a moment, her eyes. She would not disrespect him. Even if he was a brat. She looked at him again. "Let's talk."

"No."

"Yes. You have been wanting to talk, for days."

"No."

"Let's do this right now, and get this over with. Just you and me. In private."

Carlos shook his head. "No. I am not talking about this right now."

"What was I called in here for, then? You are just going to send me on my way, without resolution?" She took a step backwards. Her chin went up, and stillness settled over her. Carlos saw it and groaned on the inside. On the outside, he wouldn't give in. "No closure?" Her voice was sad. "That's not cool."

Carlos glared at her. He shrugged again. "Whatever..." He cocked his eyebrow at her, daring her to dispute what she herself taught him.

Marina's eyes pooled again. She gasped, inside. Outside, her voice broke. *"Carlitos, no seas asi, papi..."*

Jackson couldn't stop himself, any longer. He turned on his friend. "Yeah, man, don't be like that! What's up with that?"

"Jackson!" The name escaped everyone's throat at the same time.

Marina looked at Carlos, her gaze tracing over every feature. *This isn't happening to me...* Her heart felt like it was breaking. She prayed it didn't show. *Oh, God...* Her hazel eyes searched his. "You haven't even made love to me, yet..."

Carlos froze. He watched in shock as she tore her eyes away from his. His body screamed in bewilderment, at the intimate challenge. It took all of his might to keep himself from lunging after her, and sweeping her away, in front of everybody present. Nobody would dare stop him. Not her fathers, nor her brother, nor his.

Her hair whipped about her face, as she strode to Joe. Holding her arms out for the baby, Marina pressed Max to her chest, speaking softly to the baby, smiling at him, making the young pirate groan silently. She turned her back to the room, her chin firmly on top of the baby's head. They couldn't see her face. Tears spilled from her eyes. In a moment, she was gone.

Thoughtful silence fell on them.

Behind his Captain, Giancarlo began taking bets, with a grin. His eyes sparkled wickedly, as he made known where his money was going.

Some sighed, some chuckled, some groaned.

Carlos' false pride reared up, momentarily blinding him. It hushed his breaking heart.

Marina spent the next couple of hours exploring her own personal space, courtesy of Don Carlos Gaitano y Mendoza. Letting Max crawl on the sand, she sat on the shore, in front of her tent. Her mind raced with what had happened, going over and over what was said, and left unsaid, again and again. She was sad. Very sad. But a stronger feeling than that, stirred in her heart, making trouble with her emotions. She was mad. Maybe not as furious as Gaitano was. But angry enough that she wasn't going to feel pity for him. With that resolution firm in her mind, she decided to enjoy the rest of her day.

Larissa showed up soon afterwards, unaware of anything wrong with her friend. She took her son from the other girl's arms, and they walked, side by side, back to Villa Azul, where, by now, a whole different scene was playing out. The house seemed to have come alive with voices. Rich laughter, the tinkling of glasses, signs indicating that there was an occasion being celebrated. As earlier, all the windows were flung open, refreshing the inside. Around the foyer wall, Marina stood, stunned, as the scene unfolded before her. Villa Azul seemed to be full of people.

Marina's moms were there, having settled themselves into one of the seating arrangements, consisting of pillows. With them, were Salomé, Rouge, Storm, and María Isabel. They beckoned, waving happily at Marina, for her to join them. Marina waved back, quickly locating the men. They lounged next to the ladies, in a different arrangement, absorbed in conversation. She found Carlos, as he pretended not to see her.

Larissa laughed softly, urging her on. "Come on, honey, let's go sit with the females."

Marina nodded, her beautiful hazel eyes cloudy with worry. Dragging her fingers through her hair, she followed her friend. "What's the occasion?" she asked softly, catching her reflection as she passed by a mirror. Her father was right. She looked like a wild woman. Island life had given her a beauty she would have never achieved otherwise, where she came from.

Larissa's smile lit up her face. "*La Diosa del Mar*, alliances with the captured Spaniards, freed slaves..." she let her voice trail off, her laughter tinkling, to the delight of her squealing baby son. They reached the group.

"Hello, baby," Shayla called happily, reaching out with her arms, for Max.

"What have you been up to?"

Marina smiled back, her eyes adoring her mothers. Shayla was wearing a flowing, gauzy number in white, softly skimming her body, her arms bare. Her rich, dark hair was caught up under a white turban of the same material, wound with pearls, like Suleiman wore his. At her ears, the pearls Indio bought Salomé, for her, the stunning bracelet commanding attention at her wrist. "Nothing much, Mom," Marina answered softly. "You look ravishing, by the way."

Shayla smiled at her, as she crooned to the baby in her arms. "Thank you, baby. You look beautiful, yourself, in a wild, primitive way," she laughed softly. Marina grinned.

"What about me?"

Marina turned to smile at the woman who gave birth to her. She was wearing something similar to Shayla's, but in black, without the turban. Her beautiful white-blonde hair was caught back in a loose braid, falling down her back. From her ears hung the breathtaking earrings that were her gift from Carey. Marina shook her head playfully. "No, sorry," she apologized, laughing, "you don't look ravishing at all. You are *spectacular* today, Mami," she told her, with awe in her voice.

Sloane held her daughter in her arms for a moment, transmitting motherly love and support. "How has your day been, today?" She gazed into her daughter's hazel eyes. "Papi told me you had a bit of a rough time this morning," she confided, steering her daughter to sit amongst them.

Marina nodded, meeting her mother's gaze, woman to woman. "I did," she admitted. "Let's see how it goes."

Suddenly, the men greeted her. Marina bantered with them, for a while, noticing Carlos' lack of participation. Finally, she sank down again, grateful for the amount of foliage integrated into the interior design of the place.

Don Carlos' voice rang out, his voice laced with humor. "Aguilar!" he called out.

Marina smiled to herself. "Don Carlos!" she answered.

"How do you like your new tent, *hija*?" The man chuckled to himself, as he caught his son's interest at the endearment. Neither Carlitos nor Indio had ever had to compete with anyone for their father's attention and affection. Much less, any female. Their mother was sole queen in their world.

Marina laughed at him. "I love it, Capitán!" Her heart beat with love for her man's father. "Are you bribing me?"

Don Carlos was shameless in his reply. "Absolutely!"

"What is the job description, sir?"

The older pirate laughed, enjoying the game. "It entails, being in charge of all my business transactions. A position of importance and confidentiality."

"Sounds like a lot of work, sir."

"It is," he admitted, "quite more than what you have been doing, so far." He laughed again. "Come, Aguilar, leave my ungrateful son's employee, and come work for me. I can pay you more."

Marina looked into the pirate's face. Out of the corner of her eye, she thought she caught the ungrateful son, rolling his eyes. She pressed her lips together, fighting the urge to look at the son, once more. "I am tempted, Don Carlos," she finally admitted. "I promise I will think about it." She could see the man was serious.

The pirate winked at her, and sank back down, joining the men, once more.

The women laughed.

Sloane gazed at Marina in silence, for a moment, taking a good look at her daughter. Finally, she sighed. "It's a good offer, isn't it, baby? You love life here."

Marina nodded slowly, without making eye contact. "It's a very good offer. I don't think I will ever get a better business proposition, except from Papi, maybe, or Cat."

Shayla nodded. "Are you seriously going to think about it?"

Marina laughed softly. "Seriously? Yeah..." She looked at her mothers. "I've got to wait and see what happens next, before I make my decision."

Just then, Caribe joined them, a large pile of papers in his hands. "Ladies!" he called out, happily. "Would you like to take a look at the adventures your daughters have been having?" he asked, mischievously.

Salomé laughed. "You watch yourself, boy!"

Larissa's eyes lit up. "I, for one, would love to see what you girls have been up to, while you were away."

Jackson joined them, slipping next to Storm. He casually threw an arm around her shoulders, whispering in her ear, making her squirm and smile. He smiled into her eyes and turned back to the women. "I want to see, too. I totally missed out on Carey."

María Isabel laughed and excused herself, leaving her companions to surround the native boy. She walked past the men's area, on her way to get some wine to serve, as a prelude to the feast her husband had prepared for her guests. Suddenly, her son joined her, steering her to another area, where he made her sit down, flinging himself on his back, next to her, his head firmly on her lap. She smiled down at her boy, raking his hair back from his forehead, looking deep into his eyes. "Carlitos," she murmured. "What is wrong, *papito?*" she asked gently, almost crooning.

Her son sighed, closing his eyes for a moment, before opening them again, his turquoise pools looking right into her sea-green eyes. "I am confused, Mamá," he admitted softly. He frowned to himself. "I feel as if I were the one who did something wrong, and I can't take it back..."

María Isabel murmured to him gently, her eyes searching his. "I heard you were very harsh with that girl," she informed him, "almost cruel."

Carlos nodded, a sad smile hovering around his mouth, as he gazed into his mother's beloved face. "Yes. I was," he admitted. "Almost cruel..." His ears strained for the sound of Marina's voice. "Marina is a *bruja*..."

María Isabel chuckled. "You are spellbound, *bebé*..."

"I can't fix it, right now."

"And, why not, *hijo?*"

He didn't stop to think. "I am not ready."

His mother nodded slowly. "But are you ready to lose her?"

Carlos frowned, falling silent. His mother continued to caress his face and stroke his hair, providing comfort to her child.

From where she was, Marina caught sight of mother and son. Her heart clenched in a fist, with longing. *He won't speak to me, and I can't live without him.*

Turning her head, she concentrated on the conversation going on around her. "And where was this?" Shayla was asking.

Marina shook herself out of her thoughts, mentally hurrying to catch up with her companions. She looked at the drawings in her mothers' hands. "La Gitana," she answered softly. There they were, doing forms on deck, leading the men, in one drawing. The other one was of Salomé and herself, lounging, having a girls' day out. Caribe had caught the play of light and shadow on their faces, and on their clothes, as they lay, draped on the pirate's bed. Their faces were turned towards each other, laughing at some private joke.

Marina laughed happily, delighted with the quality of the drawing. Impulsively, she hugged Caribe. Her voice was a soft exclamation of admiration. "Dude! You are way better than a camera!"

Salomé hugged him next. "You rock, *papi!*"

Jackson looked at the drawing silently for a moment. Across the way, undetected by the engrossed group, the pirate's eyes flickered with curiosity, at what held their attention and gained their admiration. Finally, Jackson groaned. "I'll never be this good."

Storm stroked his back. "Sure you will. If you really want to, you will be able to." She winked at him, as he turned to smile at her.

Rouge looked at Caribe with newly found respect. "I heard you were good, baby, but these are outrageous!"

Caribe winked at her. "Just wait."

Marina stood up, suddenly restless. She couldn't sit still, any longer. Head bowed, she didn't see the men shoot covert looks at her. "Caribe is an awesome artist," she told the pyrate.

María Isabel kept silent, as she felt her son tense next to her, his head carefully held in her lap. Looking down, she saw his hooded eyes, peering through his lashes at the girl. It seemed to her, he groaned softly. Biting her lips to keep from laughing out loud, she rolled her eyes, and glanced at the endless high ceiling of bright blue sky suspended over the courtyard. She sighed, and kept watching, silently.

The next drawing was of the girls working on the ship, next to the men.

Their mothers stopped to study this one.

Shayla spoke first. "You look like you're pulling your own weight, here." Salomé laughed. "We were."

"You girls work hard on this island, don't you?" observed Sloane. She held up the next drawing. It was of Arrecife. The perspective was from the ship, as Caribe had seen the sailors abandon ship and splash happily to the beach. Sloane smiled. "This must be playtime."

Marina laughed. "It was awesome! All those days on the ship, and all of a sudden, firm land," she said, her face lighting up with the excitement of the memory. "Arrecife is the coolest beach on the whole ocean. We had a great time."

Jackson gave an exaggerated sigh. "Let me guess. You got to run around this cay." He grinned as his sisters nodded eagerly. "Who gave the battle cry?"

Marina looked down, as Salomé laughed. "I did."

Caribe chuckled. "Marina did."

Salomé agreed. "Marina."

Jackson laughed. "How was it?"

Marina grinned at him. "Just awesome." She didn't see her mothers look at each other.

He held her eyes, and smiled gently at her, nodding slowly. "Cool..."

Caribe called their attention, just then, to a packet of drawings, tied together with string. "This," he said mysteriously, "is my pride and joy. This is what happened at *El Luto...*"

María Isabel's fingers froze inside her son's hair, in mid-stroke. She pulled his head out of her lap, swinging him into a sitting position. "Carlitos," she said softly, urgently, "go get a bottle of wine, *hijo*," meeting his eyes as he turned to look at her. "Caribe is showing them some drawings. I would also like to see them. Come serve us," she said, looking deep into his eyes. He held her gaze for a moment, before nodding. She smiled at him, standing up to join her guests. "*Gracias, papi...*" And she left. Her son, left alone, turned to go get a bottle of wine.

Sloane looked at her daughter. "Wasn't that the dance?"

Marina nodded. "The one and only." She frowned slightly at the memory.

Shayla looked at her daughter. "Didn't all kinds of things happen there?"

Salomé nodded. "All kinds of things."

Jackson grunted. "Sounds suspicious, if you ask me."

Storm nudged him with her elbow, her voice low and melodious in his ear. "No one is asking." He grinned.

Caribe cleared his throat. "I have something to say..." he began, before stopping.

Salomé encouraged. "Oh, please, baby, say it. Whatever it is, it's okay."

Caribe chuckled to himself. "I draw, exactly what I see."

The girls looked at him in shocked silence, before glancing at their mothers. Salomé grinned. "What he means, is, he has some graphic stuff, I guess."

Shayla nodded. "Uh-huh..." She looked at Caribe. "How graphic, baby?"

Marina jumped in, her mind searching desperately for every time she had seen Caribe sketching furiously. "The thing is, Caribe is *everywhere*, so the truth is, we have *no* idea of what he's seen, or where he's even *been*, for that matter..."

Sloane slid her eyes over her, for a moment. Her turquoise pools, however, as opposed to the pirate's stormy ones, were calm and serene. "Sure, *mami*." She turned to Caribe. "Let's see."

María Isabel joined them, as Caribe handed them the first page. Sloane and Shayla looked at a cave full of pirates, dressed up for an occasion. They were all wearing black. Torches flickered along the cave walls, and musicians tuned their instruments in a corner. The women gasped at the clarity of the drawings. You could almost hear the murmur of voices, the musical notes, the laughter.

The next picture showed Salomé and Indio against the wall, dressed alike. Shayla's eyes filled with tears, at her daughter's beauty, next to her man.

"You look like twins, baby," she laughed shakily.

Larissa shook her head, awestruck. "You can almost see your chests rising, these are so good." She turned to her friend. "Salomé, you make such a good couple. Breathtaking on the outside and absolutely beautiful on the inside. Both of you. Together, you are powerful, to the extreme. I think you are doing the right thing, honey."

María Isabel nodded in agreement. "I know you are."

Salomé smiled. "Thank you. Your support means everything in the world to us." She laughed softly. "I'm scared almost out of my mind," she admitted shakily, "but I do love that boy so much..." The women sighed, petting her in comfort.

The next picture showed Marina, across the room from Carlos. Both their hands were outstretched, fingers yearning to touch. They were laughing silently at each other. Sloane gasped, at the love in both their faces. "Marina..." she caught herself, suddenly. Her mind switched gears. "You look beautiful, precious," she breathed. "You are more ravishing than any of the girls in my shop." Her deep turquoise eyes sought her daughter's hazel ones. "Come work for me, *mami*, I'll pay you more than Don Carlos---"

"I heard that!" Don Carlos called from around the plants, making the whole group laugh.

Carlos joined them, right then, extending a bottle, with a smile. "More wine, anyone?" he asked politely.

They all happily extended their wine glasses, ready for a refill. Except Marina. She held hers out, thoughtfully. Carlos filled their glasses with a smile, and a few murmured words. When he got to her, he poured without looking at her, flirting with the lady pyrates. Marina frowned as he avoided eye contact. Suddenly, she pushed the bottle off her glass before he was done, looking away when he frowned down at her. She turned to Caribe, curious at what the next drawing would be. Carlos finished pouring, and went to stand quietly to one side.

The next series of drawings were of Lola. Caribe had done great justice to the woman's generous breasts straining against her old dress. The moms raised their eyebrows at each other. Shayla laughed. "This must be that dancer, you girls told us about?"

The story was clear. Lola arrives. She hits on Carlos. Carlos stops her advances. The women face off. And then the pirate.

Jackson stopped the flow of papers, looking at the one in his hand. He didn't know why, but his heart beat just a little bit faster, at the sight of the blond man. Finally, he could speak. "Who the hell is this?"

The answer came back, low and subdued. "Xavier."

Jackson was scared, and he didn't know why. He didn't appreciate it. "Who the fuck is Xavier?"

For a moment, nobody could speak, the horrible memory fresh in the minds of those who had been present.

Storm reacted first. "He is a pirate that sails the same waters we do." She shook her head sadly. "He is not a very nice man." She looked into Jackson's eyes, as he turned his head towards her. "Unusually cruel, even for a pirate," she said softly.

Carlos' eyes slid restlessly, back and forth, among the women. He looked at where the men were. Indio met his eyes, expectantly.

Carlos flicked his eyes at him. In a moment, Indio had joined the group. Carlos looked back at the men. He signaled Giancarlo with an almost imperceptible move of his head. Don Carlos and Don Miguel glanced at each other, making sure each had seen, precisely what they were pretending they hadn't.

The next drawing was of Lola dancing her heart out, to one, very unhappy, scowling pirate.

Next, came Marina. And suddenly, the drawings took another flavor. Now, they were disturbing, erotic, breathtaking, as they stirred the senses. They told the story of Marina's dance. The women crowded around the drawings, gasping at the details.

Shayla cleared her throat, first. "Is this what I think it is?"

Salomé nodded happily. "Marina gave Gaitano a lap dance."

Next to them, their fathers groaned at the words, making the older Gaitanos laugh.

Shayla held her hand out. "That's my girl," she said softly.

Marina slid her some skin. "Boy didn't stand a chance," she laughed, tossing her hair over her shoulders.

Carlos reacted at her words. On the outside, he rolled his eyes. Behind her back, of course. On the inside, he grew warm at the memory. His mind took off in an inevitable direction. *I want another dance.*

Sloane laughed wickedly. "You have to show me how to dance like that, *mamita*, for Papi."

María Isabel's laugh matched hers. "Carlos asked me to dance for him like that, already. Of course," she added mischievously, "he got to see it, live..."

From next to them, the men laughed. Don Carlos blew them a kiss, through the sunny air.

The following drawing showed the pirate audience.

Storm shyly pointed herself out, leaning against the wall, beautiful in black, smiling at the proceedings. "That's me. I got to see everything live, also," she teased.

Marina gasped. "I never saw you!" Storm smiled. "You were kind of busy..."

Marina blushed, suddenly aware of the pirate somewhere behind her. "Stop... please..." Giancarlo and Indio looked at her with interest.

Jackson growled. "You weren't too shy to jump on Gaitano's lap---"

"Jackson!"

He ducked his head, bombarded on all sides, by his name. "All right, all right!" He rolled his eyes, hiding a grin, winking at Marina to show her he was playing. The men couldn't help laughing. Jackson bit his lips, wiping the smile off his face. "Then, what happened?"

The pictures successively showed Marina. Undulating for the pirate, pressing his face against her chest, dropping down on his lap, walking away from him, and throwing a last look over her shoulder. Silence fell over them, as the drawings changed hands. By the time they reached Giancarlos', he happily passed them on to Solomon, between a couple of potted palms. The young African, in turn, was more than pleased to share the amazing record of events with the elder Gaitanos, who in turn, passed them to the visitors.

Sloane and Shayla looked in dismay at the next drawings. Lola screeching and attacking. Marina slapping her with all her might, hair flying around her face. The effect was provocative, as Carlos could appreciate, even from where he stood, looking over Jackson's shoulder. Storm and Rouge laughed. Salomé and Marina looked at each other.

Sloane gasped. "Marina! You didn't!"

"She started it!"

"I don't care who started it!"

María Isabel decided to step in. The words, soft as they were, were escalating into something unnecessarily bigger. "Sloane," she soothed, putting her arm around her son's girl's mother. Her friend. "I was there," she whispered, laughing softly. "Lola would have seriously hurt Marina. Claw her face, maybe even scratch her eyes out..." she shrugged, making Sloane smile. "She was creating a scene." She looked into the turquoise eyes, so like her son's. "Marina did what any of us would have done, under the circumstances."

Shayla brushed her hair away from her face, with her healing hands. "What did she say to you, baby?"

Marina let out a harsh laugh. She didn't see Carlos flinch. On the inside. On the outside, he remained like stone. "*Puta.*"

Shayla pressed her lips together for a moment. "You did good, baby," she assured her. "I would have kicked her skanky ass all over that cave."

Next to them, the men roared with laughter, the drawing already in their possession.

"I wanted to," Marina informed them. "Gaitano wouldn't let me."

Salomé shook her head at her. "You would've killed her, *mami...*"

"What the fuck?"

"*Jackson!*" Shayla scolded her son. "What is wrong with you, boy?"

Jackson shook his head. In his hands was the next drawing. In it, Xavier was approaching the group, an evil joy reflected in his smooth face. His dark eyes seemed to burn in his face. "What's up with this guy?" He looked at Marina suspiciously. "You didn't lap dance for this guy, did you?"

The women gasped. His mother put his hand to his head, shoving it to one side, in reprimand. Behind him, Carlos tensed.

Marina shoved him. "No, but he wanted me to!" She was furious. Her brother was calling attention to all the things she didn't feel like elaborating on at the moment. "*Jax!*" She gasped for air, for a moment.

He growled at her. "You know I'll find out!"

She nodded once. "He offered to buy me. He offered..." her voice broke. "Ships." She shook her head, turning to look at where the men were. Meeting Don Miguel's eyes, she saw a warning flicker in them. She bit her lip, and reached for the next picture. It was of Xavier, smiling at Carlos, across a length of steel. All around them, every pirate had their swords drawn, pointed at the blond trouble-maker. On either side of Carlos, his father and his uncle, representing. They looked menacing, and dangerous. Marina pointed this out to Jackson. "And this is what he got for being such a jerk." She frowned. "Why are you freaking out over this guy?" she asked carefully.

"I'm not sure," Jackson answered slowly. "It's like I've seen this guy before or something..." He held up the drawing, the better to look at it, more closely. "Actually," he said, finally, "what it is, he looks just like that bitch."

Salomé frowned. "What bitch?"

Jackson rolled his eyes. "You know, that bitch... the one you worked for, before the raids. The Swan..." He looked right into his sister's green eyes. "Xavier looks just like Dominique Swan." He shrugged. "I've never seen the guy, but by just looking at these, it seems to me like he could be related to her."

All those familiar with both Dominique Swan and Xavier, froze. They felt as if they had suddenly got caught in a very, extremely cold, ice shower. It made sense. Time seemed to restart.

A drawing surfaced, different from the rest. It didn't portray action, as much as it did emotion. Deeply erotic, it was intensely disturbing. In it, Marina was held down on Carlos' lap. He was busy eating her mouth. She seemed to be straining against him with her body, even as her mouth seemed to be responding to his. One of his hands held hers behind her back. The other firmly grasped her breast, cupping it inside her bustier. Strong, dark fingers grasped his wrist, hard, showing how Indio stopped Carlos from humiliating Marina in front of the pirates. The drawing was so explicit in details, it told the whole story. As the paper got passed around, nobody spoke. No words were needed.

The last drawing was of Carlos' back, leaving the cave, Marina wrapped around him. Tears shone on her face, and her middle fingers were raised.

Carlos moved around, refilling the wine glasses. Once again, he ignored Marina. She slowly moved farther away from him. There he was, once again, flirting with the lady pyrates, this time, Salomé joining in the fun. Marina screamed inside. *This isn't happening!* She went to her mothers, and sank down at their feet, her heart heavy. Blinking back tears, she looked up as a movement caught her eye.

Solomon stood a distance away, slowly waving his arms, high in the air, trying to get her attention. Their eyes met. Solomon smiled at her, over the distance. Without making a sound, he slapped his hands to his side and bowed to her, slightly. Marina frowned at him. He beckoned with his head. She began shaking hers. He stopped her with his eyes. Once again, he motioned as if he were slapping his hands to his side. This time, he bowed a little deeper. He grinned at her, as he watched her face light up. Finally.

Marina murmured to her mother. "Tie my hair, Mami?"

Sloane stroked her hair, her fingers already in it. She began braiding. "What's up, baby?"

Marina laughed softly. "Solomon just asked me to play."

Shayla gasped, looking over at the African. "Be careful, baby..." she murmured.

Marina shook her head, as her mother laid her haphazard braid over her shoulder. "It's okay, Mom. I just need to kick someone's ass."

The women's hands grasped each other blindly, as their daughter stood slowly, and quietly went to join the young African. Dumbfounded, they watched as Marina reached him. She looked up at him for a while, finally falling into his arms, in a deep embrace. The Boatswain returned it, before putting her firmly away from him. They seemed to be lost in their own world.

Marina smiled at him, relief flooding her. *"Gracias, Salomón..."*

Solomon nodded, winking at her. "You look like you need the exercise," he said, turning to walk away from her.

Marina followed him, laughing. "You look like you're going to drop, before I get a chance to show you what I've got!"

He laughed over his shoulder at her. "You ain't got anything!" he retorted, imitating Jackson, perfectly. He beckoned her with his head, once again.

Marina laughed, and jumped on his back. Solomon carried her easily, straight through the house, to the astonishment of everyone present. Before anybody knew it, they went out the back door, to the yard.

The men left behind, looked at each other. Suddenly, there was a mad scramble, as some of them took off after the couple. Leading the pack was Carlos, followed closely by his father and hers. The women looked at each other.

Giancarlo sighed dramatically, pleased to be left to entertain the ladies, along with Jackson. "I have to apologize for the Captain." He rolled his eyes humorously, before letting them sparkle at them with mischief. "He has an aversion to his accountant and his Boatswain fighting..." he broke off, for another dramatic sigh, "a sport they seem to be quite fond of. It drives Gaitano crazy," he added wickedly.

The women smiled, knowingly. They settled down, to wait for the fight to be over. Marina would need healing.

Outside, the men stopped in their tracks, looking after Solomon and Marina. The couple were headed to the bamboo grove.

Pablo put a hand on Carlos' shoulder. "*Oye, papi*, what're you going to do, man? You think you can stop them?"

Carlos glared at the visitor. "I know I can."

"Oh, yeah?" Pablo laughed, letting go of him. "And then, what?"

"Yo, Carlitos!" Joe chuckled, keeping a wary eye on their daughter. "You're sure you want to do this, right now? You won't even talk to her!"

Carlos growled, as he walked past them, his eyes fixed on his Boatswain and his accountant. "I don't want her hurt."

Pablo grinned at the older Gaitanos, as they caught up. "*Oye, papi*, the only one hurting Marina, is you."

Don Carlos agreed with a laugh. "Pablito's right, *hijo*."

"What goes around, comes around," Don Miguel grumbled.

Carlos stopped and looked at all of them. His face was as dark as thunder. "Why does she have to fight Solomon?" he asked finally.

Joe chuckled. "Have you ever had a girlfriend?"

The younger Gaitano frowned. "I have had women."

Don Miguel laughed, as he exchanged glances with his brother. "It's not the same thing, *papi*."

"When a girlfriend, or a sweetheart, or a wife, gets to know you after a while," Joe explained patiently, "they don't react kindly to being hurt."

Don Carlos grinned. "She *has* to fight Solomon, Carlitos. There is nothing you can do to stop her."

"Why is that?" his son asked, curiosity getting the better of him.

Pablo chuckled, as he walked past him. "It's *your* ass she wants to kick," he called over his shoulder. The Gaitanos hurried to catch up with him.

The pair stood under the shade of the bamboo grove. The small clearing they chose was filled with melodious creaks and groans, from the huge stalks swaying in the wind. Except for the bell, they sounded like a ship out at sea. At their feet, a carpet of dried leaves, and soft grass. Above them, dappled sunlight, and elusive patches of blue. They looked at each other, circling warily.

Marina sighed, clenching and unclenching her fists. She didn't take her eyes off him. "What's my motivation...", she taunted, cocking her head to one side, mockingly. "Solomon..."

He laughed. "Your boyfriend's not handling things very well."

Marina grinned. "Agreed."

"If it were me," he continued slowly, still circling her, "I would be going to the ends of the Earth... to stay with you... and know your time..." In a blur of movement, his hand came up to her face, pushing it to one side.

Marina shook her head and smiled, her fists clenching and unclenching, faster. "Thanks, Solomon."

"Right now, he won't speak to you." He reached out and pushed her face to the side again, harder.

Marina had to stop, so as not to stumble. She eyed Solomon suspiciously. "No..."

He laughed. "How does it feel?" He reached out slowly.

Marina slapped his hand away, her chest rising with excitement. Her hazel eyes flashed at his amber ones. "It sucks."

Solomon reached out once more, just to get his hand slapped away again. "After all the work you do for him..." He switched on her suddenly, circling her in the opposite direction.

Marina followed his lead. "Yeah, what's up with that?"

They didn't take their eyes off each other, as the Masters approached.

Joe laughed at them. "Sorry to interrupt all the fun, kids..." he told them, "but is this necessary?"

They answered at the same time. "Yes!"

Joe held up his hands. "Just checking, just checking..." He took a step backwards and bowed to them with a smile.

Pablo stepped in between them. He smiled, looking from one to the other. "What's the occasion?"

Solomon chuckled. "Marina needs to hit someone."

Marina narrowed her eyes. "I need to hit *you*," she warned him.

He threw back his head and let out a deep, loud laugh. Looking into her eyes, he winked at her. "You wish..." he taunted softly.

"My desire," Marina reached around her father in a round kick. Solomon quickly slapped her foot away. She laughed at him, impressed by his surprised reflex. "You have been practicing," she smiled at him, her voice filled with approval.

Solomon touched his heart. "I have," he admitted. Then, he smacked his lips and laughed, circling her with intent purpose. "Kicking *your* butt..."

Marina's laugh rang out in the soft air, touching all their hearts. She didn't see Carlos flinch, as he stood with his father and uncle, watching her, unobserved. "In your dreams," she scoffed at the African.

Pablo cut in. "This fight, of course, needs to be supervised," he looked at Solomon, "for my daughter's safety."

Solomon nodded, without taking his eyes off her. "Of course." He laughed. "I would think you would be more concerned about *my* safety."

Joe chuckled as he exchanged glances with Pablo. "*Your* safety..." Pablo laughed with them. "Truthfully, I *am* more concerned about you."

He waited for the moment to pass, and turned a litte serious. "This is to be a fair fight, the motive clear, nothing personal." He looked at each of them, as he got their full attention. "No shots below the waist, from either of you," he warned. "No headshots..."

Marina groaned. "Awww..." she teased, "but he's got such a big head, too..."

Solomon laughed at her. "Sorry, baby..."

"Stay away from her breasts. No shots to her chest."

He turned to Pablo, fighting to not grin. He lost. "I'll try."

Pablo looked at him long and hard. Finally, he lifted a hand slowly and pointed a finger right at the young African, before turning to his daughter. "Is there anything you need?"

"Yeah." Marina didn't stop to think about it. "Nobody stops this fight."

Pablo faced her. "*I* stop this fight," he said in a menacing voice, "if I see fit..."

Marina swallowed, knowing with all her heart, that her father meant it. He wouldn't hesitate to stop them, at any cost, if he felt they got out of hand. She nodded. "Okay, Papi." She looked back at Solomon again. "Just let me kick his butt, first."

Pablo smiled. He saluted them, and they bowed at him. He stepped out of the way, with one last warning. "Fight fair!"

Marina stepped up and slapped Solomon, her braid flying to land over her opposite shoulder. Just as quickly, she danced out of his reach. "Solomon..." she sang out, shaking her hips at him. "Come out and pla-ay..." It was their mating call. Their own, private, personal, get-ready-to-rumble ritual.

Solomon rubbed his face. He stopped. She stopped. They faced each other. They bowed. Then they assumed the position. Finally, they fought.

From the shelter of the bamboo grove, the Gaitanos watched the sailor and the girl. Carlos seethed inside, his feelings battling one another. He felt guilty, because he was the cause, and he felt jealous. His Boatswain got to play with his girl. He did not. He was furious.

Don Miguel whistled softly, wincing at every blow given and taken. "Carlitos," he rumbled softly, "does Marina fight with Solomon often?" he asked curiously. "It seems to me, almost as if they are dancing---" He flinched at an especially hard kick Solomon delivered to Marina's ribs. He held his breath as Marina gasped, before laughing at the African.

Carlos gritted his teeth. "Too often, for my taste." He growled. "I'm beginning to think they enjoy it."

Don Miguel chuckled. "Oh, they definitely do," he said, waving a hand at the sparring couple, "even a blind man can see that." He turned his head then, smiling to himself, pretending not to see his nephew scowl at him.

Don Carlos looked thoughtfully at his son. "Carlitos, it's you she is that angry at." He laughed softly. "Out there, she is pretending it is you she has in front of her."

Carlos frowned. "Then why is she fighting Solomon?" But he knew the answer. He just needed to hear it.

Don Miguel turned to him, his energy rolling gently over him. *"Cuidado, Carlitos,"* he warned softly. "You sound like a jealous husband. You sound like you care..." he rumbled gently.

Don Carlos shook his head with a smile. "Solomon, she can hit." His eyes met his son's stormy pools. "Marina will never fight you. You are everything to her. Are you willing to lose that?"

Carlos stood still, his mind twisting and writhing with the thoughts overloading it. "I will *not* lose her," he informed his father in a low voice. "But I can't talk to her, yet. I have a lot to think about."

Don Carlos nodded slowly, and pointed out the fight. "Then, I suggest you get out of her sight," he suggested softly. "Marina knows you are here. At this rate, she is going to kill Solomon." He met his son's eyes again. "Get out, *papito*. Let the poor girl breathe..."

Carlos sighed. Papá was right. He glanced at the fight for a moment, and his eyes accidentally met hers. She looked at the scowl on his face, and pressed her lips together. Without breaking eye contact with him, she took a step back, and moved forward like lightning, fists and feet flying, making the African grunt. She danced away, quietly catching her breath. Carlos felt shock threaten to overcome him. She looked at him again. To cover his confusion, he raked his eyes insolently, up and down her body. She turned away in anger, blindly lashing out at Solomon. Turning away, himself, with that very same emotion, Carlos left. He was jealous. He was so jealous, that for a moment, he wished he were Solomon.

Marina and Solomon fought until Pablo stopped it. He saw fit. But at least, he let them fight. Neither won, and there was no loser. Just two, very badly, extremely hurt people. Friends, bonded for life, by love and violence.

Marina groaned softly. It had been a good fight. But it had been a real one. She could barely move. Her whole body screamed in pain. Her face throbbed, where Solomon had gotten her, a couple of times. Her knuckles were numb. Her sides seemed to squeeze her with every breath. All she wanted was to pass out for a couple of hours, and wake up, better. But she wouldn't be better, if she didn't take care of her wounds, now. She groaned again.

The tent Don Carlos gave her faced north, so it was in the sun, for most part of the day. The inside seemed to be subtly illuminated. It had a completely calming effect. Marina let herself fall on her beautiful, sea-colored recliner, with a big sigh. She closed her eyes, blinking away the tears. Wiping her face with her hands, she propped her head with a couple of pillows, and gazed out over the water. She felt better, but she hurt no less. And she couldn't stop thinking about the pirate.

Carlos Gaitano. Suddenly, he stood at the entrance of her tent. The sun shone behind him, silhouetting him against the bright blue sky and sparkling ocean. Behind him, the rocks gleamed as darkly as his features.

Marina sighed. "You're blocking my view."

The pirate took a step inside. Marina tried not to move. He laughed softly. Reaching her, he put a basket in front of her. Passing her, he turned and lay down in her beautiful, coral hammock. Marina ignored him and looked inside the basket. It held a couple of ointments and a few pain killers. She smiled to herself, as she tended to her wounds. Don Carlos had thoughtfully provided her with a nice-sized mirror. This gift was now before her, assisting her with her healing. She thanked his son, as she turned her back on the mirror and faced him. The only indication she had that he had even heard, was a glint in his eye. Looking over her shoulder, she tried with all her might, to reach a few bruises on her back. Giving up, she turned on her stomach, and propped her chin on her hands, staring out over the ocean. Her body soaked the pain, absorbing it completely, before releasing it. She took a deep breath, and let it go, shakily. Suddenly, she felt his hands on her back. Startled, she started getting up. He hushed her, and untying the flowered fabric around her breasts, bared her back. Rubbed ointment on it. Marina sighed.

Carlos looked at the bruises in the soft light, and blinked. He shook his head. She was crazy. *What am I thinking of?* He sighed and pressed harder, kneading her bruises, making her gasp. This was hurting her.

Marina moaned, and snuggled deeper into the recliner, sinking into the soft cushions. She knew he was teaching her a lesson. It just happened to be a good one.

Carlos shook his head. *Something's wrong with this girl. I like it.* He laughed at himself. He massaged the ointment unto her back, her arms, the backs of her legs, after he managed to take off her pants. His hands skimmed around her waist, toying with the top of her panties. Distracted by the sight of his large brown hands against the soft white material, he didn't see her smile to herself. His hands glided down her hips, barely touching. Finally capturing them, he turned her over. On his knees, now, next to her, he gazed down at her. Marina looked back at him through hooded eyes, keeping him screened by her eyelashes. Before she realized what he was doing, he had her hands in one of his, over her head. His free hand caressed her face. She gazed at him, a knowing look in her eyes. He chuckled, connecting with her at a very deep, intimate level. His hand trailed down her throat, her chest, between her breasts. He stopped. Marina squirmed. He laughed. He ducked his head, to hers. His voice was hot and low in her ear. "You want to fight?"

Marina licked her lips. "Never."

Carlos licked her jaw line before he stopped, his mouth hovering over hers. "Neither do I." He licked her lips, once, in a broad sweep, from side to side. She froze, and looked into his eyes. Shadows shifted, deep inside them. He lowered his head again, kissing his way down her throat. When he got to her chest, his mouth captured a breast. Marina bit her lip to keep from crying out, from the sensation. His swirling tongue and suctioning mouth invaded her senses. She felt like drowning. The pirate let go of her hands. Her fingers buried in his hair, grasping his head, keeping him close to her. When he couldn't breathe anymore, he dragged his mouth to her other breast, doing some more of the same. Marina drew his head up to hers, their eyes locking. Carlos smiled, gazing into the shadows of her hazel pools, like smoke on water. Straddling her, he put his hands on either side of her, to hold his weight, as he lowered his hips down unto hers. Her fingers twirled and wrapped in the strands of his thick hair, wanting to tug, but holding, instead. His sex connected to hers, and he could feel her warm folds receiving him, through the fabric of her panties. He gasped, his hands on her hips now, his breath caught in his chest, his voice husky with barely restrained passion. "All I want," he informed her, "is to spread you under me, and sink myself between your legs."

Marina's heart stopped for a moment, before starting up again. She dragged his head up to look at her, even as he pressed down into her. Her mind gave the answer that her voice could not. *And all I want is to wrap my legs around you, while you do so.* Instead, she held his gaze for a moment, before pushing against him. "Right here, and right now, you are not."

Carlos pressed his lips together, and nodded. *I love a challenge, mami.* He got off her, but not before he ground his hips against hers, for a moment. His voice was in her head again, the words low and sexy in her ear, a promise, strumming a chord deep inside her, like molten lava. "Not here, not now..." He made it sound like a cherished promise. Marina closed her eyes, as she felt herself get wet. Gaitano kissed her. Hard. Not out of love, or desire, but out of anger, and desperation. Marina pushed him away again, dragging her face away from his. She stood up, putting distance between them. Carlos sank in her hammock, once more. He propped pillows behind his head and folded his hands on his stomach, one foot on the floor, idly swinging him. He watched her, not trusting himself to not do anything else. Marina hastily put her pants back on, and tied the flowered fabric back around her breasts. Her movements were stiff and slow. She glared at him. He laughed softly, dying for her to ask for his help. She didn't. Instead, she sat carefully on the edge of the recliner, her back to him, and looked out over the ocean again, her fingers tearing through her hair, getting the tangles and snarls out.

"Marina!"

Carlos froze. He couldn't see the owner, but he knew the voice. He squinted his eyes, and saw her visibly relax.

Marina laughed as Caribe came into view. "Hey, what's up, baby?"

The dreadlocked young man laughed. "I came to see how you were."

She shrugged. "I'm okay."

Caribe stepped to the entrance of the tent, catching sight of the pirate in the hammock. He stopped in his tracks. "Gaitano..."

Carlos nodded, his eyes alert. "Caribe..."

The native boy looked from one to the other for a moment, trying not to miss anything. "Am I interrupting something?" he finally asked.

Marina laughed and shook her head. "No, not a thing." She glanced at the pirate, before grinning up at her friend. "He's still not talking to me."

Caribe laughed. "I don't think the man needs words---"

Marina shrugged. "Whatever. Gaitano brought me painkillers and ointments. I feel much better."

Caribe looked at her, skeptical. "You don't look much better. Actually," he teased, "you look like you got your butt kicked."

"Ha!" Marina laughed. "You should see Solomon. For every one of my bruises, he must have two or three."

Caribe shook his head. "I can't make up my mind, whether you are a tough guy, or just some crazy woman."

"I'm a tough guy!"

"No," he disagreed sadly, struggling not to laugh with her. "The more I think about it, the more convinced I am, you are just crazy." He glanced at the pirate, making sure he was paying attention. Gaitano was not missing a single word.

Marina shrugged again. "Maybe. But if being crazy is what gives me the rush I get, I will keep my madness, thank you very much..."

"So, getting beat up gives you a rush?" Caribe inquired. He crouched down to be at eye level with her, peering at her bruises. He reached out and cupped her face with his hand, his thumb gently stroking the dark welt under one eye.

Marina winced. She started drawing back from him, and instead, held his hand close to her face, snuggling against it, making him smile, his heart melting for her. He glanced at the pirate, rolling his eyes. Gaitano smiled. He couldn't wait to be alone with her again. Marina sighed. "I wouldn't know," she answered, "because I didn't get beat up."

Caribe laughed. "So, what do *you* call it?"

"I got *worked*, baby, but not beat up."

"Almost," Caribe insisted.

She grinned. "Solomon's gotten good, hasn't he?"

"Better than you expected, I'm sure," he teased.

She nodded. "That's true. I'm surprised and very proud of him." Her hands skimmed over her bruises. Tears came to her eyes, as her body screamed in pain. "Solomon really hurt me, this time," she admitted softly.

Caribe glanced at Gaitano again. This time, the pirate frowned. For all her fronting, he had known she was hurt, but not as much as she was admitting to Caribe. The dreadlocked boy frowned. "Are you all right?" He caught her face between both his hands, making her look at him.

Marina nodded. "Yeah... no... I will be..." She laughed softly, shaking her head at herself. "It's the rush. The fight just makes my body rejoice. All my chemicals start flowing. Excitement, anticipation, adrenaline..." Her eyes sparkled for a moment, as she sought the words to describe her reasoning, to justify her actions. "All that gives me a rush." She looked deep into Caribe's eyes. "A deep, intense, gratifying rush."

Caribe thought for a moment. "But why fight? Can't you get that same sensation doing something else? Why with pain?"

Gaitano kept as quiet as he could, as he stilled the hammock and stopped swinging. *Yes*, he thought to himself. A sentiment he had heard Salomé express once, came to mind. *Enquiring minds want to know...*

Marina sighed. "Why fight?" she repeated, and shrugged. "Because I can, for one. But mainly because it is physical. I don't have to think, or reason, or figure out, or anything. It is primal. Good stuff." She smiled. "Doing something else?" She glanced over her shoulder at the pirate before she could stop herself. Their eyes met. Her heart skipped a beat, before thundering away. She looked back at Caribe, smiling sadly. "Fighting has been the only physical activity available to me. I mean, as far as physical contact. I get a similar rush from running, but not as good, and not as long."

Caribe chuckled. "I get a rush from running, too."

She nodded. "Isn't it fantastic? No drugs, natural high, just from your body doing its own thing..."

The dreadlocks bounced gently. "Like when you dance in the village..."

Marina laughed. "I get a bigger rush from that, than from running. But not as big, as when I fight, so there must be something to the physical contact..."

"Why pain, and why Solomon?"

"You know, I must be a masochist, because, I swear, when I get hurt in a fight, my whole body goes, *Yeah, baby, bring it on! Give me more!*" She shook her head, laughing at herself. "Solomon... I *love* fighting Solomon. My relationship with Solomon is like my relationship with Uncle Jesse. He's Snake Coltrane, the tattoo artist," she explained, absently reaching behind her shoulder to stroke the mark she shared with her family.

"Tattoo artist?" Caribe repeated.

Marina nodded. "Yeah... the guy inflicted pain, and my body enjoyed it. We are connected, baby." She spread her hands, as if that explained everything. "Solomon hurts me and my body thrives on it. The pain doesn't let me think about anything else, so I just focus on it for a while. It keeps things simple. Besides, my life, exciting as it has been, lately, is so sedentary, that I welcome the violence Solomon has brought into it. It keeps me balanced." She shook her head, absorbing her own words, as her heart poured itself out. "Solomon isn't only my fighting partner, he's my friend. We are definitely connected." She sighed. "Cool stuff."

Caribe took her face between his hands again, turning it from side to side, examining her bruises more closely. The ointments the pirate had provided were working already. She didn't look too bad. Just as if she had had a tough time. "Once the rush is gone..."

Marina laughed. "Then I need drugs for the pain, because that is the only thing that remains. Rest and sleep, to help with the healing process. Until I fight again."

Carlos growled softly, to himself. *That is not happening.*

Caribe let go of her face and shook his head. "I don't know what it is, I hope your parents realize it, but there is something terribly wrong with you."

Marina laughed at him. "They realize it. Why do you think Papi supervises the fights? He thinks I'll get such a rush someday, I'll get myself killed." She looked longingly at the water. "Now, I just want to get clean..."

The young man held his hand out to her. "That's exactly why I came. Don Carlos provided you with your own private, bathing spot. I have come to escort you." He glanced over her head at the pirate. Gaitano had stopped swinging, and he still wasn't moving. Sighing, he looked at Marina again. "Come with me."

Marina looked down at his hand for a moment, before taking it. "If you know where I can get clean, right now, I'm following you to the ends of the earth."

Caribe laughed. "Were I to be so lucky," he teased. And they were gone, leaving the pirate alone.

Carlos sighed, letting out a deep, shaky breath. Caribe's gentle interrogation had given him an insight to Marina, he would have never had, otherwise. She made him crazy. He couldn't wait to see her again. Later couldn't come fast enough. He looked out over the ocean for a while, and then, he too, was gone.

Marina sighed. Caribe looked at her and grinned. She looked much more refreshed, and relaxed, not to say beautiful. Her private bathing spot had consisted of a little pool, at the bottom of a natural waterfall. Caribe had stopped on their way into the jungle, to grab a cloth sack. It held everything she wanted and needed, to pamper herself. Caribe had dropped her off, so to speak, and left her to her own devices. When she finally called for him, she was grinning like a fool, her clothes stuck to her in places, her hair sleek against her head, as she finished massaging the last lotion into it. It was a nice experience.

Gaitano hadn't been there, when they got back, but some gifts awaited her. A beautiful dress, from Salomé, had been spread out on her recliner, matching panties to one side. Handsome black leather sandals sat on the sand, next to the table. The table held her own jewelry, the silver coins she wore at El Luto, and small glass jars containing kohl for her eyes and stain for her lips. Marina had rushed Caribe outside, to wait for her, while she got dressed in the privacy of her own tent. A few minutes later, she had called him inside, once again, grinning like a fool. He couldn't help but laugh. It was as if it were a different woman, standing before him.

"Gaitano's going to freak," he informed her.

Marina nodded. "That's kind of the idea." She pointed at herself in the mirror. "Do you see this? Dude, Salomé rocks!"

Caribe's dreadlocks swayed around his face as he nodded. "She does."

The dress was breathtaking. It was made of deep, black silk, as dark as the middle of the night. Embroidered on it, in beautiful turquoise thread, were fish, swimming in the sea of black, delicate seaweed swaying from the hem, bubbles indicating movement. It was a work of art. Marina figured it must have taken Salomé a pretty long time to make this number for her. The design was a basic tube, fastened at the side by a row of ties. The effect was very sexy. Something Caribe didn't miss out on. He pitied the pirate.

Marina laughed wickedly. "Look, what else I got." She sighed happily. "Indio must love me..."

Caribe looked. In her hand, there was an eagle feather. She held it out to him, and a strand of her hair. He quickly tied it in. Looking at the effect, he nodded. "Looks good." She thanked him with a smile, holding out her last gift. It was a peace pipe. He took it, and lit it. "Tastes good." He passed it.

Marina held the smoke deep in her lungs, before blowing it out slowly.

She put down the peace pipe, and smiled at Caribe. "Let's go."

"Marina makes me crazy," the pirate admitted.

The men grinned. They were lounging in one of the areas of Villa Azul, enjoying the sundown, as it cast deep shadows inside the house.

Pablo laughed, and leaned towards the younger Gaitano, confidentially. "*Oye, papi*, you make her lose her mind." He shrugged, and clapped the pirate on the shoulder. "Fair is fair. She *has* to make you crazy."

"Marina is doing a fine job of just that," Don Miguel rumbled, laughing silently at his nephew. "The poor boy is losing *his* mind. Yesterday, he almost lost his *life*..." he let his words trail off, letting them sink into all their minds. "You know, Carlitos? You better find some resolution, before you go on another adventure. This visitor has you so that you can't even think straight, while she's around. What kind of life are you going to have, if she leaves on the next storm? You will be nothing but insufferable..." He laughed. "Marina making you crazy? Damned good job of it!"

The pirate rolled his eyes, as his mind screamed at him that it made sense. He looked right into Pablo's eyes. "Marina knows what she's doing..."

Pablo chuckled. "I hope so, she is a grown woman..." He shook his head, laughing. "If not, I'll return her. I want my money back."

Carlos laughed. He couldn't help it. "*Tranquilo, viejo*," he said, glancing at his own old man.

Don Carlos smiled affectionately at his son. "I wonder if they would take *you* back," he murmured. "You may have expired, by now, *papi*. That would be too bad. I could use the money. Maybe take María Isabel somewhere..." he looked at Pablo. "Half the money is the mother's, right?"

Marina's old man was having a grand time. "It's a shame, but, yes, it is. Something about having to carry them for nine months---"

Don Carlos snapped his fingers suddenly, as if a light bulb had gone off in his head. "Pain! They get it for the pain part of the whole deal."

Pablo agreed. "That's right. It hurts, they get half."

Carlos shook his head at both of them, wondering how he had gotten himself into that situation. He looked back at the only man, besides himself, Jackson, and Joe, that had any power over Marina. Of course, he wasn't counting the violent love she shared with Solomon, their fights. He sighed. "Marina and I are connected, I believe," he said softly, "in mind, heart and soul. In body..." he trailed off, thinking carefully. "I don't know yet," he confessed, "but if I'm reading the signs correctly, Marina is as attracted to me, as I am to her."

Pablo held his gaze, nodding with a smile. "I understand," he answered, with infuriating calm, "Jackson already explained it to me."

Gaitano frowned. "Explained what?"

Pablo laughed. "That it wouldn't be rape." He laughed again. The pirate couldn't hide his reaction, quick enough. Pablo shrugged. "Whatever makes *mi nena* happy." Their eyes held. "If you are it," he said slowly, "then, I want you for her."

"What if she doesn't want me?"

Pablo exchanged a look with the older Gaitanos. They laughed heartily. It was a man thing. The knowing came with age. Marina's dad looked right at him. "My daughter wants you."

Joe laughed. "Carlitos, all my little girl wants, is you."

Don Carlos nodded as his son looked at him. "She does."

Don Miguel agreed, when it was his turn. "Marina wants you."

Carlos looked at each one of them, back and forth, a couple of times, finally, nodding with a smile. He visibly relaxed. There was just one word, to express how he felt. And he'd heard it enough, to feel comfortable around it. Now, he used it. "Cool."

And then, Marina walked in.

"How do you feel?"

Marina smiled. "How do *you* feel?"

"I am alive. I am thankful."

Marina laughed silently. He chuckled. They were laying on a long piece of furniture, head to head, against each other's shoulder. "Your guardian angel must love you," she sighed. "I was getting ready to put an end to it all, in that bamboo grove…"

Solomon exploded. "In your dreams!" The pillows beneath them shook with their laughter. "You, my friend, are lucky Pablo stepped in…"

They laughed some more and fell silent for a while, each lost in their own thoughts.

Marina had joined the party for a while, mingling, getting compliments on her fight, on her dress. Especially from the men. Although, as she approached, Gaitano had suddenly found somewhere urgent to go. Crestfallen, she had put on a big smile, not fooling them. Her fathers, his father, his uncle. The men had proceeded to take care of her, keeping her laughing, until she put the whole incident behind her. Now, she was giggling, as she imagined what they looked like, Solomon and herself, head to head, both with bruises.

Solomon chuckled with her, his voice rumbling. "I know what you are thinking."

"I'm sure you do."

"We must look a sight, you and I."

"Exactly."

Solomon sighed. "I am sorry I hurt you."

"I am sorry I hurt you, baby."

"I am sorry I took you on La Gitana."

"That, I am not sorry about."

"Was it worth it?"

"More than worth it. It was one of the most incredible experiences of my life."

Solomon stayed silent for a moment, absorbing her words. "I am still sorry I took you against your will, and scared you."

"And I am sorry I kicked your butt on La Gitana, in front of the whole crew."

Solomon laughed with her. "I am glad you did," he admitted finally. "I wear my fights with you, like badges of honor..."

Marina gasped. "Solomon..."

Embarassed, he explained. "I love Tae Kwon Do. You are my Master."

Tears pricked her eyes, but she smiled. "Solomon..." They moved at the same time, sitting side by side. They looked at each other.

Solomon laughed at her. "Gaitano is an idiot!" he said softly. Marina smiled and kept silent.

Sloane looked at her daughter. The dress Salomé made for her was stunning. She had lost weight, since she had gotten to Encantada. Amazingly, her daughter could now make any of the models at her shop run for her money. Sloane's partner in her thriving, ever-increasing endeavor, however, had always been Salomé. Marina had shown not much interest, being more in tune with Pablo and the complex dealings of running a business. She had gotten her B.A. and was halfway through her Master's Degree at a university they all attended, close to home. It had been a freak thing that they had wanted to spend a silly weekend on Spring Break with people mostly younger than they were. All her babies had wanted was sun and fun. And now, her birth daughter wandered around Villa Azul, like a beautiful ghost, not being able to stay in one place. She sighed. And then she made up her mind, and excused herself from her companions. Crossing the gravel path that ran down the middle of the house, between the front and back entrances, she joined the men.

Said men, were lounging lazily in the afternoon sun. They looked up as Sloane approached, her beautiful hair tied up in its loose braid, whipping around her face. She was almost trembling by the time she got to them. Until she saw what they were looking at. The same thing she had been observing herself, which sent her over to see them. Marina and Solomon. She glanced at them. The older Gaitanos and Pablo and Joe had condescending smiles for the daughter.

The pirate had come back, however, and the expression on his face was quite different. He was slouched in a hammock, his arms behind his head, his eyes slit, his body thrumming with contained jealousy and restrained anger.

Sloane had no time for the boy. She stood in front of them, hands on her hips, chest rising with emotion. Pablo scowled. He seldom saw his wife like that, much less in front of company. Sloane pointed to her daughter, whom they were already watching. "Do you see Marina?" she demanded. "Do you see my daughter?"

Carlos scowled ferociously, and kept swinging idly. She couldn't be talking to him. He couldn't keep his eyes off her daughter.

Pablo and Don Carlos looked at each other, before turning back to Marina.

They shrugged. "She's with Solomon..."

Sloane crossed her arms and tossed her head, her beautiful silver earrings glinting in the fading sun, her ocean eyes flashing blue fire. "Marina is the most beautiful I have seen, in years."

The men stared at her. All but Carlos. He was busy, shooting daggers at Solomon. Pablo smiled. "I agree. Bruises, black eye, and all. *Mi hija* isn't usually, this relaxed, and wild..." he glanced at the pirate in the hammock, before looking back at his wife. "Marina is the most beautiful I have seen, in years, also..." He took her hand and kissed it.

His wife faced the Gaitanos. "I am going to offer my daughter a very juicy job opportunity, which..." She raised her eyebrows at their shocked expressions, "she..." She also glanced at the pirate in the hammock. "will not be able to..." Her eyes met with those of Gaitano, *Padre*. "...resist..."

Don Carlos, almost choking in his haste to appease her, took her hand, much as her husband had just done. *"Sloane, mi corazon, por favor, no seas asi..."*

Pablo laughed and shook his head. "It won't work, *amigo*." He laughed again. "It has never worked for me."

Don Carlos looked at his friend and winked at him. "You are not a Gaitano..."

Sloane stamped her foot. "Carlos! I am serious!"

"Of course you are, *princesa*. I know, because a chill runs through my blood, as we speak. At this moment, I can not imagine life without Marina." The pirate sighed. "Regardless, of what damage my wayward son has done to any chances I have of having that brilliant girl take care of my business."

Pablo chuckled. "That's exactly what she's going to school for. Marina is going to run mine. Good thing I'm the father, *viejo*," he teased. "I saw her first."

"I am her mother." The voice was low and intense. "I brought her into this world." She looked at each of them. "In our world, you have been dead, for hundreds of years." Her voice was deadly quiet. "Happy as Marina is here, do you think for one moment, that if she had to choose, she would stay?"

Carlos froze. Marina couldn't go. He was smart enough to accept it would completely unbalance his life, as he knew it.

Don Carlos looked sad, as he realized the gravity of Sloane's words. "Would you do that?" he asked slowly. "Would you make her choose?"

"If I thought it was in her best interest, in a heartbeat."

Shocked, Don Carlos frowned at this mother, lashing out for her daughter. "Take away her free will?"

"If I had to."

"At the cost of her own happiness?'

"Marina? Look at her! *Mi hija* does not look very happy right now, does she?" She turned to look at the younger Gaitano. "I don't know what happened. My baby is a woman, now, and she can handle herself. But something's wrong, and if I'm not mistaken, *you,* my love, are the cause of it." She glared at him. *"Fix it!"* Turning once more to the rest of the men, she threw her parting words at them, to mingle with the rays of dying sunlight. "I will *not* leave my daughter here, on this island, to have her heart broken!" And with a toss of her platinum braid, she left them alone, once again.

"Marina!"

Marina's head shot up, a smile illuminating her face, as she spied who was calling her. "Don Carlos!"

Don Carlos grinned. "*Ven, preciosa,*" he beckoned at her.

Marina glanced at Solomon. "The big boss is calling," she laughed softly. Solomon nodded. "Go take care of your business." He held his hand out. She slid him some skin. "Later, baby."

"Later."

Don Carlos waited for her to reach them. As she approached, his son suddenly found something to do, once again, going to join the females in their group. He hid the scowl from his son's accountant/girlfriend. "*Marinita...*"

Marina smiled at the endearment. The last time she had heard her name like that, it had come from her own father's mouth. She walked into his outstretched arms, sharing a warm embrace. Looking into his eyes, she hesitated. "I haven't had the chance to thank you for my beautiful tent." Her voice broke as she glanced at his son.

Don Carlos slipped an arm around her shoulders, turning her around gently, and walking her away. "You like it, don't you?" he smiled at her.

"Very much!" she nodded happily. "Did you design it yourself?"

He frowned for a moment, then nodded. "Yes. All alone. Did I do a good job?"

"Awesome! I have never seen anything like it."

They strolled slowly, around the perimeter of the courtyard, through arches, under verandas, going around, within full view of the proceedings. They stopped on the opposite side of the house, and watched from a distance, silent for a moment.

Don Carlos cleared his throat. "It is I, who should be thanking you. I have not had the chance to show you my gratitude, properly. You have saved my family's business, so to speak. You could not have come at a better time into my son's life." He sighed, as they watched. The females were hysterical, laughing at something the pirates were saying. Don Carlos sighed. "Your arrival has had a monumental impact on this island's economy. My sons were not aware of the extent of the treachery and the thievery they were being subjected to." He shook his head. "Too young, too careless..." He took a deep breath, suddenly smiling at her. "I have a surprise for you."

Marina arched an eyebrow at him. "A better job offer?"

He laughed. "No, *hija*, you are not getting a better job offer, than the one I already extended. Although I am willing to compromise, if it means it would make up your mind, and you stay..."

Marina looked down, and around, not wanting to meet his eyes for a moment. "I just can't give you an answer, right now."

Don Carlos smiled. "I am not asking you for an answer, right now. Relax... take your time..." He made her look at him. Once he had her undivided attention, he dangled something, before her face.

Marina's eyes focused on the object. It became a small, beautiful silver cross with rows of turquoises. It reminded her of the Navajo jewelry of the Southwest. Suspended from a black leather cord, it gleamed in the fading daylight. It was exquisite. She was speechless, for a moment. When she could finally speak, she gasped. "For me?"

Don Carlos chuckled, turning her around to face the mirror on the wall next to them. "Lift your hair," he said softly. Marina obeyed, making the silver coins in her ears tinkle. He began tying the necklace around her neck. "This," he explained slowly, "belonged to Indio's mother. His father and I were as close as Joe and Pablo. As close as Carlitos and Indio. His mother came into our lives, just as you have come into theirs. Two years after Indio was born, they perished, on a sea voyage. María Isabel and I were taking care of him at the time. He was the same age as Carlitos, so it worked out for us. She had set this aside for him, on the day he was born." Their eyes finally met. "Indio wants you to have this, as a token of his appreciation."

Marina blinked back tears. "Thank you. I don't know what to say---" She was cut off, by a burst of laughter, from across the way. They both watched in the mirror, as Carlos entertained the ladies. Marina's voice broke, as her eyes flooded again. "Your son is breaking my heart!"

Don Carlos chuckled. "No, *divina*," he crooned using an endearment he had heard his son use, "he is breaking his own heart." He squeezed her shoulders reassuringly. "*Ven*. You look beautiful. My son is not worth your tears." Shuffling her along gently, he started walking her back.

Marina frowned. As they slowly approached the front of the house, there seemed to be a lot of activity. The closer they got, the clearer it became. Servants were rolling in a piano, on wheels. Everybody turned to watch. She turned to Don Carlos. "Who plays the piano?"

Don Carlos laughed. "Joe."

Marina gasped, a smile lighting her face. "Wait till you hear him."

Just then, a commotion formed at the doorway. In came four pirates. The crew of La Gitana cheered. Marina recognized the rest of the Council. She stood with Don Carlos, quietly, to one side, as introductions were made all around, between her family, and the four guests. Once the formalities were done with, the pirates looked around them, restless. Spying Don Carlos and Marina in a corner, they headed towards them. Solomon went to stand at Marina's side. Giancarlo and Rouge followed in the wake of Suleiman's flowing robe. Don Miguel almost ran to catch up, Salomé at his side. Carlos hesitated, unbelieving, as he watched the scene unfold before him.

Across the way, Marina's family looked on, in silence, wondering. Jackson couldn't keep quiet any longer. "What's going on?"

Storm hushed him. "That's the Council," she explained quietly. "They came from Carey to meet here at Encantada." They watched as each pirate addressed Marina.

Shayla put a hand on her son's pyrate girlfriend. "Storm, baby, is there any particular reason why they all wish to speak to Marina?"

Storm smiled at her, affection glowing in her face for this new-found family.

"Marina's work for the Gaitanos has affected all of us," she said, throwing the pirate next to her, a glare, her sunlit eyes shooting sparks at him.

Carlos met her gaze and sighed. It seemed as if he couldn't do right, today. He turned to the rest of the family. "If you will please excuse me, for a moment." Without waiting for a reply, he turned and left them, going to join the rest of the pirates.

Larissa laughed, her green eyes sparkling excitedly, as she looked at her friends. "Your daughters have been making friends."

Pablo shook his head. "Many."

"Pirates are not quite the company we expected our children to keep," murmured Sloane, watching their daughters among the pirates. There were no alarm bells ringing in her head, or warning lights flashing in her eyes, and her heart stayed calm, inside her chest. It was just that those were her babies, and the men were... *pirates*!

María Isabel smiled. "You have to excuse my son," she said softly. "Carlitos believes Marina is a *bruja*." She laughed. "A witch. Not for real... he is bewitched..."

Jackson stood up, suddenly. "I'm going---"

Storm reached out with a hand, and just as quickly, yanked him back down to sit next to her. Her soft scolding voice had more effect than any shout. *"Jackson!"* Everybody turned to look at her, their attention caught by her warning tone. "The Council has important things to discuss with Marina."

Joe looked at the rest of the family. "Anybody for some blues?" Not waiting for an answer, he took Shayla's hand and wandered towards the piano.

Marina watched, saying nothing, as the pirates stood to face her. Four ships. That was a lot of work. It would take some time. But that wasn't what was making her heart sink. She didn't want to know what was. Her voice was husky, as she greeted them. *"Chymera, Kalahari, Ocean Wind, Black Mermaid..."*

"You look beautiful," Jai-Ling told her, taking her hand and kissing it, "as usual."

Marina laughed. "Thank you, as do you." She winked at him. "You have never seen me working, or working out, exercising with the sailors."

Jai-Ling nodded, smiling. "I have heard about your workouts." His eyes fell on her bruises. "You look like you have been fighting, Marina Aguilar."

She grinned. "I have been."

"I hope your foe looks worse than you."

Marina laughed again, slipping an arm around Solomon, next to her. She cupped his face in her hand, turning it from side to side, for the newcomers to examine. "Judge for yourself..."

The pirates laughed. Jai-Ling shook his head, smile condescending. "He does," he agreed softly. "I would be most interested in seeing you at work... and at play."

Marina gazed into his serene Oriental features for a moment, not sure if he was teasing. "I will never fight you, Jai-Ling. What I do must be child's play to you." She gazed over to where her family was. "I don't even think that my Masters would take you."

Jai-Ling bowed to her. "I would still like to watch you..."

Marina let go of Solomon and bowed back. "It would be my pleasure, Jai-Ling..."

"Our lives have drastically changed since we met."

Marina turned to look at the next pirate. She wondered if they could see her blushing, beneath the bruises. "Suleiman... I am honored. How so?"

"Trade is better now, on this part of the world, for those of us," he looked at his companions, "who have crossed the *Sea of Darkness*..." The dying sun caught on his curved sword, sparking pink and orange at them. His melodious voice soothed them. "We are establishing routes. The mindless thievery..." he searched for words. "The lost honor among these Caribbean pirates, the treachery going on in Carey, has all but stopped."

"Excellent news!" murmured Don Carlos.

"The ripple effect," Salomé said softly. They all turned to her.

"What is that?" Indio asked.

Salomé tossed back her long black hair with a smile. "When you throw a stone in the water, it creates a ripple. These go out and grow, touching everything it comes in contact with. That image is used to illustrate cause and effect." She shrugged. "Marina did good for you." She spread her hands. "It just got bigger and better..."

Don Miguel's energy rolled over the group gently, as he chuckled. "Marina's ripples have the effects of tsunamis."

The pirates laughed in appreciation, spiking the curiosity of the rest of the people in the house. They all agreed with the older Gaitano. Carlos hid a smile as he watched, quietly.

Sultan stepped up. "Since we met you..." he smiled, keeping them in suspense. He approached Marina, with a heavy wooden chest in his arms. Depositing it at her feet, he took her hand, much as Jai-Ling did, and kissed it. "We are all wealthier." He winked at her. "There must be something to all those numbers."

Marina looked down at the chest at her feet. "What is this, Sultan?" she asked softly.

Rouge shook her head. "It is a token of our appreciation, honey, from all of us. A little something to show you the difference you have created in our lives." She smiled at her. "Don't be embarrassed, we won't ask you to open it now." With a graceful wave of her hand, she had one of the servants come and take the chest away, to where her parents were. "Something for you to play with when you're alone..."

Marina grinned in relief. "Thank you."

Giancarlo chuckled. "Once you open it, we'll probably never see you again," he teased.

Solomon put a hand on her shoulder. "Please, Marina, don't open it." They laughed once again, happy to be together, comfortable in each other's company.

Jack stepped forward, his smile a ghost of what it usually was. He took her hand in his. "Marina---" he stopped, and looked into her eyes, sighing.

"Jack!"

"Marina..." he tried again, squeezing her hand. He shook his head and locked eyes with her, once more.

"Jack?"

"He is coming."

Marina felt herself go still. Her head began buzzing. All eyes were on her.

She shook her head, as terror gripped her heart. "No, he's not."

The fiery head nodded sadly. "Yes, he is."

Marina looked around her, wildly. Yes, indeed. All eyes were on her. The pirates seemed to suddenly become statues. Those who knew and those who did not. Rouge's bottom lip quivered, tears pooling in her eyes, as they met hers. Salomé's hands covered her mouth as, over them, tears streamed from her liquid green eyes, down her face. Carlos and Indio looked carved from stone. She turned back to Jack, tears stinging the back of her eyes. "No, he's not!"

Jack sighed, pressing his hand to his heart. "Marina Aguilar, it brings me such sorrow, and causes such conflict in my heart, to bring you this warning, but..." he took a deep breath, as tears stung his own eyes, while he gazed into hers. "Xavier---"

"*No, he is not!*"

Everybody turned to stare. Silent, until now, the younger Gaitano had been unnoticeable, as he had stood watching over the proceedings. Now, his heart wrenched in his chest, for the woman before him.

Don Carlos stepped in between them, as he caught Marina's family beginning to stand up. He smiled at them, and turned his back on them, scolding the pirates. "We have guests!" he hissed. "Control yourselves! All of you!"

Without thinking, Rouge grabbed Salomé and Marina, each by the hand, and stood behind a small wall supporting an arch. There, the sisters fell against the pyrate, reeling from shock. Rouge put an arm around each of them, and stroked their backs, soothingly. Tears poured down her own face, as terror gripped her own heart. "Hush! Your family will hear you, and there will be a lot of explaining to do!" she murmured at them, as they quietly, ferociously, fought their tears. "You don't want to worry them! This is between us pirates, right?" She made them look at her. "Because, whether you realize it or not, you girls are now pirates. Like it or not, you have been for some time." Reluctantly, they nodded, wiping their faces, their eyes haunted, when they finally looked at each other. "Put on your smiles, ladies, and go face your folks." Her voice was husky as it dropped to a lower tone. "Nothing has happened here." Without warning, she pulled them out of their shelter, and sent them back, making them catch their breaths, slowly.

Carlos watched them come. Their eyes were too bright. As Marina reached him, he stretched out a hand, to hold her arm. "Marina..."

"Gaitano..." She jerked away from him.

"Marina..." He grasped her once more, harder. Her words shocked him to the core.

"Lola doesn't bother me."

Desperately, his eyes sought hers. "Marina..."

Emotionless, Marina looked straight into his eyes. She felt empty. He couldn't help. Without looking away, she yanked her arm out of his grasp, and pushed against his chest with both hands, making him stumble backwards. Without saying a word, she walked past him, towards her family, her sister at her side. When they reached them, their family just looked at them, but they couldn't speak. Suddenly, their brother, their knight in shining armor, leapt to his feet, one of Caribe's portraits in his hand.

Jackson stood in front of his sisters, blocking their path. "It's *him*, isn't it?"

They tried to play dumb. "What?" But the piece of paper said it all. It held a vivid, detailed sketch of Xavier.

Jackson shook his head, waving the paper in front of their eyes. "What's up with this guy, ladies?" His tone grew low and dangerous. "What's up with Xavier?" He looked from one to the other, his eyes finally landing on Marina. He looked at her in silence, for a moment. "Is he coming for you, or something?" He caught the twitch on the side of her face. "That's it, isn't it?"

Marina just looked at him, dazed. "I don't know what you're talking about..."

He scowled at her, his voice a low growl. "You know I'll find out." Marina bowed her head and stayed silent.

Salomé hit her brother, and hissed at him. "They do not need to know!" Out of habit, they all turned to look back at their parents. From the piano, Joe and Shayla had stopped what they were doing, to look over at them. From the pillows strewn on the floor, the Aguilars were now gazing at them. Their children looked at each other, and turned on some smiles.

Pablo sighed, shaking his head. "Do we get an explanation now, or do we get one later?"

They answered, all at the same time. "Later."

Pablo nodded, scowling at them like when they were children. "You know I will."

The grown children nodded.

Larissa laughed. "You have them well trained!" she said softly, in admiration.

Pablo shrugged. "Well, you know... once they're in their twenties, they run on their own..."

María Isabel nodded. "I am impressed!"

The grownups laughed. The children did not.

Joe began to play the piano. Salomé glided towards him, leaving Marina alone.

Marina smiled at her parents, at Jackson and Storm. She reached for Max without thinking, automatically. Larissa gave him up gladly, glancing at the pirates. Then she drifted away, restless, aimless. The baby snug in her arms, she wandered around, unsettled. Her thoughts screamed at her, not letting her think. She never saw the pirate following her with his eyes, making sure he knew where she was at all times. Standing a short distance away, she looked at the happy people in front of her, now facing Salomé and her parents. She watched as Sloane peeked into the chest next to her. It seemed to her as if her mother went pale, before closing the lid. Her eyes were huge in her face, as she looked at her husband. Pablo quickly put an arm around her, and pulled her close to him, his beautiful dark head against her sleek golden one, whispering in her ear. Next to them, Jackson and Storm held a low conversation. The men had formed a group right by them, starting a lively game of dominoes, with the incredible carved ivory pieces made by Silas. Everybody settled down comfortably, casually listening to the piano player and his singers. They were all facing the front of the house now, the last vestiges of daylight visible beyond the balcony, behind the piano. And throughout it all, Caribe, in the sidelines, eyes intent, pencil flying, recording the events. The soft breeze became a gentle wind, tinkling the windch imes over their heads. Tiki torches had begun to spring up in strategic places in the courtyard, so as to keep the light going inside Villa Azul.

Joe glanced at his daughter fondly, as his wife cuddled up to him. They had been singing very softly for a while, not getting more than the occasional glance. "Salo," he rumbled softly, smiling when his beautiful daughter turned her head to look at him. "Are you up to some Alicia Keyes, baby?"

Salomé laughed, tossing her head. Marina drew closer, a little curious. "I'm always up to Alicia Keyes, Dad." Her eyes raked over the room. Signaling her parents silently, she glanced at the pirate staring at her oblivious sister. "What would be appropriate?"

Shayla's soft tone was a warning. "Now, guys..."

Joe chuckled. "What else?" His fingers stroked the keys lovingly, beginning softly and slowly.

Salomé laughed again. Commanding attention, she stroke a pose. "Where I come from," she began slowly, in a sultry voice, "women have a place!"

Shayla laughed, hands in the air. "Amen!"

Slowly, everybody lowered their voices, paying attention, as they continued their game, their drawing. Pablo and Sloane smiled, knowing the treat they were in for. The pirates kept playing, enjoying themselves. John Kline had slipped in quietly at some moment in time, joining them, after kissing his wife and locating his son.

"In society," Salomé continued, "at home... in the world!" she exclaimed softly.

Marina reached her, bouncing Max gently. "Salo, no!" she hissed.

Salomé ignored her. "But in truth, we have no place, unless our men recognize..."

Jackson looked at Storm and winked at her. "I recognize..." he said softly.

Storm smiled. "You give me my place," she murmured in agreement.

Marina hissed at her sister again. "Salo..."

Caribe appeared magically at her side, his pad of paper and charcoal pencil, clutched in one hand. "Marina," he said softly, reaching for the baby, "I'll take Max."

Marina looked at him for a moment, not comprehending. "Caribe..."

"You're getting upset," he murmured in her ear. "Give me the baby. His father's here. It'll be okay."

For the second time that day, Marina handed her charge over. Her eyes searched his, wildly. "I'm freaking out," she whispered.

"I know," he whispered back. And turning away from her, he went to deposit Max with his father, where the men were laughing.

Marina sighed, as the first notes floated in the air. After them, Salomé's voice chased, giving significance to where before there was only noise.

"You could buy me diamonds, you could buy me pearls, take me on a cruise around the world..."

Marina's voice came out, a shaky wail. *"Salomé!"*

Shayla's rich voice drowned her out, as she did the chorus for her daughter. *"Baby, you know I'm worth it."*

Salomé snapped her fingers in time, swaying like a lounge singer. Eyes closed, she embodied the diva, caught up in her art. *"Dinner lit by candles, run my bubble bath, make love tenderly to last and last..."*

Shayla followed her daughter's lead once more. *"Baby, you know I'm worth it."*

Joe looked up from the keyboard and happily blew Marina a kiss. She groaned, as she realized, all eyes were on her. Including the Gaitanos. Sighing once more, she sat by Joe on the bench, head down, hair covering her face. This was happening, whether she wanted it to, or not.

"Wanna please, wanna keep, wanna treat your woman right. Now just don't, better show that you know she is worth your time."

Marina buried her face in her hands for a moment, hiding. *This is not happening to me.*

"You will lose if you choose to refuse to put her first. She will if she can't find a man who knows her worth."

Carlos felt himself go still, as he'd seen Marina go, on a few occasions. Salomé's voice was rich and vibrant, beautiful and seductive. *She's trying to tell you something,* he thought to himself. As to confirm this feeling, Salomé looked over them, scanning their faces, until her cat's eyes connected with his ocean ones.

"'Cause a real man knows a real woman when he sees her, and a real woman knows a real man ain't afraid to please her."

Carlos sighed. *I have to fix this.* There was no reproach in her eyes, but something more like a plea.

"A real woman knows a real man always comes first; a real man just can't deny a woman's worth..."

Marina's head shot up, as tears stung the back of her eyes. "I have to go," she murmured at Joe. Without waiting for an answer, she stood up from the bench, and wandered to an arched doorway. Leaning against it, her back to the courtyard, she looked out, towards the ocean.

"Going..."

Carlos looked around sharply. The voice was dripping with pent-up feelings, reproach almost beyond control. His eyes met Jackson's tiger eyes.

"Hold... 'Cause if you treat me fairly, I'll give you all my goods, treat you like a real woman should."

Shayla stood by her daughter, snapping her fingers and swaying in time.

"Baby, I know you're worth it."

Carlos glanced back at Salomé. Her eyes had never left him. He felt a sudden sense of urgency. *I really have to fix this,* he groaned inside.

"If you never play me, promise not to blow, I'll hold you down when shit gets rough."

"'Cause, baby, I know you're worth it."

The pirates held their breath, as they had at *El Baile del Luto,* as if in the throes of a real-life passion. They all watched as Marina shifted restlessly, her back still turned towards them, leaning against the opposite side of the doorway. *"She walks the mile, makes you smile, all the while being true... Don't take for granted the passion she has for you..."*

Marina straightened herself from the doorway, taking a step outside. Tears continued to threaten. She felt as if she were in school, being punished in front of the class. *I need fresh air.* She stepped outside, drifting towards the verandah encircling the house.

"Going..." Jackson's voice was stronger. He felt Gaitano look at him sharply. Nonchalantly, he wadded a piece of paper he had in his hands into a tight ball, sliding to the front of his seat. Storm squeezed his shoulder in warning. *"You will loose if you choose to refuse to put her first… She will if she can't find a man who knows her worth…"*

Gaitano's heart felt heavier in his chest, with every note. The message was definitely for him. He watched in dismay as life went on around him, nobody seeming to notice.

"'Cause a real man knows a real woman when he sees her, and a real woman knows a real man ain't afraid to please her…"

I have to get out of here. And with that thought, Marina pushed herself off the railing she was leaning on, and leapt down the steps of the balcony. Her sandaled feet sank gratefully into the cool sand, as she left behind, Villa Azul.

"A real woman knows a real man always comes first; and a real man just can't deny a woman's worth…"

"Gone!" Jackson aimed and threw the wad of paper, at the pirate's chest. In one swift motion, Carlos batted it back to him. Jackson caught it smoothly and threw it back at the pirate, getting to his feet. Standing up, the pirate joined him. Their chests rose heavily, as they faced each other.

A surge of intense energy lashed out, sending shock waves through them. *"Sit the hell back down!"* The tone was low, and rumbling, but the effect on its recipients was monumental. Glaring at each other, Carlos and Jackson sat back down, furious for different reasons. Don Miguel recalled his energy, easing the atmosphere a little. "Now, boys," he warned in a soft condescending tone, that set shivers down their spines, "play nice."

Sloane gasped, smiling at her husband. "Where was Don Miguel when these kids were growing up?"

Pablo raised his eyebrows, in appreciation. "We could still use him, whenever they're all at home at the same time." They laughed softly.

Throughout the whole exchange, Salomé's sweet voice had kept singing the song, making a plea. She caught Gaitano's eye once again. *"No need to read between the lines, spelled out for you… Just hear this song 'cause you can't go wrong with your values…"*

Shayla joined her and their voices soared in wonderful harmony. *"A woman, woman, woman, woman's worth."* The room held its collective breath.

Salomé reminded them once more. *"'Cause a real man knows a real woman when he sees her..."*

Don Miguel turned to his nephew. His words slow and measured. "Carlos... Juan... Miguel..." He waited for the young man to look at him. "Is that your happiness, crossing the sand, disappearing into the night?"

"And a real woman knows a real man ain't afraid to please her..."

Carlos stood up, once again. "You are right, Tío..."

"A real woman knows a real man always comes first..."

"I am going to find my happiness." Carlos looked at Indio. Indio nodded, his eyes fixed on his brother. "Take care of us," the pirate told the brave. And then, he, too, was gone into the twilight.

"A real man just can't deny a woman's worth..."

Marina took a deep breath. She had thought ahead, when she didn't finish her peace pipe, earlier with Caribe. Now she did. Slowly, she felt herself relax a little. She didn't want to think about anything but the dying light, and the ocean in front of her. She sighed. The rollercoaster of emotions she had been on, almost since the day had started, was now taking a toll. Raking her fingers through her hair suddenly, she flung her head back, tears slipping out. She felt like screaming. When she looked ahead again, there he was.

"I said, you are blocking my view," she growled at the dark silhouette.

He chuckled. "There's not much of a view left, at this hour."

"It's still my view."

He crouched down until he was eye level with her. "I have a better view."

Marina didn't say anything for a moment. Finally, curiosity got the best of her. "Where?"

He shrugged and spread his hands, his movements careful. "I can't explain to you, right now, but I can show you."

She shook her head at him. Her tear-filled voice broke. "Why should I go with you?"

Carlos shrugged again. "You don't have to," he murmured. "If I were you, my rage would be so deep by now, that I definitely wouldn't go with me." Looking down, he let his knuckles graze sofly the back of her hand. Startled, she jerked it back. He sighed. "We have to talk."

"Oh, so *now*, you're ready..." Her eyes shot daggers at him. "What if I don't want to," she taunted.

"You don't have to," he repeated. "Just listen." Sighing, he straightened up, holding out his hand. "Come with me..."

Marina looked down at his hand. "No."

Carlos' eyes bore into hers, through the last veil of dusk. "Yes."

Marina stood up. "No!" Feeling as if her beautiful tent were closing in on her, she pushed past him and stepped outside. Over the horizon, the sun was sinking quickly, a big red, liquid ball. She stared at it for a moment, caught up with the beauty of it, her heart sinking with it. She turned to the man who was now standing next to her. "You can't make me."

"Yes, I can." His eyes shot purple sparks from the sunset rays. "I won't, though." He began walking backwards, towards the jungle. "I just don't want to be alone tonight," he admitted.

"I don't either," she confessed miserably.

His eyes pleaded. "Come with me..." He held out his hand, as she followed in a daze, looking down at it.

Her hazel eyes searched his. "I am not happy..." she wailed quietly.

He stopped, making her almost stumble, as she halted suddenly, so as not to touch him. "Neither am I..."

Marina's hand drifted toward his, before she caught it. "So, we'll just be two miserable people?" She squeezed her eyes shut, choking on a sob.

Carlos reached for her hand, meeting it halfway. "No," he said slowly. "We will make each other happy..."

Marina searched his eyes for a moment. Then she put her hand in his.

Someone had thoughtfully placed a tiki torch at the entrance of the path into the jungle. Carlos grabbed it, and went in a little ways, before veering off towards the beach again. They trudged through the sand in silence for a few minutes. When Marina finally looked up, they were in front of the ancient lighthouse.

Marina stopped and looked up at the stone structure. She had come only once before, Carlos had brought her, but it had been lighter than it was now.

She glanced at the pirate suspiciously. "I thought you said this was abandoned."

Carlos nodded. "I did. It was." He tugged at the heavy door, making it creak and groan. Right inside, was a small table with candles and matches. He stopped for a moment, to light a candle.

"Is this your place?" she asked, as he reached for her hand once more.

"Kind of," he answered evasively, stepping unto the first step. He tugged at her hand.

The spiral staircase curved against the inside of the smooth stone walls of the lighthouse, leaving empty space in the middle. The railing was a small stone wall, curving with the stairs. They began chasing their own shadows up. After a while, Marina just stopped looking around, and settled for following the man's back. Finally, he stopped. She waited until he moved ahead, to finish her last stairs. There was a small clearing, with holes cut out in the stone, facing the ocean. It was dark by now, though, the only remainder of daylight, a pale line laying directly on the horizon. To the side, there was another heavy door. Carlos opened this one also, and preceded her into a room. Marina followed, and stood still as he shut the door behind her. Without saying a word, the pirate circled the room, lighting all the candles. These were set at strategic places, the better to highlight certain aspects of the airy space. By the time he was back at her side, Marina was in shock.

The room wasn't very large, being right under the top of the lighthouse. But it was quite spectacular. Someone had taken great care in decorating it. An eclectic mix of art pieces and artifacts spoke of travels to foreign lands. The walls were hung with mirrors and colorful canvases depicting life at sea, life in the village. A portion of the round wall was dedicated to pencil sketches. On closer inspection, they became portraits of the both of them. The pirate and herself. Carlos Gaitano and Marina Aguilar.

Marina stopped. Carlos stood by her side, quietly gazing at the gallery. Marina shook her head, amazed. There was one of the last time they went to Arrecife. It was of when they were basking in the sun, lost in an embrace, their arms tightly wrapped around each other.

They had never seen Caribe, but he had obviously happened upon them. Another was of the morning after El Luto, Marina wrapped in a sheet, asleep, her head in the pirate's lap. His fingers were in her hair, his gaze out over the ocean, traces of a sleepless night around his eyes. Next to that was one of their laughing reflections in the mirror behind the bar at the Siren's Lair, Max between them. There was one of them doing forms aboard La Gitana, and yet another of them dancing with the natives. There was even one of the pirate holding her hand up high, slipping on the turquoise beads, in front of a cave full of pirates.

These were all beautifully placed around what in her father's culture is known as a *coqueta*, a vanity table. Rustic, made of bamboo, it had a glass top with beautiful crystal cut perfume holders, with glass stoppers. The mirror was strategically placed, so as to reflect the bed behind it, and the ocean view beyond it. The bench was low, with a woven seat. Next to that, were a couple of shelves, filled with books. Besides that, was a beautiful desk, carved out of driftwood. The top was made of a small sheet of glass. It held a globe, maps, and books. The chair was covered in a leopard skin. A small area had been filled with baby toys. There was a chest full of rich fabrics, and exotic blankets and rugs. A small table under the windows held an assortment of spy glasses and kaleidoscopes. A beautiful crucifix hung over the door. Next to that, a collection of tribal masks from Africa. The hammock in this room matched the leopardskin at the desk. And in the middle of this room, this incredibly beautiful showroom, was the bed. Queen size, four poster, it was made out of carved logs. Suspended from the ceiling, there were cascades of gauzy black mosquito netting, draping over the bed, giving it total, and absolute privacy. Facing the bed, the beautiful carved frame mirror Carlos bought her in Carey.

Marina sighed, looking around her in a daze. "Whose place is this, Carlos?"

The pirate looked around him, just as impressed as she was. He hadn't gotten a chance to see the end result of the lighthouse's transformation, until then. "It is ours."

Marina shook her head, not understanding. "Ours?"

Carlos looked at her, and nodded. "If you'll have me."

"Have you?" Marina tossed her head and walked away from him a few steps. "You weren't even talking to me!"

"I was in shock, Marina, please forgive me..."

"You are a brat!"

Carlos stayed silent for a moment. He had to think about it. Finally, he agreed. And he saw a way towards redemption. "Yes, I am," he said softly, "and you are the only one who understands me---"

"I don't get it," she interrupted, rudely. "What got you so upset?" she asked. "That I am a visitor, or that you didn't know that I am a visitor?"

Carlos pressed his lips together, and nodded. This was as good a place to begin, as any. "Neither," he began, putting out some candles. "Both," he shrugged, finishing his circuit, and going towards the hammock. The pillows on this one matched the one on hers, over by Villa Azul. Sweeping most of them away, Carlos flung himself into the hammock, swinging himself slowly. "That you didn't tell me you were a visitor..."

It was Marina's turn to shrug. "When? Where?" She went to the bed, and sat on the edge, raking her fingers through her hair. "How was I going to tell you, Carlos? Our time together is always so limited. Most of it is spent working. It seems to me, as if ships haven't stopped coming to Encantada, for a while!"

Carlos frowned. "You're right. You have been working steadily for days, now."

Marina sighed, rubbing her hands over her face. *"La Sirena, Sea Gypsy, La Gaviota, La Diosa del Mar, Ocean Wind, Kalahari, Chymera, Black Mermaid..."* She sighed again. "It doesn't end..."

Carlos sighed. "I know what you mean." He swung himself absently, all of a sudden lost in thought. "Have you ever wanted to just... change? To do something different, spend time with other people..."

Marina began laughing. The irony was not lost on her. Finally, she controlled herself. "This is it, baby," she explained sadly. "This is exactly that, for me. The only thing is, I never asked for this..."

Carlos frowned. "Is it a bad experience?"

"No," she admitted. "Not all of it." She laughed softly. "Some parts, I could do without."

Carlos chuckled. "I am sure..."

"Some parts have been terrifying---"

"How did you get here?"

Marina turned her head to gaze at him. His eyes met hers steadily. He was genuinely interested. "It was an accident."

He stayed silent for a while, just swinging and searching her eyes. He sighed. He would have to keep up his end of the conversation if he was to find out anything about this woman. "An accident..." he frowned. "Was anyone hurt?"

She shook her head sadly, her words barely audible. "Not yet..." She pushed herself off the bed and went to stand in front of the mirror, close enough so she could see out the window. Over the ocean, the light had faded until only the memory was left. Stars in the sky shone brighter and stronger, as the night progressed. "Not that kind of accident," she explained, turning around to face him once more. "It was a mistake," she shrugged, beginning to walk around the room again, slowly. "We were on Spring Break. That's a celebration among late teenagers and people in their early twenties, who are in school for a higher education. They go to the beaches of the country in droves, half naked, for a week or so, out to have..." she laughed to herself, shaking her head at the image she had created for herself. The pirate listened to her in silence. "...a very good time." Her eyes met his with wicked amusement, as she smacked her lips. "Fun... and sin... in the sun "

Carlos smiled slowly. "Do you, Marina... partake of any of this sin in the sun?"

Her eyes sparkled as she laughed. "No... I would like to, with you, though," she murmured before she could stop herself. He grinned. She shrugged. "Sorry, just the fun!" She reached down and picked up a kaleidoscope, turning it over in her hands slowly, the brass cylinder shining in the candlelight. Momentarily distracted, she changed the subject. "A visitor must have brought these over. You must have gotten them from Leila."

The pirate was impressed. "How did you know?"

Marina smiled, pointing it at him. "I collect these, myself. Do you realize they haven't even been invented yet?" Sighing, she continued her story. "Actually, we are a little bit older than that crowd. We just went to watch, so to speak. Lose ourselves in the anonymity of a sea of strangers." She aimed the kaleidoscope at the candle flame, and put her eye to it. She gasped softly, as she began turning it slowly. Smiling at him, she put it down and picked up another. "We live together at home, and at school. We have our own place which we share with Xaira, Derek and Tyler. They're our best friends. The three of us are studying hard, so we can take over our parents' companies, when the time is right." She shrugged. "We needed a break." Putting the second kaleidoscope to her eye, she gasped again. When she looked at him, it was with the thrill of a small child. "You've got to check these out, baby, they're awesome!" Taking the both of them, she passed them to him, waiting for him to catch up, as she picked up a third one. "Salomé and I were invited on a boat ride to a small island, for a picnic. There was supposed to be a whole group of people going. *Jackson* was supposed to be going. He got detained, however, and never showed up. Once Salomé and I found ourselves on the boat, we realized it was just us, with these two guys we knew from school, but not very well, and not personally. So, we get to the island and we play it cool for a while, but then these two jerks went on the boat to have some alcohol, and do some drugs..." She peered into the new kaleidoscope and sighed happily, passing it to him.

"When you say drugs, do you mean as in the peace pipe?"

Marina laughed. "Oh, no, baby, the peace pipe is medicine." Another kaleidoscope caught her attention, and she investigated its interior for a moment. "I mean, *drugs*, like you have no business taking when you are out on the ocean, under the sun, in the middle of nowhere, alone with a couple of women." She looked straight into his eyes. "The kind of thing that warps your mind and makes you think wrong, decide worse, and go ahead and do stupid shit. *That's* what I'm talking about..."

Carlos just looked at her. "Did you kick their asses?" he asked, genuinely curious.

"No… We just showed them a couple of really cool pieces of driftwood we found. They didn't bother us after that."

"What did they do?"

"They abandoned us there…"

The pirate frowned. "You were *marooned?*"

"We found a cave in the cliffs on the other side of town." She gazed into the last kaleidoscope and handed it to him. "That night there was a storm…"

"So is the cave the gateway?"

Marina thought about it for a moment, searching his turquoise blue eyes. "It must be," she finally agreed. "The next morning, we woke up in Encantada." She gathered all the kaleidoscopes out of his hands, and placed them carefully, back where they belonged. She looked out the window again for a moment.

Carlos sighed as he gazed at her back. The candlelight shimmered on the black silk of her dress. The embroidery stood out, as it accentuated her figure. His eyes caressed her curves, meeting hers when she finally turned around again. "What is your very first experience in Encantada?"

"Caribe."

"I am jealous."

Marina tossed her head back with laughter. "No, you're not! You are a brat!"

Carlos laughed with her, taunting her. "Come here and say that."

Marina shook her head. "No, *amigo*, I'm not making it that easy…"

He shrugged, enjoying playing with her. "I try…"

"Nice try…" She went back around the bed, to the *coqueta* behind it.

Drawing the bench out to sit on it, she smiled, making herself comfortable. Looking in the mirror, she caught him gazing at her across the length of the bed. He smiled back. She picked up the first bottle of perfume, holding it up to the candlelight, admiring the beautifully cut glass. "Caribe came looking for us," she explained. "We thought we had been saved…" Unstopping the bottle, she breathed deeply from the fragrance. It was intoxicating. Musky and secret. It made her think of sex in the dark, under sheets. Meeting his eyes in the mirror, she arched an eyebrow at him, holding up the bottle for him to see better. The pirate had the decency to shrug, shamefaced. She put the bottle back, picking up another, never breaking eye contact with him. When she finally laughed, it was soft and husky. "Are you trying to seduce me, Carlitos?"

Carlos nodded happily, winking at her. He looked like a young boy who just discovered what it was all about. "I can only try, Marina..."

The perfume in her hands made her frown. "This one reminds me exactly of Mami," she murmured, a puzzled frown creasing her forehead.

The pirate nodded, swinging happily. "It was her choice."

Marina didn't say anything, for a moment, thinking. Suddenly, she remembered. "Did my moms help you hook this place up?"

He nodded again, secrets twinkling deep in his eyes. "And mine..."

She sighed. "That's what all those meetings were about, at the Lair, and everything..." She shook her head at herself in the mirror. "So, they've been doing this for a while?"

"They have put a whole lot of effort into it, Marina. For you, for us..."

Marina stared at him. "Okay," she said slowly. "Let's see how this turns out..."

His eyes narrowed at her in the mirror, as he warned her. "I already placed my bet with Giancarlo."

She laughed wickedly. "So did I."

Surprised, he didn't say anything for a moment. He couldn't tell if she was playing with him or not, only that she delighted in saying certain things to get certain reactions. Happy, he reminded her what they were discussing. "What happens when Caribe finds you?"

"He takes us home to Leila, shows us around town, a little bit, and takes us home to Leila again. This time, we have all the right questions, and are ready, kind of, to hear all the right answers."

"How did you take it?"

"Not very well at all." Suddenly restless, she stood up from the *coqueta*, almost dropping the bottle of perfume in her hand. She seemed to glide around him once more, this time to the desk, right next to the hammock. "We pretended we were living a dream."

"When did it get any easier?"

Marina frowned, thinking. She reached over the beautiful glass, to spin the globe. "Salomé met Indio. That took care of it for her. And she started working for Dominique Swan. All of a sudden, she had a job and a boyfriend." She brought her hands together slowly, almost caressing the globe to a stop. Turning it in her hands, she found the Caribbean. Her fingers seemed to caress the sea. "I began taking care of Max. And Juan and Jaime," she grinned. "It definitely kept my mind occupied. But meeting *you...*" She turned her head to look at him. The pirate froze. Their eyes locked. "Meeting you in my pool ---"

He smiled, shaking his head. "*My* pool---"

Marina looked away, shaking her head. "It was bad enough, because it brought home where I was. Reality check. And then you brought the books, and I was home. This is what I know. Books and numbers. This is what I am going to school for. Numbers are in my blood. And that is when it got easier for me. As far as I was concerned, I was just biding my time, until it was time to leave. Having Jackson show up made it all fun and exciting, and the three of us were on an adventure together. And then," her eyes searched his again, "you wanted to take this one step further."

Carlos understood. "I asked you to be my makeout partner."

She nodded. "I was eager and willing. But now, if I decided to leave, it wouldn't affect just me, any longer. Next thing I know, I'm aboard *La Gitana.*"

His heart seemed to sink at the soft accusation in her eyes. "I leave you no choice."

"None," she agreed. "And then, at *El Baile del Luto*, I get these," she said softly. Raising her left arm, she rolled the turquoises back and forth on it, the rich color tumbling against her sunkissed skin. "Now, you are almost my man..."

"I want to be---"

"Why?"

Carlos just looked at her. His eyes ate her up, her face searing into his memory. "Why not?" He swung harder, exasperated. "You should see all this from my perspective. You show up in my life, as an answer to a prayer. I didn't ask for you, either. I asked for a sign." He looked beyond her, out to the blackness over the ocean. "I have been tired with my life for a while. Something was wrong, or missing. I couldn't decide which." He sighed, remembering. "I was away in Carey when you came in on the storm. I had just discovered the discrepancies with the books. I couldn't figure out what was going on, but it made sense in some other things not adding up. And then I get told that I stand to lose Encantada. So I come back, to straighten my mind out. I come home to discover that Indio can barely think straight, his mind is on the new girl in town. Next thing I know, I find you in my pool..." He looked at her again. " I stopped asking why, a long time ago, Marina. Instead, I started giving thanks..."

Marina thought on his words for a moment. "I never thought of staying, Carlos. The job offer Don Carlos is teasing me with is more than tempting. It would be an incredible experience for me to go work for him. It would do amazing things to my career, so to speak." She looked at him again. "But I need to be clear on what and whom am I staying for, if it were to come to that. It's just not on my agenda."

The pirate nodded, making the hammock stop. Climbing out, he walked around to the other side of the desk, making her turn to look at him. Reaching below it, he came up with a bottle of wine, and two glasses. Their eyes met. They smiled. He poured the wine for them, handing her one of the glasses. He held his up to the candlelight, never looking away from her eyes. "To storms," he said softly, "and the impact they have on our lives..."

Marina's heart skipped a beat, as she felt herself falling into the twin pools of his eyes. She couldn't breathe. "To storms," she whispered. She was going to drown. They touched rims, and drank from their glasses.

Carlos sighed in appreciation and finally looked away, going back to the hammock. He sank into it gratefully once more, pushing himself off with a boot against the corner of the bed, swinging happily. "Tell me about the men in your life," he said suddenly, unexpectedly.

Marina almost choked. Her eyes watered, and she gasped for air. When she could finally breathe, she took a small sip, swallowing carefully. She blinked the unwanted tears out of her eyes, before meeting his amused ones. "The *men* in my life?" she repeated, dismayed at his nod. "Okay," she said slowly. "Where do I begin?" She thought for a moment. "Pablo is *mi papá*. My father, my dad. I come from him. He has my heart. Pablo Aguilar is the kind of man I want, *exactly*, for myself. I swear, I want one, just like him. Papi is my king." She waited for him to nod. "Joe is my dad. He has helped raise me. He is also my father. My guide. He is Dad. He is the king's right hand, his brother. Second only to Papi, I owe him the same respect." She took another sip of wine, rolling the taste around in her mouth before swallowing. She felt good. Comfortable. Relaxed in his company. "Jackson is my brother. He is the Banks' and the Aguilars' firstborn, coming via Joe and Shayla. I had a crush on him when I was a little girl, and almost died when I was told I could never marry him. Jackson told me I had something with him no woman he could end up with, would ever hope to have. I was his *sister*. I shared childhood memories and milestones with him. We did everything but get romantic together, and nobody could ever take that away from me, no matter what."

Carlos thought on her words. "He is right."

Marina smiled. "He is. So, I'm cool..." She waved her hand in the air. "Then there are the twins, Catamaran and Deveraux Azure. We call them Blue and Cat. They're our older cousins on Dad's side, sons of Lisa, his older sister. Papi and Dad raised them from babies, because their parents lost their lives soon after they were born. Cat's my godfather. And my boss. I do the same thing for him that Indio does for Giancarlo at the Lair. I am a bartender at his club," her voice trailed off as tears stung her eyes. "And then there's Uncle Jesse. He's married to Dad's younger sister, Rain. He's a tattoo artist going by the name of Snake Coltrane. I adore him..." She sighed. "Then there's Derek and Tyler, our housemates. They are the sons of my parents' lawyer, Shane Butler. Really cool guys. You'll like them," she added, unaware of the tense she just used. She sighed again. "Jackson, Salomé, and I are best friends." She looked off into space, murmuring to herself. "*Athos, Porthos, and Aramis...*" Sighing, she dragged her fingers through her hair. "And of course, Xaira, who is like our baby sister and also shares house with us would be *D'Artagnan*," she murmured to herself.

Carlos frowned. "Who are they?"

Marina laughed, delighted. "A French writer wrote a masterpiece about swordsmen. *The Three Musketeers.* It is a story about devotion and skill, and all kinds of guy stuff. Alexandre Dumas wrote this extraordinary tale between 1844 and 1845. Hasn't happened yet." She smiled. "Their motto was *"One for all, and all for one."*

The pirate laughed. "That sounds about right. Jackson wants to jump on me over you!"

"Of course he does!" She smiled to herself, at something only she could see. "I'm his baby, his little sister, his best friend!" She nodded to herself. "Jackson wants to see me happy..."

"*I* will make you happy," he growled at her.

"You have been making me unhappy all day long! That's all Jackson has been seeing!"

"I have been making *myself* miserable!"

Marina stared at him, aghast. "And what need did you ever have to go and do that?"

"I thought you had made a fool of me..."

"No, you just made a fool out of *yourself...*"

He glared at her. She glared right back. "What about the men in your life, here in Encantada?"

"With or without you?"

The pirate thought for a moment. Already her brow was smoothing over, caught up in their conversation. He felt his begin to relax, also. "Without counting me."

Marina laughed. "That's easy," she scoffed, snapping her fingers. "Caribe, Max, and Indio. In exactly that order." She thought some more. "Don Carlos, Solomon, Giancarlo, and Juan and Jaime."

She looked at him. "It depends on their order of importance, and how much time I spend with them. Don Miguel..." She shrugged.

"Who's the most important?"

"Caribe." She answered automatically, smiling as he frowned. "If it weren't for Caribe, I couldn't be here." She laughed softly, pushing herself away from the desk. Brushing past him, she walked over to the baby toys. She picked up a stuffed bunny, made of real wool. "Max... keeps me anchored. Whenever I am with him, I have no time to think about myself. It's all about him. I am his protector and his caregiver. I am in charge, and responsible for him. I just get on *mamá* mode..." she shrugged. "When I have Juan and Jaime also, forget it! We are not going anywhere. There is more than enough available at my place to keep us all busy." She picked up two more stuffed toys and held them all in her arms. Hugging the three toys against her chest, she snuggled them, for a moment. "I love being with the babies!"

Carlos smiled. "That is something we need to talk about."

She slid him a look, out of the corner of her eye. "Not right now!"

He nodded in agreement. "What about Indio?"

Marina dropped her toys, and pushed them back into their corner, with her foot. "Indio's my dog..." She smiled. "He's my buddy. My sister's boyfriend. He's the one I get to talk most of the numbers, with. Indio listens to me, and that's pretty cool. Besides, he can hang with the fact that we are visitors..." She peered at him from under her eyelashes. "Solomon is my fighting partner. He understands when I need to get hurt, and when I need to hurt someone back. He's always willing to hurt me. That's pretty cool," she sighed happily. "In exchange, I get to let go. It's a fine relationship. Solomon keeps me balanced."

"You realize I can make Solomon go away, and you would never see him again, don't you?"

Marina stared at him aghast. *"You would do that?"* Shaking her hair out of her face, she put her hands on her hips. "That's like cutting off your nose to spite your face!" She shook her head, disappointed. "Your own Boatswain... and just so *I* don't get to play with him." She looked at him steadily, trying to comprehend. "Why would you do something like that?"

The pirate looked at her steadily. He decided to confess. "I am jealous."

"That is *your* problem," she informed him, eyes shooting sparks at him.

"No more fighting."

"Sorry. It's in my blood."

"No more fighting," he repeated, his voice a warning growl.

"Says who?"

"*I* say..."

Marina shrugged. "Don't give me a reason to fight, then." She walked to the opposite side of the hammock. "It is not what I would rather be doing..."

Carlos smiled slowly, understanding the implications, wanting to make sure. "What would you rather be doing?"

Marina smiled to herself. "Not fighting..."

The pirate laughed. "May I not fight with you?"

She laughed into his eyes. "Maybe later." She ducked under the hammock, going back to sit on the edge of the bed.

"Tell me about your first man..."

Marina shook her head, not believing she had heard right. "My first man?"

"Your first partner... boyfriend... lover..."

Marina laughed. "You mean my only..." She felt herself reeling back with the memory. Shaking herself, she rubbed her arms hard, bringing herself back fast. She looked at the pirate, in dismay. "There's not much to tell..."

Carlos smiled. "Tell me, as your best friend. I shall pass no judgment on you. I am just curious..." he said softly.

Marina nodded. "I haven't been with anyone, in years." She frowned. "When I was a teenager, I wanted to learn how to do..." her eyes flew to his, "certain things." She raked her fingers through her hair, distracting them both, momentarily. "It had been established that it couldn't be with Jackson, so I settled for the next best thing. One of Jackson's best friends."

"What's his name?"

"*Sheik...*" Taking a deep breath, she let it out shakily. "We hung out for a while, clear that we were way too young for anything remotely serious. But we really loved and respected each other. He was a cool guy. And that's as far as it got. We were friends, who fooled around a couple of times. Mainly just holding hands and smooching, without anything hard core. He taught me a couple of things, and that was it."

"How did it end?"

Marina gazed at him sadly. "Sheik lost his life. He was a really nice, confused guy who made a few bad choices, and found himself at the wrong place, at the wrong time." She sighed. "After that, I haven't found anybody I want to spend any time with, so I concentrated on my education, and on my father's business." Tears stung her eyes, making her blink them back. "His older brothers are still in our lives, though. Kahn, Raj and Omar. All three work for Cat."

"Do you miss him?"

"Terribly..."

"Any other lovers since Sheik?"

"None..." She blinked back tears. "We weren't really lovers, though. We just loved each other..." She searched for words. "We weren't together enough, sexually, to have been lovers..."

Carlos nodded. "What do you want to do with the rest of your life?"

Marina shrugged sadly. "I don't know," she admitted. "I thought I knew, all the way down to when I'm a little old lady." She laughed. "Not anymore, though. Now, I have no idea what I want!"

"So, what was your life plan, until now?"

"Until now?" she repeated in wonder. "Go to school, get a degree, and go to work for Papi. Find Mr. Right, or pray that he finds me, hook up..." She leaned back on her hands, gazing up at the source of the cascades of netting around the bed. "Eventually get married, and have a kid or two, if things go well. Have a dog, a nice house, a couple of cars..." Catching his frown, she waved her hand in dismissal. "But way, deep down, inside, I have always asked myself if

I'll achieve all of these goals, or if I will lack in one or more of them."
She looked at him. "It's kind of scary, to think about it."

The pirate agreed. "Life can be scary, at times. It's up to us to tackle it in whichever way we see fit. That defines us as the kind of person we are..."

Restless, she tossed her head back, her hair flying around her face. "What do *you* want to do, Carlos? Think about it," she said softly. "For the rest of your life... what is the one thing you would like to do?"

The pirate looked at her steadily. "Live happy."

Marina stared at him. He wasn't trying to convince her of anything, and he certainly wasn't lying to her. His face was smooth, but for the shadow along his cheeks and his jaw. Hands behind his head, he was the perfect picture of rest and relaxation. His eyes were warm, burning with a steady blue fire. Her heart felt as if it were melting in her chest. She nodded. "Me too, papi," she murmured. "Live happy..."

"I want to see all of you," he said, suddenly. She was still upset, he could see that. He needed a way to distract her quickly.

Marina gazed back at him. "What's in it for me?"

The pirate smiled. "You won't know until then..."

She nodded. "I want to see all of you too, but..." she smiled at his confused expression. "I like a challenge." She came nearer. "Let's play a game."

"A game?" Curiosity got the best of him.

She nodded again. "A game." Smiling at him, she gazed deep into his eyes. "It's called *Truth*." She had his full attention.

"*Truth?*" He didn't care what it was called, as long as he got to see her. "How do you play?"

Marina laughed. "Very carefully..." Her eyes sparkled wickedly. "You get to ask one question at a time, and you are supposed to get only, and nothing but the truth. The person has the option to not answer, however, but then, they have to take off a piece of clothing..."

Carlos grinned. "Let's play, baby..." Abandoning the hammock, he refilled their glasses of wine. Outside, a wind had begun blowing, sending shadows chasing each other along the rounded walls.

Coming back, he handed her a glass, raising his silently. She touched hers to his, and they drank. He sank down on the beautiful leopardskin chair, facing her. "You should start," he suggested. "I have on more clothes than you."

Marina laughed again. "Okay, I will." She looked into his eyes, searching. "Have you ever had anything with one of the lady pyrates?" She smiled, as he almost choked.

Carlos sputtered for a moment, before he realized she was serious. "Anything?" He shook his head happily. "No, mami, nothing at all…"

"Ever?"

"Never." He leaned back, enjoying himself immensely. "No marriage, no child, no love affair, not even a kiss on the cheek…"

Marina frowned. "Not even Rouge?"

He rolled his eyes. "Of course, Rouge, as far as a kiss on the cheek… only…" He took a good look at her. "Are you jealous, Marina?"

She shrugged. "Not of Rouge."

He laughed. "You shouldn't be. Rouge and Giancarlo have loved each other deeply, since we were all wild teenagers, hanging out. They are now coming together, fulfilling this love they have both denied each other their whole lives. Rouge is a lady at heart, though," he explained. "Once they get together, it will be a very powerful union. There are pirates in these waters that aren't very happy about it. They need to move with caution. Neither is willing to get the other killed, because of someone's envy and jealousy. So they play it cool, as you like to say. Staying away from one another is tearing them apart, though. They can't live without each other."

Marina nodded, thankful for the insight. "I can tell." She gazed at him for a moment, letting her eyes caress the lines of his face, the darkness of his hair. "What would you do if you were Giancarlo?"

A small frown appeared on his brow, and was just as quickly erased. "If I were Gian?" He raised his eyebrows at a private thought and sighed. "As deep as his feelings are for Rouge, I would have already hooked up."

"She's that good a catch?"

The pirate whistled under his breath. "United, they will form an empire."

Marina shook her head, smiling. "And have incredible looking children together."

"Very rich children together."

"I understand all the caution," she told him, "but I, as you, would have already hooked up, also."

Carlos smiled at her, true affection for her shining in the depths of his eyes. "Lady pyrates are not my type."

"Good. I'm not the lady pyrate type."

"That's what I like best about you." Their eyes locked. "My turn." He smiled as she took another sip of wine. "Before you met me," he began slowly, "were you planning on going back home?"

"Yes."

"Are you still planning on returning?"

Marina hesitated, feeling like a deer caught in headlights. "It's hard to explain..."

"Try."

She opened her mouth to speak, but closed it, afraid the wrong words would come out. Instead, she slipped the leather sandals off her feet, and sat back. "I don't know how to answer that, right now. You better ask me later."

Carlos nodded. "All right. It is your turn, then."

Marina smiled. "Were you with anyone when we met?"

"No one at all." He smiled, relaxed. "How about you?"

This time, it was she who rolled her eyes. "In my dreams..."

"Do you dream about me?"

Marina stared at him for a moment, choosing her words carefully. "I have dreams with you in them..."

Carlos laughed. "That's not what I asked. Now, answer the question..." he coaxed, as he would a child.

Marina looked down, thinking hard. Then she looked at him again, shaking the hair out of her face. Without saying a word, she took the eagle feather out of her hair and put it on the bed next to her. "I have the right to remain silent..."

The pirate shrugged. "That suits me fine." He chuckled. "The sooner I get to see you."

She smiled. "What is the most important thing to you in life?"

"The most important?" he repeated.

She nodded, eyes wide. "The *most* important."

"God."

Marina shook her head, not believing she had heard right. He hadn't even thought about it. Finally, a man who understood how things worked. Smiling into his eyes, she held her hand in front of him. Quietly, they slid each other some skin. "What's next?" she asked. "After God, in your life. Here, on this Earth, with all its physical boundaries and chains, what is the most important thing in life?"

Carlos looked at her for a moment in silence. Then, he sighed. Reaching down, he began taking off his boots. "Health," he said softly. Once the boots were off, he slipped off the scabbard with his sword in it. "Family." His knife was next. "Love." Muscles rippled, as off came the white shirt. "Life." He reached for his pants.

Marina snapped out of her trance, putting her hand over his. "Hey, baby! Whoa!" She laughed at the expression on his face. "What do you think you're doing?"

He smiled. "None of those things are the most important." He shrugged. "I just wanted to have as many clothes on, as you do." He winked at her.

She gasped. "You are a very sneaky pirate."

Laughter burst out of him. Finally, he looked at her, fire raging in his eyes, as they slipped down her body. "Sneaky wasn't the word I was thinking of," he informed her.

Marina leaned back on one hand, and took another sip of wine, without taking her eyes off him. "Nasty?" she raised an eyebrow.

This time, he drank from his wine, trying to stop laughing. "That wasn't the word I was thinking of, either." He grinned. "Close, though..."

Marina rolled her eyes and shook her head. Finally, she looked at him, grinning. "You..." she told him, "are such a boy!"

Carlos laughed. "I'm honest."

"You sound just like Jackson. You, all, are tweaked. It must be the testosterone. There's only one thing on your minds."

"Notice I haven't taken anything else off."

"To my dismay," she laughed.

"Well, at least you're honest."

She nodded. "Notice *I* haven't taken anything else off..."

He laughed. "We can remedy that."

She laughed back. "You can try."

Carlos winked at her. "How bad do you want me?"

Marina froze. *Oh, no, you did NOT just ask me that!* She shook her head. She tried to answer the question. A couple of times. But no words would come out of her mouth. She watched him cock an eyebrow at her, definitely amused. Finally, she took off one of the silver coin chandeliers that hung f rom her ears. Leaning over, she dropped it in his lap. "I have the right to remain silent..." she said softly.

Carlos loved it. He laughed, picking the earring up in his hand, making it tinkle in the candlelit room. The wind outside was a little bit stronger, actually blowing a couple of unlucky candles out. Shadows grew deeper, and fiercer. They kept their eyes on each other. "Since you met me, have you even thought about going back home?" He laughed, as the other earring came flying at him. "Hasn't this just absolutely changed your life?" He caught the bracelet neatly in midair. "Marina..."

"You do not play fair!"

"What is your life plan now?"

She reached down and took off her anklet. "This is it!" She threw it at him.

Carlos caught the flying coins and grinned. "You still have jewelry on," he pointed out.

Her hand flew to her chest. "Don Carlos just gave me this," she said in dismay, fingering the beautiful beads in the cool silver. "I don't want to take it off, yet. It's from Indio," she explained. Holding out her other hand, she let the turquoises roll to her wrist. "These, you will have to take off yourself ---"

"Never," he growled. Carlos took her hand, bringing it to his lips. "I am not," he told her. "When I put them on you, I meant it." He stood up suddenly, towering over her.

Marina slid back on the bed, until she was in the middle. She leaned back on her hands, looking up at him, chest rising, eyes glittering. "I thought you did."

Carlos laughed. "You established the rules..."

She nodded. "I did. I'm not playing anymore..."

He put a knee on either side of her legs, and crawled slowly, as if he were stealthily stalking her. Catching sight of tremors, he laughed wickedly. " *I* am." Reaching her hips, he began lowering himself on her, one arm on either side of her head. "What do you feel for me?" he asked, his voice husky.

Marina gasped, helpless, as she watched him come closer. "What---"

Without warning, he reached down and undid the first tie on her dress, right under her arm. "Too slow," he laughed, his breath warm in her ear.

Marina gasped again, as she felt the fabric sag on her chest. Automatically, her hands went up to catch it. "I---"

"Are you going to leave me, to work for Don Carlos?" Reaching down, he undid the last tie, on her thigh. The dress slid on her body, gratefully. Carlos groaned.

"I should!" she hissed at him, trying to push him away. "What do you feel for me, Gaitano?" she challenged.

The pirate threw his head back and laughed. Pulling back, he towered over her as he straightened up, keeping her firmly between her knees. Looking at her again, he reached down, slowly undoing the buttons of his pants. "I have the right to remain silent..."

Marina slapped at his hands, as they reached for her again. "Whatever!"

Catching hers, he held them over her head, lowering his chest down on her. He rubbed luxuriously against the soft silk. "Are you still planning to go back home?"

"I don't know," she wailed under her breath, turning her face away from him. She squeezed her eyes shut, as the pirate, reaching down, undid another tie.

"How bad do you want me, Marina?", and he undid the last tie. Marina took a deep breath. His hand caught her face and turned it to look at him. The pirate gazed into her eyes for a moment. "I want you..."

"And I, you," she whispered. And then she couldn't speak anymore. Her mouth was too busy, overwhelmed by his.

Marina sighed shakily. Her senses screamed as he stroked her chest. Straddling her once again, he sat up, looking down at her. His hands reached for her once more. Catching the soft folds of her dress, he peeled it off her, even going as far as raising her hips to slip it out from under her. Without looking, he let it fall, a shimmery pool of silk next to the bed.

Carlos groaned as he looked down at her. Moving to one side of her, he began rubbing her whole body. He smiled, as she purred, arching against his hands, eyes closed, smile dancing on her lips. He laughed, as she absently reached for him, tugging at his pants. He stopped what he was doing for a moment, and soon they were on the floor, next to her dress. As he turned towards her, she sat up, and put her hands on his shoulders. Gladly, he switched positions with her, until he was on his back, her soft hands rubbing his whole body. He laughed with the abandon of a boy, he couldn't help himself. His eyes sparkled at her. He groaned again. "I have never wanted anything so bad," he admitted huskily.

Marina arched an eyebrow at him, her hands swirling patterns on his chest and belly. "A woman?" Dipping her head, her tongue explored his navel for a moment.

Sliding his fingers inside her hair, he raised her head, to look at him. "No, not just a woman," he smiled into her eyes.

Marina smiled back knowingly, and put her hands over his. "Never?" Guiding his hands, she brought her head down again, this time lower. Without saying another word, she took him in her mouth, delighting in his moans. Taking her hands off his, she let his hands guide her, as she devoured him. *I have never wanted anything so bad.* The pirate's hips bucked against her face, his groans snatched by the wind whipping around the room. The shadows on the walls were graphic, leaving nothing to the imagination, as the woman feasted on the pirate. Her moans matched his, as her lips and tongue drained him of all thought, leaving him a quivering mass of pure feeling.

Not being able to stop himself any longer, the pirate moved, dragging her off him. He switched their positions once more, taking off her panties, and placing himself between her legs. Spreading them, he looked at her across the length of her torso. "Never," he answered huskily. His hands caressed the backs of her thighs, as he peered down at her. Her legs began shaking. Catching them, he dipped his head, his tongue doing a long and slow exploration. Marina moaned. He chuckled, and blew on her, watching her skin react to his caress. She started thrashing. Catching her, the pirate held her tight against his face. He pleased her. His tongue teased and tickled the very center of her being. His lips explored the core of her sex. Her fingers tangled in his hair, holding him fast against her, as her body responded to him. Feeling herself melt, she dragged him up, her body marveling at the feel of his, rubbing against her. His mouth took hers, before he raised his head, his eyes locking with hers. "How bad do you want me, Marina?"

Marina shook her head, at a loss for words. "I don't know," she admitted.

Spreading her legs wider, she tried balancing him between them.

The pirate raised himself on his arms, getting into position. His sex nudged hers gently, seeking the wet heat that so anxiously awaited him. He groaned, as he teased her, dipping gently into her folds, before retreating. Carlos felt her tense beneath him, starting to reach for him. "How bad, Marina?" He held himself off her for a moment, long enough for her to buck her hips against him.

Eyes flashing, she went to push him off her, as she caught his smile. She growled at him, and he caught her hands over her head, his breath intoxicating, against her mouth. Tears came to her eyes, as she felt him nudge against her once more, this time, leaving the tip of his shaft inside. Marina didn't move. She couldn't. All she could do was look up at him. "I want you so bad, Carlos Gaitano," the husky confession tore out of her throat, before she could stop it, "that I will die, if you don't make love to me..."

Carlos chuckled softly, "I feel, Marina Aguilar," giving her a little bit more, "I will die, when I do..."

Marina gasped, freeing her hands to cup his buttocks, holding him against her for a moment. She gave herself even more, tears escaping. "This is all I want!" she cried softly.

Carlos pressed slowly into her, steadily gaining entrance. "Am I hurting you?"

She cried out again. "Just, please, don't stop..." Gripping him hard, she raised her hips to meet his, whimpering in his ear.

Carlos chuckled again. "I couldn't if I wanted to." He lowered his chest on hers, the feel of her nipples exciting him more. "I'm taking you, baby," he growled, making her gasp as he sheathed himself inside her, in one swift motion. Her nails dug into his back, making him smile. "Right here... right now..."

They made love. They looked into each other's eyes, as she contracted around his sex, soaking deep inside her body. They bumped bellies gently, lips glued together, eyes never leaving each other. They breathed deeply, murmuring each other's names. Lips stroked and hands caressed, as their private parts mated, one kneading, the other squeezing. Carlos gently scratched the shadow on his face all over hers, making her laugh softly. Marina wrapped her arms and legs around him, kissing him deeply, as her body shuddered under his. She held him tight, trying to fuse into him, their hearts blending together, beating atop one another. The pirate pleasured himself. He excited her. His body knew what it wanted, seeking depth, heat and moisture. She moaned. He groaned. She licked the hollow of his throat, making him shiver. He moved faster, making her insides melt. The gates opened up, the wave taking them, both. Carlos squeezed her tight, holding her still against him, as his body released his desire into hers. His world tipped, making him lose his balance. Marina gasped his name as he fell against her, her mouth seeking his, so as not to put into words, her thoughts and her feelings. For a while, neither could move. Only their mouths. They kissed until they couldn't breathe. Then, finally, he slipped out of her.

Covering her face with kisses, the pirate excused himself, and had to pry her arms from around his neck, leaving her side for a moment. Marina followed him through slit eyes, admiring the shadows cast on his body, by the candles. She watched as he went to a table by the door, where there was a bowl, a pitcher of water, and some towels. Taking one, he poured some water into the bowl, and dipped the towel in it, wringing it out. Then he took another towel, keeping it dry. Splashing water on himself, he rinsed off, and dried himself with a separate towel. Turning back to her, suddenly, he grinned, as he caught her looking at him.

"Like what you see?"

"Very much..."

Gaitano laughed, posing and flexing for her, as he went from candle to candle, blowing them out. Marina whistled in response to his antics, her hair flying about her head as she waved her arms and blew kisses at him. Once done, the room was left with starlight. Dark enough for secrets, but clear enough to see each other. Finally, reaching her, the pirate threw himself against her, tackling her back on the bed. First, he used the wet towel, wiping her clean. Then, he used the second towel, wiping her dry. Keeping her legs spread, he went exploring, until they were both ready again.

This time, it was different. Their senses pounded until they were out of control. This time, they put the love aside. Keeping out the emotional, it was all physical. Pure raw sex.

They fucked. Their bodies writhed, slapping rhythmically, as their hearts pounded in their chests, against each other. She bit his shoulder, and he pulled her hair. They snarled, panting nasty words in each other's ears. The sweat on their skin let them slide smoother, against one another. Marina, once again, wrapped her arms and legs around him, and held on for the ride. Or for dear life. The pirate relentlessly pounded her into the soft mattress. She caught his mouth, ravishing it, capturing his eyes with hers. Groaning, he closed his eyes, slanting his mouth against hers. Pulses raced. Senses soared. Dragging his mouth from hers, he laughed, before searing a hot, wet trail down her chest. They bit and clawed each other. She moaned, as Carlos clamped his mouth down on her breast. Eyes closed, sucking as hard as he dared, he didn't see the tears fall. Bucking beneath him, Marina tangled her fingers in his hair, dragging his mouth off her. Locking eyes, she realized, he was consumed with passion. Winking at her, the sea robber reached down between them, firmly putting his thumb on her clit. The woman jumped. The pirate laughed. Didn't miss a beat. Still pounding into her, Gaitano began a circular motion on the core of her sex. She clawed at him, as he took her breath away. His voice in her ear dripped pure lust and unrestrained desire. *"Suave, mami..."* Marina gazed into his eyes for a moment, responding, stroke for stroke. Her lips parted with naked pleasure. He licked his, leering at her through a screen of eyelashes. Glimpsing the primitive response in his eyes, she rolled her hips. He whistled under his breath and laughed. Motivated, she did it again. Delighted, he gave her more. Faster. Harder. Suddenly, his mouth was next to her ear. Whispered instructions and husky words of encouragement filled the dark. Inspired, she lowered his head to her other breast. Once again, he sucked hard. His thumb kept rubbing. Marina cried out. Carlos Gaitano rocked her world. Clinging to him, she gasped, as she reached orgasm. Again. Shuddering mightily, he reached his own. With her. Inside her. Wrapping his arms around her, he let himself go. The pirate howled at the wind, in the starlit room. The woman beneath him screamed his name.

    "I don't want to be alone tonight..."
"Marina..."
"Stay with me..."
"...divina..."
"Por favor..."
"...muñeca..."
"Carlos..."
"...preciosa..."

Sleep evaded them. Giving up, they indulged themselves in the new world they had just created for themselves. Darkness embraced them. The pirate and his woman couldn't get enough of each other. So, they didn't settle. They kept exploring, and continued discovering. It was the tip of the iceberg. Their love and desire for each other consumed them both, irrevocably connecting them for life. They felt it and rejoiced, hands and mouths expressing what words could not. By the time the night was over, they were just beginning.

The sun came tentatively, not wanting to intrude. The room lightened slowly, revealing to Marina treasures she hadn't seen the night before. She sighed, looking around her in wonder. There were deep window seats cut into the walls, looking out on a small balcony that went all the way around the lighthouse. Leaving the bed quietly, she went to stand by one of the windows. The sky clung to the last vestiges of darkness. Over the horizon, a crimson line appeared, heralding dawn. Marina sighed again. It had been the night of her life. Feeling her skin prickle, she turned around.

Carlos gazed at her steadily, leaning back on his elbows, eyes hooded. His smile was slow and seductive, pouring into her veins. "What are you doing up?"

Marina smiled back, trying not to melt in the process. *"Ocean Wind, Chymera, Kalahari, Black Mermaid..."*

The pirate threw back his head and laughed. "Wrong, mami, not today..." He chuckled, shaking his head, beckoning at her. "Come here, little girl..." He opened his arms, as she crawled on the bed, towards him. Finally capturing her, he laid her head over his heart. "Hear that?" he whispered. "That is what you do to me, baby, that is what it sounds like." He stroked her hair. "That also means that you are not going anywhere today. I have been planning this for a long time," he admitted. "We are taking the day off. We deserve it. We have a lot to talk about." He smiled, as she sighed in his arms. "If I were you, however, I would get up as soon as possible, and put something decent on..."

"Why?" she murmured.

"Indio will be here any minute."

Marina jumped. It sounded like a crash outside. At the moment, she was sitting on the edge of the bed, facing the mirror from Carey. The pirate sat between her legs, letting himself be pampered as she shaved him. He laughed. "Come in, papi!"

The door banged open, making her jump again. A grunt, a few stomps, and a thump. The brave entered the room, dropping the chest, from last night, next to them. Marina raised her eyebrows at her friend, and smiled, blowing him a kiss before turning back to her task. "*Buenos dias, papi,*" she murmured.

Indio pressed his lips against her forehead, before dropping to the window seat nearest him. He took a deep breath, his night black hair stirring in the morning breeze. The sun kissed him, making him feel warm inside, as he observed his brother and his girl. "*Buenos dias,*" he answered. He grinned. "You are glowing!" he told her.

Marina laughed. She felt good. Carlos' warning had given them enough time to change the bed, and throw open all the windows in their hideaway. The sun had come in first, followed by the ocean breeze. She had spontaneously fashioned a toga, out of a beautiful white silky fabric he found for her, in the chest by the bed. At his insistence, she had put all her jewelry back on. He had helped her pin her hair up, a little, loose free strands framing her face. She had looked so good to him, he had kissed her breath away. Now, she smiled at her sister's boyfriend. "I hope so," she laughed, "it *feels* like I'm glowing..." Turning back to the pirate sitting between her legs, she caught his eyes in the mirror, smiling secretly as she caressed his face.

The pirate's eyes smoldered back at her. "You *are* glowing, mami," he confirmed with a wink.

"*You* look like you have just been brought back to life!" the brave laughed.

Carlos nodded at his brother. "I have been. Before tonight, I was one of the living dead." Taking Marina's hand, he brought it to his mouth, kissing it passionately, as he met his brother's eyes over it. "Now, I am alive..."

Indio nodded. His brother had found his own. "I came to bring the Council's gifts to Marina." He winked at her. "You have all day." Turning back to his brother, he became all business. "Who's going to help me with the Council's ships, while you two play today?"

Gaitano looked at his accountant. "Who can do your job, besides Indio?"

"Pablo." She didn't miss a beat. Passing the razor carefully over his face one last time, she wiped his face with a wet towel. He murmured his thanks, and then they both turned to their guest. Marina looked at Indio. "Papi taught me to do the books. I can send him a note on what to do." At the men's nods, she left her place on the side of the bed, and glided to the desk. "He will do this in a heartbeat, no questions asked." She scribbled on a piece of paper, read what she wrote, and folded it, handing it to Indio. "My dad will do a better job than I do. You can trust him with your eyes closed."

Indio nodded. "We do." His smile faded, as he searched deep into her eyes.

Marina felt a trickle of fear drip down her spine, rapidly cooling her extremities. "What?" she asked softly.

Indio took a deep breath, his eyes capturing hers. "He is coming, Marina." He turned to his brother. "Jack will not let it go. I have never seen him like this. He is concerned to the extent of being afraid. Jack!" He tore his eyes away from his brother. "I don't want to scare you, baby, but we have to talk about this and prepare for it." He sighed sadly. "Not today, but as soon as you get down from this tower." He held out his hand, before letting it drop to his side helplessly. "Xavier is coming..."

Marina shook her head, blinking back tears. "Thank you, baby. I will discuss this with Carlos today."

Indio stood up, turning to leave. Hesitating, he took her hand, pulling her into his arms. There, he held her for a moment, catching a silent sob with his chest. He crooned to her in what must have been his mother's language. Marina squeezed her eyes shut, trying to keep in the tears. His voice murmured in her ear, like the wind whispering in the bamboo grove. "You really are glowing..."

He pressed a kiss to her face, before meeting his Captain's eyes. A flicker, a nod, and he was gone.

Marina sat in the window seat Indio just vacated. She looked out over the ocean for a while, sunlight caressing her profile. Taking a deep breath, she turned, meeting her Captain's eyes. "Gaitano?"

"Aguilar?" He was met by silence. Sighing, he went to sit at the desk, closer to her, but not touching. "Are you afraid?"

"Yes!"

"Good!" Thunder crossed his features, his scowl fierce. Marina felt a shiver run through her. "That means that you'll be careful." He sighed again, as she scowled back at him. "What are you afraid of?"

"That he'll get me."

The pirate threw back his head and laughed. When he looked back at her, his eyes had frozen into ice lagoons. "That is not going to happen."

"What if?"

He stared at her. Obviously, she wasn't going to settle for vague reassurances. "Okay," he agreed slowly. "I'll play." His eyes wandered over her face. "What if he comes to get you?"

"Jack says he is."

"Okay, he is," he agreed, keeping her focused. "What if he gets to you, Marina? What do you think his intentions are?"

Marina bit her lip, frowning, as she thought hard, remembering. She looked out over the ocean for a moment, basking in the blessed sunlight, before turning back to the pirate, whose company she kept. "Xavier is going to try to humiliate me. Get back at me for

El Luto. He's going to want a lap dance..." she broke off, shuddering with revulsion at the thought.

Hiding his reaction, Gaitano sent the globe spinning, secretly rejoicing at her disgust towards the blond pirate. "What if he were to..." he broke off, frowning, trying to put his thoughts into words that wouldn't send her into panic. "...convince you to do just that. What if you had no other option?" He searched her eyes. "Would you do it?"

Marina scowled, shaking her head, the coins in her ears tinkling strongly in the sunny room. "If I had no other option? None whatsoever?" she laughed, making her scowl disappear. "In a heartbeat!" Her eyes flashed. "I mean, we are talking about a dangerous individual here, aren't we?" She looked at him, suspiciously. "Just how dangerous, by the way?"

Gaitano shrugged, keeping his eyes locked on hers. "Xavier is a pirate. A little more ruthless than the average one, I'll grant you that. But he is just a man, and as a man, he has his weaknesses."

Marina nodded. "Indio."

The pirate frowned, puzzled. "Indio?"

"Indio." She glanced out over the ocean. "I don't know what happened between them, but I am under the impression that they have tangled before."

"They have."

"Recently?"

He frowned, shaking his head. "No, not recently..." He sighed, running his hands through his hair. "A long time ago..."

Marina thought for a moment, his words echoing in her mind. "Were you all teenagers together?" she asked carefully, turning to look at him, again.

"Yes."

"Hanging out, having wild times...?" She sighed, as he nodded. "Who was in your group?" She counted them off with her fingers. "You, Indio, Giancarlo, Rouge..."

"Jack, Jeremiah, Morgan and Xavier."

"Jack, as in the bearer of bad news?" She sighed, as he nodded. "I never heard of Jeremiah, though..."

The pirate smiled at the memory. "Jeremiah was an African, like Solomon. An incredible human being who brought into our lives, instead of taking." His eyes met hers. "He lost his life while we were still very young." He answered the question in her eyes. "His ship went down under mysterious circumstances. We never knew exactly what happened."

Marina stayed silent for a moment, waiting for him to finish his memory. "What about Morgan? Where is he?"

The pirate laughed. "*She*," he answered slowly, "was the cause of the bad blood between Xavier and Indio."

"So, it's all about a woman?"

"Not exactly, but a woman was the cause…" Distracted, he passed his hands over his hair, once again. "We were all pirates in training. Young, ignorant fools. Ruthless and reckless." His eyes met hers. "As deadly a combination as you can get." He took a deep breath. "Morgan was beautiful," he sighed, rolling his eyes and whistling under his breath, making her smile. "Clear, fair skin, hair as black as night, eyes the color of a cloudless summer day. A teenage Larissa, with blue eyes. Xavier was crazy about her." He frowned, remembering. "Even from before we were teenagers. She was the love of his young life." He stopped, losing himself in the memories.

"Was she a nice girl?" asked Marina softly.

"Very nice. Inside and out. She was the peacemaker. If any of us was upset or angry at another, Morgan would fix it. We all adored her. But as time went by, and we grew older, Xavier's crush became an obsession. Soon, it was overwhelming for her. The more she resisted his advances, the more…" he frowned, searching for the right words, to express what he wanted to convey.

"He lost it?" Marina offered softly.

The pirate focused on her again, and nodded. "Is that how you say it, where you are from? He lost control…"

Marina nodded, wrapped up in his story. "He totally lost it, huh?" She took a deep breath. "What did he do to her?"

The lines in his face settled, as if he were a statue. "He took her."

"Abduction or rape?"

"Both."

"How old was she?"

"Seventeen." He sighed. "There was a lot going on in town that day, and we just disappeared. Took the day off, hiding from our parents. Went to the ruins, the mountains, the lake on the other side of the island, everywhere we could, where we could not be found easily." He leaned forward, his elbows on his knees, searching her eyes. "The problem was, Morgan couldn't find us, either, and instead, Xavier found her. So, while we were all gone, having fun, Xavier decided to have a good time with Morgan." Marina watched closely, as he clenched and unclenched his fists, the blood rushing in and out of his knuckles. "When we got back from our escape, we couldn't find them. So, we went looking for them." He took a deep breath. "Indio found them, but it was too late. By the time he got to them, the damage was done." He shook his head again. "Indio walked in on them as they were getting dressed. Xavier was ecstatic. Happy, laughing, celebrating, he was babbling about marriage and children. Totally oblivious of the girl."

"Lost touch with reality?"

"Demented. That's what alerted Indio. Morgan, he says, was broken."

"Broken?"

The pirate nodded sadly. "Indio says her hair was mussed up, and her clothes looked as if they had been torn off her. She was scratched, bleeding, bruised, and half naked. Meanwhile, Xavier was spouting poetry at her. So, Morgan let him have it."

"She kick his ass?"

"No. She wasn't very big, and strong as she was, she didn't have your training. Morgan's weapons were not her fists. They were her quick mind and her sharp tongue. She proceeded to unman Xavier. Shredded him to pieces."

Marina thought she understood. "In front of Indio."

Gaitano nodded again. "Indio was there. So, as Morgan proceeded to tear into Xavier, she was doing it, holding him up to Indio."

"And there was no comparison."

"None. Basically, she let Xavier know that he could never be a real contender for her heart, because she didn't feel he was the man for her. She just didn't like him like that. But at that moment of deep pain and intense anger, she insulted him. Accused him of wanting to be like us, and never being able to measure up---"

"Like you... a pirate?"

"Like us... Gaitanos."

Marina gasped. "Was she with either of you?"

"No, no, not like that. But at that moment, she made him think that. Said some incredibly vicious things---"

Taking a deep breath, she protested. "The girl was just kidnapped, and raped, probably brutally --"

"Morgan told Xavier that Don Carlos had chosen Indio over him."

She frowned, not understanding. "What has that got to do with it?"

"Xavier's parents were sailing with Indio's, when their ship went down. The only reason my parents hadn't taken Xavier with Indio, was because his grandparents were in town, at the time."

Marina's hands drifted up of their own accord, before coming down to rest on her head. She gasped. "But, that's just fate! Is he blaming Indio, because Don Carlos made him a Gaitano and not him?"

"Yes. Morgan also chose that moment to reveal her true feelings for Indio."

"She had a crush on him?"

"Big one. They were secret makeout partners."

"Forbidden love?"

"Not at all. They just hung out. We were kids. We only had each other. We couldn't wait to become adults, and find real potential lifemates."

"What did Indio do, after all was said and done?"

"Indio thrashed Xavier. Severely. Almost killed him. Also put the word out on what he had done to Morgan." He shook his head again, frowning at the memory. "There was an investigation, but Morgan suddenly disappeared."

"Mysteriously?"

"Very. So, Indio went back to have a talk with Xavier. A few hours later, Xavier is gone." He sighed. "We didn't see him again, for a few years. When we finally did, he was the man he is now. Or at least, in the making."

Marina vacated the window seat, and began walking carefully around the room, trailing her fingers along his jaw, as she passed by. "So, Indio's on Xavier's bad list, on all counts." Her mind spun out of control. "Xavier also lost his parents at sea, but Indio is the Gaitano. Xavier adored Morgan, but Indio was her secret makeout partner. Xavier takes Morgan, and she declares her love for Indio. Of course, that's not enough. Indio beats the hell out of him, and mobilizes an investigation of the events, causing Xavier to leave town. That must have turned his whole world upside down, changing completely, his life as he knew it. All, before he's twenty. So, your brother is responsible for whatever it is that has happened to him. Indio makes Xavier a victim and a wanted criminal at the same time. It must have been overwhelming." Stopping at the kaleidoscopes, she picked one up, holding it up to the bright sunlight. "Indio is the one I want at my back when I see Xavier." She handed the kaleidoscope to her pirate. "Xavier is afraid of Indio."

Gaitano frowned, peering through the lens. "What about me?"

Marina looked through another, and handed it to him. "No, he's not scared of you, at all." She sighed, looking at him. "He can't wait to get his hands on you." An eyebrow arched. "Or yours."

"What if he gets close enough to you?"

"He probably will."

"What if he does? What value do you have for him?"

"I am your accountant."

"He can have whoever he wants, to do his books. Why you?"

"I am the Gaitanos' accountant."

Carlos shrugged. "Xavier is a wealthy man by his own merit."

"But is he an honorable man?"

"Not at all."

"Then, you have something he doesn't."

"Still..."

"Check it out, Carlitos. Xavier got to *El Luto*, right after Lola and I met. You totally dissed Lola, for me, thank you very much," she said, blowing him a kiss. "Then, after I dance for you, you claim me. In front of all your pirate buddies, dogs and bitches, your business acquaintances, and your parents, your uncle, and my sister. Serious stuff. All this, in a cave full of pillaging and plundering witnesses." Marina held his gaze. She saw in his ocean eyes, the exact moment when the truth of her words hit him. Something flickered, before he extinguished it. "It's all going to depend on the intensity of his antagonism, the degree of jealousy, envy, rage, hate, whatever, towards you. God knows where he's at, on that. What if he just has to have me, over that little soap opera?"

"What if?" he replied, genuinely curious, not knowing what a soap opera was.

Marina shuddered, wrapping her arms around herself. "I can't bear the thought of that, baby, it freaks me out!" she cried softly. "But who's not to say, he just has a hard-on for you, and he just wants to mess with your mind? Where I come from, it's called *head games...*"

"What if you have to dance for him?"

"Then, I will beg for God's forgiveness. And yours. After that, I would need to soak for a few days, to wash myself."

"Why do you react so strongly towards him? Even before you knew anything about him?"

"The man is pure evil."

"How evil?"

Marina smiled to herself. "Xavier will do anything, within his power, to fuck you, any way he can."

The pirate didn't blink. "Why is that?"

"He wasn't offered to be a Gaitano?" she shrugged. "It doesn't matter. Xavier is going to take what the Gaitanos have. I'm just a casualty." She looked him straight in the eye. "Xavier doesn't care about me. At all. He had never laid eyes on me before that night, and by Morgan's description, I am not even his type. But right now, you've got me, so therefore, he wants me." She sighed, shaking her head. "Not me. He wants what you have. If not the wealth, at least the name and the power.

"What if he comes and gets you? Makes you dance? Gets back at you? What do you think he's going to do?"

"Besides making me dance, if it comes to that? At least, slap me back. I think he likes it rough." She shuddered.

"What would you do to save your life..." he said slowly, watching her flinch, "...if it came to that?"

"Just about anything," she admitted. "How bad could it get? Worst case scenario, he puts his hands on me and slaps me around a little. I can take that. If he were to touch me, as a man, I would have a problem with that. I would allow it, however, if it meant saving my life or anybody else's." Walking back to him, she sank to a crouch in front of him, taking his face between her hands. "Carlitos," she murmured. "Xavier wants *you*, not me. He's just trying to use me, to get to the Gaitanos. By me, he will never succeed, but this is beyond my control. I can't do this alone, papi." Her voice broke, as tears stung her eyes. "I just can't do it."

The pirate stared. Only in her strange language could he express the reassurance they both needed. Taking her in his arms, he held her against his chest, their heartbeats blending. "I've got you, baby..."

They spent the day together, as they had no other. The lighthouse room was their refuge. In it, they talked to each other, listened, and learned from one another. They formed an alliance that would never be broken, surpassing the distance in time, between them.

Marina explored everything in the room, marveling at her discoveries, as a child would. The gift from the Council turned out to be a veritable treasure chest, taking her breath away. As her mother had done, the night before, she had only opened the lid and glimpsed inside, before she gasped, slamming it shut. In just that way, she shut out the image impressed of her mind, of coins, and jewelry, and priceless artifacts. She glanced at the pirate and shook her head. "This is the kind of stuff that makes me believe I'm in a dream. Nothing is real. I am going to wake up in my own bed, with nothing more exciting to look forward to, than classes and homework."

The pirate laughed. His eyes blazed with carefully controlled passion. "When you wake up in your own bed, next time, I should be right beside you..."

Marina froze, caught in the clear blue gaze of his loving eyes. No words came out, there was nothing to say. A strange feeling invaded her body, as if it had been poured over her head. Warm, fuzzy, it left her breathless. So they left it at that, because they were still not ready to talk about the future. Instead, they frolicked and played, distracting themselves.

The bed held the most interest for them, being the center of the room and of their attention. In it, they rested, played, discussed important matters, and made love. Never having had so much time together alone before, they made it last. And from their desire to learn everything there was to know about one another, and being together, came the most amazing conversations either of them could have ever imagined.

"Where are your parents from?"

Marina hesitated. She was loathe to overload him with information or details he couldn't grasp, or couldn't handle, so she had to tread carefully. "Mami is from California. Her business has to do with clothing and women's apparel. That is how Salomé got into it. Through her, because of her, with her."

"Your mother is very beautiful," the pirate sighed happily, his eyes caressing her own face.

Marina rolled her eyes, before laughing at him. "Sloane is the most beautiful woman in the world. To me..."

"Where did you learn Spanish? Where is Pablo from?"

Marina hesitated once more. She was a little rusty on her history, and she needed to proceed with caution. She thought carefully before answering him. "Papi is from a small island, here on the Caribbean Sea. Originally, that is. He was taken to the States when he was young, and he made his life there, keeping his roots intact."

"Where is he from?" he asked again.

Marina was silent for a moment. Then, she answered softly. *"Boriken..."*

Gaitano sat up from his reclining position in the bed, his eyes wide in his face. "*Boriken*? I have been there! Many times, as a matter of fact..." He looked into her eyes, searching. "It is beautiful there," he said softly.

She nodded slowly, agreeing. "It is the most beautiful place on Earth."

Her hand reached out for his, capturing it. She looked down, rubbing his knuckles softly with her thumb.

The man gazed at her, bewildered by her cau tion, but respectful of it, trusting in her. "Is San Juan still the capital?"

Looking up suddenly, she smiled. "San Juan will always be the capital."

"How do you like it?"

"I adore it."

"Do you get a chance to visit often?"

Marina shook her head sadly. "Not often. Life is too busy. Occasionally, do I get a chance to visit my relatives."

"Is *El Morro* still standing? *Fuerte San Cristobal?*"

Marina nodded, tears shining in her eyes. "People visit them to learn about history."

Gaitano frowned. He chose his next words carefully. "Are there any *tainos* left?" He watched with dismay, as she threw her head back and laughed, tears escaping her eyes.

Marina shook her head at him, still laughing softly. "*Tainos?* No, papi. The *conquistadores* made sure there was not a single, living one left." Her voice broke. "They did away with the whole race. Pablo's people," she shrugged, fire blazing in her swimming eyes, "*my* people, are a mix of the Spaniards, the African slaves, and the *tainos* that populated the island when the *conquistadores* arrived."

The pirate felt his heart squeeze inside his chest, at the pain in her eyes. Lifting her hand, he pressed his lips to it, before rubbing his face against it. "Is it still under Spanish domain?"

A sob escaped her throat, as she tried to laugh again. "No, baby. It has been an American territory since 1898."

Gaitano felt the blood leave his face. His voice was barely audible. "*Since* 1898?..." And he could say no more.

"What about discoveries?"

Marina turned to look at him. They had spent the rest of the morning indoors, and were now lounging on the balcony that surrounded the lighthouse. It was a beautiful day, clouds wispy and far away, sky crisp and clear, sun strong. The wind blew the hair around their faces as they sat side by side, their backs solid against the stone structure of the lighthouse. Their knees were drawn up, Marina's toga tucked between her legs. They had entertained themselves, passing a spyglass back and forth. Now, their eyes were glued to the horizon, where a mysterious spot had appeared. "Discoveries?" she repeated slowly, glancing at him.

The pirate pressed his lips together and nodded. "Discoveries." He was never going to have a grasp of her world, if he didn't plunge head first into it.

Marina nodded. "Okay, discoveries." She took a deep breath. "For one, almost the whole world is mapped. There are many places, remote, deep, high, whatever, that no man has ever visited, still, but for the most part, we know where is what." Taking the spyglass he handed her, she peered into it. It seemed as if the spot was getting larger, but for now, it was nothing more than just that. A spot. Sighing, she handed the spyglass back. "I think the most amazing advances in our time is travel. Means of transportation. There are machines in my world that would probably give you nightmares," she smiled sadly. Absently, she reached for the stack of papers next to her, weighed down by a nautilus shell. Taking the charcoal pencil he retrieved from his pocket, she proceeded to sketch busily, putting in visual form, what she found difficult to describe. It had been her way of communicating to him, the wonders of her world, and it was easier for him to absorb, than her words were. In a few moments, she had a gallery of cars, motorcycles, trains, buses, bicycles, cruise ships, and airplanes.

The pirate gazed at her as he put his spyglass down, and took the paper she offered. Sighing happily, he made himself more comfortable, and turned to study the paper. Shock registered deep in his eyes, but the smile never left his mouth. He made a couple of questions, and grunted with satisfaction at her answers. Finally, he turned to her. "What about space travel?" he asked, taking a wild guess.

Marina laughed, shaking her head at him. "Oh, ye of little faith..." she teased. Sketching furiously this time, she produced sky rockets and satellites, and a lunar landscape. "We have space museums, where you can go and see amazing things. We have huge telescopes that bring down planets to your backyard, in incredible space observatories, with scientists working busy, praying for some sign of life out there."

Gaitano laughed happily, enjoying every moment with her. "What about the ocean?"

Marina waved her hand, scoffing. "You mean that little pool, way over there?" At his raised eyebrows, she laughed, her heart singing. "They've gone deep into the ocean, and have come up with some incredible things. There are fish at the bottom of the ocean, who carry their own little lanterns around, so they can see, it's so dark down there." She glanced at him. "Did you know that?"

He shook his head quickly, his eyes eating her up. "I would have never guessed," he answered, his hand caressing her cheek. He felt himself grow hard as she snuggled again st it, peering at him through her lashes. When he spoke again, his voice was hoarse. "Let's make out." Swinging his body around suddenly, he entered their room through the window. Turning, he held his arms out for her. "Let's make love..."

Marina smiled, shaking her head at him, but the tingles in her body overwhelmed her. She followed him, without a thought. "Are you sure you want to do this?" she teased. "You know I can't get enough of you."

In a moment, the pirate had her on her back, gazing up at him, making his pants grow even tighter. He captured her face between his hands, making her arch her neck back. His tongue ran a slick path from the hollow of her throat to her chin. He chuckled as she squirmed under him,. "That's the idea..." Softly, he ground his hips against hers. Marina squirmed harder, until he captured her mouth. Then she melted under him. The pirate groaned. He couldn't get enough of her, either. Their clothing seemed to disappear, and suddenly, it was he who was on his back, the woman straddling him. He grinned, as he lifted her hips, impaling her on him. "Your turn." He laughed, as she gasped. "Show me what you feel for me, baby..."

Marina smiled. Getting into the rhythm, she began riding him, his hands alternately cupping her breasts and coaxing her hips. Throwing her head back, she laughed happily, squeezing him deep inside her. He laughed with her, as she undulated her hips on him. "Is all this for me?" she whispered.

The pirate groaned, the smile never leaving his face, his hands solid on her hips now, his eyes on the connection of their bodies. "All for you."

Marina laughed again, teasing him. Her hands were on her thighs, and her fingers brushed against their private parts, seemingly accidentally. She bit her lip as she heard him draw in a sharp breath. He mustn't know that it was taking all she had, to keep from openly fondling herself and him. But, oh, God, that is exactly what she wanted to do. Instead, she shook her head and dragged her fingernails down his chest. "Just me?" she taunted, freezing, as she realized what the words were, that escaped her mouth.

The pirate's arms came around her suddenly, holding her close against him. Before she knew it, he had her on her back, and he was happily making himself comfortable between her legs. It seemed to her, he never missed a stroke. Just as happy, Marina wrapped her arms and legs around him. Suddenly, he began pulling out, torturing her slowly with the intimate caress. Wildly, she contracted around him, trying to keep him in for as long as she could. Chuckling softly, he suspended the moment, just leaving the tip inside her. His laugh was low and husky in her ear, making her tingle all over, drenching them both as she shuddered. "Just you..."

Marina sighed, letting out a shaky breath. Her restless hands caressed his waist, his hips, fingernails scratching softly. Her lips were parted, and her hazel eyes looked straight into his. Her voice came out a hoarse whisper. "Then, give me some."

The pirate laughed again. Without warning, he slammed into her. Marina gasped. Her fingers tangled in his hair, keeping his head close to hers. His voice poured over her, like thick honey. "You can have it all, mami..." He kissed her desperately, as he established the rhythm of their grateful bodies.

Marina pulled back, to look deep into his eyes. Her eyes sparkled with the desire her bruised mouth tried to convey. "I just want *you*, pirate..."

Gaitano gazed at her. This was it, for him. As far as he was concerned, he was home. Nothing else would do. His rhythm changed, just a little, making his strokes longer and deeper. The woman beneath him moaned with satisfaction, eyes shining with endless desire. He realized, every cell in his body, accompanied with every thought in his head, was devoted to her. "How bad do you want me?"

Her mouth smiled, as she drew him down on her chest, meeting him stroke for stroke. Her voice in his ear was intense with the sincerity of her words, low and husky with overwhelming passion. "I want you so bad," she whispered shakily, "that this is where I want to be."

"How long?" he challenged.

Marina didn't think. "For the rest of my life."

The pirate laughed, his heart soaring. And then, he confessed. "I also want to spend the rest of my life with you." Not waiting for a reply, he ducked his head, his mouth ravishing hers. While inside her head, Marina screamed and jumped for joy, on the outside, her body expressed for him what words could not. When they finally came, together, bodies slippery with lust and desire, slick and sticky with satisfaction, they knew. A decision had been made. The words would come later, but their minds knew what their hearts showed them. For now, their bodies shuddered from their mutual orgasms, reaching for each other, eyes closed as they caught their breaths, mouths meeting hungrily, sealing their intentions with a kiss. They sighed happily, in each other's arms. There would be no turning back. Nothing and no one would stop them.

Marina gasped.

They had taken a short nap, and had just wakened, refreshed and excited, anxious to continue discovering each other. They had dressed; Marina opting for pants and a top this time, hoping for some time away from the lighthouse. She had silently followed the pirate down the circular stairs. At the bottom of the lighthouse, on the table by the door, had been bags containing bread, fruit, and fried fish, and beautiful dark glass bottles of drinking water. Indio was taking care of them. They had taken the picnic upstairs, and back outside, where they had been hanging out, before making out, and making love. Now, the visitor couldn't believe what she was seeing. While they had been busy, engrossed in lust and sex, the dark spot on the horizon had come much closer, growing significantly larger.

Heart racing, Marina's mind began quietly freaking out. *Oh, my God!* Her eyes flew to the pirate next to her.

Carlos glanced at her, a smile playing around his mouth. He didn't address her unspoken question, and instead, made himself comfortable, sitting down. He pretended not to notice the dismay in her eyes, his body language inviting her to join him. She dropped down next to him, and looked back at what she knew now was a ship, headed towards Encantada. Without saying a word, they shared their meal quietly. Once they were done eating, collecting all their trash, and disposing of it, they sat back, enjoying their bottles of water, sharing a spyglass. He stopped her as she went to hand it back to him, making her look through it again. "What do you see?"

Marina's lips parted, as his voice filled her senses, low in her ear. "A ship..."

"What color?" He wrapped his arms around her suddenly, swinging her unto his lap, then accomodating her between his legs.

She sighed happily, leaning back against his hard chest. "Gray..."

"What about her sails?"

"Gray..."

"Flags?"

"Many."

"Do you recognize any?"

"Some." She bit her lip, concentrating. She had never seen anything like it. And it was definitely coming closer. "Spain, France, Italy... Are those others, African flags?"

He rubbed her arms, proud of her. "Some... What else can you tell me about this ship? Anything outstanding?"

"Jolly Roger... Looks kind of like yours..." she added suspiciously.

"What type of ship is it?"

"A very big ship."

The pirate laughed softly, letting it rumble in his chest, making her head bounce against it. "Who's the brat now?"

The woman smiled to herself. "It's huge..."

"What type?" he insisted gently.

Marina fell silent for a moment. Finally, she gasped softly. "A galleon!" The pirate lauged quietly. "Good girl... Now, look closely."

"Okay..."

"What impression do you get from the ship? Can you see anyone on board?"

"Not really. Very few men. It looks like just the basic crew it needs, in order to sail."

"Excellent! Now, how about any weapons?"

"Cannons..."

"What impression do you get from the ship?" he asked again, his hands absently caressing the curves in his possession.

"That it's empty. It's fast, as if it were light..."

"Go on..."

"So, if it's not bringing any cargo," she wondered out loud, "is it taking any?"

"Maybe..."

She frowned. "I have no knowledge of any merchandise being dispatched anywhere."

The pirate at her back laughed softly, stroking her hair, now. "What if it's not merchandise?" he asked mysteriously.

"What else could it be?"

"Can you make out a name yet?"

"Not yet."

"Look for one. It's almost here."

"It's hard, it's so big, and so dark... Oh! I think I see something..." she whispered, peering closely. She hadn't seen them, until the galleon had turned a degree, and sunlight bounced off the silver paint outlining the black letters. Now, she could read the ship's name. She sighed. *"La Prision..."* Reaching behind her, she hooked a hand behind his head, bringing him down to nuzzle against her, while his hands kept busy. "Carlitos," she breathed, "is it a *prison ship?*"

The pirate pressed his lips to the side of her neck, breathing deeply of her essence. "Yes, Marina. It is a prison ship, coming to take the people Pedro Escobar is holding, from the raids we conducted some days ago."

She smiled. "Bye-bye, Dominique Swan," she whispered, "you bitch!"

He chuckled. "If it hadn't been for that bitch, and for Salomé suspecting her, we would have never found out what was going on ---"

"It's not over," she warned softly, keeping her eye on the ship.

"No," he admitted. "Not yet, but almost..."

All of a sudden, she gasped. *"*Carlitos! Carlitos!" she cried, trying to bury herself into him. "There's somebody there, and he's looking this way!"

Carlos grunted as she knocked the air out of him, holding her tight to stop her squirming. *"Suave, mami,"* he rumbled in her ear. "What does he look like?" He held her tighter, trying to still her agitation.

Marina pressed herself firmly against his chest, and gasped. She needed to slow her breathing, so she wouldn't hyperventilate. She had felt as if she were spying on the ship as it drew nearer, but nothing had prepared her for the sight of the man looking through a spyglass back at her. "He's big," she answered softly. "He's looking at us, so I can't see his face very well."

"What is he wearing?"

"Pants, no shirt, boots---"

"Rolled down, with big silver studs on the sides."

"A sword at his hip---"

"In an old, worn, leather scabbard."

"A cross around his neck---"

"Gold, on a black cord."

"Gold hoops in his ears..."

"Black hair?"

"Tanned skin." To her surprise, the man on the galleon lifted his hand. Beneath her back, she felt the rumble of silent laughter. Disgusted, she handed the spyglass back to him. "I think he wants to talk to you." Standing up, she went to move away from him, wrapping her own arms around herself.

He laughed aloud, this time, taking the spyglass from her, and joining her at the railing. "I want to talk to him." Looking through the scope, he lifted his hand in greeting.

Still disgusted, Marina crossed her arms and rolled her eyes, tapping her foot impatiently. "So, is this a friend of yours?"

The pirate chuckled. "Do you know my full name, *querida?*"

Marina felt tingles at the endearment. She scowled. "*Carlos Juan Miguel Gaitano y Sandoval...*"

"My father is Carlos, his oldest brother is Miguel," he explained, amused, "his other brother..."

Marina sighed, as the men proceeded to make signs at each other. "Let me guess. *Tio Juan?*" Even more disgusted, she shook her head and turned to go back inside. "I'll let you two boys talk..."

His arm snaked out as she brushed past him, to climb back in the window.

His voice in her ear was low and seductive, as he dropped the spyglass, with one last wave. "Marina..." his lips brushed the side of her neck, "...want to run, mami?"

Marina fell against him, relieved that he wasn't turning his attention away from her. "Yes, please!"

The pirate kissed her cheek. Holding her in front of him, he sent her inside, first. Throwing back his head in silent laughter, he rolled his eyes at the bright blue sky, behind her back. He patted her on the butt and followed her inside. Marina never saw the love in his eyes.

They ran. Gaitano took her through parts of the island she had never seen before. Long stretches of sand dunes, thick segments of jungle, rows of waterfalls. And throughout the whole trail, Marina couldn't get his words out of her head.

They had sprinted down the stairs, anxious to be outside of the round walls. The pirate had stopped her, as they were getting ready to take off.

"We need to talk about what will be better for us," he informed her casually, "staying here in Encantada, or going back to your time." Pretending not to see the shock in her face, he turned her towards the trail. "What are the pros and cons of each place, *divina*? Think about it, and let's get together on it."

And without saying another word, he had taken off, leaving her no option, but to follow him.

This is getting serious. I love it... She loved Encantada. But she was a new millenium woman. Finishing her college education would secure her future, but so would staying in Encantada, and working for the Gaitanos. Going back home, she was looking at a future of working for Pablo, and eventually running his hard-earned company. Staying in Encantada, she would be sharing her life with the man she loved. There wasn't much to think about.

Now they were doing forms next to some waterfalls. Mist surrounded them, refreshing them and cooling them down, even as they worked out. It was an orgasmic experience. They grinned at each other.

The pirate took her hand and rubbed it against his cheek, before pressing his lips to it, kiss lingering. Although his voice was low, his glowing blue eyes spoke volumes. "You have a life here, in

Encantada. You have a job most grown men would kill to have. You have friends and family, so to speak. The association and protection of the Gaitano family. You have been here a few weeks, and already you have a few homes. You have babies to keep you occupied, and men who would follow you anywhere. You have the most powerful family, in the Caribbean, at your beck and call; and the most brave and dangerous pirates, to ever navigate the Sea of Darkness, at your feet." Shaking with passion, the younger Gaitano closed his eyes, scratching the shadow on his face over her hand, breath shuddering in his chest. "You have wealth, above and beyond any other single woman, or married, for that matter, on this island." He laughed softly, raising his face to look deep into her eyes. "Here in Encantada, Marina Aguilar..." he whispered, kissing her hand again, "you have me... Carlos Juan Miguel Gaitano y Sandoval... "

"For how long, pirate?" she whispered back.

"For as long as you will have me..."

"How long before you get tired of me and discard me---" Suddenly, the breath was knocked from her.

"I may be a pillaging and plundering pirate," he growled, his arms tightening around her in a vise grip, "but I do not play games. I will never discard you, *preciosa*. I give you the respect you deserve." To which she had nothing to add, because he was right. He did respect her. Kissing her on the cheek, he let go of her suddenly, making her stumble against him.

Marina caught herself, hands solid against his chest. She gasped, a rush of desire invading her. "As long as you give me my place, pirate," she growled. "We'll see..." And she kissed her pirate, making him melt against her.

That evening, they joined the villagers in their native dance. Her family rejoiced at seeing her, and so happy at that, reaching out to stroke them, as they danced by. Indio and Storm joined them. Giancarlo and Rouge greeted them, dancing with them. Their village friends recognized their union, leaping and dancing around them. It was a celebration. Carlos and Marina danced their hearts out.

From across the way, the older Gaitanos watched, quietly, letting the rhythm of the drums invade their bodies. They sighed collectively, making themselves more comfortable. Silas and Jimmy chuckled as the spectacle unfolded before them. No matter how many times they had come here before, it was different each and every time. Tonight, it was special. Things were going to change in Encantada, as a result of the new alliances.

A peace pipe appeared out of nowhere, and slowly made its round, each grownup drawing deeply from it, before passing it on. Don Miguel faked out his sister-in-law, María Isabel, pretending to skip her and passing it over to his brother, Don Carlos. María Isabel, in turn, snatched it away from him, with a laugh, and a scolding shake of her beautiful dark head. Carlitos' mother took a deep drag, before passing it on to her husband. Who, turned and passed it to his other brother. Juan held it for a while, before passing it back to Miguel. One last round and the peace pipe disappeared just as mysteriously. A few minutes later, they were all relaxed, smiling at the dancers.

"How was your trip?" Don Carlos asked his younger brother.

"Fine," the newcomer laughed. "Ocean has been friendly, these days."

"Will you be staying a while this time, or will you be leaving right away?"

Juan grinned, shrugged. "*No se, viejo*. Depends on what's going on..."

"You should stay, Juanito," María Isabel said softly. "You should be here when Carlitos reveals all his achievements."

Juan laughed, his eyes caressing his nephew. "Actually, it so happens, I have to stay here anyway. I came as fast as I could, trying to get here before Xavier."

His brothers sighed, and looked at each other. "How far behind you, is Xavier?" Don Carlos finally asked.

The younger brother shrugged. "A couple of days maybe." He fell silent, waiting for an explanation. None came. Finally, he couldn't stand it any longer. "Is anybody going to tell me what is going on?" He sighed, as his brothers looked at each other and shook their heads. Looking back at the natives, he sat, deep in thought. Finally, he laughed, shaking his head. "It's about the girl, isn't it? Is that the accountant I keep hearing so many things about?"

Don Miguel's laugh rumbled deep in his chest. "Marina Aguilar has progressed to be much more than Carlitos' accountant."

Juan grinned at his older brother. "I can see that..." He watched the couple for a little bit longer. "She's his girlfriend, isn't she?" His nephew and his accountant were busy seducing each other with their movements, unaware of the dancing around them. "How does she really feel about him?" His family laughed.

Don Carlos waved his hand in the air, dismissing the question. "The girl is crazy about him!"

"What about Carlitos?"

"He adores her," his mother confirmed.

"Is it a good union?"

Don Carlos laughed. "It is so good, that we should seriously consider doing business with these people."

Don Miguel turned, and arched an eyebrow at his brother. *"¿En serio?"* he asked, curious.

Don Carlos answered, with a nod. *"En serio."*

Don Miguel took a deep breath of air, expelling it slowly, thoughtfully. "I agree. It would protect both children," he finally said.

"I agree," María Isabel added, softly.

"If it is such a good idea," Juan wanted to know, "what is the problem?"

His brothers looked at each other, laughing once more. Don Carlos turned to his younger brother, mischief dancing in his eyes. "Juanito," he said softly, out of Silas' and Jimmy's hearing, "do you remember when you were a little boy, and I used to take you to Leila's hut, in the village?" He waited for Juan to nod. "Do you remember the stories she used to tell us?"

Juan smiled at the memory. "She told us a million of them..."

"Do you remember the stories about the visitors?"

"Of course. She had met one once, when she was a little girl, and none since." He turned his head to look at his older brother. "You told me you had never met any, yourself."

It was Don Carlos' turn to grin. "Those were Carlitos' exact words," he chuckled. "I hadn't, at the moment." He waved his hand again, signaling the dancers. "I certainly have, since then." And then, he had the satisfaction of watching his younger brother's jaw drop.

Juan gasped. "You are playing with me, Carlos! I am not believing this!" He turned to look at his other brother. "*¿Es verdad, Miguel?*"

Don Miguel nodded his head happily at the visitors. "You have before you, Marina Aguilar. Extraordinary girl. That is the one with Carlitos. She comes from an extraordinary family. Her father, Pablo Aguilar is a businessman. He grew up with his best friend, an African named Joe Banks. They met two beautiful women who were best friends themselves, and got married. Pablo got lucky in business, and bought some property, building homes for Joe and himself. The couples eventually had three children between them, raising them together, sharing the parenting equally."

"How do they get here?"

Don Miguel's energy wrapped around them, his voice vibrating through their senses. "Freak storm. The girls were marooned in their time, got caught in a storm, and woke up in Encantada. Salomé is the dark-skinned one, with the beautiful olive eyes. She catches Indio's attention, while Carlitos is still in Carey."

Juan smiled proudly at his other nephew. "She is stunning." His family murmured in agreement. "Indio looks ridiculously happy." They laughed.

"He is," María Isabel sighed, fondly.

"When Carlitos gets back from Carey," continued Don Miguel, "he finds that Indio can't think straight. So he gets curious as to the cause, and that's when he meets Marina."

"Did he fall head over heels for her?" Juan teased.

Don Carlos laughed. "Not at all. It seems to have been very gradual."

Don Miguel agreed. "He mentioned the discrepancies he had found in his books to her, the day they met. Immediately afterward, he hires her as his accountant. Kidnapped her, and took her to Carey to present her findings to the Council."

"Aaaah," said Juan in understanding. "*That* is how they come to show up at *El Baile del Luto*."

"So, you've heard?"

Juan laughed again. "Of course! I'm sorry I missed it. I was held up in San Juan and couldn't make it in time. Carey is still buzzing about the Gaitanos' accountant!" He shook his head in admiration for the couple, seeing them in a new light. "I saw Lola. She was devastated! Told me all about it..." He rolled his eyes. "She wants the accountant of La Gitana imprisoned for attacking her."

The Gaitanos who had been present at El Luto, laughed. Don Carlos smacked his lips, eyes glinting with mischief. "You have never seen such a catfight," he informed his younger sibling.

"Stop! Carlos!" María Isabel laughed. She turned to her younger brother- in-law, gazing at him fondly. "Lola would have seriously injured the girl if Marina hadn't..." she struggled for a word, and failing, burst into laughter, "beat the hell out of that imbecile tramp!" The men laughed with her.

"I heard it was more than that, though," Juan finally said, after the laughter had subsided a little. "Is it true that Carlitos recognized her...?" He smiled, as they all nodded at him.

"In front of everyone present," Don Carlos said in a low voice, shaking his head at the memory.

Don Miguel's energy covered them like a blanket, keeping them warm and fuzzy. "Everyone was there," he sighed, looking into his youngest brother's eyes. "And in front of every pirate present, young and old, male and female, local and foreigner... our wild, carefree nephew recognized the young woman as his official..." then it was he, struggling for a word, finally shrugging, "companion, I suppose."

Juan nodded thoughtfully. "What did he use?"

"A string of turquoises he got from Indio." María Isabel sighed happily at her recollection of the events.

"So, Indio approves this union..."

They all nodded once more. "Indio is crucial in this relationship," Don Miguel explained softly. "Without Indio, it would have never happened."

Juan frowned. "I met up with Carlitos a couple of months ago, though, and he never mentioned his accountant. I suppose he hadn't met her yet. So I imagine they haven't known each other long. Isn't it too soon?" He looked over at his brothers as they both shook their heads.

Miguel waved a hand at the couple. "Not at all. It is as if they have been moving towards each other their whole lives." He sighed. "They have just found each other."

"Who are the other people with them? Is their whole family here?"

Don Carlos chuckled. "Basically..." He let his eyes caress his friends, happily expressing themselves among his villagers. "The girls came through first. Then, their brother joined them. That would be the exuberant young man dancing with Storm," he pointed out unnecessarily. "When Carlitos abducted Marina to take her to Carey for his presentation in front of the Council, Jackson, Salomé's brother, goes back and gets the parents. He brought them back through, to Encantada."

Juan stared, aghast, just as María Isabel had, when told. "So, they can come and go as they please?" His dark hair caught the reflection of distant tiki torches, as he shook his head, incredulous. A tell-tale shiver told of the fear that struck his pirate heart. His brothers reached out to stroke him, reassuring him immediately.

"*Tranquilo, Juanito*," Don Miguel rumbled. "We are not in danger of an invasion. These are our friends. The daughters are on a mission. Their family is here, offering them support, ensuring their safety."

Juan's voice was almost drowned by the native drums. "Amazing..." He shook his head. "Incredible..." He sighed. "The women are beautiful." His family laughed again.

"They are," agreed María Isabel, before any of them could comment. "They also call themselves professional women. Sloane is the gorgeous blonde dancing with her husband, Pablo Aguilar. She has her own company, related with women's apparel. Shayla, Joe Banks' wife, Salomé and Jackson's mother, is a baby doctor!" she informed him, deep admiration in her voice. "Joe is a teacher of physical education, who reads stories to children, on his time off. Salomé works with Sloane, Jackson is studying business and art, and Marina is an accountant, who takes care of babies---"

"Enough!" Juan exclaimed in a low voice, raising his hands and shaking his head. He turned to look at his brothers. "I agree," he said softly. "This seems to be bigger than a mere union between Carlitos and his accountant girlfriend. Papers need to be drawn up. They both need to be protected, in case the relationship doesn't work out." His family murmured in agreement. "I am assuming he will marry the girl..." Silence followed his words, for a moment. Finally, they all nodded.

María Isabel felt she could express it better. "I don't think either of them would have it any other way, Juanito. This is more than an infatuation for them, boys," she verified for them. "This is true love..."

The Gaitano brothers nodded, watching affectionately over their boys and their girls.

"What about Indio and Salomé?" Juan asked, finally.

"That is another reason we need to do business with this family," Don Carlos informed his brother.

Don Miguel grunted. "These children are forming an empire, without realizing it. They need to be protected."

"I see," Juan nodded. He looked around at them, holding out his hand. "Let's do it..." Each one of them slid their hand against his. A few minutes later, the older Gaitanos and the lady Sandoval were gone.

"In my time, you would be able to indulge in any form of transportation imaginable, except for a rocket ship into outer space. With your kind of money, you would have much more available to you than most people. You could go all over the world in a fragment of the time it would take you to do it now, in your Golden Age of Piracy, navigating the Sea of Darkness. Also, you would experience firsthand our amazing means of communication. You, Gaitano, could live in the most sophisticated abode, with the latest high-tech toy available to you, while I serve you in my Victoria's Secret lingerie," she murmured in his ear, as they finally left the waterfall. They had all gone splashing there after the dance, and now they were each making their own way home. The couple waved goodbye to her family, disappearing down the jungle trail, their arms around each other.

Carlos groaned. He had gotten a crash course in the wee hours of the morning, on the art of seduction by Victoria's Secret. Marina had happily illustrated apparel he had never even dreamed of. He was definitely interested as he looked into her eyes, blazing with mischief. He held his hand out in front of him. "Good one, baby," he murmured back, winking at her. His girlfriend slid him some skin.

"Nobody's home!" Marina called up to the ceiling.

They were lying next to each other on the big bed, surrounded by a cloud of black gauze. Around the room, candlelight flickered inside beautiful glass lamps. The door was open to the landing, the better for the breeze to cool the stone room. Now, there was somebody banging on their door. Marina smiled as the sound echoed up the stairs.

Carlos laughed quietly next to her. "I don't think they're going away," he said in a stage whisper. They grinned at each other.

Marina shook her head sadly. "It looks like they're not." Laughing, she leapt out of bed, and left the room through the window, to the balcony.

The pirate followed her. "Should I boil some water, *querida*?" he offered. "*Gracias, papi,*" she threw over her shoulder. "Let's give them one last chance." Reaching the front of the lighthouse, she called down at their unexpected company. "Go away! We don't want any!" She smiled down at them.

Illuminated by tiki torches were her brother and sister with their respective companions, and Caribe, in tow. They all craned their necks to look up at them.

Salomé cupped her hands around her mouth. "I want to see your room! Mom told me all about it! I haven't seen it yet, girl!"

Indio laughed, capturing her hands. "She's just jealous, because I got to see your room, first!"

Jackson stepped up. "We miss you, baby, we just want to hang out for a little while!"

Storm pulled him behind her, laughing as his arm snaked around her waist. "The truth is Jax wants to make sure Carlos isn't holding you against your will!"

"And why should we let you in, intruding on our privacy?" Marina called down to them, laughing at their antics.

"We bring you gifts," Salomé sang to her.

"We bring you entertainment, baby! We thought you would like to listen to some music!"

Marina turned to Carlos, with the delight of a child. "I hear a guitar!" she gasped.

Carlos nodded. "So do I," he murmured, intrigued. Looking at their unexpected visitors, he laughed.

Caribe held up his hands. "I am just here to record the events," he explained with a shrug.

The pirate smiled down at them. "Please," he beckoned, "come, join us!"

Moments later, they were all spread out around the room. They had come with baskets of fruit and bottles of wine. The guitar had materialized in Jackson's hands. Caribe had immediately made himself comfortable at the window seat, the breeze blowing at his back, stirring his dreads. His pencil began to fly on the paper in his hands. Storm threw herself on the bed, purring on the leopardskin bedspread they had found in the chest their mothers had left for them. Salomé claimed the *coqueta*, and Indio took over the desk. Jackson threw himself into the hammock. That left the corner with the baby toys, for the host and hostess.

"What are you guys up to?" Marina asked with a smile, as the pirate next to her took her hand in his.

"We just wanted to see how you two were doing," Jackson answered. Storm sat up on her elbows, stretching her long legs in front of her.

Tonight she was dressed as the sisters, low-slung cutoff pants, and flowered fabric around her breasts. Beautiful gold bracelets graced her upper arms, and feathers dangled from her ears. Around her neck hung a lion's claw, like Sultan's. Jackson seemed enthralled. Her almond shaped lioness eyes twinkled with mischief as she tossed her head. Full of braids again, she looked very exotic and cute. "You have to excuse Jackson," she laughed, with a wave of her hand. "*We* is too many people."

Salomé gasped as she studied the drawings around the mirror. "Yo, this is awesome, boo!" She laughed at her sister's reflection in the mirror. "I'm jealous, Marina," she sang out. Her eyes flashed green fire at Caribe. "Y'all better have some drawings of me and Indio, boy!" She smiled as everybody laughed around her, and tossed her long silky hair, turning her cat eyes on her boyfriend. "Baby, why don't you make a room for me like this? We've been together longer," she pouted, blowing him a kiss.

Indio watched her, mesmerized, before shaking himself out of his reverie. Then, tossing an orange back and forth between his hands, he turned to his brother. Finally, he threw it at him. Carlos caught it neatly and grinned. The brave couldn't help but smile back at him. He shook his head. "You had to go and spoil it, didn't you?" he rumbled. "She was so happy at my place." They all laughed.

Marina turned to her brother, eyes sparkling with excitement. "Where did you get a guitar, Jax?"

Jackson waved a hand at her, eyes alert on her face, looking for signs. "I've got connections," he laughed.

Storm rolled her eyes. "Giancarlo hooked him up," she told the sisters confidentially. The females smiled. The males chuckled.

"Too bad you don't have drums," Marina mourned softly.

"Actually, Dad and Papi are having a set made, as we speak," her brother informed her. "They should be ready tomorrow, or the day after."

Marina gasped in delight, and glanced at Salomé for confirmation. Her sister nodded. She laughed happily. "All right! I guess we'll be jammin' soon..."

Caribe spoke up then, since nobody else seemed to notice the pirates' confused expressions. "They get together and play rhythms and start chanting," he told the locals. "Basically, they just make a lot of noise." The pirates nodded in understanding.

"So, what's up?" Marina asked.

"Well, I originally wanted to play some music," Jackson answered. "But," he continued mysteriously, glancing at the pirates, "I think I'd rather listen to these guys, first."

Next to her, the pirate froze. "What do you mean?" he asked her brother cautiously.

Jackson smiled. "It's out, dude. A little bird told me all about those sexy sea shanties y'all sing, when you're out on the ocean..."

Salomé spluttered, as she tried to choke back a laugh. *"Sexy sea shanties?"*

Next to her, the brave grumbled. "Would this little bird of yours happen to own a whorehouse?" he wanted to know.

Storm waved a hand at him. "Oh, don't play," she laughed, including the Captain, "you both sing good, and you know it." The pirates began to protest, but she shushed them both, holding her hands out to them and closing her eyes, shaking her head.

Caribe shrugged, as the sisters looked at him for confirmation. He nodded, glancing at them before turning back to his sketch. "They do. I have heard them sing." And if looks could kill, he would have been dead, from the daggers shooting out of the pirates' eyes.

Jackson cracked up, laughing silently, holding his stomach and pointing at his brothers-in-law. "You think my sisters are going to take no for an answer?" He strummed the guitar, in challenge. "I'll bet that anything you can sing about, I can do a modern version of the same..."

Indio rose to the bait. "You are on!"

Marina smiled as Carlos sighed. Their eyes met. "You are so busted," she laughed at him. "Go sing me a song, baby..."

The brothers did. They sang their hearts out. Sexy sea shanties. Indeed. They sang the bawdiest tales the girls had ever imagined. Marina blushed during the most graphic descriptions, only to gain a wink from her lover. Salomé just cracked up, delighting in the men's expressions. They sang of love, in any way possible. Love found, love lost, everlasting love, one-night-stands, real love, imagined love, harems and masturbation, the most pure expression of self-love. Their audience laughed until tears rolled down their faces. And true to his word, for every song the pirates entertained them with, Jackson responded with a humorous rap. The girls screamed with laughter. Caribe's dreadlocks rioted around his head, as he tried to sketch, even as his shoulders shook from amusement. The pirates chuckled with appreciation at Jackson's comebacks.

They had a very nice time together. At that moment there were no differences between them. Not in sex, age, or race. They were not pirates, nor visitors. Only grown children with a lot of love between them, looking for a good time together. Young adults in age, but nothing more than big kids hanging out. "Marina," the pirate smiled at her, "in your time, what song would best describe the way you feel about me?"

Marina froze. To say she was surprised at the question was an understatement. Shocked was more like it. But she recovered beautifully. "That's easy," she tossed her hair away from her face. "It's called *Everything I Do*, and it's sung by a guy named Bryan Adams."

Jackson strummed the guitar, cocking his head at his sister before turning to the pirate. "Let me demonstrate," he offered. Then, he proceeded to sing the chorus. *"I would fight for you, I'd lie for you, walk the wire for you, I'd die for you... everything I do--- I do it for you..."*

The pirate listened attentively, letting the words flow through him. When Jackson was done, he raised an eyebrow at Marina. "Really?" he murmured, bringing her hand to his lips. His eyes blazed into hers. "All that?"

Marina blushed. She nodded, aware of all eyes on them. "All that."

"I like Bryan Adams."

"So do I."

"So, how do you *really* feel about me?"

"I really love you," she confessed, pressing his hand against her lips.

"You realize we have witnesses," he pointed out, reminding her of where they were.

"I realize."

"I really love you," he confessed.

Marina's heart stopped. She looked into his eyes and began drowning. Forcing herself out, she began breathing again. She smiled. "Cool." Steadying her heartbeat, she turned to Jackson. "Bryan Adams rocks," she sighed. "Play the one from *Don Juan De Marco*," she requested.

Jackson grinned. "Quite appropriate," he murmured.

Salomé laughed softly. "You're sly," she whispered.

"Who's Don Juan De Marco?" Indio asked.

"He's not even a real person," Salomé explained. "He's a character."

"Like Silas?"

Salomé laughed out loud. "No, like people in Shakespeare's plays, or someone in a Greek tragedy, or comedy."

"So, what's special about him?"

"He's a cool character," she answered him. "The actor who plays him name's Johnny Depp." Lowering her voice, she turned to Storm. "Very cute. Very sexy."

"*I* am cute and sexy," Indio informed her.

Salomé blew him a kiss. "You sure are, baby."

Jackson interrupted their banter. "You'll like this one," he winked at the pirates. Striking a pose, he began playing, the music filling the round stone room with haunting notes. His head bowed over the instrument, candlelight danced along his cornrows, glinting off his earrings and the cross around his neck. Storm sighed. Salomé and Marina smiled at each other. Then, Jackson's rich voice spilled into the room, husky and seductive, filling their senses. The pirates listened attentively, as he inquired whether they have really ever loved a woman. "You are sly," the pirate smiled at her, admiration in his eyes. This time, he brought her hand to his heart. He confessed again. *"I really love you."*

Marina stroked his face and winked at him. *I can't live without you.*

"What other characters has Johnny Depp played?" Caribe asked casually.

Jackson stopped his strumming, slapping his hand against the strings and silencing them. He laughed. *"Captain Jack Sparrow!"*

This time, Carlos' curiosity was piqued. He frowned. "Captain Jack Sparrow?"

Salomé nodded. "That's right. He's a pirate just like you."

"What happened to him?"

"His ship's name was the *Black Pearl*," Marina offered with a laugh.

Salomé nodded. "This character had a mutiny on the ship, and lost it to his First Mate," she explained, smiling apologetically at the brothers. "They marooned him, and he got tweaked from the sun, but he managed to survive, and at the end, he gets his ship back. Cool stuff."

The men were silent for a moment. Finally, Indio broke the silence. "So, is Johnny Depp a good actor?"

Salomé laughed. "Very good."

"So, is that the kind of people you admire, where you come from?" Storm asked softly. "Actors?"

The siblings laughed. Jackson was the first one to be able to answer. "It's easy to admire actors, because they create an art form for us, where they portray characters in situations, we would otherwise never encounter," he explained, careful to not overload them with stuff they wouldn't understand. "We also admire other people that are of public domain. Like presidents, sport stars, astronauts, inventors, musicians..." He smiled at the pirates. "For example. We had a president recently that was very controversial. He did a lot of good for the country, but in the end, he got caught with his pants down." He looked at the brothers, the way men look at each other, sharing men secrets. "It didn't matter all he did. That unemployment was down, that the world was at peace, this president had pretty much everything under control," he shook his head mournfully. "But after all was said and done, all that mattered, all that people remembered..." he paused, taking in a dramatic deep breath, and rolling his eyes, "was that the guy got caught with his dick in a mouth that wasn't his wife's---"

"*Jackson!*" his sisters shrieked at him.

"What?" he asked, feigning innocence. The pirates laughed.

"So, what do you admire about him?" Carlos Gaitano wanted to know. "He was a good president!" Salomé exclaimed defensively.

"What was his name?" Indio asked.

"Bill Clinton."

Carlos turned to Marina. "Was he a good president?"

She nodded. "Very good. He was young, and handsome, and charismatic. He did a lot of good." She shrugged. "He just got caught. Didn't make him a bad president, or a bad guy. Didn't undo all the good he did. Just made him lose the presidency. Of course, he *lied* about it," she explained, glancing at the ceiling. "But we haven't had one as good since," she rolled her eyes, "the next one, made war, so..." she shrugged again, smiling.

"Well, what I admire the most," Jackson laughed, "is that he had the balls to get his dick sucked in the Oval Office, and then had the face to deal with the public."

"You are crude," Storm informed him. Marina and Salomé rolled their eyes in agreement.

Jackson wiggled his eyebrows at his date. "Just the way I am, baby," he teased.

Storm shook her head at him, playing along. They had been hanging out for a few days, and she had already experienced firsthand what an extraordinary gentleman Jackson really was, as opposed to the character he was playing now, to his sisters' outrage and amusement. "I like it," she told him.

"I know," he smiled at her, eyes crinkling at the corners.

"Who else do you admire?" Indio asked.

"Michael Jordan!" Marina offered.

"Who's Michael Jordan?"

Jackson sprang out of the hammock, putting the guitar where his body had just lain, swinging gently in the breeze that cruised around the room. "Dude!" he said, pretending he was dribbling, and shooting at an invisible basket over Caribe's head. "Michael Jordan is only the single, most amazing athlete of our time. The guy is an angel. He flies..." He went off, playing one-on-one with an invisible friend.

The girls eagerly proceeded to explain the mechanics of basketball, and what Michael Jordan's amazing contribution had been to the sport. And in that manner, the pirates learned lessons on a range of people, centuries beyond their time, ranging from Arafat to Ozzie Osbourne. From Mark McGwyer, to Martin Lawrence. Jesse Jackson preaching love, Jesse James designing motorcycles. John Travolta and John -John Kennedy.

And the pirates understood. The world was not only beyond their aquatic boundaries. It was way beyond their imaginations.

Soon after, the guests left, after much more laughing and sharing wine. Nobody overdid it, though. Not the ones that had to walk home, not the ones that got to stay home. They just finished the night happily, glad to have spent the evening together. As the last one went out and the door closed behind him, the couple turned towards one another. They had found out a lot about each other tonight. Carlos and Marina smiled.

"Look at us..."

Marina looked. She moaned. Candlelight flickered around the room, in the beautiful glass lamps. Shadows danced with the wind on the walls. The pirate held her in his arms, like a guitar, her back against his chest. His arm sustained part of her weight, as his left hand cupped her breast, her nipple peeking between his fingers. Her hair was loose and wild, around her body, clinging to them. She was riding him, sitting on his lap, impaled on his sex, his powerful thighs holding her. His right arm rested on her hip, his hand busy strumming her clitoris as if it were the chord of a musical instrument. The shadow on his face absorbed the light, just as the sweat on his skin reflected it. His eyes were closed, his mouth against her ear. She shivered. Mesmerized, she couldn't look away. They were on the edge of the bed, facing the mirror. The glass reflected them beautifully, framing them in their lovemaking. His tongue snaked out, tasting her skin, from her shoulder to right below her ear. She shuddered. Their eyes met in the mirror. He fondled her shamelessly, controlling her body as she never could. She gasped. He chuckled. Her arm snaked out to hook around his head, bringing her face next to his. Their rhythm grew a little bit faster.

"Look at us," she echoed in a husky whisper.

The pirate laughed, hugging her in his embrace, guiding her to her orgasm. He held her eyes in the mirror. "*Eres mia,*" he told her. And then he repeated it, just to make sure she didn't misunderstand. "You are mine..."

Marina whimpered at her approaching climax, not being able to think straight anymore. "No," she informed him in a ragged whisper, "*you* are *mine...*" Carlos pressed his face against hers, passion overwhelming him, as he devoured her through the looking glass, his heart surrendering to hers. He smiled, as he felt her contract around him, making her smile back. "*Bruja...*" he accused softly. Marina laughed. And then, banging harder, they came. Gasping, the wave swept them from the inside, outwards. Grasping each other, their heads turned and their mouths met, tongues mating, as the rest of them. Clutching, nails dug in, adding a sting. Ending their kiss, they looked into each other's eyes, through the glass in front of them. They laughed. The pirate bit her shoulder. Burying her fingers in his thick shaggy hair, holding his head against hers, the woman kissed his face. Sighing and moaning, their orgasms overtook them and sent them over the edge, leaving their reflections shuddering in the mirror.

"I need to see Caribe."

The pirates turned to look at her. They were on the balcony of the lighthouse, looking out over the ocean. The Captain, his Quartermaster, and the accountant. Since early morning, ships had been sailing steadily into Encantada. Pirates and merchants from the neighboring islands, coming in for the convention. Marina felt a small sinking feeling, as she realized just how many visitors would be in Encantada in the next few days. It was on.

"Why?" Gaitano wanted to know.

"You realize the *White Ghost* will be joining us."

The brothers looked at each other over her head. "We are counting on it," Indio said carefully.

"I think I have information, from when we went to Carey, that will help eliminate possibilities." Her eyes scanned the ocean, restless. "I need to see Caribe," she repeated softly, and went back inside.

The men looked at each other again, shaking their heads and chuckling. Indio smiled at his brother. "You are *so* whipped," he taunted softly.

Carlos growled. "Get out of here! Go get Caribe for the girl!" Indio laughed.

Caribe came. Indio was back with him, half an hour later. They brought breakfast. The pirates lounged inside, watching the couple outside on the small deck. There were still ships coming in.

Marina and Caribe embraced, kissing on the cheek. Smiling at each other, they sat to share a mango, and drink fresh juice out of the beautiful dark glass bottles Silas sent them. Finishing their breakfast, they cleaned up with damp towels Indio had provided them. Finally, they looked at each other.

"What's up, baby?" he asked, fondly.

Marina gazed at him with affection. "I call, you come," she teased. "I like that."

"Sending Indio on horseback was a nice touch."

"Only the very best for my baby..."

"What's on your mind?"

"Remember *El Baile del Luto*?" she asked with a wry smile.

Caribe rolled his eyes, his dreadlocks shaking around his head, as he laughed quietly. "How could I forget? I only have a record of the events!"

"Exactly!"

"You need something?"

"Why, yes, baby, how kind of you to offer..." They laughed softly at each other. "Remember when we first got to the cave?"

Caribe nodded, thoughtfully. "You went around, shaking hands."

"I did. I was making personal contacts. You were right next to me..."

"Sketching the pirates' faces..."

"That's right, baby. Now, what I want for you to do is, since you have all the paperwork, match the faces to the text. All the notes I scribbled down. Names, ships, port'o'calls, everything!" Marina turned to look at him, fire flashing out of her hazel eyes. "We need to eliminate everybody who couldn't possibly be the *White Ghost*, in order for them to catch him!"

Caribe reacted to the passion in her hushed voice, his heart bursting for love and gratitude for her and her friendship. "What can I do?"

"Make me a book. Something nice. Special. Professional. Sketch the pirates the size of a full page. On the page opposite that, write down all their information, in a nice, beautiful script. Put the pages together, as if it were a book," she instructed him, waving her hands in the air to demonstrate what she wanted done. "Take it to John Kline, and ask him to bind it for you, the most beautiful way possible. Tell him what it's for." She nodded to the ocean. Still, ships coming in. "By the look of things, there will be a meeting tomorrow of the powers-that-be. On your way out, ask Carlos and Indio when it will be. What time, where." She smiled ruefully. "They won't ask you why you want to know. I already told them I had something that could help. Once the book is done, bring it by, for me to look at, real quick." She laughed. "Only because I don't think I'll get a chance to, once it is in the pirates' hands." She took his dark hand in hers, and brought it to her face. "Thank you, baby." She kissed it, and smiled at h im.

Caribe laughed, stroking her face. "You call, I come." And he was gone.

Marina felt the murmur of voices behind her, as Caribe requested the information she needed. Indio peeked his head out to kiss her good-bye, and it was quiet again. Carlos came outside to join her. Finally, he couldn't resist it any longer.

"Marina, let's run..."

Sighing, she smiled up at her man. "I thought you would never ask..."

They spent the whole day together. Again. Alone. It was their last day off before they went back, to not only face daily life in Encantada, but also, the wave of tourists they were getting, due to the much anticipated *Pirates' Convention Expo. Caribbean Edition.* Marina smiled to herself. It was overwhelming. So, instead, she focused on the back of the man in front of her.

Today, he led her through more familiar territory. Back home, so to speak. They skirted the outside of the village, and into the mountain. Forms were done by the ancient ruins, the jungle steaming around them. They cooled down in their pool. The one they met in.

"If we stay here in Encantada," he began casually. Marinas' eyes flew to his. *We...* And as if he read her mind, "we don't actually *have* to stay in Encantada, if you don't want. We could have houses on every island in the Caribbean, if you so desire. God knows, I can afford it," he smiled ruefully, shrugging. "Or, I could build you a hut on Arrecife..."

Marina's heart stopped. She forgot to breathe. Tears came to her eyes. He caught her as her knees failed her. Holding her close, Carlos glided her away in the water, towards the deep, dancing secret circles in the lagoon, until her heart beat again. Until she gasped for air. He made her look at him. They smiled at each other. Marina had no words for what she felt in her heart at that moment. So instead, she held up her hand. The pirate grinned. He slid her some skin.

Grabbing her against him, suddenly, he began swimming with her, arms and legs wildly wrapped around him, as she tried not to drown by laughter. Reaching the other side, he kissed her. Hard. Hungrily. His voice was husky in her ear.

"Right here, right now..."

Marina moaned, spreading her arms out on the ledge behind her. He laughed, anxiously grasping her hips. She winked at him, blowing kisses at him, shaking her breasts at him as they floated in the water, making waves. Her mind whispered an old song in her ear. *Come on and rock me, baby...*

The pirate laughed. He was *whipped.* So... he took her. In the water. Right there in their pool. Not with violence. Just in an exciting way. He played with her, until she was laughing with him. In his arms, Marina screamed. He loved making her scream. Whether from laughter, or in orgasm, it didn't matter to him. As long as she screamed with pleasure. This was what he wanted for the rest of his life.

"In my time, they can see hurricanes coming."

The pirate froze, next to her. *"They can see them coming?"* He couldn't believe it.

Marina nodded. "Hurricanes are nothing but wind storms, born in Africa. Once they hit the Atlantic..." she shrugged, "...they gather the power and momentum, speed and force, because there is nothing out there to stop them. They encounter no land until they reach the Lesser Antilles in the Caribbean, and by then, for the most part, they are monsters. Hurricane season is around five months long, I think," she said, frowning thoughtfully, "from June to October," she waved her hand in the air, emphasizing the importance of her words. "It helps to know what's coming your way."

Gaitano shook his head in wonder at her. "How do you know so much?"

Marina sighed dramatically, rolling her eyes at him, with a smile. "I have family in Boriken, remember?"

In a boyish gesture, he bit his lip, to keep from laughing out loud. "I remember..." He settled on a smile.

"Do you know anything about them?"

"I learned about the one in 1515, that caused the death to many *tainos*." He frowned, trying to remember. "In 1530, three storms in 6 weeks blew down half the houses in San Juan, and tore the roofs off the rest. In 1537, three hurricanes in two months, caused many slaves and cattle to drown."

Marina looked at him, in awe. "How do *you* know so much?"

He laughed at her. "I am a sailor, remember? Besides, living in the Caribbean, you have to learn about the hurricanes." He looked into her eyes, searching for her reaction. "San Mateo struck in 1575 and 1615 brought the most severe hurricane the island had seen in forty years."

"I know a little bit, too," she offered, shyly. "I had to do a paper for the university, about the history of tropical storms and hurricanes in the Caribbean, and their impact on the islands. After writing and rewriting the material, I learned most of it," she explained. Taking a deep breath, she concentrated. "In 1767, plantations were destroyed and livestock drowned. October 14, 1780 saw the most devastating hurricane of record up to date. *El Gran Huracan*. After a while, people named them, depending on what day they fell on, according to their almanac. In 1804, *San Mateo II*. 1825, *Santa Ana*, very violent and very destructive. 1837, *Los Angeles*; 1851, *Santa Elena* or *San Agapito*; 1867, *San Narciso*; 1876, *San Felipe I*; 1899, *San Ciriaco*; 1928, *San Felipe II*; 1931, *San Nicolas*; 1932, *San Ciprian*; and in 1956 *Betsy* or *Santa Clara*. That was the last one named with a saint."

"How can they see them coming?"

"When the season begins, they, the people that are in charge of these things, already have a list of names in alphabetical order, to give these storms, in order of appearance. The storms are monitored by satellites up in space. There are people trained to fly right over them, in airplanes." She waited, as the pirate thought on her words, for a moment.

"And then, what do they do?"

"Well, the center of the hurricane is called the eye. The winds rush around it, in a circular motion," she explained, demonstrating with her hands. "How large it is, depends on each individual hurricane. These men, in these airplanes, drop instruments into the eye, that measure real important stuff," she smiled, seeing the understanding in his eyes.

"Like what?"

"Size, strength, speed," she shrugged, "everything you need to know, basically."

"And once this information is gathered..." he raised an eyebrow at her.

She shook her head at him, laughing. "Why, it gets imparted to the public, of course." She sighed. "They warn people that the hurricanes are coming."

"They actually have time to warn people?"

"Yes!" she whispered urgently. "First, they announce an advisory. That's like, *Hey, people, by the way, in a few days, there will be a hurricane coming your way, just for your information.* Then, they send out a hurricane warning, which is more like, *Okay, people, you need to prepare yourselves for this one, make sure you have and do everything you need to be safe, or get the hell out!* So, it's really good to know what your hurricane season looks like." She gazed deep into his eyes. "In 1918, in Boriken, more people died, as a result of a tsunami, on the southwestern side of the island. The ocean had receded, and people walked out on the sand, marveling at what the water had left them. When the ocean came back, it wiped them all out. Nothing like that ever happened again, however. Nowadays, though, in *my* time, I mean," she added hastily, "they see tsunamis coming from miles, and/or days away. They really screwed up with a huge one that hit

Indonesia at the end of 2004. It killed thousands of people, because some jerk wouldn't give the warning." He winced. She tore her eyes from his, to look out over the ocean. "My father remembers *David* and *Federico* in 1979." They had reached the base of the lighthouse. "Check this out." Grabbing a sharp piece of driftwood, she began tracing patterns in the sand. "In September, 1989, there was a huge storm named *Hugo*." She drew the size of her father's native island, and the size of *Hugo*.

The pirate shook his head in disbelief, his eyes searching hers. "That is incredible!" he murmured, in awe. "What happened?"

Marina chose her words carefully. "Do you know that beautiful rainforest on the northeastern side of the island?"

Carlos nodded. "Over by *Loquillo*'s domain."

Tears sprang to her eyes, admiration for this man overwhelming her. She laughed. "I knew you would." She sighed. "It stopped Hugo. Took the wind out of his sails, so to speak."

"It must have been devastating."

"To some," she agreed. "To others, it was a fresh beginning." She turned to smile at her pirate. "Pablo tells me, Hugo stripped the bark off the trees in that rainforest," she told him softly. "He saw it himself. He went up that mountain with a group of friends, a couple of nights later. It was full moon. He says the trees were so bare it looked like an enchanted forest. The tree trunks shone like silver in the moonlight. The hurricane cleared the atmosphere over the island, you see. The air had never been so clean. You have never seen so many stars. But it could have wiped out the whole island," she said, "obviously," pointing out her drawing in the sand.

"God is merciful," he whispered.

"He is," she whispered back, squeezing his hand. Then, she continued. "In 1995 it was *Luis*. People put signs in their windows, *Go away, Luisito, we don't want you here*. Just as the first winds began reaching San Juan, he turned a sharp right, at a ninety degree angle, and headed straight north into the open Atlantic Ocean, missing Boriken, completely."

"That sounds like a miracle."

"It was."

"What's your explanation?"

Marina smiled at him. "Thank you for asking. People were warned, days ahead of time. They had plenty of time to prepare." Her eyes twinkled at him, stirring shadows in their depths. "I believe that the power of prayer convinced Luisito to go another way."

Carlos thought for a moment, silent, pondering her words. He was still trying to come to terms with the history lessons he was receiving on things that hadn't happened yet. Finally, he took a deep breath. "How big was Luis?"

Marina showed him. She nodded. "Luis was bigger than Hugo."

Shock flashed behind his eyes, like lightning reflected on water. The pirate let out a low whistle. "Yes, he was."

"Then, there was *Georges* in 1999, who surprised the hell out of everyone, coming in the opposite side of the island..."

"Sneaky Georges..."

"Yes! And then, in 2004, *Jeanne* didn't do much damage in Boriken, but almost totally decimated what we know as Haiti, on the western side of the Hispaniola."

"*Bojio*," he murmured.

Marina frowned. "Isn't *bohio*, a hut?"

"Yes," he agreed, "but the natives refer to that side of the island, as home, because that's where they live."

Now, she nodded, smiling. "That makes sense."

"Your hurricane lore is very interesting."

"I made sure I knew all about them. Dad's older sister Lisa and her husband, Blue and Cat's parents lost their lives in one, right after the twins were born. So, hurricanes have impacted us directly."

The pirate reached out to stroke her. "I am sorry for your loss."

"My point is, Gaitano, if you and I are here, together, as a couple, and something happens..." she shrugged. "We are young, we are together, whatever, right? But..." she saw the pirate shake his head as he saw from where she was coming, "what if---"

"*When---*"

"Then, it won't be just the two of us anymore, baby."

"We'll be a ---"

"Not alone anymore, and responsible for..." she saw him shake his head with a smile, as he saw where she was coming from. But Marina couldn't think about it, much less say it, "...keeping safe. Now," she urged softly, "having the option of settling in for a surprise attack by a hurricane, or being able to prepare for it, and, if necessary, move away from its path, which would you prefer?" Reaching out, she took his face in her hand, making him look at her. "Don't answer now," she whispered. "Think about it."

Marina gasped. "Is this your place?"

The pirate chuckled, delighted with her reaction. "Do you like it, mami?" he asked, teasingly.

Marina laughed with joy. "I'll trade you..." she offered.

They had spent a short while at the lighthouse, but the sight of neverending ships coming into the island, was unsettling. Marina was preoccupied, and that disturbed him. In order to distract her, he had made her collect all her toiletries and offered her a surprise. She had gladly gone with him. Carlos noted that she didn't ask him where he was taking her anymore, but instead, followed him blindly, with the delight of a child. She trusted him implicitly. He liked that. So, being obnoxiously mysterious, he led her down the beach, around Villa Azul, to the jungle behind it, and up a cliff. They reached a small landing, overgrown with vines. From there, they turned to survey the scenery around them. Below them was Villa Azul, so clearly, you could look down on the courtyard. Straight ahead, was the ever changing ocean, with its maritime traffic. On the other side of some sand dunes from Villa Azul, was the tent Don Carlos had gifted her with. A short ways down the beach was their lighthouse. Finally, he pulled aside some vines, and led her inside what she now realized was a cave. Up on a ledge by the entrance, were matches and candles. The pirate lit one and went inside for a moment, indicating her to wait outside. Soon afterwards he invited her to join him. Holding her breath in anticipation, Marina stepped inside. To her, it was like Ali Baba's den of thieves. You couldn't tell, at first, but it was more evident, as you went in.

It was the most amazing place Marina had ever been in. There was the sound of water, everywhere. Falling, running, dripping.

Liquid noises filled the cavern. Appropriately, there were stalactites hanging from the ceiling, with corresponding stalagmites on the floor. There were tiki torches placed in opposite corners of the room, casting eerie shadows on the wall. Marina murmured with delight, as she took her time, looking about her.

It had been cool, as they had come in, at the entrance. However, it grew comfortably warmer, as you approached the center. From the drier walls hung opulent Persian carpets. Antique, in her time. And in his, she realized, eyes wide as saucers. Laughing at herself, she made herself relax. The furniture was exquisite. Beautiful bamboo, with decadent pillows made of luscious fabrics from the Orient, for cushions and backrests. Low tables with different sized chests on them, and gorgeous cut glass vases filled with seashells and dead coral branches, were located in strategic places. There wasn't a hammock, she realized, because the ceiling was too high. However, incredibly, there were potted plants. Against one side of the room, was a beautiful bamboo bed, complete with posts and mosquito netting draped over it. On the walls behind it, were slabs of wood with papers tacked unto them. On closer inspection, Marina perceived they were sketches. Varied ones.

Two were about him. A formal portrait of the crew in command of La Gitana: Carlos, the Captain; Indio, the Quartermaster; Giancarlo the Sailing Master; and Solomon, the Boatswain. The other sketch was of him with Indio, caught in an intimate moment, the brothers laughing over a shared secret.

Two were of her. In the first sketch, she had Max in her arms, his little back against her chest, and they both had their eyes closed, identical smiles, faces lifted up towards the sun. In the other, she was fighting with Solomon. Caribe had caught her beautifully, in the middle of a lightning kick to the African's ribs. Fists clenched, face set, eyes fierce, mouth twisted in a taunting smile, you could almost see the sheen of perspiration on her skin. To one side of these, separate, was another set of sketches. Her heart skipped a beat. Of them.

There were three. In the first, their heads were bowed together, as they worked on Gaitano's books, doing numbers. The second was a semi -formal portrait they had playfully posed for at the entrance of El Baile del Luto, dressed in all their finery. They looked like VIPs at the Vampire Ball. Absolutely stunning. The last one was graphic. It was in the middle of the notorious lapdance. Marina faced him, knees on either side of him, as he slouched on the pirate throne. Her fingers were buried in his hair, as she grasped his head back, chin pointed at her chest. His hands gripped her hips, her butt tight on his thighs. His eyes were closed and his lips were parted, an expression of pure lust in his face. Above him, Marina's hair fell over her face on one side, revealing her expression on the other. Her eyes were also closed, lips also parted. Her chest seemed to heave, coins in her ear seemed to be playing music.

Marina bit her lip. Caribe had caught her, trembling with desire. There was no denying the passion the couple felt for each other. Marina sighed. Turning her head, she shared a long intimate look with her pirate. Finally, she grinned. "I am *so* busted," she laughed softly. Then she winked at him.

Carlos Gaitano chuckled. "You are..."

Marina kept exploring. On the far side of the cave was a waterfall. Nice and neat, it reminded her of the manmade falls you found back home as part of the decor of some business buildings. Only this had been made by no man. She stepped closer. A small cloud of steam seemed to come from it. Straight up above it was a natural skylight, through which sunrays poured in, at this hour of the day. Marina reached out curiously, with her hand, to feel the water. It was very warm. She frowned, looking for a source. The waterfall seemed to spring straight from the wall. At the bottom of it, there was shallow water. Like a kiddie pool. And that's where it seemed to end. On instinct, Marina turned her back to the waterfall, and faced the entrance of the cave. Right in the middle of the space in between, there seemed to be a small pool. She had caught sight of it from the corner of her eye, when they first came in. However, the bigger, more visible items in the cave had distracted her immediately. Now, she headed straight towards it. It also had a natural skylight right above it, seeming to illuminate the beautiful bright blue water. There was a little movement to it, and it also seemed to be emitting a vapor. Without thinking about it, she dropped to her haunches, and stuck her hand in the water, only to draw it back immediately. *It* was *hot*. Straightening up slowly, she turned to look at him, her voice hushed with awe. "*Dude!* You have a shower *and* a jacuzzi!"

Carlos shook his head and laughed. He had no idea what she was talking about, but he liked the way it sounded. He especially liked the reaction it got from her. It could only mean good things for him. He was right. Once he told her what his intentions were with her, she was delirious with joy, as he guided her through the most decadent afternoon either of them had ever had.

First, they went to the waterfall. Having discarded their clothes long ago, they just stood there soaking, smiling at each other through the curtain of water. The sunlight kissed their wet bodies, making them glisten in the gloomy cave. Marina taught him how to use the hair products John Kline had so painstakingly prepared, especially for her. She loved the way he let himself get absorbed by such a menial task as untangling her hair. Once he was done, and the last was rinsed away, she did the same for him. He loved it. The feel of her fingers massaging his scalp, the smell of the fragrance in his hair. He loved all of it.

The last suds disappeared, she wasn't quite sure exactly where, yet, and Marina dropped to her knees. Leaning back on the wall behind him, he closed his eyes, letting the water cascade past him, clearing her backside, keeping them in a small, misty pocket. The pirate groaned as her mouth engulfed him. Knees cushioned by a sandy bottom, she was comfortable. So, she didn't stop until she pleased him. His knees buckled, and she pretended to catch him before he fell on her. Laughing, they both stumbled out of the waterfall, grinning like fools.

From there, they went to the pool in the middle of the room. Soaking for real, facing each other, arms draped over the edge, heads thrown back, eyes closed, expressions of pure bliss on their faces.

Marina moaned softly, her muscles relaxing in the hot water. It was *exactly* like a jacuzzi! Only without the bubbles. "So, Carlitos..."

The pirate's moan echoed her own. "So, Marina..."

"Nice place you got here, babe," she sighed.

He sighed back. "Why, thank you, darling..."

"Do you mind if I ask you a question?"

"Not if you don't mind me asking you one."

"Where does all the water come from, and where does it go to?"

"What is this contraption for?"

Marina's eyes flew open, meeting his. She looked at what he held in his hand, and smiled. It was the razor John Kline had made for her. Suddenly, there was a little devil on her shoulder, whispering in her ear, what to do. Marina gave him a slow, sexy smile. She saw interest sparkle in his eyes. "That, baby, is for taking care of business..." Giving him a saucy grin, she climbed out slowly, resting her backside on the edge of the pool, feet dangling in.

The pirate's breath caught in his chest. His eyes followed, mesmerized, as water cascaded off her shoulders, down her chest, between her breasts, over her belly... He licked his lips, his eyes hooded. His hand automatically went to his hardness, beneath the water, a slow smile spreading on his face. "Taking care of business?" he murmured.

Marina saw the muscles flex in his arm, and laughed wickedly. Reaching out with her foot, she brushed his hand, underwater. Now, she had his full attention. Withdrawing her foot, she spread her legs. The pirate leered at her. Framing her sex with her hands, she seduced him with her voice. "That little blade you have there in your hand," she explained softly, "is for shaving a woman, in such a place, that it will heighten the pleasure, and enhance the enjoyment of herself and her partner, during sex..."

"Aaaah..." Carlos understood. Giving himself one last squeeze, he glided towards her, hand outstretched, caressing her from her ankle, to her inner thigh. There, he let his fingers dangle caressingly, over her sex. He glanced at her face, their eyes meeting. "Trust me?"

Her nod was automatic, her laugh was husky. "Absolutely, baby..."

He wet his lips and glanced down at her womanhood again, sighing dramatically, making her laugh. "Then, permit me..." Reaching out with both hands, he grasped her upper arms, easing her back, his lips pressed to hers. When he had her lying down, he looked into her eyes. "Don't move..." he cautioned.

Marina sighed and nodded, closing her eyes. She trusted him implicitly. She heard him splash in front of her. Soon, his fingers were gliding over her, soapy, caressing gently. Then, she felt him get to work. Her fingers grasped the rock she lay on. She sighed. "Water..." she reminded him.

Carlos smiled, engrossed in what he was doing. He had never shaved a woman down there. Hell, he had never known a woman to shave down there! He laughed to himself. *Mine does.* He sighed happily. "This cave is halfway up this cliff. So, basically, high up as we are, we are still underground, as far as the hill is concerned," he explained. "An underground spring feeds the waterfall. That is why the water seems to come out of the wall."

"The shower," Marina murmured dreamily.

"So, that water hits the cave floor and just seems to disappear, right?" Without looking away from what he was doing, he sensed her nod. Gently, he continued shaving his woman. "Actually, it runs under the floor, and comes out here," he explained, "and from here, it disappears under the floor again, entirely. The water comes out, a little ways down the cliff. Water is always circulating here, in this pool."

"Jacuzzi..." she sighed happily.

"I discovered this place when I was a teenager. One day, I had a disagreement with my father. Moved right on in. Indio with me. My mother almost died," he chuckled at the memory. "Of course, I patched things up with my *viejo*, almost immediately, in fact. But..." he sighed, finishing up carefully. "I just couldn't bring myself to leave here. This was home. Mine. So, my parents built Villa Azul down below, so they could stay close. I have lived here, ever since. Indio eventually moved out. Now I am a man, and all parties involved are comfortable with the arrangement. Especially, since they spend most of the time in their house in Carey. We are barely in Encantada at the same time, as we are on this occasion. Me..." he laughed, eyebrows raised, his expression that of the teenager he was reminiscing of. "Would you leave here?"

Marina smiled. "I don't blame you. I'll trade you," she teased, "my hut in the village, and my tent by Villa Azul, for this place---"

"No."

"I'll throw in my share of the lighthouse room, and half of what's in that treasure chest the Council gave me!"

Gaitano laughed, rubbing his thumbs over her newly shaved skin, feeling for rough spots. Carefully, he went over the whole area again. "I love a desperate woman."

"Share?"

"I'll think about it," he teased her.

"Do all of you live like this?"

The pirate smiled. He knew exactly what all she was talking about. "Not at all. Indio has a house in town."

"Been there. With Salomé. Chilled. Cool place."

He grunted. "It's easier for him to be close to where he is needed. Until now, he hadn't found anyone he wanted to be secluded with. Time will tell whether he will stay there," he murmured thoughtfully. Now, he was almost done. "Solomon lives in a treehouse in the middle of the jungle. Giancarlo lives in a beautiful house on the top of the mountain, complete with Moroccan arches, Greek mosaics, Italian marble, Spanish tiles, and Roman statues."

Marina's eyes flew open. "You are kidding me!"

"Not..."

She sighed. "Rouge must love it up there."

He laughed. "Actually, she does." Finishing, he rinsed her off, and inspected her one last time. Slipping his hands under her buttocks, he turned her, so that the sunlight, coming in the opening overhead, hit her directly, making her glisten.

"I love it here..."

"I know you do, baby..."

"Share?"

The pirate swallowed. Licked his lips. "Share..." He couldn't take his eyes off her. Then, he couldn't get his mouth off her.

Carlos ate her. He had taken care of business. His business. For himself. And now, he enjoyed the results. He devoured her, making her scream. Just the way he liked it.

"Stay with me..."

Marina clung to him. The voice in her ear invaded every pore in her body. "I will..." she promised. Her hips rose to meet his, lifting from the soft mattress.

Locking his arms on either side of her head, so that he hung suspended over her, he looked down at her. His face glowed with pleasure. He rotated his hips against hers, making her moan. "I need you..."

Marina nodded, reaching up to stroke his cheek, brush his hair away from his face. "I absolutely need you..." she smiled. She contracted around him.

He laughed. "I would very much like it if you would be my life partner, Marina Aguilar..."

Marina smiled again. Grasping his hips, she pulled him deep inside her. "I can't live without you, Carlos Gaitano..."

The pirate nodded. He felt himself sink into her, his body taking over. The rhythm changed, he was not in control anymore. Marina, beneath him, moaned in pleasure, exciting his senses even more. Their voices mingled with all the water sounds in the cavern. Their space was limited by the netting encompassing his bed, enshrouding them in a world of their own. "I have never brought anyone here," he confessed in her ear.

Marina hugged him tight, tears stinging the back of her eyes. Passion overwhelmed her. "Thank you, baby..."

Then, he confessed again, this time, looking deep into her eyes. "I love you..."

Marina's body seemed to bloom. Her heart stopped, reminding her to breathe. Then, she sighed deeply, happiness flowing through her. She nodded, sinking into the deep turquoise pools of his eyes. "I love you..."

They showed each other just how much.

That night saw them back at the lighthouse. Thankfully, the last of the ships had come in. They treated themselves to a beautiful sunset, the ocean undisturbed by anything but the change of color. They had a quiet dinner, thanks to Indio. Together, they disposed of their trash, and cleaned up. Finally, they made their way to the hammock, the woman comfortably settled between the pirate's legs.

Carlos reached out with a foot and pushed against the bed, setting them rocking gently. Her head lay on his chest, turned, the better to hear his heartbeat. He brushed the hair away from her face, caressing her cheek. She was lost in thought. "How are you doing?" he inquired gently.

"Sad..."

"Sad?"

"I don't want this to ever end," she confessed huskily, "I don't want to go back to civilization." She moved, until she was looking up into his eyes. "I want to stay with you, like this, forever," she whispered passionately.

The pirate's heart thumped in his chest. "I would like that, also, *divina*," he murmured, humoring her.

Marina sighed deeply, rolling her eyes humorously. "Not very practical, though, is it?"

Carlos shook his head, playing along. "No, not at all."

"They would miss us, and then they would start wondering where we were..."

"They would send out a rescue party..."

"This island's big, but it would only be a matter of time before they found us..." she smiled, at the image she was conjuring.

Gaitano smiled with her. "Eventually, they would find us," he agreed. "We would be found out, our hiding place discovered..."

"No privacy..."

"I would die," she admitted, laying her head on his chest again. "There is only one way to stop that from happening."

He sighed. "There is," he murmured in agreement. "We will have to leave here before they come..."

Marina smiled. "Damn them!" she whispered. They laughed quietly. Settling down again, they each got lost in their own thoughts. "You know, Carlos, this thing about Xavier is killing me."

The pirate nodded, taking a deep breath, controlling his muscles so that they didn't react to her words. "What are you thinking?"

"I have to face him," she said simply.

The pirate nodded again, giving her a squeeze. "I agree," he rumbled softly. "You won't be alone, though..."

Marina laughed softly. "I should hope not!" She sobered again. "At least, Indio at my back."

"What about me?"

"You, I'd rather have where I can see you, at all times. You know, it's *you* he really wants..."

"So, how do you want to do this?"

"Very carefully." Marina thought about it for a moment. "For real?" She buried herself into him. "We'll know when the time comes..."

The pirate sighed. Wrapping his arms around her, he held her close. Marina was right. There was no way to prepare. Whatever was going to happen, would just happen.

Later, when the moon had crossed the sky, and was shining at them from the opposite side of their tower, he reassured her. It was dark and fresh in their room, the wind whipping around it, boundless. They sought each other's warmth, comforting themselves with each other's body. They made love in the dark. Slow, and silent. Their mouths moved, wordless, giving each other pleasure. Their hands stirred their senses, until they were wrapped up in themselves, floating in their own dimension. There, they consummated their love, sealing what they had known, what they had tried to tell each other while they had been secluded. Their bodies knew, their minds told them, and their hearts confirmed it. They were meant to be together. They didn't know why, where, when, or how.

But they would work that out. They had found each other, and that's all that mattered. Carlos Gaitano and Marina Aguilar would be together for the rest of their lives.

Pablo Aguilar sighed. They were all sitting at the Siren's Lair, getting ready to begin their day. All but their grown children. The last twenty-four hours had been hectic, what with all the visitors sailing into Encantada. Now, they were gathered to form a game plan, about what was to happen next. He looked at the Gaitano brothers. Having them together, it was easy to see why these men ruled these waters. In their middle age, they were young, strong, and impressive. They were smart, educated, well-mannered, handsome. And rich beyond belief. It was evident that their men respected them, and even more, loved them. Having spent time with two out of the three, he, too, along with Joe, and their wives, respected them and loved them. Never mind that his girls were crazy about their boys. But, time was running out for them here, in Encantada. Now, they were on the horns of that ever present obstinate animal, a dilemma.

"Pablo… What are you thinking?"

Pablo turned his head to look at Don Carlos, the heart and soul of the Gaitano dynasty. His friend was smiling at him, like he knew. Pablo sighed again. "Just wondering, Carlos…" He smiled as his friend raised an eyebrow at him. "How many of us are going back home?"

Around the table, everyone sighed. Joe lifted a hand, and let it fall, helpless, back down again. "We weren't counting on this, *viejo*," he said mournfully.

"What? On being in such excellent company?" Don Carlos teased.

"Carlos!" María Isabel scolded softly. "Always the clown!"

Her husband laughed, reaching for her hand, and bringing it to his mouth for a kiss. "You are right, mi amor," he murmured. "I apologize, my friends," he said, lips still smiling, eyes still twinkling. "But you have to see the irony, in that..." he gestured at his family, "we did not expect this to happen, either. Or do you think we came here to lose our boys?" He took a deep breath, smile fading, from amused to sad, shadows shifting deep in his eyes. "One would have been bad enough, Pablito," he turned respectfully, to Joe, "Jose," glanced at the women, "but both?" He held up two fingers in front of his face, shaking his hand to emphasize his point. Then, the pirate burst out laughing. "*Carlitos*, you can have, but *Indio*, I am attached to and quite fond of---"

"Carlos!"

"*Storm* is not even my daughter, so you can have her, also---"

"*Carlos!*"

The brothers Gaitano roared with laughter. María Isabel jumped to her feet, beautiful night hair flying around her face like a mantilla. Towering over her husband, she put a hand on her hip, while the other grasped her husband's face to look up at her, her smile betraying her. Sloane and Shayla looked at each other, shook their heads, and rolled their eyes, smiles spreading on their faces. María Isabel sat back down, shaking her head and clicking her tongue in mock admonishment. Pablo and Joe chuckled, shaking their heads.

"*No deal!*" Shayla laughed at the pirate. "Indio's with Salomé," she said, shaking her head, her hands in the air. "*We* get Indio!"

"I'll take Carlitos," Pablo shrugged. "I'll take *anybody* that will pay Marina, keep her busy *and* make her happy!"

More laughter.

"Laugh all you want," María Isabel sang ominously, "it is not going away..."

"No," Juan snickered, hiding behind Don Miguel, "it looks like at least half of them will be staying here..."

"Juan!" María Isabel wrung her hands in the air, almost choking with amusement, as she rolled her eyes.

By now, there were tears of laughter in the Gaitano men's eyes, and they were gasping for air, arms folded over their middles, hands holding their sides. They had the same sense of humor. It was genetic.

"The truth is, we won't even know for sure what is going to happen, until an agreement is made between..." Sloane said softly, her soothing voice commanding attention, as she looked straight into Don Carlos' smoky eyes. "...my *nena* and your *nene*..."

Don Carlos smiled, wiping the tears from his eyes, shoulders shaking in a last chuckle. Taking her hand, he kissed it. *"Si, Sloane, mi corazon, eso es asi..."*

Sloane relaxed, smiled. "We will just have to wait and see..."

"I do believe an agreement must have already been made, however," offered María Isabel provocatively. She laughed wickedly as they all turned to look at her. "Carlitos and Marina are going to stay together..." she predicted.

They all sighed, nodding their heads in agreement.

"But where?" asked Shayla.

Joe shook his head. "You mean *when?*" He frowned, suddenly thinking of something. "Do we even know the boys will go through, to our time?"

Everybody fell silent for a moment, lost in thought. Finally, Shayla rolled her eyes. "Of course they will, Joe!"

Joe turned to his wife, a frown creasing his brow. "How do you know?"

"Well, Jax went through, from this side to ours, didn't he?" she asked, waving her hand in the air, as if he should have known.

Their companions followed them with their eyes, as if at a tennis match.

Joe gaped at her, getting a round of smiles. "Yeah! But Jax is originally from our side!" he grunted.

Shayla winked at María Isabel. "They'll go through, Joe..." she sang out to him, closing her eyes and shaking her head with a wave of her hand, dismissing him.

Sloane nodded. "I agree. They will. It's about the cave, and being in it when the storm hits..."

All heads nodded. Some shoulders slumped.

Don Miguel's energy rolled out over them, finally, consoling. "It is all about *them*," he reminded them. *"Carlitos and Marina."* His voice soothed, as it embraced them. "If I didn't know any better, I would say we are all caught up in the middle of a real life love story." He sighed, frowning thoughtfully. "Indio and Salomé already know what they are going to do. And Jackson and Storm," he laughed at the thought, "are having a *very* good time together." He rolled his eyes, making them all laugh. "They must be soulmates. I would not be surprised if it evolved," he added thoughtfully. "But..." he sighed dramatically, eliciting smiles. They understood. *"Carlos Gaitano and Marina Aguilar..."* He shook his head with a chuckle.

Carlos looked around him. The streets were filling with pirates. All sizes, ages, and nationalities. There was color, sounds, and smells everywhere. He glanced at Marina as a particular, foul smelling sailor approached. The man seemed amused at her outfit of pants and flowered top. He wasn't leering or making fun of her, though, his smile respectful.

Marina stopped, as the pirate stood in front of her. "Hi!" she smiled.

The pirate smiled back. "You must be the accountant," he rumbled, glancing at Gaitano.

She nodded. "I am."

All of a sudden, he didn't know what to do with his hands. He held one out, thought better of it, took it back, shuffled his feet, and finally, shrugging, let it fall to his side.

Marina laughed. Looking deep into his eyes, she took his hand in both of hers, squeezing it, and shook it slowly. "I am Marina Aguilar, accountant of La Gitana," she told him softly.

The man sighed, all reservation melting away. He grinned self-consciously. "I am John," he sighed, squeezing her hand in return, before letting it go. "I need a place to get clean and a place to sleep..."

"I understand," she said softly. "I would be glad to help you. You need to go back the way you came," she directed him gently, pointing him towards the docks. "Find Indio Gaitano or Jackson Banks. They are in charge of the sailors," she glanced at Carlos, who nodded quickly. "They will find you a room where you can store your belongings, and that you can call yours during your stay here."

The sailor heaved a sigh of relief. "Thank you." He smiled. "As soon as I'm clean, I will kiss your hand," he offered shyly.

Marina squeezed his hand, laughing. "Make it my cheek, and you've got a deal."

"Deal!" he laughed.

Marina frowned at him, looking straight in his eyes, and pointing a warning finger at him. "Promise?"

The man laughed harder. "Marina Aguilar, I will move heaven and earth to keep my promise..." His eyes met Gaitano's in silent man-to-man communication. They grinned at each other. The sailor winked at Marina, and disappeared, back the way he had come from.

Marina sighed. She turned to her pirate. "Are we in trouble for being gone these last couple of days?"

He laughed. "No, not at all. Everything is running smoothly," he reassured her. He brushed the hair away from her face, eyes twinkling mischievously. "Do you want to go back to the lighthouse?"

She grinned at him. "Would if I could, baby..."

"Gaitano!"

They both turned to look at where the voice came from. Headed towards them, was a group of men. Unlike the one that had just left them, these were already cleaned up, having arrived earlier, obviously. The trio of men were grinning from ear to ear.

Next to her, the pirate laughed, delighted to see the men. *"Fenix!"* he cried out, what must have been the name of their ship.

Marina stepped aside, as the men seemed to collide, melting into warm embraces. She stood quietly as they slapped each other on the back, held each other's faces, tousled each other's hair, and looked into each other's eyes.

Finally, Carlos turned to her. His eyes sparkled with happiness. "Marina, meet my friends, the Hawthorne scoundrels, I mean, *brothers*," he laughed, winking at her.

Marina smiled. "Hi! I am Marina Aguilar---" In a moment, they surrounded her.

"Marina!"

"Aguilar!"

"The accountant!"

"Is it true?"

"That you beat Lola?"

"That you danced on his lap?"

Marina gasped, blindly reaching for her pirate's hand. *"Capitán!"*

"All right, men," he laughed, pushing them away from her. "The answer is yes. Actually, she almost *killed* Lola," he chuckled, "and yes, she most *definitely* danced on my lap..."

"You did?"

"So, it's true..."

"Do you have a sister?"

Gaitano laughed again. "You guys are a little late. Sister's spoken for. Indio saw her first." Taking Marina's hand, he brought it to his lips. "Never mind them, *mi amor*, they are jealous..."

The men laughed, letting Marina know that they had, indeed, been playing with her. She sighed with relief and smiled, as she said good-bye to the newcomers, turning to leave her man with them. "'Bye, boys..."

Carlos pulled her against his chest as she pushed past him, dipping his head to murmur in her ear. The Hawthorne brothers watched as she nodded at his words, before he sent her off with a pat on the butt. He turned to them with a smile. "Now, boys..."

They turned to him, identical grins splitting their faces. "That's the one, huh, Gaitano?"

"The mother of your children?"

"Way to go, Carlitos..."

Laughing in male camaraderie, they wandered off.

Marina walked slowly, almost shuffling her feet, letting herself get lost in the ever growing crowd. People smiled and said hello to her, left and right, as many friendly faces, as there were unknown. Her outfit gave her away. The notorious accountant of La Gitana was reputed to take care of business in flowered fabrics and boys' pants, so she was easily recognizable. People stopped her. To greet her, to meet her, shake her hand, kiss her cheek, ask her for directions, instructions, advice, and thank her. It was overwhelming. But she waved back, shook hands, answered questions, and offered solutions, making sure that everybody that walked away from her, did it with a smile. At this rate, the walk to The Sirens' Lair seemed never ending. Gaitano and the Hawthornes had walked past her a while back, disappearing into the increasing multitude. Now, she looked in the shop windows, marveling at the beautiful displays that had been made for the occasion of this convention.

Somebody's watching me.

Marina stopped short, wondering where the thought had come from. She had never been one to fall into paranoiac delusions, but she couldn't convince herself that her skin wasn't tingling, when it was. Pretending to be more tired than what she actually was, Marina stretched. She stood in front of the picture window she had been admiring, and stretched, long and hard, looking into its reflection. Quickly, she scanned the crowd around her. Nobody was looking at her. Eyes closed, turning towards the street, face turned towards the sun, she lifted her arms, her hands reaching for the air, making her bare belly smooth and flat, as the pants rode down and the top rode up. People kept walking around her, some ignoring her, others greeting her, those who knew her, chuckling. Marina smiled, lowering her arms slowly, until they were at chest level. Elbows out, she twisted her waist from side to side, silently reaching out with her energy. She hadn't the capability or control Don Miguel had, but she had the ability to sense things. Good and bad. It had never failed her yet. This was bad. Suddenly, her eyes flew open. Time seemed to stop. People were still wandering, all around her, but this time it was different. This time, she was looking right into a set of pale, washed-out eyes. Refocusing her eyes, she quickly adjusted her vision, so they zoomed out and she could see more. Rapidly, she assessed the package they came in. Weather beaten face, filthy brown hair under a disgusting bandanna, white shirt black from grime, dusty pants, scruffy boots. Satisfied, she watched as the man recoiled in shock, when their eyes fleetingly met. Pretending to smile to herself, as she looked all around, surveying the whole crowd, Marina did one last stretch, and turned away.

Dude, you've been made.

Walking on, Marina let herself get lost in thought. She knew she was the object of curiosity and of fascination of many. People stared, whispered, ogled, pointed, looked for her, at her, and talked about her. But none of that fazed her. She was a stranger in a strange land, and that came with the territory. However, until now, nobody had looked at her as if they were memorizing her every move. That unsettled her. It could only mean no good.

Suddenly, Marina felt herself hauled off the street, as she passed an alley.

She screamed.

Oh, my God!

No sound was audible, though. There was a hand clamped over her mouth, and an arm crossed over her chest, in a strong hold. She felt herself stumble as she scampered backwards, being dragged away as she was, making her attacker manage her weight. Trying not to panic, she took a deep breath, willing herself to calm down. Her heart wouldn't listen, though. It thumped against her chest, like wild mustangs through a desert canyon. A faint roar began in her head, quickly getting louder, threatening to consume her. She dug her fingernails into the arm that had moved up around her neck, only to be treated to an amused laugh. The voice in her ear was hoarse and strange. She had never heard it before, but it sounded familiar.

"You must be the Gaitanos' accountant," it rasped in a low, amused tone, "and such a pretty thing, too." It laughed. "I'm sure they won't miss you ---"

Oh, yes, they will!

Marina didn't stop to think, anymore. A wave of cool washed over her, and she reacted, just as she had been trained to do. Raising one knee, she stomped on his foot, at the same time she jabbed her elbow into his side, with all her might. Her would-be captor let out a whoosh of air, in pain. Slipping out of his hold, she turned to face him, hair flying around her head, fists up in a fighting position. She didn't stop to look at him, just proceeded to attack him. Surprised, the man took a step back. Marina pursued him with a flurry of kicks and a barrage of punches, fury driving her towards him, as he shielded himself, his strong thick arms protecting his surprised face from her onslaught. She didn't hold back. He stepped back again, this time, holding out a hand in disbelief. Stepping forward, she punched him with all her might, sending him stumbling back, until he slipped and fell on the seat of his pants. Without waiting to see what he was going to do, Marina turned and walked away.

Dios mio...

Tingling from emotion, she finished her walk. Her strides were long and Marina didn't look at anybody anymore. Nor greeted anybody. Smiled at no one. Her fists clenched and unclenched with every step she took. By the time she reached the Sirens' Lair, she was shaking. Banging in the front door, all heads turned to look at her. Scanning the place, she quickly located Carlos Gaitano, Hijo. He was sitting at his usual spot by the corner of the bar, the Hawthorne brothers nowhere in sight. All eyes followed her as she quickly crossed the room, reaching her lover. Without saying a word, she threw herself on his lap, flung her arms around his neck and buried her face in his shoulder.

To say the man was surprised would be an understatement. Shocked, his arms went around her, trying to still the tremors coming off her body. "*Marina!* What happened---"

The front door flew open again, making all heads turn and look.

Seeing who it was, tears came to her eyes. "*He attacked me!*"

"Who?" asked Carlos, bewildered, turning to look from one to the other.

The man kept coming nearer, making her squirm in his lap.

"*He* did!" she cried, tears stinging her eyes. All eyes turned to the man.

Juan Gaitano shrugged, and grinned, wincing from the pain. "I had to see for myself, if it was true," he explained helplessly. "I have never met a woman before, who could defend herself with such a talent," he said, awe in his voice.

Beneath her, the pirate shook with amusement, as he began to chuckle. "You should have known better," he admonished softly. Rocking Marina for a moment, he held her tight, trying to still her trembling. "*Divina,*" he murmured, "remember that man looking back at you from *La Prision*?" Gently, he turned her face to look at his uncle. "Marina Aguilar, meet *Juan Gaitano...*"

Marina glared at the man standing in front of her, through tear filled eyes. Now she could see it all. The turned down boots with the studs, the gold cross on the black cord, the earrings, the beautiful bronze skin topped by the night black hair... "*Not* nice to meet you!" she informed him, eliciting laughs from those, present.

The youngest of the older Gaitano brothers had the decency to look shamefaced. Looking straight into her eyes, he smiled. "Marina Aguilar," he began formally, "I would lie, if I were not to say what an incredible honor it is, to finally meet you..." Stepping closer, he held out his hand to her, eyes never leaving her face.

"You scared the hell out of me," she told him, still glaring.

Juan nodded, pleased. "I realize it, and for that, I am deeply sorry. I wanted to see firsthand," he explained, smiling mischievously, "the girl who fights men. I must admit," he confessed, "I didn't believe a single word they told me. I thought my brothers were making a fool out of me..."

"No, Juanito," Don Miguel rumbled, from behind the bar, "you just made a fool out of yourself." More laughter. The older pirate turned to the young woman in his nephew's lap. "I hope you hit him hard, mamita," he smiled at her.

Marina nodded. "I kicked his ass, Don Miguel..." The older, and younger, Gaitano brothers howled. Her trembling stopped, almost completely, but for the occasional shiver.

"That will be, what, Juanito?" Don Carlos teased. "Your first black eye in ten years? And from a *girl*, too," he added mournfully, shaking his head. Even more laughter.

Juan nodded with a smile. "It has been an honor," he told Marina, eyes never leaving her face. He looked deep into her hazel eyes, stormy with indignation. "If my nephew here messes it up for you," he asked, "would you marry *me*?"

Marina didn't stop to consider it. The man in front of her was a Gaitano, and she was used to them, by now. "*Maybe*," she growled at him. "I'll *think* about it---"

Juan laughed, delighted. "We have the same genes," he murmured. His hand stayed, held out to her.

Marina looked down at it. She glanced at Carlos. He shrugged, struggling not to laugh out loud. She looked back at the Captain of *La Prision*, and put her hand in his. "Don't *ever* scare me like that again," she warned, meeting his gaze. Then she bestowed him with a wicked smile. "Thanks for the rush..." she whispered to him.

Juan Gaitano kissed her hand. "Thank you for the lesson..." he whispered back, winking at her. And he was gone.

Marina hugged the pirate again, pressing her chest against his. "He scared me, Carlitos," she whispered in his ear.

"I know," he whispered back. Taking a deep breath, he held her closer, stroking her back. With every breath, her heart beat a little bit slower, until it matched his own heartbeat. He felt her melt against him with a big sigh. He grinned. "Feel better?"

Marina nodded, breathing deeply of him. "Yeah... Thank you, baby..."

Carlos stole a kiss before gently getting her off his lap with another pat to the butt. "Anytime, *mi corazon*..."

Before Marina could ponder on him calling her his heart, the door banged open for the third time. In marched her siblings, with their respective partners. These, came in bearing baskets of fruits, loaves of warm bread, and bottles of fresh juice, and water. Laughing happily, they grabbed a table, moving it right next to the grownups'. Marina and Carlos moved to join them. All the grown children greeted their parents and prospective in -laws, and they all settled down for breakfast. Grace was said, bread was broken, and bottles were passed around. Everyone smiled.

"Dudes!"

Marina's family turned to look at her. Parents, siblings, Carlos and Storm. Her tone was soft, full of wonder.

Salomé and Jackson replied automatically, at the same time. "What?"

"Carlitos?"

"Yeah?"

Her voice dropped to a conspiratorial whisper. "Lives in the *Bat Cave!*"

"*Not!*"

They all turned to stare at the pirate. His family looked at each other. The visitors had certainly lost it!

Carlos frowned for a moment. "Well, there really aren't any bats, but..." He shrugged. "Yeah..." he grinned, "whatever she said!"

"With a shower and a jacuzzi!"

Salomé and Jackson stared at each other openmouthed, before laughing. "*Not!*" Their parents looked on with interest.

Pablo smiled at the young pirate. "You know, Carlitos, now that I think of it, I have never seen where you live..."

Carlos laughed. "Marina should marry me," he said softly, "she absolutely *loves* where I live."

Marina grinned, nodding. "Absolutely."

"It's that good?" her mother wanted to know, teasing.

"The very best!"

"What got you, baby?" Shayla asked with genuine interest.

Marina sighed, and looked at the females sitting at her table. "Ladies..." she said, as she squeezed some lemon into her juice. Prolonging the suspense, she took a sip, licked her lips and sighed with contentment. "...the boy has *running... hot... water...*"

The ladies shrieked. The men laughed.

"And if you stay in Encantada," Carlos continued in a conversational tone, without looking at her, entertained with a slice of mango, "you get to *live* in the Bat Cave."

Marina gasped, eyes wide as she turned on him, bursting into laughter. "That is not fair, you said you would share!"

Their breakfast companions followed them with interest, looking from one to the other.

The young pirate shrugged. "All's fair..." he drawled provocatively.

Marina crossed her arms and looked at him through slit eyes. Finally, she pointed a finger at his face. "You're on, dude!" The pirate grabbed her finger and pretended to eat it. She looked him up and down. "In *my* time, the third millennium, with your money, you could design your *very own Bat Cave*, complete with *Bat Mobile, Bat Plane, Bat Cycle, Bat Speedboat...*" She arched an eyebrow at him.

Carlos thought for a moment. Finally, he let his head fall forward, shaking it in defeat. Looking up, the corners of his beautiful eyes crinkled with a smile. Pressing his lips together, he held out his hand.

Winking at him, Marina slid hers against it. *You are just a boy.* Then, they both turned to their respective meals.

Their family looked at each other in puzzlement.

Finally, Joe spoke up. "Could somebody please explain to me what's going on?"

Laughing as she bit on a slice of orange, Salomé raised her hand, waving it wildly in the air as if she were in school. Orange juice dribbled down her chin, and she wiped it off with the back of her other hand. "Oo! Oo! I know! I know!"

Joe glanced towards the ceiling, and waved for her to proceed. "Salomé..."

"If I'm not mistaken, they are doing the pros and cons..."

"Of what?" he asked with interest.

Behind his back, Shayla and Sloane rolled their eyes in amusement. This time, Jackson's hand shot up. The Gaitano family chuckled.

Admitting defeat with a big sigh, Joe finally laughed with them. "Jackson..."

Taking a drink of water, he wiped his mouth with a towel. He looked at their parents. "Staying in Encantada, or going back to the future..."

Silence followed his words. But not for long.

Don Carlos burst out laughing. "I'll pay for Carlitos' passage!" The table roared. His son rolled his eyes and shook his head with a smile.

They ended their breakfast on a very lively, upbeat noise, immensely enjoying each other's company. Then, the Gaitanos, as well as the Aguilars and the Banks --- and Storm --- hit the streets.

Pirate's Convention Expo: Caribbean Edition. That's what they called it, because that's what it was. Pirates from surrounding islands, native to the waters, converging in one place, where there would be expositions of merchandise, crafts and wares, made by them, achieved because of them, available to them. There were sailors everywhere, pirate and not. The mood was sunny and happy. Everybody seemed quite relaxed.

Marina stared in awe, as the main street stretched out in front of them. The strip between The Siren's Lair and Kline's General Store was transformed. Every store front had undergone a makeover. Each had a fresh coat of paint in a luscious tropical color. The windows had been embellished with eye-catching displays of the goods sold inside. The sidewalks had been swept, and adorned with benches for people to sit on, while they waited outside the stores. There were even potted plants. In front of each particular store, there was a table laden, with a sample of their merchandise. At each table were people looking, inspecting, buying, or moving on to the next table. As the group walked by, they would make eye contact with the store own-ers. From each and every single one of them, they got the thumbs up sign. Going down a side street, they found themselves in what had become the town plaza. The church was to one side. Pedro Barbosa's office with its unique landscaping was nearby. There was a large empty space in the middle, where different events were to take place. Bordering everything were tables upon tables of arts and crafts, from the local sailors, the villagers, and the newly freed African slaves taken from *La Diosa del Mar.* There were fabrics, and masks, and crude instruments, and tribal jewelry. It was awesome.

As they found themselves in front of the church, Padre Ignacio came out to greet them.

"Gaitanos!" he cried happily, eyes crinkling at the corners.

The men greeted him back, waiting patiently as the women flocked around him. Marina didn't join them.

Noticing her, the priest broke away from the female attention he was subjected to, and turned towards her. "Marina!"

Carlos sighed, as the woman next to him froze. He was aware that she had some serious issues with the priest, that hadn't been resolved yet, since she hadn't even seen him, once they got back from Carey. The situation called for some quick intervention. "Padre Ignacio..."

Unaware of the storm brewing, the priest stood in front of her, smiling hopefully, as the two families looked on with interest. "Marina..." he trailed off, as he took in her expression. Reaching into his pocket, he drew out a small box. Taking one of her hands, he placed the box in it. "This is for you..." Searching her eyes, he pressed his gift into her hand, and sighed. "I know I screwed up, with you---"

"Yes, you did."

Among her companions, eyebrows raised, lips pressed together, and heads shook.

Padre Ignacio sighed again. "I can only ask God that you find it in your heart to forgive me---"

"It's not the *forgiving* I'm having a problem with!" She shook her head at him with a grimace. "It's the fucking *forgetting*," she growled.

Sloane and Shayla's heads whipped around to glare at her. Pablo and Joe whistled under their breaths.

Padre Ignacio nodded, his brown eyes mournful. "I understand---"

"I don't think so, Padre." Her eyes flashed. "Regardless of the outcome of your little show of force, you have *no* idea of what you did to me!"

Carlos coughed, thinking it was as good a time as any, for him to step in. "Marina, it was my fault! Padre Ignacio was only following orders!"

Marina shook her head stubbornly. "He's a big boy. He could've said no." Lowering her eyes, she studied the box in her hand, sadly. Finally, she looked back at the priest. "Thank you, Padre Ignacio. I will always remember you." Glancing at the building behind him, her mouth twisted into an amused smile. Her eyes, shining like smoky precious stones, found his. "I will *never* enter *your* house of worship again."

The females in her family gasped, while the men stood around and shared looks. The Gaitanos shook their heads and chuckled.

Carlos looked at the priest, shrugging apologetically. "Sorry, Padre. I guess it was a really bad idea..." He turned to Marina. Taking the box from her hand, before she did anything with it, he slipped it into his pocket. Then, he brought her hand to his lips. "Marina Aguilar," he announced, in front of their families, "I will build you a church!"

Marina's smile came, like the sun bursting through clouds. Her eyes thanked him, capturing his. Her hand caressed his face. The pirate gazed back at her with deep affection. He turned his head to kiss the palm of her hand. They thanked the priest, and moved on.

To one side of the plaza, tiers of seats had been built. Already, they were occupied, by what seemed to be a select few pirates. Joining them, the families assembled in the crude, primitive bleachers, and smiled at each other, settling down into pleasant conversation. Soon, the empty space in the center began filling with wandering sailors. They walked around aimlessly, greeting each other, glancing at the bleachers.

"So, what's on the agenda today?" Shayla asked.

Marina looked at her. "You have an *agenda*?"

Salomé laughed, falling into their teenage patterns of speech. "*Dude!* Where've you *been*? There's a full *program*!" she teased.

Marina felt herself blushing, and turned to Salomé. Lowering her voice, she brought her head closer to her sister's, until they were touching. Her words were for Salomé's ears only. "I have been busy, being *ravaged* by a pirate..." she drawled in a whisper.

Salomé pulled back to look into her sister's eyes. "How was it?"

Marina let her feelings show in her face. She sighed with pleasure. "*Spectacular!*" The sisters smiled, their hands sliding against each other.

Indio grunted. "*I* am spectacular," he murmured, fighting to keep a straight face.

"I'm *sure* you are, papi," Marina reassured him, laughing softly.

Salomé winked at him. "You *are*," she confirmed. Then, she turned back to her sister. "What are you going to do?"

Marina looked deep into her eyes, becoming quiet. There was no easy way to answer. Finally, she sighed. "I don't know!"

Next to her, the pirate's voice rumbled in his chest. Carlos raised his eyebrows and looked at Salomé. "If Marina doesn't ask me to marry her by tomorrow," he warned in a hiss, "I am going to *freak*!"

Salomé and Marina gasped, eyes wide, hands going up to cover their open mouths. Then, they giggled. It wasn't what Carlos said. It was the way he said it. Finally, they settled down, eyes watering, and shoulders shaking.

Marina grinned at her sister. "Salo!"

"What?"

"Remember Sandra Bullock in *Miss Congeniality*?"

"Yeah..."

Marina laughed wickedly. Eyes glittering with mischief, her voice came out in a soft singsong. "He thinks I'm pretty... He wants to kiss me, and make sweet love to me... He wants to marry me..."

Over their heads, the brothers grinned at each other. Beside them, all the parents looked at each other, before turning to face them. The mothers raised their eyebrows, but the daughters just shook their heads, gasping for air. The pirates chuckled. The fathers grinned.

Pablo cocked his head to one side. "You're not going to share?" he asked, smiling to himself as the young women shook their heads. They had been doing that to him, since they were months old.

Joe leaned forward, elbows on his knees, hands clasped together, studying them closely. The sisters laughed harder, as their dad shook his cornrowed head, diamond stud in his ear, catching the bright morning sunlight. Finally, he pointed a finger at them, brown eyes crinkling at the corners. "You know I'm going to find out," he predicted in the warning of their youth.

"Joe," Sloane said casually, eyes scanning the sailors in the middle of the plaza, "you know that the kids have a right to their secrets..."

"That's right," Shayla agreed, "but if you announce to them that you're going to find out, then we won't be able to sneak up on them and catch them doing something..."

The Gaitanos laughed. By now, their sons were shaking their heads, and their girlfriends were drying the tears on their faces. They were all having a good time. Suddenly, Caribe appeared in their midst.

"Are you ladies ready?" he asked them.

Salomé nodded with a smile. "Ready, Freddy..."

Marina frowned. "Ready for what?"

"Forms," Caribe answered, waving a hand at the men, who had magically assembled into formation. "Come on." And without waiting for them, he went to join the men.

These, were now looking their way, grinning. Unnoticed by the families, they had started a soft chant. It had begun low, but the power of the rhythm had taken over. *"Marina-Salomé! Marina-Salomé!"*

The sisters looked at each other and smiled. Next to them, Jackson and Storm looked at each other and high-fived. These, started chanting back. *"Jack-son! Jack-son!"*

Jumping to his feet, Jackson kissed Storm on the forehead. "Later, baby..." And he too, went to join the men.

Salomé stood up first. "Let's get this silly thing done with..."

Marina glanced at Carlos. He shrugged at her and nodded at his men. No words were said. Marina answered with glowing eyes. Going past him, she let her fingers trail lovingly over his face. Behind her back, the pirate looked at Indio. He raised his eyebrows, and shook his head, taking a deep breath. Indio's eyes reflected sunlight, crinkling at the corners. *Definitely whipped.* The brothers grinned at each other and followed their women. Their parents shook their heads.

Giancarlo appeared, in midst of the pirates, and stood in front of their men, addressing the few spectators in the bleachers. His white shirt was bright in the morning light. His black pants --- loose, because he did forms with his men --- tucked into shiny boots. Today, he had a bandana covering his thick black hair. His earrings shone in the sunlight --- everybody's did --- sparkling, as he turned his head. *"Good morning!"* he cried, looking happy and relaxed.

The pirates greeted him back, some not as polite, all in good fun.

"The brave and dashing crew of *La Gitana* of *Capitán Carlos Gaitano...*" he broke off with a huge grin, while the men in the bleachers began stomping their feet as they booed and hissed. The Sailing Master raised his hands, laughing with them, finally quieting them down. "We are gathered here to demonstrate a martial art form brought to us, indirectly, by Master Aguilar and Master Banks. Please watch carefully," he instructed the pirates. Then, he turned to take his place with the rest of the crew. The visiting pirates watched as he went to take his place with the rest of the sailors, followed by Carlos, Indio and Solomon.

"*La Gitana!*"

"*Aguilar!*"

"*La Gitana!*"

"*Banks!*"

They began. The families looked at each other and smiled. Then they turned back to watch their grown children. Who performed beautifully, by the way, among the crew of *La Gitana*. To the amusement of the visiting sailors. Everybody laughed for different reasons, soon to be seen.

Giancarlo stepped up again, not even breathing hard, and faced the visiting pirates once more. "That is what you *see*," he laughed at them. "This," he added mysteriously, "is what you *don't* see..." Turning to Joe and Pablo, he bowed. "Masters..."

Joe and Pablo grinned at each other.

Joe turned to Shayla. "I guess that's our cue..." And he was gone.

Pablo laughed at his wife. He shrugged apologetically, smile wide, eyes sparkling slits. "This is my school..." Gone.

Those, left at the bleachers watched, as the two men plunged into the crowd, threading their way among their children, and ruthless pirates. They would tap one and another consecutively, right and left, pairing them off. Salomé with Marina. Jackson with Caribe. Carlos and Indio, Giancarlo and Solomon. Then they went on to the rest of the crew of the pirate ship their children had allegiance to. Done, they went to stand at opposite sides of the small plaza. Finally, giving command, they observed the people in front of them fight.

The visiting pirates roared. They had never seen anything like that.

Sloane turned to María Isabel, frowning. "Are they upset, or do they approve?"

María Isabel laughed. "Approve."

"Well, they certainly sound excited," Shayla pointed out.

Don Miguel's voice rumbled. "They think it is a joke," he chuckled. "Fools!"

And he was right, the pirates did, but only because the fighting was more of a demonstration.

The Hawthorne brothers arrived, in time to contribute to the hilarity. "You know, Gaitano, it really isn't fair..."

"The girls look like they're *dancing*!"

"Show me a *real* fight!"

Everybody laughed. Giving up, the crew stopped fighting, and fell back into formation.

Giancarlo stepped forward for the third time. *"Fenix scoundrels!"* he laughed, affectionately. "You are right. The girls look like they are dancing, but only because they are sisters, fighting each other. What you don't know," he said, dramatically, "is that these girls will fight *any... man... here!*"

And, of course, all hell broke loose.

Shayla and Sloane grasped hands, hiding smiles behind their free hands, even as their eyes gave them away. Don Carlos and Don Miguel burst out laughing. Storm stood up and began dancing in place, throwing kisses at Jackson's sisters in female moral support. Pablo and Joe shook their heads. They felt as if they were in the middle of a set-up. It smelled of Giancarlo Ilarraza.

The owner of The Sirens' Lair laughed at the siblings. "Would you like to place a bet, gentlemen?"

Laughing, the men reached into their pockets. "Let us see."

"The girls will definitely lose!"

"There is no way in this world..."

Salomé reached for Caribe's hand. "Let's go, baby," she murmured. "Let's make us some money." She turned to wink at him.

"Just fight me for real, papi, so that I can show them what we can do."

Caribe winked back. "My pleasure..."

Stepping to the center of the plaza, they faced each other. Everybody around them fell back. Carlos and Indio went to join the Hawthorne brothers, followed by Giancarlo and Solomon.

Indio laughed. "Are you making fun of my girl?" he teased, slapping hands with each of them.

"She is *not!*"

"Where was *I?*"

"She is *beautiful!*"

"Did you expect otherwise?" Indio laughed.

"No."

"Not really."

"Not after meeting the accountant."

The Gaitano brothers laughed. Indio pointed at Salomé and Caribe fighting. "Watch and weep..." he predicted.

They watched. Caribe and Salomé genuinely fought. But for some reason, they also seemed to be dancing. Whether it was familiarity from working out together, or extreme care of not hurting each other, it was hard to tell. But the Hawthornes were not convinced.

"Very nice..."

"Quite entertaining..."

"Unremarkable, though..."

Indio laughed. "You are right. Not good enough."

"Too... artistic!"

"Not violent enough."

"They seem to be holding back..."

Carlos chuckled, shaking his head. He looked at his brother. "They are right---"

"Besides, isn't that Leila's kid?"

"How about they fight someone else, like..."

"...*Solomon?*"

The Gaitanos froze. This was too good to be true. Giancarlo had to restrain himself, so as not to swoop down on them, like a hawk. Behind the clueless brothers, Shayla and Sloane covered their faces with their hands, shaking their heads. Don Miguel and Don Carlos had their arms around each other, shaking with silent laughter, tears escaping down their faces. Juan shook his head. He had heard about the infamous fights between the accountant and the Boatswain.

"Gentlemen," Giancarlo smiled, playfully rubbing his hands together, "I will bet you that one of the Aguilar-Banks sisters will dare to take our Boatswain, Solomon, in a real fight---"

"*Not!*"

"They are so pretty and... *girly...*"

"*Neither* of them would take on your Boatswain..."

"Want to bet?"

All heads turned to look at *Carlos Gaitano. Hijo.* His voice was low, and mocking. Challenging. The reckless brothers rose to the bait.

"I will bet that neither of them could compete with Solomon, and of course it would have to be Marina, since Salomé already fought..."

"You are just playing with us!"

"I will put my bet on the Boatswain!"

Carlos grinned. Playing the trick on the Hawthorne brothers was worth going back on his word about Marina and Solomon's fights, and making an exception. "You're on, gentlemen!" he smiled, bowing at them. "Giancarlo will work out the details with them." He laughed wickedly. "And with you..." Turning away from them, he called out. *"Marina!"* In a moment, she was at his side. Smiling, she greeted the grinning Hawthornes. Carlos' eyes crinkled at the corners as he looked into hers. "The scoundrels believe that this was all for show," he began softly. "They claim that neither you nor Salomé would fight a man for real." Keeping eye contact with her, he saw the moment she understood where he was coming from. Her smile hit her eyes, first. "A man like *Solomon...*"

Marina fought to keep as straight a face as possible. "Do I *have* to?" she asked softly. Her body began to tingle.

In the bleachers, Don Miguel and Don Carlos bent over with silent laughter, wiping away their tears. Sloane and Shayla squeezed each other's hands. Storm shook her head, braids flying back and forth around her face.

Carlos nodded solemnly, putting a reassuring hand on her shoulder. "I am sorry, Aguilar. My friends here," he waved a hand at them, "will make me a laughingstock of these waters, if you don't do this small favor for me---"

"But what if he *hurts* me?" Marina asked, eyes wide and glassy, as she glanced at Solomon and shivered. The clueless brothers would never know it was from pleasure.

"I know, I know," Carlos said consolingly, "but please do this for me," he pretended to plead, "and I promise you will *never* fight Solomon again..."

Marina bit her cheek, to keep from laughing out loud. "Okay. Just please, don't let him embarrass me," she sighed.

Carlos laughed. "I promise that, too. Thank you." Taking her hand, he kissed it. Their eyes laughed at each other. He glanced at the plaza, where the men were waiting for instructions. Marina nodded. She was almost as good as Indio as communicating with him without words. She walked away, sent with the now expected pat on the butt. Reaching Caribe, they exchanged words and laughs. Marina turned her back to the villager. The dreadlocked boy put his hands in her hair and quickly braided it. Finally, she began walking around, smiling and slapping hands with every single one of his men. He watched the whole thing. Turning to the Hawthorne brothers, he smiled. "Gentlemen, please place your bets with Giancarlo."

The men eagerly did so, anxious to have a tale to tell.

Carlos turned to his accountant, now standing alone in the center of the plaza. All the men stood around the perimeter, knowing smiles on their faces. *"Aguilar!"* he called out to her. She waved happily at him. "Whenever you are ready..." She nodded.

Approaching the bleachers, she began to dance, shaking her hips and waving her arms. "So-lo-mon!" she sang out, finally making eye contact with the African, "come out and pla-ay..."

The pirates roared with laughter. Her mothers gasped, before dissolving into helpless laughter themselves. The men of La Gitana cheered her. Her fathers sighed with patience. The Hawthorne brothers hooted. The Gaitano brothers howled. Storm laughed silently, before mimicking her behind the pirates' backs. Rouge joined them just then, a puzzled frown on her brow, even as she smiled. She took her place quietly next to Storm, and waited to see what was happening. María Isabel sighed, a huge smile on her face. She could not have asked for better, for Carlitos. Caribe and Jackson shook their heads and high-fived. Salomé danced out to slap hands with her sister, and danced her way back. Indio cheered encouragingly at Marina. Giancarlo glided from pirate to pirate, taking their bets. And their money. It was a full blown setup. And they were all in on it.

Solomon glanced at his Captain. He grinned when his Captain nodded. Climbing down the bleachers, to the tune of catcalls and hoots of laughter, he blocked everything out and just saw Marina. Now he was standing in front of her. They went through their ritual. She slapped him. He slapped her back. The crowd screamed. They grinned. Then they circled each other warily, their eyes never leaving one another's. Quick as lightning, his hand came out and pushed her face to the side. She smiled at him. They were in their own world. "Haven't seen you in a while, Aguilar," he teased, "where've you been?"

"*Vacation*," she shrugged. "You see," she pushed his face back, "those of us that bust our butts working, get certain *privileges*..." They switched, circling each other in the opposite direction. "*Slackers* are destined to *never* have any time off to have fun..."

Solomon grinned. "Then I guess you won't be seeing me for a while, if I go on vacation for the equivalent of my labor..."

Marina laughed. "Now, you're just wasting my time, son!" Her punch flashed out, catching him on the shoulder before she drew it back. "What's my motivation?" she challenged.

Solomon looked straight into her eyes. His words were for her ears alone, as his taunting melodious tone reached her. "*Xavier...*"

Marina froze. A single drop iced her way down her spine, stopping at the waist of her pants. A stillness came over her and she could only see Solomon.

They faced each other. Standing perfectly straight, they slapped their hands to their sides. Then they bowed at each other. Her fathers ran to them, hastily establishing ground rules. They nodded. They began.

"Show me!" Solomon said, a fierce scowl on his face. "You are my Master! Show me how you would save your life from this heathen!" And he rushed her.

Marina blocked him as best as she could, giving him some ground. She danced around him, getting back into fighting stance. *"Fuck Xavier!"* she growled at him. And with no more words between them, they fought.

The pirates couldn't get enough. The Hawthorne brothers were shocked. The Gaitanos' accountant gave as good as she got. Rouge joined them, inquiring about their reckless bet. Caribe got busy with paper and pencil. Jackson stayed close to his dads, supervising the fight. From around the plaza, the villagers and the ex-slaves cheered the combatants on. Carlos watched, quietly, as everybody screamed around him. Finally, he sighed. He couldn't object to this fight. Not because it wasn't real. It most definitely was. And they were hitting hard, too. But it was more like a show of skills. Solomon had become quite good. Jealous that he didn't have that relationship with the woman, he was still proud of both of them.

The fight was a success. Joe stopped it before it was possible to call a winner. The pirates got the point. The contenders bowed. Stepping towards each other, Marina and Solomon hugged, nuzzling each other. She warbled softly in his ear. He murmured comfortingly in response and rubbed her back. They were in their own private world of strength, skill, and pain. Love and respect shrouded them like a cloak.

The Hawthorne brothers paid Giancarlo with the same good humor they had shown throughout the whole thing.

"I would have *never* guessed!"

"Our *sister* has to learn this!"

"Marina can probably *beat* Solomon, too, huh?"

Giancarlo turned to face the bleachers. Catching Rouge's eye, he winked at her over the distance, making her smile. Then, he waved a hand at Marina and Solomon, who were now in each other's arms. "As you can see, friends, the art of Tae Kwon Do, is not to be taken lightly. If any of you are interested in signing up for classes for you and/or your men, please contact my associate, Jackson Banks." He turned back to the plaza behind him, signaling Joe and Pablo. "Now, please relax and enjoy, as the Masters themselves demonstrate how it's really done..."

Pablo and Joe fought. It was spectacular. After everything was said and done, every single pirate present signed up for classes for themselves and their crews. It was a success. The *Pirates' Convention Expo* was off to a great start.

Marina smiled at the pirates, slipping an arm around Giancarlo's waist and kissing him on the cheek. She scanned the crowd restlessly, making sure of establishing eye contact with every pirate there. Even the one from this morning. *Gotcha!* Pretending not to notice the startled man, she grinned at the Hawthorne brothers. "Nice taking your money, boys..."

"You are not what you appear to be!"

"I knew Gaitano was too happy to make a bet!"

"I will never make fun of Carlitos again!"

Laughing, Marina left them, and went to join her family. Reaching Salomé's side, they slid hands against each other. "What's next?"

"Villagers dance, welcoming the visitors."

"We don't have to do that, do we?"

"No, babe. We're sitting this one out."

"Max!"

Marina's head jerked up at the sound of the greeting. Larissa had just reached the bleachers, and was scanning the growing crowd. Marina stood up, so she could be seen better. "Baby Boo, I've been looking for you!" she sang down to them, laughing when the baby jumped in his mother's arms.

Spotting her, Larissa rolled her eyes, sighing in relief. She met Marina halfway, quickly transferring the baby to her. "So, you've been gone a while..." she teased. "How was it?" Marina couldn't speak. She searched for words, but they failed her. Larissa raised an eyebrow at her, smiling knowingly. "Very much and a lot?" Marina could only look into her eyes and smile. Larissa nodded. "Uh-huh, I thought so. I always wondered, you know, but I always knew." She glanced at the pirate in appreciation. "All you have to do is to take a good look at him…" She laughed. "Marina, I'm happy for you. Good job, girl!" Impulsively, she hugged her friend. "I hope it goes as well for you, as it has for John and I," she whispered fiercely. Pulling back, she kissed her son and winked at her. "See you in a couple of hours…" And she was gone. Baby in her arms, Marina went back to join her family. Faded eyes under a disgusting bandana followed her every movement, marking where she was.

A faint beat filled the air, soft at first, filling the senses. The sun shone down on the plaza, making it the center of everyone's atten tion. In it, the villagers got ready to dance. The bleachers kept filling. Down below, Carlos Gaitano scanned the crowd. His family watched as he searched for his accountant. No, his girlfried. Finding her, he made his way through the pirates. María Isabel nudged her husband, nodding towards their son. "Where is this going to end?" she murmured.

Don Carlos sighed, as he watched. "It looks like it is just beginning, *mi amor*."

Their son made his way among the people. It took him longer than he would have thought, since everybody wanted to speak to him. Finally, playfully moving Salomé aside, Carlos reached Marina and proceeded to embrace her and the baby at the same time.

"Max!" he laughed, as the baby took his face between his tiny hands, peering into his eyes. Gurgling softly, Max pressed his face against the pirate's, asking for a kiss. Carlos obliged, his eyes soft like pools in sunl ight, and then pretended to eat him up, making the baby squeal with laughter. Finally, he looked at the woman in his arms. "How are you doing?"

Marina smiled. "Good… Did you make money off the scoundrels?"

He grinned. "Absolutely." He searched her eyes. "Did Solomon hurt you?"

"Yeah…" She grinned. "It was fantastic."

Carlos laughed. "You know, there is something terribly wrong with you."

"I know."

"I like it."

This time, her smile was private. "I know..."

"I'm jealous," he confessed in her ear. Closing his eyes, he held Marina and Max tight again, close to his heart. "Ready to talk about a baby?"

"Soon..." she replied.

Carlos nodded. He sighed.

The drums sounded louder now, the air around them throbbing with the beat. Slowly, the plaza filled with villagers. White smiles shone out of beautiful dark faces, in every shade imaginable. The bright fabrics clothing them granted a soothing treat to the eyes, bursting in a riot of colors. They danced. The visiting pirates cheered enthusiastically, all good sports, enjoying the entertainment. After the locals, came the newly freed slaves. These, performed magnificently, chanting and singing in their own native tongue. The sight was heart-wrenching, there were so many of them. But, standing tall and dignified, wearing their pride like cloaks, the Africans expressed gratitude, in the face of sadness and tribulation. It was a humbling experience, watching them. They had been taken, beaten, enslaved and transported. They had faced torture, hunger, misery and fear, in hands of the now defunct slavedriver. Terror had ruled their hearts throughout their unsolicited trans Atlantic voyage. And here they were now, praising God, or their ancestors, or both, for their good fortune in having made it alive.

Tears came to the sisters' eyes. Salomé pulled on Gaitano's shirt with one hand, even as she wiped her face with the other. "Are they okay?"

The pirate loosened his hold on the woman and the baby enough to reassure her. "Yes, Salomé, yes, they are." He sighed. "We cannot give them their old life back. But we can make this new one, the best possible for them."

She sniffled. "That's good enough."

He nodded. "We live in a place where it is easy to erase past mistakes. This tropical paradise is abundant with new opportunities for a better life..." he trailed off, looking at Marina again.

Marina wiped her own tears. "I come from a place where there is no slavery," she answered meeting his gaze.

Carlos did not answer. There was nothing to say. Max chose just then, to step in, making sure their attention was all on him. Turning from one to the other, he kissed them each in turn, even going as far as reaching out for Salomé. Laughing, they went down the bleachers to join their families.

Once down on the ground, they wandered around the perimeter of the plaza, stopping at the different tables on display. The crowd had dispersed along with them, drifting toward the booths that were at the corners of the plaza. The Gaitanos and their visitors strolled along, taking their time, enjoying the sights and sounds, the sun on their faces.

The first booth they came to was one of information. That was where the pirates could sign up for their own Tae Kwon Do classes, or for a tour of the upstairs of the dress shop now belonging to Liana, Dr. Kyle Richardson's exotic sweetheart. This last part was seen to by Jackson, as requested by the local brothel owner, Giancarlo Ilarraza. That was also where they could request a change to a particular ship they would rather work on. Or a hut down by the beach, or in the new sailors' village on the outskirts of town. The lines were long. So, smiling, the families waved at Jackson, and walked on.

They passed tables laden with an assortment of beautiful wares. Stunning household items like pots and pans, cast in the shiniest copper and bronze. Hand-made floppy dolls for little girls, with button eyes. Carved wooden animals and pull toys. Canvases with beautiful oils of ships.

The next booth belonged to Leila and Don Manuel. The families greeted each other lovingly and enthusiastically. Caribe motioned to Marina. Excusing herself with a murmur, she handed Max to Gaitano, and followed him to the back of the booth, which was its entrance. There, the dreadlocked young man pulled out a heavy, leatherbound book. Moving a stack of beautiful, bright fabrics to one side, he opened it for her.

Caribe smiled. "Here's what you asked for."

Marina gasped. The boy had created a masterpiece. Grasping a bunch of pages between thumb and forefinger, she quickly passed them, scanning them in silent wonder. Faces flashed before her eyes. Pirates, and their entire crews. On the facing pages were list of names and dates, in a beautiful manuscript. Her eyes flew to his laughing golden ones. "Dude, you rock!" They high -fived.

"Where are you going to be, later?" he asked.

She thought about it for a moment. "Maybe up in the village. Haven't been there in a few days, and the place is probably all musty. I want to at least clean it, before I leave it, so somebody else can use it."

Caribe nodded. "Cool."

Suddenly, something caught Marina's eyes. She spread the book open, and frantically signaled at a particular sailor. "Caribe, who *is* this?" she gasped. *"Who is this?"*

Alarmed, Caribe put an arm around her shoulder, quickly glancing behind his. His eyes met Gaitano's. The pirate frowned. Spinning her around, he held her tight against him, his voice low. "What's wrong?"

Eyes wide, she edged the panic out of her voice. "What ship? Which crew?"

Caribe's frown equaled Gaitano's. "Xavier's..." He watched tears spring to her eyes, before she fought them off.

Marina bent at the waist for a moment, shaking her head. Then she took a deep breath and straightened slowly. Turning on a bright smile, she turned and looked over the table, out at the crowd. Smile frozen, she scanned slowly, like the periscope of a submarine. Her glance went right over him, like a speed bump. *There you are!* And her heart threw itself against her chest, trying to get out, but her smile never wavered. She turned to Caribe, when she finished looking at everyone. "Look behind Don Manuel, to the left, but *don't* look," she murmured.

Caribe laughed, taking her cue, and scanned the crowd, a little bit quicker than she had. When he finished, he turned towards the back of the booth, his eyes wide. "Marina---"

"Sssshhh," she shook her head at him. "I don't think he's here yet, 'cause this guy hasn't taken his eyes off me all morning." Her eyes locked on his. "He'll be here soon." She sighed, biting her lip. She closed the book, passing a loving hand along the leather cover. Suddenly, she straightened. Looking back at Caribe, her mind began churning. "Has your father seen this?"

Caribe shook his head. "No. I did all the work myself. It wasn't hard, it was half done, already. You had notes on everybody, and I had a drawing to match."

"Has he seen anything about El Baile del Luto?"

Caribe shook his head again. "Not at all. I keep everything at my place." He grinned. "Don Manuel and Leila have been very busy getting reacquainted..."

"You got a drawing of Xavier here?"

Caribe nodded, this time. "I have everybody here." Passing the pages quickly, he located it.

Marina looked at the sketch. Caribe had caught beautifully, Xavier's stunning face, and the wicked gleam in his dark eyes. The smile twisting his mouth was condescending. Firelight seemed to play in his white hair. *He looks like the* Vampire Lestat. Marina looked up at her friend, her smile sad. "Call your dad over here."

Caribe froze. Something told him that this moment would determine the fate of many people. But he obeyed, driven by the fear that struck his heart. Forcing a smile on his face, he called at the man in front of them. *"Papá!"* His father turned around with a smile of his own. Caribe beckoned him over.

"Marina!" Don Manuel exclaimed happily. "I haven't seen you since last time you joined us dancing."

Marina nodded, smiling in return. Standing in front of the book so that he couldn't see it, she got right to the point. "I need you to see something, but I can't have you react in any way, shape, or form." Turning quickly, she reached for the book, holding it up to the open page.

Don Manuel's smile had gone from genuine to perplexed. In truth, the man looked years younger, than when she had first met him. Leila's loving hand was evident in his whole appearance and demeanor. He was groomed, his beautiful dreadlocks framing his handsome face. His eyes fell on the sketch of the pirate. His knees failed him, and he stumbled. His mouth open and shut like a beached fish, eyes transfixed on the face in front of him. Tears sprang to his eyes. He looked at Marina in puzzlement.

Marina and Caribe held him on each side, as Marina slammed the book shut, and threw it back on the table. She planted herself firmly in front of Don Manuel, looking into his eyes. "Do not speak of this to anyone, please," she murmured urgently. "It will be over soon. This man shall pay for his sins." She looked at Caribe. "Meet me at home, later. I'm sure the pirates meet tonight?" He nodded, his arm around his father, who was now wiping his eyes and shaking his head, regaining his composure. "*Ciao*, baby," and she slipped outside.

"*Ciao*," he called after her. Fear had left his heart, leaving an empty space. It quickly filled with liquid hatred.

Marina reached Gaitano, and flashed a smile at his amused face. "*Max!*" She reached for the baby, who was already lunging into her outstreched arms. Marina nuzzled him. Finally, she glanced at the pirate. He still had the same smile on his face.

"Are you going to tell me what all that was about?" She shook her head, laughing at the baby she held. Carlos reached out and took her face in his hand, turning it so she was looking at him. And in the manner of her fathers and her brother, he echoed the beloved warning. "You know I'm going to find out," he cautioned softly.

A trickle of fear slid down her spine. His words! Her nipples got hard, her panties got wet. His voice... Inside, she moaned. *There's definitely something wrong with me.* On the outside, she nodded. They moved on.

The next booth was obscured by the people standing in front of it. Children. All ages, all sizes. The smallest ones in their mother's arms, or on their father's shoulders. The center of their attention was none other than the captured seamen from *La Diosa del Mar*. The very distinguished Don Andres Segarra y Collazo and Don Luis Vega y Ramos, of the mountain colored eyes. They each had a hand puppet, and were in the midst of telling a wild action adventure story.

Salomé tugged on Gaitano's sleeve. "How about them? How are they doing?"

The pirate chuckled, holding Max's hand in his, as they walked along. "See for yourself," he invited.

The sisters looked hard. The men were laughing, obviously treating themselves, as well as the children, to their storytelling. They were clean, as were their clothes, and nicely groomed. The Captain and his Quartermaster looked well taken care of. They seemed relaxed and happy.

Salomé nodded approvingly. "They look good, at least, so they must be feeling okay."

"They are fine," he reassured her.

Joe turned to his group with a huge smile. "This is where I get off, dudes. See you all, later." And quickly threading his way through the kids, he went to join the Spaniards. His daughters and Storm happily blew kisses at him, as well as his daughters' mothers. The families kept walking, but not until they watched him grab a hand puppet, and join the men in their wild tale.

"Accountant!"

Marina stopped. Scanning the people around her, she spotted the pirate coming her way. She recognized him almost immediately. "John!" She laughed.

Unbelievably, it was the same person of earlier this morning. He grinned. The man's eyes twinkled with amusement. His rich brown hair was still wet from a recent wash and bath, catching bands of sunlight as he moved. His cheeks were still pink from his shave. Clothes were clean, and boots were shining. It barely looked like the same man, except his size was unmistakable. The group stopped as Marina approached the pirate, baby held fast in her arms. Smiling down at her, he seemed sheepish, all of a sudden. "I need more help," he murmured.

Marina laughed. "First things first," she told him, offering her face.

The pirate sighed in relief. "Thank you," he chuckled, kissing her cheek.

Gaitano laughed. "John! It's you!" he teased. Holding out his hand, he introduced himself with a wink. "Carlos Gaitano."

John shook his hand warmly, grinning back. "I know."

Marina looked into eyes the color of bronze. They sparkled as if made of sunlight. She felt her heart swell. There was something about him that tugged at the deepest corner of her mind. There was a reason why she was meeting this man, but... She sighed. Its meaning would reveal itself in due time. It wasn't a bad feeling. But she needed to have met his acquaintance for some reason, yet undisclosed. Marina felt him searching her eyes. She smiled. He smiled back. They connected. Relieved, she let out a deep breath. "Now, how can I help you?"

The pirate bowed. "Why, thank you, Marina. Where can I find a place that can tell me where everything is?" he asked. "Where can I get my bearings?" He frowned, searching for words. He sighed, glancing from her, to Gaitano, and back. "Where," he included the younger pirate, dropping his voice lower, "could I get some---" he stopped himself, dismayed. Frowning again, he shook his head. Finally, he just shrugged helplessly. "I have been on the ocean for a real long time..."

The couple smiled.

Marina bounced the baby, shaking her head in amusement. "Sexual release?" she offered tentatively.

He let out air from his lungs, an expression of relief washing over him. "Please!"

Gaitano laughed. "The local brothel is The Siren's Lair, in town, except they've been kind of cleaning up their act, a little bit, lately."

Marina turned to look at him. "Really? How so?"

"They want a different crowd coming in, so they moved the girls elsewhere, that's all," he explained.

She nodded, smiling. "Well, I think that's really cool."

John nodded thoughtfully, sure he knew what she meant. "So do I," he offered. "Keeps things separate and doubles the business."

Carlos nodded. "Exactly." He pointed out the first booth. "My Quartermaster, Giancarlo Ilarraza, owns the Lair. Tell him we sent you."

"I appreciate it," the older man grinned.

Marina put her hand on his arm, meeting his eyes again. The feeling got better and stronger. "Tell him Marina said to treat you to the cleanest, prettiest girl he's got, and she'll take care of it."

"And then," Carlos added, "if you would like a thrill, of a different variety, you should visit our local dress shop, my guest, of course…"

John frowned again. "Dress shop?"

Marina rolled her eyes, and shook her head. "There are girls, there, doing things to each other, that don't mind men watching…"

The man's eyes widened, as his eyebrows shot up. He choked on a laugh. "Girls do things to each other?"

Marina made a disgusted sound. "So I've been told." She kept shaking her head. "I don't get it."

The men exchanged looks, bonding over her head. John laughed. "And who do I contact for that particular tour?"

Marina rolled her eyes again, and took a deep breath, letting out a big dramatic sigh. Max looked at her curiously. "My brother, Jackson Banks." She nodded towards the booth. "He is the savage sporting the cornrows in his head, gold rings in his ears, and a small gold cross around his neck. Tell him Marina sent you."

Chuckling, the pirate ducked his head again to kiss her cheek once more. "I thank you." Shaking Carlos' hand once more, he walked away.

The couple watched as he stopped to greet the older Gaitano brothers. The men embraced and slapped each other's shoulders, in old camaraderie. They exchanged friendly words, and parted ways.

Marina approached the men in her group thoughtfully. They turned to look at her. She hesitated for a moment, but decided to inquire anyway. "Don Carlos, do you know John?"

"Very well."

"Do you trust him?"

"With my life."

She nodded, smiling. "Cool."

The last booth had a long line of people wrapping around it. All nationalities, all ages. At the table sat one Dr. Kyle Richardson, offering a free clinic. He waved at the group, his face bursting in a smile.

Shayla turned apologetically. "I stay here. See you all, later," and she too was gone.

The remaining family members looked at each other.

"Sun is getting high," Pablo announced. "How about we all take a break?" Everybody agreed.

"I guess I'll go and keep Jackson company then," Storm said. She turned to Salomé. "When is your thing?"

Salomé turned to her with a smile, just as Indio began leading her away by the hand. "In a couple of hours, in front of the dress shop."

Storm nodded, waving to them as she walked away. "See you then," she called over her shoulder, disappearing into the crowd.

Marina frowned. "What thing?" she called after her sister.

Salomé laughed. "Meet me there!" And she too, along with Indio, disappeared.

The parents waved their goodbyes, along with the older Gaitano brothers, leaving her standing alone with Max and Carlos.

The pirate turned to her. "Hungry yet?"

She shook her head. "Not really, but I have got to set Max up."

"Where do you want to go?"

"Back to the Lair, for now. Jimmy usually hooks us up with some bread and fruit and water, and we just go someplace quiet."

He laughed. "Not quiet today, is it?"

"No," she agreed. "But maybe..."

The breeze whispered, stirring the orange pink blossoms around them, mixing them with fuschia and purple, as the bougainvillea swayed. They had just finished a nice, light lunch, and were now sipping from their bottles of water. The sun felt warm on their faces as they sat together, happily, watching the baby play at their feet.

The pirate turned to her and grinned. "Makes you want to stay here, doesn't it?"

Marina smiled. She didn't ask what. She knew exactly what he was talking about. "Would if I could..."

He laughed. "You're not a very social person, are you?"

"No, not really. Sometimes, I get overwhelmed. I'd rather be alone, most of the time."

He nodded. "Good. So do I."

"Yeah, but your place rocks!"

"It is your place too, now," he reminded her.

"Do you ever get overwhelmed?"

"Sometimes," he admitted.

"What do you do?"

"Go home."

Marina grinned. "See what I mean?" She nodded. They had achieved the level of comfort with one another in which they either looked into each other's eyes without saying anything, or they barely even looked at each other as they spoke softly, enjoying the quiet, away from the bustling town. Below them, the docks were swarming with newly arrived pirates. There seemed to be about half a dozen ships still coming in.

Marina swallowed. *I have to know.* Glancing at Carlos, she let her eyes ravage him. The bright sun seemed to sink into his black locks at the same time it struck lights off them. The midday light made his tan golden as it caressed his beautiful chiseled face. His earrings sparkled in the sunlight. There was the beginnings of a shadow on his face. Marina sighed. He looked so good, she could eat him up with a spoon. His beautiful ocean eyes were squinted as they surveyed the activity in the harbor. She swallowed again. She just had to know.

Taking a deep breath, she made herself look away as he turned his head to look at her. "Did you mean it?" she gasped. *I've really got to know...*

"About me freaking out if you don't ask me to marry you?" The pirate did not miss a beat.

Marina's eyes flew to his face, suddenly meeting his. She froze, as he looked away. Something tightened in her chest. She had never seen him so troubled, so unsettled before. When her voice finally came, it was little more than a hoarse whisper. "Yes..."

"*Yes!*" A frown crossed his face. Blindly, he reached for her hand, gripping it desperately when he finally found it.

"I don't want you to *freak*," she wailed softly, tears stinging her eyes.

Carlos' head snapped back to look at her. "So, ask me..." he drawled, in a dangerously low voice. "Make sure you mean it." His warning was a growl. "Don't play with me, Marina..." He went still as death. "Either spend the rest of your life with me, or get out of my life." Beautiful deep sea blue eyes darkened with the storm raging inside him. His hand squeezed hers rhythmically, in a silent beat, only he could hear. Marina's free hand went up to her chest, pressing hard, fighting to keep her heart from pounding its way free. The pirate shook his head at something only he could see. "I can't live without you," he confessed.

"I would die without you..."

"But?"

"We've only known each other---"

"For weeks!"

"A few, right? But how can you be so---"

"I am sure."

"From the bottom of your heart?"

"To the depths of my soul!"

"You fill me..."

"Do you have any doubts?"

"No. My soul recognizes you. My body adores you. My mind is full with thoughts of you. My heart stops and pounds for you..."

"You love me."

"I do."

"I love you."

"I want to stay with you."

"My way."

"Which is?"

"I have been your boss, and your friend. Makeout partner, boyfriend, lover. I will only stay with you as your husband..."

Marina shook her head slowly, overwhelming joy engulfing her. "Marry me, Carlos?"

Carlos' hand kept squeezing hers as his eyes caressed her features. Relief flooded his face. "Marry me, Marina..."

She bit her lip and nodded. "When?"

He frowned for a moment, thinking. Something he had heard Jackson say, once. Tomorrow? No. "Yesterday," he finally murmured. Locking eyes with her, he brought her hand to his lips, kissing it longingly.

Marina smiled. "I'm crazy about you..."

Carlos nodded. "And I, you..." Eyes twinkling with mischief, he rubbed the back of her hand over his face, scratching it with his shadow. Kissing it again, he finally let her go.

Without saying another word, they picked up their things, and Max safely riding on the pirate's shoulders, they headed back to town.

"Marina! Hurry!"

Marina looked around her wildly, searching for her sister. "Salomé?"

Said sister was jumping up and down, waving her arms in the air, in front of the dress shop. "Hurry!"

Marina sighed, shaking the hair out of her face. She turned to the pirate next to her. "Watch the baby, baby?" she murmured as he took Max from her. Blindly, she went to join her sister.

Inside the dress shop, there was a bustle of activity. There were women of all ages, all sizes, and all colors. Standing around, preening before mirrors, talking to each other, pacing restlessly. Liana, the brand new proprietor of the dress shop, and soon to be Mrs. Kyle Richardson, the doctor's wife, orchestrated the whole thing. And in the middle of it all, Sloane Aguilar.

Salomé grabbed her hand, pulling her into a room behind a curtain. "Here, put this on, quickly, they are getting ready to begin," she said, throwing a dress at her, and leaving her alone, suddenly.

Marina sighed. "How the hell did I get conned into a fashion show?" she muttered under her breath. Salomé, being her sister, knew better. Shaking her head, she quickly stripped off her pants and top, and stepped into the dress that had been given her. Shimmying into it, she realized it was a sarong. Comfortable as a bath robe, it was made of shimmery pearl colored liquid satin. Gathered at the bust, it added support and cleavege where before there was none. Gathered again, gently, at the waist, it draped sensously on her hips. Without looking at the mirror, Marina smoothed her hands over her body slowly, caressing the material into place. The dress complied, settling on her curves with murmured whispers and sighs. Sinful. Marina felt naked.

Out of nowhere, Salomé peered around the curtain. "By the way, there's a toy box over there, so you can dress for this outfit..." She took a good look at her sister, suddenly rendered speechless. "You... oh, Marina... you... look... stunning!"

Marina grinned. Still without looking. "Stop!" She sighed, running her hand down the dress one more time. "I hope Carlitos likes it..."

Salomé swallowed. "Oh, baby, he's gonna *freak*." She winked at her sister. "Trust me." Laughing happily, she waved a hand at a wooden box on a table. A candle burned softly next to it, making the weathered wood shine enticingly. "Knock yourself out." Frowning gently, she scolded softly. "But hurry! You're the last one out. Don't lose sight of the last girl before you, and you'll be fine," she assured. And just as suddenly, she was gone.

Lowering her eyes so she wouldn't catch sight of herself in the mirror. Marina crossed the small room to the wooden box on the table. Flinging the lid open, she was greeted by a piece of cloth. The same fabric as the dress. Marina held it up thoughtfully, turning it this way and that, for a moment. It was a plain, shimmering pearl square. Finally, her face brightened. Qu ickly putting up her hair, wrapping it around itself, off her nape, she proceeded to work on the fabric. Folding it in half diagonally, she held the folded edge to the back of her neck. Flipping the opposite corner over her forehead, she proceeded to mold the fabric to her head, allowing a little room for her hair. She then tied the remaining opposite corners in a double knot on top of her head, pinning the third one, so that there were three peaks sticking out. Coaxing them gently under the fabric, she made them disappear, leaving only sleek and smooth lines. The effect was magical. Where the hair around her face softened her features, the pure lines of her turban put these same features on prominent display, in a most flattering way. Girl next door goes cosmopolitan. Marina still wouldn't look at herself.

Peering into the box, she finally opted for spilling its contents on the table. Candlelight sparkled off a variety of jewelry, ranging from ethnic to gems. Marina went through it all a few times, before she finally made up her mind. Quickly slipping some things on, she was ready. Everything felt exactly right. Taking a deep breath, she was ready. Then, she looked in the mirror.

Marina's heart skipped a beat. The woman staring back at her took her breath away. The line of the turban around her face brought out, well, *her*. Hazel eyes shone brightly in a sun kissed face. The sarong shimmied and shimmered in all the right places. She shifted her weight slowly, watching the fabric flow on her. It screamed sex. Biting her lip, she sighed happily, raising her eyebrows at her reflection in the mirror. Salomé was right. *Carlitos is definitely going to freak...*

Beautiful hammered silver disc earrings swung happily from her ears, chunky turquoise drops suspended from them. A larger disc and drop graced the top of her chest, suspended from black cord, framing Indio's silver and turquoise cross. A bracelet consisted of a cuff of the same discs, held together, side by side, with smaller drops falling softly over the inside of her wrists, brushing gently against the tops of her palms, and over the backs of her hands. The same, but longer by a whole silver disc and nugget, graced an ankle. Indio's bracelet, the one Carlos used to recognize her before a cave full of pirates at El Baile del Luto, on the Caribbean island of Carey, had never been seen off her left wrist, since that fateful night. Marina sighed. There was no denying it, it was a fact. She looked hot. She took a deep breath. Definitely sexy. Disturbingly so. Good for her. Quickly turning away from her reflection and hurrying after the last girl in front of her, Marina left the dress shop.

Stepping outside into the suddenly brighter than hell sunshine, she seemed to screech to a halt. Stopping in her tracks, as graceful as possible, rope sandals and all, she began to walk slowly, blindly, adjusting her eyes. Finally, she could at least recognize Carlos, gaping at her. Quickly, she bathed herself in cool, visualizing, casting herself instantly into the role of the most beautiful woman in the world. After all, she looked like a movie star.

The effect was instantaneous. She hid a smile as she saw his bright sea water eyes widen. By the time he reached her, she felt like

Helen of Troy. To Carlos, she looked just as beautiful. Marina decided to keep it light, pretending she didn't see the effect her change of looks had on him. Which happened to be kind of difficult, since the man was stunned. The impact had rendered him speechless.

Marina laughed at herself. "I can't see, baby," she confided shyly. "Will you walk me out of here, please?"

Without any words available to him, the pirate could only nod. Shifting Max to his opposite hip, he held out his arm to her. Marina smiled at him, her eyes sending wicked thoughts his way. Relaxing, he grinned, walking her slowly between the people lined up, shoulder to shoulder, on both sides of the street. An improvised catwalk.

"I want to cry," he whispered hoarsely.

Tears came to her own eyes at his heartfelt words. Blinking them back, her breath shuddered in her chest. Impulsively, she pressed her lips passionately against his shoulder.

Out of the crowd, flowers were thrust at her. Well, not really flowers. An improvised bouquet of bamboo shoots, tied together with hemp rope.

Juan Aguilar's eyes twinkled merrily over the delicate leaves. "Would you still consider my offer?" he asked mischievously.

"You're too late," she informed him, accepting the offered bamboo with a smile.

Juan winked at her. "I tried..." And he melted into the sidelines.

The crowd murmured. The effect was complete. Marina had totally forgotten the custom of most major designers, and their runway shows. Most major designers accustomed the last dress to be the same. Of course, she didn't think about it. Not even when her family and his collectively gasped at them as they approached, only to turn back the way they had come, towards the dress shop. Not when her fathers looked at each other and tears came to her mothers' eyes. Not when his parents blindly reached for each other's hands. Not even when her brother and sister did, either. Nor when his brother broke into a smile before he began chuckling. But she should have known. Even if she wasn't as into Sloane's line of work as Salomé was, she should have known. The pirate holding the baby, instead of hampering the look, enhanced it. How could she have forgotten? She had learned to crawl, walk and run on a catwalk, had grown up among the most beautiful women in the world, and was raised on runway shows. How dare she forget? Most major fashion designer runway shows ended with a wedding dress.

At her side, the pirate resembled a dazed groom. Marina looked like a bride.

Max was safe in his parents' general store. Happy and exhausted from a full day of fun and lots of attention. Most everybody had disappeared save for the steady stream of visiting pirates swarming in the streets. *The Pirates' Convention Expo* was off to becoming an unprecedented success.

The pirate had led her by the hand down the alley that ran along the Sirens' Lair. Just being off the main street muffled the noise a little bit, so that they could speak a little bit more comfortably. Next to them was an old wooden barrel, the lid askew, the better to catch rain water. A soft drip sounded as if fell from the gutter of the building, unto the lid of the barrel, to be immediately soaked by the ancient wood. It was also cooler here in the shadows, away from the direct sunlight. The couple smiled at each other.

The pirate reached out with his hands, burying his fingers in her hair.

"What happened?" he murmured, smiling into her eyes.

Marina shook her head, not understanding. "What do you mean?"

"A few minutes ago, you were as exotic and mesmerizing as any tropical queen," he informed her. Dragging his fingers out of her hair, he ran his hands over her shoulders, and down her arms.

Marina slipped her hands into his, palm to palm, raising them slowly, fingers interlocked. "And now?" She felt herself grow warm as his eyes caressed her, taking in her regular outfit.

"Now," he teased with a drawl, raising their hands over her head, "you are wild and mesmerizing..."

She smiled. "One out of two isn't bad," she murmured.

"Mesmerizing is good," he agreed, ducking his head to rub his shadow over her face. "So is wild..."

Marina closed her eyes and breathed deeply. Her only reality consisted of the side of the building against her back, his hands holding hers over her head, and his warm breath on her neck. She shivered. "I can do exotic, more often, if you like," she offered huskily.

"I like," he mumbled between the hot kisses he was pressing on her chest. Marina laughed as he let her hands go, allowing her to slip her arms around him. She raked her fingers in his hair, finally keeping his face pressed against her beating heart. Closing her eyes for a moment, she felt him steal a kiss. She basked in it.

Carlos deepened his kiss. She felt good in his arms. Made him feel like a teenager, of not so long ago, pressing her against the side of the building, giving her a taste of the passion she inspired in him. Oh, yes, she felt really good.

Marina raised her face skyward. *Gracias, Dios mio...* Propelling herself off from where she was leaning, she made him dance in a circle with her, until his back was to the street and she faced it. Then, slowly rubbing her soft cheek against his scratchy one, she propped her chin on his shoulder, and slowly opened her eyes. Her heart stopped. *Oh, my God!* Just as slowly, she closed her eyes again, dreamily. Taking a deep breath, she reined herself in, almost completely shutting herself down. Her reasons were clear. Marina wasn't about to let her body betray her fear.

Carlos frowned over her head. Something was wrong. Something happened. Marina's stillness had crashed down on her, causing her heart to go from silent, to thunderous. It was the only indication of life in her. "What's wrong?"

There's this guy that's following me, and it's really creepy, 'cause he's been doing it all morning, and I'm terrified, because I think he's spying on me for Xavier! Marina shook her head. Making herself snap out of it, she took his face in her hands, and suddenly overcome with passion, she pretended to eat him with her kisses. "Nothing, baby," she murmured, swinging him around gently, held tight in her arms, so her back was to the street, and he faced it. "Somebody walked over my grave, is all..." She stopped kissing him suddenly, and pulled away from him, making him open his eyes.

Carlos looked down at her. If only they weren't out in public... "I want you so bad, I could do you right here and right now," he assured her in a seductive whisper, winking at her shocked expression.

Marina smiled. "How crude." She licked her lips, distracting him.

"You like it!'

"I love it!"

Carlos grabbed her by the hips, grinding them against his, and looked over her head, scanning the street behind her. People walked, ran, and rode to and fro, in steady streams. But only one man stood at the head of the alley, staring at them. It was his turn to go still.

Marina moaned, quickly distracting him again, playing a nymphomaniac overcome with lust. She didn't want the pirate focusing on her watcher. Raining kisses on his face, she felt him relax suddenly.

Carlos caught her mouth with his. He had made himself open his eyes again, even as he was being kissed passionately. There was nobody there now. He forced his muscles to loosen up even more. Playfully, he ended the kiss and threw his arm around her shoulders, steering her back into the heart of things. As soon as they reached the street, they stopped.

"Caribe!"

The dreadlocked young man stopped in his tracks, and turned to look at them. So preoccupied was he, that he hadn't even noticed the couple as they emerged from the shady alleyway he was crossing. "Hey!" He quickly glanced at Marina. For some reason, although her mouth was bruised from kisses, her eyes were wide in her face, and it wasn't from passion. They flickered. His heart squeezed. "What's up?"

"Take Marina for a run."

They stared at the pirate. Caribe couldn't believe it. He knew for a fact, that Marina's passion for running was one of the things, besides her fighting Solomon, the pirate was trying to come to terms with, not very happy about it. "You are serious? Why?"

Carlos glanced down at Marina, searching her face. His hand absently stroked her hair. "Marina needs a break. I want her out of town."

Inside, Marina gasped, her heart racing. For a moment, she was speechless. Then she decided, she didn't want to know any more. Switching channels in her head, she flashed him a smile. "Why, thank you, papi, I could use the time away from here. I guess you're going to be busy."

The pirate nodded. "Pretty much."

Reaching up, she stole a kiss. Looking into his eyes, she winked at him. "Later..."

Carlos winked back and nodded. Their eyes flickered at each other, and she turned away.

Caribe slid hands with him. *"Adios, Capitán..."*

The pirate nodded. *"Adios, Caribe.* Take her home and look out for her." He lowered his voice. "Don't let her out of your sight. I'll be by later, tonight."

Caribe nodded, and also turned away. Grabbing Marina's hand, he began dragging her through the crowd.

Left alone, Carlos Gaitano, Hijo, quickly scanned the crowd. *Aaaah, there he is.* Quickly and silently, Carlos crept up behind the man he had spied at the head of the alley. The stranger was actually hu rrying, trying to catch up with Caribe and his girlfriend.

"Charlie!" Carlos cried happily, clamping his hand down on the man's shoulder. "I haven't seen you in ages!"

The man spun around quickly, eyes wide and startled in his grimy face. "I-I think y-you got the wrong m-man, Captain," he stammered.

Carlos studied him closely, even as he frowned, feigning puzzlement, letting his hand fall off the man's shoulder. "Well, I apologize, my good man, but I could have sworn I knew you from somewhere. Got you mixed up with someone I run into in Carey..."

The man paled, and swallowed visibly, his eyes almost tearing. "Not me, Captain. I have never seen you before---"

Carlos grinned, slipping his arm firmly around the man's shoulders. "Good! The name is Gaitano. Come. I'll show you around." And turning him around, he headed back towards the Lair.

Dismayed, the man looked over his shoulder, wondering the amount of trouble he was going to get into for losing sight of the girl, at this most critical moment. But he couldn't deny the man who just ruined his mission without seeming suspicious. "Th-thank you, C-Captain. I have never b-been in Encantada be-before."

The pirate grinned. "Of course not, my good man. I would have remembered you." He glanced at him, catching a shudder race through the man's body. "Now that I have met you, I will never forget you." He laughed wickedly. "Come. Be my guest." He glanced behind them also. "There is nothing back there except the natives. Everything you could possibly want or need is this way. Come."

They ran. Breath huffing in rhythm, as their feet pounded on the sandy trail. They swam. The pool beckoned to them as they neared it, so that the detour was decided with silent agreement. The cool blue water refreshed them, washing away more than sweat and dirt. Feeling better, they finished their run, stampeding into the village. Parting ways, they went to their respective huts to get clean.

Marina was wrong. Her hut wasn't musty at all. On the contrary, it had been recently cleaned and aired. Fresh flowers in the black glass bottle could have been anyone. But children's scribbles on papers tacked to the wall, could only come from Leilani's siblings, Ali and the twins, Juan and Jaime. Marina's heart melted. The place looked, smelled, and felt great. Smiling to herself, she crossed the floor and out the back door, to her beautiful yard. There, a tub of sun warmed rainwater stood by the steps. Marina smiled. She must be truly loved. So many people watching out for her. Quickly stripping off her clothes, she jumped in. All she wanted was to wash the day away.

"So what do you really think?"

Marina sighed at her dreadlocked friend. "I already told you, baby, I think these are fantastic."

They were sitting at her small table, heads together as they looked at the book he had made for her. They hadn't danced with the natives tonight, opting for hanging out together, instead. They had shared a little food, and a lot of laughs, their friendship strong and solid between them. Caribe relished this moment with Marina, almost above all others, because he knew that it would be one of the very last times he would hang with her, before she united her life with the pirate's. And the way things were going, that seemed to be pretty soon. "Could I make a living in your world, doing what I do?" he asked suddenly.

Marina's heart skipped a beat. "You are interested in my world, Caribe? For real? Since when?"

"Since I've known that it's possible to come back."

Marina did quick mental calculations. "So, you've been thinking about this for weeks?"

Caribe nodded, smiling happily. "If I can make money and survive in your world, and be able to come back to my world, I would have the best of both."

"Isn't that something you would want to share with someone, though?"

"Of course. There is no one, though." He smiled at her startled look and answered the question in her eyes. "Of course I would love to have someone." It was his turn to sigh. "It's just not going to be anybody from here."

Marina thought about his words, but her heart burst with happiness for him. "Dude, you will make one of the most awesome boyfriend, lover, husband, father, whatever, any girl could ever wish for."

"I want to do something with my life. I want to know the world, you know?" He searched Marina's eyes. "There's got to be more out there than just pirates." His hands lifted for a moment, as he gathered and organized his thoughts, before they fell back on the tabletop again. "I don't feel like sacrificing myself any longer. I enjoy what I do, don't get me wrong, I know I am of value to those I respect and love." He sighed. "But I'm also ready for much more. I want to go to school. I want to develop my drawing and explore other art forms. I want to meet real women." He shrugged. "Women like you and Salomé."

Marina put her hands on top of his, squeezing them gently. "You know what, baby? You're the man with a plan. You've obviously given this some thought, and I agree with all my heart, that your way is the best. Do it. I have a girl back home that lives with me. It's a long story, but she's like my younger sister. Her name is Xaira, and she is absolutely beautiful. Extremely talented, and artistic, and sexy. I think that if you were to meet, she will fall madly in love with you before you both know it. Go for it, Caribe. This is your time to shine."

Caribe nodded. "I will." He turned his hands over, catching hers, and brought them to his lips, kissing each one in turn. Soft candlelight reflected in his eyes, happy that he had confided in her. "I have to go. The Council and the main pirates will be meeting soon, with the men in charge."

"In charge of what?"

"In charge of deciding if Gaitano keeps Encantada or not."

"Who are they?"

"I don't know."

"Find out."

Caribe laughed. "Are you worried?" he asked, incredulous.

Marina grinned. "Not really. I guess I just want to know who affects my life directly. And anything that happens to Carlos Gaitano…" she shrugged, "is definitely going to affect me."

"You know he's serious about you. I have never seen him like this, in my whole life."

She nodded. "We are getting married."

"I know. I think everybody knows."

Marina smiled. "Maybe, but you are the first one I am telling. Carlos Gaitano and I are getting married. Nobody knows yet…"

Caribe laughed happily. "I understand, and I am deeply honored. I hope to be present."

"You have to be. How else am I ever to have a record of the event?" She answered his unspoken question. "Don't know when, yet."

"I will be there."

"Good." Putting her hands flat on the table, she stood up. "Right now, you've got to go." Caribe followed her to the door, where she put the book in his hands. "Do me proud, papi. Represent."

Caribe nodded. "I will." They embraced in parting, holding each other tight. Ducking his head, he kissed her on the cheek and climbed down the steps, quickly swallowed up by the darkness.

Caribe hesitated. It was more quiet over here by the docks, than in the heart of town where revelry and noise abounded. He could hear soft laughter and a murmur of voices behind the closed door on the top floor of the warehouse. Taking a deep breath, he knocked. The door swung open immediately, and a familiar face peered out at him.

"Caribe!" The greeting was warm and friendly, as the Boatswain smiled at him, teeth bright in his beautiful African face.

Caribe grinned back, stepping inside, feeling the door shut behind him again. "Solomon!" They slid hands against each other.

Solomon nodded at the book in his arms. "What have you got there?" Caribe slipped on his most serious face, even as his eyes twinkled merrily.

"The accountant sent me to the people in charge. She feels this must be of some value to them."

"Knowing the accountant, it must be, then." The Boatswain motioned at a large table where the rest of the pirates were sitting.

Smiling, Caribe approached the table slowly. His artist's eyes avidly took in the details, knowing that he would be interrogated on them. Candlelight flickered all around the room, as the men spoke urgently. The whole Council was there, including Rouge. Also present, were the captured seamen from *La Diosa del Mar*, Don Andres Segarra y Collazo and Don Luis Vega y Ramos. The Hawthorne brothers were there, and so was the huge imposing pirate Marina called John. And then, there were the Gaitano men. The older three brothers, Don Miguel, Don Carlos, and Juan, were in the middle of it all, and with them, the second generation, Carlos and Indio. The pirates looked up as the village boy approached them.

"Caribe!" Don Carlos beckoned him to approach them. "What have you got there, son?"

Caribe stood in front of them, looking at them carefully. They had all fallen silent as he drew near, all eyes on the book in his hands. "I bring you a gift," the dread finally said.

"A gift?" Don Carlos repeated, interested. "And who is this gift from?"

Caribe took a deep breath. "Marina Aguilar, accountant of La Gitana."

The pirates smiled. Chuckles rumbled in deep chests at the mention of the name. None more interested than the Captain of La Gitana, now silent and very watchful as he followed the younger man's moves. "I asked you to keep an eye on her," he reproached softly.

"Jackson's got her."

Don Carlos laughed softly. "A gift from Marina!" he exclaimed in a low voice. "May we see this gift?"

Caribe nodded. Without saying a word, he placed the book in front of them. The men crowded around, curiosity high among them. He opened the book slowly. Noises of wonder and approval filled the air, as the drawings seemed to come to life in the flickering candlelight. "When we were in Carey," Caribe began softly, "there was one thing that came out, that preoccupied our accountant more than anything." His hand caressed the front page before he turned it, revealing the crew of La Gitana. Facing the page was a log of the dates and port'o'calls the ship had been in. "The White Ghost." He glanced at Rouge. The woman looked up at him with startled eyes, not being able to hide a shiver. Giancarlo slipped his arm around her in a protective gesture. "While we were at El Baile del Luto," Caribe frowned, remembering something, "before the entertainment," he couldn't help but flash a smile at Carlos, "Marina went about meeting some ships' Captains and crews, taking down notes on where they were, when." He passed another page. "It's all here."

Rouge stared at the pages before them for a moment, before turning wild eyes on Caribe. "How is that going to help with the White Ghost, honey?" she asked, her voice trembling.

"Process of elimination." He flipped through the book to the last page. "Here are all the dates and places the White Ghost has struck that we know of. You're supposed to check these dates against where everybody has been at those moments in time." He sighed, and flipped the book back to the portraits. "Everybody she has met is here."

The Gaitano men looked at each other. "This is amazing, Caribe," Don Carlos told him, awe in his voice. "You have done a good job. You and Marina, both." He shook his head, amazed at the vivid drawings before him. "What drove either of you to create such a thing?"

Caribe shrugged. "I just like drawing, and this has kept me busy for a while. Marina..." He looked around the table once again, meeting everybody's eyes, and shook his head slowly. "Marina thinks you can catch this guy, if you can figure out who he's not."

"I suppose there's a name to this process?" Don Miguel rumbled in a low voice.

Caribe nodded. "Cross-referencing." He pushed the book towards them. "It might take a little while, but it can be done."

Juan's hand went out, flipping another page. "Who of us can do this?" Caribe motioned with his head at Carlos and Indio. "*They* can. She says that they both have done the books with her, so between them, it should take them no time at all."

Juan turned his head to look at his nephews. "Is this true?"

The young men looked at each other for a moment, eyes locked together, before turning back to their uncle.

Carlos cleared his throat. "Yes. It is true. We both have been actively involved with every step of Marina's bookkeeping."

Indio nodded in agreement. "If she says we can do it, we most certainly can. She has taught us a lot."

Don Carlos put both his hands on the table, pushing himself up, so he was standing. "All right then," he said, glancing at the men next to him. He looked at his sons. "It looks like you boys have some work to do." Turning back to the dreadlocked native, he smiled warmly. "Thank you, Caribe. We greatly appreciate everything you have done for us, son."

Caribe smiled at the patriarch, meeting his eyes. "Thank you, Don Carlos, it has been an honor for me to work for Marina and Carlos, and to be of help to the Gaitanos."

Don Carlos reached out with a hand and stroked his cheek, as he would have his son's. "You are your father's son, with your mother's heart. God bless you, Caribe."

Tears stung the back of his eyes, but he maintained his smile. "Thank you, Don Carlos." He blinked, and looked at the pirates again. "One more thing." He reached over and flipped some pages in his book, until he found what he was looking for. Spinning it so that it was facing the younger Gaitano brothers, he pointed at a particular sailor. He met Carlos' eyes, as the pirate looked from the drawing, back into his eyes. "This person has been following Marina all morning."

Carlos and Indio froze. They looked at each other, their eyes communicating silently, before they turned back to Caribe. "How do you know?" Indio inquired softly.

Caribe's mouth twisted sardonically. "She told me. I saw him." He looked pointedly at the brothers.

Indio frowned. "I noticed nothing. It's been a busy day."

Carlos sighed. "She didn't tell me. But I saw him." Before he could stop himself, he blurted out what everybody was thinking. "What does she think?"

Caribe laughed and stepped back, shaking his dreads, his hands in the air. "What else?" He met his eyes. "Xavier will be here." And without saying another word, he nodded to the pirates, and left the warehouse, sliding hands with Solomon as he went out the door.

The remaining pirates looked at each other. Rouge roughly brushed the tears that spilled from her eyes. Giancarlo held her against him, murmuring in her ear. Solomon scowled, as he approached the table and glanced at the book. Don Miguel and Don Carlos let out deep breaths, as they flipped pages. Carlos and Indio looked at each other again, communicating silently. The captured Spaniards sat quiet, respectfully not even looking at one another. The Hawthorne brothers stared. John frowned, deep in thought. The rest of the Council kept quiet, watching things unfold.

Juan stood up suddenly, and pushed himself off the table, letting his chair fall with a bang on the wooden floor. Restlessly, he started pacing back and forth, no longer the younger, wayward, jovial brother of the Gaitano clan. Moving like a caged wildcat, he exuded strength and power, transformed into the man of authority his position commanded him to be. Here was Juan Gaitano, Captain of La Prision. The jail keeper and justice of the peace of the seas. And he was furious. Finally, he stopped, eyes wild as he stared at the pirates looking back at him. His voice, when it finally came out, was a mute roar. "How safe is Marina Aguilar?"

Carlos stood up. "I will kill Xavier before he takes her."

"Yes!" Juan agreed with him. "And so you announced to him in a cave full of witnesses!" His laugh was short and hard. "Do you think you are dealing with a stupid man? He will go around you, now that he's been warned."

Indio stood up, side by side, next to his brother, supporting him. " Tio Juan," he said softly, "we will defend Marina with our lives---"

"That may not be enough!" he roared at his nephews.

"Juan!" Don Miguel stood up, holding out a hand towards his brother, and the other towards his nephews. His energy lashed out, whipping at the men until they trembled where they stood. His voice dropped, until it was pure ice. "Let the boys handle their business," he warned softly.

Carlos clenched his fists at his side, his eyes glowing like blue flames. "We are talking about the woman who is to be my wife," he said slowly. "I will kill Xavier!"

Don Carlos then stood up, clapped his hands together and rubbed them in a gesture meant to distract. "If I know Marina Aguilar, she might just kill Xavier first." The pirates chuckled, and the mood lifted. The pirate slid the book across the table at his sons. "Get to work boys. Let us know what you find."

Indio nodded. "Right away, Papá."

Carlos glared at his uncle for a moment longer, before finally relaxing as he met his father's loving eyes. "Whatever you say, Papá."

The Gaitano men sat back down. The rest of the pirates resumed their conversation. Carlos and Indio quickly began to work with paper and pencil, heads bowed together, the precious book between them. Solomon and Giancarlo joined them, hoping to speed things up. The Hawthorne brothers sat with Juan Aguilar in one corner, while the Council convened in another. John conversed with the older Gaitano brothers.

Finally, the verdict was read. Speculations were said. Decisions were made. The room fell silent, and everybody looked at each other in silent agreement.

John slammed his hands down on the table, and stood up, commanding attention. They all looked at him. "Gentlemen," he glanced at Rouge and smiled, bowing his head respectfully, "princess," making her smile, he looked around at them, "we have work to do."

Marina smiled, as she crouched behind the hibiscus bushes. She sang out softly. "Humpty Dumpty sat on the wall, Humpty Dumpty had a great fall..." Scampering like a crab, on the balls of her bare feet and the palms of her hands, she went around the last shrub and came up behind the twins. "All the king's horses and all the king's men..." She pounced on them, making them scream with laughter. "Couldn't put Humpty together again!" Marina gasped, not being able to stop laughing herself. She rolled on her back, holding a squirming baby in each arm, scrambling all over her as they tagged team and held her down.

Ali came up skipping the path they were in, and watched, thoughtfully. "You're a good mommy," she finally announced.

Marina sat up, hugging the twins to her. "Why, thank you, baby, so glad you think so!" The twins smooched her, pressing small open mouths to her cheek, cool and wet. Marina widened her eyes at them, rubbing noses with one at a time. "Juan! Jaime!" she squealed at them. They squealed right back, making their older sister dissolve into giggles.

It was a beautiful morning. A fresh breeze whipped around the back yard, rustling the leaves in the avocado and mango trees. Vines swung from the higher branches of a breadfruit tree. Beautiful red hibiscus dripped from the tops of their bushes, bowing their petals. Hummingbirds zoomed amongst the bright yellow kind, called *canarias* in her father's native island, because of their extraordinary color. In a far corner of the yard, bamboo creaked like galleons. From the next yard over, part of the umbrella of a flamboyan in bloom, dripped red petals in a shady canopy over her own yard. It was a gorgeous day.

"Hi! Looks like you're having fun!"

Startled, Marina looked around and right at Leilani. "Oh, hi, mami! You scared me," she admitted with a laugh.

Leilani smiled. "Sorry..."

"What brings you back so soon?"

The native girl pointed over her shoulder. "Caribe says I must come and stay with the children. You are needed in town."

Marina looked at the dreadlocked young man standing behind the girl. "I am?"

Caribe nodded. Without saying a word, he beckoned her with his head, for her to join him. Turning, he walked away from the children, into the middle of a bright sunny spot surrounded by luscious birds of paradise.

Marina relinquished the twins to their sisters, and stood up slowly. "Excuse me," she murmured and walked towards Caribe. "Caribe?"

"*Buenos dias,*" he murmured, putting a hand on her shoulder and kissing her cheek. And without saying another word, he handed her some papers.

Marina took them, suspicious, her eyes sliding over him. She made herself look. Of course they were sketches. The first one was a blow-up of Max, apparently gurgling on somebody's lap. He seemed to be chewing on the hilt of a sword. Marina couldn't smile. The second one was as if a camera had zoomed out a little, and Marina could see more of the surroundings. The person was obviously a male, the shirt opened at the chest, and a heavy belt at the pants. The strong hands held the baby lovingly, certainly not harming it. The baby himself seemed okay with the person holding him. Around them were tables and chairs, a bar at their backs. Marina closed her eyes and swallowed, as she tucked the paper behind it and revealed the third picture. She opened her eyes. And then she wished she hadn't. The third paper revealed the whole picture. Now, she could actually see whose lap Max was in. Who was holding him with such tender care, as if it were the father himself. But it wasn't John Kline. Oh, no. It was *him.*

Caribe caught Marina as her legs buckled and she stumbled, horror cloaking her like a sheet of ice cold water. She went numb, even as he dragged her back up. His beloved voice warned in her ear. "The children are watching."

Marina caught herself, calling on all her powers to bring herself together. "How could this happen?" she choked out, not being able to hide the terror in her voice.

Caribe shook his head. "We don't know."

"But is he in grave danger? And who the hell is *we?*"

"Everybody's there. Not really. He's not hurting Max."

"What about Larissa?" she wailed, hands flying to her mouth as her shocked eyes brimmed with tears.

"Larissa is furious. They took him out the back door, as she was busy tending customers up front. John's with Pedro Barbosa, keeping an eye on the sailors' huts, so he doesn't even know yet. She's been banging on the Siren's Lair for a while now, but they won't let her in ---"

"Won't let her in?" she repeated, horrified, gulping air so she wouldn't burst into sobs.

"He insists that you are the only one he will relinquish Max to..."

Stunned, Marina looked at the paper in her hand. On a closer look, the pirate seemed to be playing with the baby in his lap. Closing her eyes, she turned her face heavenward. *Dios mio, Padre amado, beloved Father, give me strength.* Eyes flying open, she looked at Caribe. "I'm going to freak," she informed him softly.

Her friend nodded solemnly. "I'm sure you are."

"But I have to take care of some business."

"Yes, you do."

Marina glanced at the paper in her hand, again. *"Fucking Xavier!"*

Caribe nodded in agreement. *"Fucking Xavier!"*

Marina looked at him, and beckoned with her head, for him to follow her inside her hut. "Come. *Visteme despacio, que tengo prisa.*"

Caribe frowned, as he followed her inside. "What does that mean?"

"Dress me slowly, because I'm in a hurry."

He shook his head at her. "I can translate it, but what does it mean?"

"It's something that Pablo learned in history class in Boriken." Marina shrugged. "I need to do things right the first time." Striding to where her fabrics lay, she frowned, as she went through them. "I want black," she announced. There was only one black fabric with luscious aquatic color designs brushed on it in exotic dyes. It was shorter than the normal sarong. She turned to Caribe. "Do you have anything in black?" she asked.

Caribe nodded and disappeared out the front door, running across the dirt lane to his own hut. He was back out in seconds, a bundle under his arm. Reaching her side once more, he thrust the clothes at Marina. "Here!"

Marina took them. While he was gone, she had hurriedly replaced what she was wearing with the black fabric. Tying it like a sarong anyway, it hung at midriff. Other than that, she was only in her panties. Now, she was looking at black pants, a black shirt, and a black leather belt with a simple, heavy silver buckle. Quickly, she donned the outfit on. Everything was oversized, so she had to adjust here and there. With the help of a mirror that had appeared magically while she had been absent, she finally achieved the look she wanted. Finally, she turned to Caribe. "Now, I'm ready."

Caribe shook his head. "You need to relax, first." Locking eyes with hers, he drew out a peace pipe from behind his back, lit it and passed it to her. Marina dragged deeply and passed it back to him. Her muscles loosened. He tamped it out with a smile, and put it away above the window frame over the table. "Now, you're ready."

Marina nodded.

Saying goodbye to Leilani and Ali and Juan and Jaime, the pair headed into town.

They weren't in a hurry. They had to tread carefully.

Caribe looked at her. Poor visitor. So much fear and pain. From the little he knew and could comprehend about her world, it was much more civilized than his, if not completely, at least for her. He shook his head. So much love and happiness. Marina had traveled time, to meet her soulmate, the love of her life. Thankfully, her love was reciprocated, making her into the woman she was now. Marina was one of the best friends he ever had. His heart swelled with love for her.

Marina sighed sadly. Fucking Xavier! How dare he come into her life in this outrageous dramatic manner! Her day was supposed to have gone well. It started wonderful! First, Carlos had visited her at dawn, and made sweet love to her in her own hut, before creeping out with passionate wet kisses and whispered promises in her ear. By the time Leilani had dropped off the kids, she had been up for a while, clearing out her backyard, and was absolutely glowing. It should have continued that way! But no! Here comes Caribe, the bearer of the worst news ever! Marina shook her head. Poor Caribe. She apologized silently, glancing at him. *I'm sorry, baby, I didn't mean it, I love you so much, but I'm just so scared!* She looked away as his eyes met hers. Now, she felt her dark side. Her thoughts were bordering on evil. Even though the day was cloudless and bright, she felt her darkness emanating from the inside out.

Silently, Marina reached for his hand. She needed the support. Caribe glanced at her and winked. Just as silently, he locked fingers with hers. *He* needed the support.

There were few people out on the street, definitely not as much as there were yesterday. Most of the visiting sailors weren't even up yet. Many were at the plaza by Padre Ignacio's church, where there would be more activities, later. Right now, the pair was thinking about no one else, as they strode hand in hand into town, but the woman before them.

Larissa stopped pacing as she caught sight of them and looked from one to the other. She stood still, waiting for them to reach her. The tears had dried on her face, leaving silver snail tracks. The glitter in her emerald green eyes was sparked by terror and fueled by white hot fury.

"Larissa..." Her voice broke. Marina stood in front of her, and her eyes immediately flooded with tears.

"Marina... Oh, no, honey, don't," she crooned, flinging her arms around the younger woman, even as she choked on a sob. "Hush! Max is all right, honey, he's not in any danger."

"I am so sorry," Marina wailed softly. Her sole impulse was to let go, to wander out into the middle of the street, racked by sobs, wailing and screaming, and tearing at her hair. Instead, she gathered her thoughts and stashed that image of herself into the back of her mind, recalling her tears and stifling her sobs. "I am deeply, incredibly sorry, from the bottom of my heart."

"Hush!" Larissa ordered, taking her face between her hands, and peering deep into her eyes. "Maximillian is not hurt in any shape, way, or form." She glanced pointedly at the papers in her hand. "They just won't give him to *me*." Her voice broke, and she took a deep breath to steady herself. "Only you, honey." She frowned, and stamped her foot. *"Fucking Xavier!"* she whispered fiercely.

Caribe and Marina agreed silently. The dread pulled urgently on the accountant's hand. "We have to go," he murmured.

Marina blinked her tears away and looked at Larissa. *God help me, how will I ever make this up to you, and how will you ever forgive me?* "I have a plan," she said softly, her voice husky with unshed tears. "You have to come with us, and this is what we are going to do." Quickly, she outlined her idea to them, giving Larissa the exchange of words they were to have. "When you come in, just scowl at him as ferocious as you can, so he can't see, oh, please, make sure he doesn't see the color of your eyes, Larissa."

Larissa frowned. "Why?"

"Because otherwise, none of this is going to work." Marina shook her head. "Trust me. I'll explain later. Right now, there is a baby we have to go get."

The three made their way down the street, one goal on their mind.

"Mrs. Gaitano! Mrs. Gaitano!"

The trio stopped, as a group of women stood in their way, all gazing expectantly at them.

Marina shook her head. "I am sorry, ladies," she said softly. "María Isabel Sandoval is Mrs. Gaitano."

The females smiled, and tittered. The spokesperson of the group was a ravishing blonde with crystal clear blue eyes, her beauty dimmed only by the plain clothes she was wearing. "Not *that* Mrs. Gaitano. *You.* The *younger* Mrs. Gaitano."

Bewildered, Marina began shaking her head in protest. "I am sorry, I---"

"Mrs. Gaitano is kind of busy at the moment, ladies," Larissa stepped in, always the lifesaver. "She has some urgent business to attend to right now, but she will be glad to speak to you tomorrow."

The young woman blushed, suddenly aware of their urgency. "Why, of course, Larissa. Thank you, Mrs. Gaitano," she added shyly, waving to her friends to let them by.

The three friends continued down the street, holding hands, Caribe in the middle. The people they encountered took one look at their faces, and let them by, shaking their heads, whispering after them. They didn't speak to anybody, their minds set on their destination.

Suddenly, Marina stopped, bringing her companions to a halt. Something teased her vision, at the corner of her eye. Turning her head, she caught sight of the pirate.

"*John!*"

The man walked towards them, apparently in a state of confusion, hooding his eyes so as not to reveal his razor sharp mind. He slid his sight over them, taking in their tear stained faces, the locked fingers. "Accountant!" he rumbled, ducking his head to kiss her cheek. His heart lurched in his chest, for reasons yet unknown to him. "I am lost today," he explained. "I am looking for the Gaitano men, and I can't seem to find any of them."

Marina looked at Caribe.

Caribe nodded. "They're at the Lair."

John frowned. "All of them?"

Caribe sighed. "Every single one of them."

Impatient, Marina looked up at the giant pirate. "John, have you heard about me?"

"About you?" he repeated, not understanding.

"Yes. Do you know who I am, and what I do?"

The pirate nodded, being more truthful than she could ever imagine. "Yes."

"Do you trust me?" she demanded.

"Implicitly," he answered.

"I---" Marina looked up into his bronze eyes, and stopped. He seemed to reel her in, to his very soul. She went gladly. Taking a deep breath, letting out a shaky sigh, tears stung her eyes again. "I need help."

John stared at her. "Are you in trouble?" he asked, finally.

"Maybe. But I'm taking care of it. I just need some back up."

John nodded slowly, strange lights flickering in the depths of his eyes. "I've got your back," he finally agreed.

Marina held her hand out to him, eyes searching his, before taking him in. Today, John was even more intimidating than ever. His size, just as with Don Miguel, was only part of it. Today, the man was dressed as the Gaitano brothers did when they were representing. A sword at one hip, a pistol at another, the man presented an imposing figure. Yes. John would do quite nicely. Silently, the pirate put his hand in hers, their fingers locking. Now, there were four of them, walking side by side, hand in hand, until finally they reached the Lair. Slipping down the alley, Marina splashed some rainwater on her face, and through her hair.

They stood right outside, hesitating. Pulling her hands together, Marina drew them in a circle around her. "Excuse me, but I have got to pray," she explained quietly. Out of respect for her, her companions bowed their heads. "*Padre Amado*, Heavenly Beloved Father, I ask You for strength in this moment of great need. Please keep me calm and my mind clear, that I may resolve this injustice and take care of this matter once and for all. I open my heart, my mind, and my soul to You, Father, that You may guide me through this. Please make me your instrument. Please send an army of angels to assist me. Please hear my plea and take care of me. I ask this of you in the name of your only Beloved Son, Jesus Christ, who with You lives and reigns, with the Holy Spirit, forever and ever..."

"Amen."

They looked at each other.

Marina turned to Larissa. "You wait here. Caribe will let you know." Larissa nodded.

Taking a deep breath, Marina faced the door. Guarding it was a very disgusting sailor. The man was leering at her, his eyes insolently undressing her, his tongue all but falling out of his head. Marina sneered at him. "Do you know who I am?" she asked, half expecting him to reply, *The Executioner.* Anita Blake, Vampire Hunter, of the Laurell K. Hamilton series, was her all time, for as long as she lived, undisputed hero.

But no. "The accountant," the man smiled, waggling his eyebrow, in the same singsong tone of voice, as he would have used had he been saying *Oo-la- la*!

Big mistake. Anita Blake wannabe chilled him with a look, making the poor soul's smile fade, and shivers run down his spine. All of a sudden, the man stumbled and turned horrified eyes on her, as if she were the devil himself, holding his hand to his face, as he blinked un controllably at his sudden tears. Over her head, Caribe and John looked at each other, momentarily shocked. She had backhanded him, fist closed, with all of her might. Hard enough to daze him. Marina shoved the man to one side, making him fall. "Get out of my way, boy," she drawled in her teenage language. "Don't make me smack you again."

Caribe was the first one to react. His left hand flew to his mouth, eyes roaring with mocking laughter at the man, over it, while his right hand snapped in the air. He looked like any typical third millenium young man, making fun of someone. "You better run and hide, boy," he crowed.

John shook his head and chuckled. "What the lady wants, the lady gets." The three turned to the front door, but not before glancing at each other, eyes communicating silently.

Marina turned quickly to Larissa. "How do I look?"

Larissa crossed her arms, and looked her up and down, approvingly. "Like you're going to kick ass."

Marina nodded. "Good. I am." She turned to the men accompanying her one last time. "Now," she said in the softest voice possible, "quiet as mice, let us not be detected right away, we need to see what we are getting ourselves into."

The men nodded. They slithered in.

They stopped right inside the entrance, letting the door fall quickly shut behind them. Their eyes gradually adjusted to the scene before them. The members of the Council sat at a table. The older Gaitano brothers lounged behind the bar. To one side were the Hawthorne brothers, laughing and apparently having a good time, as if nothing were going on. To the other side, Carlos and Indio stood side by side, surveying the scene, seemingly made from stone. By their side, flanking them, were Salomé and Storm. Giancarlo, Rouge and Solomon sat by themselves at another table. Pablo and Joe sat quietly in a corner. Behind them, Jackson paced restlessly, like a caged black panther. He was wearing a deep scowl.

Marina sent her sensors out hesitantly, not wanting anyone aware of her presence yet. Quickly, she scanned the scene one more time, before looking at the center of everyone's attention. Taking a second look, she realized she only knew half the people present. The other half pertained to a scraggly bunch of sailors, dirty and tired, obviously just having sailed in. These poor, misguided souls seemed to be guarding, of all things, the half of the people present that she did know. Of course, her people seemed a bit amused. At least the ones that weren't scowling, like Jackson.

Still not moving from their position by the door, the trio, after surveying the scene, assessed the situation.

Marina made herself look at the man sitting in Carlos' chair, by the bar. The Vampire Lestat. Fucking Xavier. And Max. Inside, she was thoroughly disgusted. Outside, she remained motionless.

Oh, come on! Give me a break!

Max was ecstatic. He had made a new friend. Actually, he seemed to have learned a trick or two while Caribe had been out getting Marina. This particular trick was heart stopping.

The pirate held a dagger in his hand, twirling it in front of the baby's face. Rays of sunlight sparkled off the sharp blade, bounced off the bejeweled handle, sending prisms to the wall. Max sat expectantly, both chubby hands in the air, eyes fixed on the blade held by the man whose lap he was now occupying. Xavier murmured to him, eyes sparkling, a genuine smile lighting his breathtaking handsome face. From where Marina stood, he seemed to give a command, urging the baby to lunge for the dagger. If Xavier held the dagger by the handle, and the baby went for the blade, he would snatch it away repeatedly, until the baby learned not to lunge. If the pirate held it by the blade, the baby was allowed to grab the handle, the beautiful gems sparkling between his tiny fingers. Then, he was praised effusively. This was repeated, until it was learned. By the end of the lesson, Max wouldn't even move, unless it was the colorful, jewel encrusted handle sparkling before his face. The pirate snuggled him madly, stroking his baby hair and kissing the top of his head. Xavier was right to be proud. Dangerous, foolish, insane as it had been, he had taught Max a lesson on self control and good judgment.

Okay, so you're good with kids. Marina took a deep breath, closing her eyes for a moment. In her mind, she filled her body with good air and white light, from the soles of her feet, up to the top of her hair, until she found herself in a bubble of her own makin g. *Visualize.*

Marina opened her mind to her inner eyes, and began designing a scenario.

Xavier sitting in the chair, no Max. Not inside the Siren's Lair. Out in the open. Not the beach. The desert. Wide, flat, open spaces to each side, with wonderful, majestic colors. No aqua or turquoise hues. Everything in reds and browns, and incredible purples. Mesas and rocks. And Xavier. In an office chair. Facing her, sarcastic smile marring his pure masculine beauty. They were on a huge flat slab of rock, like those found in the Road Runner and Coyote cartoons. Xavier laughed. Marina laughed with him. Poor soul. He couldn't see the things she could. His chair had wheels. In her mind, Marina reached out with some energy and gave him a little push. The fool held his hand out to her, thinking she was playing, not noticing that he was farther away from her. Absolutely clueless.

Marina smiled and opened her eyes. Silently, she reached for her companion's hands, and squeezed them. From either side of her, they both looked down at her. She looked at each of them, her heart in her eyes. She took a deep breath. "Okay, guys," she said softly. Letting go of their hands, she took a step forward.

Caribe sidled away, to be closer to the pirates from La Gitana. Reaching the table where Giancarlo, Rouge and Solomon were seated, he grabbed a pad of paper, and wildly began sketching.

Silently, John put a hand on Marina's shoulder, squeezing gently before taking it back. "I'm right here..." he said softly.

Marina nodded. She took another step forward, her eyes now fixed on Max and the pirate, who were no longer playing. *Baby Boo...*

"Houston!"

Marina searched wildly, until her eyes met Jackson's. "We have a problem..."

Marina swallowed and nodded at him, quickly looking away. She needed to be careful. Slowly, she headed towards the corner where he was with their dads. John kept close behind her. The pirates that knew her followed her with their eyes. The pirates that didn't couldn't tell that she was inside yet. Salomé and Storm joined them. Carlos and Indio followed. They couldn't take their eyes off the unfolding scene.

"Category: *Rock Albums of the Eighties*. Title: *Foreigner 4.*"

Marina's family turned their heads to look at her. Her eyes remained fixed on the pirate Xavier.

"Song referring to mental entertainment."

Jackson's breath came out in a rush. "What is *Head Games*?"

Marina nodded. She looked around at her family. Frowning, she realized something was wrong. "Where are our moms?"

"At the warehouse," Storm answered quietly.

"Sloane, Shayla and María Isabel?"

Pablo spoke up softly. "*Si, mamita*, all your moms."

"They're having a girls' day out," Salomé explained softly.

Marina nodded and looked around them one more time, making sure she had everyone's undivided attention. "I am going to fuck with this guy's head until he's tweaked to hell," she said quietly. She glanced at her father. "Papi, he's going to hit me, but only because I slapped him at El Baile del Luto. So, please, don't come to my rescue. It would ruin everything. I'll take care of him." Turning her head, she looked at Indio. "I need you at my back, papi. Xavier is scared of you. John can stand quietly to one side." To Salomé and Storm. "We're the Powerpuff Girls today, ladies..." She looked at them until they nodded.

Carlos reached for her hand. "What about me?"

Marina met his eyes, carefully retrieving her hand. "You have to trust me and stay out of trouble. Don't mess this up for me, Carlitos, please, I need you to be a good boy and play along." She shook her head as he began to protest, making him fall silent. "Remember Bryan Adams?" He frowned. He nodded. "Just keep in mind what I would do for you..."

"What about us?" Joe asked.

"Did you get those congas Jax was telling me about?" They nodded.

"*Muchachos*," Marina smiled at her dads, "you are going to play your asses off."

"You're going to dance for this guy?" Jackson hissed at her.

"No! She's not!" Carlos thundered quietly.

"Oh, don't be difficult!" Salomé exclaimed, just as quietly.

"Stop!" warned Storm.

Marina shrugged. "I've got to go." Raising her hand, she slid hands with everyone around her, including her reluctant lover. Meeting Caribe's eyes, she signaled to the door. Nodding, he stood from the table where he was sitting at, and went to do as he was asked. Without saying another word, she began walking quietly away. Indio and John followed slowly, Salomé and Storm right behind them. The rest stayed where they were, for the moment, waiting to see what would happen. The older Gaitano men made eye contact with her as she approached. The Council followed her with their eyes. Finally, she was looking into bottomless black eyes. Marina took a deep breath, forcing herself to make eye contact with Max, instead. She prayed her voice didn't break and betray her. "Baby Boo, I've been looking for you..."

Max was squealing and bouncing on the pirate's lap, trying to get away.

Xavier smiled. "Accountant! How nice of you to join us!" He waved a hand at everyone present. "We have been expecting you."

Marina smiled back, but her eyes said it all, as they looked into his. Her voice was quiet. "Give me the baby."

Xavier gave Max one last kiss on top of his raven head, and gladly handed him over. "Why, of course. That was the agreement." Suddenly, he frowned, as he got a good look at Marina's companions. Rising to his feet, his sword clinked at his side. He wasn't wearing a pistol. The bejeweled dagger was held loosely in his hand. "In what capacity are you here, John?"

John shrugged, aware and grateful that Marina was surprised by the question. "I am here as the accountant's friend."

"Not in any official capacity?" Xavier insisted.

"Yes!" Marina told him. "He's *officially* my friend!"

"Not that I am aware of," John rumbled in his chest. He raised an eyebrow at the younger man. "Should I be... Xavier?"

Xavier laughed, insolent. "I am not sure..." He turned back to Marina. "Aguilar..."

Marina met his gaze steadily, Max held tight in her arms. "Xavier..." Looking around her, she searched for Caribe. She found him. He nodded. Marina called over her shoulder. "Morgan! Come get your son!"

Everybody stopped and stared. They seemed to freeze.

Marina looked at Xavier through her eyelashes. He sat with a thump on his chair, a dazed expression on his face. *Another little push. The wheels glided soundlessly beneath him. Still clueless.*

Larissa appeared magically next to her. She looked like a wild woman, glaring at the pirate, hair in her eyes. She tossed her head, dismissing him, and took her baby. "Walk me outside, please, Indio," she said suddenly, exactly as she had been coached to do. "I have to find Jeremiah."

At the Council's table, tears stung Jack's eyes. Rouge gasped softly, and Giancarlo closed his eyes in shock. From behind the bar, the older Gaitanos frowned in disbelief.

Indio felt his blood run cold. It was all he could do not to choke. Instead, he nodded and led her outside, coming back inside as quickly as he could. On the way back to Marina, he stopped and looked at his brother. "Does she know what she's doing?" he asked, a little worried.

Marina's dads looked at each other, eyes communicating silently. "What the hell is she doing?" demanded Jackson softly.

Carlos shrugged, eyes glued on the scene unfolding before them. "She is playing head games."

Indio grunted and went back to Marina.

Xavier looked dazed. For a moment. But then, he shook his head, turning the charm back on. He had imagined it. Surely he was hearing things. A smile played on his lips. "You lie," he announced to no one in particular. "They never found her body." He laughed at Indio's exclamation of pain. His eyes searched for and found the accountant. Getting to his feet, he took a step towards her and slapped her.

Marina had braced herself, the moment he stood up. As soon as she felt his hand against her face, she realized he was holding back. Not hurting her, he was exerting power over her. What Marina wasn't ready for, was what he did next.

Xavier quickly wrapped an arm around her waist, pulling her towards him. He buried his fingers in her hair, yanking her head back, making her look at him, until it hurt. Then he kissed her.

Marina was stunned. Xavier was kissing her. In front of her friends, family and her man, he was kissing her. There was nothing she could do, either. The pirate was holding her in such a manner, that all she could do was hold on for dear life, lest she fall flat on the floor, and break her back. Meanwhile, Xavier was kissing her. Not at all unpleasant, quite skillful, sensual. He ate her mouth as a lover would.

"Oh! Come on!" Jackson shouted his protest.

The older Gaitano brothers agreed. *"Xavier!"*

Carlos rolled his eyes and shook his head, as her dads looked on with interest.

Caribe's pencil flew over the ever present paper in his hands. "Let her go, Xavier," Indio ordered quietly.

Just as abruptly, Xavier ended the kiss, gently sucking her lower lip into his mouth, making eye contact with her. He let her go suddenly, helping her up until she was standing straight. Then, he laughed. His eyebrows arched, as if he were a young boy, up to mischief. "*Three* ships for the accountant of La Gitana."

The men roared with laughter. Xavier's scruffy sailors as well as the men from Encantada. For different reasons, of course.

"Since she last saw you, Xavier," Don Carlos called to him from behind the bar, "the accountant has become quite wealthy by her own merit."

That got Xavier's attention. "Is that a fact?" He reached out to stroke Marina's hair. She pulled back carefully, not wanting him to touch her again.

"Yes, it is," Carlos answered, approaching the group with caution. "But you don't want her, anyway."

Xavier laughed, his eyes wary. "And why is that?"

Carlos reached the table where his crew sat. Grabbing a chair, he turned it around, straddled it, and rested his arms on the back. His eyes were twin glaciers as he appraised the blond pirate. "For one, you are not even her type."

"You are?" Xavier was amused.

Carlos smiled mysteriously. "The accountant of La Gitana prefers Africans."

Silence followed his words, as everyone held their breath. "Africans?" Xavier echoed. Surely Gaitano was playing with him.

"Why, yes, Africans," Carlos laughed. "It is only a matter of personal taste," he shrugged. "The accountant has been quite honest with me about the men in her life. Samuel Jackson and Michael Jordan are only a couple of the black men she enjoys."

Salomé and Storm looked at each other. Indio and Caribe grinned. The visitors glanced at the ceiling and shook their heads. Head games indeed.

Marina rolled her eyes, trying to control her smile. She shot Carlos a look. "You forgot Will Smith."

The pirate nodded his head at her. "Of course. *The Fresh Prince of Bel-Air*. How could I forget?"

Xavier frowned. "The fresh prince of where?"

"Not where, Bel-Air," Marina sighed. She took a step forward, getting his full attention. "What do you want, Xavier?"

"You."

"Why?" She waved a hand over her shoulder. "Gaitano doesn't want me anymore."

"She lies!"

Attention shifted to the intruder. The man sidled around the group, making his way to Xavier's side. He faced the group, emboldened by his Captain's proximity, and raised a hand, pointing at Marina, and the pirate sitting a distance behind her.

Carlos stood up, holding to the back of the chair, so as not to tip it over. "Who are you, sir?" he asked. But of course, he knew. It was the guy from yesterday.

"I have seen them myself, Xavier!" The disgusting wretch hissed. "The Captain took her down the alley, and did everything but pull down her pants!"

"How dare you!" Marina turned on him. Better to act the outraged female, than to laugh in his face.

Carlos shook his head with a smile. "Charlie!"

The man cringed. But then he turned on Marina again. "She lets him do anything he wants to her!"

Xavier turned to her, interested. "She does? *Anything?*"

Marina shrugged. She let wicked thoughts sparkle in her eyes. "He may not be black, but he's cute."

Salomé and Storm glanced at each other, eyes laughing. Indio glanced at the ceiling. Caribe sketched furiously, smile splitting his face. Jackson snorted in disgust. Pablo and Joe shook their heads. From their corner of the room, the Hawthorne brothers hooted with laughter. Giancarlo and Rouge laughed.

"My Boatswain and my accountant can't keep their hands off each other," Carlos told Xavier, sinking back down in his chair. "Ask anyone here."

The room held its collective breath.

Xavier thought on his words for a moment. He knew for a fact Gaitano knew her better than anyone.

Marina pushed again. Xavier was so preoccupied, he never felt it. Behind him, a line was divisible in the distance.

Solomon glanced at Carlos. His Captain signaled him with his eyes, and a nod of his head in Marina's direction. The Boatswain sighed. He wasn't sure what Gaitano expected of him, but he was supposed to do something. Quiet as a jungle cat, he got up from the table he was sitting at. Slowly, he made his way to Marina. Casually, he slipped his arms loosely around her, drawing her back against his chest.

Marina glanced at the beautiful black arms wrapped around her, and relaxed, leaning her head back against the Boatswain's shoulder. She locked eyes with Xavier. A chill ran down her spine. There was no depth to them. Only reflection. Fucking Lestat.

Solomon ducked his head down to hers, his breath warm on her cheek, his words for her ears only. "You okay, mami?"

Marina smiled slowly. "I got it, babe," she murmured. Solomon laughed softly.

Xavier stared. The Boatswain and the accountant seemed to be very well acquainted. He marveled at the boldness of the female. "So, it's true?"

Marina licked her lips. Solomon took her hand and slipped it behind his neck, his hands going back to her hips. The caress appeared to be much more intimate than what it really was, from Xavier's viewpoint. From where Carlos sat, he could see the Boatswain's hands barely skimming her curves. Turning her head, Marina smiled up into Solomon's eyes. Solomon smiled back and pressed his lips against hers.

Xavier shot a glance at Carlos. It must be true. Gaitano was smiling. Meeting his eyes, he cocked his eyebrow at him. "So, the accountant is actually a slut..."

"No!" Charlie shouted. "They are faking it, Xavier! The accountant fights the Boatswain. Her lover is Gaitano!"

"Oh, shut the hell up!" Salomé turned on him, hair flying around her face. Solomon squeezed Marina one final time and pushed her away from him.

Marina turned on the filthy sailor. "You!" she accused, not screaming at him. "Followed me all morning, yesterday." She cocked her head to one side, as if she were studying a specimen. "What the hell were you thinking of?" Not letting him answer, she turned back to Xavier. "I realize you probably have a lot of people who do your dirty work for you, but this guy's really not very good at all. I *saw* him following me," she informed him. Indignant, she turned back to the man Carlos called Charlie. "You..." she said slowly, "are a *stalker*!" Coming another step closer, it gave her great satisfaction to see the man flinch.

"Is this true?" John rumbled from next to her.

The sailor was gasping for air by now. His eyes darted from Marina to John, and back to Xavier. He looked as if he were to drop from a heart attack, at any moment. Desperately, he turned to his boss. "I have seen them myself, Captain," he insisted. "The women in town are calling her Mrs. Gaitano."

"Is this true?" John repeated, to the man's increasing dismay. "Were you stalking the accountant, Marina Aguilar?" He willed the man to look at him. "And, did you remove the baby from the premises?"

"That makes you a stalker *and* a kidnapper!" Marina cried indignantly. If she could have killed him with a look, she would have done so, gladly. Satisfied, she watched him flinch.

"I thought you were here, unofficially," Xavier reminded John.

"And so I am," the older pirate answered. "I am just making sure I get the story straight."

"I said," Marina reminded Xavier, "that officially he's my friend. End of story." She took a deep breath, making the silver and turquoise cross ride on her chest as it rose. "What do you want, Xavier?"

"You."

"Three ships are not enough!"

"How many do you want?"

"I don't want any ships!"

"Houses, then."

"You don't need an accountant!" Tossing her hair back, she shot daggers at him with her eyes.

Xavier chuckled. "Maybe not."

"I'm sure you don't need a woman, either."

"Besides, you don't want this one," an amused voice called out from behind Marina.

Everybody turned to stare at Carlos. Of course, he fell silent as everyone's attention fell on him, like a cloak.

Xavier grinned. "And why not?"

"Africans aren't the only men she likes. The list is endless."

Xavier shrugged. "For what I have in mind, might as well if she has a little experience."

Carlos clenched his fists, but his smile remained glued to his face. He laughed. "You couldn't keep up with her," he taunted.

"Gaitano lies!" wailed Charlie. His eyes shone suspiciously. *"The accountant is with no man but him!"*

"Yo, man! That is enough!" Jackson stepped forward. His father's hand shot out and landed on his shoulder, gripping him hard, detaining him before he could go any further.

Marina moved to stand in front of the sailor. "What I do, and who I do it with, are none of your business! Who the hell do you think you are, anyway?" She turned back to Xavier. "I don't want anything from you. Besides, I don't belong to the Gaitanos, for you to be doing business with them, for me. I don't even work for La Gitana anymore, anyway."

The room fell into a stunned silence. You could practically see the wheels in everyone's minds turning.

"Since when?" Charlie sputtered, indignant at the woman's insistence at being less associated with the man, than she actually was.

Nobody was more surprised than the Captain of La Gitana. Outside, he didn't let on, keeping his feelings and thoughts under control. Inside, he was shocked. *Yes, since when?*

"I now work for Don Carlos Gaitano y Mendoza, Captain of *La Sirena*." She smiled, aware of Carlos' sigh of relief behind her. "He offered me more money," she explained with a shrug. "You can't afford me."

The older Gaitano brothers looked at each other.

"Let her be, Xavier," rumbled Indio in warning. "There is nothing for you here."

Ignoring him, Xavier laughed. "I'll bet I can," he challenged softly, mocking.

"Go away, Xavier," she warned softly. "Go home, or go back to under whatever rock you crawled out of. Just go."

"Not until you dance for me."

"Dance for you?" Marina repeated in dismay.

"She would love to," Salomé stepped in, tossing her hair. "And once she does, man," she smiled sweetly, "you are so out of here."

"Go away, Xavier," urged Storm softly. "You are a smart man. Go away."

"Not without the accountant," Xavier answered ominously.

Behind Marina, Indio laughed. "You'll take her out of here, through me."

Xavier laughed back. "So be it."

Marina didn't take her eyes off him. She could see what nobody else could. *Indio scares the hell out of you, tough guy...*

The air itself seemed to shift. Everyone present was caught up in the current running through the room.

Marina could almost feel the warm wind in her face. It seemed to her the sun beat down a little bit harder on the slab of rock they found themselves on. Xavier smiled at her across the distance. Marina smiled back. She pushed again. The pirate was suddenly farther away from her. The line behind him grew closer. Xavier had absolutely no idea.

Marina met his eyes. It was up to her, how this was going to go. "I will dance for you." She looked around at the men in her family. Spying the drums next to them, she forced a smile. It never reached her eyes. "Hey, guys, how about some *reggaeton?*"

Without saying a word, they nodded. Taking off their shirts, Pablo and Joe sat at the drums, hands caressing the skins. Jackson joined them and they murmured between them. Slowly, the dads began to play, their hands sure and confident, as they began beating a rhythm.

Marina knew what she was doing. Xavier wanted her to dance. She was going to dance for him in such a way, that he would remember it for the rest of his miserable life.

Reggaeton was the perfect choice. This outrageous genre of music was a mix of reggae, as its name implied, rap, and hot tropical beats. The songs ranged in lyrics from violent, condemning accusations and exclamations, alluding to weapons, lawbreaking, and general mischief, to sweet, passionate declarations of love and lust, depending on who the artist was. Some songs were usually accompanied with a vulgar, sexual dance called *perreo*, derived from the Spanish word *perro*, meaning dog. This dance was commonly executed in a semi crouch, with a lot of bumping and grinding, reminiscent of dogs having sex. Basically, freak dancing. Not the prettiest, most ladylike dance. It was confusing for the males who couldn't differentiate between girls who were advertising, from the girls who just let the music take over them. As guys, all they saw was bouncing, gyrating butts. These females, however, turned the obscene movementes into, definitely, the most suggestive and arousing. All undulating hips. The men in her father's country enjoyed it no end. To them, it was as close as they could get to having sex with clothes on. And truth be told, there were actually some really nice songs out there, no matter the commercial aspect of the almost pornographic dancing, so different from the movements of those who just gave themselves up to the music. The Aguilars and the Banks had gone on vacation to Pablo's native island the summer before, and had been exposed to it, during their whole stay. The moms could gladly do without it, thinking it gross and demeaning. The dads and the kids got a big kick out of it, enjoying the nicer lyrics, and the throbbing beats that got under their skin. Since then, they tended to jam at home, at least once a week, when the moms were out of the house. Now, the room seemed to pulse, as the men began playing louder.

Jackson moved between them, dancing in ancient rhythm, his eyes never leaving the blond pirate Xavier. His voice was rich and vibrant as he began singing, softly at first, slowly growing louder and more confident. Of course, the words were in Spanish, his accent flawless. Joe and Pablo joined him, singing the chorus, allowing him to harmonize. His sisters and Storm began swaying, letting the music fill them, moving slowly around each other, their bodies doing what they needed to do. Around them, everyone seemed to relax and sit back, enjoying the show. They had never heard or seen anything like it. They could barely comprehend the words, not because of the Spanish, but for all the slang. But it didn't matter. They understood the intention.

Marina slipped off her shirt, pulling it out of the heavy leather belt, tossing it blindly, not looking to see where it fell, or who caught it. She didn't care. Her shoulders and arms were bare, beautifully tanned. Whatever happened, she looked good. The breathtaking colors against the black fabric tied around her, stood out beautifully in the bright morning sunlight filling the room.

"Look, Xavier!" howled Charlie. "They all belong to the same tribe! She is marked, just like them!" he wailed, pointing at the men playing and singing. He turned to her sister. "They both are!" They all shared the same tattoos. Bewildered, he looked at Rouge's First Mate.

Storm glanced at Jackson and seemed to blush. "I haven't gotten mine yet."

Marina and Salomé glanced at each other, ignoring the sailor, pretending they didn't know what he was talking about. But if Xavier's eyes held fire, they would have burned off their tattoos. Before he could act on the sailor's words, or say anything about it, the girls went closer.

Salomé grinned as she lifted her arms over her head, making her flowered top strain against her breasts. "Surely three ladies dancing are better than one," she taunted him.

Storm joined her, shaking her hips, tossing her hair. "You think you can handle this, Xavier?" she asked, hands cupping her breasts before gliding down to rest on her hips.

Xavier laughed. "I can take anything you've got to give me." His eyes met Marina's. "I didn't think you would make it this special."

"I have to," she smiled. "It's not your fault your sister messed things up for you."

She spun his chair around, making him disoriented.

By now, Xavier's men were distracted, focusing more on the girls' bodies swaying and moving to their men's music. They were not paying attention at all to the exchange of words. However, the Council, the Gaitanos, the crew of La Gitana, the Hawthorne brothers, John and Caribe were caught up in the throes of a live drama. Mesmerized, enthralled, they could taste the tension, breathe the danger.

Xavier stared at Marina. "Mess things up for me?" he repeated.

Storm and Salomé danced in circles, crossing each other behind his chair, and coming back on opposite sides of Marina.

Marina smiled. "Sure. If y'all hadn't gotten so greedy, you would still be doing what you were doing."

Xavier laughed, but only with his mouth. His black eyes went from shiny onyx, to thick bottomless tar pits. "Greedy?"

Marina turned it on, even as her words cut him. "She let herself get caught, Xavier. Stupid, don't you think?"

A twitch appeared in the corner of his eye. Squeezing his eyes shut, he made it disappear. When he opened them again, they were amused. "Whatever are you talking about, you silly little girl?"

Marina met his eyes and gave a throaty laugh. "Oh, baby, she got caught with more guns than there are people on this rock."

Xavier chuckled. "Dominique was always one to exaggerate."

The Gaitano men froze. Jackson had been right. John's eyes met Juan Gaitano's.

"Bad habit," Marina smiled, in agreement. "Unfortunately, she lost it all."

"All?" repeated Xavier. His voice was level and cool, but he lifted his hand and massaged his forehead before raking his fingers through his white blond hair.

She nodded, enjoying the edge she had over him. "The dress shop now belongs to Liana, Dr. Kyle Richardson's fiancee. I understand she's been slaving there for years. The upstairs, where the girls perform, is at the moment, run by Jackson Banks, for Giancarlo

Ilarrazza. Salomé Banks is the head designer for the downstairs, supervised by Sloane Gaynes." She was careful to give her mom's maiden name, so he wouldn't make the connection. Xavier may be crazy, but he wasn't stupid.

"And where is my dear sister now?" Xavier asked curiously.

Marina shrugged, turning around for a moment and shaking her butt at him, before smiling into his eyes. "On *La Prision*, waiting for Don Juan Gaitano to sail. You might want to talk to him about it."

Xavier raised an eyebrow at her in amusement. "I may just do that," he murmured, glancing at Juan standing next to his older brothers. Juan met his eyes, still as a statue.

The room seemed to sway and pulse with the beat of the drums. Jackson's voice held laughter, as he got caught up in the scene unfolding before them. The louder his dads played and he sang, the better Marina could keep the situation under control.

Salomé and Storm danced up to Xavier, momentarily distracting him. They shook their breasts before his eyes, swiveling their hips, seeming to offer him thigh. The smile never left his face.

Marina observed him closely through her eyelashes. She knew he was a monster. But now, his beautiful face lit up with the most gorgeous smile. He was just, well, a *guy*. She could handle that. Dancing away from him in a moment, she pretended to let herself get lost in the music. Her body moved automatically, intuitively, to the familiar rhythms and words. That left her mind free. Quickly scanning the room, she looked around her for anything she could use. There didn't seem to be anything. Most of the chairs were occupied, and there was nothing lying around. The men she knew could easily overpower the men Xavier had brought with him. There might be a little blood shed, but it could be done, with the least pain possible. But it shouldn't have to go down that way. Although all the men she knew in the room were armed, including her family, there wasn't really anything that she could use.

"Now, what would Jack say?"

All eyes turned to the Captain of the Black Mermaid. He said nothing.

They all looked back at the Captain of La Gitana.

Marina glanced at Carlos, puzzled. His words brought her around to face him for a moment. *Who is Jack?*

"Who is Jack?" Xavier wanted to know.

Carlos laughed. "Only one of her lovers."

Xavier laughed with him. "You seem to be quite tolerant of your accountant, Gaitano. Who is Jack?" he repeated.

"Captain Jack Sparrow, Commander of the *Black Pearl*."

The women looked at each other and smiled knowingly. The reference to their modern day *Pirates of the Caribbean* was totally lost on the real ones present.

Salomé laughed. "Gaitano's right, Aguilar," she sang out. "What would Jack say?"

Storm moved past the pirate. "Jack won't be happy..."

Marina laughed. "No," she agreed graciously. "He won't be happy at all."

Xavier cocked his head to one side, his eyes hungrily roving over her fluid body. "Who is this Captain Jack Sparrow?" he asked. "I have never heard of the *Black Pearl*."

"You wouldn't," Marina informed him. "My man is one of many disguises." She neared Xavier, almost within touching distance. Almost. "Disguises?" he echoed.

"Many," Marina agreed. Reaching out with a hand, she touched him, stroking his face, making him look at her.

She pushed again, following the chair. Behind him, she could see vast emptiness.

Xavier went to catch her hand again st his face, but she took it away. He sighed, frustration welling up inside him. "Captain Jack Sparrow..." he murmured.

"His real name is *Johnny Depp*," she murmured back.

Suddenly, Xavier wasn't playing anymore. "Come here," he said. Snatching her, he planted her firmly on his lap.

Carlos laughed, his tone belying his true feelings. "She will never sit on your lap the way she has on mine," he taunted.

Xavier laughed back, preoccupied with the woman's warm behind on his thighs. He didn't see Gaitano slip off his sword and let it fall to the floor. "I am sure she will…" His hands began roving.

Marina cringed inwardly, but it was all up to her. Catching her sister's eye, she motioned her. Salomé nodded, and quietly went behind Xavier, even as Storm danced wildly in front of him, distracting him. Marina began squirming, making sure that the pirate wasn't thinking with the head on his shoulders, any longer, but rather with the one between his legs, instead. She felt his hands on her hair, caressing. He took a deep breath, letting it out slowly, and his thighs seemed to quiver beneath her butt. Smiling, she met Carlos' eyes. He wasn't happy, even though the smile hadn't left his face. Surreptitiously, he put his foot on his sword, and slid it forward a little bit, calling her attention to it. She winked at him. Moving her hands to the heavy buckle on the huge belt around her hips, she undid it slowly, making sure to not call attention to her movements.

Xavier's hands started wandering over her. Caressing, he was careful not to paw her. His thighs seemed to shake more. He grabbed a handful of her hair, burying his face in it. "You smell so good," he breathed. Brushing it aside, he traced the tattoo on her back. Hesitantly at first, with his fingers. Then, with his tongue, tasting her. Closing his eyes, he opened his mouth and pressed it against her skin, as if to suck the ink from her. Hard enough to hurt. He was marking her. Tired with her back, he turned her head and kissed her again. And again. Surrendering her mouth, he went back to her tattoo.

Carlos clenched his fists, beginning to rise. From behind the bar, his father and uncles scowled at him, giving him warning looks, signaling behind the pirate and the woman, for him to be still. Tio Miguel's quiet energy enveloped him, making him relax. Pablo and Joe played stronger, Jackson sang louder. The words and music seemed to fill their heads and their bodies.

Marina kept squirming on Xavier's lap. She wasn't speaking anymore. Instead, she softly sang along with Jackson, further distracting the man under her. Suddenly, slipping his hands under her arms, he cupped her breasts and hauled her back against his chest. Taking advantage of the movement, Marina opened her belt and quickly flung the ends back behind her, urgently waving them.

Salomé stepped up right behind the chair and grabbed them, her mouth next to the pirate's ear. "How do you like all the attention, handsome?" she whispered in a sultry voice, making him smile. Her body shielding her hands, she tied the belt again, behind the chair, loose enough so that the pirate wouldn't feel the trap. Quickly, she lifted her hands and began caressing his face, stroking his hair, staying behind the chair, so none of his men would see what she had done.

Behind her, the older Gaitano brothers looked at each other with raised eyebrows. From their corner, the Hawthorne brothers quietly fondled their swords, wondering where this would all lead up to.

"Let her go, Xavier," Indio said, taking a step forward.

Meeting his eyes, Marina shook her head at him, the fake smile glued on her face. Bringing her hands up, she put them over the pirate's to cup her own breasts. "Let me finish my dance, baby," she said.

Xavier groaned. "No..." He held her tighter, his hands squeezing gently, molding her breasts as if they were memorizing their dimensions. The feel of them was almost overwhelming.

"What do you mean, no?"

Xavier's voice was husky in her ear. Storm was dancing before him, filling his mind with all kinds of thoughts, at the same time that Salomé's slender fingers wreaked havoc with his senses as they combed his blond white hair, and caressed his face. His thighs were tense beneath Marina's buttocks. Her breasts filled his hands. "I can't move..." he rasped.

Marina felt his hardness. She smiled to herself. If that was on his mind, he couldn't be thinking straight. *You are such a guy!* "What's the matter, baby?" she teased. "Getting a little excited?" she laughed softly, reaching up to caress his face as he buried it in the side of her neck.

Xavier chuckled. "I really don't want my men to see me like this," he confessed in her ear. "I will not be able to walk..."

Marina turned her head to look at him, rapidly being pulled into his bottomless black eyes. *God, you are gorgeous!* "You wanted me to dance," she reminded him.

Xavier kissed her again. Ending it suddenly, he squeezed her tight before letting her go. "Dance for me," he urged with a smile.

Jumping off his lap, Marina turned to face him. From the corner of her eye, she caught movement. Caribe was coming closer. As was Indio. But so intent was the pirate on her and the other females that he didn't notice. She danced, her eyes never leaving his face. "I know something nobody else knows," she taunted gently.

Xavier smiled into her eyes, raising an inquisitive eyebrow. "And what would that be?" He sighed deeply, relaxing under Salomé's ministrations.

"I know you have been busy..."

"I usually am."

"And that you have been traveling extensively."

Interest flickered in his eyes, but he shrugged anyway. "I usually do."

"You leave your mark everywhere you go..."

He chuckled. "We all do."

"Yes," Marina agreed, coming closer. Looking deep into his eyes, she smiled, entrapping him. "But none are called the *White Ghost...*"

Stepping up to him, she gave him another spinning push. She saw the bewildered pirate look back at her, still not aware of the chasm yawning behind him.

Xavier froze. His hands lay on his thighs, unmoving. The twitch reappeared at the corner of his eye. *"Marina..."* His name on her tongue was a soft, controlled threat.

"I know, but nobody else does," she said urgently.

He frowned, puzzled. Around them, the drumming and chanting and singing continued. He was unaware of anything but the accountant before him. "How..."

"You've been careless, Xavier," Marina smiled. "Just like your dear, dumb sister..."

Behind the bar, the Gaitano men looked at each other once more. Hearts beat harder, breaths came faster. Caribe's pencil flew, catching every look, every emotion. Indio and John exchanged looks. Carlos froze. Nobody else was close enough to hear, but they could all sense the change in the air.

Xavier smiled. "Careless... no..." he said thoughtfully, "not at all." He shrugged. "I like to leave my mark wherever I go, but the *White Ghost*..." He shook his head with a laugh.

"I know, Xavier," Marina sang out with a smile. "I could even prove it, if I wanted to..."

"You could not," he finally said, chilling her to the bone. "Even if I were..."

"Doesn't all that blood on your hands bother you?"

Xavier looked steadily into her eyes. He was good at hiding emotions.

Suave and cool, his face remained as if carved from stone. But he wasn't *that* good. They say that the eyes are the windows of the soul. Well, there didn't seem to be anybody home. It seemed to Marina as if he waged a personal war, as heavy ominous shadows shifted in their depths. But there was something wrong. Something missing. And suddenly, she realized what it was. Sanity. There was none. Complete lack of, instead. The boy was as psychotic as they come. And right before her eyes, she saw him lose his grip. In the deep recesses of her mind, she shuddered with apprehension.

Xavier shrugged. "Why? They were only natives. The only thing they have in common with us is that their blood is just as red..."

"Doesn't it bother you? All the people you have massacred? All those women? What about the children?"

"I have not lost any sleep over it, if that's what you mean..."

It was Marina's turn to shrug. "Whatever, baby," she soothed. "Just admit that you don't need an accountant." Her movements slowed down. Not much, just a little. Enough for her to concentrate on the conversation. "You don't want me, you just want to fuck with Carlos Gaitano."

"Marina!" Carlos called out. "Leave this loser, and come back with me."

Xavier laughed. "The accountant is not interested in you right now, Gaitano!"

Carlos laughed with him, ignoring his words. "Marina..." he said, "I promise you that I will take you to *Loquillo's* beach after this is over."

Marina's heart flip flopped and tears stung her eyes. He wanted to take her to her father's home town, in his time. Gaitano loved her! It gave her the strength she needed. She smiled at Xavier. "Actually, now, I am *very* interested."

Xavier's hands clenched into fists on his thighs. Salomé's hands raked through his hair, and Storm's hips wiggled before his eyes, thoroughly distracting him. He turned black eyes back on Marina. "So, you *are* a slut..."

Marina shrugged again. "If it makes you happy..." She stepped closer. "You don't want me," she smiled, "you could care less about me."

"Leave her alone, Xavier," Carlos warned.

Amused, Xavier glanced at him. "What are you going to do, Carlos? Would you start a war between us, over a..." he sneered, wild laughter dancing in his eyes, "female?"

Carlos raised his eyebrows, smiling. "Not just any female..."

"So, what are you saying?" Xavier asked belligerently. "Are you so consumed with her that you would break our rules? What would your men say about that?"

Carlos threw back his head in laughter. "My men adore her! Their wealth has increased, since they've met her. They would gladly leave me, and follow the accountant to the ends of the earth!"

Xavier shook his head, amazed. "You lie..."

Carlos shrugged. "Ask them," he invited.

Xavier pressed his lips together and nodded. "Who, in this room, would leave Captain Carlos Gaitano, and follow the accountant..." he licked his lips, meeting her eyes, "...Marina Aguilar?"

Nobody moved at first. Then, Solomon stepped forward. He smiled mockingly at the blond pirate. "Gladly," he rumbled, laughter in his voice.

Slowly, hands raised, men came forward.

Captain Jack of the Black Mermaid walked over to them. His fiery hair blazed as he passed through beams of sunlight pouring in a window. "If I were to follow anyone," he informed the unwanted instigator, "it would be the accountant, Marina Aguilar."

Rouge joined him, Giancarlo at her side. "Aye!"

Amazed, Xavier glanced at the rest of the Council. They all nodded. He glanced back at Marina.

"You just want to fuck with Carlos," she repeated.

Xavier shrugged. "Actually, I would love to." Behind him, the Gaitano men looked at each other in shock, before glancing to John and Indio. The blond pirate grinned, making Marina's blood run cold. "There is nothing I would like better, than to *fuck* with Carlos."

Marina stared at him, stunned. His meaning was clear. She glanced at her sister. Salomé's eyes were wide in her face as she looked at her over his head. "For real?"

Xavier laughed. "Why not?" He glanced at the man in question. "He is tall, dark and handsome. Besides, Lola tells me..."

"Now you're just pissing me off!"

"...that when they were together all those years ago, he was quite an accomplished lover..."

Marina's heart dropped to her stomach, where it froze. *Cabron! Hijo de puta!* This wasn't happening. She had to remind herself to breathe. "You mean to tell me the *White Ghost*..."

"Likes sex more than just about anybody he knows..."

"The exterminator of just about every other small island of these waters is a---"

"No, I'm not!" He sighed. "Just because I indulge in some male companionship occasionally, in the absence of women, does not make me that. But..." he admitted with another shrug, and a twinkle in his eye, "I would give anything to fuck Carlos Gaitano, any way I can." His dead eyes caressed the younger Gaitano insolently, before meeting hers. "It has been my life long dream. If I can't possess his life, I will own his death. Otherwise, I will gladly settle for his body..." He laughed suddenly, sending chills down everyone's spines. "If he bends over, all the better, unless he would rather suck my dick!"

Marina felt she was going to be sick. Except for Storm and Salomé, everyone within hearing distance seemed to turn to stone.

Stunned, her voice came out in a shocked whisper. "Dude, that's my man you're talking about..."

Xavier laughed. "I'll share, Aguilar. We'll have him together. I'll make you my queen..."

Suddenly, power shifted in the room. The crew of La Gitana moved stealthily around the room, as if acting on some unspoken command. Quickly, they surrounded it. Bewildered, Xavier's men looked around them, but it was too late. They were too slow, too tired, not smart enough. The Council flowed like liquid stealth, containing the room without aids of weapons. The Hawthorne brothers had stopped laughing, and joined Salomé, placing themselves strategically behind the disturbed pirate. The older Gaitanos watched quietly, approval in their eyes. Pablo and Joe continued drumming and chanting. This time, it was different. They were still playing, but Jackson was improvising, and they were following. The song was scathing as it relayed what was going on, provocative, providing a twisted soundtrack to the events unfolding. Jackson kept singing, making a mockery of the situation. Rage churned in his tiger eyes.

She shook her head. "No, you don't understand. Charlie was telling you the truth. I *am* with Carlos Gaitano. I am going to marry him..."

"Marry him?" Xavier exploded into laughter.

Marina felt herself go deadly still. She clued him in, her voice quiet and full of passion. "I live for his kisses. I die for his touch. I would kill for his love." She growled at him. "You are *not* going to screw this up for me!"

His eyes went wild, as a feverish glow filled his face. "I'll have you both! How excellent!"

"No..."

"I will just have to get a bigger bed!"

"No!"

"The three of us together should be quite a thrill..."

"Shut up!"

"Maybe he can hold your hair back, as *you* suck my---"

"Shut the fuck up!"

"Or maybe you would like us both, one at each breast at the same time..."

Marina shook with rage. *"Xavier..."* she warned, swallowing her tears.

Xavier's men stood still, shocked, not sure what to expect, quite confused. The Council members and the rest of the men in the room acquainted with her rumbled softly, their protest and outrage slowly getting louder.

"No? Maybe you would prefer something different," he smiled, as Marina began shaking her head. Her hands went up to her face in disbelief. He licked his lips. "I've got it! How about if Gaitano holds you in his arms while I take you from behind..."

Salomé grabbed handfuls of his hair and pulled his head back. *"Mother fucker..."* she said in a strangled whisper.

Xavier looked up into the outraged green eyes and blew Salomé a kiss. "Indio looks real good, too," he taunted her. Salomé yanked his head from one side to the other, before she let him go, thoroughly disgusted. He went to stand, suddenly finding himself immobilized. Looking down at the belt around his middle, he realized his arms were pinned with it. He arched an eyebrow at Marina. "Games, ladies?" Suddenly, he threw himself against the leather holding him, thrashing and roaring with rage.

Moving smoothly, Indio grabbed the discarded dagger from where it had fallen next to the chair. Quick as lightning, he stood behind the pirate, instead of Salomé, a handful of hair in one hand, the bejeweled weapon in the other. Under the blade, Xavier's pulse was almost visible against the shining steel. "Do you realize, I have never actually scalped a man before?" the brave inquired conversationally. "I have always wanted the opportunity. Good thing Papá taught me how."

Xavier took a deep breath. He smiled. This was much more fun than he had expected. Then he shrugged. Turning back to Marina, he made as if nothing were happening. "So, what do you say, accountant?"

"No..." Marina whispered, clinging desperately to her sanity. She could feel it slipping away, with each word.

"Yes..." he hissed at her.

Marina stopped moving. She wasn't playing anymore. "I will kill you..."

Xavier laughed. "Better yet," he taunted, "you hold Gaitano in your arms, while I fuck him from behind..."

"*Shut up!*" she screamed at him. "*Shut the fuck up!*" Blindly, she turned around, facing Gaitano. Without thinking, she walked towards him, reached down and grabbed the sword from the floor, already out of its scabbard. Trembling, she turned to the blond pirate, the sword held out in front of her. "*Stop!*"

The room froze. Pablo and Joe stopped playing suddenly. Jackson fell silent. Storm stopped dancing. Salomé stepped back, as Indio's eyes flew to Marina. They were both shocked. John put a hand on Marina's shoulder, not restraining, just ready for anything.

"*Xavier!*" Charlie cried, his voice laced with panic.

Out of nowhere, Solomon came up behind him, holding him still in his massive arms, before the man could go to Xavier.

Meeting Marina's eyes once more, Xavier laughed. "What are you going to do?" he taunted. "Kill me? For real?" He glanced at John. "Are you still here unofficially?" he demanded, the sneer on his face transforming his features.

John just looked at him. Around him, he was aware of Gaitano's and Xavier's men fidgeting.

Marina stepped closer, until the tip of the sword was over his heart. Her voice was deathly quiet. "I am going to marry Carlos Gaitano. I am going to have children with him---"

"*Children!*" exclaimed Xavier happily. His eyes were wild now, the madness within shining out. "Which would you prefer, Aguilar? Boy or girl?" He laughed, hysteria creeping into his voice. "Imagine that!" he wondered softly. "A little girl to pet, and caress, and..." he leered at her, "... *lick*!" His laugh couldn't chill them more.

Salomé screamed. "*You sick fuck!*" She started crying, her chest heaving with sobs. Storm looked on, shocked. Salomé reached around Indio and smacked him on the side of the head, almost getting his throat cut in the process. "*Shut up! You are nothing but a fucking animal!*"

"How can you say that?" Marina demanded. She was slowly and steadily losing it. "You seem to be good with children," she said, bewilderment creeping into her voice. "Watching you with Max, I thought you liked them!"

Xavier ignored her. "How about a little boy, Marina?" he taunted. "You think I want to fuck with *Carlos*?" He laughed, as if he were Lucifer himself. Suddenly, he tried lunging out of the chair, pulling his head back so as not to slash his own throat, arms straining against the belt. He sat down with a thump as Indio yanked him back.

"Shut up, Xavier," Marina warned him. "You just better shut the fuck up..."

"Let me tell you, what I will do... when you have a little boy..." And lowering his voice, so only she, and those immediately next to him, could hear, he proceeded to describe in graphic detail all the perverted things he would do to a little boy born from Marina Aguilar and Carlos Gaitano.

Marina's body seemed to hum, her heart throbbing against her chest. Her vision narrowed, so she could only see the pirate sitting in the chair. *Surrendering herself to a higher power, she shoved with all her might. Xavier's chair rolled backward, increasing speed. Suddenly, he went over the edge, and he was gone.*

"I told you I would kill you!" Carlos Gaitano shouted from behind her. That was her cue.

Marina took a step forward, breaking through fabric, through skin, into muscle. Before her eyes, a beautiful red flower bloomed on Xavier's white shirt. She felt as if she were underwater. Eyes open wide with shock around her, mouths moving in terror. She saw nothing, heard nothing. In fact, the room roared. Xavier's men turned to her, shouts of fear and outrage directed at her. The room quickly filled with the sound of swords singing as they were drawn out. Even the jewel encrusted ones of her dads. Marina remained absolutely clueless. The only reality in front of her was the sword in her hand. She didn't recognize her own voice, dripping ice, making her own blood run cold. "You just had to go there, didn't you?" Numb, she took another step and shoved it in further, watching mesmerized, as the flower grew bigger, brighter, more wet.

Xavier's mouth moved, but nothing came out. He laughed at her, excitement shining in his eyes, along with admiration. Finally, he gasped. "You look so beautiful. I'm grateful I got to hold you, and touch you, and kiss you... Carlos hated it..." His whisper gurgled in his throat. *"Bitch!"*

Marina lunged forward with all her might, until the sword would go in no more. Her body thrummed as she held on to her anger with her whole being. *"Hasta la vista, baby."*

And then, Xavier made sure Marina Aguilar would remember him for the rest of her life. He reached up and caressed her face before his hand dropped helplessly on his lap. Movie star smile lighting up his gorgeous face, he looked straight into her eyes, holding her captive. And then he did it. Left Marina Aguilar with the nightmare that would haunt her for as long as she lived. Xavier died.

Looking into his eyes, she saw them dim. And then he was just completely gone. Still looking back at her. Still smiling. Inside her mind...

Marina freaked.

All hell broke loose.

The older Gaitano men jumped over the bar. Indio let go of the dead pirate and ran around to her. He grabbed her and yanked her away, making her let go of the sword. It vibrated as it stuck out of Xavier's chest. It didn't seem to bother him, though. Not at all. Shocked, Xavier's men roared their rage, rushing the men from Encantada in a blind fury. Pablo and Joe took up their own swords, reaching their daughters' sides, Jackson next to them.

"John! John!" screamed Charlie. "You allow this?" Tears streamed down the man's face. Blubbering, he shook an accusing finger at Marina, stepping towards her.

Pablo grabbed Marina, beginning to steer her out. *"Vente, mamita,"* he ordered. "Hurry! Let's get out of here, *nena."*

"No! You can't take her!" screeched Charlie. *"She has to be punished!"* He stepped towards Pablo and his family, howling to the wind. *"You can't take her!"*

Slowly, Pablo turned and stared at the men. Pushing his daughter behind him, his hand went up to his chest, a look of disbelief on his face. Before their eyes, his whole demeanor changed. His posture, his look. It was as if he were a different man, entirely. Suddenly, his accent was heavy and thick. "Are you talking to me?" he asked incredulously, reminiscent of Robert De Niro in *Taxi Driver*. "Are you talking to *me*?" he repeated, facing the hysterical sailor.

"*Yes!*" the man screamed. "*You can't take her!*"

Pablo held out his sword, sighting the man down its edge. In one fluid moment he was Al Pacino in *Scarface*. Now, his voice was just like Tony Montana's. "*You wanna fuck with me? Okay. You wanna play rough? Okay. Say hello to my little friend...*"

Charlie froze. The blade glinted in the sunlight pouring into the room as it came closer. The lapis lazuli winked pure blue in the handle seen between Pablo's dark fingers. "*John!*"

Marina shook her head, dazed. Her voice was a strangled whisper in her father's ear. She sounded to him just as if she were five years old again. It broke his heart. "*Papi*," she wailed softly, tears choking her voice, "*I want Mami...*"

Turning back to his family, Pablo began ushering them out. "*Vamonos!*" He turned to his hosts. "With, or without," he sneered, "your permission, I am taking my family."

Joe looked back at the chaos around him. "*Storm!*"

"*She is not your family!*" Charlie sputtered.

Joe turned stone eyes on him. "Yes." His voice was cold as ice. "She is."

He grabbed Rouge's Quartermaster's hand. "Come on, baby, we're not leaving you here."

"*Pablo!*" cried out Don Carlos in shock. "Don't go, Pablito!"

Pablo shook his head at his friend. "I have to, Carlos."

"You don't understand!" cried Charlie. "*The accountant just killed Xavier!*" He turned to John, tears streaming down his face. "What are you going to do?"

"No! *You* don't understand!" Pablo's words froze him. "I am leaving here with my whole family right now. Whatever mess you pirates have, is all yours. You can wipe your own asses."

Joe put his arm around Salomé and ushered Jackson and Storm out. Indio joined him. Caribe followed. Reaching for Marina's hand, he began pulling her out. "Let's go, baby, let's get you out of here. Come with Dad, *mamita.*"

Stunned, Marina followed.

Turning to the room, Pablo addressed those present, his sword held out in front of him. "Now, I am leaving with my family, and *nobody* is going to stop me," he told them ominously. He looked around him, backing away slowly.

"Pablo!"

Pablo shook his silver streaked jet black head. "You don't understand..." His voice was a warning growl. *"I will... kill... for my daughter..."* And he was gone.

They ran. People turned and stared, rushing out of their way, as they pounded down the middle of the street. Eight figures in the bright sunlight, three women and five men, escaping as if the Devil himself were behind them. As if their lives depended on it.

The Sirens' Lair roared. Xavier's men were quickly overcome amidst the mayhem.

The man now known as Charlie was completely hysterical. His eyes overflowed with tears, streaking his grimy face. Snot dripped from his nose. His voice was hoarse from tears. His body racked by sobs. *"Murderer! Murderer!"* he screamed at the door, straining against Solomon's hold on him. He cried as if his world had come to an end. Turning back to John, his cries were reproachful. *"You are letting her get away! They are taking her!"*

"Silence!" John thundered. The room came to full attention, everyone suddenly quiet. He turned to the sniveling man. "The accountant is not going anywhere," he told him, glancing at Carlos for confirmation.

Lips pressed together, Carlos shook his head, rubbing his eyes. He could not believe what had just transpired. But the truth was, it had, regardless of whether he believed it or not. *Fucking Xavier!* "Marina Aguilar, the accountant of Don Carlos Gaitano y Mendoza, for La Sirena, should be at this moment, heading towards her mother's arms. She will not be leaving Encantada." His eyes searched for his own father's and connected, quickly finding solace in deep gray eyes, the color of steel weapons.

The Hawthorne brothers stepped up to John. "What a mess, huh?"

"The accountant is quite daring and bold, Gaitano."

"What do you want us to do, Dad?"

Suddenly, the door opened. Pedro Barbosa strode in, closely followed by Silas and Jimmy. The room seemed to part as he entered.

Trapped in a spray of sunlight beams, Xavier sat. Still looking. Still smiling. Still dead.

Pedro Barbosa came to a halt before the very recently deceased pirate. The blood had stopped spreading on his shirt. Taking a deep breath, he crouched in front of Xavier, looking into his eyes. Straightening up, he looked around him. Charlie began warbling, but he quieted him with a look, pointing a warning finger. He finished moving in a full circle, making sure he made eye contact with every single pirate in the room. Finally, he looked at Carlos Gaitano. He was the one closest to the dead body. "Who saw exactly what happened here?" He frowned warningly at Charlie. "I'm not asking what happened, I don't want to know," he advised them. He wasn't their friend right now. "Not yet." Pedro Barbosa was the law. He turned his head to inspect the crime scene once more. "Better still," he added thoughtfully. "Who *heard* what transpired here?"

The older Gaitano brothers raised their hands, expressions a mix of condolence for the accountant's heartache, but pride and joy at her strength and determination. Pedro Barbosa observed this and took note of it, unaware of who the recipient of their feelings was.

Juan Gaitano spoke up. "We did," he said, eyes locked on the lawman's. "Saw and heard everything."

Pedro Barbosa nodded. He looked at Carlos Gaitano, Hijo. The younger pirate shook his head.

"Saw, kind of heard, not sure."

Looking around at the Council, he breathed deeply as they looked at each other. "All right, guys, I don't have all day. We have to clean up in here," he added, pointing at Xavier.

Rouge's words echoed Carlos'. "Same here. We saw everything, but we didn't quite catch all that was said." She pointed a thumb over her shoulder, signaling Xavier's sailors. Horror was still fresh in their eyes, shock clear all over their faces.

Pedro Barbosa took note of this, also. "Let me ask this..." he said slowly.

"Who is missing from here? Who else has been here and left the scene?"

"The accountant!" screeched Charlie.

Pedro Barbosa turned on him, thunder in his face. *"Not another word out of you!"* He turned to Solomon. "Get him the hell out of here! Throw him in the cell, I'll be right there."

Solomon grinned. "Glad to." And grabbing the stalker by the scruff of his neck, he escorted him out, kicking and screaming.

"One more time, who's not here?"

The Gaitano brothers looked at each other. Don Carlos stepped forward. "The visitors."

"All of them?"

"Without the mothers," Don Miguel explained. "So..."

Exasperated, Juan butt in. "The two fathers and the three kids!"

Pedro Escobar glanced around the room and narrowed his eyes at him. "Who else?"

"Indio, Caribe and Storm."

Pedro Escobar nodded. "Now we are talking." He smiled, satisfied. "And where may I find our dear visitors at this moment?"

Don Carlos sighed. "We're not sure, but we believe they are headed to our warehouse at the docks, to join the women." He shrugged. "They are certainly not fleeing."

Pedro Escobar nodded again. "All right." He turned to the younger Carlos. "I want you and the Council to escort these men to La Prision, until further notice." He turned to the older Gaitanos. "You gentlemen, if you please, come with me..." And he was gone.

The Gaitano men shook their heads at Carlos as he began to protest.

Then, they too were gone.

The women looked at each other. They had been enjoying some time alone, away from the madness in town, when they heard pounding on the stairs. Next thing they knew, their door was being pummeled as if with a battering ram. Jumping to their feet, they ran to it, hearts in their throats.

"Who is there?" demanded María Isabel.

"Mamá, it's me."

Frowning with bewilderment, she glanced at her friends. "Indio?" Opening the door, she quickly searched his eyes. Something flickered in their dark depths. It took her breath away. *"Qué pasó, papito?"* she gasped, her hand going to her heart.

Indio looked at his mother. The one who raised him, who called him hers. Tears stung his eyes. "Marina needs to speak to her mom." He looked steadily at her. "Right now."

María Isabel glanced behind him. Her friends' husbands stood with heads bowed, their children around them. Storm was included in the group that huddled together. Right behind Indio stood Caribe, eyes wide with shock, a bunch of papers gripped tightly in one hand. María Isabel reached inward and drew strength. "Why, of course." Turning to Shayla, she said quietly, "Maybe we should wait outside?" She didn't want to offend, so she made it into a question.

Shocked, Shayla just stared at her.

Sloane searched for her daughter and found her, locking eyes. With a gentle movement of her head, she motioned for Marina to join her. Turning around, she returned to where they had just been. She made eye contact with her daughter once more.

Marina broke away from her group, and walked up to Shayla. Tears brimming in her eyes, her voice came out hoarse. "I need to talk to Mami..."

Shayla crossed her arms. "I am also your mother, Marina del Sol..."

Marina shook her head. "Just for a moment," she pleaded, choking down a sob. "Please, Mommy, just for a moment..."

Shayla put a restraining hand on her shoulder, calming her down. "I understand, baby, but you are *not* going to leave me out of this one." She looked deep into her other daughter's eyes. "You have ten minutes alone with your mother, and then Mommy's coming in."

Marina nodded.

Shayla followed María Isabel out, and they shut the door behind the young woman.

Marina took a deep breath. Crossing the room quickly, she dropped to her knees before her mother. Bracing her hands on either side of Sloane, Marina looked deep into her eyes. Panic seemed to fill her. "Mami..." she choked. Cleared her throat. Gasped, shaking her head.

Sloane didn't know why. But she wanted to die. She sure did. Like no other time previous to this, in her whole life. Looking deep into her daughter's eyes, she gathered strength. Reaching out, she began stroking her daughter, brushing her hair out of her face, rubbing her arms. *"Qué pasó, Marinita?"* murmured the mother.

"Mami..." whispered the daughter. She began leaning forward, as if in slow motion, falling into her mother's waiting embrace. A sob escaped her throat, racking her chest. She tried again, as her mother began holding her tighter, squeezing. "Mami..." and then it came. The torrent of inconsolable, uncontrollable tears. Tears made for drowning. Her voice was the wail of a tormented soul. *"I just killed a man..."*

Sloane's heart skipped a beat, but her arms kept squeezing. She mustn't falter. Not now. If she needed to carry her daughter, so be it. Brushing the hair back from her tortured daughter's face, she pressed her mouth to her ear. "Hush, now, darling..." She began rocking her. *"Calla, bebé..."* She kissed the young woman in her arms, breathed her fragrance, her own tears running. "Cry your heart out, for a while, until your mind and body stop hurting," she whispered, "and then you can tell Mami all about it…"

Marina nodded, doing just that. Crying her heart out. She slid down her mother's front, arms clinging, hands grasping. Finally, she laid her head on Sloane's lap, and sobbed as if she hadn't cried in ages. Sloane tossed her head back, blinking fruiously at her own tears.

That is how Shayla found them when she finally came in, at the end of her self-allotted time. Quickly, she joined them, concern in her voice. "Oh, baby, what happened?"

Sloane met her eyes. "She killed a man."

Shocked, she looked at her soul sister in disbelief. Outside, nobody had said a word, so she wasn't prepared. Shaking her head, she looked down at her other daughter. "Can she talk yet?"

Sloane shook her head. "No, she's still crying. But she's slowed down some."

"Who did you kill, baby?"

Marina forced herself to come to a stop. Hiccuping, she looked through a veil of tears, at her mom. "Xavier," she whispered, not wanting to say his name too loud.

"Why, baby?" Sloane asked. Marina shook her head.

Shayla shook hers. "Somebody is going to do some talking around here." Leaving Sloane and Marina for a moment, she went back to the door. Flinging it open, she faced the intruders, and María Isabel. She had had no luck with Indio, either. Shayla made the announcement. "Everybody, get your butts in here, right now!" She held the door open as they all filed in. Pablo and Joe stood to one side, their children next to them. Jackson had his arms around Storm. Indio slipped his around María Isabel's shoulders. Caribe looked at Marina as if his heart were breaking. "Does anybody have anything to say?" asked Shayla softly in the hushed room. They all looked at her. But nobody moved. No one said anything. Dismayed, she looked at each of them. Then her eyes fell on Caribe's papers. Her eyes met his. "I guess it's up to you, huh, baby?" She glanced down at his hand. "Did you get it all down?" Her heart went out to the dreadlocked young man as he nodded miserably. "May we take a look at these?" She held out her hand, taking the bunch of papers from him.

"I only have a few you can look at, though. I need to work on them," he explained in a hushed tone.

Sinking down on the antique sofa next to Sloane, Shayla patted the space on her other side. "Come, María Isabel. Let us find out what happened..."

María Isabel squeezed Indio before letting go. She went to join her friends. Pablo and Joe moved to stand behind their wives. Jackson knelt down beside Marina and wrapped his arms around her. Storm draped herself on his back, caressing Marina next to him. Indio knelt behind his mother, draping his massive arms over the back of the sofa, and crossing them over her chest. He kissed her temple, her cheek. María Isabel grasped his wrists, bringing them up to her mouth, one at a time, in a tender kiss.

Jackson sighed, shuddering with tears. Blinking them back furiously, he shook his head, clearing it. Storm straightened up, allowing him to do the same. On his feet, he faced his moms. They looked at him expectantly. He took a deep breath. "I'll sing about it," he offered with a shrug. "I couldn't speak the words..."

The women nodded.

"Go ahead, baby," Sloane encouraged him.

Jackson cleared his throat, forcing the tears away. He began drumming a beat on his thighs, setting the rhythm. Eyes closed, rocking in place, he hummed, haunting notes filling the sun drenched top floor of the Gaitano warehouse. His beautiful voice embraced them, as he began a melodious chant.

"Al bebé se llevó, ese pirata maldito..."

Nobody spoke as everyone stared at the sketches. No explanation was needed. The story was clear.

"So he took the baby, that damned pirate," Shayla translated softly. She pointed out to one of a blubbering Charlie. "What's *his* problem?"

Salomé sighed. "Marina and Carlos were pretending that they'd split up or something. They were playing." She shrugged. Her eyes were distant. "But this guy had been stalking Marina all yesterday morning, and she had seen him. So he knew they were actually together, and he was having a heart attack over it, because Marina and Carlos kept denying it." Salomé stopped, taking in a deep, shuddering breath. Tears rolled down her cheeks. Swimming eyes fastened on her sister. "When Marina and Carlos finally admitted it..."

Sloane reached out with a hand and cupped her beautiful troubled face, rubbing tear tracks into the beloved dark skin. "Keep going, baby," she urged softly, encouraging her other daughter to continue.

"Xavier lost it!" she wailed softly, sobbing for a moment. Everybody remained silent, as she controlled herself. It was as if the wind had been taken out of her sails. Her voice dropped, emerald ice glowed in her eyes. "When Marina told him she was marrying Carlos and having his children, he snapped."

"A bailarle la obligó, ese pirata maldito..." called out Jackson, completely lost in his melodious storytelling.

"That damned pirate made her dance?" Shayla asked, incredulous.

Storm reached out with a hand, appeasing Salomé. "I'll tell them, if you want..." Salomé nodded, squeezing her hand. Storm did. The moms sat stunned. They had gotten to the last pages. Xavier sitting in the sunshine, deceased. Their men ushering their children out. Pablo Aguilar as Tony Montana.

"Como a un perro lo mató, a ese pirata maldito..."

"You killed him like a dog..." Shayla reached out and scratched Marina's head. "I would have killed him too, baby. I sure would have," she choked, shuddering at the visual image she had after being told what Xavier had said.

"I would have too, mami," agreed Sloane, hugging her.

María Isabel nodded. "Xavier was referring to my grandchildren, also," she said, her voice dripping ice. "I would have killed him with my bare hands, myself."

"Mirándola a los ojos murió, ese pirata maldito..."

"He died looking into your eyes?" Sloane asked. "Oh, baby, that damned pirate..."

They sighed. They cried. They stayed by Marina's side.

Pedro Escobar sat on the edge of the bench, arms crossed, feet planted firmly before him. The Gaitano men waited. They were outside, in Pedro Escobar's amazing rock garden, sitting at a mosaic patio table, complete with benches. They faced each other across the beautiful tiles sparkling in the sun. John stood quietly next to them. Solomon mirrored him on the other side of the table. The sun was straight overhead by now, and the bright blu e sky was absolutely cloudless. It was a beautiful day. Deceiving day. Full of pain and shadows no one could see.

Pedro Escobar cleared his throat. He looked straight at Don Carlos Gaitano. He sighed, letting his breath out softly. "What happened?"

Don Carlos took a deep breath. "First, Xavier abducted Max."

To say Pedro Escobar was shocked, would be an understatement. His hooded eyes flew open, his eyebrows arching in surprise. "Max?"

They all nodded. "He had one of his sailors follow Marina around, yesterday morning, while we were all down at the fair," Don Carlos explained. "This reptile knew about Max. That is the one you are holding in your cell, we are talking about." He shook his head, lost in thought. "Marina danced for him. She was playing..." he trailed off, searching his memory.

"Head games," provided Juan.

Don Miguel smiled, his voice rumbling deep in his chest. "Marina Aguilar is a master at head games."

Pedro Escobar nodded. "I see. And what kind of head games was Marina Aguilar playing?"

Solomon laughed. "The very best!"

The brothers chuckled. Juan held up his hand, laughing at the lawman. "Allow me," he said graciously. "Marina Aguilar got the pirate Xavier to admit to a couple of things." His eyes shone. "Some very crucial things."

"Like what?" inquired Pedro Escobar.

But the Gaitano brothers would say no more.

John turned to the Mexican. "Xavier admitted to being Dominique Swan's brother. He didn't deny knowing about the weapons, instead joking about it. He wanted to know where she was. Marina told him *La Prision*, waiting for Juan Gaitano to sail."

Pedro Escobar turned to Juan. "Did he say anything to you?"

Juan shrugged. "Not to me. He told Marina he would talk to me, but he never got around to it." He laughed wickedly. "Xavier had to leave suddenly."

His brothers smiled.

Don Miguel chuckled. "Xavier finally said the wrong thing to the wrong person." His laugh wasn't happy. It was that of a netherworld.

"What did he say?" the Mexican asked.

Don Carlos told him, his heart feeling heavier in his chest with each word.

Pedro Escobar sat stunned, absorbing all he had been told. Taking a deep breath, he shook his head, letting it out slowly. "You are all witness to this?"

They nodded their heads. "Marina Aguilar killed Xavier?"

John's voice rumbled around them. "Marina Aguilar got the pirate Xavier to admit he was the White Ghost."

Pedro Escobar lost his composure. He couldn't help himself. Tossing his head back, he pressed the palms of his hands into his eyes, before dragging his hands down his face. "Xavier was the White Ghost?"

They all nodded again.

"She actually gathered together some proof, that he was the only one around the areas where all the crimes were committed."

Pedro Escobar sighed. "Did Xavier know this?" They shook their heads.

"Not at all," answered Don Carlos.

"Marina Aguilar is a master at head games," repeated Don Miguel. "You all swear to this?"

They nodded.

"I have never heard or seen anything like it, Pedro," said John. "It was an incredible experience to see this girl's skill..."

"Marina studied psychology at school," Don Carlos explained. "Pablo told me. Besides her studies in numbers, she balanced her education with the study of the human mind."

Juan laughed. "In other words, she fucked with Xavier's mind until she was leading him around like a puppy."

Pedro Escobar nodded thoughtfully. "Does Carlitos know what Xavier said about..." he trailed off, blushing, but met them head on, "children..."

They all shook their heads.

"He knows it was something bad," provided Don Miguel.

"But he didn't actually hear," confirmed Juan. "The visitors... the men were playing drums and their son was singing, creating a diversion for Xavier's men."

Don Carlos breathed deeply. "I did." His eyes met Pedro Escobar's. "I heard every word." His voice growled in his throat. "I would have killed him myself."

They all nodded.

"Are you planning on telling him? I am sure he is curious about what the trigger was..."

They all shook their heads.

"You all agree," Pedro Escobar intoned, "that the actions of the accountant Marina Aguilar, of," he frowned, intent on getting it straight for the record, "*La Sirena* de Don Carlos Gaitano?" He smiled when Don Carlos nodded. "Were of those of self-defense, as she saw her life, and that of her loved ones, especially the intent of harmful assault on children ---" They didn't let him finish.

"Aye!"

Pedro Escobar stood up. "Maybe we should find Marina Aguilar, and tell her she is absolved of any wrongdoing."

"Aye!"

"Marina!"

Everyone turned to look at her. They could all recognize Carlos' voice.

Tears brimmed in her eyes once more, and her bottom lip quivered. Marina shook her head, snuggling deeper into her mother's side. The tears had subsided, to be replaced with a vacant look in her eyes. No one was speaking.

Jackson turned to the door. "Go away! Marina doesn't want to talk to you!"

Carlos Gaitano shook his head. "I'm not speaking to you, Jackson. I need to talk to your sister!"

"Go away!" Jackson repeated, in a warning growl. "My sister can't see you right now."

The young pirate's shock was almost palpable, even through the thick wood of the door. He ignored Jackson. "Please, Marina, come out."

Marina shook her head desperately. Like a wild animal, she looked around her, searching for a place to hide in. A sob caught in her throat. "I can't..." A rumble of voices was distinguishable through the door. Marina looked absolutely miserable. "This is totally going to ruin Carlitos. What are they going to say when they find out?"

Caribe frowned at her. "Marina," he said softly. "You know, *they*?" He waited for her to nod. "It's John..."

Marina stared at him. "John?" she repeated.

Caribe nodded. "Yes, mami, John."

More pounding on the door. "Marina! Please!"

"Go away!" Jackson shouted. "She doesn't want to play right now!"

"Open the damn door!" Carlos shouted from the other side. "Right now!"

Jackson straightened up, tiger eyes glowering, rage and fear for his sister marring his beautiful face. "Oh! I'll open the damn door right now, alright! How's that, dog?"

"Jackson!"

Joe and Pablo grabbed him, each dad by the arm, holding him back.

Storm shook her head at him. "Jackson, no!" Her hand reached out to caress his chest. "Don't do it, dude," she said softly. "Don't pick a fight with Carlos." She signaled at Marina. "He's as much of a victim as she is."

Indio shook his head in agreement. "Not the time to get into it with my brother, Jackson." The pirate's brother and the accountant's brother faced off. In the bright daylight, sunbeams slid down straight hair, and hid among the cornrows. "Wait a little while," he warned softly.

The moms rolled their eyes.

"What we should do," suggested Sloane in a deceptively soft tone, "is maroon the two of you together on a deserted island, and let you kill each other."

The dads grinned.

"I agree," chorused Shayla and María Isabel.

Salomé shook her head at her brother. "You guys have to grow up. Marina doesn't need this crap right now."

Jackson sighed. They were right. Although he wanted to beat the hell out of the pirate at times, he was a good friend. The best. And his sister's man. They loved each other deeply, and passionately. They would be uniting their lives soon. Marina wasn't his to protect any longer. His baby sister now belonged to Carlos Gaitano, and the pirate belonged to her.

On the other side of the door, the men looked at each other. The older Gaitano brothers shook their heads, eyebrows raised half in amusement. Carlos was not amused. The cornrowed man was nothing but a pain. The idea of fighting him did not appeal to him. On the contrary, he was trying to avoid a real, physical confrontation, any way he could. Jackson loved provoking him, however, and right now was a perfect example of one of those times. He stepped away from the door, shaking his head and scowling fiercely, all at the same time.

Juan chuckled. He lifted his left hand and wiggled his fingers at him. A smile split his face from side to side. "I hear she doesn't see a ring on her finger," he taunted his nephew.

Carlos, Padre, grabbed his son as he lunged at his brother. "*Tranquilo, Carlitos,*" he soothed, trying unsuccessfully to keep the laughter out of his voice. "Juanito speaks the truth, you know..." He looked at his older brother. "Miguel," he sighed deeply, rolling his eyes, "I suppose it is up to you..."

Don Miguel frowned. His hand went up to his chest, and he shook his head. "Who, me? No, not me..."

Don Carlos would not take no for an answer. "Do it." He smiled wickedly. "They won't dare say no to you..." he laughed.

Miguel sighed, shaking his head. Looking at the rest of them, he could see they were all urging him. He took a deep breath. Letting his energy roll out in waves, he called her, his tone deep and warning. Like a storm out in the middle of the sea. *"Marina... Aguilar... de Gaitano..."* He looked around and shrugged at his companions, his palms held out helplessly, indicating he hadn't known what else to do.

A wail burst out from the other side of the door.

The men groaned and laughed, shaking their heads. "You scared her, Miguel," Juan pointed out needlessly.

"Marina... Aguilar... de Gaitano..."

Marina burst into tears, her blood running cold. Her name had been pronounced as if it were a death sentence. She began crying like a little girl. Her companions moaned. Her voice came out in a helpless wail. "He's scaring me..."

María Isabel shook her head, disgusted. "Oh! For the love of God!" Standing up, she left the warmth of her friends' company, and strode to the door. Angrily, she flung the door open, revealing the anxious pirates on the sunny landing. *"Miguel!"* Hand flashing out, she softly smacked her older brother-in- law on the side of the head. "You just scared the life out of her!" she admonished. Hand on hip, foot tapping, like Shayla before her, she jerked her head towards the room. "Everybody in. Right now."

Silent as a shadow, Indio placed himself in front of Jackson, so that when Carlos came in, he was standing between them. Raising both arms until they were level with his shoulders, he pointed a finger at each of them. He turned his head to look them in the eye, one at a time. "Not here. Not now." He looked at them one more time. Finally, he relaxed his hands and lowered his arms. Then, staying between his brother and Marina and Salomé's brother, he crossed his arms over his chest.

Marina stood up, as did everyone around her. Her sad eyes went from Carlos, to his relatives, to Solomon, Pedro Escobar, and John.

John stood for a moment, still as a statue, staring at Marina. His eyes went over her, taking in the shock she found herself in. If he didn't hurry, she would be scarred for life. "Marina!" he rumbled, approaching her, getting her full attention. "Let me introduce myself. Formally." He smiled, bowing his head at her. "My real name is John." He took a deep breath, not taking his eyes froim her. "John Hawthorne..."

Something flickered in Marina's eyes. "Hawthorne?" she repeated softly. "As in the Hawthorne---"

"Scoundrels?" John smiled at her nod. "Yes." He shrugged. "They are grown children. But they do work for me, however," he added with a wink. He realized Marina was just staring at him, so he decided to move it right along. "My sons are private investigators. They are the ones in charge of uncovering any crimes being committed in these waters," he explained. "I am the man in charge of making sure everything is running along in a nice, safe, healthy environment. I am the man..." he trailed off, frowning, words evading him.

Marina nodded. "You are the man," she told him. "Do you decide if Carlos keeps Encantada or loses it?"

"That's me. Of course he keeps it."

Marina felt the people around her smile. "What happens to me, now?"

"You are free to go."

"You understand---"

John shook his head at her, smiling affectionately. "You understand..." he laughed, shaking his head in disbelief. "I was there!" He stroked her hair. "You are free to go!" Turning around, he signaled the men that had come in with him. "Gaitanos..."

Carlos turned to his mother, as his company filed out. "Mamá! Take her to my place. Spend the rest of the day there. All of you, females. I will be there, later." His eyes met Marina's, but she didn't seem to be there. There was nothing more he could do for her right now, but leave her alone. Sad, he turned away, and left.

It turned out to be exactly what the doctor ordered. The women had a blast. By far, one of the most memorable afternoons in their whole lives. Rouge had been sent by the men to join them, and heal herself in the process. Thus, Carlos Gaitano's home was invaded by a formidable army of females, united by ties of blood and love. The cave throbbed with their energy.

Oohing and aahing, they flocked from spot to spot, admiring everything, from the furniture to the sketches on the wall, and of course, the majestic bed.

Shayla's eyes lit up with mischief as she regarded her baby daughter. "You done good for yourself, girl!" She sighed happily, kissing Marina on the cheek. She cocked her head to the waterfall flooded in sunlight. "Shower?"

Proud, Marina smiled. She felt lighter. "Yeah..." She raised her eyebrows. "Hot," she whispered.

From the waterfall, Salomé laughed happily, her hand in the flow of water. "Hot, Mom!" she called out.

From their place by Caribe's drawings, Rouge and Storm shook their heads.

Storm laughed. "The boy is... *whipped!*" she announced.

Rouge agreed. "I have *never* seen Gaitano like this. It is awesome!"

Shayla laughed and took Marina's hand. She signaled to the small pool in the middle of the cave, bright sunlight spotlighting it. "Jacuzzi?"

Marina nodded. "One and the same." She began leading her mom in that direction.

"I must have you all know, that Carlitos has actually been planning to have us... *females,*" María Isabel rolled her eyes, laughing silently at her absent son, "spend a nice day together, here in his cave, for quite a while now. So, he has provided us with some products for us to entertain ourselves," she explained, lifting a medium-sized burlap sack, bulging with the items it held. In a moment, she was surrounded as if she were offering bird feed, and the women were pigeons. Out came shampoos, conditioners, fragrant soaps, sponges, rags, brushes, makeup and colognes.

Sloane walked away from the group for a moment, and stepped into the small pool. The water reached her upper thighs, soaking at her clothes as it lapped around her in its silent circulation. The sun poured down over her, as if she were the star on a stage. Her hair gleamed almost white, her skin like honey. Her eyes sparkled bright turquoise, like warm shallow waters. In contrast, the lapis lazuli that hung from her ears, was more like the cooler depths of the ocean. Raising her arms, she put her hands together as if in offering and raised them over her head. Eyes closed, her head tipped back, she took a deep breath, her lips moving in silent prayer.

Heavenly Father I thank you for the blessings you have bestowed on me. I thank you for the everlasting mercy you have shown us, keeping our daughter from harm. Please forgive her for what she has done. It was your will that she come here. I thank you for the man you have rewarded her with, the man of her dreams, the companion of her life. We have seen their love for each other grow until it has consumed them both. I thank you for putting Marina in Carlos Gaitano's life. Amen.

Yes. The women definitely had one of the best days of their lives.

Carlos Gaitano and Marina Aguilar spent one of the worst nights of their lives. The nightmares came. As expected. In droves. They had decided to spend the night at the lighthouse, instead of the cave. Marina didn't want her screams, when they came, bouncing around her head. Instead, she wanted them snatched by the wind and taken away, so she could pretend nothing happened. And throughout it all, Carlos holding her, soothing her, mouth pressed against her ear, breath warm on her face, arms wrapped tightly around her. And rocking. That, she would later remember. That every time her own screams woke her up, or pain tore through her chest with such a force that she would be racked by sobs, he was there. Carlos. Rocking her in his arms, making the pain go away. And Xavier. Fucking smiling dead Xavier. Making Xavier go away.

Marina looked up as a shadow crossed over the sun on her upturned face. Sighing, she closed them again, blocking out the faces hovering over her. "Go away," she mumbled, "don't want any..." Taking a deep breath, she moved her arms carefully. They were each cradling a sleeping baby twin. "Get out of my sun..."

Salomé laughed. "Get up, baby, we're leaving!" she announced happily.

Marina opened her eyes again and smiled. "No, we're not! Where are we going?" She sought for balance in the hammock as the twins were removed from their place on either side of her.

Indio grinned at her, gently draping a sleeping baby over his shoulder. "We are sailing in half an hour. Get ready," he told her.

Carlos went to stand by him, the matching twin draped over his own shoulder. "We will take Juan and Jaime home." He smiled. "Go wash the sleep out of your face, and get ready." He raised his eyebrows as she started to protest. "I hooked up some drugs for you, so your voyage will be a pleasant one," he teased. "Dr. Kyle gave me some medicine for you, so the motion of the ocean doesn't bother you," he explained, winking at her.

Marina sat up and gasped, a hand to her chest. "I thank you." And the men were gone. She turned to Salomé, who held out a hand to help her out of the hammock. Gratefully, she took it, and stood before her sister. "Why are we sailing?"

Salomé shrugged with a smile. "Well, you know how the *viejos* went with the older Gaitanos to Carey? Oh! And Jackson and Storm..."

Marina nodded. "They wanted to go sailing before they went home. Don Carlos and María Isabel invited them to Carey for the weekend. Jackson and Storm went along for the ride..."

Salomé nodded excitedly. "Well, we're supposed to meet them out there..."

Marina shook her head, puzzled. "Where?"

Salomé shrugged. "It doesn't matter. The storm is coming up in a few days, and then they are out of here." Her eyes locked with her sister's.

Marina nodded. "You're right. I'll meet them anywhere on the Caribbean Sea or on the Atlantic Ocean, that they wish..."

"Exactly. So, come on. It should be fun. The four of us, the crew necessary to sail, and..." her eyes sparkled with mischief, "Solomon... for you to play with."

Marina breathed a deep sigh, a big smile spreading on her face. "I love Carlos..."

Carlos' wish for their voyage came true. Beyond pleasant, it was absolutely memorable. They had left La Gitana and taken El Tiburon instead. During their three days out on the ocean, they did their share of chores and exercise. Accompanied by a school of dolphins the whole time, the sisters and the men entertained themselves. Then there was also plenty of time for resting. The days were bright and sunny, the wind strong and friendly. Finally, they were there.

"Arrecife!"

Marina and Salomé sat up straight, startled at the unexpected call.

"Arrecife?" Marina echoed. Salomé nodded with a grin. Marina frowned. "So, we're not going all the way to Carey?"

Salomé shrugged. "I guess not." She looked meaningfully at her sister. "Besides, you don't want to go to Carey, do you?"

"No, not at all," Marina admitted. "I am not ready yet..." she shrugged. "There you go, then," Salomé reasoned. "Let's go upstairs, and see what's up."

Smiling, Marina followed her older sister.

Upstairs, they were already anchored, and the crew was almost all gone. Standing on the side, hanging unto some ropes, were Carlos and Indio, the boat swaying under their feet. Marina and Salomé joined them, grabbing unto them, one hand held out for balance. Squinting against the sparkling water, they could make out the people already on the shore. Anchored a short distance away was La Sirena. The sisters grinned.

"¡*Viejos!*" exclaimed Marina happily under her breath.

"Last one in..." sang Salomé softly, and she disappeared. Indio followed.

Carlos and Marina looked at each other.

The pirate smiled. "Good morning," he greeted softly, looking into her eyes. He ducked his head for a kiss.

Marina smiled, melting inside. "Good morning..."

Carlos straightened again, and signaled at their companions swimming away. "Shall we?"

Marina nodded. "Let's." They dove off together.

From shore, *los viejos*, the old people, looked on. "They made good time," observed Don Carlos proudly.

"Yes, they did," agreed Don Miguel.

"El Tiburon is much faster than La Gitana," commented María Isabel.

"They are good sailors, our boys," added Juan.

"Is this place a regular stop for them when they go to Carey?" Joe wanted to know.

"You read my mind, papi," Pablo thought out loud. "It seems remote to me..."

"Not really," answered Giancarlo. "Only when they want to play for a little while."

"It's a favorite place," explained Rouge, "for..." she searched for the words, her face suddenly brightening, "hanging out!"

"I wonder if they have any idea what they are coming here for..." Sloane murmured.

"Now, girl, don't you worry about a thing," Shayla reassured her, her eyes glued on the four figures. "I am sure they have no idea."

Storm smiled. "Absolutely none."

Jackson squeezed her hand. "Clueless."

As they all watched, Salomé dove in, followed by Indio. They set a steady pace towards them. Carlos and Marina seemed to hesitate, however. They watched as the couple turned towards each other and kissed. Then, they followed their brother and sister. The two couples swam closer. Everyone's heart jumped with excitement.

"Mira lo que nos trajo el mar!" exclaimed Pablo happily, eyes crinkling with mischief as they met his daughter's. "Look at what the sea has brought us!"

"The ocean has blessed us," added Sloane, holding out a towel and wrapping it around her daughter. She kissed her and drew back to look into the beloved hazel eyes. "It's scary out here, isn't it?" she murmured.

Marina nodded. "It helps to be connected, that's for sure," she grinned. Mother and daughter laughed.

Shayla hugged both her daughters. "How was your sail?"

"Awesome!" laughed Salomé. "The weather has been wonderful!" The moms nodded.

"How about you, Carlitos?" his father asked fondly.

"I agree with the girls," his son answered. "It was smooth sailing out here."

"Y tu, papito?" Don Carlos looked at Indio fondly.

Indio nodded, the love for his father shining in his eyes. "We had fun," he agreed.

"We had fun," echoed Solomon, who had made it ashore sometime before they did.

"Don't you just *love* it here?" demanded Marina suddenly, laughter dancing in her eyes. She lifted her face up to the sun, arms spread wide on either side of her. "Isn't this the *coolest* sandbar on the whole ocean?"

"This place rocks, yo!" agreed Jackson.

Everybody stood around for a moment, just looking at each other.

Marina looked around her, suddenly realizing something. "This looks like a family meeting!" her soft tone accusing, even as she laughed. "What's up?"

The parents smiled.

Sloane stepped forward. "Well, *mi amor*, you know we are leaving soon," she began, waiting for her daughter to nod. "Some decisions have to be made, and we know you and Carlitos are still going through the pros and cons thing..."

"It's not an easy decision to make," Marina felt she had to defend herself.

"Oh! No doubt, baby!" Shayla agreed.

"We would never rush you, mamita," soothed Joe. "You take your very own, sweet time, baby girl. It is we, who have to go."

"And for that reason, Marina, it is that we are here together," her mother rushed on, "and we were just wondering, baby, if it were any way possible, and didn't interfere with your plans..." she gazed at her daughter's eyes. "Marina, we would love to see you married before we go."

Carlos' and Marina's heads whipped around to look at each other. Their hands blindly sought one another. *"Yes!"* they shouted, making tears come to their mothers' eyes.

"When and where?" Marina asked excitedly.

"Here and now, baby," Shayla informed her.

"We brought everything to throw you a wedding right here, if you agreed," explained María Isabel.

"Oh, please say yes!" pleaded Giancarlo laughing. "It might be what it would take to convince this woman to marry me!"

Rouge rolled her eyes at him. "I haven't needed convincing in years, Gian!" she informed him. "I just haven't been ready..."

"Who would marry us?"

"Tio Juan!" laughed Indio.

"Juan is justice of the peace," explained Don Miguel. "At least, that is his job description."

Juan stepped up to Marina, hand to his heart, taking her free hand and bringing it to his lips. His eyes sparkled with mischief. "I will marry you one way or the other..."

Marina laughed. "I would love to!" She looked at her man. *"¿Si, Carlitos?"*

He nodded. *"¡Si!"*

"Perfect!" María Isabel clapped her hands. "We will get everything ready."

"You kids go for a run!" Sloane shooed them away.

Grinning, the kids did. They looked like a pack of wild animals, as they pounded on the sand, away from the parents. Solomon and Caribe joined them.

Giancarlo laughed at the men. "What can we do to help?"

Rouge smiled at María Isabel. "Carlitos is actually getting married!" she said in wonder. "If I weren't seeing it, I wouldn't believe it!" She glanced at the Italian Sailing Master. "Now, I'll marry Giancarlo," she said softly. "Now that he will not be the only married one in his crew. That he can see what it's really about, and not just a way to have me in his bed every night."

"Good girl," said Shayla.

"Giancarlo and you are going to have a wonderful marriage together," Sloane said.

María Isabel nodded. "We will have plenty of time to prepare for that one. Right now, it's all about Carlos and Marina..."

God had never made a more beautiful day for such a deserving occasion.

Tents had been set up while they had been out on their run. Tables laid out with food and plenty of drink. What seemed to be gifts, in a pile, to one side. Everybody was ushered to a couple of tents, the girls separate from the boys. Inside their tent, the girls grinned at each other, before turning to their moms.

"This is nice," sighed Salomé.

"Yes, it is," agreed Shayla, wringing out a towel in a bowl of water. "Now, no talking, and just get ready." She took her daughter's face in her hand and began wiping her down.

Sloane mirrored her actions. "This is the second biggest day of your life," she murmured, as she ushered Marina out of her clothes.

Marina laughed softly. "When's the biggest?"

Sloane looked into her daughter's eyes. "The day your first child is born."

"But seeing as how we are worlds---and centuries---apart from any convenience we ever imagined we'd have available for either of your weddings," Shayla explained, "we decided to improvise."

Marina beamed. "Thanks, Mom!"

"I hope you do the same for me, when it's my turn," pouted Salomé.

"Of course, baby," soothed Sloane. "Maybe yours can be in our time, won't that be fun?" she asked, raising her eyebrows and opening her eyes wide.

"What are we doing for rings?" Marina asked suddenly.

"It's taken care of," answered Sloane.

"That's Giancarlo's and Rouge's gift to you," Shayla explained. "Flowers?"

"Rouge and Storm are scavenging as we speak," her mom answered again.

"Dress?"

Salomé turned to her sister, eyes brimming with love. "I made the dress," she said softly. "Indio decorated it."

Marina gasped. "No!"

Salomé nodded. "Yes..."

Marina turned to her moms. "Show me..."

The men's tent went in much the same way. Water was provided for the runners to freshen up. They changed clothes, drank water, munched on some fruit. Caribe busied himself with a stack of blank papers, and a few pencils, readying himself. Solomon preened in front of the mirror, smoothing his hands over his black leather vest, gold arm bands shining against straining muscles. He looked like Sultan's younger brother, a fact that escaped no one. Indio busied himself, braiding feathers and strings of beads into his long straight hair.

Don Carlos turned to his birth son. "How are you feeling, Carlitos?"

Carlos smiled at his father through the mirror propped on the table he was leaning on. He stood shirtless, new black pants already tucked into soft leather boots, hair wet and curling around his head, a razor in his hand. Eyes glowed like deep turquoise pools caught in sunlight. Finishing the last stripe left on his cheek, he put down the blade and splashed water on his face. Blindly grabbing a towel next to him, he pressed it against his face for a moment, before scrubbing his face dry. Then he turned to Don Carlos, smiling. He looked radiant. "Never better, Papá…"

Juan rolled his eyes, grinning. "Are you sure you want to marry this girl, Carlitos?"

Carlos snapped the towel at him. "You lost. Go away," he laughed.

"You look good, papi" Don Miguel reassured him.

"Welcome to the family, son," smiled Joe, shaking his hand and pulling him into a deep embrace. Letting Carlos go, he turned to Indio, laughing, doing the same. "And you, papi…"

Pablo waited for Carlos to look at him. Then, holding out his arms, he beckoned with his head. "*Ven aca, papi,*" he murmured. The pirate stepped into his arms, returning the embrace. Not many words were needed. Tears came to Pablo's eyes. "You know, I love you, and I trust you…" he hesitated. Carlos nodded. "But what's more important, *mi nena* loves you and trusts you, and you are just plain crazy about her, so," pulling back, he smiled into Carlos' eyes, through his tears, "I'll be fine."

Carlos chuckled. *"Gracias, Papi…"*

"Come, Carlitos," Don Miguel urged him. He held out a brand new shirt, of the finest silk.

Carlos approached his uncle, slipping his arms into the sleeves. Turning to the mirror, he buttoned it partially, slowly. Next came a new clean bandanna for his hair. It framed his face beautifully, his earrings sparkling in his ears. Finally, his sword.

Indio slipped a string of turquoises around his neck. "Happy day," he rumbled deep in his chest, love for his brother in every cell of his being. The splash of color matched his eyes.

Carlos nodded in approval. The brothers embraced and kissed. Then he turned to the men in his company. "I'm ready."

Marina looked at herself in the mirror that had been so thoughtfully provided. The dress was a plain white shift, hanging to above her knees. It fell loosely and comfortably around her. The straps were thin, allowing for bare chest and arms. The whole thing was adorned with shells and beads, in a subtle, tasteful manner. Marina's smile spread slowly, as she studied herself. Her hair fell loose around her face, bold turquoise earrings peeking through. They had found some makeup and had brushed some kohl on her lashes, making her eyes stand out more. That was it, though, leaving the rest of her natural. Shells on hemp string hung from the neckline of the dress, and from the hemline. Indio's turquoises still graced her left arm, as did his mother's cross, her chest.

Marina nodded in approval. There had never been a more beautiful wedding dress. "I'm ready."

Marina stepped out of the tent, blinking against the bright sunlight. Immediately, she had a dad on either side of her. Smiling, they offered her their arms. Smiling back, she took them. They walked her away.

Up ahead, there was a canopy. Under it, all her loved ones stood, looking at her. Her moms and sister rushed past her to join the people under the shade. To one side stood María Isabel, Rouge and Storm. To the other side, stood Indio, Jackson, Don Carlos and Don Miguel. Solomon and Giancarlo accompanied the women. And in the middle of them all, Carlos. In all his brand new, pirate finery, eyes glowing like the middle of the sea.

Caribe moved stealthily, pencil flying over his paper, catching her attention from the corner of her eye. From over Carlos' shoulder, Juan beamed at her. Finally, she reached them. Marina looked up, up, up.

Carlos had never been taller, broader, stronger. Never more handsome or more sexy. Reading her thoughts, he grinned. Half-turning to his uncle, he laughed, never taking his eyes off her. "You better hurry, Tio..." Taking her hand, he locked his fingers with hers, raising it to his mouth, pressing a kiss on it. Then, he led her out from under the shade of the canopy, letting themselves be bathed in sunlight. They glowed. He nodded at his uncle.

Rolling his eyes, Juan shook his head. Squinting, he followed them out, leaving the rest of the wedding party in the shade. Taking Marina's free hand, he pressed Rouge and Storm's arrangement of bleached driftwood branches and gull and pelican feathers into it. She laughed. Clearing his throat, he began.

"We are all gathered here on ---" he stopped for a moment, looking around him. Finally, he shook his head, "---this God for-saken sandbar---"

"*Arrecife!*" the Gaitano men shouted from under the canopy.

Carlos and his uncle looked at each other and laughed. Marina shook her head with a smile.

"To witness this man and this woman join their lives together by the power the law gives me, before God and before man, in mat-rimony." He smiled, as the watched the couple get lost in each oth-er's eyes. "This commitment is not to be taken lightly," he warned them softly. "There are things involved here, that do not come into the picture with just any other commitment. Such as," he continued infuriatingly, answering their unspoken question, "time and distance, power and wealth..." Gone was the happy-go-lucky, teasing, outra-geous young uncle. Here was the Captain of La Prision, the youngest Gaitano brother with all that his name and station in life implied, the justice of the peace of the pirates' Caribbean. He cocked his head to one side, studying them carefully. "How committed are you really?" he wondered aloud, eyes going from one to the other. "What is your ultimate sacrifice to be with each other?"

Marina's eyes widened with shock. "I killed a man," she gasped. The look in Tio Juan's face said, *so what*. That wasn't what he was talking about. She searched his eyes for a moment, and then turned to the man before her. "I renounce," she said clearly, for all to hear, "to any power, wealth, property, or anything else of significant mate-rial value that you may have acquired before this day---"

"What about the riches I've acquired because of you?" Carlos inquired, genuinely curious.

Marina shrugged and shook her head impatiently. "They mean nothing to me!" she exclaimed, oblivious to the Gaitano men grinning under the canopy. "I'll take your name, but all I want is you."

"What if I had nothing to offer you?"

She shrugged again. "I've got plenty to offer you."

"How about when I get old..."

"You'll be fabulous. I'll have to put a collar and leash on you." Her heart sighed at his smile. "Besides, *I'll* be older."

"Sick?"

"I'll take care of you."

"Will you have my children?"

"I can't wait!"

"All I want?"

"We'll negotiate."

"Do you accept me with my family and friends?"

"Absolutely."

"Would you give up fighting Solomon?"

Stunned, Marina couldn't speak. She knew he got jealous, but only because he couldn't share her need for occasional violence with her, as the Boatswain could. Tears stung the back of her eyes, and before she could stop herself, she glanced at the canopy. Her fingers tightened around his, clutching tight, as did the ones holding her beach bouquet. Everyone stared back, solemn, still. She had eyes only for Solomon. There was a single ripple over his massive muscles, as he held his breath. His eyes locked with hers. They communicated silently. A shadow seemed to pass over both their faces. She turned back to the pirate in front of her. "Are you asking me to?" She searched his eyes. "I would--

-" she choked on the words.

"No!" Carlos was almost sorry he had brought it up, but he had to know. He had never seen his Boatswain almost getting ready to cry before, either. "The woman I fell in love with, prefers Africans, and fights my Boatswain." He sighed in relief as the guests laughed softly. "As long as it's just Solomon you play with..."

"Just Solomon…"

"Any special requests?"

"Yes." She looked him right in the eye, without blinking. He met her gaze steadily. "Don't ever hit me. Never in anger, for as long as you live. Not even once. Respect me. Trust me. Always be truthful, honest with me. I've got your back, now." She watched the play of light in his eyes, as he nodded. "Don't… ever…. cheat on me…"

Licking his lips, the pirate nodded. "Same goes for you, *divina*…" Thunder clouded his face for an instant. "Don't you ever cheat on me…" He held up his hand in front of her. Not wanting to put down her bouquet, she slid the back of hers against it.

"It will never happen," she reassured him. "Carlitos…" Smiling, she shook her head at him. "Let me break it down for you, *mi amor*. As a friend, you kick ass."

The pirate smiled back. "You're the best."

"You're a great boss."

"You're my top employee." He glanced at his father. "Or were…"

"We can totally hang…"

His eyes crinkled at the corners as he smiled. "We get along fine." He glanced at the Gaitano men, amused.

"Sex rocks…"

His head whipped around, and he gave her a low wolf whistle, eyes shooting sparks at hers. "You have shown me Heaven…"

"And I want to have your baby…"

"And I want to be your baby's daddy…"

Marina gasped. "Jackson taught you that!"

Carlos laughed. "Of course he did."

"I knew it!"

"What do you want from me?"

"After today, your name. Other than that, just you, papi, just you…"

"Mind?"

"I thrive on your mind…"

"Body?"

"I immensely enjoy your body…"

"Soul?"

"I rejoice in your soul..."

Under the carp, their parents gasped.

"That's exactly the same way I feel about you, Marina..."

"Just you..."

Carlos squeezed her hand. "I just want you..." He held her eyes for a moment longer. Then, he turned to his uncle. "We are ready..."

Juan rolled his eyes and shook his head. Turning to Indio, he held out his hand. Indio dropped two rings into it. Holding one in each hand, he held them up. They were perfect, matching, thick silver circular tubular rings. The smaller one, he held out to his nephew. "Carlos, put Marina's on her finger," he instructed. Then, he handed her the larger one. "Marina, puts Carlos' on his finger." He waited for them to obey, and dusted his hands. "My job here is done." He raised his hands in the air, then made the sign of the cross over their heads. *"Los declaro marido y mujer..."*

Marina looked into twin seas. *Man and wife...*

Carlos winked at her. *Finally!*

They kissed.

Juan turned to the canopy, and hesitated. Then he grinned. "Gaitanos!" he exclaimed, getting their full attention. "Do you, along with Giancarlo Ilarrazza and Solomon, Rouge and Storm, and Caribe, accept the Aguilar Banks---"

The company in the shade exclaimed with appreciation.

"In business and in wealth, in sickness and in health, as trusted partners, friends and in-laws---"

"Aye!"

"Aguilar-Banks?"

"Aye!"

"I declare you associates and friends, through space and time, for life!"

Startled by the cheer, a flock of seagulls soared, crying hysterically into the bright, cloudless sky.

The rest of the afternoon was a blur for the bride. She made an effort of trying to observe everything as if she had a camera. But if you were to ask her about it soon afterward, she couldn't tell you a single thing. It wouldn't be until she saw the album Caribe made for her with his sketches, that Marina would be able to recount in vivid detail, every single detail about their wedding.

There was food, there was music, and there were papers. That was the general impression. Foodwise, their was a picnic laid out with a banquet of fruits, and bread, and fresh fish fried over a fire. It was awesome. The crew of La Sirena and of El Tiburon, mingled and shared, along with the Gaitanos and the Aguilar-Banks tribe. Music was more *reggaeton*, under totally different circumstances. Beautiful love songs to sensuous beats. Made for good background music, and good dancing. Joe and Pablo singing backup to Jackson's strong, beautiful voice. The fathers beat the skins, and the son danced and swayed to their songs. Good stuff. Then there were all the papers, all the *viejos* had dreamed up together. All kinds of stuff about business, and work. Things about assets in his time, and investments her parents were going to make for them in hers. Then there was something about Pablo and Don Carlos making a company for them, that would cover both their butts, but was to be designed more in benefit of the children they would have together. These children, just like the ones Giancarlo and Rouge were destined to have one day, would also be very cute and very rich. *Los abuelos* were looking out for their future. Something like that...

And then, there was Salomé's voice in Marina's ear. She was kind of busy at the moment, gazing into her brand new husband's dreamboat eyes. So, high on love and lust, she couldn't be really sure, but she was pretty sure it was Salomé. Anyway, the voice said, "You get a three-day honeymoon in the luxury of your own Captain's cabin, in which seeing the light of day is optional. You will have discreet, anonymous room service, which will leave your meals at your door, so you never have to leave the comfort of your own room. All this will be provided to you by Indio Gaitano, and the crew of El Tiburon. We're driving. Enjoy..." And then it was gone, so she really wasn't sure, but the part about Indio Gaitano kind of clinched it.

The food was delicious, but they ate light. There was wine, but they only had one glass. They disappeared into one of the tents, and changed back into their respective clothes. Then, kissing their family goodbye, they walked into the ocean and swam back to El Tiburon. Meanwhile, on Arrecife, the celebration continued.

El Tiburon moaned as the pirate chased the accountant into his cabin. She stopped, short of his bed, and whirled around, hands raised in the air, mouth open, ready to scream with laughter. He grinned and slammed the door behind him. Peeling off his pants, he approached her. Marina stared. Marina swallowed. Finally, she looked up at him. Then she couldn't see him, because she closed her eyes. He was kissing her, like it was the last time he would kiss her, for as long as he lived. Later, she wouldn't be able to explain to herself how he did it, but he peeled off her pants without her noticing it. It only came to her attention when he was deep inside her a minute later. Once she wrapped her legs around his waist, he completely forgot to free her breasts. By then, the pirate could barely remember his own name. But he did his job, and he did it well. Now, he was the husband. And as his wife melted under him, her fingers in his hair, and her mouth kissing him and kissing him, and she just wouldn't stop, squeezing him deep inside her, Carlos Gaitano loved every minute of it.

"We have to go…"

The Aguilar-Banks children froze. It didn't matter which parent had said it, they had all heard it.

The Siren's Lair droned softly around them. The Pirates' Convention Expo was long over, and everybody had sailed on. Now, they were sitting at a table with the Gaitanos around them, discussing their immediate future.

Salomé shook her head at her parents. "No way! Has it been a month already?"

Shayla put her hand over her daughter's. "Yes, baby. It's been more than a month already, precious, it's been about six weeks. We have to get back."

Jackson looked down at a table. "So, when do you have to go?"

Joe reached out and squeezed his shoulder. "Tomorrow…"

The three of them stared at him, identical dismay on their different faces. "Tomorrow?"

"Any of you ready to come back?"

"Do we have a choice?" Jackson demanded.

His father grabbed his face in his hand and turned it to look at him, but in a gentle manner. "You are a grown man, Jax. You always have a choice…"

Jackson nodded, smiling at his father. Then, light shifted in his eyes, and he slid them over Storm, licking his lips like L L Cool J. Finally, he looked back at his father, upgrading his smile to a grin. "I think I'll catch the next one, Dad…"

Smiling, Joe turned to Salomé. "What about you, baby girl?"

Salomé smiled back. "Well, we're kind of hanging right now, and why fix what's not broken, right?" Then, just like her brother, she also upgraded her smile. "But I think Indio secretly wants to go back with me."

Indio smiled and grunted.

Sloane laughed. "Take your time, kids, no rush, make sure..."

Pablo turned to his pride and joy. *"Oye, nena, y ustedes..."*

"We don't know yet," Marina moaned.

Carlos frowned in agreement. "We don't know yet."

Pablo sighed. Then he raised his eyebrows hopefully. "You have until tomorrow..."

The Gaitanos laughed. Don Miguel's energy rolled out like a nice warm soft blanket. María Isabel's laughter was music to their ears. Juan reached out and high-fived Pablo in male camaraderie, his shoulders shaking as he chuckled. Don Carlos shook with silent laughter. "I have an idea." Everybody turned to look at him. "Let us, immediate family, all go," he suggested in a deep, mind seducing tone. "When the storm starts..." he looked at each and every one of them, "let's see who stays and who goes..."

Astounded, the younger generation stared at each other, smiles spreading slowly on their faces. They communicated with their eyes and came to a final silent agreement. Finally, they faced the parents.

"Aye!"

The next day was heavy with rain. Dawn came, cool and metallic, smelling of wet. The wind whispered that it was on its way. Sunshine was opaque and dim, like the memory of sunshine.

At Villa Azul, glasses tinkled as the visitors spent time with their guests. Joe played soft background on the piano, making it sound like a cocktail lounge. Everybody was happy and relaxed. The women laughed at mysterious secrets of their own, as Marina and Salomé sat surrounded by the men, in an intense revelation.

"This was it," Salomé intoned in a low voice. "This was the reason why we crossed over---" she hesitated, startled, and cast an apologetic glance at her sister, "in time, of course, I mean, we're not dead," she mumbled under her breath. Looking up, she tried again. "I think I was brought here to bust Dominique Swan. It was pretty bad what she was doing. Carlos and Indio were going down like a plane shot out of the sky…" she shook her head, exasperated as the Gaitano men looked at her with puzzled expressions. "But we got her, you raided the hell out of Encantada with amazing results, and Carlos keeps the island." She nodded, looking around at all of them. "And meeting Indio, for sure," she sighed. "That's what I came here for."

She was rewarded with solemn silence.

Jackson laughed, and leaned forward, moving to the edge of his seat, hands clasped between spread knees. "I came here to defend my sisters' honor…" He shook his cornrowed head. *Not!* He smiled around him. "I came here to learn business from Giancarlo Ilarraza, and art from Caribe. I'm not done, yet." He too, sighed. "I came here to meet Indio and Carlitos, to pave the way for our *viejos*." Grinning, "Which means, because of me, there is now a *Gaitano-Aguilar-Banks* alliance." Laughing, he ducked his head as he got booed by the vast majority. "For real," he added, totally serious, even though the smile never left, "I came here to meet---" he shook his head, "know Storm. This girl is teaching me things about myself. I like who I am with her, whom I never knew I could be," he explained softly. "Storm is hooking me up with Jackson," he shrugged his shoulders, holding out his hands, "you know what I mean?"

All nodded, and slid their hands with his.

Marina took a deep breath as all eyes turned to her. "Besides meeting Carlitos," she winked at him, "I came here to take care of babies, while their moms produced more." Her eyes took a faraway look. "I came here to show Carlos and Indio what was being done to them, and help them recognize the signs, show them what to look out for, and take better care of their business." She took in a shuddery breath. "I must have come here to unmask Xavier…"

"To *rid* us of Xavier," rumbled Don Miguel gently.

"To *kill* Xavier…" Don Carlos said, a ferocious mix of relief and anger at the recently defunct pirate.

Marina shook her head at them. "So, is my job here done?" she asked them. "If so, then what now?"

As Salomé before her, she was greeted with silence.

Juan was the first to break it. "That part of your voyage is done, yes. But look at it as your…" he trailed off, looking up at the silver sky above their heads, searching for the words, "introduction here, so to speak. You came here to meet, fall in love, and marry Carlitos, and in that manner unite the Gaitanos with the Aguilar-Banks. That is accomplished." He searched her eyes. "And now that the beginning stage is over, you embark on a new journey, as one of the Gaitanos. Here? There?" He shrugged, shaking his head. "It doesn't matter where. Now you have a life together."

Everyone concurred. "Aye!"

Marina closed her eyes in contentment, as Carlos ducked his head, his breath warm on her ear.

"*Querida*," he murmured, "go play with Solomon..."

Her eyes flew open. "You want me to fight Solomon?"

He chuckled, like rich fresh honey. "No, I want you to *play* with Solomon. *Pretend* fight. Stay where I can see you..."

Marina nodded, eyes dancing with laughter. Her mouth made a perfect circle, and she glanced skyward. "I get it, you boys are going to talk..."

Carlos grinned. "You had it right, the whole time," he teased, "I want you for your mind." Laughing as she stood to leave them, he spanked her softly as she walked away. He watched as she called Solomon over and explained to him what was going on. They saluted, and began slow motions, a variety of kicks and punches and blocks. Then he turned back to his group.

Salomé sighed dramatically. "All right, I'm going." She smiled at them, as she also took her leave. "I'm gonna go hang with the females for a little while..."

The men remained, talking to each other, discussing business. Their business. The union of the Gaitanos with the Aguilar-Banks. And as Joe continued playing the piano, and Marina and Solomon danced around each other, in the ancient art of Tae-Kwon-Do, Caribe continued to sketch, the men kept planning, the women kept laughing, and the sun sank, letting darkness embrace them.

By the time they got to the cave, the wind was blowing strong. Laughing, the group of people ducked inside, quickly lighting the tiki torches on the walls. They sheltered from the incoming rain, joking and laughing, singing and dancing. They were all there. Three sets of parents, two uncles, one friend, a brother with his girlfriend, and two sisters with their men. There were fifteen people in that cave when the storm began.

It started. There was a mad scramble of hugs and kisses, as final decisions were made. They could feel it creeping over the water. Running out of the cave, eight people scrambled down the path along the cliff, laughter mixing with tears. Inside the cave, seven people remained, laughing softly, crying quietly, marveling at their voyage.

And then it happened. A warp in space flowed in from the ocean, skimming over the ferocious waves on the open sea. The people in the cave stood at the opening, watching it come. The ones who had seen it before, smiled as if at an old friend. The ones who hadn't, marveled at it. And then, it was done. All that was left was the wind and rain. Happy, exhausted from excitement, the people in the cave went to sleep.

Reaching their respective abodes, a little sad, but reassured, the people who ran out of the cave went to sleep.

Pablo Aguilar sat up and stretched, yawned, rubbed his eyes. Light came into the cave, displaying his sleeping companions. They, too, were beginning to stir. Overhead, a plane droned. He grinned, and went exploring.

The morning light revealed his attorney's effort at a Welcome Back gift package. There were baskets with toiletries and fresh towels. A few clean T- shirts. A styrofoam cooler with bottles of water and juice swimming in half-melted ice. A humorous Hallmark card. And the cell phone. It was fully charged.

Grinning, Pablo stepped outside, ignoring his amazed companions. He pressed a button on the cell phone and held it to his ear.

"Pablito!"

Pablo smiled, his heart jumping in relief. "How're you doing, papi?"

"You mean, how are *you* doing!"

"I'll bet you barely slept last night."

His friend chuckled over the air waves. "How well, you know me..." His voice got suddenly drowned out by the noise of a motor starting. "Do not move," it suddenly laughed in his ear. "I'll be right there!"

Pablo laughed, shaking his head. "Shane, Shane, Shane..." Tears came to his eyes, and he swallowed. "You know I love you, right, papi?"

"Same here, Pablito..."

Pablo blinked back his tears. "We got company---"

"I can't wait to see the girls! How did it go? Are they glad to be back?" Pablo laughed, shaking his head. "I'm afraid it's not the girls, Shane."

Dead silence reached him from the other end. Other than the noise of a boat's engine. Then, "You sound okay with that."

"I'm fine." More laughter.

The puzzlement on the other side was so thick you could cut it with a knife. "So, Jackson couldn't wait to get back to third millennium civilization?"

"Not Jackson, papi."

Dead silence again. Finally, a choked whisper. "No way..."

"Way..." Pablo nodded at his lawyer, even if his friend couldn't see him. He laughed. "I have brought back..." he chuckled some more, "actually, he insisted..." He took a deep breath. He couldn't believe it himself, it was so extraordinary. "Our children call him HRC." He didn't wait for the question. His voice dropped to a conspiratorial whisper. "His Royal Coolness himself ---"

"No way!"

"Way, papi..." He sighed. "We have come back accompanied by---

"No way..."

"... the most distinguished..."

"Please, stop, you're killing me..."

"King of the Pirates, Don Carlos Gaitano y Mendoza..."

"No way..."

"... and the fabulous María Isabel Sandoval de Gaitano..."

Translations

a la orden (ah la OR-den) - at your service
"A usted, caballero" (ah oos-TAID, cah-bah-JEH-ro) – To you,
    gentleman
abuelos (ah-BWEH-los) – grandparents
amado (ah-MA-doh) – beloved
amigo (ah-MEE-goh) – friend
Arrecife (ah-reh-SEE-feh) – reef
azul (ah-ZOOL) – blue

baile (BAH-ee-leh) – dance
bebé (beh-BEH) – baby
bruja (BROO-ha) – witch
Buenas tardes (boo-EH-nas TAR-des) – good afternoon
Buenos días (boo-EH-nos DEE-as) – good morning

cabrón (cah-BROHN) – bastard
callejón (cah-yeh-HONE) – alley
Carey (cah-RAY) – sea turtle
cuidado (coo-ee-DAH-doh) careful (command)

del Mar – of the sea
Dios mío (dee-OHS MEE-oh) – my God
diosa (dee-OH-sa) – goddess
divina (dee-VEE-nah) – divine
duelo (doo-EH-loh) – mourning

en serio (en SAIR-ee-oh) – seriously
Encantada (en-can-Tah-dah) – enchanted

eres mía (air-es MEE-ah) – you are mine

Gaitano – (gah-ee-TAH-noh)
Gaviota – (gah-vee-OH-tah) Seagull
Gitana – (hee-TAH-nah) Gypsy
gracias – (GRASS-ee-ahs) thank you

hasta la vista (AHS-ta la VEES-tah) – see you later
hermano (air-MA-noh) – brother
hija (EE-ha) – daughter
hijo (EE-ho) – son
hijo de puta (EE-ho deh POO-tah) – son of a bitch
hombre (om-BREH) – man

Indio (EEN-dee-oh) – Indian; native

Joyas (HO-jas) – jewels

las, los (the)
Loquillo (loh-KEE-joh) – crazy; cacique (taíno chief) who ruled
    the northeastern corner of Borikén (present day Puerto Rico)
    during the Spanish colonization. He was best known for his
    resistance to the conquistadores, thus earning him his name.

Mamá (ma-MAH) – mother, mom
Mami (MAH-mee) – mommy
mami (MAH-mee) – term of endearment reserved for loved females
mamita (mah-MEE-tah) – diminutive for "mami", term of endear-
    ment for a girl child
Mano (MAH-noh) – short for "hermano" (brother); bro
mi amor (mee ah-MORE) – my love
mi corazón (mee cor-ah-ZOHN) – my heart
mía (MEE-ah); mío (MEE-oh) – mine
muchachos (moo-CHA-chose) – guys; young people
mujer (moo-HAIR) – woman
muñeca (moo-NYEH-cah) – doll

nada (NAH-dah) – nothing
nena (NEH-nah) – baby girl
nene (NEH-neh) – baby boy
no sé (no SEH) – I don't know
no seas así (no SEH-as ahs-SEE) – don't be like that
nos vamos (nos VAH-mose) – we're leaving

oficial (oh-fee-see-ALL) – officer; official
oye (OH-yeh) – listen; hey

Padre (PAH-dreh) – Father
Papá (pah-PAH) - Dad
Papi (PAH-pee) – Daddy
papi – (PAH-pee) – term of endearment reserved for loved males
papito – (pah-PEE-toh) – diminutive for papi; term of endearment
     reserved for a boy child
por favor (por fah-VORE) – please
preciosa (preh-see-OH-sa) – precious, beautiful
princesa (preen-SEH-sah) – princess
prisión (pree-see-OHN) – prison
puta (POO-tah) – short for prostituta (pross-tee-TOO-tah), prosti-
     tute, whore, slut

¿Qué pasa? (keh PA-sah) – What is the matter? What is going on?
     What is happening?
Querida (keh-REE-dah) Querido (keh-REE-doh) – wanted; darling,
     beloved

Salomé (sah-loh-MEH)
¡Salud! (sah-LOOD) – Cheers!
Suave (soo-AH-veh) – easy, gently, softly

tetas (TEH-tahs) – teats, breasts
tiburón (tee-boo-ROHN) – shark
tranquila (tran-KEE-lah) – tranquil, peaceful; as a command,
     "Relax..."

tu madre (too MA-dreh) – your mother

ustedes (oos-TEH-des) – you (plural)
ven – command meaning "Come"
viejo (vee-EH-ho) – old man
viejos (vee-EH-hos) – old folks

The Pirates

La Gitana:
    Carlos Gaitano – Captain
    Indio Gaitano – Quartermaster
    Giancarlo Ilarraza – Sailing Master
    Solomon – Boatswain

The Council:
    Don Miguel Gaitano – La Gaviota
    Jai-Ling – Ocean Wind
    Sultan – Kalahari
    Suleiman – Chymera
    Jack – Black Mermaid
    Rouge – The Sea Gypsy (Captain)
    Storm – The Sea Gypsy (Quartermaster)

La Sirena
    Don Carlos Gaitano

La Prisión
    Don Juan Gaitano

Xavier

The Visitors

The Aguilars:
    Pablo – Father
    Sloane – Mother
    Marina – Daughter

The Banks:
    Joe – Father
    Shayla – Mother
    Jackson – Son
    Salomé - Daughter